Warrior

Karen Lynch

ISBN: 0997990104
ISBN-13: 978-0997990102

Cover Designer: Nikos Lima

For my readers

Thank you for coming on this journey with me and for helping
me realize my dream.

Acknowledgements

Thank you to my family and friends for always being so supportive. There are so many people who help make these books a success. I want to thank my PA and amazing proofreader, Sara, my editor, Kelly, and my cover artist, Nikos. And last but not least, my two beta readers, confidantes, and author BFFs: Ednah Walters and Melissa Haag. Couldn't do it without you ladies.

CHAPTER 1

"I'LL GUT THIS bitch if you take another step, Mohiri."

I fingered the hilt of my sword as I studied the vampire pressed back against the wall with the human girl dangling by her throat in front of him. The girl's face was a mask of terror when the vampire's claws drew blood from her throat. I could feel her staring at me, silently pleading with me to save her.

I kept my attention on the vampire. "If you think the human will save you from me, you are sadly mistaken, my friend."

He shifted from one foot to the other, his eyes darting around for another means of escape. He knew what I was, and he also had to know there was no way he was leaving this place alive. I had to convince him not to take the girl down with him.

From another part of the house, a scream rang out and was quickly cut short.

The vampire's eyes widened, and the hand around the girl's throat shook. "You protect humans. You won't do anything that will hurt her."

My gaze locked with his. "I do protect them, but I'm a hunter above all else. Seeing her blood on your hands will only make me hungrier for the kill."

He swallowed hard, glancing at the door four feet away from him.

I made the decision easier for him and moved two feet in the other direction. I even lowered my sword to let him think he had a sporting chance.

The girl cried out as he threw her at me. I caught her with one arm and set her aside.

The vampire sped toward the door. He was fast – at least fifty years old.

I was faster. My sword sliced through the side of his throat. He croaked and clamped his hand over the wound, but not before blood sprayed across

3

the Victorian-style wallpaper and the pale blue carpet.

The girl screamed.

I went after the vampire, who staggered to the door. Bringing my sword up, I skewered him through the heart with enough force to embed the tip of my blade in the wall behind him. I yanked it free, and he crumpled to the floor.

Chris appeared in the doorway, his own sword dripping blood. "That's the last of them. I found a human male upstairs. He's lost a lot of blood, but he'll live."

"Good."

We'd discovered four teenagers in the nest of seven vampires. That two of the humans had survived was a small miracle.

The girl whimpered.

Chris stood his sword against the wall and approached her slowly. "It's okay. You're safe now."

She threw herself at him, wrapping her arms around his waist as she sobbed. Chris gave me a helpless look, and I shrugged. There was nothing I could do for the girl he wasn't doing already.

I pulled out my cell and nodded toward the door. "Looks like you have the situation under control. I'll call Denis and tell him to send a cleanup crew."

The night was warm and muggy when I left the house and called the local unit to give them the address. I also let them know we had a couple of human teenagers needing medical attention. I waited for ten minutes until they pulled up in front of the house, and then I walked down the street to where Chris and I had parked our bikes in the driveway of an empty house.

Pulling off my bloody T-shirt, I found a clean spot and wiped my face. I used the shirt to wipe down my sword before I stowed the weapon away in the sheath that ran along the bottom of my seat.

I was donning a clean shirt when Chris walked up to me. "Why is it they never cling to you like that?" he asked as he went to his bike.

I laughed at his sullen expression. "Must be your smile that draws them to you."

He yanked off his shirt. "It wouldn't kill you to comfort them every now and then."

"But you are so good at it." I sat on my bike and waited for him to clean up. "I keep them alive and kill the bad guys."

I didn't need to add that I had no clue how to handle an overwrought teenager. Unlike Chris, I didn't associate with humans on any kind of personal level. They were my job. I protected them and kept them safe from the monsters they didn't know existed. As a warrior, it was better to remain detached. Closeness created emotions, and emotions created distractions. Distractions got you or the people you were protecting killed.

Chris scoffed and mounted his bike. "Beer?"

"Sounds good."

Thirty minutes later, freshly showered and changed, we walked into the bar down the street from our hotel. We found a table against the back wall, and I sat facing the door. I liked to know who – or what – was coming and going from a place while I was there.

A pretty blonde waitress came over to take our drink orders, and her red lips curved into an inviting smile when she looked from Chris to me.

"What can I get for you gentlemen?"

We ordered whatever they had on tap and a couple of burgers. The waitress lingered at the table for a moment before she went off to put in our order.

Chris leaned back and ran a hand through his blond hair. "I'd call that a good night's work."

"Yes."

My eyes swept the bar. At a corner table a young couple was making out, oblivious to everyone around them. I wouldn't have noticed them if I hadn't caught the gleam of silver in the male's eyes. Incubus. Most of the sex demons were careful not to harm humans when they fed from them, but there were some who loved the thrill of the kill. I wasn't sure yet which way this one swung.

A laugh drew my attention back to Chris. I shot him a questioning look.

"You are so predictable, my friend." He inclined his head toward the incubus. "We haven't had our first beer, and you're already looking for your next fight."

"Just keeping an eye on things."

The waitress returned with two glasses of draft and set them before us.

Chris picked up his beer and drank deeply. "Relax. I saw the two of them in here last night. If he was going to hurt her, he would have done it by now."

He was right. An incubus intent on killing his victim would do it within a few hours. He certainly wouldn't come back for a second date.

I gave the pair one last glance then turned my attention to my beer. I preferred a nice aged Scotch, but the rich lager was good for quenching thirst. I downed half the contents before I set the glass down and stretched out my legs beneath the table.

Chris looked at me as if he was waiting for me to say something. When I didn't, he said, "So, you want to stick around here for a few days?"

"I don't mind staying here for a day or two. They're having a problem with lamprey demons in Bywater, and I told Denis we'd give them a hand."

"That wasn't exactly what I had in mind," he replied dryly.

I let out a laugh. "What's her name?" Chris only suggested we take some downtime after a job when he'd met a female he wanted to get more acquainted with.

He grinned over the top of his beer. "Nora. She's a student at Tulane, and she invited us to a party at her sorority tonight."

"I think I'll pass." Intoxicated coeds were not my idea of an entertaining night. I could think of more pleasurable ways to spend an evening. An interesting book, a good game of poker, a bottle of Macallan, to name a few. Or a beautiful female friend who knew me well, in and out of the bedroom.

"Let me guess your plans for tonight. Prowling the streets to keep the good people of New Orleans safe, or staying in your room with a book?"

I suppressed a chuckle. He knew me too well. "Neither, actually. Viv's in town."

"Ah, the lovely Vivian. It's been a while, hasn't it?"

"Two years."

"That long?" He smiled over the rim of his glass. "I guess I won't be seeing you for breakfast then."

"Probably not." Or for lunch, knowing Viv.

Our food arrived, and as we ate, we talked about the job we'd just finished. A week ago, we'd gotten word of an increased vampire presence in New Orleans, along with a rash of missing persons, mostly teenagers. New Orleans was already a hub of supernatural activity that kept the local unit busy, so Chris and I had come to help them out with the vampire problem.

It had taken us three days to find one of the elusive vampires and trail him back to the nest in the Garden District. It didn't require much guesswork to know what had happened to the previous owner of the old house the vampires had claimed for their own. We'd watched the place for a day and then made our move.

I hadn't expected to find human survivors, and that made the job even more satisfying. I'd told the vampire I cared about the hunt more than the humans, but that was a lie. Nothing was more important than protecting human lives.

Chris crumpled his napkin and tossed it on his empty plate. "I was thinking we could head west when we leave Louisiana. There's always something going on out that way, and we could pay a visit to Longstone while we're there."

"How long has it been since you were home?" Longstone was the Mohiri stronghold in Oregon where Chris grew up. His parents moved to Germany a few years ago, but he still had family at the stronghold.

"I haven't been back since my parents left, almost three years."

I pushed my plate away and reached for my beer. "Sounds like a plan. We can stop over at Westhorne on the way."

His phone buzzed, and he smiled when he looked at the screen. "Right on time. I need to go meet my date." He stood and threw some money on the table. "Say hello to Vivian for me."

"Will do." I pulled out my phone and texted Viv, asking if she was up for some company.

I smiled when she replied immediately. **Do you need to ask?**

Tossing some cash on the table, I stood and headed for the door. **See you in ten.**

Vivian's suite was on the top floor of the Ritz-Carlton, and she answered the door wearing a white silk robe, with her long, blonde hair loose around her shoulders.

"Nikolas!" She pulled me into the room, hugging me before she'd even shut the door. "It's so good to see you."

Chuckling, I hugged her back. "Great to see you, too." I pulled back and looked down at her short robe that came to mid-thigh. "If I'd known you'd greet me like this, I would have come to visit you a lot sooner."

A throaty laugh slipped from her. She pulled my head down to hers for a slow, languid kiss that was sensual, but also warm and familiar. My other sexual encounters were just about mutual pleasure. Vivian Day was more than that. She was a good friend whose company I enjoyed, and there were no strings attached. She wanted to be tied down even less than I did, if that was possible.

Breaking the kiss, she took my hand and led me into the living room of her suite that had a great view of the French Quarter. She sat on the couch and made me sit beside her.

She arranged her robe around her legs. "I couldn't believe it when I heard you were in New Orleans. It's been too long."

"It has. But then you're the one who's always off on some mission for the Council whenever I'm on your side of the world."

"Maybe if you'd agree to work for them, we'd see each other more."

I stretched out my legs. "I love you, Viv, but I have zero interest in working for a bunch of bureaucrats. I respect the Council for what they do, but I prefer to work my own way."

She gave me a knowing smile. "Still haven't outgrown that little aversion to authority."

I laughed. "And you still know me better than anyone."

I'd known Vivian most of my life, our friendship going back to my early years in England when my sire was leader of Hadan Castle. Vivian and I had trained together, and the two of us had been competitive, driving each other to work harder.

She got up and went to the bar. "Drink? They didn't have any Macallan, but they brought up a bottle of Bowmore."

"Only if you're having one."

"Of course." She poured two drinks and came back to the couch, handing one to me. "I can't believe it's been two years. I remember when I couldn't imagine not seeing you every day."

"What was it you said back then? When we became warriors, we'd go off and hunt together, just the two of us."

Her eyes sparkled with laughter. "That's because I was afraid you'd beat me in vampire kills if I left you alone."

I sipped my drink. "And it had nothing to do with the huge crush you had on me?"

"Ha! If anyone had a crush, it was you. You were a lovesick fool that first time."

"I was a horny teenager, and the prettiest girl I knew wanted to have sex with me."

When she'd come to me one day and told me she wanted her first time to be with her best friend, my sixteen-year-old self had needed no persuasion. We still laughed over how awkward the two of us had been that first time.

She burst out laughing. "I'll never forget the look on your face when I asked you. You went from shocked to 'let's do it' in about five seconds."

"Three. I was trying not to look too eager."

"God, we were something." She took my free hand and laced our fingers together. "Sometimes I miss those days. Life was a lot simpler back then."

"Are you being nostalgic, or is something going on?"

"I'm great, just a little weary, I guess. I've been on the road for almost a year. You know how it is."

"I usually get back to Westhorne every month or two."

The life of a warrior often took you away from home for long periods, unless you were mated. Mated couples tended to stay closer to home, at least for the first few years. I couldn't stay in one place for a long time. Neither could Viv, which was one of the reasons both of us were happily unmated, much to our mothers' mutual despair.

She swirled the amber liquid in her glass. "I was surprised to hear you no longer work solo, and that you and Chris have been partnering on a lot of jobs."

"Yes. It keeps the Council off my back. Well, almost."

The Council of Seven was the ruling body for our people, and most of them had their own ideas about how things should be run in the field. They liked everyone to work in teams, and it annoyed them when someone didn't follow their protocols. I wasn't on their list of favorite people, and I didn't lose any sleep over it.

"So where is your partner tonight?" she asked with a smile that said she could already guess what Chris was up to.

"Sorority party."

She laughed. "Let me guess, not your thing?"

"You could say that. And I wouldn't pass up a chance to see you."

Her eyes softened. "You always say the sweetest things, Nikolas Danshov."

I finished my drink and gave her a small smile. "Keep that to yourself. I have a reputation to protect."

She grinned. "I'm well aware of your reputation, and I'll do what I can to keep it safe. But it's going to cost you."

"What's it going to cost?"

She stood and took my glass, setting it on the coffee table with hers. Then she reached for my hands and tugged me to my feet.

She turned to the bedroom. "I'm sure I can think of something."

*   *   *

"She's good, isn't she?" Chris inclined his head toward the small group of trainees practicing their swordplay. Most of them were skilled with the weapon, but the blonde moved with a lethal grace that I'd seen only in more experienced warriors. Next to her, the other trainees looked like children with toy swords.

I watched the girl's opponent lunge at her. At the last second, she parried and slipped her blade behind his, sending his weapon flying away from him.

I nodded. "She'll make a fine warrior."

The boy she'd disarmed retrieved his sword and turned to say something to her. He noticed us watching them and flushed. The other trainees stopped their practice and turned to see what their friend was staring at.

I inclined my head at them in acknowledgement.

Chris smirked. "Your adoring fans. Maybe you should give them a lesson while we're here."

"I'll leave that to the real trainers." I shouldered my bag and resumed my walk to the main building. Some people were cut out for teaching; I was not one of them. I had neither the patience nor the inclination toward that vocation, though I had a ton of admiration for those who did. There were few jobs more important than molding our youth into warriors capable of defending themselves when they went out into the world.

A grinning red-haired warrior left the building as we neared it. "About time you two showed your mugs around here. How long are you back for this time?"

"Couple of days," Chris said. "Thought you and Niall were still in Ireland."

"Nah. Got back last week." Seamus's eyes gleamed. "Brought back a couple of bottles of good Irish whiskey. Stop by later and we'll catch up."

"Sounds good." Anything that involved Seamus, his twin, and a bottle of whiskey promised to be entertaining.

Chris and I entered the building and went directly to the south wing. People greeted us as we passed, but we didn't stop to talk. I said good-bye to him at his door and stepped into my own apartment, dropping my bag on the floor. After a month away, it was nice to be back in my own place.

My gaze swept over the living room, taking in the dark colors and the simple yet comfortable décor. Aside from the portrait of my parents, there was no art on the walls. My collection of antique swords hung on one wall, and above the mantle was a pair of Flintlock pistols that had belonged to Alexander II – a gift from my sire who had received them from the emperor. There was a full bookcase and a state of the art audio system, but no television. I preferred it that way.

Kicking off my boots, I tossed my jacket on the back of the leather couch and headed for the shower to wash off the grime of the road. Ten minutes later, I emerged with a towel around my hips and put on my favorite sixties rock mix.

I was tempted to drop the towel and crash on the bed for a few hours, but I knew Tristan would be by when he got word we were here. I pulled on a T-shirt and a pair of sweats, grabbed my Slaughterhouse-Five paperback, and stretched out on the couch to read until he dropped in.

A little over an hour later, a knock came on the door. I called out for him to enter, and Tristan walked in wearing a wide smile.

"Heard you were back," he said, sitting in the leather chair across from me.

I sat up and laid my book on the couch beside me. "You're getting slow. I expected you half an hour ago."

He laughed and settled back in his chair. "Council business. You know how it is."

"No, I don't, and I'm happy that way."

Like any government, the Council spent half their time embroiled in debates and wrapped up in meetings. Some days, Tristan spent more time talking to the Council than he did running the affairs at Westhorne. Where he got the patience to handle them day after day was beyond me.

"Well, it shouldn't come as a surprise to you that we were discussing your latest job. They aren't happy you and Chris went into that nest in New Orleans without backup."

I had never explained my actions to the Council, and I wasn't going to start now. But Tristan was my friend, and I respected him too much to not tell him what he wanted to know.

"I would have invited Denis's team along, but you know how busy those guys are down there. Chris and I did our due diligence, and we knew exactly what we were facing when we went in. A nest of seven vampires is nothing we haven't faced before."

Tristan nodded. "The Council says you should have followed protocol and called in one of the teams from Houston or Atlanta once you located the nest."

"We could have, but we would have been too late to save those two human teenagers. And saving human lives *is* our first priority, is it not?"

"It is." His fingers tapped out a rhythm on the arm of the chair. "I'm required to tell you that you are too valuable to risk your life needlessly. And that you must follow procedure next time you are in a similar situation."

"Noted."

"Now that we have that out of the way." He smiled and leaned forward, resting his elbows on his knees. "How was New Orleans?"

"Busy. We helped Denis's people with a lamprey infestation, and we raided a gulak operation that was breeding bazerats. They could use some more people down there."

"I'll bring it up to the Council."

"Good." I knew Denis would have another team at his disposal by the end of the week.

Tristan gave me an amused look. "Surely it wasn't all work and no play. It is New Orleans after all."

I shrugged. "We ate, we drank, we listened to some good music. Chris got to know the locals a little better."

The two of us laughed because we knew how much his nephew loved getting to know the locals. Chris treated the females well, and he never made any promises he couldn't keep. He'd left a trail of pining hearts from the Atlantic to the Pacific.

"I heard Vivian is there for two weeks. Did you see her?"

"Yes. We spent some time catching up. It was great to see her again."

He smiled fondly. There were few who knew Viv and didn't like her. "Why didn't you stay on a few more days with her? You didn't need to rush back here."

I raised an eyebrow at him. "Careful. You are dangerously close to sounding like my mother."

My mother had two missions in her life: protecting humanity and seeing me happily settled. After almost two hundred years, you'd think she would let the second one go.

"Irina wants her son to be happy. It's what every parent wishes for their child." Sadness flickered in Tristan's eyes, and I knew he was thinking about Madeline. Over fifty years had passed since she'd left, but she was never far from her father's thoughts.

"I *am* happy," I grumbled.

He chuckled and looked around. "How long are you planning to stay this time?"

"Three or four days and then Chris wants to visit Longstone. From there, who knows?"

"Sometimes I envy you, my friend."

"I keep telling you to come with us. Claire is more than capable of managing Westhorne in your absence." And the Council would learn to deal with it. They deferred too much to Tristan as it was. The Seven ruled together, but at times they treated him like their unofficial leader.

"One of these days I'll take you up on that." He ran his hand through his blond hair. "How would you feel about postponing your trip to Oregon? We've received word of a possible vampire problem in Maine, and I was hoping you would look into it."

"Maine? That's werewolf territory. Vampires usually avoid that place like the plague."

"True, but there have been a number of disappearances in Portland in recent weeks. Four human girls have gone missing with no trace, all close to the same age. The authorities there have no evidence or leads. I might have dismissed it if we hadn't also gotten word of several dead bodies with animal attack listed as the cause of death."

"Do we have anyone in Portland now?" We didn't keep a permanent Mohiri presence in Maine because it was usually very quiet there.

"Erik's team is in Boston and they've been monitoring the situation, but they haven't found anything. We considered the possibility that the deaths could have been caused by a rogue wolf, but the werewolves would have dealt with it by now."

I rubbed my jaw. "Erik's good. If he can't find any leads, what makes you think I can?"

Tristan smiled. "Because you are the best at finding things when no one else can."

"Now you're just trying to butter me up."

"Is it working?"

"Maybe." He *had* piqued my curiosity, and he knew it. Mysterious disappearances in a quiet place like Portland, that was the kind of job I couldn't resist. "I'm sure Chris won't mind waiting a week or so to visit Longstone."

"Good." He clasped his hands together. "Perhaps you should take a team with you, just in case."

I laughed at his not-so-subtle attempt to get me to comply with the Council's wishes. "I don't think that'll be necessary. I'm sure this is nothing Chris and I haven't handled before."

"Famous last words, my friend."

The corner of my mouth lifted. "You'll see. We'll be in and out of Maine in no time."

CHAPTER 2

"LOOKS QUIET HERE, Nikolas."

I glanced at Chris and went back to studying the occupants of the club. He was right. This crowd was mostly college students who were more interested in dancing and hooking up than doing something nefarious. But Intel had identified this club as a place of interest because it was close to where the teenage girl had disappeared last Saturday. And our guys were rarely wrong.

"Let's give it another ten minutes, and then we'll head out."

Chris nodded and turned away to do another slow circuit of the room. "I'll meet you back here in ten."

I leaned against the wall, ignoring the restlessness plaguing me since we'd arrived at the club an hour ago. Five days in Portland without a lead on the vampires who'd taken those four girls. The vampires were still in the city; of that I was certain. There'd been several other deaths since we'd arrived in town, vagrants who did not make the five o'clock news. These vampires were good at staying out of sight even as they made their presence known. What I wanted to know was what had brought them to Portland, and why were they still here?

My thoughts were interrupted by an attractive blonde who approached me wearing an inviting smile.

"Hi. Want to dance?"

I stared at the girl, not because of her question, but because my demon suddenly stirred as it detected the presence of another Mori. Chris was too far away for it to be him, so that left the blonde girl. But she was young, and there was no way a Mohiri teenager would be out alone in a club. Plus, we had no strongholds in Maine.

The sensation began to fade, and my eyes were drawn instead to a dark-haired girl passing behind the blonde. I could only see the other girl's back before she entered the ladies' restroom, but she looked young. I watched the door, waiting for her to reappear.

The blonde girl made a sound, reminding me of her invitation to dance. I declined and went back to watching the restroom, not wanting to miss the dark-haired girl when she came out. As far as I knew, there were no female warriors working in Portland at the moment. So why would one of them be here, partying with human college students? And why was she here without her team, especially with all the vampire activity in the area?

A few minutes later, I frowned when the restroom door opened and the girl came out. She was younger than I'd expected, and pretty. She wore little makeup, and there was something about her expression, a wary innocence that made her look out of place here. She was too young to be a warrior and too old to be an orphan. *Obviously human.*

Behind the girl, two blondes left the restroom arguing loudly. The brunette shook her head and gave an eye roll that made the corner of my mouth twitch. I was curious about her even though she was not Mohiri as I'd suspected, and I watched her stop to let the other women pass her.

One of the blondes screamed an obscenity and gave her companion a shove just as they moved past the girl. Her friend stumbled backward, flailing her arms and colliding with the dark-haired girl. I took a step away from the wall as the two of them fell. The girl hit the floor hard, and I heard her grunt in pain as the heavier blonde landed on top of her.

I started toward them as a man grabbed the blonde's arms and lifted her off the girl.

"Is she all right?" someone asked when I reached the girl and looked down at her dazed expression.

I bent and waved a hand in front of her face. "Are you okay?"

She blinked and tried to sit up. "Um, I think so," she replied in a low, husky voice that made my breath catch.

I reached for her hand to help her up, and as soon as our fingers touched, a warm tingle shot through mine. My Mori quivered with recognition and...excitement? There was no doubt in my mind that the girl was Mohiri. But how was that possible? How was I able to sense her one minute and not in the next? And how could I have gotten this close to her and not sensed anything until we touched? Most importantly, what was she doing here instead of living in a stronghold?

The girl dropped my hand and looked up at me, her cheeks pink and her full lips parted in a timid smile. Her eyes met mine, and I sucked in a sharp breath as I stared into beautiful green eyes framed by long dark lashes. If the eyes truly are the windows to the soul then I knew I was looking at one of the purest souls I had ever seen. I was only dimly aware of my Mori pressing forward and the strange fluttering sensation coming from the demon. All I could focus on was the feeling that I'd somehow met this girl before, even though I knew it was impossible. I never would have forgotten those eyes or that face.

Realizing we were only inches apart, I took a step back. She looked away, and I felt strangely bereft and more than a little confused by my reaction to her. I'd seen thousands of beautiful women in my life, and not one of them had drawn me in the way this slip of a girl did.

Her eyes lifted to mine again, and she smiled. "Sorry, I must have banged my head harder than I thought."

The wave of emotions that slammed into me nearly drove me to my knees. Something base and primal welled up inside my chest, and I was gripped by an almost uncontrollable need to touch the girl.

What the hell? I clenched my teeth as I fought the insane urge as well as my agitated Mori. I hadn't lost control of my demon since I was a child, and it shocked me to my core that I was fighting it now.

It took me several seconds to realize the girl had left, and I looked around in time to see her disappearing into the crowd.

Who is she? Mohiri, obviously, but what was she doing here alone? She was at least seventeen or eighteen – too old to be an orphan. More importantly, why were my Mori and I so damn affected by her?

Something caught the light at my feet, and I bent to pick it up. As soon as I touched the warm silver cross, I knew it was hers. The cross was old, and something told me she would be upset if she lost it.

It wasn't hard to guess where she'd gone, and when I stepped out onto the deck, I found her alone at the rail, staring out into the night. She rubbed her temple, and I wondered if she had hurt herself when she fell.

The sight of her brought on another disturbing jumble of emotions – want, protectiveness, desire, fear – and I started to turn around and go back inside. I couldn't deal with this now – whatever this was. I'd find Chris, have him talk to her and find out her story.

A soft sigh drew my attention back to the girl, and my gut clenched at how small and vulnerable she looked out here alone. Something about her tugged at me in a way I could not comprehend, and I found myself walking toward her.

"I believe this is yours."

She gasped and spun, staring at the broken necklace hanging from my fingers. Her hand went to her neck, and then she reached for the necklace cautiously as if she half expected me to grab her.

"Thank you," she said softly as she tucked it away in her pocket.

I studied her face, confused by what I was sensing and feeling. She was definitely Mohiri, of that I had no doubt, but her Mori was so quiet it seemed to be asleep. When two Mohiri get within a few feet of each other, our demons sense each other. My Mori was desperately trying to reach out to the girl's Mori, but it wasn't getting a response. I was mystified by my demon's strong need to connect with this particular Mori, and by my own attraction to the girl.

"Are you done?"

Her blunt question shook me from my musings, and I stared at her in surprise. Tonight I had been approached and flirted with by more women than I could count, but this girl plainly wanted nothing to do with me. For some reason that thought did not sit well with me.

"You're a bit young for this place," I said sorely.

Her chin lifted. "I'm sorry but I don't think that is any of your business."

"You can't be more than seventeen or eighteen," I countered, intrigued by the emerald fire in her eyes. "You shouldn't be here alone."

"You're not much older than me. And I'm not here alone."

"I'm older than I look," I replied, unsure if I was annoyed with her or myself for feeling this unreasonable swell of jealousy at her words. I didn't know a thing about this girl; why should I care if she was here with another male?

I ran my hand through my hair and gave a silent groan of frustration. *What the hell is wrong with me tonight?*

"Nikolas," called Chris, and I turned to see him in the doorway wearing an amused expression. "Ready to move out?"

"No," I almost said, because I was suddenly reluctant to leave this mysterious girl who drew me like a moth to a flame. I didn't even know her name, for Christ's sake.

But I would. She was a young Mohiri out in a part of the city where vampires prowled. It was my duty to protect her and to discover who she was and what had brought her here. The glint in her eyes told me she was not going to be forthcoming with me if I asked her straight out. There was a wariness about her that said she did not trust easily.

"Be out shortly, Chris," I told him, though I'd already decided we were not leaving. We were going to stick around and watch the girl to make sure she was safe here. Then I was going to follow her home and find out who she was. It had nothing to do with the strange protective instinct she stirred in me. I was a warrior, and she was my responsibility.

My mind made up, I strode to the door, turning to her before I reentered the club. "Stay with your friends. This part of town is not safe for a girl alone at night." Not that she needed to worry. Chris and I would make sure she and her friends got home safely.

"I'll keep that in mind," she said quietly.

Chris grinned at me when I joined him inside. "You sure you're ready to leave, my friend?"

"Not quite." His grin grew, and I scowled at him. "It's not what you think. She's Mohiri."

"What?" His eyes widened. "She can't be more than eighteen. What is she doing here?"

"That's what we're going to find out." I scanned the crowded club for anyone who looked like they could be with the girl, but no one stood out. "She said she's not here alone. I plan to watch her and her friends, and make sure she gets home before I start asking questions."

Chris looked behind me at the girl still standing on the deck. "You know, she reminds me of someone, but I can't put my finger on it."

"I know what you mean. It feels like I've met her before, but I'd remember her if I had."

He gave me a sly look. "Memorable, is she?"

"She is different," I admitted. Then I got down to business. "Let's split up. I'll watch the girl, and you keep an eye out for trouble."

"Sounds like a plan."

He melted away into the crowd, and I settled back into the same shadowy corner I'd inhabited before the girl caught my eye.

Less than a minute later, she entered the club and passed by me without looking in my direction. My eyes followed her as she crossed the room and joined two teenage boys at the edge of the dance floor. The tall, dark-haired one grinned affectionately at her when she stood beside him, and she gave him a sweet smile in return.

Something dark and savage reared up inside me, making my entire body stiffen and my hands clench into fists at my sides. My Mori growled, and a fierce possessiveness roared through me.

Mine!

Mine? What the –? I forgot how to breathe as the truth slowly filtered through the turmoil of my emotions. *It can't be.*

Solmi, my Mori insisted angrily.

"*Khristu!*" I sagged against the wall as my strength deserted me.

She was my mate.

Mate. The word sounded foreign, alien, as it repeated in my head. How was this possible? In my almost two hundred years, I must have met a thousand Mohiri women, with not a single potential mate among them. What were the odds of me finding one in a night club, in a city I hadn't been to in fifty years? I wouldn't even be here now if I hadn't been doing a favor for Tristan.

My gaze travelled across the club, drawn to the girl. As soon as I found her, my heart thudded against my ribs, and I felt the swell of raw emotions again. *Mate.*

I tore my eyes away from her. I knew males who had bonded – Tristan was one of them – but I'd never asked them what it felt like. I hadn't wanted to know. We were taught about bonding when we were children, but nothing in my education had prepared me for this barrage of emotions for someone I hadn't known existed thirty minutes ago. I'd talked to her for all of five minutes, yet every detail of her face from her emerald green eyes to her full pink lips was etched in my memory.

Pushing away from the wall, I moved through the crowded club until I found a spot closer to her and her friends, but out of sight. This close, I could hear her laugh when her dark-haired friend said something to her. The sound was warm and rich, and it sent heat straight to my groin. *Jesus.* I took a deep breath and released it slowly. I was behaving like a goddamn teenager.

Stop it, demon, I commanded, and then I realized I was actually talking to my Mori. Who the hell did that? But from the moment I touched the girl, the damn demon had been straining against me and flooding me with irrational emotions.

I set my jaw and pushed all those thoughts aside. No matter what was going on with me, the girl was a young Mohiri who should be in a stronghold, not out here in a club. She had to be an orphan; that was the only explanation for her presence here. But why hadn't she shown any sign of recognition when we were together, and why was her Mori so quiet? If she was an orphan as I suspected, how was she in control of her demon at all? I had too many questions, and she was the only one who could answer them.

My phone vibrated, and Chris's name flashed on the screen.

"Find something?" I asked him.

"Just got word that someone reported a body in the parking deck down the street. Thought we should check it out before the police arrive. I can go if you want to stay and watch the girl."

I looked at her again. She was dancing with her friends, and they didn't appear to be leaving anytime soon.

Suddenly, fresh air and distance from her sounded like an excellent idea.

"She'll be okay here for a few minutes. I'll meet you outside."

Chris was waiting for me when I got to our bikes parked behind the club in the employee lot. He was quiet as I donned my harness and sword. When I looked up, I found him watching me.

"What?"

He shook his head. "I don't know. You seem distracted."

"I'm fine."

He didn't look convinced, but he didn't push it. That was one of the things I liked about Chris. He knew when to let something go and move on.

Normally, we'd walk the short distance to the parking garage, but we needed to be in and out before the police got there. We used our Mori speed to get us there in less than thirty seconds. The body was on the second level, between two cars, and thankfully, whoever had reported it hadn't stuck around to wait for the authorities.

Chris went to examine the body. It was a young man in his early twenties, wearing a college letterman jacket. I could smell the blood before Chris rolled the body over to expose the neck wounds.

"Body's still warm. He hasn't been dead long." Chris stood. "Definitely vampire. Looks like our guys were right about… Where are you going?"

"Back to the club for the girl." I cursed myself for leaving her unprotected. Hadn't I been the one to tell her this place wasn't safe for her? I should have stayed with her and let Chris investigate the body. But I'd let emotion overrule my common sense and left her alone. Now that I knew there was a vampire in the vicinity, all I could think about was getting back to my orphan and keeping her safe.

My orphan? I shook my head. Jesus. I was already feeling possessive, and I didn't even know her name.

"Nikolas." Chris's voice was laced with amusement. "Are you planning to enter the club looking like that?"

I glanced down at my leather harness, and my jaw clenched. Chris was right; I *was* distracted.

"I'm going to scout the area while you cover the girl," Chris said before he headed off in another direction, no doubt having a good laugh over my odd behavior. Wait until he heard the girl was my mate. He'd probably fall on his sword from laughing so hard.

Potential mate, I reminded myself. Discovering you had a bond with someone didn't mean you had to take it further. People had been known to walk away from bonds before they had a chance to grow. I liked my life the way it was, and I had no desire to add a mate to it.

Hell, maybe I was wrong about the whole thing anyway. A bond was a two-way thing, so the girl should have felt something. But she hadn't shown a hint of recognition.

Then what the hell is wrong with me?

A muffled sound from the alley beside the club pulled me from my thoughts as I reached my bike. It was probably nothing, but with a vampire in the area, I had to check it out.

I stepped into the alley just as a terrified female voice floated toward me. "No!"

That single word made ice form in my veins. My first instinct was to run to her, but almost two centuries of hunting made me move slowly into the alley to assess the situation before I acted on it.

I almost forgot every one of my years of experience when I saw her. The vampire had her pressed against the building with his mouth at her throat. Her eyes were closed, but the terror coming from her was almost palpable.

Red tinged my vision, and I had to force myself to think clearly and weigh my options. I could reach them in a second, but if the vampire was mature, he would rip her throat out before I got him away from her. If she was going to make it out of this alive, I had to approach this like it was just another job.

The vampire murmured something. Then his head jerked up, and he stared at the girl. It was time to make my entrance.

"Now, that is no way to treat a young lady." The thought of any young Mohiri in the hands of a vampire angered me, but seeing this vampire touch *her* awakened something feral and dark inside me.

The vampire spun until he was backed against the wall with her body shielding him. "You are very brave, my friend, but you will move on if you know what's good for you."

"I have been told that I don't heed orders well." I walked into the light so the vampire could see me. Few vampires would stay and face an armed Mohiri warrior. If this one had any sense of self-preservation, he would release the girl and run.

The vampire let out a frightened hiss. "Mohiri!"

One of my rules was to never take my attention away from a vampire, but it required all of my self-control not to look at her. I could not afford to lose my focus now.

I laughed, feigning a calm I didn't feel. "I see there is no need for introductions. Good. I hate to waste time on formalities."

The vampire's clawed hand went to her throat. "Stay back or I will rip her apart."

I couldn't stop myself, and my gaze flicked to her face. The fear and pleading in her eyes made my Mori push closer to the surface. It wanted out, but I had to play it cool. The moment the vampire realized the girl was more than a job to me, he would use that to his advantage.

"A bit melodramatic, don't you think?" I said lightly as I took a step toward them.

His voice rose. "Her death will be on your hands, Mohiri." He closed his eyes briefly, and my body coiled to attack when I saw a thin rivulet of blood trail down her throat. The smell of her blood was stirring his bloodlust, and the look on his face made it clear how much he wanted her.

My Mori saw it too, and it seethed beneath my skin, its voice melding with mine. "Do it and it will be your last act, vampire."

"Brother, how like you to sneak off and sample the sweets by yourself. And look at the trouble it has brought you."

I looked up at the second vampire standing on the fire escape. *Damn it. I should have known he wouldn't be alone. Sloppy, Nikolas.* I flexed my jaw. I hadn't been thinking straight ever since I'd met this girl. If I didn't get it together, I'd get us both killed. Fortunately, two vampires was nothing I hadn't faced before. My fear was the risk to her.

"Come now, Joel," said the vampire holding her. His voice grew cocky with the arrival of his friend. "You know I always save some for you."

Joel laughed. "I think I deserve a little more than a nibble this time. Mmm…she looks like a tasty little bit."

"This one is mine," said the one holding her.

Over my dead body.

"No!" She jerked away from him, and her eyes found mine.

Before I could move in, the vampire yanked her back against him, and his friend landed beside them. It looked like they were going to try to fight their way out of this. Worry for her safety ate at me as I drew my sword, but I kept my face impassive.

The first vampire sneered at me and voiced my fears. "You can't take us both and save her. She will die, and your efforts will be for naught."

I met his challenging stare. "Then I will have to settle for killing only you."

His smile faltered. "Bold words for one outnumbered."

"Sara?" called a male voice, and all four of us looked toward the alley entrance. I sniffed the air and smiled as my Mori picked up a new and unexpected scent. Werewolves.

"Sara, where are you?" yelled a second male.

The recognition on her face told me she was the Sara they were calling for. My sense of smell was stronger when my Mori was near the surface, which must be why I hadn't scented them in the club. It seemed my orphan was full of surprises.

I laughed at the shock on the vampires' faces. "Do you smell that, my friends? I believe the odds just changed."

Joel nudged his friend. "Come, brother. There are sweeter meals to be had."

"No. I want this one."

I bit back a growl at the possessiveness in his voice. "Release her or die, your choice. And you'd better make up your mind soon."

"Sara, damn it, where are you?" her friend called, closer this time.

The vampires shifted nervously. Sara cried out, and I tensed to spring.

One of the boys shouted. Then a loud growl echoed down the alley.

I waited for the vampires to release Sara and run. No prize – even a young Mohiri – was worth staying and facing an armed warrior and two werewolves. As soon as the vampire let her go, I'd grab her and pull her to safety.

A werewolf pounded into the alley. He was huge for a young wolf, and his sights were on Sara.

The vampires cried out, and the one holding Sara jumped for the fire escape, his arm still locked around her waist.

No! I lunged for them, but the second vampire, the one named Joel, used the distraction to swing at me with his claws. He nicked my side and jumped back out of the range of my sword. He was old and fast, and the arrogant smirk on his face said he thought he could take me alone.

Any other time, it would have been my pleasure to fight him, but my only thought now was getting to Sara. If that vampire got away with her…

I tightened my grip on my sword. No. I wouldn't let that happen.

Joel snarled and came at me again in a blur of movement. I spun away from his attack and brought my sword up, laying open his shirt and scoring his chest. He grunted and danced away again.

Sara's scream tore my eyes away from him. I looked to my right to see the other vampire halfway up the ladder to the first landing. He was kicking frantically at the werewolf latched on to his leg. Sara fought the vampire wildly, but he was determined to hold on to her. A few feet away from them, the second werewolf stood watching his friends and looking unsure of what to do.

Joel came at me again, and I parried his attack just in time. He stumbled back, holding his hand over his bleeding shoulder.

"You're good, Mohiri, but you aren't good enough to save her," Joel taunted as he darted back and forth out of my reach. "Eli is going to have so much fun with her. He loves pretty young things, especially brunettes, and I've never seen him this hot for one. He'll make her scream."

Enraged, I struck at him again. This time my blade sliced through muscle and bone, severing his left arm just below the shoulder. He screamed and grabbed his stump.

I risked another look over my shoulder, and my heart lodged into my throat. Eli had escaped the werewolf, and he was halfway up the fire escape with Sara still in his clutches. The werewolf was climbing after them, but he was too slow. He'd never catch them in time.

My Mori needed no urging, and it sent fresh waves of strength through me. I moved and my blade was at the vampire's throat before he knew what had hit him. His head flew into the brick wall as his body crumpled.

I spun to the fire escape before the body hit the pavement.

God, no.

Eli and Sara were only feet from the roof, with the werewolf too far below to catch them. In another second, Eli would reach for the roof, taking her with him.

Without thinking, I pulled a knife from my harness and threw it at the vampire.

Eli screamed and stopped climbing. He reached for the silver knife buried deep in his side, but he couldn't get to it while holding Sara and the ladder.

I drew out a second blade, prepared to throw it.

The vampire's eyes fell on me and moved to the werewolf advancing on him. Determination crossed his face as he abandoned the knife and grabbed the ladder rung above his head.

I pulled back my arm, but stopped mid-throw when Sara reached down and yanked the knife from the vampire's side. *What is she doing?* I thought, a second before she plunged the blade into his shoulder.

Pride surged in me. She was a fighter.

The vampire screamed and almost lost his grip on her. She dangled precariously three stories above the ground.

I've got you. I raised my throwing arm again and stopped. Sara's body was shielding most of Eli's, and with them struggling, I could too easily hit her instead.

Her eyes met mine, and I saw the raw fear and resolve on her face.

"Do it!" she screamed. Her voice broke. "Nikolas…please."

Hearing her speak my name felt like she had reached her hand into my chest and squeezed my heart. I couldn't look away from her as I released the knife.

The vampire cried out as the blade found its mark in his other shoulder. Struggling frantically, he snarled at Sara.

Then he released her.

CHAPTER 3

I DROPPED MY sword and cradled my arms to soften the impact of her fall. My arms closed around her, and I held her against my chest as I breathed hard to maintain my cool. The feel of her soft body against mine awoke something other than protectiveness inside me. In that moment, I didn't want to ever let her go.

A low growl nearby reminded me we were not alone. One of the werewolves crept closer to me. The other had shifted back to his human form and was racing down the fire escape.

"Sara!" the dark-haired boy yelled before his bare feet hit the ground. He ran to us and held out his arms for her. "Is she...?"

I made no move to hand her over to him. "She passed out, but she's okay."

The boy let out a harsh breath. "I don't know how to thank you." He reached for her again. "You can give her to me."

The affectionate way he looked at her made me want to crush her to my chest. There was no way I was handing my...orphan over to a naked male, even if he was her friend.

"You might want to get dressed before she wakes up," I suggested dryly.

"Shit!" The boy and his friend ran to the mouth of the alley. I heard them talking in hushed voices as they pulled on their clothes.

I studied the dark lashes and pale skin of the girl in my arms, and breathed in her scent that was a mix of sunshine and spring rain. Never had I found those scents overly appealing, but on her the combination was alluring and sweet at the same time. My eyes moved over her lips, and I had to resist the sudden urge to taste them.

She looked so young and innocent, and I would have given anything to have shielded her from the evil she'd faced tonight. She'd been incredibly brave, but I worried about how she would be affected by all of this when she woke up.

The attack wasn't the only thing she'd have to cope with. Her lack of fighting skills proved she was no warrior, or even a trainee. She *was* an orphan, and she was in for an even bigger shock when she learned the truth about what she was.

I still had no idea how she had survived this long on her own. I'd need to call for someone who had experience dealing with orphans and helping them acclimate to their new life. Paulette worked with the most difficult cases. I'd call her.

"I'll take her now." The dark-haired boy approached me slowly as if he half expected me to run away with her.

I reluctantly placed her in his outstretched arms, and then I cursed myself for the sudden rush of sentimentality. I should be off tracking down that vampire, not standing here acting like a lovesick boy.

"Thank you again," her friend said thickly. He held her like she was a porcelain doll that might break if handled too roughly. I got the impression that *none* of them knew what she really was.

And none of them had any business being here. What was the pack thinking, allowing their pups, and what they obviously believed to be a human girl, out at night with vampires roaming the city?

I was furious at them and at myself for letting the vampire get away. I snatched up my sword and sheathed it, then reached for the fire escape. Silver wounds slowed a vampire down, but a mature vampire could still cover ground quickly.

"Take her home," I growled over my shoulder.

"Where are you going?" the red-haired boy asked.

"Hunting." I started up the ladder without looking back. "Get her out of here."

On the roof, I found the vampire's blood trail. I called Chris to let him know what had happened, and he said he'd try to pick up the trail on the ground. I let my Mori come closer to the surface to enhance my senses. I could already see and hear far better than a human, but the more my demon emerged, the easier it was to smell the vampire's blood.

I followed the blood trail across the rooftops of four buildings before it disappeared. At the last building, I made my way to the ground, but the trail was cold. Chris was a good tracker, and if the vampire was anywhere in the area, he would find him.

I swore softly. I should have handed the girl over to her friend as soon as I'd caught her and then gone after the vampire. A warrior fresh out of training would have done this job better than I had tonight. I wasn't used to failure, and I didn't like it one bit.

My mood was dark when I started back to the bikes. But instead of going behind the club, I stood in the shadow of a building where I could observe Sara and her friends, unseen. She was awake and sitting on a bench with the werewolves on either side of her. My gut twisted when I saw how lost and scared she looked, but there was nothing I could do for her now. I'd find out where she lived and send someone to collect her. It was better that way.

I watched them stand and walk to a blue Toyota parked on the street. Easy enough. I'd catch the license plate when they drove past me.

Sara and the dark-haired wolf got in the car. The redhead stood outside and made a phone call, most likely to his Alpha if his unhappy expression was any indication. The news that vampires had attacked someone in werewolf territory was bound to get the pack riled up, and Maine had the largest werewolf population in the country.

The boy hung up and got into the back of the car. I waited for them to drive away, but they sat there talking. After a few minutes, worry began to gnaw at me. Why hadn't they left? Was something wrong? She'd looked okay as they'd walked to the car, but there was no telling how an ordeal like that would affect her.

Before I realized what I was doing, I left the shadows and strode toward the car. The werewolves jumped out of the car and intercepted me before I reached it.

"I thought you left," the dark-haired boy said harshly.

"I came back."

He scowled. "About that. What is a hunter doing around here? This is not Mohiri territory."

Instead of answering him, I looked past them at the girl approaching us. She was pale, but otherwise she looked unharmed, and I couldn't help but admire her resilience.

"Hello again. You seem to have recovered quickly from your adventure." When she didn't reply, I waved a hand at her two companions. "So, these are the friends you spoke of earlier. It's no wonder you were attacked, with nothing but a pair of pups to protect you."

"Hey!" the redhead protested angrily.

She pushed between the boys, clearly not happy about my criticism of her friends. "It's not their fault. How could they have known something like this would happen?"

"How indeed?"

A frown creased her brow. "What do you mean? What's going on here?" She turned to the dark-haired boy. "Roland? Do you know this guy?"

This guy? My demon and I had been in turmoil since we met her, and she had no clue who I was or my connection to her.

Roland shook his head. "I've never seen him before."

"But you know something about him? What does Mohiri mean?"

"I am Mohiri," I said, drawing her attention back to me.

26

She gave me an appraising look. "And you hunt vampires."

"Among other things."

I studied her in return. Most people would be in a quivering heap after experiencing what she had been through. I could see she was still shaken by the attack, but she wasn't at all intimidated by the sight of an armed warrior.

She looked unsatisfied by my answer. "What about your friend from the club? Is he a hunter, too? Why didn't he help you?"

"Chris scouted the area for more hostiles while I handled the situation here." Considering she'd only seen Chris for a moment in the club, it surprised me she remembered him after everything that had happened.

She shook her head and gave me a wry smile. "So what happened? Did you get the short straw or something?"

"Or something." If it were only that simple.

The redhead spoke up. "What about the other vampire? Did you get him?"

"Chris is tracking him."

Roland stared at me with a mixture of disbelief and alarm. "He got away?"

"He's injured, so he won't get too far," I said to assure Sara more than her friend. "Don't worry. He won't stick around here now that he's being hunted."

Roland did not look convinced. "We should put some distance between us and this place all the same."

They should have left when I'd told them to go. There was no telling how many more vampires were in the area.

"You live in Portland?" I asked.

The three of them shook their heads.

"Good. The farther you get from the city, the better. It's not safe here right now." I didn't want her anywhere near this city with that vampire out there, injured or not.

"No shit." Roland took her arm. "We need to get out of here."

He tugged her gently toward the car, and I stayed where I was, feeling a mixture of relief and dejection. I shook my head to clear it. The bond was new, and I didn't think it should affect me like this so soon. I was closer to Viv than I'd ever been with any other female, and I'd never felt anything like this for her. It made me feel naked and vulnerable, and I didn't like it.

Sara pulled away from her friend and spun back toward me. "Thank you…for what you did. If you hadn't come when you did…" Her voice broke, and she appeared to be fighting back tears.

Her green eyes met mine, and I felt myself being pulled into them. My protective instincts flared, and for a moment, all I wanted to do was pull her to me and wrap her in my arms.

I caught myself before I took a step toward her. *What the hell am I doing?* I needed to put as much distance between us as possible. I definitely should not be entertaining any thoughts of holding her. The sooner she got out of here, the better it would be for both of us.

"Just doing my job."

I regretted my cold words as soon as they left my mouth, especially when she flinched and hurt crossed her face.

"Oh…okay, well, thanks anyway," she said quietly before she turned away to join her friends.

I watched her walk to the car, waiting for her to turn around and look at me again. But she got in the car, ignoring me as if I didn't even exist.

Probably for the best. I melted back into the shadows and watched them drive away, ignoring the part of me that wanted to jump on my bike and follow them. I caught the license plate and pulled out my phone to shoot off an email to one of the security guys at Westhorne. It wouldn't take Dax long to track her down. I'd call Paulette and let her know we had a new orphan that needed help, and then I could get back to business as usual.

* * *

"Seems our boy likes pool."

I watched the young blond vampire we'd been following enter the pool hall as if he hadn't a care in the world. If he'd paid attention to his surroundings, he might have noticed he'd had a tail for the last five blocks. Today's vampires were less vigilant than those created a century ago, which was why most of them did not live to maturity. Their increased strength and speed made them feel invincible, and that made them cocky and careless. It also made for easy hunting.

Chris or I could have taken this one down at any time, but I was hoping he'd lead us to his friends first, namely the vampire I'd let get away last night. Vampires rarely traveled alone, and the odds of two different groups of them showing up in Portland at the same time were slim.

We were halfway across the street when a gray sedan pulled up and four males got out. Downwind from them, I picked up the scent easily this time. They stood in front of the car and quietly watched us approach.

"It looks like we aren't the only ones on the hunt tonight," I said.

The largest man, a tall stocky one with reddish-brown hair, nodded. "So it would seem. We don't see your kind here often. What brings you to Portland?"

"We heard about the human girls that went missing here recently, and we suspected vampires." I gave the entrance to the pool hall a meaningful look. "Appears we were right."

The man, who appeared to be the leader of the group, crossed his arms over his chest. "We sent some of our people to check out the disappearances. They couldn't pick up the vampires' trail, so we thought they'd moved on."

"This lot is good at covering their trail...except for the one we followed here," Chris said.

"You mean the one *we* followed." A dark-haired man who couldn't be much older than twenty sneered at us. "We'll take care of it from here."

Ignoring him, I addressed the older man. "You can have the vampire after we ask him a few questions."

The young one took a step forward. "This is *our* territory, and we'll decide how to handle the bloodsucker."

"Like I said, you can do what you want with him when I'm done." I couldn't help but notice the young wolf bore a slight resemblance to Sara's friend, Roland.

"Listen here. You don't —"

"That's enough," barked the leader, putting an arm out to restrain the hothead.

"But Brendan —"

"I said *enough*, Francis." A low growl entered his voice, and the younger man backed off, glaring at us. The older man didn't act like an Alpha, but he was definitely someone with authority in the pack. The Beta, most likely.

The other two males kept silent, apparently content to let their leader do all the talking. He studied me for a long moment. "What information do you hope to get from the vampire?"

"I hope he can lead me to the vampire who got away from me last night." I saw no reason to keep anything from them. Mohiri and werewolves were not friends, but we had a common enemy.

The man's expression told me he knew exactly what vampire I was referring to, but he wouldn't speak of it. Werewolves were almost as secretive as my own people, and if Sara was a friend of the pack, they would protect her as if she was one of them. Would they feel the same way when they learned what she was?

"We'll give you thirty minutes with him."

I nodded. "Fair enough. We'll send him out the back when we're done."

The man stepped aside, despite the muttered objections of his young pack member, and Chris and I walked past them to the entrance of the pool hall. Chris opened the door, and loud music assailed us along with the smell of sweat and beer.

The interior of the club was dimly lit except for the lights hanging over the pool tables. Along one wall ran a long bar that was already crowded, and small tables filled the rest of the floor. It was only nine o'clock and the place was over half-full.

It took me less than thirty seconds to locate our target. He stood at the end of the bar near a dark hallway, talking to a brunette in a low-cut blouse and a short, leather skirt that left little to the imagination. She might as well have rung a dinner bell. The vampire was practically salivating over her.

My eyes met Chris's in silent communication. He nodded and began to make his way around the room, while I set off in the other direction. Fortunately, the vampire was too wrapped up in procuring his next meal to notice us. He wasn't a match for either of us, but the less attention we drew, the better.

The vampire looked up when I was six feet away, and something in my expression spooked him. Fear flashed in his eyes, and he took a step back, but Chris came up behind him and grabbed him by the arms.

"Not a word," I heard Chris whisper to him.

I smiled at the female. "Would you mind giving us a few minutes? We have some business to discuss with our friend."

She tossed her hair over one shoulder and looked me up and down. "Baby, I'll give you anything you ask for."

I slapped on the bar to get the attention of one of the bartenders. He came over, and I handed him a twenty. "Give the lady whatever she wants to drink. Keep the change."

"Thanks, man." He turned to the brunette. "What's your poison?"

She leaned against the bar, putting her breasts on display. "I'd love a White Russian."

Chris made a noise and smirked at me over the vampire's shoulder.

My lips curved, and I nodded toward the hallway that led to the restrooms and the back exit. Wordlessly, Chris forced the silently struggling vampire to the end of the hallway.

Once we were away from the humans, I pushed the vampire against the wall, easily holding him there. "I'm going to ask you some questions. Whether or not you walk out of here will depend on how you answer them."

He swallowed convulsively and nodded.

"Where is Eli?"

"Wh-who?"

I shook my head slowly. "Wrong answer."

He hissed in pain when a knife suddenly appeared in my hand, the blade pressed lightly against a spot under his ear. It was barely touching him, but the silver made a wisp of smoke rise from his singed skin.

"Let me ask that question again. Where is Eli?"

"I don't know," he squeaked, trying to lean away from the knife. I pressed harder and he whimpered. "I'm not lying! I haven't seen him since last night. No one has."

"Who is no one? How many of you are here?"

His eyes were fixed on the hand holding the knife. "T-ten."

Ten vampires was an unusually large group to be travelling together.

Something important had drawn them to Maine and had made them willing to risk discovery by the werewolves. There was much better hunting to be found in larger cities like New York and Philadelphia.

I thought of the four missing human girls, and then another face filled my mind. I remembered Sara's terror as Eli held her against him. If I'd been just a few minutes later, she might have suffered the same fate as those other girls.

The thought of her at Eli's mercy made my hand tighten on the knife. A thin rivulet of blood ran down the vampire's throat.

Chris laid a hand on my arm, and I eased the pressure on the knife. A dead vampire could not answer questions. And I had promised the werewolves the kill. As much as I hated letting a vampire walk away, I was a man of my word.

"What are you doing in Portland?" I asked harshly. "Your kind isn't usually stupid enough to walk into werewolf territory."

His eyes widened, telling me he had been unaware of that fact. "Eli didn't tell us why we're here. We just go where he tells us to go."

I wasn't surprised by his answer. Most vampires worked together out of necessity, not loyalty. "How long have you been in Portland? Why are you here?"

"We got here three weeks ago, and we haven't done much but hide out in the place Eli found for us. He goes out with Joel, but I don't know what they're doing. He…."

"He what?"

The vampire cleared his throat. "He brought some human girls back to the house, but he kept them to himself."

I knew the answer before I asked my next question, but I had to ask it anyway. "Are the girls still alive?"

Terror flashed in his eyes. "No. Eli killed them, not me!"

Experience told me I wasn't getting anything useful out of this one - except for maybe one thing. "Where are you and your friends holed up?"

The vampire stared at me but didn't answer. I suspected it was fear for his own life and not loyalty to the other vampires that kept him quiet.

"Here's the deal, and it's the only one you'll get. You tell us where your friends are, and we'll let you walk out that door. Or you can choose not to answer, which is not in your best interest. Trust me."

Doubt and hope filled his eyes. "You'll really let me go?"

I lowered the knife. "I give you my word as a warrior that you'll walk out that door unharmed. But if I see you again, you won't fare as well."

His eyes darted to the door, and he nodded jerkily. "Okay, I'll tell you. We're staying in a place on Fletcher Street." He rattled off an address. "That's all I know. I swear. Can I go now?"

I released him and stepped back, clearing a path to the exit. "Go."

The vampire lunged for the door and pulled it open. Without a look back, he ran outside into the alley at the rear of the building. As the door closed behind him, I heard a chorus of growls followed by a muffled scream.

Chris blew out a noisy breath. "Ten vampires?"

"I know. Something is up, and we're going to get to the bottom of it."

"We should call in a unit for this one," Chris said as we headed for the front exit. "Unless you're in the mood to piss off the Council again."

I laughed, remembering my last talk with Tristan. "Let's call Erik. His team is closest."

Chris made the call. "They'll be here in two hours."

We left the building and headed back to our bikes. My mind kept replaying what the vampire had said about Eli and the teenage girls, and the more I dwelled on it, the more I wanted to hit something.

"You want to tell me why you're in such a black mood tonight?"

I gave Chris a sideways glance. "I'm not in a mood."

He made a sound suspiciously like a snort. "How long have we known each other? You have the coolest head of any warrior I've ever met, but you almost killed that vampire back there. What was that about?"

"I'm mad at myself for letting Eli get away last night. That's all." The real reason for my agitation wasn't something I wanted to discuss, even with Chris. The sooner we dealt with the situation in Portland and sent our people to get Sara, the sooner I could put this behind me.

My Mori growled unhappily. It had been doing that a lot since I'd let Sara drive away with her friends last night. Mori demons were driven by instinct and emotion, and all mine could think about was its mate.

Potential mate, I reminded us both. I couldn't deny there was something about the girl that drew me in like no one ever had. Was it the innocence I'd seen in her eyes? Or her blind trust in me in that alley?

Or was it because of how right it had felt to hold her in my arms?

It doesn't matter what it is. There was no place in my life for a mate, no matter what I was feeling. My Mori would just have to get over it.

My phone rang and Dax's number flashed across the screen.

"Dax, what do you have for me?"

"I traced the license plate to a Judith Greene in New Hastings, which is about an hour north of Portland. She has a son named Roland, who attends St. Patrick High School. I searched the school records and found two girls named Sara. I'm sending you their pictures now."

A photo appeared on the screen of a blonde girl named Sarah Cummings.

"Not her," I said.

It took a minute for the second picture to arrive, and I recognized the face immediately. I stared at Sara Grey's green eyes until Dax spoke.

"Is it her?"

"Yes. Do you have an address for her?"

Dax chuckled. "Do you even have to ask?"

Seconds later, a text arrived with her address. "You need anything else?" he asked.

"No, that's it. Thanks."

"Anytime."

Chris leaned in to look at the face on my phone. "Ah, Dax found your little orphan."

I closed the picture. "She's not my orphan," I grumbled, ignoring my Mori pressing forward insistently. *Mine*, it growled.

"So, are we going to pick her up?"

I stared down the dark street instead of looking at him. "Since when do you and I bring in orphans?"

"It's been a few years, but I've handled orphans once or twice." He fell silent for a minute. "Anyway, we're here and she knows you. You already have a connection with her."

"Connection?" Was it that obvious?

Chris laughed. "Yes, that happens when you save someone's life. Look, I can handle the girl if you want me to. Or are you thinking of calling in someone?"

"Paulette has the most experience. I'll call her tomorrow," I said as our bikes came into view. The least I could do was give the girl a few days to recover from her ordeal before we sent someone in to turn her world upside down.

Opening the GPS app on my phone, I entered the address for the house on Fletcher Street. I hoped Erik didn't take too long to get here because, right now, I was in the mood to make a different kind of house call.

CHAPTER 4

WELCOME TO NEW Hastings. The sign flew past as my bike roared along the almost deserted road, and I smiled grimly, not expecting a warm welcome when I got to my destination. After the way we'd parted, Sara wasn't going to be happy to see me. The memory of the hurt in her eyes as she'd turned away from me had stayed with me all weekend.

I still wasn't sure what I was doing here. I'd picked up my phone half a dozen times yesterday to call Paulette, and each time something had stopped me from making the call. It could have been the waves of anger coming from my Mori every time I thought about having someone else make this visit.

Or it could have been the questions burning in my mind ever since Friday night. Sara was definitely Mohiri, and we had a bond. I could feel it; my Mori could feel it. Why, then, hadn't she shown a hint of recognition or a sign she'd felt *something*? The more time that passed, the more I had to see her again to make sense of it all.

And how the hell had she survived alone all these years? I could see the werewolves keeping her safe from predators, but how had her demon not driven her insane? Could it be related somehow to the reason her Mori was so quiet? The more I'd thought about it, the more I wondered if her Mori could be sick. I'd heard of it happening, and there had to be some explanation for all of this.

The idea of Sara or her Mori being sick sent a chill through me. *It's not that,* I reassured myself. An ailing Mori would cause the person to fall physically ill. Our symbiotic relationship gave us our demon's strength, but also their weakness. If her Mori was sick, she would be too, but she'd looked healthy when I met her in the club.

My Mori fluttered excitably a few seconds before I rounded a bend in the road and spotted the girl on the bicycle. I didn't need to see her face to

34

know who she was.

What in God's name is she doing out here alone? We were on the outskirts of the small town, and I hadn't seen any houses or buildings for the last few miles. After what had happened Friday night, I was shocked to find her out alone, even in daylight. Most people in her situation would still be terrified from an experience like that.

I passed her and started to ease off the gas, but the fear I saw cross her face changed my mind. This wasn't the best place to talk to her anyway. I figured she was heading home, so I decided to go on and wait for her.

It wasn't difficult to find the three-story brick building she lived in. I parked the Ducati in front of the coffee shop next door and leaned against the front of the shop to wait for Sara. Ten minutes later, she appeared at the end of the waterfront and pedaled toward me. When she was a few hundred yards away, I felt her presence and my Mori pressed forward happily.

Sara obviously didn't share the sentiment, and she wore a scowl when she stopped in front of me.

"How did you find me?" she asked curtly.

I couldn't help but admire her spirit. "What, no hello after everything we've been through together?"

Something like annoyance flashed across her face. "Hello. How did you find me?"

Sensing that the direct approach was the only way to go, I said, "I tracked your friend's license plate."

Her eyes widened. "Why?"

When I'd decided to come here, I thought I'd known exactly what to say to her. But facing her now and seeing her confusion and alarm, I knew this was not going to be as easy as I'd planned. I stepped away from the building. "We need to talk."

"Talk about what?" There was a slight quiver in her voice, and her shoulders tensed as if she was going to run.

"You look ready to flee. I don't bite, you know."

"Yeah, that's what I thought about the other fellow."

Her wry humor took me by surprise and pulled a laugh from me. She was smaller than the average Mohiri female, and she didn't have any physical strength or fighting ability based on what I'd seen the other night. But she had fire, and there was nothing cowardly or weak about her.

"You sound like you're well recovered at least." I'd worried she might be traumatized once the reality of what had happened set in, and I was relieved to see her looking whole and well. She was wary of my reasons for being here, and I couldn't say I blamed her.

"I'm not here to harm you, and we really do need to talk."

"What could we have to talk about?" Her brows drew together. "I don't even know your last name."

I smiled. "It's Danshov, and your last name is Grey. Now that we're acquainted, can we talk?"

She chewed her lower lip, and for a moment I thought she was going to say no.

"Okay."

"Is there somewhere we can talk privately?" The conversation we were about to have was not one I wanted other people to overhear.

She looked around. "We can go down to the wharves. They're usually pretty empty this time of day."

"That will work."

I waited for her to put her bike up. She was quiet when she came back and started walking with me toward the wharves. I wondered what she was thinking, and how long it would take her to ask me the point of my visit. She didn't strike me as a person who would wait long for answers.

For my part, I was curious about how a Mohiri orphan ended up in a small town in the middle of Maine. I'd done a little digging this morning and found out that the Alpha of the Maine pack lived in New Hastings. One of her friends was the Alpha's son and the other was his nephew. Sara was in with the most powerful werewolf pack in the country.

"How long have you been friends with the werewolves?" I asked as we strolled along a long, empty wharf.

There was a brief pause before she answered. "A long time."

"And your parents don't mind?" I already knew she lived with her uncle, who was her legal guardian, but I wanted to get her talking about her parents.

She tensed up beside me. "It's just me and my uncle, and he likes my friends, but he doesn't know what they are. He doesn't know about any of this."

"Do you mind if I ask about your parents? How did you come to live with your uncle?"

"My parents are gone. My mother left when I was two, so I don't remember her." Her voice held an edge of anger, but I sensed deep pain in her too. "My dad died when I was eight. Uncle Nate is his brother."

Her answer confused me. Orphans were always the offspring of a male warrior and a human female, but according to her, her father was human. It was conceivable for a female warrior to be away from a stronghold long enough to have a child, but our mothers were very protective of their young. I couldn't see one of them leaving her child unprotected with a human, even if he was the father.

"Do you know your mother's maiden name?"

She stopped walking and stared at me suspiciously. "Why do you want to know about my parents? What do they have to do with anything?"

"Answer my question, and I will answer yours."

She walked away, and there was no mistaking the bitterness in her voice this time. "Her name was Madeline. I think her maiden name was Cross or something like that. She abandoned us. I don't really care who she was."

I stared after Sara as the meaning of her words hit me full-on like a freight train. *It can't be.* Madeline had always been selfish, but even she would not abandon her own daughter.

Sara stopped walking and faced me. "What's wrong?"

It hit me then why Sara had looked familiar to Chris and me. She bore a resemblance, not to her mother, but to her grandmother, Josephine.

Khristu! She's Tristan's granddaughter.

I struggled to keep my expression and voice neutral even though I was reeling inside. "Madeline Croix? That was her name?"

"It could be. I'm not sure." She frowned nervously. "Why are you looking at me like that?"

I glanced away from her, trying to think of how to proceed. I'd known I was going to have to explain certain things to her, but the bombshell she'd dropped on me had thrown me for a loop. Madeline was alive *and* she'd had a daughter.

"I just haven't heard that name in a while," I said. "If she is the Madeline I knew, it explains a lot to me."

"Well, it doesn't tell me anything, so why don't you fill me in? You said you would answer my question if I answered yours."

"I will." I started forward, waving at some overturned wooden crates. "Let's sit. This is a good place to talk."

We sat, and I turned to look at her. The move brought me close to her, and my eyes were drawn to her mouth. My body grew warm, and my Mori shifted excitedly at her nearness.

Khristu, get a grip.

I raised my gaze to hers. "You didn't know who the Mohiri were before the other night. How much do you know about us now?" I figured the werewolves had told her what they knew, which wasn't a lot.

"I know you guys are vampire hunters, and you and the werewolves don't like each other. That's pretty much it." She shrugged, but the interest in her eyes told me she was more curious than she let on.

"I imagine your friends don't talk about us any more than we do about them. Would you like to know more about the Mohiri?"

"Yes," she replied without hesitation.

Her answer pleased me more than I wanted to admit. "You seem very familiar with the real world, but how much do you know about demons?"

"Nothing, except to stay as far away from them as possible."

"What if I told you there are thousands of types of demons, and that vampires are one of them?"

She frowned, and there was a note of fear in her voice when she spoke. "I'd ask you if you are deliberately trying to scare the hell out of me."

I rested my elbows on my legs. "I am not here to frighten you." I didn't want to upset her either, but she had to hear this if she was to understand the rest of what I had to tell her. I could already tell from her reaction to my question about demons that this wasn't going to go well.

She looked down, and I followed her gaze to the hands clenched in her lap.

"Do you still want to hear about the Mohiri?"

Green eyes met mine again. "Go ahead."

"You sure?"

She smiled, and it was like the sun breaking through the clouds. I had to look away so she couldn't see what I was feeling. Hell, *I* didn't know what I was feeling.

I began to recite the story I had learned from my sire when I was young. "It all started two millennia ago when demons learned how to leave their dimension and walk the Earth in corporeal form. Most of them were lesser demons, and they were dangerous, but not a major threat to humanity. But then a middle demon called a Vamhir appeared. It took a human host and gave the human immortality…and the thirst for human blood."

"The first vampire," she said in a hushed voice.

I nodded. "The demon soon learned how to make more like him, and before long there were thousands of vampires. The Earth's population was small back then, and ancient civilizations were virtually defenseless against the vampires' strength and bloodlust. If left unchecked, the vampires would have eventually overrun the earth and wiped out humanity.

"So the archangel Michael came to Earth to create a race of warriors to destroy the vampires. He took a middle demon called a Mori and put it inside a human male, and had the male impregnate fifty human women. Their offspring were half human/half demon and they had the speed, strength, and agility to hunt and kill vampires. They were the first Mohiri."

I watched the play of emotions across her face: revulsion, amazement, disbelief.

"The Mohiri are demons?" she asked hesitantly.

"Half demon. Each of us is born with a Mori demon in us."

"You mean you live with a demon inside you like…like a parasite?" Her face paled, and she pulled back several inches. If I had any question about whether or not she knew what she was, her reaction answered it for me.

"Exactly like that. We give the Mori life, and in return, it gives us the ability to do what we were created to do. It is a symbiotic relationship that benefits us both."

She stood abruptly, and I thought she was going to run. Instead, she walked to the edge of the wharf and stared at the water.

"You're not planning on jumping, are you?" I asked lightly, trying to allay the fear I sensed in her.

She looked at me, and my gut twisted at the confusion and anxiety I saw in her eyes. "Why are you telling me all this?" she asked in a small voice.

Her distress drew me like a magnet, and I moved to stand in front of her.

"Because you need to hear it."

Her eyes widened. "Why? What does this have to do with me? Or my parents?"

"I'll get to them in a minute. First, tell me, haven't you wondered why you're different from everyone else you know?"

Before I told her what she was, I needed to know what she felt around me. Bonds were not one-sided. I could sense her Mori, and all mine wanted to do was touch her. How could she stand this close to me and look so unaffected? Even if she had no idea what she was, she should feel *something*.

"D-different? I don't know what you mean."

"I think you do."

She shook her head. "Listen I —"

My eyes locked with hers. I felt for the new bond stretching between us and pushed against it gently. Immediately, her demon responded and reached out to me. My Mori fluttered happily, and I felt a deep sense of satisfaction. She might not recognize our connection, but her Mori did.

Suddenly, it was like a wall slammed down between us, pushing me away from her. I barely had time to react before she spun away from me, her eyes dark and frightened.

"Sara?" I reached a hand toward her.

"I have to go." She moved past me without looking in my direction.

I sighed. "Running away won't change anything, Sara."

She ignored me so I tried another approach. "I didn't take you for a coward."

She stopped walking but didn't look at me. "You don't know anything about me."

"I think we both know that's not true," I said to her back.

Her eyes were ablaze when she turned to confront me again. "What about my parents? Did you know them?"

"Not your father. But I knew Madeline Croix for many years."

Disbelief crossed her face. "You're only a few years older than me."

"I'm older than I look."

The fire left her eyes. "So what are you trying to tell me? How do you know Madeline?"

There was no easy way to say it; she was going to find it hard to take no matter how I put it. Sara had to hear the truth about her mother so she could accept who she was.

"I watched her grow up."

Her head moved from side to side, and denial filled her eyes as she stared at me. I watched emotions cross her face as she processed my words. I wished there was something I could do or say to make this easier for her.

"No!" She turned and fled.

"Sara," I called, but she ran faster. "Damn it," I muttered, going after her.

I moved past her and stopped. As she collided with me, her palms pressed against my chest to steady herself, and I felt their heat as if they were touching my bare skin. A wave of need pulsed from my demon, but I refrained from touching her. She was as skittish as a colt. The last thing I wanted to do was frighten her more than she already was.

A gasp slipped from her. "How –?"

"Demon speed, remember?"

"Someone could have seen you." She backed up, pressing her lips together.

"You and I both know that people see only what they want to see and believe what they want to believe. But just because a person chooses to not believe something, doesn't mean it's not real."

The double meaning in my words was not lost on her, and she wrapped her arms around herself defensively.

"How can you be so sure?" Desperation filled her voice as she fought the truth. "There must be more than one Madeline Croix."

"I was sure of what you are before I heard her name. As soon as I saw you the other night, I knew." I stared at the water, afraid of what she might see in my eyes. "My Mori recognized yours."

"What?"

"Mori can sense each other when they are near. It is how one Mohiri always recognizes another." *And my Mori would know yours anywhere.*

She started to shake her head.

"They are never wrong," I said with gentle firmness.

"I…"

I searched her eyes, looking for recognition in them. "You felt it, didn't you?"

Her lower lip trembled, and I finally saw what I was looking for. When she gave a tiny nod, an emotion I couldn't define made my chest constrict.

Solmi, my Mori growled softly.

"This can't be happening," Sara whispered.

I gave her a small smile. "There are worse fates, you know."

"You're telling me I have a demon parasite inside me, and I'm supposed to be okay with that?" Fear colored her voice, but I knew it was only fear of the unknown. She would lose that when she got to know her people and accepted what she was.

"It's not as bad as you make it sound," I said.

She winced, her internal struggle visible on her expressive face. "No, it's worse."

I felt the urge to comfort her, but there was nothing I could do that wouldn't scare her away. Paulette would have known exactly what to say.

"I know this is strange and frightening, but you are not the first orphan we've found. You will adjust as they have."

"Orphan?"

"It's just a term we use for young Mohiri who were not born to our way of life," I explained when she recoiled. "They have no idea who they really are until we find them."

Her eyes widened. "Then there are others like me?"

"Not exactly like you. The others have been much younger." By at least ten years. It shouldn't be possible for her to be standing in front of me, but she was. One more piece of the mystery surrounding her.

"What does that matter?"

I searched for the gentlest way to explain it without frightening her more. "Our Mori need us to survive as much as we need them, but they are still demons, and they have certain impulses and wills of their own. We learn from an early age to control those urges and to balance our human and demon sides. Otherwise, the Mori will try to become dominant.

"Orphans who are not found young enough to be trained grow up with deep mental and emotional problems, tormented by their demon sides. The worst cases become severely schizophrenic and end up in institutions…or they kill themselves."

She shuddered, and I could only imagine what was going through her mind in that moment.

"How old was the oldest orphan you ever brought in?" she asked.

I thought about the blonde trainee at Westhorne. "The oldest reclaimed was ten, and she was the exception. The others were no more than seven."

"Ten?"

"I know what you're thinking; I see it in your face. You *are* Mohiri. I know that with one hundred percent certainty." I took a step toward her, and my Mori tried unsuccessfully to reach out to hers. "What I don't know is how you learned to subdue your demon without training. I've never seen control like yours. Your Mori is practically dormant."

When she retreated again, I didn't follow. She needed space, and I wouldn't push her.

"Is that why I'm not fast or strong like you?"

"That and we reach maturity around nineteen or twenty. You should already have noticed some of your abilities starting to show by now, but you'll have to learn how to use your demon side to enhance your physical abilities."

Her face blanched.

"Are you okay?"

She shook her head slowly. "No. It's just so much to take in."

"It will take time."

My words failed to comfort her, but she appeared to collect herself. "So, what else can you do besides move really fast and catch people falling off buildings? What other powers do you have?"

I tried not to think about her falling in that alley. "Powers?"

"You know, can you compel people like vampires do or read minds or heal things? Stuff like that."

Her expectant expression drew a laugh from me. "No special powers or compulsion or anything else. We have the speed and strength to fight vampires. That is all we need."

"Oh."

"You sound disappointed."

"No, I'm just trying to understand it all." Her eyes moved slowly over my face. "How old are you? And I don't mean how old you look."

Her gaze snared me, and I almost forgot to answer. "I was born in eighteen twenty."

Her jaw dropped. "Am I...?"

"Yes. Once you reach maturity, aging will stop for you, too." Growing old and dying were two things most humans feared. Knowing she would never have to worry about that should ease her mind a little.

"Oh." Her chin quivered, and I was surprised to see something akin to sorrow fill her eyes.

"That upsets you?"

She nodded and rubbed her shivering arms.

Concern filled me, and I moved to give her my leather jacket. "You're cold."

"I'm fine, thanks." Her shoulders heaved as she took a deep breath. "What if I don't want to join the Mohiri?"

My Mori growled unhappily.

"You don't join. You *are* Mohiri."

She lifted her chin. "What if I don't want to live with them, and I just want to stay here? You said yourself that I can control this demon thing better than anyone you've ever seen, so I don't need your training."

I knew my next words would hurt, but she had to understand what all of this meant for her. "You don't belong here anymore. What will you tell people when you stop aging? What will you do when everyone you know here grows old and dies? You need to be with your own people."

She flinched. "These are my people."

"That's because they are all you've ever known. Once you get to know the Mohiri —"

"No!" Anger burned in her eyes. "I knew a Mohiri, remember? All she did was abandon me and my father. My *loving* Mohiri mother deserted us, and my dad was murdered by vampires. Where were my people then?"

Stunned by her outburst, I stared at her. "Vampires killed your father?"

Her laugh was bitter. "Pathetic, isn't it? You'd think someone like me would be a lot less likely to be taken in by a vampire, considering my past and my genes. Some warrior." She started walking at a fast pace toward the waterfront again.

I walked beside her. "That vampire, Eli, knows what you are now. He'll be looking for you. Vampires love nothing more than draining Mohiri orphans. We deprived him of that pleasure, and he will not forget it."

She stumbled slightly, but didn't stop walking. "I thought you said he wouldn't get away."

"He was more resourceful than most." I cursed myself again for letting the vampire escape and for being the cause of the fear that had crept back into her voice.

"Well, if he does come back, he'll think I'm in Portland, right?" she said hopefully. "There's no way he would know to look for me here. Besides, this is werewolf territory and the werewolves are doing sweeps of Portland to find the vampires."

"The werewolves might not catch him either." Eli had evaded the pack for the last three weeks. He might not be stupid enough to come this close to the Alpha, but I'd seen how much he wanted Sara.

She glared at me. "Are you *trying* to scare me?"

"No, but I will not lie to you either."

When we reached my bike, she faced me with her shoulders back and her arms crossed. "I don't want you to think I'm not grateful for you saving my life because I am, more than I can say. But your way of life, your people – I don't belong with them."

Her statement made waves of agitation roll off my demon. I wasn't too happy either. But short of forcing her to go with me, there was nothing I could do.

Solmi, my Mori insisted. It wanted its mate, and it sent me a vivid image of me carrying her away.

Ignoring the demon, I pulled out a small card and handed it to her. "This is my number. Call me if you need me or when you reconsider your options."

She took the card and looked at it for several seconds before she put it in her jeans pocket. "I won't reconsider."

The set of her jaw told me she wouldn't be easily persuaded, and I would not force her to leave. Something told me she would never forgive me if I did. I'd never cared much about people's opinions, but the thought of this girl hating me did not sit well with me.

"One more thing." I took a small sheathed dagger from an inner pocket of my jacket and held it toward her. "You may feel safe here now, but as you found out Friday night, danger can find you when you least expect it."

She shook her head, but I put the knife in her hand before she could pull it away. I watched her unsheathe the dagger and study the silver blade with open curiosity. Seeing her holding one of my weapons gave me an absurd rush of pleasure. I grabbed my helmet and donned it before she could see the smile tugging at my lips.

I mounted my bike and turned my head toward her. "I'll be seeing you, Sara."

Very soon.

CHAPTER 5

RIDING AWAY FROM Sara, I wasn't prepared for the mixed feelings that assailed me. I'd expected my Mori to be upset, but it surprised me to realize I didn't want to leave either. When I'd decided to come here today, I had only wanted to make sense of what I was feeling and to clear my head. If it wasn't for the bond, she'd be just another orphan.

I laughed at my pathetic attempts at denial. There was nothing average about Sara Grey. I could blame all of this on my demon, but the truth was, I'd noticed the girl before I'd touched her and felt the bond. And the more I got to know her, the more intrigued I was by her. She looked so small and defenseless, yet she possessed inner strength and courage. She'd had no idea what she was, but she had not only survived her demon, she had somehow mastered it. In my whole life, I had never met anyone like her. Her vulnerability and fear made the warrior in me want to protect her, while her soft curves and sweet voice stirred me more than I wanted to admit.

I swore harshly. How the hell had this girl managed to get under my skin so effortlessly? She didn't want anything to do with me, yet I couldn't stop thinking about her. I tried to recall some of the beautiful women I'd been with, but all I could see was *her* face.

I'd convinced myself I had to come here to get answers, and that I should be the one to tell her what she was. After all, it was part of my job to protect our people, and she needed my protection even after I broke the bond.

But seeing her today… The bond was too new for me to be having such a strong reaction to her. And yet, I was a thought away from turning this bike around and going back to her.

Exhaling loudly, I focused on other things, such as the fact that I had to tell Tristan about Sara. He was going to be beside himself when he learned he had a granddaughter. My mind was still trying to grasp that Sara was

45

Madeline's daughter. Madeline was a lot of things, but I never would have believed her capable of deserting her child and leaving her unprotected in a world so dangerous to our kind.

Before I told Tristan about Sara, I needed proof of her identity. By the time I made it to the town limits, I'd called Dax and put him to work looking into Sara's background, particularly her parents' marriage and her father's death. If there was anything to uncover, Dax would find it.

That left me with one job to do. If Sara would not leave Maine, I'd make Maine safe for her. I would scour Portland until I was confident there wasn't a vampire in the city and Eli was no longer a threat to her.

Saturday night, we had cleaned out the house the vampire had sent us to, capturing two vampires and disposing of another three. If our informant had been honest with us, there were at least two more vampires running around Portland along with Eli, unless the three of them had turned tail and run.

But I'd seen Eli's hunger when he had to let Sara go. His was not the face of someone who was going to give up easily. I'd seen it before, a vampire fixating on a human to the point of obsession. And Eli had to know Sara was Mohiri after being that close to her. Vampires loved the taste of our blood, and the younger the Mohiri, the purer the blood.

*　　*　　*

I spent the rest of the evening helping Erik and his team set up the new safe house we had established in Portland. The discovery of so many vampires in the city had necessitated a Mohiri presence for the time being. We still had no clue what had drawn Eli and his brethren here in the first place. We had the two vampires from Saturday night on lockdown, and a few days without feeding would make them talk if they knew anything.

The next morning, there was a voice mail from Dax by the time I got out of the shower. I returned his call, and he confirmed what I'd already known. Daniel Grey had been married to a Madeline Croix until his death ten years ago. There was even a black and white photo of the couple that had accompanied an article in the *Portland Press Herald* about his grisly murder. Strangely though, Sara was not mentioned in the article.

After I hung up, I sat on the bed, thinking about the conversation I'd be having with Tristan soon. My thoughts inevitably turned to Sara, and I wondered how she was faring after our talk yesterday. Would she be less resistant to the Mohiri if she knew she had family among them? She'd been very defensive when I'd mentioned her leaving and adamant that her family was here. I was afraid any more revelations might be too much for her.

Chris was in the kitchen making breakfast when I went downstairs. We lived mostly off restaurant and bar food on the road, and both of us enjoyed a home-cooked meal when we could get one. Luckily for me, Chris liked to cook and he was good at it.

He shot me a questioning look when I walked into the kitchen, and I knew he was waiting for me to tell him where I'd disappeared to yesterday. We'd been friends a long time, and there wasn't much we kept from each other. But I found myself reluctant to talk about Sara.

"Did you call Paulette to take care of your orphan?" He slid scrambled eggs and sausage onto a plate and held it out to me.

I took the plate and sat at the counter. "No. I decided to take care of it myself."

He spun around, sending bits of egg flying off the spatula in his hand. "You did?"

I dug into my eggs, ignoring his stare. "It was your idea."

"Yes, but I didn't think you'd take me seriously." He glanced up at the ceiling as if he suspected I had her locked away upstairs. "What happened?"

I gave him a wry smile. "She wasn't exactly happy to see me or to discover what she is. And she was more than clear that she is not leaving Maine."

"What did she —?"

I pointed at the stove. "Your eggs are burning."

"Shit!" He grabbed his smoking pan of eggs and started scraping them into the garbage disposal. He filled the pan with soapy water and turned back to me. "We'll have to send Paulette to talk to her. She's the best with orphans. We can't leave the girl here unprotected."

"I have no intention of leaving her." I carried my plate to the sink and washed it.

Chris's brows drew together. "What aren't you telling me?"

I dried the plate and put it away, listening for other people in the house. "Where are the others?"

"They went to Boston early this morning to grab the rest of their stuff. Why?"

I picked up my cell phone and walked into the living room. "Because I'd rather keep this conversation between the three of us."

"The three of us?"

I sat on the couch, and he sat across from me. "You, me, and Tristan," I said before I dialed the number.

Tristan picked up on the second ring. "What did you find?" he asked when he realized who was calling.

"More than we expected." I looked at Chris, who was watching me with open curiosity. "It *was* vampires who took those girls. There were ten of them holed up in a house, and we took care of five of them. We have two locked up, and we're looking for the last three."

"Ten. That's an unusually large number. Did you find out why they were in Portland?"

"Not yet, but we will," Chris answered.

There was a short silence on the other end of the line. "Why do I get the feeling there is more to this than you're telling me?" Tristan said.

"There is." I took a breath. "We found an orphan. We saved her from the vampire we're hunting now."

"Is she okay?" Concern flooded Tristan's voice. "Have you called Paulette? What about the girl's mother? Did she survive the attack?"

I waited for the barrage of questions to end. "She is unhurt, and her parent was not involved in the attack. We ran into the girl at a bar on Friday night."

"A bar?" Tristan echoed incredulously. "What on Earth was a child doing at a bar?"

"That's the thing." Chris leaned forward with his arms resting on his knees. "She's not a child, at least not a young one. She's seventeen."

Tristan inhaled sharply. "How is that possible? You're sure she is Mohiri?"

"I've never been surer of anything in my life," I replied, drawing Chris's scrutiny again. "I've been around her several times, and I was able to sense her Mori each time. I went to visit her yesterday, and I learned some things about her that, frankly, shocked the hell out of me. I had Dax look into her background to confirm what I suspected before I told you."

I took a deep breath. "Her name is Sara Grey, and her father was human. Her mother is Mohiri."

Tristan and Chris inhaled sharply at the same time.

I continued before either of them could speak. "Her father was killed by vampires ten years ago. Her mother left them when Sara was very young, and Sara had no idea what she was until I told her."

Chris frowned. "How do you and Dax know her mother is Mohiri if Sara didn't even know?"

"I knew when I heard her mother's name." I stared at the phone. "Tristan...Sara is Madeline's daughter."

"Madeline?" Tristan said in disbelief. "How...how do you know this?"

"Sara told me her mother's name was Madeline, and Dax found a picture of your Madeline with Daniel Grey." I looked at Chris, who still stared at me with his mouth hanging open. "And Sara bears a resemblance to Josephine."

Chris found his voice again. "That's it! I knew she looked familiar. Madeline's daughter? Damn."

"Nikolas, you're positive about this?" Tristan's voice shook, and I could only imagine what he was feeling. I was there when he'd found the note Madeline had left him before she took off. I'd helped him search for her for over a year, and I'd seen his fear and worry for his only child. Madeline was a trained warrior when she left, but she'd never been out in the world alone.

I'd watched as the years passed and the hope of her coming home slowly faded from his eyes.

After several decades went by without a word from her, he had accepted that she could be dead, and he'd resigned himself to being the last of his line. Now to discover his daughter was still alive – or had been seventeen years ago – and she had married and given birth to a child...

"Without a doubt, she is Madeline's daughter, your granddaughter," I said.

"Oh dear God," Tristan whispered hoarsely. "Madeline."

Chris and I said nothing for several minutes while Tristan recovered from learning Madeline could still be alive, and that he had a granddaughter.

Tristan cleared his throat. "Is Sara with you? May I speak to her?"

"She's not here. She refused to leave her home."

I could hear Tristan's footsteps as he paced around his office.

"We can't leave her unprotected. Did you explain how dangerous it is for her?"

"Yes, but she is determined to stay. She has no warm feelings for her mother, and I think she blames Madeline in part for her father's death. She wants nothing to do with us."

Tristan stopped pacing. "I'll come there and talk to her. Maybe if she knew she had family here, she would be less frightened of us."

A laugh escaped me. "She's not afraid of us. Trust me. I'd say it's closer to contempt."

There was a brief silence before Tristan spoke again. "You said she's seventeen and she had no idea she was Mohiri. How has she survived this long without training?"

"I don't know, but her control over her Mori is unlike anything I've seen. If I hadn't sensed it, I would have thought she was human."

"If I didn't know you better, I'd think that was admiration I hear in your voice," Tristan said.

I didn't try to deny it. "It's hard not to admire someone with that kind of strength. She is surprisingly composed, considering all she's been through. In some ways, she reminds me of you."

"My granddaughter," he said in wonder. "I'm going to call for the jet. I'll be there this afternoon."

My eyes met Chris's as I shook my head. "I don't think that is a wise idea. Sara's strong, but she was overwhelmed when I talked to her, not that I blame her after the last few days. She holds a lot of resentment for her mother, and I think meeting Madeline's family would be too much for her right now. It might drive her further away."

"Are you suggesting we leave her there?" Tristan asked sharply.

"No. We'll give her some time to process everything before we talk to her again. Chris and I will watch over her, and we're not her only

49

protectors."

"What do you mean?" Tristan asked.

"When I met Sara, she was with two members of the Maine pack – the Alpha's son and nephew. She's close to the wolves, and the two I met were very protective of her. She lives in a small town called New Hastings, in the heart of pack territory an hour north of Portland."

"Werewolves?" It took Tristan a minute to recover from his shock. "That's Maxwell Kelly's pack."

Chris spoke up. "You know him?"

"By reputation only," Tristan said. "He's a strong Alpha and widely known for his hunting skills. I've heard other packs send their wolves to him for training. His pack is one of the first in the country to live among humans instead of segregating themselves. He is also territorial. I'm still trying to grasp how those vampires managed to elude his pack for weeks."

"The vampire who attacked Sara was their leader," I replied. "He's proving to be adept at hiding and covering his tracks. But if he's still here, we'll find him."

Tristan expelled a long breath. "I feel better knowing my granddaughter is under Kelly's protection, but I won't rest until she is here with us. Please, keep her safe."

Chris nodded solemnly. "I'll guard my cousin with my life."

"As will I," I vowed.

"Thank you. I don't think I could entrust her safety to anyone else." Tristan's chair squeaked when he sat again. "This is… I can't tell you what this means to me, knowing I have a granddaughter. I just can't understand how Madeline could abandon her own child. I knew my daughter could be selfish, but she was never a bad person. If she didn't want the child, why didn't she send her to me?"

"I don't know." I had wondered the same things. Madeline could have easily picked up a phone and let Tristan know about the girl. Why she hadn't done that was a question only she could answer.

Tristan's tone changed, and he was all business. "What is your plan? Will you have Erik's team hunt the vampires while you two watch over Sara?"

"Chris and I will take turns keeping an eye on her." I looked at him, and he nodded in agreement. "We'll have to keep our distance though, because she won't be happy if she knows we're hanging around."

"Perhaps I should ask Paulette to join you," Tristan suggested. "There's no one better at handling orphans, and a female might be less threatening to Sara."

He was right, but I was reluctant to bring anyone else in. A few days ago, I'd planned to turn Sara over to Paulette, but I couldn't do that now.

"Nikolas?" Tristan said.

"Let's hold off on Paulette for now. I've already explained things to

Sara, and I think bringing in someone else might be too much for her. Chris and I can handle things here."

No one spoke for a long moment. Finally, Tristan said, "Okay, if you think that is best. I trust your judgement."

"Thank you." His faith in me made me feel a moment of guilt that I hadn't told him everything. But a bond was a deeply personal connection between two people, and Tristan would understand my wish to keep it private. I'd have to tell Chris, but the fewer people who knew about it the better.

"We'll take care of the vampire problem here," I said. "Between us and the werewolves, Sara will be well protected. Hopefully, she'll be more open to us in a few weeks after she's had time to take it all in."

"And if she isn't?" Tristan asked, worry in his voice.

"We'll stay as long as it takes. She won't be alone, Tristan." I leaned back against the couch. "Sara is strong-willed, but she's also intelligent and curious about the world. I believe she'll want to know more about her people when she's less wary of us."

"I hope you are right."

So do I, I silently agreed with him.

Tristan made an aggravated sound. "I have a Council call in two minutes, but I'm afraid my mind won't be on business today. I'll check back with you tomorrow."

"I'll talk to you then."

I hung up and silence hung heavily in the room. Chris stared at me for a long moment before he finally spoke.

"All right, what are you holding back? I know you better than anyone, and I can tell there's something you're not saying. It has to be bad if you didn't want Tristan to know."

I got up and walked to the window. Peering out at the quiet street, I thought about how to tell him what he wanted to know. It was harder than I'd expected to come up with the right words.

"Why don't you want anyone else to visit Sara? You've never shown interest in orphans before. I would think you'd be happy for someone like Paulette to take over."

"Sara's not like other orphans."

"Because she's Tristan's granddaughter?"

Goddamn, this was not easy. But I had to tell him about the bond, unless I planned to walk away from it. Remembering how difficult it had been to ride away from her yesterday, I knew leaving was no longer an option.

I turned from the window to face him. "Because she's my mate."

"*What?*" Chris stared at me like I'd lost my mind. "*Mate?*"

"Yes."

His mouth opened and closed a few times, and I realized it was the first time I'd ever seen him speechless.

He shook his head. "You were distracted at the club. I suspected you were taken with the girl...but bonded? Why didn't you tell me?"

I frowned at him. "It's not an easy topic to bring up, and I wanted to be sure of the bond before I said anything."

Understanding dawned on his face. "That's why you went to see her instead of calling Paulette."

"Yes."

"Damn." He released a loud breath. "I don't even know what to say."

His face told me what he couldn't put into words. I had never spent longer than a week in a relationship, although enough women had tried to entice me to stay. The harder they tried, the more determined I was to remain single. Chris thought it was hilarious, and he'd always said someday I would meet the *one*, and he hoped he had a front row seat for the show. I don't think either of us expected me to actually find my bond mate. He was almost as stunned as I had been.

"There's not much to say. Sara is my mate."

Mine, my Mori insisted.

Yes. The moment I admitted the truth to myself, the knot in my stomach eased, and my chest felt oddly light. She was mine. She might despise me and everything I stood for, but I'd do whatever it took to protect her.

Chris cleared his throat. "Does Sara know about the bond?"

"She feels something, but she doesn't know what it is." I rubbed the back of my neck. "She's been through too much; she's not ready to hear about this."

"I agree. She was raised as a human, and she needs time to adjust to our way of life before she learns she is bonded to someone. That is, unless you decide to break it before it grows."

I looked out the window. I could end this now and Sara would be none the wiser. I'd be free to go back to my life, and she could go on with hers. But when I thought about doing that, my Mori growled and an unpleasant sinking feeling settled in my gut.

"I don't think I can."

"Wow." He let out a puff of air. "Well, I can see why you didn't want to tell Tristan."

I shot him a questioning look.

He laughed. "He just found out he has a granddaughter. I'm surprised he didn't insist on coming here. If he knew you and she were bonded, he'd be on his way to the airport right now."

I scowled as I went back to sit on the couch. "I'm not sure whether or not to be insulted by that statement."

Chris grinned. "Well, you haven't exactly hidden the fact that you don't want a mate. The only woman I've ever seen you show any affection for, besides your mother, is Vivian, and she is as bad as you when it comes to commitment. I think if Vivian had shown any real interest in settling down, you would have run far and fast."

"This is not the same," I practically growled at him.

His expression grew thoughtful. "Are you sure you're ready for this, Nikolas?"

"Is anyone ever ready?"

"You know it's not going to be easy for you to stay away from her once the bond grows. You'll need to be near her, and it'll become increasingly difficult to see her around other males."

"I know." I groaned inwardly. Mohiri males always felt the bond more intensely than their mates, and they tended to become possessive of their female until the bond was complete. I'd seen it enough times, but I'd never expected or wanted to experience it myself. I'd only known the girl for four days, and already she occupied my thoughts more than any woman had.

Chris kicked his feet up on the coffee table. "We've both seen bonded couples and how stormy their courtships were in the beginning. If my new cousin is half as stubborn as you, I expect fireworks – and not the good kind."

I glowered at him. "You're enjoying this, aren't you?"

His eyes flashed with amusement. "More than you could possibly imagine. So when are you going to tell your mother you've met your mate? She'll be overjoyed."

I rubbed my face. "*Khristu*, don't even mention my mother. I have enough to deal with."

Laughter filled the room. "I'm just going to buy some popcorn and sit back to enjoy the show."

"Remind me again why we're friends," I said, earning another laugh from him.

"Because no one else can put up with you. And because I like to piss off the Council almost as much as you do."

The front door opened, and Erik's team filed in carrying duffle bags and weapons cases. Erik dropped his bags in the hallway and joined us in the living room. At five-eleven, he was tall for a Korean, but shorter than most Mohiri males, a fact that left him in a perpetual state of annoyance.

He scowled as he sank into a chair. "We're cleared out of Boston. I think Raoul's team is moving in there tomorrow. My guys are going to stow their gear, and then we're going to start checking out the spots in Portland where those suckers could be holed up."

"Sounds good." Erik was meticulous when it came to doing a grid search, which was one of the reasons I was glad to have him here. If Eli was still in Portland, Erik would flush him out. This was one time when I couldn't afford to leave a single stone unturned. Sara's life could depend on it.

"Anyone check on our guests this morning?" Chris asked. "They must be getting thirsty by now."

Erik nodded. "I looked in on them before we left. The female is still holding up, but the male looks ready to crack. In a few days, he'll tell us whatever he knows." His gaze flicked between Chris and me. "Are you two going to join us in the search, or do you have something else in the works?"

"Both. Chris and I have another job." I told Erik about Sara and who she was, omitting the part about the bond.

Erik let out a low whistle. "Tristan's granddaughter? I'm surprised he's not here already."

"I made him see it would be better if he let us handle this. Chris and I are going to split our time between watching over her and dealing with the vampire problem."

Erik gave me a look much like the one Chris had given me earlier. "*You're* going to work with an orphan?"

I shrugged, ignoring Chris's knowing smile. "This is a special case."

A red-haired warrior named Carl entered the room. "We picked up some activity at an abandoned apartment building on Franklin. Could be demons, or it might be vamps."

Chris, Erik, and I stood at the same time. Erik went to his duffle bags, and I grabbed my jacket and sword that were lying on the dining room table. I checked my inside pockets for knives as I turned to the others.

"Let's go hunting."

*　　*　　*

I stood in the shadows between the two buildings across the road from St. Patrick High School and watched students spill through the front doors. It wasn't until the last few trickled out that I saw the face I was looking for.

Sara walked slowly down the front steps of the school with her eyes downcast. She could have been alone for all she seemed to notice the people hurrying around her.

Someone called her name as she walked toward the street, but she didn't seem to notice. She looked tired. What was wrong with her? Was she ill?

A movement behind her caught my eye, and my body tensed when I saw someone running toward her. I relaxed when I recognized her werewolf friend, Roland.

He caught up to her and grabbed her by the arm. I wasn't prepared for the jealousy that burned in my stomach, and I took a step toward them before I came to my senses.

I exhaled slowly and wondered for the hundredth time if it was in my best interest for me to be here checking up on her. Chris had offered to come, but I'd wanted to see for myself she was okay. Or maybe I just wanted to see her.

Roland said something to Sara, and she shook her head. He frowned and gestured toward the school. She shrugged and answered him, but whatever she said only made his brows draw together more.

I wanted to know what they were talking about, but I wouldn't listen in. It was one thing to watch over her, and another to invade her privacy.

Sara resumed walking, and Roland stared after her, worry creasing his brow.

I waited for him to turn toward the parking lot before I followed Sara at a distance. I wasn't surprised when she went straight home. On Tuesday when I'd been here, she'd done the same.

She disappeared into her building, and I found a spot across the waterfront where I could see her apartment. A few minutes later, curtains on the third floor moved as a window opened. Sara appeared in the window, staring at the bay for a long moment before she turned away.

I stayed for two hours, and then I walked to where I'd left my bike on the next street over. There was no need to stick around here all night. My time was better served in Portland, helping the others in the hunt for Eli.

* * *

When my phone vibrated, I knew who it was before I looked at the screen. "What's up, Chris?"

"The male vampire finally cracked," Chris said. "He told us about two places where Eli could be hiding out. I thought you might want to be there when we check them out. How soon can you get here?"

"About an hour."

"Ah. How's our girl?"

"The same." I watched the lone figure walking on the wharf, the wind tossing her dark hair around her face. Even from a distance, my demon-enhanced eyesight could see how pale she was, and the way her shoulders hunched. An aura of loneliness surrounded her, and she looked like someone who had lost her best friend.

This was my third visit to New Hastings since I'd talked to Sara on Monday, and each time she looked no better than the last. Had learning what she was really affected her that deeply, or had something else happened to douse the fire in her eyes? Her pain called to me across the invisible thread that stretched between us, and each time I saw her, it got harder not to go to her. Chris was right. Staying away from her was going to be an impossible task.

My fingers tightened around the phone. "I hate seeing her this way."

"Nikolas, eventually she was going to realize she was different, and she would have had no idea what was going on. That would have been a lot more frightening than what she is going through now."

My grip on the phone eased. "You're right."

He laughed. "I'm always right. Now are you going to spend all weekend there, or do you want to help us take down that vampire?"

I cast one last look at the girl on the wharf and turned toward my bike that was parked out of sight around the corner. "I'm on my way."

It took me less than an hour to reach Portland. Chris and Erik were waiting for me, and the first place we hit was an apartment in South Portland. There were signs someone had been there recently, but it looked like it had been empty for several days. We left it undisturbed except for several surveillance cameras we installed behind the ceiling fixtures.

We had better luck at the second location, a house in Westbrook.

"Look at this," Chris called from the master bedroom.

I entered the room where he'd spread out a bunch of photos on top of the dresser. In every photo was a blonde teenage girl, and there was a name and address on the back. A quick computer search revealed four of the photos were of the missing girls. The other three girls were alive and well.

"Looks like we interrupted Eli before he could get to all the girls on his list," Chris said.

I studied the photos. "I wish I knew why he singled out these particular girls."

The other vampire with Eli had said he preferred brunettes like Sara. So why were all the girls in these pictures blonde? Understanding Eli's motive for being in Portland would make it a lot easier to hunt him. The fact that he'd taken time to make a list of females was troubling. It was premeditated behavior instead of impulsive, and a vampire with that kind of patience was a very dangerous one.

Eli might have come to Portland looking for these girls, but he'd found Sara. And he wanted her. I'd seen it in his eyes. The chances of him finding her an hour away among the pack were slim, but not impossible. The vampire had proven to be more resourceful than most.

I shared my fears with Chris. "One of us should stay in New Hastings until this is over. I'd do it, but Sara will notice me if I'm there every day. I don't think that will go over too well."

Chris nodded. "We'll alternate days. Don't worry. We'll keep her safe."

*   *   *

On Wednesday, I went with Erik, Andrew, and Reese to check out two closed up buildings on the waterfront that were perfect for vampire nests. The first one we searched was clear, but we came across a couple of ranc demons hiding out in the second one.

The short, dark-skinned demons squeaked when four Mohiri warriors interrupted their meal, a small bucket of pig's blood from one of the local butchers. One of the demons jumped to his feet, kicking the bucket and causing blood to slosh out onto the floor.

"We've hurt no one." His catlike eyes glowed in the darkened room. "We're just passing through."

I barked a laugh. Ranc demons were mercenaries for hire, and they never went anywhere without a purpose. The odds of them just "passing through" Portland were slim, especially given the sudden increase in vampire activity. No, they were here for a reason.

"Why don't I believe you?"

"It's true," the second demon said in a calmer voice. He waved his arm at the old office they had holed up in. "It's just the two of us, and we'll be off as soon as we finish our meal."

"I see." I strolled around the room. "Where are you two coming from?"

"Boston –"

"Canada –"

The two demons glared at each other.

"Let's try this again." I crossed the room to tower over the diminutive demons, and they craned their necks to stare up at me. "Why are you in Portland? And if I don't hear something that sounds like the truth, there will be two fewer demons in the world tonight."

"We answered a call," the nervous one blurted, ignoring the scorching look his friend gave him.

"What kind of call?" Erik asked.

"My brother and I are trackers," the quieter demon replied. "We got word there's a bounty on someone, but that's all we know. We were supposed to get more information when we got here, but we haven't been able to contact the one who sent out the call."

"Who put out the call?" I demanded.

The demon shrugged. "Some vampire, that's all we know. But you can bet we weren't the only ones to get it."

Coldness settled in my stomach. It didn't take a genius to figure out who was behind this. If Eli had called in trackers, he was serious about finding someone. And my gut told me it was Sara. It could be the bond making me overreact, but I wasn't taking any chances either way.

I needed to call Chris and let him know what we'd learned. Pulling out my phone, I headed for the door, leaving Erik to decide what to do with the two demons. The phone vibrated before I could make the call, and my steps faltered when I saw Chris's number. My first thought was that Sara was in trouble.

"What's up, Chris?" I asked more calmly than I felt.

"Good question," said an angry female voice.

I smiled as I walked outside. "I told Chris you'd recognize him if he got too close."

"Great. You won the bet. Buy him a beer or whatever." Her voice rose. "I thought we had an understanding when you left here last week."

I leaned against the front of the building. "And what understanding would that be?"

She huffed. "The one where you go your way and I go mine, and we all live happily ever after."

"I don't recall that particular arrangement. I believe I told you I'd be seeing you again." I knew my response would anger her. She'd made it clear she wanted nothing to do with us the last time I talked to her, which was why I'd told Chris not to let her see him. But I hadn't told her I was leaving because that would have been a lie.

The line went silent, and I thought she'd hung up on me. "Sara?"

When she spoke again, her voice sounded strained instead of angry. "What do you want from me, Nikolas? I told you I just want to be left alone."

I sighed and raked a hand through my hair. The last thing I wanted was to frighten her after all she'd been through, but she needed to know she could be in danger. "We got word of increased activity in Portland, and we have reason to believe the vampire might be searching for you."

"I don't know anyone in Portland, so there's no way he can trace me here, right?" she asked, a hint of a tremor in her voice.

"There's more than one way to track someone." *But they'll have to go through me.* "Don't worry. We'll keep you safe. Chris will stay close by until we handle this situation."

"I don't need a babysitter. I'm not a child."

I pictured her fiery eyes and flushed cheeks. "No, you're not." Pushing away from the wall, I walked the length of the building. "But you are not a warrior either. It is our duty to protect you even if you don't want our protection."

I expected her to argue again. Instead she said, "How close is he planning to stay? He's kind of conspicuous, and I can't have my uncle or anyone else asking questions."

I frowned. "Conspicuous?"

She sighed loudly. "If you guys wanted to blend in, you shouldn't have sent Dimples here. The way some of the women are staring at him, I might end up having to protect him instead."

The idea of her protecting my warrior friend from the ladies made me almost laugh out loud, but I didn't think she would appreciate that in her current mood. "Ah, I'm sure Chris can take care of himself. He'll be in town in case we suspect any trouble is coming that way."

"Fine. But as soon as this is cleared up you guys have to go so I can try to have a somewhat normal life again."

"Sara, I —"

There was a muffled sound, and then Chris chuckled. "I never thought I'd say this, but I think you've finally met your match, Nikolas."

I was still smiling about her "Dimples" comment. "I think you may be right."

"I can see why you asked Tristan to stay away. She really doesn't want us around."

"I wish I could give her more time to get used to us, but we've had a new development." I filled him in on what we had learned from the ranc demons.

"Are you sure Eli's looking for Sara? All the other girls were blond, even the three he didn't take. Maybe it's one of them he's after."

"I pray to God you're right, but you didn't see his face, Chris. He almost died trying to take her with him when he could have just run." My hand tightened on the phone as I remembered Eli's raw lust and hunger when he'd held Sara. "I can't let him get near her again."

"We'll keep her safe," he vowed. "She's with one of her werewolf friends now, and I put a tracker on his truck so I can find him again." There was a clicking sound and a short beep. "Looks like he's driving her home."

"We can't let her out of our sight until we get this vampire," I said.

"Other than school, she doesn't go that far. I don't think we'll have any trouble keeping an eye on her." I heard him shift position. "I'm on my way to her place now."

"Okay."

He laughed. "Don't worry, Nikolas. I've waited a *long* time to see a female lead you on a merry chase, and no one is going to spoil my fun."

CHAPTER 6

I PULLED MY bike in next to Chris's and shut it off. Music and laughter filled the air, along with the crash of waves below the lighthouse. The party was in full swing, and a couple of boys stumbled as they approached the parking lot. One had car keys in his hand, and neither he nor his friend looked fit to drive. Why humans thought they could drink themselves into this state and still function correctly was beyond me.

I veered to intercept them. "Hold up, guys. You're not planning to drive, are you?"

"Nah, just getting some beer from my buddy's trunk," said one of them. Judging by his slur, the last thing he needed was more alcohol.

I watched them grab a case of beer from a car and head back to the party. I followed them at a slower pace. When I'd talked to Chris earlier, I'd been surprised to learn he was at a party. Since the night at the club two weeks ago, Sara hadn't left the house much, except for school. I was glad she'd recovered enough from the vampire attack to go out with her friends again.

There was no sign of Chris or Sara when I reached the party, but I knew they were there because I could sense her nearby. I saw her two werewolf friends standing with a group of teenagers, and I scanned the crowd for her face. A white van blocked my view, so I walked around it to stand near the lighthouse.

My chest rumbled in displeasure at the sight of Sara in another man's arms. They were dancing and laughing together, and she smiled at the blond man in a way she had never smiled at me. I was still getting used to the intense protective urges she awoke in me. This surge of possessiveness was something new. I'd known the bond would grow the more I saw her, but I hadn't expected *this*, at least not so soon.

Was the blond guy her date? The idea of her with someone else made my gut clench, but I knew it was a possibility. Sara was seventeen and beautiful, and she'd had a life before I found her. There was no reason why she wouldn't date.

"Hi. Are you one of Dylan's friends from Portland?"

I tore my eyes from Sara to look at the tall girl with short, dark hair who had walked up to me.

"No." I had no idea who Dylan was, and I didn't care, unless he was the blond man dancing with Sara. My gaze went back to them.

"Oh." The girl moved closer. "You want to get a drink or maybe dance?"

"No, thanks."

I promptly forgot about the girl when Sara's partner dipped her, making her laugh. My jaw tightened, and my Mori made angry noises, wanting me to go up to them and pull her away from the guy. There was nothing suggestive in their movements, but it was impossible not to see the man was interested in more than dancing.

As the song ended, her body tensed and she began to scan the crowd for someone. My pulse leapt. Was it possible she felt my presence the same way I sensed hers?

I got my answer when her eyes landed on me and she frowned. Then she pulled away from her dance partner and stalked off in the other direction with the blond man following her. They spoke, and he went to the white van while she stayed where she was. I approached her, and she turned to glower at me.

"What are you doing here?"

I smelled beer on her breath, and I glared after the man. If he returned with more beer for her, he and I were going to have a talk. My gaze returned to her, and I noticed she was flushed and slightly tipsy. We were very tolerant of human alcohol, and I wondered how much she had consumed to make her this way.

"Obviously protecting you from yourself," I said. "Are you drunk?"

She drew herself up. "No, I'm not drunk! And even if I was, it would be none of your business."

"You are my business. Whether you like it or not, you are one of us and we protect our own." *I protect my own.*

Her eyes blazed. "First of all, I am nobody's *business*, and I don't belong to you or your people or anyone else. This bossy act might work on little kids, but it won't work on me, and if I want to party with my friends or drink or do *anything* else, I will."

She spun away, stumbling, and I grabbed her arm to keep her from falling.

"You *are* drunk."

Before she could retort, her friend returned.

"Everything okay here?" he asked.

Sara smiled at him. "Peachy. My…cousin was worried that I might be drinking too much. He's a lot older than me and way too uptight."

I almost snorted at her description of me. Only a blind man would believe there was anything familial between the two of us, at least on my side. She felt something too; she just didn't know it yet. Or she didn't want to admit it.

Her friend wasn't buying her explanation.

"Cousin, huh?"

"Distant cousins, practically unrelated," I responded, and the look in his eyes told me he understood my meaning.

He looked between Sara and me. "Listen, if there is something going on between you two, I –"

She made a derisive sound. "Yeah, not in this lifetime." Turning to him as if I wasn't there, she said, "I think I'll go see what Roland is up to. Maybe I'll see you again later."

She stalked off toward the beach. I wanted to go to her and make sure she was okay, but I decided it would be wise to give her a few minutes to cool down first. A smile curved my lips. She was beautiful even when she was furious.

"You're not really her cousin, are you?"

I looked at the blond man, who was still standing nearby. "No."

He nodded and stared after her. "She's something else."

"Yes, she is," I said more to myself.

The man surprised me when he held out his hand. "Samson."

I shook his hand. "Nikolas."

"Can I ask what the deal is with you and her? She didn't mention a boyfriend, and you don't exactly seem like her type."

"What type is that?"

He grinned. "I'm not sure, but I hope it's blond drummers. No offense."

"None taken." I couldn't help but like the guy, even if my Mori wanted me to hit him for touching Sara. "I'd better go check on her."

Samson chuckled. "Good luck with that."

I saw Chris as I approached the bluff overlooking the beach, and I knew Sara had never been out of his sight even when she was out of mine. He gave me a look that said "better you than me" and pointed at a lone figure down the beach away from the fire. Not that I needed to be told where she was; I could sense her from here.

I watched her from a distance for a few minutes before I joined her. She didn't look up as I neared, but she knew I was there despite my quiet approach.

"Please go away," she said quietly. "I promise I won't have any fun or fall into the ocean in my drunken state if you'll leave me alone."

I hated the sadness in her voice and knowing I had put it there. She'd looked so happy and carefree with Samson, and it bothered me that she reacted the opposite way to me. She didn't know what we were to each other, and it was clear she was still upset by the things I'd told her last week. I wished there was something I could say to take away her pain, but all I could do for now was try to reassure her.

I sat beside her, and my Mori almost purred with happiness at being so close to its mate. After watching her from a distance for so long, a feeling of contentment settled over me at her nearness.

"I've heard that some orphans take the transition to the Mohiri life well and others struggle to adapt. Eventually, they all come to love our way of life."

She didn't look at me. "Maybe that's because their life before wasn't that great. It's got to suck being a little kid with a demon wreaking havoc in your head. But I'm not like them."

"No, you're not." If she only knew how different she was.

"Why?"

I thought about the best way to answer her. "You are very strong. I don't mean physically. Like I told you before, you have amazing control over your Mori; it's almost effortless."

She shifted restlessly, and I wondered if her Mori was reacting to being so close to mine. If so, was she even aware of it?

"You don't seem to have any trouble with yours," she said.

"I've had many years to learn this much control, and it's still not as good as yours." If she only knew how much I'd struggled with my Mori as a boy, and how hard it was to restrain the demon when she was near. It would never harm her, but it couldn't understand why we weren't trying to claim our mate.

"Oh." She rubbed her knees nervously. "But you do control it, right? You're not going to go all Linda Blair on me, are you? Because I've had all the craziness I can handle for one year."

I laughed at her ability to find humor in the situation. "I don't think you have anything to worry about."

She turned her face toward me, allowing me to see the sadness that still lingered in her eyes. "How long is this going to go on? I just want to go back to some semblance of a normal life."

"Sara —"

"I know what you're going to say. How normal can it be when I'm immortal and everyone else is not? Why can't I have it for now, at least until I have to leave?" she asked desperately.

I sighed softly, hating that I was going to crush her hopes of having a normal life. But if she was ever going to accept that she couldn't go back to the way things were, I had to be honest with her. About the danger, at least.

"That might have been possible before the vampire found you. You don't know what they're like; once they decide they want something, it's like a predator scenting their prey. And you are the one that got away."

She trembled, and my arm ached to wrap itself around her shoulders. But I knew my touch would not be welcome.

"The werewolves don't think the vampires will enter their territory," she said.

"I hope they're right, and I wish I could tell you this will all go away, but I won't lie to you. I believe you are in danger here, and I won't leave you unprotected as long as that danger exists."

She stood. "Just do me a favor and don't act like every person you see is out to get me. It is possible that some boys might actually like me." She walked around me and headed back to the party.

"*Ya znayu*," I said softly. *I know.*

She looked back at me. "Did you say something?"

"I said I'm sure they do."

I stayed there for a few minutes after she'd left. Chris would keep an eye on her, and I didn't want to upset her more. I wished I knew what to do or say to make her world right again, but I was at a loss.

When I returned to the party, I found a spot in the shadow of the lighthouse to stay out of sight. Sara was with her two werewolf friends and she wore a smile again, though it wasn't as bright as the one she had before I'd made my presence known.

I knew I should probably go. She was safe here with her friends and Chris, and I only managed to distress her. But every time I thought of leaving, I couldn't make myself walk away.

"She's really gotten to you."

I'd been so focused on Sara that I hadn't even heard Chris approach. He stood beside me and watched her with her friends.

"I've never seen you look at a female the way you look at her."

I glanced over at him. "What way is that?"

He smiled. "Like a blind man seeing for the first time."

I scoffed, but I had no rebuke because I was afraid he might be right.

"How bad is it?" he asked with more seriousness. "I'm not going to have to restrain you if she goes near another male, am I?"

Sara laughed at something Roland said, and my chest warmed in response. "It's stronger than I expected it would be this soon," I admitted. "I don't think I realized how strong until I saw her with the other guy."

"I guess it's true what they say. The bigger they are, the harder they fall." His voice didn't hold any of his usual humor. He laid a hand on my shoulder. "Maybe you should stay away for a while, until she's more willing to accept you. The more you see her, the harder it will be to keep your distance from her."

I nodded stiffly. "I know, but I can't stay away with Eli stepping up his search for her."

That was only part of the reason. Being near Sara eased the slowly tightening coil of tension inside me. I'd heard from bonded males that just touching their mates was enough to calm them when they were upset. It wasn't as if I could walk up and take my mate's hand. She'd probably break her fist on my nose.

Chris and I split up. He mingled with the crowd, while I stayed out of Sara's sight. A few females came up to me and attempted to start a conversation, but I discouraged them as nicely as I could. I had eyes for only one female. My Mori wouldn't have endured me being with someone else anyway now that it had found its mate.

It was around eleven when I felt the first drops of rain. I'd been watching the clouds move in for an hour, so I wasn't surprised when the sky suddenly opened up and sent a torrent of rain down on us. Some of the females squealed, and everyone raced for their vehicles. As I watched Sara and her friends run to an old red pickup, I moved toward my bike, intending to follow them.

Chris met up with me in the parking lot. "She's fine. Stop worrying. She's safe with the werewolves, and I heard the boys talking about a party in the Knolls. It's just a few miles from here, and it's where the pack lives."

He was right. As much as I wanted to make sure for myself that she got home safely, it would only invite trouble if we followed her into the pack's home for no reason. Normally, I wouldn't worry about upsetting a few wolves, but this pack cared for Sara, and her friends were protective of her. I didn't want to change that.

But if I ever suspected she was in danger, I'd go through the entire pack to ensure her safety.

Chris shook out his wet hair and pulled on his helmet. "I found a pretty decent pub the other day. Let's grab a beer and dry off."

I agreed because there was nothing else for me to do in that moment. Chris led the way to a small bar near the waterfront. We grabbed a booth, paid for two beers, and talked in low voices about the situation in Portland. My eyes kept going to the clock on the wall, and I couldn't help but wonder what Sara was doing. I was so used to her being at home where it was easier to watch over her, and I didn't like not knowing where she was.

Chris groaned. "You're killing me, Nikolas. If I ever find a bond mate, just shoot me right away and put me out of my misery."

I smiled into my beer. "When this happens to you, I'm going to enjoy your suffering as much as you are enjoying mine. Maybe more."

He let out a snort. "No way. I'll stick to human women for the next hundred years or so, just to be safe."

"For a guy who dates so many women, you're going through a lot of trouble not to settle down."

"Oh, it's no trouble." His eyebrows lifted suggestively. "I happen to love human women, and they're less aggressive than our females."

"Mohiri women aren't that aggressive, unless you're talking about someone like –"

"Celine?" he finished for me with a smirk. "Remind me again, how long ago did you and she hook up? And she still tries to rekindle your little romance whenever she sees you."

I chuckled. "Celine is in a league of her own."

I thought about the raven-haired beauty I'd met while on a job in New York City back in the twenties. Celine Moreau was a superb warrior and just as skilled as a lover. She'd made no secret of the fact she wanted me in her bed. It had been a pleasurable week for us both, and then we'd parted ways. I'd seen her many times since then, and we were on friendly terms, but I had no interest in picking up where we'd left off. Celine pursued me only because she was used to men adoring her and she couldn't conceive of one not wanting her.

My thoughts turned back to Sara. I couldn't have bonded with someone more opposite of Celine. Sara wasn't afraid to express herself, yet she seemed to try to *not* be noticed. And unlike Celine, Sara had no interest in me.

The irony of the situation was not lost on me.

My phone vibrated on the table, and I frowned at Erik's name on the screen. He wouldn't call this late unless he'd found something important.

"Nikolas, we have trouble," he said as soon as I picked up. "We got word of a strange animal spotted near the university in Gorham. Reese went to check it out. He says based on the tracks and the witnesses' descriptions, it was a crocotta."

My blood chilled. Crocotta were vicious creatures that resembled giant hyenas and always traveled in small packs. They were better than bloodhounds at picking up a scent and tracking it. If there were crocotta in or near Portland, they had been brought in to find someone specifically.

I immediately thought of Eli. The Attic had been full of college students the night we were there, and it made sense that Eli would assume Sara was also in college. So the first place he would look for her was the university.

"Thanks for letting me know," I said with forced calm. "Keep me posted if you find anything else."

"What's wrong?" Chris asked as soon as I hung up.

"There was a crocotta spotted near Portland. You know there's only one reason someone would bring those things here."

"Jesus."

"Chris, check the tracker you put on the truck. Where are they?"

He pulled out his tracking monitor. "I told you she's in the…"

His brows drew together, and my chest tightened with dread. "It looks like the truck is stopped on Fell Road, about a mile from the Knolls."

I was out of my chair and halfway to the door before he called after me. He caught up to me at the bikes.

"There are lots of reasons why they could be stopped on the road," Chris said as I straddled my motorcycle.

"She's in danger. I feel it in my gut, Chris."

"Okay. But you have to think like a warrior now, not a mate. Crocotta are intelligent and they like to surround their prey. If we rush in there together, they'll have the upper hand. We need to split up and go in from different directions."

He held up the monitor that displayed a map of the town and a blinking yellow dot that was the truck. It didn't take long for us to determine the fastest routes there. A minute later, I was speeding toward the Knolls and praying we were not too late.

It took eleven minutes to reach the turnoff to Fell Road. As I slowed for the sharp right turn, the unmistakable screams of crocotta reached my ears.

"Hold on, Sara." I hit the gas and shot down the road toward the screams.

I let out the breath I was holding when I sensed her presence. It was faint, but she was nearby and alive. It grew stronger as I sped around a bend in the road and the truck came into view.

I sized up the situation as I raced forward. In front of the truck, Chris fought with two crocotta, and a few feet away, the werewolves battled one between them. A fourth crocotta stalked toward the truck. There was no sign of Sara, and I hoped she was safely locked inside the vehicle.

A growl rumbled in my chest as my eyes narrowed on the creature threatening my mate. I reached down, unbuckled my sword, and gripped the hilt without taking my eyes off my prey. Instead of slowing, I sped up, and my bike plowed into the crocotta with a satisfying crunch.

A second before impact, I leapt from the bike and spun in the air, landing on my feet with my sword in hand. I went after the creature trapped under the bike. It struggled frantically when it saw me, and it managed a weak scream before I severed its head.

Bloodlust filled me as I turned to Chris and the two crocotta he battled. I strode into the fray and brought my sword down across the flank of the closest creature. It cried out and spun around to face me. I didn't give it a chance to attack. I drove my sword into its wide chest, killing it instantly.

Seconds later, Chris and the werewolves finished off the last two crocotta, and the night was silent except for the werewolves' panting and the light rain.

I looked at the black werewolf. "You know these woods?"

He nodded.

"Go make sure there are no more crocotta nearby."

He hesitated and glanced at the truck.

"I'll take care of her. I promise you."

He nodded again, and he and his friend dashed off into the woods. I turned to the truck, and my breath caught in my throat when I saw what I hadn't noticed at a distance. The hood and driver door were crumpled, the windshield looked ready to fall in, and the roof was shredded with jagged pieces of metal sticking up. Through the cracked window, I could make out someone sitting in the middle of the cab. *Sara.*

In three strides, I was at the truck and pulling on the handle of the driver's side door. The damage to the door had wedged it, but nothing was going to stop me from getting inside that cab. I gripped the edges of the door, where it twisted away from the frame, and ripped it off the truck.

"Easy, man. You'll frighten her," Chris called as I threw the door away from me. His warning registered in my brain, but I almost lost it when I took in Sara's ghostly pale face splattered with blood. Her green eyes were dazed, and the knife I had given her was coated with blood in her clenched hand. I could see no injuries, and I prayed the blood on her belonged to the creature she had fought.

My hand trembled from a mixture of relief and fury when I cupped her cold face and made her look at me. The pain and fear in her eyes made my heart constrict, and my words came out harsher than I meant them to.

"It's okay, Sara. They're all gone. Are you hurt anywhere?"

She didn't answer, and I worried she was in shock. I snapped my fingers in front of her eyes, and they lost the glazed look.

"Sara, can you hear me?" I asked with more gentleness.

"Yes." Her voice was little more than a hoarse whisper.

Relief coursed through me. I let go of her chin and covered the hand still clutching the knife so tightly that her knuckles were white.

"You're safe now, *moy malen'kiy voin.* Let the knife go." The endearment slipped off my tongue easily, though I'd never spoken that way to another person.

She relinquished the weapon to me, and I threw it on the floor before I took both of her hands in mine. I studied the blood-splattered interior of the cab, and anger surged in me again when I looked up at the shredded roof where the crocotta had tried to get to her.

"You fought them off? By yourself?"

"J-just one," she croaked.

I let out a short laugh and shook my head. "Just one? *Khristu!*"

Crocotta were savage fighters, and she had fought one with a knife while trapped in this small space. Pride filled me, and I tugged gently on her hands.

"We need to get you out of this thing. Do you think you can stand?"

She nodded, and then she let out a cry of pain. The agony on her face awoke something dark and violent within me.

"What is it? Did it hurt you?"

She nodded weakly and closed her eyes, but that didn't stop the tears from spilling down her cheeks. "G-guess I'm not much of a fighter after all."

The urge to kill something rose up inside me, catching me off guard. I had to fight to maintain a calm expression so I didn't frighten her more.

Get it together. The last thing she needs is to see you lose it.

"Stay here," I managed to say.

I ducked out of the cab and stormed away from the truck. My mate was hurt. Her cry of pain echoed in my head, and all I could see was blood. The smell clung to my nostrils, fueling the fury building inside me.

I almost ripped the storage compartment off my bike in my search for the can of gunna paste I kept there. The medicine was carried by all warriors because it was a pain reliever as well as an accelerant for our natural healing abilities.

I swore loudly when I couldn't find the can of paste, and I almost punched Chris when he nudged me aside and dug through the compartment. His hand reappeared holding the metal cylinder, and I reached for it, but he held it away from me.

"Give me the goddamn can, Chris." I advanced on my best friend.

"I will tend to her," he said.

"The hell you will. I'll take care of her."

"Nikolas, you need to calm down," he ordered in an even voice. "If you go over there like this, you'll frighten her. Is that what you want?"

His words pierced my anger. "No, I don't want that."

He nodded. "She'll be okay. Just get it under control while I do this."

I stood rigidly beside my bike while he went to the truck. I heard the soft murmur of voices, and a few minutes later, Chris reappeared with Sara in his arms.

I started toward them, but stopped when he set her on her feet. She clung to him for support while he examined the injury on her arm and explained about crocotta venom. She looked weak, but her face was no longer twisted in pain, thanks to the gunna paste.

When Chris turned her and pulled up her coat and shirt to reveal the scratches on her back, a deep primal rage erupted inside me. It pulsed red behind my eyes, and my body trembled as my Mori fought for dominance. Only Chris's words about frightening Sara kept me rooted to the spot and fighting with every ounce of willpower to control my Mori's rage.

"These are a little deeper but nothing life-threatening," Chris said loudly, and I knew he was trying to reassure me as much as her.

Sara looked at me, wearing a confused expression, but all I could do was stare back at her. Chris smiled and said, "I have a better bedside manner than my friend."

"He looks angry. Is he mad at me?" she asked.

Chris shot me a warning look. "No. He's upset that we were too late to stop you from getting hurt. He's worked himself into a bit of a rage, and he just needs a minute to calm down."

She looked away from me. "A rage?"

"Yes, it happens when…" He glanced at me again as if he was unsure of what to tell her. "It's a Mori thing. You'll learn about that stuff soon."

"Oh." She looked around fearfully. "Where are my friends?"

"They are making sure there are no more crocotta hiding nearby." Chris whistled softly. "Six of them. That is an unusually large pack. Someone is very serious about finding you."

I clenched my hands into fists at the thought of what would have happened if Erik hadn't called me. If we hadn't gotten here when we did…

"Finding me?" Sara asked in a small voice.

"The crocotta are trackers," Chris told her. "Someone sent them after you, probably with orders to retrieve you."

"They…almost killed me."

He helped her into her torn, bloody coat. "The thrill of the hunt got the better of them. Good thing they're not as good at killing as they are at tracking."

She started to shake, and her hand flew up to cover her mouth. "I think I'm going to be sick," she uttered before she rushed to the other side of the road and threw up.

The sight of her in so much misery snapped me out of my rage, and I started toward her.

Chris held up a hand and mouthed, *Wait.*

"I'm good," I said in a low voice.

The anger was gone, replaced by the need to comfort the girl who was quickly becoming the most important person in my life. I still wasn't sure how I felt about that, but right now, all that mattered was her well-being.

She finished retching and stood facing away from us, shivering with her arms wrapped around her. She looked so small and vulnerable that my chest ached.

I pulled off my leather jacket and walked over to drape it across her shoulders.

"I'll get blood all over it," she argued weakly.

I gently turned her to face me, wrapping the jacket around her to make sure she was covered and warm. The jacket swallowed her. The sight of her in it made my Mori happy and stirred more than my protective instincts.

I released her and took a step back. "I think it can stand a little blood."

"I... Thank you," she said softly.

I was glad to see she was no longer shivering. "Are you still in pain?"

She shook her head. "I'm much better, thanks."

She looked past me, and I watched her face as her gaze moved over the dead crocotta and landed on the destroyed truck. Her eyes widened when she saw the extent of the damage for the first time.

"Only someone with warrior blood could have survived that," I told her.

"I'm not a warrior."

"So you keep telling me," I challenged softly.

The play of emotions across her face made me want to pull her to me and comfort her. I went to busy myself by checking on my bike. Sara was injured and most likely suffering from mild shock; she didn't need to deal with my lack of control on top of that.

"Sara!"

Her friend Roland ran toward her, and I was glad to see he had found his clothing. When he reached her, he moved to hug her, but she held up a hand to stop him. His smile was replaced by concern. "Are you hurt?"

"Yes, but I'll live," she replied.

"I nearly lost it when I saw it attacking you," he said in a shaky voice. "I studied crocotta, but I never thought I'd see them around here. Fuck! They were strong. You were incredible, fighting it off like that."

Yes, she was, I agreed.

"I wouldn't have lasted much longer without you guys." She glanced around. "Where is Peter, by the way? There's no way I'm going out there looking for him again."

Roland laughed. "He went to find his clothes. There was no one home when he got there, so he grabbed a lug wrench and headed back. He was coming up the road when he saw us getting attacked."

Sara was quiet for a moment. Then she turned to me. "How did you know?"

"One of our men called to tell me a crocotta had been seen in the Portland area," I said. "I knew that they could track you, even if the vampires couldn't."

"But how did you know where we were?"

Chris chuckled. "I put a tracker on your friend's truck at the pizza place a few days ago." Her eyes widened and he said, "You didn't think I was going to run around town all week looking for you, did you?"

Roland looked angry, but we would not apologize for taking a measure that had ended up saving their lives. I'd do it again, as many times as I had to, to keep Sara safe.

Their friend Peter ran up to us. "I think we got them all. No worries about one of them reporting back to whoever sent them." He stared at the truck. "Damn! What the hell happened to the truck?"

"You three are like a disaster magnet." Tonight had proven that this town was no longer safe for Sara. The best place for her was Westhorne. Surely she would agree after what had happened here.

I rooted in the compartment on my bike for my phone before I remembered it was in my jacket pocket. I walked over to Sara and retrieved my phone. "I'm going to call for a pickup," I said to Chris.

Sara gave me a puzzled look. "A pickup for what?"

"Not what, *who*," I answered. "Look around. It's not safe here for you."

Her lips pressed together, and she moved closer to Roland. "I'm not going anywhere."

It bothered me that she moved toward another male for support, but I pushed it aside. Her safety was more important than my jealousy. "Be reasonable, Sara. You need to be with people who can protect you."

"We can protect her." Roland hugged her against him with one arm.

"I can see that," I replied dryly. "Why is it both times she's been attacked were when you've been *protecting* her?"

Roland's eyes narrowed. "Are you implying something?"

Was he serious? "Look around you."

He scowled at me. "No one could have expected a large pack of crocotta to show up like that. And you couldn't have held off that many alone either."

"No, but if she was with her own people, she wouldn't have had to worry about that."

"Her people?" he repeated angrily, and I could tell I had touched a nerve. "We're her friends. We care for her more than a bunch of strangers."

"They wouldn't be strangers for long," I argued. "And she can train to protect herself."

"Stop it!"

I looked at Sara, whose eyes were flashing angrily.

"Stop talking about me like I'm not even here," she yelled at us. "I'm not leaving New Hastings, so drop it."

Her short outburst seemed to drain her, and the fire went out of her eyes as she sagged wearily against Roland. I immediately regretted upsetting her.

"Sara, I think you should come home with us tonight," Roland told her.

She looked at the dead crocotta. "But you guys got them all."

"Yes, but you're covered in blood and your clothes are all ripped up. You don't want Nate to see you like this."

She looked down at her ripped and bloody clothes, and sighed heavily. "You're right. Nate can't see this."

I wasn't happy about her refusal to leave, but I thought it was a good idea for her to stay with the werewolves tonight. Of course, I had every intention of going with her. My Mori was quiet now, but neither of us was going to let her out of our sight tonight.

I looked at the truck and the mess of crocotta parts. "Is there anyone around here who can clean this up before the locals see it? If not, we'll bring in someone."

"Yeah, I'll call someone." Roland pulled out his phone and made a call. When he hung up, he said, "My cousin Francis will be here in a few minutes with a crew to take care of this. We'll take Sara to my house."

"Chris and I will come with you to make sure there's no more trouble," I said, expecting an argument.

Roland shook his head. "There's no need for that. She'll be safe in the Knolls."

"Forgive me if I have my doubts. We will accompany you."

I was surprised when Sara didn't protest us going with them. But one look at her face told me she was too tired to fight me on this.

Her brow furrowed, and she looked at Chris. "How did you get here so fast?"

"My bike is half a mile down the road. When I heard the crocotta's hunting calls I decided to come in on foot to surprise them." He arched an eyebrow at me. "I had no idea some people would come roaring in, making enough noise to wake the dead."

She gave him a weary smile. "Thank you."

Chris grinned. "And I thought small town life was boring."

Roland's cleanup crew didn't take long to get to us, and within minutes, a pickup and a car pulled to a stop in front of us. I recognized the driver of the car as the hotheaded werewolf Chris and I had seen in Portland. He ignored us, drawn instead to the six crocotta corpses on the road. He swore repeatedly as he studied one of the creatures.

Two more men piled out of the truck. One of them let out a whistle and looked at Sara's friends. "You guys did this?" he asked incredulously.

Peter grinned. "Yes, with help."

Francis and the others finally noticed us, and their faces twisted into scowls. "What are they doing here?" one of the guys asked. I expected Francis to have something to say after our encounter in the city, but he only glared at us.

"They helped us fight the crocotta," Peter told them.

Sara looked like she could barely stand, and every second these guys talked was one more she would not be resting. "If you guys don't mind, Sara is hurt."

Francis turned to her. "You're hurt? Do you need to go to the hospital?"

"No hospital," she said firmly.

"Maybe you should get checked out," Roland told her.

Chris stepped forward. "She'll be okay. I gave her something to help with the pain and to speed up the healing. Trust me. It's a very powerful medicine. The Mohiri have used it in battle for centuries. With her own accelerated healing, her injuries will go away in a few days."

Francis stared at Chris. "Her accelerated healing?"

"It's a long story," Sara and Roland said at the same time.

Francis gave his keys to Roland. "Take my car. I'll stay here with the boys to take care of this. We'll need to call in a few more hands to get rid of all these."

Roland helped Sara to the car, and they set off for his house. I climbed on my bike to follow them. "I'll call you and let you know where we are," I told Chris, who had started down the road toward his own bike.

I parked beside the car at the house and went inside without bothering to knock. It wasn't as if they weren't expecting me. Roland and Peter were in the kitchen, and Roland pointed to the living room where Sara was curled up on the couch, still wearing my jacket.

"We should put her in a bed so she's more comfortable," I told them in a low voice.

Roland shook his head. "Sara loves our couch. She'll be okay there."

"Then get her a warm blanket," I insisted.

"Sometimes, I forget she isn't like us and she gets cold easier," Roland said sheepishly. He disappeared down a hallway and returned carrying a thick quilt, which he laid over her. She mumbled in her sleep, but did not awaken.

"Were the crocotta really sent to find Sara?" Peter whispered as I took out my phone and texted Chris to let him know where I was.

"I believe so. I think the vampire who attacked her is trying to find her."

Peter's eyes rounded. "But that was weeks ago. Why would he be looking for her?"

"Because she got away. I have no proof it's him, but I've seen vampires obsess over someone like this before. And you don't use crocotta unless you're desperate to find someone."

Roland swore. "Dude, thanks for showing up when you did. If anything happened to her…"

"I'll do whatever it takes to keep her safe." I looked at her sleeping form. "She told you about my visit to her last week?"

"Yeah, she told us what she is," Roland said. "If you think that matters to us, you're wrong."

It was good to know Sara had such loyal friends. I hoped someday she could learn to trust me as much as she trusted them.

"Dad nearly lost it when I told him about the crocotta," Peter whispered. "He and Uncle Brendan are on their way home."

"Mom will be here soon, too." Roland looked at me. "You don't need to stay. This place is gonna be swarming with pack soon, and nothing will get near Sara."

"I'll stay all the same." I left them and walked into the living room. Sara hadn't moved, and she looked innocent and vulnerable in sleep. My Mori wanted to stand over her and growl at anyone who came near her. But I knew she was among friends here.

I could have stood guard outside, but I couldn't make myself leave her. I took a spot by the window where I could see her and keep watch at the same time.

It was just after midnight when Roland's mother, Judith, came home, followed shortly after by the Alpha, his Beta, and several other pack members. I stepped outside to talk to them briefly, but I refused to leave Sara for long. The wolves gave me questioning looks, but I saw no reason to explain my actions to them.

Maxwell Kelly was a big, brawny man with graying reddish brown hair and beard who exuded authority. It was easy to see why he was the Alpha of the largest pack in the country.

"Thank you for helping my son and nephew, and Sara," he said in a deep voice. "We are in your debt."

A few of the other wolves grumbled, but a look from Maxwell silenced them. He turned back to me.

"We are not used to having your kind here. How long do you intend to stay in our territory?"

The underlying message in his question was clear. He would tolerate us because we had helped save the lives of his pups, but he didn't like outsiders in his territory.

"I'll stay as long as I need to be here. I respect your territory, but Sara is Mohiri and under my protection."

Whispers and growls broke out around us. A low growl from Maxwell cut them off.

He gave me a hard stare then nodded. "Your people are in Portland as well?"

"Yes. We brought in a team to deal with the vampire problem there. And to provide backup in protecting Sara." I shared what we had learned so far about the vampire activity in Portland.

"I'll increase patrols here and send some of my wolves to Portland," he said.

"Good. If you'll excuse me, I'll go back to Sara."

One of the younger wolves spoke up. "You can stand guard out here. No need of you being in the house."

Before I could reply, Judith said, "This is my home, and I decide who enters it. The Warrior is welcome. If you have a problem with that, you can take it up with me."

No one argued with her, and the pack left. Judith and I talked for a few minutes and exchanged phone numbers in case Maxwell or I needed to contact each other. Soon after, she retired for the night and I went back to my spot near the living room window.

A few times, Sara tossed fitfully and murmured in her sleep, but she settled down when I went to her and gently touched her face. She might not know about the bond, but even in sleep my touch soothed her.

It was in the hours before dawn when she finally stirred. Her sleepy voice broke the silence in the room. "Nikolas?"

"Go back to sleep," I said softly.

Quiet settled over the room, and I thought she'd fallen asleep again. I turned back to the window.

"Don't go," she pleaded in a hoarse whisper.

Those two whispered words affected me as nothing ever had. My chest grew warm, and I swallowed past the strange tightness in my throat.

"I'm not going anywhere," I promised. *Ever.*

CHAPTER 7

SARA WAS SLEEPING peacefully when I walked outside at dawn. I was reluctant to leave her, but she was safe here with the pack. It was clear they cared for her, and Judith had assured me last night they would protect her as if she was one of their own. The two large men stationed outside when we left were proof of that.

Chris was waiting when I quietly closed the door behind me. We didn't speak as we pushed our bikes down the driveway to the road. Sara had had a rough night, and neither of us wanted to disturb her sleep. It wasn't until we were a quarter of a mile from the house that we started the bikes and drove into town.

We found a small diner that was open for breakfast, and I sank heavily into a booth with a low groan. Physically, I was good. I'd pulled all-nighters more times than I could remember. My head was another matter.

In all my years as a warrior, nothing had ever gotten to me as much as last night had, and I felt wrung out. Seeing Sara in that mangled truck and knowing how close I had come to losing her had awakened emotions I'd never thought I could feel. Even now, the anger threatened to resurface every time I thought of her standing in the rain in her torn and bloody clothes.

"Two coffees," Chris said, dragging me from my thoughts. I looked up to see a waitress walking away from our table.

Chris gave me a wry smile. "You remember the big quake in nineteen-oh-six?"

"How could I forget?" Chris and I had worked tirelessly for three days with a dozen other warriors, combing through the ruins of San Francisco for survivors and dispatching vampires who'd sought to take advantage of the disaster. Three days without food or sleep, but we'd rescued hundreds of people from the rubble.

"We looked like hell when that was over. That's what you remind me of now."

"I feel like hell."

He stared at me long and hard. "You almost lost it last night."

I nodded wearily. "I know."

His fingers tapped on the table. "You know it's only going to get worse. The next time you might not be able to control the rage."

"I will. I have to." The last thing I wanted was to frighten her.

"Maybe you should tell her the truth, so she'll know what's going on with you next time."

I opened my mouth to argue, and he held up a hand.

"I watched the two of you last night at the party and after the attack. She might resent you for what you represent, but she trusts you. She asked for you when I went to tend to her injuries. She has to sense there is something between you, even if she doesn't know what it is."

"No, she's not ready for that." It warmed me to know Sara had asked for me, but it was too soon to tell her everything. She needed time to get to know me, and preferably in a situation where she didn't fear for her life.

He shook his head. "It's your call."

The waitress brought our coffees, and I took a drink of the strong black brew. "I have to tell Tristan about the crocotta."

Chris made a face. "Good luck getting him to stay in Idaho after this. And once he gets here and learns about you and Sara…"

I set my cup down and rubbed my jaw. "I'll just have to be persuasive."

He laughed softly. "Like I said, good luck with that. When are you going to call him?"

"In a few hours. If I wake him up, he's going to think it's an emergency, and there'll be no talking to him."

"Good idea." He sipped his coffee. "I assume you're going to stay here, for today at least."

"Yes." There was no way I could leave her so soon after the attack.

"I'll head back to Portland then and see what Erik is up to. I called him last night and told him about the attack. He couldn't believe it when I told him there were six crocotta."

I scowled at the memory of all the crocotta bodies in the road. "I think I've seen a pack that big only once before."

He gave me a grim look. "Whether it's Eli or someone else behind this, they're not messing around."

"I know."

"If it gets too dangerous and she won't leave, we might not have any choice but to make her go." He stared intently at me. "Are you prepared to do that if it comes to it?"

"She might hate me for it, but her safety comes first."

"Then we'll have to make sure it doesn't come to that." Chris pushed his cup away and got out of the booth. "I'll see you tomorrow."

I paid the bill and left the diner several minutes later. I'd seen a small hotel near the waterfront, so I decided to get a room where I could shower and recharge for a few hours before I called Tristan.

Chris knew Tristan well. After I told Tristan about the crocotta attack, it took me well over an hour to convince him to stay at Westhorne. He thought being her grandfather, he could somehow convince Sara to leave everything she knew behind. It wasn't easy, having to remind him that most of Sara's dislike for the Mohiri stemmed from her resentment toward her mother. She would not welcome Madeline's sire, even if he was nothing like his daughter. And if she was able to get past that, she would not leave her uncle.

It was almost noon when I ended the call with Tristan. My first thought was of Sara and how she was doing today. It would take her a day or two to fully recover from her injuries, and I wished I had thought to leave some gunna paste with her in case she needed it for pain.

Remembering I had Judith's number, I called her to check on Sara.

"She's doing great. She's in no pain and healing incredibly fast. I doubt she'll have any scars at all in a day or two."

I released the breath I was holding. "Is she still there?"

"You just missed her. She left with Roland. I believe he's giving her driving lessons."

"Driving lessons?" The thought of her doing something so normal after last night made me smile at her resilience. "Is she okay to drive?"

Judith laughed. "I hope so. That's my only car."

I was smiling when I hung up, relieved Sara was recovering well from last night. I spent the rest of the day combing the town and surrounding woods for any signs of trouble. I doubted there would be more crocotta, but I was taking no chances where Sara was concerned.

Several times I ran into pack members in wolf and human forms, but we acknowledged each other without any conflict. It was clear from their expressions that they were not happy about my presence in town, but their Alpha must have ordered them to stand down.

Later that night, I walked from my hotel to the waterfront to keep watch for a few hours and to reassure my Mori and myself that she was okay.

I'd expected her to be asleep, but light shone from the third floor of the building where I believed her bedroom to be, having seen her in the windows up there on several occasions. A few minutes later, the third floor lights went out and the curtains moved in one of the windows.

My eyesight sharpened, and I saw her outline clearly as she looked down at the waterfront. I couldn't see her expression, and I wondered if she was afraid to sleep, expecting another monster to come out of the darkness.

Facing that many crocotta would give some warriors bad dreams.

Every other time I'd kept watch, I'd made sure to stay out of sight, but tonight I wanted her to go to sleep knowing she had nothing to fear. I stepped into the circle of light from the street light so she could see me clearly.

For a long moment, she looked at me without moving. Then, the curtain fell back into place and she disappeared.

I stayed in the light for another minute before I melted back into the shadows.

*   *   *

I left New Hastings the next morning with the intention of returning that night, but the escalating situation in Portland demanded my presence in the city. On Sunday night, the body of a young woman was found in a dumpster near the university. Her ravaged throat told us our vampire problem had grown.

Maxwell must have gotten word of it because suddenly Portland was crawling with werewolves. There were a few clashes when our warriors encountered some of the younger wolves who didn't like our presence in Portland. I had to go out and diffuse several of the conflicts.

On Tuesday, Maxwell called and asked to meet at a small pub in Portland owned by one of his pack members. I met him there alone since Chris was in New Hastings, and I received more than one glare when I walked up to the bar and ordered a beer.

Maxwell arrived as the bartender was pouring my beer. He ordered one for himself and we sat at a booth in the back.

"My wolves don't like having your people in our territory, and frankly neither do I," he said. "But we're all hunters here, and we have the same enemy. So we need to learn to work together to deal with this situation."

I took a drink of my beer. "I agree. What do you propose?"

Surprise showed in his eyes. "I'm going to send six wolves to Portland every night. You tell me where you'll be working, and I'll focus on another part of the city. We'll cover more ground that way and stay out of each other's hair."

"Sounds good." I sat back in my chair. "I believe the vampire named Eli is behind this. He's dangerous and slippery, and I need to know if one of your wolves takes him down."

Maxwell nodded gravely. "I'll have them take pictures of their kills, although I can't guarantee there will be much left to identify."

We talked for another hour about how we could work together to avoid future problems between our people. Maxwell was overly protective of his territory, as any good Alpha would be, but he was rational and smart enough to acknowledge the Mohiri were a strong ally against the threat to this city. I respected that in a leader.

That night, there was a second vampire attack near the university, but it was thwarted by two werewolves who killed the vampire. True to his word, Maxwell had his wolves send us a photo of the dead vampire. There was just enough left of his face to know he wasn't Eli.

That same night, Erik and I took out three young vampires we had cornered behind a night club. They couldn't have been more than a few weeks old. When they said they didn't know who Eli was, they were almost too terrified to speak, let alone lie to us.

We were killing vampires, but there was no sign of Eli, and it frustrated the hell out of me. My instincts told me the bastard was still here and he was up to something. I'd seen vampires obsess over a prey before, but why would he risk his life by staying around here with so many hunters in the city? I wouldn't be happy until I put a blade through his demon heart.

I was in a black mood when I finally left Portland late Wednesday afternoon to ride to New Hastings. I didn't realize how worked up I was until I got closer to the small town and the tension began to leave my body. It still stunned me how strong the bond had grown in just a few weeks, and how I could miss someone after only three days apart.

It troubled me as well. As a warrior I didn't have many weaknesses, but Sara made me vulnerable in ways I'd never thought possible. My feelings for her and my need to keep her safe were things an enemy could exploit. Chris had been right the other night when he said I needed to think like a warrior and not like a mate when it came to protecting her. Emotions in battle made you sloppy and distracted, and that could get you killed.

I thought my imagination was playing tricks on me when I sensed Sara on the outskirts of town. Then I rounded a bend in the road and saw a lone figure riding a bicycle past the city limit sign. What the hell was she doing out here alone, especially after the attack a few nights ago? Where was Chris? And the werewolves who had sworn to watch over her?

I let off the gas and kept pace behind her for the three miles to her building on the waterfront. She knew I was there, but she didn't look behind her once, and she didn't change her speed. I wasn't sure if that was because she trusted me or because she believed she was safe in broad daylight.

I saw her shoulders tense when we reached the waterfront, and I knew she was going to try to slip inside before I could confront her. Keeping her in sight, I rode ahead and parked my bike in front of her building. I was standing by the corner, trying to rein in my anger when she rode up. Seeing her soothed my Mori and me, but that didn't diminish my fear at her disregard for her own safety.

I didn't give her a chance to speak as I moved toward her. "Did you not learn anything the other night? Are you *trying* to get yourself killed?"

"Of course not," she retorted, though fear flashed in her eyes as she dismounted and walked her bike toward the building.

"No?" I hated my hard tone, but I was too wound up after the last few days to soften it. "Do you want to tell me where you had to sneak off to that was so important?"

"No." She shifted from one foot to the other. She was hiding something.

"There is nothing but woods for miles south of town. What were you doing out there?" And where the hell was Chris? How could he let her go off on her own like that?

Her brows drew together. "How did you find me anyway? Did you put one of those trackers on my bike, too?"

"No, but maybe I should."

Her eyes darkened with indignation. "No, you should not! I'm not helpless, you know, and I don't need you guys following me around twenty-four seven. I took care of myself pretty well before you came along."

A part of me understood her anger and frustration. I wouldn't be happy if someone entered my life and tried to restrict my freedom in any way. A larger part of me was infuriated that she refused to see reason, and my words came out mocking. "Yes, I can see how well you do on your own. I'm amazed you lived this long."

She drew back. "I'm sorry I'm such a *trial* to you, but no one is asking you to stick around here. You can go back to doing your warrior thing – hunting vampires or whatever you do – and forget all about me."

I could sense she was hurt by my words, but all I could think of was keeping her safe. When she tried to march past me, I blocked her, grabbing her bike so she couldn't move. I leaned down, and her scent surrounded me. "If I was a vampire, you'd be dead – or worse."

Her body stiffened, and I heard her sharp intake of breath. As she lifted her eyes to mine, her warm breath caressed my throat. For several seconds, I forgot everything but those soft lips inches from mine.

She averted her gaze. "Does it even matter?"

I blinked as her words pierced the spell she'd cast over me. "What?"

"You said that day on the wharf that you can't save every orphan. What difference does one more make?"

The suggestion that her life meant so little, that she was nothing more than a job to me, made my chest tighten. If she only knew how precious her life was to me. How did I make her understand that I only cared about her welfare and happiness?

She pulled away from me. "Do you mind letting go of my bike? Nate will be home soon, and it's my turn to make dinner."

"*Khristu!*" My grip tightened on the handlebars until I thought the metal would bend. How could someone make me want to shake them and kiss them at the same time? "Do you not understand the danger you're in? I know you want to believe you're safe here surrounded by your werewolf friends, but someone went to great lengths sending that pack of crocotta to find you. If it is that vampire, he won't give up."

This time she couldn't hide the fear that crossed her face, and guilt stabbed me for making her afraid again.

I laid my hand over her smaller one. "If you are honest with yourself, you'll admit I'm right. I can protect you if you'll let me."

I felt her tremble, saw the uncertainty in her eyes, along with some other emotion I couldn't read. Just when I thought she was going to admit I was right, she pulled away.

"I really need to go inside now," she said quietly.

I stepped back to let her pass and followed her as she wheeled the bike around the building to the back door. I watched her fumble for her key. "You can run away from me, but you can't run from the truth. The werewolves can't protect you forever, and eventually, you'll have to leave New Hastings. What will you do then?"

She froze for several seconds, and I knew my words had hit home. There was a slight tremor in her voice when she spoke again.

"When that happens it'll be my problem, not yours." Opening the door, she shoved the bike inside. "I don't want you following me around anymore."

My hands clenched at my sides. "And I don't want you to keep putting yourself in danger. Seems like neither of us will get what we want."

The door closed between us. I went back to my bike, pulling out my phone as I walked. I dialed Chris's number, and he answered on the third ring. From the rumbling in the background he was on his bike.

"What's up?" he asked.

"What's up is that I just found Sara riding her bicycle a few miles outside of town. Why weren't you watching her?"

Chris sighed loudly. "I've been driving around for the last hour looking for her. Is she okay?"

"Yes, but anything could have happened to her out there." I paced in front of my bike. "How could you lose her?"

"She gave me the slip," he replied sheepishly. "I followed her home from school, and I thought she was still inside. A couple of girls from her school showed up, and they kept coming over to talk to me. I couldn't get them to leave. Then one of them mentioned seeing Sara riding away on her bike. She was gone by the time I went to look for her. She's been so predictable this whole time, and I never thought she'd take off like that. I'm sorry, Nikolas."

I pinched the bridge of my nose. "Don't worry about it. We'll just have to keep a closer eye on her."

"What was she doing outside town on her bike anyway?"

"She wouldn't say." I looked up at her window. "I think she's hiding something."

"Like what?"

I straddled my bike. "I have no idea, but I'm going to find out. You want to come back here and watch her place while I go check it out?"

"I'll be there in five minutes."

As soon as I saw Chris riding down the waterfront, I set off for the area south of town where I'd found Sara. I drove up and down the empty stretch of road, but there was nothing but trees and rocks in sight. No houses, businesses, or buildings of any kind. I did find an old gravel road that was so overgrown it was little more than a track. I followed it for a mile where it ended at an abandoned mine that didn't look like it had been disturbed in years.

After an hour of searching, I had to admit there was nothing suspicious in the area. Was it possible that Sara had just been out riding her bike? I quickly banished that thought, remembering her nervous reaction when I'd asked what she was doing out here.

There was another possible answer, one I hadn't wanted to entertain. It could be that she had met up with someone, a male she didn't want anyone to know about. The thought of her with another man made my stomach burn like it was filled with acid. I had to remind myself that she was oblivious to my feelings and to the bond, and it was only natural that she might be seeing someone.

I shook off the jealousy as I rode back to town. To Sara, I was the warrior here to protect her, nothing more. Despite her knowledge of the world, she wasn't ready to cope with the intense emotions of a bond mate. Hell, most Mohiri females who grew up knowing about bonding were unprepared to deal with it at first. I'd do my damnedest to shield her from that until she was ready to know the truth.

* * *

The sound of a phone ringing woke me early the next morning, and I rolled over in my hotel bed to grab my cell phone off the nightstand. I scowled when I glanced at the alarm clock and saw it was only six fifteen. I hadn't gone to bed until four because I'd been keeping an eye on Sara's building, and I could have used a few more hours of shut-eye.

A groan slipped out when I saw my parents' faces on my phone screen. Why on Earth were they calling at this hour? Hoping it wasn't bad news, I got up and pulled on a T-shirt and jeans before I answered the video call.

My mother's smiling face greeted me. "Good morning, my son."

"Good morning, *Mama*," I replied, slipping into my native tongue. "Is everything well there?"

She nodded and brushed aside a lock of dark hair that fell loose from the knot she liked to wear it in. "I should be asking if everything is well with you. We haven't heard from you in a while."

I ran a hand through my messy hair. "I'm only a few days late."

I talked to my parents once a month, but with everything I'd had going on lately, I'd forgotten to call them. Of course, there was no way I was telling my mother I'd been distracted by my mate. I hadn't gotten nearly enough sleep for *that* conversation.

"I'm on a job in Maine, and it's keeping me busy."

"I know. I talked to Tristan last night, and he told me you found his granddaughter." Her face lit up. "Such incredible news! To think Madeline had a daughter and told no one. Tristan might never have known of the girl's existence if you had not stumbled across her. It almost seems like providence, doesn't it?"

I swallowed a laugh. "You could say that."

She grew more serious. "You look tired. Are you sleeping well?"

"I sleep very well when my mother doesn't wake me at the crack of dawn," I teased.

I was rewarded with a deep chuckle as my sire sat beside her and put an arm around her shoulders. She leaned over to kiss him on the cheek, but he turned his head so their lips met instead.

My parents were bonded years before I was born, and I had grown up surrounded by their displays of affection. Both of them were great warriors and loving parents, always ensuring that one of them stayed with me when the other had to travel. They had pushed me hard in my studies and training to prepare me well for the dangers I'd face as a warrior.

"Good morning, Nikolas." My sire smiled into the camera, and it was almost like looking into a mirror. We were so alike in appearance that strangers often mistook us for brothers.

"I told her it was too early, but you know how she gets when she wants to talk to her son."

"Mikhail, shush!" She shouldered him then gave me a stern look. "Perhaps if my son came to visit more than once a year, I would not miss him as much. Or maybe if I knew he was finally ready to settle down and give me my own grandchild…"

My sire laughed, and I knew what my expression must be. I rubbed my jaw, which was in need of a shave, trying not to think about what my mother was going to be like when she found out about Sara.

"Tristan told us about the situation you are dealing with there," said my sire, coming to my rescue. "Wouldn't it be easier to convince the girl to go to Westhorne."

I let out a short laugh. "Trust me; it's easier to fight a dozen vampires than to convince Sara to do anything. She doesn't exactly have the highest opinion of us." I told them how Madeline had abandoned Sara and then Sara's father had been killed by vampires.

"That poor girl." My mother's eyes glistened. "Surely, she must see now that it's too dangerous for her there."

I shook my head. "She lives in the heart of werewolf territory, and she's close to the pack. She thinks they'll protect her, and I can't make her see reason."

My sire laughed. "Someone you can't command? I may have to meet this girl."

"A female immune to my son's charm? Impossible," my mother chimed in.

I scowled at the pair of them. "Go ahead and laugh."

"I'm sorry, Nikolas." My mother's lips twitched, and she pressed them together. "What can we do to help?"

"Nothing." I thought about Sara going off on her own yesterday and a sigh of frustration escaped me. "Unless you can tell me how to talk to someone who has a total disregard for her own safety. A few days ago, a pack of crocotta attacked her, and yesterday, she slipped away when Chris was watching her to go off doing God knows what. She refused to tell me where she went, and she got angry at me when I confronted her about it. How am I supposed to protect her if she won't listen to me?"

My parents exchanged a look, and my mother gave me an indulgent smile. "I think, my son, that you've forgotten what it is like to be young and reckless."

"And to challenge authority," my sire added.

"I might have broken a few rules, but I —"

Their laughter filled my hotel room, and it was a full two minutes before either of them could talk. My mother wiped her eyes and leaned back in her chair.

"My darling boy, there wasn't a rule you *hadn't* broken by the time you reached puberty."

"I wasn't that bad."

"Really?" She arched an eyebrow. "How many times did you sneak out to watch the warriors train after I forbade it? How many times did you injure yourself playing with your papa's swords even though you were warned against it? We went through more gunna paste than five warrior units together."

"I wanted to be a warrior. What was wrong with that?"

"You were ten, a little young to be a warrior." My sire nudged my mother. "Irina, how old was our son the day he decided he was ready to join the warriors on patrol?"

Her eyes sparkled with laughter. "Thirteen."

I remembered that day well. I had wanted so much to be a warrior like my parents, and I'd spent every hour I could with the warriors, watching them train and listening to their hunting stories. I started practicing with knives when I was ten, years before my formal training began, and by the time I was twelve, I was already proficient with most of the weapons used by the warriors.

The warriors' stories of the world had enthralled me. I had never been outside the walls of our stronghold, and I longed for the day I could go out and see the world. I started asking to go on patrols as soon as I was skilled enough to ride a horse and hold a sword at the same time, but the warriors told me I wasn't ready. I knew better – or I thought I did.

One day, I hid inside a supply cart going to an isolated village suffering from an especially brutal winter. It took three hours to reach the village, and by the time we got there my whole body ached from huddling in the cart. I knew by the warriors' hushed voices that something was wrong, and I climbed out to see the villagers gathered around seven bodies laid out in the village square. Two vampires had attacked in the night and killed six people before an archer took down one of the vampires. The other had fled.

We helped the villagers bury their dead and stayed the night with them. The warriors were furious when they discovered I had stowed away, and they gave me a severe tongue lashing. That was nothing compared to the scolding I got from my parents when I returned home the next day.

For weeks, I'd dreamed of the bodies lying in the bloody snow. Seeing up close what a vampire could do lit a fire in me, and I began to train with a new intensity. By the time I entered the warrior training program at sixteen, I could best all but the most experienced swordsmen.

"Your escapades were much talked about back then." My mother laughed softly, laying a hand on my sire's shoulder.

He smiled and reached up to lay his over hers. "You always had a good heart, Nikolas, and you were passionate about your dreams, but you didn't like to be told what to do. And you always felt ready to take on the world, thinking you could handle anything. Remember that the next time your orphan challenges you. Maybe you two are more alike than you think."

A faint knock sounded on their end and my mother went to answer the door. She came back wearing a rueful smile.

"I have to go. I have a new litter of weerlaks, and no one else here will handle them. They must be fed six times a day or they become difficult."

Difficult was a mild word to describe the bad-tempered brutes. Weerlaks resembled a cross between a honey badger and a saber-toothed tiger, and they were just as mean. They were always born in litters of four, and they communicated telepathically with their litter mates. They were fast, deadly, and territorial, and if trained properly, they made excellent guard animals. My mother had been raising and training them for as long as I could remember, and her weerlaks were highly sought after by other strongholds in Europe and Asia.

She blew me a kiss. "I love you. Get some sleep so you are strong enough to keep up with your charge." Laughter followed her as she left before I could make a retort.

My sire grinned at me. "I'll let you get back to your rest. I'm sure it's well deserved. Don't wait too long to call next time. You may be a great warrior, but she worries."

I nodded. "I'll talk to you soon."

Laying the phone on the nightstand, I slid down on the bed and put my arms beneath my head to stare at the ceiling. Had I been as incorrigible as they made me out to be?

I thought back to my childhood in Russia and then in England, and I came to the surprising revelation that I'd really been as bad as my parents had said. All I'd cared about back then, besides my parents and Viv, was becoming a warrior, and I hadn't wanted to listen to anyone who slowed me down or got in my way. I'd been so sure I knew what was best for me, and I took foolish risks, believing I was ready for anything just because I could use a knife and a sword before anyone else my age.

I understood Sara's behavior a little better after talking to my parents. The anger she'd directed at me yesterday was a mask for her fear. Not fear of vampires, but of losing the life she knew. New Hastings was her home, and she felt safe here with the pack. From my observations and my interactions with her over the last few weeks, I learned she was a private person, despite her friendships, and she valued her independence greatly. She saw me as a threat to her way of life and her freedom. I could empathize with that, even though it wouldn't change my plan to keep her safe.

I sighed heavily. I just wished I knew what she was hiding. Asking her about it only pushed her further away, and I wanted her to trust me, not fear me. I racked my brain for answers, but nothing came to me. Sara seemed too guileless and clean to be involved in anything criminal, and her werewolf friends obviously cared for her a great deal. Werewolves had the uncanny ability to sense malice and corruption in others. Even if the pups were too young to pick up anything, Maxwell would have caught it for sure.

Rolling over, I punched my pillow in frustration. I could make demons cower and give up their own mother, but I couldn't crack the shell of one teenage girl.

My groan dissolved into a laugh full of self-mockery. It was no wonder my parents had been so amused. They'd no doubt get a few more chuckles out of it. If I was them, I probably would too.

*   *   *

Chris and I stepped up our watch after Sara's little escapade. We no longer tried to hide our presence from her because I didn't want her taking any more risks. She wasn't happy about it. But she would have to get used to us being around. Until we eliminated the threat to her, I was taking no more chances with her life. I didn't like the situation any more than she did, and if I had my way, she'd be living at Westhorne right now where no vampire could touch her.

When I wasn't in New Hastings, I was in Portland, working with Erik to deal with the city's growing vampire problem. And it wasn't just vampires. In the last week, we'd seen an increase in demon activity in the normally quiet city.

Some demon races were innocuous, quietly living among humans who were blissfully ignorant of the world around them. Then there were the troublemakers, the ones that posed a real threat to humans. The vampire presence in Portland had attracted a number of these demons, including the lizard-like gulak thugs. Gulak demons were known to work for vampires, and they would do anything for the right price.

The werewolves were not happy about the growing demon population in their territory, not that I blamed them. Maxwell requested another meeting with me on Saturday to discuss the problem, and this time, I went to visit him at his lumber yard in New Hastings. The Alpha not only led the largest pack in the country, he also made time to run a successful business. I had to admit, my respect for him grew every time we talked.

Maxwell was waiting for me outside his office when I pulled up. He held out a hand when I walked over to join him. "Thank you for coming."

I took the offered hand that was weathered from a life spent outdoors. "I'm glad we can work together on this."

We walked into his modest office. He sat behind the worn wooden desk while I took one of the visitor chairs. As soon as we were seated, he got straight to the reason for our meeting.

"I've been here for almost fifty years, and I've probably seen a dozen vampires in my territory in all that time. In the last three weeks, we've killed twice that many between my pack and your people." He scowled deeply. "There are vampires and demons running around Portland like it's LA, and I had goddamn crocotta hunting a mile from my home."

My body tensed. As long as Sara was in New Hastings, the vampires would be in Portland. Had he called me here to ask me to take her away so his territory would be safe again? If so, he was in for a disappointment. Sara did not want to leave her home, and I would not force her to leave unless I felt I could no longer protect her here.

Maxwell rested his arms on his desk. "I know what you're thinking, warrior. In the beginning, I had my reservations about my son and nephew's friendship with Sara because she was too fragile to play with two male pups. But she'd just lost her father, and it would have been cruel to take away her only friends. I ordered the boys to never reveal what we were to her, and the three of them became inseparable. Though we don't share the same blood, I would never turn my back on that girl."

My eyebrows shot up. "Sara didn't know you were werewolves?"

"Not until the night she was attacked in Portland."

"That must have been quite a shock for her." How was it possible for a girl to know so much about the real world and not know that her best friends were werewolves? When I'd seen her with Roland and Peter in Portland, I'd assumed she knew what they were since she'd known about vampires. And she hadn't missed a beat when I'd mentioned the werewolves to her that day on the wharf.

The more I learned about her, the more I realized how much I didn't know about her. Something told me there was a lot more to her than even her friends and family knew.

Maxwell chuckled gruffly. "I'd say we were the ones taken by surprise. We thought we'd have to calm a terrified human girl, and she was only upset that we'd hidden what we were from her. Then she started talking about vampires killing her father."

He rubbed his jaw. "Did you know she was the one who found the body? She must have been only seven or eight at the time."

"I didn't know that." My chest tightened at the thought of the little girl seeing what those monsters had done to her father. I silently cursed Madeline once again for leaving her daughter unprotected and forced to cope with such a horrific ordeal. "The newspaper and police reports didn't mention Sara at all. Do you know why?"

"No, and I thought that was strange as well. It's as if someone went to great effort to hide her." He leaned back in his chair. "I couldn't do anything for her back then, but as long as she lives here, she is under my protection. I know she's one of yours, and I'm not saying this to undermine you. I just want you to know where I stand."

"I appreciate that, and I'm glad Sara has the pack watching out for her. Until we take care of the vampire problem in Portland, she's not safe."

Maxwell's mouth tightened. "No one is. That's actually why I asked you to come today. I wanted you to know I've called in wolves from up north to beef up the patrols around Portland. These guys live a little more segregated from humans, but they are some of the best hunters in the country. I've ordered them not to engage your people when they come across them, but there still may be trouble. Some of them still carry the old resentment toward the Mohiri."

I nodded. There had been a time, a few hundred years ago, when werewolves were not as civilized as they are now, and some had attacked humans. It was Mohiri duty to protect humans from such threats, which meant hunting down and eliminating the dangerous wolves. Over time, the werewolves learned to control their animal urges and had turned their aggression on vampires instead of humans. A truce had been formed between us, but there was a lot of anger and bitterness on their side. Centuries later, the old animosity remained with a lot of werewolves.

"I'll let our warriors know."

"Good." He folded his arms across his chest. "Now, let's talk about the situation in Portland and how we're going to clean up my city."

Two hours later, I left the Alpha's office, confident that between the Mohiri and the werewolves, we would soon track down Eli and any other vampires in Portland. Maxwell was a lot more strategic than I'd first given him credit for, and he knew Portland far better than I or the other warriors. Our people had better resources, so we agreed to work together against our common enemy.

It was Chris's turn to watch over Sara, but now that I was here, I wanted to see her before I headed back to Portland. As I left the lumber yard, I called him to find out where she was.

"Nikolas, anything wrong?" he asked.

"No. I just had a good meeting with Maxwell Kelly about our vampire problem. Thought I'd stop by and check on Sara while I'm here. Is she at home?"

"You're in New Hastings?" There was an edge to his voice that immediately put me on guard.

"You sound worried. Is everything okay with Sara?"

"She's fine. But…"

"But what?" I asked in a hard voice.

He cleared his throat. "You have to promise me you won't do anything stupid."

"Chris," I bit out. "What the hell is going on?"

He exhaled slowly. "Sara just left her place with the blond man she was talking to at the party on Saturday. It looks like…they're on a date."

I was unprepared for the pain that pricked my chest. I'd known there was a possibility she dated, but hearing that she was with another male was not easy.

"Are you still there?" Chris asked.

"Yes. Where are they now?"

His bike started. "I'm following them. She's safe."

"You didn't answer my question."

"Nikolas, maybe it would be better if you stayed away right now. I'll keep Sara safe."

His unspoken message was clear. Sara wasn't in any danger, and seeing her with the other man would only agitate my Mori and me. If I had any sense of self-preservation, I'd turn around and head back to Portland. It was the rational thing to do.

No one would ever accuse a bonded male of being rational.

"I can't, Chris." How could I describe my need to see her, the irresistible pull from the bond between us? A few weeks ago, I could not have imagined feeling this way about anyone.

He swore softly. "Just promise me you won't do anything to upset her." I started to speak, but he cut me off. "I mean it. Sara might be your potential mate, but she's my family, and I don't want to see her hurt."

"I'd never hurt her. You know that."

"Not intentionally, but if you react to seeing her with the other man, you might say or do something you'll regret."

"Unless I see she is in danger, I won't approach them." My hands tightened on the bike's handlebars. "No matter what I see."

After a long pause, Chris said, "They're going into a coffee shop called The Hub. Don't make me regret telling you that. I'll be at the waterfront if you need me."

I ended the call and headed for the coffee shop. A few minutes later, I parked my bike down the street and walked toward the busy shop. When I got close enough to see the couple sitting on the other side of one of the big windows, I stopped and moved into the doorway of the nearest building, close enough to see her, and far enough away that I couldn't sense her presence.

I wasn't surprised to get a call from Chris barely five minutes after I arrived, and I assured him all was well. I wasn't happy with the situation, but I wasn't going to do anything foolish. He offered to relieve me now that I'd seen her, but I said I was good.

Sara laughed at something Samson said, and I realized I hadn't seen her laugh much since we'd met, and never with me. Not that she'd had much occasion to laugh with the events of the last three weeks. It bothered me that someone else was able to make her smile when I couldn't, but at the same time, I was glad to see her happy.

Samson got up and brought her a notepad and pencil. She wrote on the pad as they talked, so she didn't see the warm affection on his face as he watched her. But I saw it clearly, and so did my Mori.

Mine, the demon growled.

CHAPTER 8

I TOOK HALF a dozen strides toward the coffee shop before I realized what I was doing. I should have turned around and gone back, but I kept walking. Once I sensed Sara, the invisible cord that stretched between us drew me to her. I knew entering the shop was a bad idea before my hand touched the door, but that didn't stop me. Ignoring everyone else in the shop, I settled in a chair that gave me a clear view of Sara on the far side of the room.

Neither Sara nor Samson seemed aware of my presence as she finished writing and handed the notepad to him. He smiled broadly, and there was no mistaking the adoration in his eyes as he said something that made her blush prettily and look down at her lap.

My fingers clenched the arms of the leather chair as I watched him flirt openly with her, and I knew I'd be across the room in seconds if he touched her. Coming here had been a mistake, but I couldn't leave if my life depended on it.

Sara said something. Then her shoulders stiffened and she stared out the window at the street. I wondered again if she could sense me as I did her, and I felt a thrill of satisfaction when her head turned and her gaze swept the room as if she was looking for someone.

Her companion shifted, and my eyes narrowed on him as his hand moved toward her arm to get her attention. My Mori pressed forward, and I fought the urge to leave the chair.

And then I felt her gaze on me, and I forgot about the other male as I met her indignant stare. Her chin lifted defiantly and her lips pressed together, telling me she was not happy with me being there. My pulse quickened in response. God, even when she was angry, she was beautiful.

She stared at me until Samson spoke to her. I felt the loss of her gaze when she turned it toward him. They talked, and she kept her face turned

93

away from me, although he looked my way several times.

I waited for her to look at me again, but she seemed determined to ignore me. It didn't bother me at first, but the longer they sat there talking as if I wasn't in the room, the darker my mood got. By the time they got up and walked out without a glance in my direction, I was ready to bite the head off the first person who looked at me wrong.

After a minute, I went outside and strode to my bike. Straddling it, I gripped the handlebars, trying to rein in the storm brewing inside of me.

"*Khristu!*" I swore loudly as I fought my angry demon. I wasn't happy either, but there was nothing I could do about it right now. I should have stayed away. I'd seen a few newly bonded males lose it because they couldn't control their demons. I would not do that to her.

I was still there five minutes later when Chris called to tell me Sara had just gotten home. Knowing she was no longer with Samson eased my agitation a little, but I still wanted to pummel something. I started my bike and headed out of town. One of Erik's guys had set up a punching bag in the basement of the safe house, and I had a feeling he was going to need to replace it after I was done with it.

* * *

Maxwell's northern wolves arrived in Portland Saturday night, and by Monday there had been two confrontations between the new wolves and our warriors. The additional wolves sent the vampires into hiding, and the city was quiet for the next few days.

Chris and I continued to watch Sara, who stayed closed to school and home. There was no sign of Samson, but I noticed her werewolf friends were sticking closer to her than usual. She didn't look too happy about their constant presence, and I wondered what was up with the three of them. They had been acting strange since they walked out of the mall on Sunday with Sara covered in what appeared to be orange drink. I'd been tempted to ask what happened, but the scowl on her face had warned me against it.

On Tuesday, Sara's uncle left on a trip. I didn't like the idea of her alone in the building, but it wasn't as if her uncle could have protected her from a vampire. Between Chris and me and the werewolves, we'd keep her safe.

I was halfway to New Hastings Wednesday afternoon when Chris called. "Are you on your way here?" he asked.

I chuckled. "You in a hurry to get back to the city?"

"No." He let out a groan. "Sara gave me the slip at school and took off."

My stomach lurched, and I hit the gas, making the bike leap forward. "Goddamn it, Chris! She's an untrained orphan. How the hell did she get away from you again?"

"I was waiting for her in front of the school like I do every day, and she must have gone out the back," he said apologetically. "Her friend Roland is gone too. Peter swears he has no idea where they went."

I sped around an eighteen wheeler. "How long?"

"About twenty minutes. I'm riding around now, looking for her. She couldn't have gone far without a bike or car."

"Are you sure she didn't go home?" I asked, though I knew better. *Sara, what the hell are you up to?*

"I knocked and there was no answer, so I went inside. She's not there."

I let out a few choice expletives.

"Listen, she probably just wanted some space," he said in a conciliatory voice. "You know she's not happy with us hanging around all the time. Peter said Roland went after her, and I doubt they'll find much trouble here in the middle of the afternoon."

"You forget that trouble seems to have a way of finding *them*," I ground out. "Keep looking for her. I'll be there in fifteen minutes."

When I got to town, I rode straight for the waterfront. The first thing I saw was Peter sitting in a car outside her building. He paled when I pulled up beside him.

"I don't know where she is, so please don't yell at me," he blurted out before I could speak. "Roland figured she was up to something, and he said he was going to follow her. He told me to wait here for him."

"Where would she go around here?"

He shrugged. "There aren't a lot of places Sara would go. She likes to go down to the wharves, but she doesn't need to sneak away to do that. I checked, and they're not down there. And neither of them is answering their phones."

"Give me your phone number," I ordered, and he rattled off the number. I punched it into my phone and called his. "Now you have my number. Call me if she shows up."

"Where are you going?"

"I'm going to ride around and see if I can find her."

I rode slowly through the streets, trying to feel her presence. With each minute that ticked by, my frustration and worry grew. Where could she have gone without a vehicle? If she was around here, I should have felt her by now. Did her disappearance have anything to do with the last time she took off, or was Chris right and she just needed to be alone?

Half an hour later, I looked at the dark sky. A storm was brewing, and a bad one by the look of it. *She's too smart to stay out in bad weather*, I told myself as I turned back to the waterfront.

Peter was still in his car, and he shook his head when I pulled up. At that moment, a gust of wind hit me and it began to rain. It was growing darker by the second.

Fear started to gnaw at me. Abandoning my bike, I began to pace. *Where are you, Sara?*

My Mori fluttered, and I sucked in a sharp breath. I spun and looked down the waterfront at the two figures emerging from the darkness. A mixture of relief and worry-fueled anger filled me, and I strode toward them, not knowing if I was going to hug her or shout at her. Maybe both.

My nose twitched when I got within a few feet of them and picked up the strong smell of fish and brine. Then I noticed the two of them were drenched from head to toe.

"What the hell happened this time?"

Roland started to answer, but Sara cut him off. "Nothing," she replied with a stubborn set to her jaw.

"*Iisus Khristos!*" I said under my breath, ready to pick her up and carry her inside whether she liked it or not. "I'll take her from here," I said to Roland.

Her tough stance faltered. "I don't think so!"

Relief flashed in Roland's eyes, even as he protested weakly. "I'm not sure that's such a good –"

"Sara and I need to talk – just talk. And judging by the look on your face, I think you agree with me."

He looked away, telling me all I needed to know.

"Roland?" Confusion and hurt laced Sara's voice when she faced her friend.

"You won't listen to me," he replied weakly. "Maybe it will be good for someone else to…"

She stared at him for several seconds before she pushed past us. "Traitor," she uttered without looking back.

"Sara, wait." Roland started after her, but I put a hand on his shoulder. I expected him to push me away. Instead, he just watched her walk toward home. "She won't forgive me for this."

"Yes, she will." It was easy to see how much Sara cared about her friends. She was upset right now, but she wouldn't hold this against him.

"Maybe I should talk to her."

"I think it would be better for everyone if I talked to her." We followed her. "Do you want to tell me where you two went and why you came back smelling like the harbor?"

He shook his head. "You'll have to ask Sara. If I tell you, she won't be happy, and I'd rather have *you* mad at me than her."

We reached the bottom of her steps, and he looked like he wanted to say something else. But whatever it was, he decided against it and ran to Peter's car instead.

I ascended the steps and reached for the doorknob, expecting to find it locked. I was surprised when it opened under my hand.

Sara was in the main hallway pulling off her wet coat and shoes, and she didn't look up when I entered. "Make yourself at home," she called coolly over her shoulder before she disappeared up a set of stairs at the end of the hallway. A few seconds later, her three-legged Beagle emerged from the living room and followed her as if I wasn't there.

I shot off a text to Chris to let him know Sara was home, and then I removed my leather jacket and threw it over the back of a chair in the kitchen. Water dripped from my hair onto my shoulders, so I went in search of a towel in the bathroom on the main floor.

I was rubbing my hair dry when a shower came on overhead. My hands stilled as my mind suddenly filled with an image of her standing beneath the steaming water.

My Mori fluttered in excitement. *Solmi!*

"*Khristu!*" I threw down the towel and stormed to the living room, trying to banish my wholly inappropriate thoughts. It was natural for a bonded male to be sexually attracted to his mate, but there was nothing normal about my relationship with Sara. She was young and innocent, and she deserved better than me behaving like a horny teenage boy.

I took a tour of the apartment to redirect my thoughts. It was a nice place, comfortable and simply decorated. Sara's uncle obviously lived on the main floor where the wide doorways provided easy access for his wheelchair. Dax's background check had revealed that Nate Grey had been in the Army until he'd been injured by a roadside bomb in Bosnia. Now he wrote military novels and was the legal guardian to his niece. From everything I'd heard and observed about him, he was a good man who cared for Sara as if she was his daughter. She might have grown up without her parents, but she had never been without a parent's love.

Studying the titles in the bookcase in his office, I noticed we shared a similar interest in books, and I grabbed one to read while I waited for Sara. But after forty minutes had passed with no sign of her, I wondered what was taking so long. The water had stopped long ago, and I could hear no sounds of someone moving around upstairs. She wasn't happy to have me here, but she wouldn't...?

I laid aside the book and noiselessly went up the stairs to the third floor that had been split into an attic and a spacious loft bedroom. On the far side of the room, I saw a bed, a desk, and a closed door to what was most likely a bathroom. There was a couch and several overflowing bookcases and not much else. On the walls hung several framed photos of her friends and one of a man who had to be her father, judging by the resemblance.

The Beagle lay on a rug by the bed, and it lifted its head to look at me when I walked over to listen for sounds on the other side of the bathroom door. Water sloshed quietly, telling me Sara hadn't taken off at least, though she was obviously in no hurry to talk either. If my headstrong mate thought I would get tired of waiting and leave, she was in for a disappointment. I wasn't going anywhere.

I walked across the room, intending to go downstairs, but I was drawn to the bookcases instead. There was so much I didn't know about Sara, and my curiosity got the better of me. Unlike her uncle's collection of books about war, Sara's was made up mainly of well-worn classics such as Brontë, Hemingway, Fielding, and Wilde. On the bottom shelf of one of the bookcases, I was surprised to discover an impressive collection of vinyl records from the sixties and seventies. I pulled out a Fleetwood Mac album and stared at it as if it would reveal the secrets of the girl I still knew so little about.

I put the album back on the shelf and turned to the stairs again when a book on the couch caught my eye. An artist's sketchbook? Unable to resist, I picked it up and opened it to a drawing of a crow perched on what resembled the desk across the room. The detail in the sketch was incredible, from the shape of the feathers down to the intelligent gleam in the bird's eyes. In the bottom right corner of the page were the initials S.G.

Enthralled by this other side of Sara, I forgot my intent to go downstairs and sat on the couch with the sketchbook on my lap. A few seconds later, a gray tabby jumped up to lie beside me, purring loudly as it began to wash behind its ears. I smiled as I turned to the next page where a drawing of the three-legged Beagle came alive on the page. After that it was Roland and Peter, her uncle, a bog creature, an imp in a ragged loincloth, a werewolf.

My hand hovered over the page when I uncovered an eerily accurate drawing of a troll, and I wondered where on Earth she had found a picture to draw from. There weren't many books that could boast a true depiction of the fiercely reclusive creatures.

I turned the page, and my breath caught at the next drawing. It was me, emerging from the shadows with a sword in hand, and I knew immediately it was from the night we met. She had drawn me strong and lethal, but there was also a calm reassurance in my expression, as if she'd had no doubt I would save her from Eli. As if she'd had complete faith in me before we –

"Hey! What do you think you're doing?"

I looked up and sucked in a sharp breath at the sight of Sara standing across the room, wrapped in a white towel that barely came to mid-thigh. Water glistened on her bare shoulders and arms, and her hair hung in wet curls around her face. Heat shot through me, and my body immediately responded to my beautiful mate.

Her voice rose. "Get out of my room and keep your hands off my things."

"You took so long I thought you'd tried to run off again," I drawled in an effort to hide my aroused state before it became embarrassing for us both. Not an easy feat with her standing there in all her half-naked glory.

An angry blush spread across her skin, and she clenched the top of the towel to her chest. "Well, as you can see, I am still here. Now do you mind leaving my room so I can get dressed?"

"Of course." I knew I was invading her space, but she looked so adorably flustered that I couldn't help but smile.

I stood, leaving the sketchbook open on the couch. "Your drawings are quite good. Has anyone ever told you that?"

She scowled at the mention of her work. "I don't show them to anyone. They're *private.*"

So many secrets. It was time to start unravelling the mystery that was Sara Grey. I'd almost forgotten the reason I was here tonight. I'd give her the privacy she wanted…for now. But we *were* going to talk at some point.

"I'll see you downstairs shortly," I said before I descended the stairs.

At the bottom, I took a deep breath and shook my head at how easily she affected me without even trying.

Rain battered the windows as I walked into the kitchen, and I felt the building shake from the gale force wind. I listened to the storm, relieved that Sara was safe here with me and not out in that weather.

It hit me then that, for the first time since we met, I wasn't worrying about her safety. I smiled wryly because I knew it wouldn't last. Best to enjoy it while I could.

My stomach growled, reminding me I hadn't eaten since breakfast, and I guessed Sara was probably hungry too. There were several restaurant magnets on the refrigerator door, so I assumed she liked them all. Pizza sounded good, so I pulled out my phone to see if they were still delivering.

Just as I was about to dial, another gust of wind hit the building. The lights flickered and went out, plunging the apartment into darkness. I went to the window and peered out, but there wasn't a light to be seen. It looked like the whole waterfront was black, which meant the rest of the town could be without power as well.

Fetching a pillar candle I'd seen on a shelf in the living room, I lit it and set it on the kitchen counter. Then I checked the contents of the refrigerator to see what I could put together for dinner. Our choices were limited with no power, so it was good that I knew how to make a decent sandwich.

I heard her coming down the stairs as I assembled our meal.

"What are you doing?" she asked from the kitchen doorway.

"Dinner. I would have ordered in, but it looks like power is out all over town. So sandwiches it is. Hope you like roast beef."

"Um, thanks… I do," she replied, clearly confused by my actions.

I hid my grin. So this was what it took to put her off her guard. If I'd known it was this easy, I would have fed her weeks ago.

Schooling my expression, I laid the sandwiches on the table where she had already placed a bag of potato chips and two glasses of soda. She sat as

I placed the candle between us then took the chair across from her.

It took me a minute to notice how quiet she was, and when I looked up, I caught her watching me shyly, her teeth tugging at her lower lip. Our eyes held each other's for several seconds before she blushed and looked down at her plate.

I stared at her, a smile slowly curving my mouth. Maybe she wasn't as unaffected by me as she let on. Pleased by the thought, I turned my attention to my own sandwich.

I let her enjoy her meal for a few minutes before I asked the question she had to be expecting. "You want to tell me where you disappeared to today, and why you came back smelling like you went for a swim in the bay?"

She stopped eating and met my gaze defiantly. "It was personal business I had to take care of…and I did go for a swim in the bay. Satisfied?"

"Not even close." I hadn't expected her to confide in me, but I wasn't giving up. Whatever she was involved in might not be dangerous, but going off alone was. I wished I knew what she thought was so important she had to risk her safety for it.

As much as I wanted answers, the stiffness in her shoulders told me I would not be getting them tonight. Watching the candlelight play across her hair as she pretended to focus on her meal, I came to a decision. We were alone and not arguing for once, and it didn't look like she was about to kick me out. Why not take this opportunity to get to know her better? I couldn't think of a better way to spend the evening.

"Aren't you going to yell at me or something?" she asked as I bit into my sandwich.

I hid my amusement. "Will it make you tell me what you were doing today?"

"No."

A part of me was happy she refused to answer because it allowed me to say, "Then why don't we just have a pleasant meal instead?"

She stared at me, but I pretended to ignore her, enjoying myself immensely. I'd thrown her off with my change of tactics, and she was trying to figure out what I was up to. Sara had secrets, but it was obvious she was no game player. I liked that about her. It was a refreshing change from most of the women I'd known over the years.

I thought about one girl in particular with bittersweet fondness. Tristan's little sister, Elena, had been beautiful and precocious, and a master at feminine games. She'd believed herself in love with me, even though I had only ever treated her as a sister, and she'd been persistent in her efforts to get my attention. Sara didn't share many traits with Elena, but she had definitely inherited Elena's tenaciousness.

"You remind me of someone I knew a long time ago," I said. "She was stubborn to a fault, too."

Her eyes narrowed. "If you say it was Madeline, I'm going to throw my pickle at you."

I thought about the girl who had been gone for many years. "Not Madeline, no. Her name was Elena, and she was actually Madeline's aunt, though she died before Madeline was born."

Sara's scowl faltered. "Was she your girlfriend or something?"

I shook my head, still lost in the past. "No, Elena was like a sister to me. She was beautiful, but willful and very spoiled."

"Are you calling me spoiled?"

Her indignant tone drew a chuckle from me, which only made her scowl. I fought not to laugh again because I suspected she really would throw her food at me.

"Okay, maybe not spoiled, but definitely obstinate."

"Pot, meet kettle," she muttered. "What happened to her?"

My humor faded. "She ignored the rules that were there to protect her and went off by herself alone. She was killed by vampires."

I remembered that dark day as if it was yesterday. Elena's friend Miriam had come to me in tears to tell me Elena had ridden out alone hours ago and wasn't back. I alerted Tristan, and we rode out after her with every available warrior. We split into four groups to spread out the search, and it was my group that found Elena – or what the vampires had left of her.

The fire was still smoking when we got there, and several of the younger warriors had retched at the sight of the body the vampires had torn apart and tossed into the fire like garbage. Her body was charred, but I recognized pieces of Elena's favorite blue riding habit and her mare tied to a nearby tree.

I couldn't let Tristan see her like that, so I'd put out the fire and wrapped her body for transport back to the stronghold. To this day, I could still smell the burnt flesh and see the bloody bits of clothing scattered over the ground. I could still see the grief etched on Tristan's face when I'd brought his beloved sister's body home to him.

A look of horror replaced Sara's chagrin. "Oh, I'm sorry," she said quietly.

"It was a long time ago." I regretted bringing it up. The last thing I wanted was to upset Sara, who had lost her father to a vampire.

"So does Madeline have any family left?" she asked, surprising me.

"She still has some living relatives; her sire, for one."

Sara made a face. "Sire? That sounds so…impersonal."

I sat back in my chair and smiled at her. She'd grown up as a human, so it would take some time for her to get accustomed to our ways.

"It's just a title. Mohiri families are as close as human families, maybe more so since we do not grow old and die naturally."

"So you and your parents all look the same age? Don't you find that weird?"

"We don't think of age the same way mortals do. Humans see it as a way to mark one's passage through life. Physically, we don't age once we reach maturity."

Her brow furrowed, and I wished I knew what she was thinking. "So, my grand…Madeline's father is still alive," she said slowly. "Does he know about me?"

I thought about Tristan, who called every other day to ask about his granddaughter. "Yes, and he is looking forward to meeting you."

I could sense her withdrawing. "He will wait until you're ready to meet him," I told her.

"A patient Mohiri, who would have thought it?" she replied dryly.

"A Mohiri has all the patience in the world when something is worth waiting for," I said as she picked up our plates and carried them to the sink.

She started washing a plate. "I guess it helps that you guys are immortal, huh?"

I moved to stand beside her, and I couldn't resist leaning in close. "So are you."

She jumped. "Don't do that!" she sputtered, and I chuckled at the blush that rose in her cheeks.

I took the plate she was washing and dried it, deliberately standing so close to her that our arms touched. Since the night I'd met Sara, my Mori and I had been in turmoil. Being near her helped, but it was never enough. Touching her, breathing in her scent, soothed my restless demon and me as nothing else could.

I was drying the last dish when I felt a shiver go through her, making me notice how chilly it was in the apartment. My Mori regulated my body temperature, but Sara's demon was too young to do that yet. Without power, it was going to get cold in here. Somehow, I didn't think she would be open to letting me warm her with my body heat, as pleasurable as that sounded.

"The temperature is going to drop a lot tonight," I said as she reached for her flashlight. "Does that fireplace in the living room work?"

"Yes, it's gas."

Perfect. I headed for the living room. "Go put on something warm, and I'll start the fire."

"So what, we're going to sit by the fire and roast marshmallows now?"

I smiled at the picture that presented. "You have anything better to do?" I called over my shoulder.

In no time, I had a good blaze going in the fireplace. Her retort about roasting marshmallows prompted me to check the kitchen cupboards, and I smirked when I found an unopened bag in the pantry. I grabbed the bag and two long metal skewers from a drawer, and went back to the living room. Tossing the bag on the coffee table, I sat on the floor near the fireplace and stared at the flames as I waited for her to return.

"Where did you find marshmallows?"

The delight in her voice warmed me as no fire could. "Top shelf in the pantry. Want one?" I asked, already preparing one for her.

"Yes!"

I held the marshmallow over the flames until it turned brown, and then I passed the skewer to her. "Here."

She smiled her thanks and blew on the glob of melted confection while I roasted one for myself. We sat in companionable silence for several minutes, and I couldn't remember the last time I had felt so relaxed and content.

When she finally spoke, her question wasn't one I'd expected. "Have you always done this – hunting vampires? Do all Mohiri become warriors?"

"Most do, though we have some scholars and artisans," I told her, pleased by her sudden interest. "Being a warrior is in our blood, what we are born to do. I have never wanted to do anything else."

"What's it like growing up there? Do you live in houses or on some kind of military base? Do you go to school or start training when you're little?"

"We live in fortified compounds all over the world. The larger compounds look like private campuses, and the smaller ones are basically well-fortified estates. It is not safe for a Mohiri family to live outside a compound because they would be vulnerable to vampire attacks," I said meaningfully. "Families live together, and the living quarters are large and comfortable. Children attend school until they are sixteen, and physical training begins when they reach puberty."

She didn't look convinced, and I wanted her to see that life with our people would be rich and fulfilling. "It's a good life. There is a deep sense of belonging among the Mohiri, and everyone who comes to live with us is happier than they were living among humans."

Sara grew silent and pensive, and I wondered what was going through her mind. When the phone in the kitchen rang suddenly, she rushed to answer it. Based on her side of the conversation, it was her uncle calling to check on her. I noticed she didn't mention my presence when he expressed concern about the storm.

No sooner had she hung up from his call than the phone rang again. This time it was Roland, and based on her comments, he wasn't happy she was alone with me.

She ended the call and came back to the living room. "Everyone's checking up on me."

"The werewolf cares for you," I said, earning a glare from her.

"He's my best friend, and he has a name, you know."

I shrugged. "We don't make a habit of being on a first name basis with weres, and I'm sure you know they feel the same about us. It's just how it is." It still amazed me how close she and the werewolves were, and how protective the pack was of her, even after discovering what she was.

Her chin lifted. "Well, *I* am Mohiri and I have loads of werewolf friends, so you'll just have to get over it."

Hearing her call herself Mohiri sent warmth radiating through me, and I didn't realize I was smiling until she snapped, "What?"

"That's the first time you've admitted what you are."

"It doesn't change anything," she replied crossly. But her denial lacked the force it would have had a few weeks ago.

"It's a start." I smiled at her, and she looked like she was going to make a retort, but she fell silent. "What else would you like to know about the Mohiri?" I hoped her curiosity won out over her determination to have nothing to do with us.

She frowned like she was contemplating what question to ask. "Who is in charge of everything? Do you have a president or a king or something?"

"Not exactly." I explained the Council and how they met every month to discuss important Mohiri business. When she asked if I wanted to join the Council someday, I couldn't keep the scowl off my face. "Never. I have no time for bureaucracy and not enough patience to endure the long meetings. I am a warrior, and that is all I aspire to be." Or it was.

"Didn't you just say you guys have lots of patience?"

"When something is worth waiting for. I care very little for political matters."

She gave me a knowing smile. "Something tells me that sentiment doesn't make you popular with the folks in charge."

"They are good at their job, and they know that I'm good at mine. We differ in opinion sometimes, but we all work to the same end."

Her hands toyed with the pillow on her lap. "What do they think about you hanging around some town no one's ever heard of, wasting time with an orphan instead of out doing your warrior business?"

Did she really believe her life meant so little to us? To me? "You think you're a waste of our time?"

She shook her head. "I didn't say I'm a waste of time, but there must be other orphans who need rescuing more than I do. And since I won't change my mind about leaving, it doesn't make sense to stick around."

Being near her and keeping her safe were the only things that made sense in my life anymore, but I couldn't tell her that. "There is an immediate threat here. We were tracking vampire activity in the area before we found you; it was what brought us to Portland that night."

My answer seemed to satisfy her because she let it go. Then her brow furrowed slightly and she asked, "Where are you from? You have this faint accent I can't place and sometimes I think you're speaking another language."

"I was born in Saint Petersburg, and I lived there for the first sixteen years of my life until my family moved to England and then America. My accent is usually noticeable now only when I'm aggravated." Which was most of the time lately.

"And what's Chris's story? Is he your partner?"

"I normally work alone, but we sometimes work as a team. Christian and I have known each other for many years." As soon as I said that, I realized it might have been true at one time, but no more. In fact, I couldn't remember the last job I'd worked without Chris.

"Christian. It suits him better than Chris."

My lip twitched. In truth, few people called Chris by his full name, and he preferred the shorter version. "I'm sure he'll be pleased to hear that."

Her eyes gleamed impishly. "Well, I aim to please."

I made a noise between a laugh and a snort, liking this playful side of her.

Her teeth worried her lower lip. "Listen, I know you'd rather be off hunting monsters even if you guys feel like you need to be here. And I know you think I'm a pain sometimes, but –"

"Sometimes?" I gave her a pointed look.

She rolled her eyes. "What I'm *trying* to say is that even though you are way too bossy and you can be an arrogant ass sometimes, I guess you're not all bad."

Surprise and pleasure rolled through me. Her statement was hardly a declaration of affection, but it was a long way from the animosity she'd shown me a few weeks ago. She didn't see me as a mate, but maybe she would accept me as a friend. I'd be whatever she needed until she was ready for more.

"I think that's the most backhanded compliment I've ever gotten," I quipped. "And I will say that you are without a doubt the biggest pain in the butt I've ever met."

"The biggest pain, really?"

She grinned at me, and I couldn't resist saying, "Yes, but I do like a challenge."

For a long moment, she stared into the flames, and when her eyes returned to mine, I saw uncertainty in them.

"I don't want to fight with you anymore," she said.

Apparently, tonight was full of surprises. "I'm glad to hear that."

Her eyes widened a little as if she'd realized what she'd said. "I haven't changed my mind or anything. I just don't want us to be at each other's throats all the time."

"You want to be friends?" I asked, enjoying the adorable look on her face as she tried to explain herself.

She wrinkled her nose. "Let's not get carried away. How about we agree to disagree and take it from there?"

"A truce then?"

"Yes – or a cease-fire," she suggested.

She could call it whatever she wanted, because I knew we had taken a step forward tonight. I didn't expect it to be all smooth sailing from here, but it was progress.

I extended my hand to her. "Okay. A cease-fire it is."

She hesitated for a second before she put her hand in mine. The familiar bolt of recognition shot through me, and I wondered if she felt it too.

Her hand pulled away from mine, and I reluctantly let her go. *Take it slow,* I reminded myself when I saw her tuck her hand beneath her leg. The last thing I wanted was to make her nervous and undo what we had started to build.

She hid a yawn behind her other hand, and I noticed for the first time how tired she looked. I didn't want to leave her, but staying would be selfish, especially when she needed sleep.

Standing, I smiled at her. "You look tired. Go to bed. I'll let myself out."

A gust of wind shook the building, and her eyes went to the window. "You can stay in here tonight – if you want to."

I couldn't hide my surprise. I knew her offer was completely innocent, but it warmed me anyway.

She blushed and averted her gaze as if she was afraid I'd see more into her invitation.

"You're already here, and it makes no sense for you to be out in that weather when you could have the couch," she blurted. "I'll get you some blankets."

I stayed where I was as she jumped up and ran from the room. A minute later, she came back carrying a quilt and a pillow, and she quietly handed them to me.

"Thank you," I told her.

She nodded jerkily. "Um, okay, good night."

She was out of the room before I could say anything else, her nervousness thick in the air. I was happy she had asked me to stay, but I didn't want her to feel uncomfortable about it.

"Sara," I called after her.

She stopped and looked back at me over her shoulder. "Yes?" she asked breathlessly.

"You're still the biggest pain in the ass I've ever met."

Her smile made my heart squeeze. God, she had no idea how captivating she was, or what she did to my insides when she looked at me like that. I heard a soft chuckle as she turned away and climbed the stairs to her room.

I stretched out on the couch and fell into the best sleep I'd had in weeks.

CHAPTER 9

"YOU'VE BEEN TALKING to Tristan again." Erik gave me what could pass for a smirk when I walked into the command center he'd set up in the basement of the safe house.

I sat on a chair and rubbed the back of my neck. "How can you tell?" I replied dryly.

He barked a laugh then turned back to his computer and began studying a map of downtown Portland. "You always look like you could use a stiff drink after his calls. Is he still talking about coming here?"

"Every day."

I understood why Tristan wanted to be here. With each day that passed, he grew more worried about Sara's safety and more impatient to meet his granddaughter. It was becoming increasingly difficult to convince him to stay away.

Sara was slowly coming to accept who and what she was, as well as our presence in her life. Though I hadn't spoken to her since Wednesday night, she didn't look upset anymore when she spotted Chris or me watching over her. Bringing someone new into the picture now, especially an overly emotional grandsire, might undo the progress we'd made with her.

"Better you than me." Erik clicked a grid on the map, and it zoomed into a section of the waterfront. His brows drew together as his eyes moved over the area magnified on the screen.

I rolled my chair closer to his. "What are you looking for?"

He leaned back and tapped his chin pensively. "Trying to figure out where all the hostiles disappeared to."

"Still no sign?"

A week ago, the city had been crawling with demons and vampires. The last four days, we'd been seeing fewer and fewer of them. I suspected the increased Mohiri and werewolf presence had driven many of them to safer territory. I didn't delude myself that all the vampires had left. They were laying low, most likely hoping we'd move on when there was no longer a threat to the city.

"Nothing." Erik scowled at the screen. "In fact, we've had a sudden increase in demon activity in Boston. Raoul asked for some backup, and I sent Andrew, Reese, and Carl to help since it's so quiet here. They should be back on Monday."

I nodded quietly. I didn't like to reduce our numbers here, but the warriors had to go where the need was greater.

"We still have a few areas to search. You want to come with us?"

"Yes." Chris was in New Hastings, and there wasn't a lot for a warrior to do in Portland when we weren't hunting.

My phone buzzed, and I looked at the name on the screen. "What's up, Dax?"

"Hey, Nikolas. I've been working on that job you gave me, and I might have something for you." Dax chuckled. "Your girl is pretty good at covering her tracks, but she's no match for me."

I pushed my chair back and stood as an unpleasant feeling settled in my gut. I'd done what I said I wouldn't do, invaded Sara's privacy. After her disappearing act on Wednesday, and her and Roland's refusal to discuss where they'd been, I decided her safety was more important than whatever she was up to. So I'd asked Dax to dig around and see what he could come up with.

"What did you find?"

"I got what I could from her browsing history. Your orphan is a busy little bee." He typed something on his keyboard. "You know, this would be a lot easier if we had physical access to –"

"No." I drew the line at going into her home and searching her things.

"It's your call. Lucky for you I am really good at my job." He typed again. "She likes to visit certain message boards, the ones where people talk about paranormal sightings, stuff like that. Did you know Bigfoot was spotted wrestling an alligator in the Everglades last week? He must be on vacation."

I laughed. "Is that all you have?"

"Patience, friend. I didn't break into her accounts because you asked me not to, but based on her history, I can tell you she mainly follows threads about vampire activity. There is one in particular by a guy named Wulfman that she visits the most, and he seems to focus on Maine."

"I'm not surprised she's reading up on vampires after being attacked by one." Sara had proven more than once she didn't let fear rule her life. Instead of cowering, she was seeking answers.

"I agree, but her interest isn't only in what's been going on there for the last month. She's spent considerable time searching for vampire activity in

Portland ten years ago. Right around the time when –"

"– her father was killed," I finished for him, a cold knot of suspicion forming in my stomach. "What did you find?"

He snorted. "I knew you'd ask that, so I dug around a bit more. She's looked up all the news reports on the killing, and she's done Google searches on Madeline and Daniel Grey. She's also googled some random things in the last month like Ptellon blood, baktu, and red diamonds. Like I said, random stuff. But most of her searches have been about her father. Does that help?"

"Yes," I said, though I prayed I was wrong and that Sara's little escapades had nothing to do with her father.

"You want me to keep looking?"

"Hold off for now." I'd already broken Sara's trust by going behind her back this way. I needed to talk to her before I decided on my next course of action. And I'd have to be careful in broaching the subject with her. If she knew I was digging around like this, she'd pull away again.

"Will do. Let me know if you need anything else."

As soon as I ended the call with Dax, I dialed Chris's number. "How are things there?" I asked when he answered.

"Good. Sara and her friends are at a party at the lake. And before you start worrying, I'm looking at her right now."

"What kind of party?" My first thought was of what had happened the last time Sara went to a party with her friends.

He chuckled. "Not what you think. It's just a bunch of kids playing music and hanging out at a house on the lake. They're not even drinking. I don't see anything out of place."

"You forget who we're talking about," I replied dryly.

It hadn't escaped my notice that Sara only chose to sneak off when Chris was watching her. He was still kicking himself for the last one, so I knew he'd keep a closer eye on her this time. But if I'd learned anything about Sara, it was to never underestimate her ability to find trouble – or for trouble to find her.

Chris scoffed. "Trust me. I won't forget."

"Well, you'll have backup today. I'll be there in an hour or so."

He grew serious. "Why? Is everything okay?"

"That I know of." I told him what Dax had found and about my suspicions. "I need to talk to Sara."

"I'll text you the address, and we can switch out when you get here," he said. "I hope you're wrong about this."

"So do I."

Erik turned away from his monitor to peer at me when I hung up.

"What?" I asked.

"Just trying to figure you out."

A laugh escaped me. "We've known each other for years, Erik. What is there to figure out?"

He shrugged. "Sixty years, give or take a few. And in all that time, I've never seen you get involved in orphan business. Normally, you can't wait to call in a team and get back to business."

"This isn't any orphan," I said, keeping my tone casual. "She's Tristan's granddaughter."

Erik snorted and folded his arms across his chest. "I've seen pictures of the girl. She doesn't look like our typical orphans, and you're in a mood every time you come back from seeing her. If I didn't know better…" He let out a loud breath. "I'm guessing Tristan has no idea; otherwise, he'd be here already."

I should have known I couldn't hide everything from Erik. He was one of the shrewdest and most observant people I knew, which was why I was glad he was heading up the search in Portland.

He held up a hand when I didn't respond immediately. "I understand why you're keeping it under wraps, and your secret's safe with me." An amused gleam entered his dark eyes. "But I don't envy you having to tell Tristan you're involved with his only granddaughter."

I almost laughed at that because "involved" didn't come close to describing my relationship with Sara. I expected Tristan to be shocked about the bond and protective over his granddaughter, but he would not come between us. The only person who could break this bond was Sara.

"Neither do I." I headed to the door. "I'll see you tomorrow."

He turned back to his computer. "Later."

* * *

I pulled into the driveway at the address Chris had sent me and shut off the engine. Music drifted to me from behind the large house, and I smiled as I pulled off my helmet. Sara and I hadn't spoken since she had declared a truce between us, and I was looking forward to seeing her again. That was, if she didn't try to shove me in the lake when she found out why I was here.

Chris met me before I'd gotten halfway around the house, and the self-recrimination in his eyes made my stomach twist with dread.

"I'm sorry, Nikolas. She did it again," he said before I could speak.

"How?" I demanded. "You weren't supposed to let her out of your sight."

He shook his head as he plunged into the woods beyond the driveway. "I didn't take my eyes off her. She and Peter were riding jet skis, and they suddenly took off across the lake. There was no way to stop her."

"Goddamn her!" I ran after him. "Which way did they go?"

"Straight across, less than fifteen miles if we follow the shore."

I swore again as I sped past him. Using our Mori speed, we could cover that distance in about five minutes, but Sara could also have a vehicle waiting for her on the other side.

What was she thinking, taking off like this again? For once, I hoped it was normal teenage rebellion and not something to do with her father. I understood her need for closure. I'd hunted and killed every vampire in Virginia after Elena was killed. But I was a trained warrior and I hadn't gone out alone. Sara probably thought the werewolf could protect her, but neither of them had any idea what they were up against if Eli or one of his hired demons found them.

My jaw clenched tightly because I was as angry at myself as I was at Sara. If she had been anyone else, I would have gotten to the bottom of this by now. But it was getting harder to think objectively when it came to her. For the first time in my life, my judgment as a warrior had been impaired, and it was not a good feeling.

"There," Chris called when we finally made it to the opposite side of the lake. "I think that's where they went."

I slowed to normal speed and looked at the two jet skis secured to the small wharf. Chris moved past me, leaping onto the wharf and reaching down to touch one of them.

"Still warm." He straightened and scoured the area. "They can't have gone far."

"Unless they had a ride." I joined him on the wharf. "Let's split up."

It took less than ten minutes to figure out that Sara and Peter were gone. I wanted to roar my frustration. They could be headed anywhere.

I called Chris to tell him to head back to the house across the lake where our bikes were. I was going to scour every inch of this town until I found her. I just prayed I got to her before someone else did. And then she was going to tell me the truth about what she was hiding. If she was going to insist on staying here, she had to be honest with me so I could keep her safe. She might fight me on it, but I'd rather risk her animosity than lose her.

Chris caught up to me as I reached the lake house, and he stopped when I moved toward my bike. "Her friend Roland is still here. I bet my wheels he knows where they went."

I headed for the back of the house and searched the partiers for the werewolf. He was standing on the wharf with a cell phone in his hand, and he looked up as I stormed across the lawn toward him. His expression told me he had been expecting me.

"Where is she?" I fought to keep my voice at a normal volume, but every minute Sara was out there was another minute she could be in danger.

Roland shook his head slowly. "I can't tell you. But Pete's with her, so she'll be okay."

"Like she was okay in Portland?" I asked harshly. "And when the crocotta attacked?"

He swallowed. "This is different. It's the middle of the day, and she'll be back soon."

"*Khristu!* When will you three get it through your heads that no place, no time, is safe for her anymore. She's an untrained Mohiri, and no match for the kind of enemies we have. The vampire that attacked her is still out there somewhere."

"But it's sunny and –"

"Any number of demons can go out in sunlight, and they would be only too happy to do a vampire's bidding for the right price."

Fear and uncertainty flashed in his eyes. "She just went to… She'll be back soon."

"What is she doing, Roland? What is so important that she had to take off again like this?"

"I-I can't say. She made me swear."

My Mori growled and pressed forward, and the effort to keep it back made me grit my teeth so hard my jaw ached. Its intent was clear, and the only thing that stopped me from shaking the truth out of the werewolf was Sara. She'd never forgive me if I hurt him. Any other time, I'd admire the unwavering loyalty the three of them had for each other, but right now, it was impeding my ability to keep her safe.

"Just tell me they haven't left town," I managed to say.

"They haven't," he rushed to assure me. "All I can tell you is that she went to talk to someone."

"About what?" My Mori eased off a bit, knowing she was still in town. "Is this about her father?"

He gave me a startled look. "No… Why would you say that?"

His expression told me I was right. "Tell me where she is, Roland."

"I can't say." His tone was apologetic, but it was clear he wouldn't betray Sara's trust. He glanced at his phone. "They'll be back soon. You can ask her then."

Oh, I intend to. I folded my arms across my chest, staring across the lake as if that would make her magically appear.

"Whose idea was it to use jet skis?" I asked, though I already knew the answer.

"Sara's. She's pretty creative."

I released an angry sigh. "So I've noticed."

Chris joined us. "What do you want to do?"

What I wanted to do was find Sara and take her straight to Westhorne. Since that wasn't an option, I'd settle for finding her and making sure she never did anything this risky again.

"I can't wait around here." I fixed Roland with a hard look. "Will you call me the second she shows up?"

"Yes."

We exchanged phone numbers, and then I strode toward the driveway, ignoring the curious stares that followed me. My face must have reflected my mood because people quickly moved out of my way.

At my bike, I looked at Chris who had accompanied me. "Roland said she didn't leave town. Let's split up and hope one of us spots her."

"You believe him?"

"Yes."

"Okay." He walked over to a dark blue Toyota and stuck his hand under the front bumper. Then he pulled out his tracking monitor and turned it on to check the signal. "Just as a precaution. If he leaves, we'll know."

"Good idea." Roland hadn't looked like he planned to go anywhere, but Sara had proven to have more than a little influence over her friends. One call from her and he'd be out of here.

Chris straddled his bike, his eyes dark with remorse. "I'm sorry, Nikolas."

I picked up my helmet. "It's not your fault. Sara had this all planned out. She knew we couldn't catch them on the lake without a boat."

"Clever girl."

"Too clever for her own good," I muttered as my bike roared to life.

We separated at the main road. I went one way around the lake, and Chris headed in the other direction. If Roland was right about Sara and Peter returning soon, they couldn't have gone too far. I might even catch them as they returned to the cottage where they'd left the jet skis.

I'd almost made it to the other side of the lake when a police car sped past me with its lights flashing. My stomach twisted, even though I knew it most likely had nothing to do with Sara, and I did a U-turn to follow the vehicle. When it drove up a ramp to the highway, I almost didn't follow because Roland had sworn Sara was still in town. But a gut feeling had me tailing them to a rest stop a few miles down the highway.

Half a dozen people were milling around when I pulled in behind the police car. They all gave slightly different accounts to the officers, but I was able to get a picture of what had happened. And it made my blood run cold. Three teenagers had gotten into an altercation with a large man wielding a knife. One of the boys was stabbed before they took off in a red Mustang. The man had jumped into a black Escalade and gone after the teens, one of whom was a female with long dark hair.

I left the rest stop, heading in the only direction the Mustang could have gone, and took the first exit I came to. At the bottom of the ramp, I found myself on a road in a small industrial area with little traffic. There was no sign of the Mustang or the Escalade, but the place wasn't that large. If either vehicle was around here, I'd find it.

As I began searching the area, I called Chris, bringing him up to speed.

"It's them. I'm sure of it. I don't know who the second boy is, possibly the person they went to see."

"You want me to head your way?"

"No. We can cover more ground this way. Is Roland still at the party?"

There was a short pause, and then he said, "His car's still at the house. Unless he got a ride from someone else, he's there."

"Good." If Roland thought Sara was in trouble, he'd go to her. So he must not have heard from her, which meant he expected her to show up there. "Let me know if he leaves."

I spent the next thirty minutes covering every road, alley, and parking lot within a five-mile radius. I saw no red Mustang, though I did pass a black Escalade with tinted windows once. The driver wasn't doing anything suspicious, but when I saw the SUV's dented fender, my body tensed, and worry flooded me again. There was a chance that Sara hadn't been involved in the rest stop incident, but with her track record, I wasn't betting on it.

What are you messed up in, Sara?

My phone rang, and my pulse quickened when I saw Roland's name. I didn't bother with pleasantries. "Please tell me she is with you."

"No, and they should be back by now." Fear laced his voice. "One of the guys heard the cops were called to a fight at the rest stop."

"I heard that too."

"That's where Sara and Pete went," he confessed, confirming my fears. "I tried calling them, but they're not answering their phones."

"Where would they go, Roland? If you know anything, you have to tell me."

"If Sara's in trouble, she'll go home," he answered without hesitation. "I'm going there now."

"I'll meet you there."

There was no sign of the blue Toyota when I got to Sara's building, and I swore as I called Chris. "Where is Roland's car?"

"One second. He's headed toward the waterfront. No wait. He just turned into the parking lot next to their school. I think it's the church."

"Got it." I did a U-turn and tore away from the waterfront.

I reached the church minutes later, and I sensed Sara as soon as I pulled into the parking lot. Relief and anger flooded me when I sped around the corner of the church and saw a red Mustang with Sara behind the wheel. I stopped the bike a few feet from the car, and my control slipped when I saw the damage to the front of the Mustang. Tearing off my helmet, I was at the car in seconds and pulling her out of it.

"Do you have a death wish?" I shouted.

"Hey!" she yelled, but I drew her closer, torn between the urge to choke her and the fierce need to hold her.

She twisted weakly, another reminder of how defenseless she was against the vampires and demons that hunted her. And now she could add humans to that list.

"Let me go," she demanded.

"Forget it. You're coming with me since it's obvious you can't be trusted to take care of yourself."

Roland moved toward us. "Now wait a minute."

I shot him a warning look. "I'll do whatever is necessary to protect her, even if it's from herself."

"The hell you will!" Sara's eyes blazed. "You don't own me."

I opened my mouth, but Peter cut me off. "Hey, this is not helping anyone. Before you all go off half-cocked, why don't you let us tell you what happened?"

Reluctantly, I released her, but I didn't move away. I didn't think I could if I tried. I forced myself to calm down and listen as she told us what had happened.

"Peter and I went to Phil's, and he dropped us off at the rest stop a few minutes before I was supposed to meet David. I went into the diner, and Peter stayed outside. David showed up and we talked, and then he left. That's when the trouble started."

"Who are Phil and David?" I asked.

"Phil is a friend, and David is a guy I know from online," she said without looking at me.

It was even worse than I'd suspected. "You went to meet a stranger from the Internet?"

She crossed her arms. "I had my reasons."

Roland exchanged a look with her. "Tell him."

She finally looked at me. "I've been looking for answers about my dad's murder for a long time. David lives in Portland and he had information for me, but we could only meet in person."

I stared at her, afraid of what I'd say if I opened my mouth. She took advantage of my silence to continue her story.

"I went outside to call Phil to pick us up, and Peter ran into the diner to get a milkshake. That's when the man grabbed me and tried to drag me to his SUV. And then the witch showed up."

"Witch?" Roland and I said together.

"Yes. I think he was African, and he was covered in strange white tattoos."

I froze. *It couldn't be.* "You're sure about him, what he looked like?"

I was close enough to feel the shiver that went through her.

"I don't think I'll ever forget that face after what he did," she said.

"What did he do?" The thought of one of those bastards touching her made my skin crawl. She didn't answer immediately, and my gut clenched. "Sara, did he hurt you?"

"No, not really. He tried to do something to my mind. It felt like something…awful got inside my head and took control of me. I couldn't move or say anything."

She shuddered, and I had to fight to not wrap my arms around her. "It was the most horrible feeling, like I'd never be clean again," she said in a trembling voice.

"Fuck! How did you get away?" Roland asked.

"I don't know. One second there was a creepy voice in my head telling me to go to sleep, and the next thing I knew the tattooed guy was screaming." She fell silent and hugged herself, as if that would protect her from the horrors she was reliving.

When she spoke again, her voice cracked. "I think… I think my Mori is dead. I felt it dying."

Solmi! My Mori reached for hers.

No longer able to resist the need to touch her, I laid a hand on the small of her back. "It's been hurt, but it's still alive," I told her softly.

She didn't meet my eyes. "How do you know?"

"Trust me. I would know if it was gone," I replied gruffly, refusing to think about that possibility.

Roland looked at me. "What kind of witch can hurt a demon like that?"

My lip curled in disgust. "A Hale witch. A desert witch from Africa. They get their power from the spirit world."

"Like a shaman or witch doctor?" Sara asked.

"Hale witches only deal in dark magic, and their power is much greater than a shaman's. A Hale witch can cripple a person with a single thought, and their compulsion is even stronger than a vampire's, almost unbreakable."

She gasped and raised her gaze to meet mine. I saw the confusion in her eyes.

"Not even the Mohiri are immune to their power. I've seen warriors brought to madness after a single encounter with a Hale witch." I thought about Desmund Ashworth, the strongest warrior I'd ever known, whose mind was destroyed after a confrontation with one of them. "Hale witches abhor demons, and they do not work with vampires. And they usually stick close to their tribal region of the desert. It would take something big to get one of them to come all the way to America."

I held her gaze. "You aren't telling us everything. Who else is after you?"

"No one. I swear, I have no idea why they attacked me," she declared so earnestly I believed her.

"What happened after you got away from the witch?" Roland asked.

"Peter was still fighting Tarak, and Tarak pulled a knife on him. I kinda lost it when I saw him cut Peter. I just jumped him and squeezed his throat until he went down. Then we took off."

Roland pointed at the dark-haired boy sitting in the front passenger seat of the Mustang. "Where does he come into this?"

"He was there at the rest stop when those guys showed up. He got blasted by the witch when he tried to stop Tarak from taking me."

My hands clenched at my sides when I thought about how close she'd come to being taken. "What were you thinking, going off to meet a total stranger in the first place with everything else that's going on?"

She took a step back from me. "I had to go. You don't know how long I've waited to find answers about my dad. I've been trying to meet with David for weeks."

"How do you know he didn't lead those men right to you?"

She shook her head. "He's an Emote, and I believe he was telling the truth. He knew things…things about Madeline."

My body tensed at the mention of her mother, and I knew I was not going to like what came next.

"Ten years ago Madeline went to see David's father to tell him she was in trouble. They were friends, and David's father gave her a lot of money to leave the country. She said vampires were after her and before she left she had to warn –" Emotion choked her, and she paused for a moment. "She had to warn my dad. A few days later, my dad was killed."

Roland paled. "Jesus, Sara."

She cleared her throat. "David wanted to meet with me because he lost someone, too. The vampires killed his father the same day they killed mine. David's afraid the vampires will come after him because of what he knows. He was hiding upstairs while Madeline was there, and he heard something he wasn't supposed to. He thinks it's why his father was killed."

Dread filled me. Vampires didn't need a reason to kill, but these deaths sounded too deliberate, too organized. "Did he tell you what it was?"

She nodded slowly. "Madeline told David's father that she knew the identity of a Master."

It was as if a switch had been flipped in my brain and all I felt was pure instinct. I lost all thought except getting Sara as far away from this place as possible.

Moving with demon speed, I grabbed her and carried her to my bike. I had only one helmet, which I shoved down over her head.

She pushed against the helmet. "Stop! What are you doing?"

I fought to maintain control as fear gripped me. "I'm getting you out of here. I can't protect you from a Master by myself. The only place you'll be safe now is at a Mohiri stronghold."

"That happened ten years ago. There is no Master after me," she argued, trying to twist away from me.

I let out a harsh laugh because after everything that had happened, she still had no comprehension of the danger she was in.

"To you ten years is a long time, but to a vampire who has lived hundreds of years, it's nothing. And what of this witch and the man who grabbed you? Either way, someone is looking for you, and we need to get you out of this town."

She tried to push me away. "I'm not going anywhere with you."

"I'm not asking," I said through gritted teeth. Chris had asked me if I was willing to make the hard decision when I knew I could no longer protect her here, and that time had come. I didn't want it to be like this, but I was out of options.

Shock and hurt filled her eyes. "So, that's it? You're going to force me to go against my will? You're no different than them."

Roland lifted a hand. "Sara, maybe he's right. I don't want you to go, but I don't want you to get hurt either." He looked at me next. "But maybe we should talk to Uncle Max first to see what he thinks."

"I see," she bit out. "So everyone gets a say about my life but me?"

I steeled myself against the angry hurt in her voice and took her by the shoulders so she was forced to look at me. "If you stay here, you or someone you care about is going to end up hurt or killed. Someone is trying very hard to get to you, and they obviously won't think twice about going through your friends to do it."

She blanched, but I didn't stop. "Next time it could be worse. They could go after your uncle. Is that what you want?"

"Of course not!" She flinched, and I hated the cruelty of my words, but I was desperate to make her see reason. Her face gave away her internal struggle, and I could see her trying to think of a way out of this. "Talk to Maxwell all you want, but I am not going *anywhere* until Nate gets home tomorrow. And if you make me go, I'll run away the first chance I get."

"Fine. You'll stay with me and Chris until then." Between us and Erik's team, the safe house was the best location for her until we could leave.

She crossed her arms. "I don't think so. I'm going home, and you are free to follow me if you want."

"That location is not secure."

Her laugh took me by surprise. "Trust me. The devil himself couldn't get into that building."

Peter cut in before I could point out just how unsafe her place was. "Um, guys, can we just figure out where we're going? Bleeding here."

Shaking my head, I called Chris to tell him to meet us at Sara's place. Then I followed her to the cars.

She pointed at the boy still sitting in the Mustang. "What are we going to do about Scott? We can't leave him here like this."

"Don't worry about him. Once we get you safely to your fortress of an apartment, we will take care of your friend." She was my only priority, and the boy would have to wait.

Her lips pressed together. "Those guys are looking for a red Mustang. We can't take a chance of them finding Scott before you come back. Besides, I think he needs a doctor."

I didn't want to tell her that if the Hale witch had gotten into her friend's head, there wasn't much anyone could do for him. I went to him and checked his pupils and pulse. He mumbled a few words and managed to focus his eyes for a second. *Lucky bastard.*

I pulled out the gunna paste I had started carrying on me since the night of the crocotta attack and made him eat some. He made a face, but he obediently swallowed the medicine.

I stood and faced Sara and Roland. "I think he'll be okay in a few hours. If he'd been permanently damaged, he'd be catatonic. I gave him something to speed healing. By tomorrow, he won't remember any of it and he'll feel like he has a bad hangover."

Relief showed on her face. "How will he get home?"

I sighed and called Chris again to tell him to come to the church instead. I handed the phone to Roland so he could give Chris directions to the other boy's house. Then he and I helped Peter into the back seat of the other car. Sara and Roland got in the car, and I drove behind them the short distance to her apartment.

I moved to help Peter up the stairs into the apartment, but Sara stubbornly insisted on doing it. Following them, I secured the door while they took Peter up to the third floor. Then I began walking through the apartment, which had too many entry points for my comfort. Did she really think she'd be safe here if someone tried to get in?

"I told you this place is safe. I warded it myself." She walked past me in the hallway and pulled a carton of orange juice from the fridge. "Anyone thirsty?"

I held back a laugh. "*You* warded it?"

"Don't look so shocked," she retorted smugly. "I told you before I'm not helpless. And I got away from those guys, didn't I?"

Roland took the carton of juice she offered him. "I'd believe her if I was you. Sara knows things, and if she says we're safe here, then we —"

The troll appeared out of nowhere between me and the kitchen, and it immediately crouched aggressively, showing its sharp teeth. Roland shouted, and the troll's shaggy head swung toward him and Sara.

Cold spread through my limbs, and I prayed the creature was as young as it looked. I had fought many things, but even I couldn't win against a fully grown troll.

"Keep her there," I yelled at Roland, trying to draw the troll's attention to me. "I'll take care of it. Damn it, I knew this place wasn't safe."

I reached inside my jacket for a knife, knowing I'd only get one chance before the troll attacked. I hoped Roland kept his head enough to get Sara out of here while the troll was focused on me.

"No!"

Sara's scream pierced the air, and the troll snarled ferociously in response. In the next instant, my heart leapt into my throat when she ran from the kitchen and threw herself in front of the creature.

CHAPTER 10

"*KHRISTU!*" WHAT IN God's name was she doing? I stared at her face, which was devoid of fear even though she stood inches from one of the deadliest creatures on the planet. A new chilling thought hit me. What if she hadn't come away from the Hale witch attack unscathed after all? Why else would she do something so suicidal?

Worry about that later. My only concern now was getting her out of here alive. If we survived this, I'd find her the best healers in the world.

Roland ran from the kitchen. "Sara, are you insane? Do you know what that is?"

She took a defensive stance in front of the troll, raising her hands to ward us off. "He's my friend! His name is Remy."

I jerked to a stop mid-stride, and my jaw fell.

"*That* is Remy?" Roland's shock echoed mine.

"Yes. Now back off, both of you," she yelled as fiercely as a mother bear protecting its cub.

If the archangel Michael himself had appeared in front of me, I could not have been more dumbfounded. My hands fell limply to my sides as I watched Sara turn to the troll and take its hand.

"Are you okay?" she asked tenderly as if she expected it to answer her.

The troll immediately stopped snarling, and it wrapped its long fingers around hers.

Roland recovered first. "Is *he* okay?" He looked at me. "I nearly had a heart attack and she's worried about a troll. A goddamn troll!"

"Roland, shut up," Sara snapped, still facing the creature. "Remy, what's wrong? Please tell me."

The troll looked at her, and I could have sworn I saw fear in its eyes. "Minka gone. Creah and Sinah, too," it replied, sending me reeling again. A troll speaking English?

"Gone? What do you mean gone?" she asked fearfully.

"Humans take them."

She gasped. "We'll find them. We'll get them back."

A dull throbbing started in my head, and I rubbed my temples wearily. I wondered vaguely when I'd last had a headache, and decided it had to be that time Chris and I battled a thirty-foot rageon demon in Nebraska in nineteen seventy-three. The serpentine demon had slammed me into the ground so hard my ears had buzzed for an hour after we'd finally killed the beast. After taking on a rageon demon, I knew there was nothing I couldn't handle.

Of course, a monstrous demon with diamond-hard scales, ten-inch claws and paralyzing venom had nothing on Sara Grey.

I almost laughed at the absurdity of the situation. "Does your uncle have any alcohol here?"

Sara turned her head to stare at me. "How will that help us?"

"It won't. I need a drink." Or twenty.

Roland looked as wrung out as I felt. "I'll help you look."

She glared at us, still holding the troll's hand. "You guys are not helping the situation. Remy's little cousins are in a lot of danger, and we have to find them."

I leaned against the wall as the pounding in my head grew worse. "We have enough problems to deal with without going out looking for missing trolls. Have you forgotten your own considerable troubles?"

Her eyes took on a haunted look. "But this is my fault. I have to help them."

The troll spoke up. "Is *our* fault. Sara warn me it dangerous but I not believe it. I need medicine for boggie."

"What on Earth is he talking about?" Roland asked. I wasn't sure I wanted to know.

Sara chewed her lower lip. Any other time, I'd find that endearing. In our current situation, it filled me with misgiving.

"Remy has this boggie friend who was sick, and they needed a special medicine that you can't get here," she said. "It only comes from Africa, and it's very hard to find – and really expensive. I found someone to get it for us, but we needed it as soon as possible so Remy gave me something to trade for it...something very hard to find."

Oh, hell no. "Please tell me you're joking."

She shook her head.

"*Sukin syn!*" I bit out, followed by some choice words I rarely used. If we survived the night, it would be a bloody miracle.

Roland frowned. "What? What am I missing?"

I paced the short hallway. "*Iisus Khristos!* You used troll bile to buy the medicine? What the hell were you thinking?"

"Oh, Sara, you didn't," Roland croaked.

"I was careful," she said. "I went through a guy I used a few times before for other things, and he's always careful. He said he went through a middle man with an overseas buyer and there was no way to trace it back to me. But a few weeks later I found out that someone was posting on some of the message boards, asking about troll bile, and I got worried. I never believed they would find us, let alone be brave enough to do something like this."

"Not brave, incredibly stupid." Whoever had taken those young trolls had just signed their own death warrant, and possibly ours as well.

Her shoulders slumped miserably, but there was no time to comfort her. I had no idea how long the trolls had been missing or when the clan would retaliate. It might already be too late to get Sara out of here.

I turned to the troll. "How long do we have?"

"Elders meet now. I come find Sara to see if we find little ones before."

Roland looked at us in confusion. "Before what?"

Sara's voice was barely a whisper. "A rampage. The elders are going to rampage."

Roland turned to me. "That does not sound good."

I laughed harshly. "There is a reason why no one – not even a vampire – tangles with trolls. If you mess with one troll, you get the whole clan, and if you harm one of their young, you die. And if a young troll goes missing, the clan rises up to find them – or who took them. Trolls are even better trackers than crocotta, and once they are worked up into a rage, they will kill anyone who has come into contact with their missing children. And during a rampage, trolls do not distinguish between the innocent and the guilty."

Sara and Roland paled. Even the troll looked scared, which didn't bode well for us.

When the doorbell rang, I answered it, knowing it had to be Chris. "Just in time for the real fun," I quipped as he stepped inside.

"Fun?" He grinned and walked past me.

And then he saw the troll.

"What…what…?" he uttered, his face draining of color.

"Here, you need this more than I do." Roland handed Chris a glass of whiskey, which Chris downed in one gulp.

"Nikolas, why is there a troll here?" Chris asked without taking his eyes off Sara's friend.

"Chris, meet Remy, Sara's partner in crime," I said wryly.

"Huh?"

I filled him in on Sara's troll friend and what the two of them had been up to. Before he could recover from his shock, I brought him up to speed on everything else that had happened in the last hour.

"This is some kind of joke, right?"

"God, I wish it was." We followed the others into the living room, and I went to stand by the window. I would not have been surprised to see a horde of trolls descending upon us.

Chris sat on the couch and smirked at me. "Your little orphan is just full of surprises. Never a dull moment."

"I'm nobody's little orphan," retorted Sara, who sat near the fireplace with the troll beside her. No matter how many times I saw them together, I still couldn't believe my eyes.

Chris chuckled. "So, what's the plan?"

"We've got to find them," Sara answered.

No one spoke, and her eyes misted. I could handle anything but her tears.

"They're only babies," she said. "God knows what those people will do to them."

"Can't he track them?" Roland asked, pointing at the troll, who shook his head sadly.

"Only elders know tracking. If I close, I find them."

That was all well and good, but we had to get close to them first. I didn't want to bring up the fact that those trolls could be in the next state by now. Anyone who would risk their lives to steal young trolls was not going to stay around their territory. If it were me, I'd be on a plane to some place on the far side of the planet.

"I'm calling Malloy." Sara pulled out her phone. "If anyone has heard about this, it's him."

"Who is Malloy?" How many damn people were messed up in this?

Sara ignored me, so Roland answered. "Buyer."

Buyer? I frowned at him, and he made a face. "Don't ask."

Oh, I'd ask all right. When this was over – if we made it out alive – Sara and I were going to have a long and very overdue talk.

I took out my own phone and called Erik. I gave him a brief overview and told him to recall his guys from Boston. Chris gave me a questioning look when I hung up.

"I called in Erik's team. It has to be a big player to risk the trolls' wrath. I guess we know who sent the witch, too. It had to be someone with a lot of power and influence to get one of them."

A soft gasp drew my attention to Sara, who had suddenly gone pale. "This is all my fault. I'm so sorry, Remy."

"It my fault, too," he told her quietly.

"I promise we'll get them back." She hugged him – and he hugged her back, making me question everything I'd ever heard about the notoriously hostile race. Before today, I'd never even seen a troll in person. Tristan had some dealings with them, but that was before my time. How the hell had

Sara not only met one but befriended him as well? Watching them together, it was obvious they had been close friends a long time. Chris was right. My little orphan was full of surprises. Thank God, there was no way she could top this one.

Movement in the hallway drew my attention. Peter entered the living room and came up short. "Am I delirious, or do I really see a troll over there?"

"Pete, meet Remy," Roland said. "He and Sara have been trading his bile for stuff on the black market. Someone tracked them down and kidnapped three of his little cousins, and unless we find them ASAP, we're all going to be killed in a really horrible way by a mob of angry trolls." He looked at me. "That sound right?"

"Pretty much."

"Oh." Peter lost some of the color he'd regained and sank down to sit on the floor.

Chris came over to stand by me. "What's the plan?" he asked in a low voice.

"There's nothing we can do to stop the trolls if they rampage," I said. "If we don't hear from Sara's friend soon, we need to get her out of here. The trolls will only go after people who've been in direct contact with their young. It sounds like they know Sara, but I won't risk it."

"She won't go quietly."

I watched her talking to the troll. "I know, but it's too dangerous for her here. Someone sent a damn *Hale witch* after her, Chris. I have no idea how she got away from him."

He followed my gaze to her. "You think she's holding out on us?"

"I hope not, but then I never expected to meet a troll today either."

Sara's phone rang. She spoke to the caller for several minutes, and when she hung up, her eyes shone with excitement.

"I got the address of a place in Portland where they might be keeping Minka, Creah, and Sinah. They're planning to fly them out tomorrow on a private jet."

She jumped to her feet. "Come on, we have to go before it's too late."

I stepped away from the window. "Chris and I will go. I think we can handle whatever kind of security they have in place."

"I'm coming, too," she said. "I got them into this nightmare, and I'll get them out."

"Forget it. It's not going to happen."

There was no way I was taking Sara anywhere near that place after today. The thought of her facing another Hale witch, or something even worse, made my gut clench.

She crossed her arms defiantly. "Stop telling me what to do. I'm going whether you like it or not."

"Like hell," I shot back, letting my fear for her get the best of me. "I'll tie your little ass to that chair over there if I have to."

Her face flushed angrily. "You can kiss my —"

Chris grinned and put himself between us. "I don't think this little debate is getting us anywhere. As entertaining as it promises to be."

My eyes stayed on Sara. "There is no debate. She stays here."

I expected her to yell at me. She tried a new argument instead.

"All right Mr. I-Know-Better-Than-Everyone-Else, what will you do when you find them? I bet they didn't teach you in warrior school how to handle a bunch of frightened troll kids."

Nice try. "Your troll friend will come with us."

"And who will stay here with me while you guys are on your rescue mission?"

"The werewolves should be able to keep you safe here for a few hours." Once I called Maxwell, this place would be crawling with pack.

"Really? And what happens if that witch finds us again?" she replied. "Wouldn't I be safer with a bunch of warriors, two werewolves, *and* a troll?"

The troll came up behind her and gave me a solemn look. "Sara come. I keep her safe."

My resolve wavered. The troll was better protection for her than all of Maxwell's wolves together. He was clearly loyal to her, and the fierce promise in his eyes told me he would guard her with his life. I didn't want to take her to Portland, but I didn't want to leave her behind either. This way, I would keep her close by without driving myself insane worrying about her safety.

"You do not leave his side."

"I won't," she promised happily.

I exhaled sharply. "Let's go."

Outside, Sara followed Roland and Peter to their car. She motioned for her troll friend to come with them, but he shook his head.

"Oh, I forgot." She glanced at Roland. "Trolls don't like cars."

"How fast can he run?" Peter asked, eyeing the troll dubiously.

Sara and the troll smiled as if sharing a private joke. "Don't worry. He can keep up." She hugged the troll and got into the back of the car.

Chris walked to his bike. I moved toward mine, but changed my mind and tossed Chris my keys to grab my stuff. I wasn't ready to let Sara out of my sight after what had happened earlier.

The three of them looked surprised when I opened the door and got in, but no one said anything. Sara looked around expectantly, and I said, "Chris will follow us."

She nodded stiffly and turned away to look out the window, still upset with me for trying to make her stay.

A smile played around my mouth as I studied her profile. She drove me crazy, challenging me at every turn. She was also one of the few people who refused to back down from me. God must have had a good laugh when he decided to bond the two of us. One thing I could be sure of: life with Sara would never be boring.

We drove for a few minutes before Peter turned in his seat and gave Sara an expectant look.

She answered with a frown. "What?"

"Really? That's all you have to say about the *troll* who was just sitting in your living room?"

She smiled and her expression softened. "I met Remy not long after I moved here to live with Nate, before I met you guys. I used to go exploring down by the old lumber mill, and one day he saw me and just decided to show himself to me. He was only a year older than me and pretty adventurous for a troll."

Adventurous was a gross understatement. Trolls did not associate with many species, let alone befriend them. According to her story, her friend Remy had to have been no more than nine years old when they met. Knowing how protective trolls were over their young, I found it hard to believe the elders had let him out alone and then had permitted him and Sara to continue their friendship.

"Weren't you scared?" Roland asked. "I would have wet my pants if a troll walked up to me in the woods when I was that age."

"You still would," Peter said, and the three of them laughed.

I didn't add that I probably would have wet mine too in her place.

"I was scared at first," she admitted. "Even back then Remy looked pretty fierce. But he knew some broken English, so we were able to talk and I found out he was as nervous as me. It was a...pretty hard time for me. I'd just lost my dad and moved to a strange place, and I was lonely. Remy was my first friend here."

Her voice quivered on the last sentence. I imagined how difficult it must have been for her back then, a little girl, grieving her father and starting over in a new place where she knew no one but her uncle. She'd been so lonely she had reached out to the first creature that had shown her kindness.

Peter's eyes widened. "But trolls don't like anyone, especially humans. They kill anyone who gets near their young. Weren't you afraid of the adult trolls?"

She laughed. "I didn't know any better at first and Remy didn't tell me. He was a lot of fun to be with. I taught him English, and he taught me all about the real world. He was the one who told me that vampires really did exist and most likely killed my dad. By the time he took me to meet his family, I didn't know I was supposed to be afraid of them. They weren't happy, but they didn't threaten me either. Maybe it's because I was a little kid or maybe they knew all along I wasn't human – I don't know. Anyway, I don't see them very often. Usually, it's just me and Remy."

Peter looked at her with something akin to awe. "Okay, you are officially the most badass girl I've ever met. To think we were worried you'd be afraid of us when you found out what we are."

"So, what does troll bile look like?" Roland asked. "Is it true it can cure everything?"

Sara chuckled. "It's kind of yellowish brown, and if it could cure everything, Nate wouldn't need his wheelchair. It could probably cure cancer if you had enough of it."

"How exactly do you get bile out of a troll?" Peter wanted to know.

"That I can't tell you. I promised Remy I'd never share that secret with anyone."

Peter's face fell. "Weren't you afraid of carrying around troll bile?"

Roland snorted. "Why would she be afraid with Remy around?"

She rolled her eyes at them. "Are you nuts? I didn't carry it around. Remy and I have a cave we hang out in down on the cliffs. It's where we go so no one can see us together. I keep the bile there."

"I heard trolls have really strong magic," Peter said. "Have you seen it?"

"Lots of times. Remy actually showed me how to make the ward for our building. Not much can get past a troll ward."

Listening to them, I began to have a much deeper understanding of Sara and why she fought so hard to stay in New Hastings, despite the vampire threat. After seeing her father brutally murdered, this place and the people in it had become her safe haven. Not only was she sheltered by the pack, she had a troll friend that could rip a vampire apart in seconds and help her ward her home with some of the strongest magic in the world. Something told me it was her friend Remy she'd been with that day I found her riding her bike outside town. No wonder she'd refused to tell me where she'd been.

We made good time on the highway, and soon we were circling a neighborhood of large houses tucked behind tall iron gates. I directed Roland to an empty lot we'd passed on the next street. It would be a good place for the three of them to stay while Chris and I checked out the house.

The troll was waiting for us. "Little ones close."

Good. The sooner we got those trolls out of there, the sooner there'd be one less threat to worry about. Then I was going to have a long talk with Sara and make her understand why she couldn't stay here anymore. Her uncle would be home tomorrow. I'd give her two days, and then we were leaving whether she wanted to or not. She'd most likely hate me at first, but I hoped she'd forgive me when she realized it was for the best.

Chris pulled into the lot and shut off his bike. "The place is heavily guarded, but nothing we haven't dealt with before. I'd say a dozen or so armed men on the perimeter with more inside the house."

"Chris and I will go in and neutralize their defenses," I said to Sara, praying she would listen to me and stay here. I saw how worried she was about the young trolls, but I couldn't focus on my job if she went in there. "Once it's safe and we have located the young trolls, we'll come back for you."

To my relief, she nodded.

Roland wasn't as happy with the plan. "You expect us to stay here?"

I understood his eagerness to see some action, but Sara's safety was my only concern.

"You can shift and be okay, unless those men are packing silver ammo, but what about Sara? Are you willing to put her in that kind of danger?"

"I…no."

I waved them closer. "There will be several layers of security. Whoever orchestrated this will not take chances with so valuable an asset and will expect trouble." I doubted they were expecting Mohiri warriors though, and we had that going in our favor. "If you hear gunshots or other commotion, stay here out of sight with your heads down. We can handle this. Is everyone clear on that?"

Sara spoke first. "Yes."

I followed Chris to his bike and donned my weapons harness. Picking up a sword, I turned to the others. "Stay here until you hear from us."

Sara clasped her hands together, and my heart squeezed at the emotions playing across her face. Her concern for us touched me, but it was the trust in her eyes when they met mine that made me want to pull her into my arms.

"Be careful," she said softly.

Don't worry. I'm not going anywhere.

"Careful, Sara, or people might think you care," Chris teased her before he tossed me a knowing look.

I followed him out of the lot. When we got to the road I glanced back, but I couldn't see Sara and the others through the trees.

"She'll be okay."

"I know." I made myself believe that because, otherwise, I'd never leave her. I was loath to let her out of my sight after all that had happened today, and I had to remind myself that the troll could protect her as well, if not better, than I could.

I called Erik as we headed for the estate, and he told me he, Raj, and Glenn were on their way. The others were held up in Boston. The five of us could handle a dozen armed humans, as long as there were no surprises waiting for us. Like a Hale witch.

We reached the property and moved silently along the fence until we came to a small gate. I snapped the flimsy lock and eased the gate open.

Whoever was in charge was either careless or they believed their armed guards could handle any intruders.

Chris slipped inside first, and he held up a hand when I followed him. Walking toward us along the fence were two large guards, each armed with a silenced SIG MPX.

I motioned to Chris, and he nodded. A second later, we were behind the two males and had them in choke holds before they could raise their weapons or shout a warning. We lowered the unconscious guards to the ground, not bothering to remove their weapons. They'd be down for hours.

Wordlessly, Chris and I set off in opposite directions. We'd worked together enough that we didn't need spoken communication at times like this. If things went according to plan, we'd neutralize the threat here and secure the young trolls before Sara and the others had time to wonder what was going on.

I took down four more guards before I came upon one that was definitely not human. I stared in disbelief at the vampire patrolling the grounds with his fangs and claws extended. A vampire working with humans?

The vampire spun as I moved toward him. "Mohiri!" he snarled and came at me with a speed that matched mine.

My sword cut deep into his side, and he hissed in pain as he lunged away from me. He hit the ground and rolled back to his feet in one fluid motion. I started toward him again, but his sudden cocky grin alerted me to the fact that we were not alone.

I leapt to the right and spun, my blade slicing through the shoulder of the vampire behind me. He opened his mouth to cry out, and I brought my sword around to remove his head before he could alert any others nearby.

The head was still rolling across the ground when I went after the first vampire, who had turned to run. I pulled a knife from my harness and threw it at the fleeing vampire. The silver blade sank into his back, and his choked gasp told me it had struck home.

As he crumpled to the ground, I strode to him and yanked my knife free. Wiping the blade on his shirt, I sheathed it and turned toward the back of the house.

A large pool came into view, along with three human guards. The first two went down quietly, but the third managed to cry out before I knocked him unconscious. I entered the house through the open French doors, only to encounter two vampires who must have heard the guard's shout.

The vampires came up short when they saw me, and their hesitation was all the opening I needed. I got one in the chest with a knife. Before he hit the marble floor, I swung my sword and gutted the second one. He clasped his stomach, trying to keep his intestines from spilling out, and his mouth opened in a silent scream as I brought my sword up to end his life.

I started to move past the bodies, but a shout had me running outside and speeding around to the front of the house to find Chris battling three vampires. Two were missing an arm and one clutched at a gash in his chest.

"Sloppy," I bantered as I jumped into the fight to take on a one-armed vampire, who barely had time to snarl at me before I beheaded him.

Chris snorted as he swung his sword at the vampire holding his chest. His blade easily parted the vampire's ribs and sliced through his heart.

"I was doing fine until you came to ruin my fun." He spun and ran his sword through the chest of the last vampire who had stupidly stood there as his brethren were killed.

Wiping his blade on one of the fallen vampires, Chris swore and looked at me. "Vampires? What the hell is going on here, Nikolas?"

Before I could answer, shouts came from the direction of the main gate. "Sounds like Erik is here. He'll handle it –"

Chris grunted and fell to the ground beside me as bullets tore up the grass around us.

I threw my body over his, not sure how badly he was hit. Bullets were not usually deadly to us, but enough shots to the head or heart could kill anyone. I scanned the grounds, and my demon sight quickly located the shooter hiding in a tree.

"Stay down," I ordered Chris. Moving fast, I was at the tree and scaling it before the male could get off another shot. I was not gentle when I knocked him out and let him fall fifteen feet to the ground. As a rule, I didn't kill humans, but I had no mercy for someone who worked with vampires.

Chris was sitting up, inspecting a wound in his thigh when I got back to him. "It's nothing," he said when I knelt beside him.

Something glinted on the ground, and I picked up a twisted piece of metal. "Silver bullets."

"I guess the humans were willing to work with the vampires but not willing to trust them." He grimaced as he used a knife to dig out the slug before he let his demon healing take over. "Fuck!" he muttered when he pried the piece of bloody silver from his leg.

"You two okay?" Erik called, running toward us.

Chris stood, waving off the hand I extended to him. "We're good. You take out the gate?"

Erik reached us. "Yeah."

I looked at the house. If the people inside hadn't realized they had company, they did now.

"We need to find those trolls before something happens to them," I said.

"How do you want to do this?" Erik asked.

"You guys take the front. Chris and I will go around the back. If you find the trolls, don't touch them. The last thing you want is their parents coming after you."

"Understood."

Chris and I set off around the house. Just as we reached the back corner, loud growls split the air, followed by snapping and barking.

"What the *hell* are they doing here?" I raced around the corner to find the werewolves locked in a battle with two vampires. The black wolf dodged the clawed hand that came at his face, and then he lunged to wrap his powerful jaws around the vampire's throat. There was a loud snap as he shook the limp body like a rag doll and tossed it aside. He turned to help his friend, but the rusty-haired wolf had already finished off his vampire.

I scanned the grounds, but there was no sign of Sara, and I couldn't sense her nearby. She and the troll must still be with the car. I stalked toward the two werewolves, intending to send them back to Sara before they got themselves hurt. I did not want to deal with an angry Alpha on top of everything else today.

A shot rang out. The black wolf staggered, and an agonized whine escaped his lips as he collapsed to the ground.

"Chris," I shouted, running for the wolves as more bullets hit the ground.

"On it," he yelled back.

I hit Peter and knocked him to the ground. It was impossible to cover both wolves, so I tried to protect their heads and upper bodies from the bullets. Silver was harmless to Mohiri, but it could be fatal to werewolves.

"Got him," Chris called a few seconds later.

I rolled off the wolves and knelt on the ground. Peter leapt to his feet, but Roland lay on the ground panting heavily. He whined when I turned him onto his side to look at his wound.

My gut clenched when I saw his bloody chest, and all I could think of was how devastated Sara would be if anything happened to him.

I pulled out my phone and tossed it at Peter's feet. "Call your father and tell him Roland needs medical help immediately."

Peter shifted and grabbed the phone. "He'll be okay though, right?"

"I don't know," I said honestly. "He's been hit in the chest with a silver bullet."

Peter blanched, "S-silver?"

"Yes. I told you two to stay put. Where is Sara?" I barked at him.

"She's with Remy," he answered shakily. "In-in there."

He pointed at the house, and my stomach dropped like a rock.

CHAPTER 11

I SHOT TO my feet and raced inside. I heard fighting upstairs, but I tried to block it out and focus on Sara. Halfway down the hallway, I felt her. I ran to an open door with a set of stairs leading down into what had to be the cellar. Uttering a silent prayer that she was okay, I descended the stairs, bracing myself for what I might find.

Nothing could have prepared me for the sight that greeted me at the bottom. I'd seen a lot of strange things in my time, but a pair of hellhounds lying meekly on the floor like house dogs was definitely not one of them. The beasts raised their heads and growled at my arrival, but neither moved to attack.

Voices floated to me from beyond a rounded archway, and relief flooded me when I recognized Sara and Remy.

"Stop!" Sara cried out, her voice shrill with fear and pain.

I ran around the hellhounds to the doorway and stopped short when I saw Sara walking calmly to a glass cage rippling with red electricity. Demon fire. Inside the cage huddled three small trolls who cried piteously as Sara neared them.

Her hands grabbed the glass bars and shattered them, making a large hole in the side. Immediately, a tiny body flew out of the cage and into her arms. Instead of hugging the troll back, Sara quietly set her on the floor and turned away from the cage.

Behind her, the other two trolls jumped from the cage and ran to Remy. Three sets of eyes widened when they saw me, and they clung to the older troll.

My only concern was the girl on the other side of the room. "Sara?" I called to her.

She turned, and I sucked in a sharp breath when I saw her eyes. No longer the emerald green I knew, the irises were completely black. A

134

demon's eyes. Recognition flashed in them, but it was not Sara who looked back at me.

My Mori surged forward, feeling hers so close to the surface, and I had to fight to keep it down.

"How did this happen to her?" I asked the troll as I walked toward Sara, my eyes never leaving her.

"Sara let demon free cousins," he answered.

"Khristu!" She had deliberately let her Mori take control of her in order to save the trolls. Knowing how Sara felt about having a demon inside her, I marveled at the sheer will and courage it must have taken to relinquish her mind and body to it. And I knew the terror she must be feeling right now, trapped inside the demon's mind.

Reaching her, I framed her face with my hands. "Look at me."

Unfamiliar eyes met mine.

"Sara, it's time to come back now," I ordered more calmly than I felt.

"Your friends need you. Roland needs you." *I need you.*

There was no reaction. She stood woodenly, her eyes blank. I'd hoped Roland's name, if not my voice, would snap her out of it. Her Mori was strong for one that had been repressed its whole life, and it was fighting to stay in control. The longer it did, the more Sara would slip away into madness.

I won't lose you. I slapped her across the face hard enough to make her head snap back.

Nothing.

Grabbing her shoulders, I shook her hard. "Goddamnit! You will not do this. Do you hear me?"

She blinked, and for a second, something stirred in her eyes. Her body twisted in my grasp, and she – the demon – tried to pull away from me.

I wrapped my arms around her. Her Mori was strong, but it was no match for me. "That's it, Sara, fight. Follow my voice. Come back to me."

She let out a growling roar as she struggled to break my hold. The demon was scared because she was fighting.

Holding her closer, I put my mouth to her ear. "You were right, Sara; you are not weak. In fact, you are one of the strongest, most infuriating people I have ever met. You fight monsters, you befriend trolls and beasts, and you face horrors that would break a lesser person. And you walk headfirst into danger to protect the ones you care about. You are loyal, stubborn, and foolhardy and, though you don't believe it, you are a warrior."

She stopped struggling and stood quietly in my arms.

I pressed forward. "Few Mohiri could have done what you did tonight, giving up yourself to save those trolls. You did what you had to do, and now you have to come back to us. To Roland."

"Roland?" she rasped.

"That's right," I said hoarsely. "Your friend, Roland. He needs you now."

She began to shake. I remembered clearly the first time I'd lost control of my own Mori. Barely five years old, I was terrified when the demon had filled my mind, taking over my body. At that age, my Mori was weak, and my mother had talked me through it. I couldn't imagine the struggle Sara was going through with her much stronger demon.

I pulled back and looked into her eyes. My breath caught when I saw green specks in the black irises.

"That's it, *moy malen'kiy voin.* Fight."

A violent shudder went through her, and when her eyes met mine again, they were the perfect shade of emerald green. "What happened to Roland?" she asked.

I wanted to crush her against me and yell at her to never do that to me again. Instead, I rubbed her arms and looked into her confused eyes. "Roland and Peter ran into some guards and Roland was shot."

"What?" Fear filled her eyes. "Is he okay?"

"He was alive when I left him. Peter is calling Maxwell."

"He was…" She jerked away from me, and I let her go. "Where is he? I need to help him."

"If anyone can help Roland, it's Maxwell. He'll know what to do."

My words were meant to calm her, but they only seemed to agitate her. Fear and desperation crossed her face, and she pushed past me and ran for the door.

"I have to find him!"

All I could do was follow her. In the outer room, the hellhounds perked up when she raced past them, and one let out a soft whine.

"Stay," she ordered as she tore up the stairs.

The hellhounds lowered their heads to the stone floor.

Shock rippled through me. No one but a hellhound's master could command the beast, yet this pair had just submitted to Sara as if they belonged to her.

I saw her go outside and say something to Erik and Raj. Then she was off and running down the front steps. At the bottom, she turned to look up at me. Her chest heaved as if she couldn't draw air into her lungs.

"I have to go to him. Please. He needs me," she cried.

I went to her. "Roland is with his people. If anyone can help him, they can." I hated hurting her, but she needed to hear the truth, to prepare herself for the worst. "The men had silver ammo, most likely to protect themselves from the vampires they were working with."

She took a step back, shaking her head frantically. "No, no, you don't understand. I can help him."

I grabbed her by the shoulders before she could run again. "He took a direct hit in the chest, Sara. The pack will do what they can for him, but this type of injury is almost always fatal to werewolves. I'm sorry."

"No! I won't let that happen!"

Sobbing, she pulled away from me, pain radiating from her. "I know I've been nothing but trouble to you and you have no reason to do this for me, but I have no one else. Please help me, Nikolas."

Her desperate plea gutted me. She had no idea there was *nothing* I wouldn't do for her.

I turned to the house. "Erik, I need your bike."

He tossed his keys to me. I took Sara's hand to lead her to the motorcycles. I gave her a helmet and grabbed one for myself. Straddling Erik's bike, I started it and waited for her to climb on behind me. She pressed herself against my back and wrapped her arms tightly around my waist.

I broke the speed limit all the way to New Hastings, even though I knew what we'd find when we got there. Neither of us spoke until we reached the Knolls.

"Brendan's. That's where they'll take him," she said when I slowed at the turnoff.

I'd gotten to know the area over the last month, so I knew where Brendan's farm was. Minutes later, we drove along the edge of the driveway, which was packed with vehicles. Lights shone from every window in the big two-story house, and a small crowd of people stood on the front porch talking. Everyone quieted and stared at us when we pulled up.

Sara jumped off the bike before I shut it off. She ran up the steps and found her way blocked by the young hotheaded wolf named Francis.

"Haven't you done enough?" he railed at her. "You are not welcome here."

"I have to see him." She tried to push past him, and one of the other men grabbed her shoulder to hold her back.

"Let me go!" she cried.

My Mori growled dangerously.

"Take your hand off her."

I forced myself to walk calmly to Sara so I didn't go over and rip the arm off the man who dared to touch her.

The man let her go and narrowed his eyes at me. The others moved closer to him, scowling as if they could intimidate me.

I tensed and prepared to pull Sara behind me in case one of them made a move toward us.

"What's going on here?" rumbled Brendan from the doorway. Several of the men hung their heads under his glare.

Sara ran to the Beta wolf. "Brendan. Please, I need to see Roland!"

The older wolf's eyes and voice were kind when he laid a hand on her shoulder. "I know how much you care about him, but you can't go in there right now. It's not safe."

"Not safe?" she repeated tearfully.

"The silver went in too deep. It's too close to his heart, and we can't get to it. He's half mad with the pain, and he doesn't know anyone right now. He'd tear you apart."

A long mournful howl came from inside the house, and every person on the porch shuddered.

"He can't heal," Brendan told her, his eyes dark with grief. "A couple of hours at the most."

A wave of her pain hit me, and I almost closed my eyes against the force of it.

"No!" She pushed past him into the house. "Roland is not going to die!"

Brendan let her go and shook his head sorrowfully. "She loves that pup like a brother. This is going to kill her."

"This is all her fault," Francis spat.

"Francis!" Brendan gave him a look that brooked no argument. "Roland is old enough to know better. Do you really think that little girl could force a werewolf to do anything against his will?"

The younger wolf had no reply to that.

"Is there no chance?" I asked Brendan, though I already knew the answer.

"None." He wiped his eyes with his shirt sleeve.

Silence fell over the porch. A few of the wolves laid their hands on the shoulders of those next to them, seeking solace in each other's touch. I'd always heard that werewolf packs were closely knit, but I'd never experienced it firsthand until today. Every member of this pack would grieve the loss of one of their own. Even Francis bowed his head in sorrow.

Another agonizing howl tore through the silence. A woman began to cry quietly.

A boy appeared in the doorway, his eyes wide with excitement. "She's gone in with Roland!" he cried in a high voice.

"Who?" Brendan asked.

"Sara. She said she's gonna save him!"

I shoved past the wolves, ignoring their shouts of outrage.

Brendan stepped aside to allow me entry, and I ran to where a crowd was gathered outside an open door on the first floor. I pushed through them, earning more than one growl until Brendan barked, "Let him pass."

I reached the room and took in the sight of the black werewolf chained and thrashing on a mattress in the corner. Sara called to him, and he went nuts, straining to break the chains that held him.

I grabbed her around the waist and pulled her from the room.

She turned and smiled at me. "It's all right. I just tamed two hellhounds, remember?"

Her eyes held mine, begging me to have faith in her. I didn't know what Sara had done to those hellhounds, but she had done something to make them her own. My gut told me I was about to find out what that was.

I released her, and she sat on the floor a few feet into the room, close enough for me to grab her if the wolf somehow managed to break his chains.

"Roland, do you know who I am?" she asked him softly.

He growled and bared his fangs.

"I see. Well, that won't do at all," she said calmly as if she wasn't sitting less than ten feet from a crazed werewolf. "I know you're in a lot of pain, and we're going to deal with that soon, but first I think we need to have a talk. Or I'll talk and you can listen. How does that sound?"

Another growl.

She shifted, settling her hands in her lap. "I know I said that Remy was my first friend here, but you were always my best friend. The best times of my life have been with you and Peter. Remember when we used to have slumber parties, and Brendan let us camp out in the hayloft that one time? We told ghost stories until we were all too scared to sleep, and we ended up sneaking back into the house after everyone else went to bed. Or the time you nipped some of Brendan's whiskey, and we got drunk for the first time. I never touched that stuff again."

Someone chuckled softly, and I looked behind me at Brendan who smiled fondly at Sara.

She continued to speak in warm, gentle tones, remembering humorous stories from their childhood and all the mischief the two of them and Peter had gotten into. Every now and then, someone else would smile and nod, and I saw how rich and happy Sara's childhood had been, despite all she had suffered.

"Roland?"

The wolf's yellow eyes were fixed on Sara. He whined, making me realize how quiet he had become. He no longer growled or struggled to break free. He was as enraptured by her voice as the rest of us.

"You were pretty shocked to learn about Remy, weren't you? But he's not my only secret. Remember the other day after the marina when I said there were things I had to tell you about me? Do you want to know what it is – what I can do?"

Secret? Marina? What was she talking about? What else could she possibly be hiding?

She got to her knees and moved toward the wolf.

In a second, I had her by the arm. "What are you doing? That's an injured werewolf. He'll rip you apart."

Her eyes never left the wolf. "No, he won't. You always ask me to trust you. Now it's time for you to trust me."

Every part of me screamed to hold on to her, to keep her safe. But her plea and the quiet confidence in her voice loosened my fingers until she pulled from my grip. I held my breath as she crawled toward the wolf, stopping just short of the mattress.

"I know it hurts a lot, but I'm going to make the pain go away now. You know I would never hurt you, don't you?"

My whole body tensed as she reached out to touch one of the wolf's paws.

"There you are," she crooned. "You had me worried there."

The wolf lifted his head and made a mournful sound before he collapsed back onto the mattress. Whatever Sara had done, the fight had gone out of him.

"Shhh," she said softly as she laid one hand over the wound on his chest.

I held my breath, waiting to see what she would do.

After a long moment, she placed her other hand on his chest. The wolf watched her trustingly, and I wished I could see her face. What was she doing?

Her hands began to glow.

What the —? I stared, transfixed, as the white glow from her hands grew brighter. Whispers broke out behind me, but I couldn't take my eyes off the sight before me if my life depended on it.

"I think this is going to require a bit more contact," she said. She began to lower herself to the mattress.

I took a step forward.

A hand on my shoulder stopped me, and Brendan whispered, "Wait."

I clenched my jaw as I watched Sara lie beside the wolf and slip her arms around his body. Her back was to us, and she looked so small pressed up against the large werewolf. My heart thudded in my chest when he wrapped his hairy arms around her. His jaws were too close to her bare throat. One bite could snap her neck.

Sara began to glow again, and this time it wasn't just her hands. Her arms and torso emitted the same white light that grew until it nearly blinded me.

Minutes passed, and Sara and the werewolf stayed in their tight embrace, bathed in light. People whispered, some sent up prayers. All I could do was watch the miracle I knew was taking place before my eyes.

At last, the light faded, leaving Sara sagging against the wolf.

"Now you know my secret," she said.

No one moved or spoke.

The bloody paw resting on Sara's shoulder flexed, showing one-inch black claws. I tensed and called on my Mori speed so I could reach her if the wolf attacked.

The wolf let out a low whine. Seconds later, the paw became a human hand.

Shouts broke out behind me, and Brendan blessed himself. "Holy Mary, Mother of God!"

I went to Sara and lifted her into my arms. I stepped back as Judith rushed over to lay a blanket over Roland, whose naked chest bore not even the trace of a scar.

"Mom?" he said sluggishly before he closed his eyes and slept.

Judith's shoulders shook as she tenderly brushed damp hair away from her son's face.

"Is Sara okay?" Maxwell asked from the doorway.

I gazed down at the closed eyes of the girl in my arms. Was it normal for her to be like this after she did...whatever that was?

She mumbled incoherently and curled into me. The emotions that welled in my chest were indescribable.

"I think she's just exhausted. Hopefully, all she needs is some sleep."

Brendan nodded. "She's earned it, poor thing. I had no idea you Mohiri could do that."

"We can't."

My words hung in the air between us. Brendan's eyes widened, and Maxwell stroked his beard thoughtfully. Behind them, people pressed as close as they dared to see what was going on in the room.

Judith stood and came to me, brushing her hand against Sara's cheek. "You brave, wonderful child," she said in a voice filled with awe. "Thank you."

Her eyes were wet when she looked at me. "Take her upstairs. Second door on the left."

Brendan cleared a path to the stairs. I followed him, carrying my precious burden, ignoring the stares and whispers around us. I didn't blame them because I was still reeling from what I'd witnessed.

Upstairs, I found Peter waiting for us in the hallway. His face was pale and drawn, but his eyes were filled with hope. "Is it true? Is Roland...?"

"He's okay," I said, and he sagged against the wall.

"And Sara?"

"She's sleeping." I carried her past him to the room Judith had mentioned. Laying her on the bed, I pulled a thick quilt over her.

"I wanted to give this back to you."

I turned to Peter, who stood in the doorway holding my cell phone. Walking over to him, I took the phone and stuck it in my back pocket.

He cleared his throat. "Thanks for what you did tonight. We would have been goners if you hadn't pushed us down."

I nodded, but I wasn't ready to let him off the hook that easily. "Why did you come there when I told you to stay put until we took out all the guards?"

"Remy said his cousins were in trouble, and Sara said they were going in. Roland and I couldn't let her go without us."

My brows drew together. "Two werewolves couldn't stop one girl?"

It was his turn to frown. "Dude, you ever try to stop Sara when she's set on something? And she had the troll on her side."

"Point taken."

He looked past me at Sara. "All this time, we never knew…"

"She's good at keeping secrets." How closely she must have guarded this one. Only the fear of losing her best friend had made her reveal her ability.

"Peter?" Maxwell called from below.

"I better go," Peter said. "Tell Sara I'll see her tomorrow."

He ran downstairs, and I stepped into the hallway to call Chris.

"Nikolas, where are you?" he asked as soon as he answered. "Erik said you left with Sara."

"We're in the Knolls with the pack."

"The Knolls?" He paused for several seconds. "How is Sara holding up?"

"She's good and so is Roland. They're both sleeping."

"But he took a silver bullet to the chest. I was there when the wolves came to get him. Even they didn't think he'd make it."

"Let's just say he had a guardian angel." I ran a hand wearily through my hair and decided this was a story that needed to be shared in person. "I'll tell you about it tomorrow. Are you still at the house?"

"Yes. The rest of Erik's guys just got here, and they're collecting the bodies for disposal. The human guards are still out. We'll call in the authorities to handle them after we're done here." Sounds on the other end told me he had walked outside. "By the way, you'll never believe what we found in the cellar."

"A pair of hellhounds?"

"How did you…?" He sighed. "Sara?"

I smiled. "Where are they?"

"Still in the cellar. We had to close them in there because they tried to follow you. I take it then we're not putting them down."

It was our policy to destroy any creature that posed a direct threat to humans, and hellhounds definitely fit into that category. They were savage beasts, bred and trained for one thing. But the two I'd encountered in that cellar were as tame as pets.

"I just tamed two hellhounds, remember?"

Werewolves, trolls, hellhounds. It seemed no creature was immune to her charm. What would it be next? Dragons?

I looked at Sara, who slept with a tiny smile on her lips. There was nothing I wouldn't do to keep it there.

"Arrange a pickup for them. We'll figure out the rest later." I lowered my voice. "Before you dispose of the vampires, take a photo of each one. I'm the only one who's seen Eli, and I want to know if that bastard is one of them."

"You think he's involved in this?"

"I don't know, but this seems like too much of a coincidence to me." I clenched my free hand. "Sara has vampires hunting her, and now we have humans and vampires working together to steal trolls that just happen to be friends of hers."

His breath came out as a hiss. "I'll take the pictures myself and text them to you."

We talked for a few minutes more about the cleanup operation, and then we hung up. I was confident Chris would handle everything in Portland, and that left me free to be with Sara. I entered the room again and quietly shut the door before I pulled a chair over beside the bed.

Her hand lay on top of the quilt, and I covered it with mine, taking advantage of the opportunity to touch her. In my youth, I'd laughed at the way my sire held my mother whenever he returned from a trip. He would raise his eyebrows and tell me that one day, if I was as blessed as he was, I would understand. I finally grasped the meaning of his words.

In sleep, Sara looked young and vulnerable, making my protective instincts flare. But I also knew that behind her innocence lay a strength she'd chosen to keep hidden from the world.

"What are you, Sara Grey?" I asked her softly. "Is that another of your secrets, or do you even know?"

The bond between us left no doubt that she was Mohiri, but her healing ability had to come from somewhere. The only race I could think of with that kind of power was the Fae, but the demon inside us made it physically impossible for a faerie to couple with one of my people. And Sara's uncle was human, which meant her father had been human as well. Maybe I should have Dax look into her father's background some more and see what he could dig up.

I started to pull my hand away, but her smaller one suddenly gripped mine. Her brow furrowed, and she murmured words I couldn't make out.

I leaned in to kiss her forehead. "Sleep easy, Sara. I'm not going anywhere."

* * *

Late the next morning, I sat in the room studying one of the pictures Chris had sent me while I waited for Sara to wake up. The dead vampire could be Eli, but I couldn't say for sure until I saw the body in person.

Chris had it on ice until I could get to Portland. Vampire bodies decomposed quickly once the demon was dead, and the older the vampire the faster the decay. But I was not leaving here until Sara awoke and I knew she had recovered from last night.

The bedclothes rustled, and I looked up to find Sara staring at me in confusion.

"How are you feeling?" I asked her.

She groaned and rubbed her eyes. "I've been better. Where am I?"

"At the farm. You weren't in any shape to go anywhere last night."

She appeared disoriented for a moment, and then her eyes filled with anguish. "Roland!"

"He's fine. He's down the hall."

I moved my chair back to the side of the bed, where it had sat most of the night, and studied her face. Despite the many hours she'd slept, she still looked tired, and that worried me.

"Is this normal after you do that? Passing out?" I asked.

"After a healing? It doesn't usually knock me out like that, but I've never healed a werewolf before. Usually I'm okay if I rest for an hour or so."

She made it sound like saving a life was a normal occurrence for her, and I had a feeling that wasn't far from the truth. "You do this a lot?"

She smiled. "More times than I can remember. I've been doing it since I was six."

So young. I was about to ask her where the power came from when I remembered something she'd asked me when I told her what she was. "That day on the wharf, you asked me if Mohiri had other powers. You wanted to know if we could heal others."

"Yes."

I wished I could give her answers, but I only had more questions after last night. One thing was clear; her ability wasn't limited to healing.

"I don't know of any Mohiri who can do what you did last night. Is that what you did with those two monsters in that cellar?"

She nodded. "I've used it before to calm animals, but I had no idea it would actually work on hellhounds. What happened to them? You didn't – ?"

"They tried to follow you, so Chris and Erik had them restrained. They'll be transported to one of our facilities until we figure out what to do with them." At her look of relief, I knew I'd made the right decision last night. "We couldn't have a pair of hellhounds running amok around Portland."

She frowned. "What kind of facility? I don't want them hurt."

"No one will harm them." I chuckled. After everything that had happened yesterday, she was worried about the welfare of two hellhounds.

Wanting to reassure her, I said, "They are yours now. Once a fell beast imprints on a new master, they are incredibly loyal. They will only answer to you."

Her eyes brightened. "That's what the witch said."

Witch? I gave her a questioning look.

"The Hale witch. He was there last night in the cellar."

My body tensed. "Did he hurt you?"

"No," she blurted. "He didn't even try to stop me. He was curious about Remy and the hellhounds, and he said a bunch of stuff that didn't make sense. Then he left."

I rubbed my jaw. Why would the Hale witch attack her earlier in the day, only to let her go a few hours later? Maybe she'd frightened him when she was able to fight him off. Hale witches were defenseless without their magic.

Talking about the witch didn't appear to bother her. In fact, aside from looking tired, she seemed well recovered, considering all that had gone down yesterday.

"A lot happened in that cellar last night." I watched her closely. "Do you want to talk about it?"

"No." She looked away, swallowing hard. I didn't need to see her face to know some of what she was feeling. I could sense her pain through the bond.

"Every Mohiri struggles with their Mori at some point in their lives," I said, remembering my own battles. "For most, it happens when they are younger and lack the training to manage the demon impulses. You have such control over your Mori that it must have been very frightening to let your guard down the way you did. But don't let your fear make you forget why you did it. You saved those trolls."

Her breath hitched, and I saw she was trying not to cry. My first impulse was to reach out to her, but I sensed she needed reassurance more than comfort.

"You are stronger than the demon. I knew that when I met you. But hearing how you fought off the Hale witch, and then last night, watching you with the werewolf, I realized you have power I can't comprehend. You saved more than one life last night. People here are calling you a hero."

She stared at the ceiling. "Some hero. Roland wouldn't have needed healing if I hadn't almost gotten him killed in the first place."

She'd made some bad decisions, but I wouldn't let her blame herself for this. "What happened last night wasn't your fault, Sara. We found out who was behind all this. His name is Yusri al-Hawwash, and he is a billionaire oil sheik who found out two years ago he has Alzheimer's. He's been searching everywhere for a cure, and he was looking for trolls long before you sold that bile. He's a desperate man with unlimited resources."

"But he would have looked somewhere else if I had been more careful," she said miserably.

"That still does not make you responsible for his actions." I leaned closer to the bed. "Look at me."

She obeyed, and the torment in her eyes made my chest ache. "Yes, you have made mistakes, but you are not to blame for the greed and actions of another. Your fault lies in taking too much on yourself. You have to learn to trust people and stop trying to take on the world alone."

I couldn't tell if my words had gotten through to her or not. She let out a deep breath. "My life was a lot less complicated a month ago. Maybe now things will start to settle down again."

I'd known this moment would come, but that didn't make it any easier. "I wish that were true, but after what I saw last night, I think you might be in more danger than we first thought."

She moved up until she was sitting with her back supported by pillows. "What do you mean? We haven't seen any sign of vampires except those working for the sheik – which I totally don't get by the way. And the sheik's witch only tried to grab me to get to the trolls."

"Think about it, Sara. The young trolls were taken around the same time you were attacked at the rest stop, which means the sheik didn't need you to find the trolls. So why did they come after you when they had what they wanted?"

I watched her closely, waiting for my words to sink in and knowing what they would do to her. I'd had all night to think about this, to fit the pieces together.

"You want to know why vampires would risk helping humans kidnap trolls? What if the vampires wanted something and they made an agreement with the sheik – a trade of some kind? You for the trolls."

She shook her head in denial. "No, the two vamps I ran into tried to kill me, not capture me." I sucked in a sharp breath, and she rushed to add, "Remy and I took care of them."

Had I heard her correctly? "You killed a vampire?"

"With Remy's help. He's scary good."

I started to say that Remy could have killed the vampires without involving her, but I wouldn't take that away from her. What was more important was making her understand the danger she was in. I didn't want to think about the number of unscrupulous people who would do anything to get their hands on someone like her.

"Even if you are right about the vampires, there is one thing you're overlooking. You have an incredible ability. If word of it gets out, the sheik will be coming after you, and he won't be the only one."

"It won't do him any good. I can't heal humans."

I raised my eyebrows, and she scowled. "My uncle is in a wheelchair. If I could heal humans, don't you think he'd be the first one I'd heal?"

I believed her, but that would not keep her safe. The fact was she was no longer safe in New Hastings, or in Maine for that matter.

"But no one else would know that. Last night was just a taste of what could happen. They will keep coming and people will get hurt. And don't forget, we still have a Master to worry about. He could come after you just to use you against Madeline."

A shiver went through her. "Don't hold back. I'm not quite paralyzed with fear yet."

"You need to hear these things, Sara," I said firmly.

She glared at me. "You're trying to scare me, to get me to go with you."

"Yes, I am. But that doesn't make them any less true."

I watched the emotions play across her face as she processed what I'd told her, and I saw the resignation when she finally came to a decision.

"I-I need to tell Nate, to explain it to him," she said hoarsely, looking away from me. "It's going to be hard for him to understand all this."

Relief flooded me. "We have some things to wrap up in Portland that will take a few days, and it should give you the time you need with your uncle. I know this is hard for you, but you're doing the right thing."

I carried the chair back to the corner and opened the door. "I swear to you that I will keep you safe," I vowed before I left the room and closed the door behind me.

CHAPTER 12

"IS IT HIM?"

I studied the features of the dead vampire that bore a striking resemblance to Eli. It had been a month since that night in the alley, but I'd never forget that vampire's face or the hungry way he'd looked at Sara. The picture Chris had sent had given me hope the bastard was dead, even though I wanted the pleasure of ending him myself. But seeing the body up close, I knew I might still get that chance.

"No." I turned away from the body to look at Chris. "It's close, but not him."

"Too bad." He motioned for two warriors to take the body away. "So what time do we depart this fair city?"

We walked outside to where our bikes sat in the driveway. "Tomorrow afternoon, Wednesday at the latest. Sara needed a few days with her uncle. This isn't easy for her."

Chris pursed his lips. "It was never going to be easy, but your girl's tougher than she looks."

"That she is." Knowing that hadn't made it any easier to leave her today, even for a few hours. I hadn't seen her since I dropped her off yesterday, but when I'd called her earlier today to let her know I'd be back this evening, she'd sounded so lost. I knew her talk with her uncle yesterday hadn't gone well. Standing outside her apartment last night, I could feel her pain, and it had been hard not to go to her.

"You heading back already? I thought Maxwell said the pack would watch Sara."

"He did, but I don't want to spend too much time away from her now." I was actually planning to introduce myself to her uncle and to extend an invitation for him to come to Westhorne with Sara. I hoped it would help him and Sara adjust to the changes in their lives. And I wanted to assure him that we would never try to keep her from her family.

My phone rang, and I pulled it out, expecting to see Tristan's name again. He'd already called me three times since I let him know Sara had agreed to go to Westhorne. The last time I'd seen him this happy was when Madeline was born.

Sara's name flashed on the screen, and my stomach instantly knotted. She wouldn't call me unless something was wrong.

"Sara, what is it?"

"Something outside." She gasped for breath, her terror almost palpable. "They're trying to get in. The ward is holding, but Nate's not here. If he comes home and…"

I swore and jumped on my bike. Chris grabbed my arm, and I almost roared at him. "Call Maxwell. Sara's in trouble."

I forced my voice to sound calm despite my heart trying to punch its way through my ribs. "We're coming. Stay right where you are, and do not hang up. I'm going to stay on the phone until we get there. Do you hear me?"

"Maybe I should call Maxwell."

"No, stay on the phone with me. Chris is calling them now."

Hearing her voice and knowing she was safe were the only things keeping me from losing it. I yanked on my helmet, activated the Bluetooth headset, and started my bike.

"I'm on my way," I said as I shot out of the driveway.

"Okay," she rasped, sounding a little calmer.

God, I never should have left her. If anything happened to her…

"What was that?" I asked when I heard a sound on her end.

"The house phone. Maybe it's Nate." I heard her run through the house and pick up the other phone. "Hello?" Then, "Yes."

There was a loud noise as she dropped the cell phone. "Sara?" When she didn't answer, I yelled, "Sara, pick up the phone."

"I'll do it!" she cried. Her words made no sense until she said, "How do I know I can trust you to let him go?"

"Sara, it's a trap. Don't leave that apartment!" I shouted. They couldn't get to her, so they were using the one thing they knew would lure her outside.

"No! I'll come," she said to the person on the other phone. Then there was silence.

"Don't listen to him. Whatever he's telling you, it's a lie."

Nothing.

"Goddamnit, Sara, answer me!" I bellowed.

There was a muffled sound as she picked up the phone. Her next words were like a knife twisting in my gut. "I'm sorry, Nikolas. I have to go."

"Do not leave that apartment. I'll be there in thirty minutes. Whatever it is, we can take care of it."

"It'll be too late. They have Nate, and they're going to kill him if I'm not there in ten minutes. I've made a lot of mistakes, but I will not let Nate die because of them."

"Sara, think about this," I implored. "They are not going to just let your uncle go once they have you. If you do this, you could die."

"He'll die for sure if I don't go. I'm not going to hide here and do nothing while he's killed. I couldn't live with that." The resignation in her voice scared the hell out of me. "You were right. All I do is put the people I love in danger. It has to stop now."

"Sara, no, listen to —"

The line went dead.

I called her cell phone, and it went to voice mail. I hit the gas and my bike shot forward. I tried her phone again even though I knew she wasn't going to answer. Sara would do anything for the people she loved, even if it put her own life in danger.

It had to be Yusri al-Hawwash. A man who would risk the trolls' wrath would think nothing of hurting Sara or her uncle to get what he wanted. I tried not to think about the other option, that Eli had finally found a way to get to her. The thought of her in his hands made the blood pound in my ears and my stomach churn violently.

I had never known this kind of fear existed until today. "God, please keep her safe. I can't lose her."

Torture took on a new meaning for me as I counted down the miles one by one. In my mind, I replayed every conversation we'd had. I saw her eyes flash in anger when we fought, and the way her face lit up when she smiled. I watched her battle a crocotta, defend a troll, heal a dying werewolf. She was unlike anyone I'd ever met, and within the span of a month, she had become everything to me.

I recognized Maxwell's truck outside Sara's apartment when I roared up. I leapt off my bike and took the stairs three at a time, bursting through the front door without knocking.

Sara's uncle and Maxwell were in the kitchen when I stormed into the apartment, and it was all I could do not to punch the Alpha for not protecting her like he'd promised.

"Who are you?" Nate Grey demanded before I could speak.

"Nikolas Danshov. I'm a friend of Sara's."

Recognition dawned in his eyes. "She told me about you." His voice grew hoarse. "Please, find her."

"I will. Tell me what happened."

He cleared his throat. "I had some appointments in Portland, and I was on my way home when two men grabbed me at the grocery store. One was German and the other was Middle Eastern. They took me to an empty building on Crescent Street where a man named Haism Bakr was waiting for us. He told me he had business with Sara, and that if I behaved myself, I'd be home in no time. I asked him what he wanted with Sara, but he wouldn't say. I knew it had to have something to do with the things she told me last night. She said she had to leave because people were after her."

His voice cracked. "Now they have her."

It was little consolation that the sheik's men had Sara and not the vampire. The sheik wanted her to try to cure him, so he'd keep her alive. If he valued what was left of his life, he'd keep her unharmed.

"What happened next?"

"Haism's men left and came back a little while later with Sara. Then Sara and Haism talked about his employer. He told her the sheik was angry with her because she stopped him from stealing the young trolls. He yelled at her, but she stood up to him. She was so brave, even when…"

Coldness spread through me. "When what?"

Nate's voice shook. "When the vampire called. She was frightened, but she never showed it to them. Haism said he was giving us to the vampire to settle a debt."

Oh God, no.

"That bastard, Haism, wanted to frighten her, to make her suffer," Nate spat. "He was enjoying himself."

My Mori roared in my head, and I promised it we would kill that man with our bare hands.

"How did you get away, Nate?" Maxwell asked.

"It was Sara. She made a deal with Haism. If he let us go, she'd give him some troll bile she had stashed away. The German man brought me home, and Sara went with Haism and the other man to get the bile."

Hope sparked in my chest. I didn't believe Haism would let Sara go when he got the bile, but she was smart and she knew we'd be looking for her. "How long ago did she leave with him?"

"Less than twenty minutes."

"They could still be here. She'll stall him to give us time to find her." I looked at Maxwell. "We need to block every way out of this town."

"As soon as Chris called, I sent the pack out. They're covering all the exits and the harbor. The whole pack knows her scent, and my best trackers are trying to pick up her trail."

"Good." I started for the door. "Let me know the second they find something."

"Where are you going?" Nate called after me.

"To get her back and to kill anyone who touched her," I vowed coldly.

I called Chris as I jumped on my bike. "Yusi al-Hawwash's men took her. They haven't been gone long, so they're still in New Hastings."

"How do you know they're still here?"

"Sara promised them troll bile. They won't leave town without it."

"Smart girl," he said. "I'll be there in five minutes. We'll find her, Nikolas."

I hung up and started my bike.

"Nikolas," Maxwell called from the top of the stairs. "Francis picked up Sara's scent on the old mining road south of town. He said it's fresh."

"I know where that is." I peeled away from the building before he could say anything else. I called Chris on the way and told him to meet me there.

I spotted a white Cadillac half a mile down the mining road. Pulling up behind it, I saw Francis crouched beside a body on the ground.

"Vampire got him." He pointed at the mutilated man as he pulled out a cell phone. "More than one by the look of it. I need to let Maxwell know."

My stomach turned to ice. Only mature vampires could walk in the daylight, even on an overcast and foggy day like today.

Eli was here.

Moving with demon speed, I donned my harness and swords. "When Chris gets here, send him to the cliffs."

"How do you know where they went?"

"I just do."

I ran into the woods. The cliffs were Sara and Remy's special place, and *that* was where she'd hidden the damn bile.

It wasn't hard to follow their trail. I stopped to study the two sets of footprints in the dirt, and my rage grew when I saw the smaller set was made by stockinged feet. A little farther on, I found where she had lain on the ground; the same place she had escaped from her bonds and run.

Moving swiftly, I came to a stream. There were blood smears on a fallen log, and I told myself she had cut her feet while running and wasn't suffering worse injuries.

I kept moving, and suddenly I could smell the ocean.

Then I felt her.

I burst from the trees and stopped dead in the middle of a small field. Ahead of me on the cliffs milled a dozen or more vampires, and in the middle of them stood Sara and Eli.

Red colored my vision when I saw his possessive grip on her arm. I pulled my swords free of the harness and welcomed the rage descending over me.

Sara spun, and her gaze locked with mine.

Solmi! my demon roared.

For a moment, the world faded until there was just her and me and the bond that stretched between us. My eyes greedily drank her in. Bruised and bloody, wearing torn, dirty clothes, she was still the most beautiful thing I'd ever seen.

Eli's shout broke the spell that held me. "He is only one. Risa, Heath,

Lorne – take care of this."

Three vampires came at me. Circling me, they stayed out of reach of my swords, looking for an opening.

My Mori boiled beneath my skin, wanting blood from those who would harm our mate.

You'll have it, I vowed as its bloodlust filled me.

A red-haired male moved toward me. His eyes darted to my left as I raised my swords, and I knew he was trying to distract me. We spun away from each other at the same time, and one of my blades cut through skin and bone.

The blond male that had attacked on my left screamed and tried to retreat, but I gave him no quarter. His face was still frozen in shock when his severed head hit the ground.

A female shrieked behind me as the red-haired male came at me again. The look in his eyes told me he was not feinting this time.

Holding my swords against me, I kicked off from the ground in a burst of speed. Flipping backward, I landed behind the charging female. She was moving too fast to dodge the male's attack, and she screamed again as his claws gouged her face.

The male tried to veer away, but he hesitated too long and my swords were waiting for him. He cried out when the first blade slashed across his chest.

Kill! my Mori growled as my second blade cut deep into the vampire's gut, eviscerating him. No longer a threat, he sank to the ground, clutching his entrails.

The female made an inhuman sound, and I spun, bringing my swords up as she flew at me. One of her eyes had been destroyed by the male's claws, but her good eye held enough hatred for both of them. Crazed, she charged like a mindless beast, and I cut her down easily, driving my blade through her heart. Before her body hit the ground, I brought my other sword down in an arc to remove the head of the male that still writhed on the ground.

I faced the remaining vampires, who watched me in wary silence. My eyes went to Sara and the vampire that held her captive. She was pale, and I could sense her fear. But pride and hope shone in her green eyes.

Eli's voice rang out sharply. "All of you! Finish him."

"Coward!" Sara screamed at him as the other vampires took a step toward me.

I prepared myself for the attack. A warrior entered every battle knowing it could be his last, and each of us had our own way of facing our possible death. For me, it had always been the knowledge that I'd lived an honorable life, keeping humanity safe from the evils that walked the Earth, and I would die doing what I had been born to do.

But that was before I found Sara, before I knew what it was to live for another person. Her fate rested in my hands now, and if I fell, she'd be lost. I would not let that happen. I'd never faced this number of vampires alone, but then, the stakes had never been so high.

Sara gasped. At the same time, every one of the vampires blanched and took a step back. I didn't need to look behind me to know reinforcements had arrived. I could smell the werewolves, and I heard the soft whisper of an arrow being fitted to a bow.

I looked at Eli, but my words were directed at all the vampires. "Let her go and we will let you live…for today."

Eli yanked Sara against him with his claws pressed to her throat. His lips pulled back into a snarl that couldn't mask the fear in his eyes. "I think not. We both know I could rip her throat out and jump before you reached us."

My breath caught when he moved closer to the edge of the cliff. He would survive a plunge from that height, but Sara might not. I had to convince him that letting her go was the only way he'd get out of this alive.

"But then nothing would prevent me from hunting you down, and this time I will not stop."

Eli sneered. "I think sweet little Sara is important to you, and you won't do anything to jeopardize her life."

I didn't respond because he was looking for a reaction to give me away.

"Nothing to say?" Eli laughed and ran his claws down her face. "Will you still have nothing to say when I taste her?"

I knew the vampire was goading me, but that didn't stop the growl that worked its way up from my chest. The sight of his hands on her was enough to drive me and my Mori insane with rage.

"Stay back, Mohiri," Eli shouted. "You *might* kill me, but not before I end her."

The only thing that kept me in control was the knowledge that Sara's life depended on me holding it together. "Let her go and you'll have a chance of getting out of this alive."

My gaze swept over each vampire. "Is she worth your life – all your lives?"

The vampire closest to Eli said something I couldn't hear.

Eli snarled at him. "She is mine, and I will not give her up! You heard the Master. Kill her or take her, but the girl is not to be left behind."

Sara's voice rang out. "Kill me then. All I ever wanted was to find the one who killed my father, and here you are. Knowing that my friends will rip you to shreds – all of you – after I'm dead is enough for me."

My shock at hearing that Eli had killed her father was tempered only by the fresh wave of fear her words sent through me. The calm acceptance in her voice filled my veins with ice.

The vampires heard it too, and I could see panic on their faces. Some of them looked around, preparing to run.

"Stand firm!" Eli shouted at them. "You would dare disobey the Master's orders?"

The vampires rushed to form a shield in front of their leader. Behind me a few wolves let out low growls.

My eyes stayed on Sara, and my body shook as I watched Eli pull her against him and put his mouth to her ear. I could not hear his words, but I saw the revulsion on her face as she responded to whatever he'd said to her.

It killed me to stand there and watch her suffer his touch, but I was acutely aware of how close they were to the edge of the cliff. Eli was as fast as I was, and he'd be over the cliff with her before I could reach them.

"I'll kill you!" she cried suddenly, trying to pull away from Eli.

He laughed, and Sara stopped struggling. Her eyes met mine, and I saw the resolve in them. She was planning something.

I wanted to shout at her, to tell her no. She had no chance, surrounded as she was by so many vampires.

Eli wrapped his arms tighter around her waist. "Maybe I'll keep you until I find dear Madeline. I've never had a mother and daughter at one time."

Instead of cowering, Sara taunted him. "You sick bastard! I'm going to enjoy watching you die, Eli."

Some of the vampires turned to stare at her. Eli sneered and spoke loud enough for all to hear. "You're brave enough to say that now, but soon you will beg to die. I will use you and drink from you over and over until I have had my fill. And when there is nothing left, I will send you to be with your dear father."

Blood roared in my ears, and my body felt like a spring coiled too tight. My control was about to snap.

Eli jerked and made a choked sound. He stumbled back from Sara, clawing at the hilt of the knife she had buried in his chest. The same knife I'd given her that day on the wharf.

No one else moved.

Every pair of eyes was riveted on the girl who stood quietly, her face serene as she watched the vampire who had terrorized her gasp his last breath.

I was moving toward Sara before Eli hit the ground. The vampires recovered from their shock, and half a dozen of them came to intercept me. One went down before they could reach me, an arrow protruding from his chest. Chris was as deadly with a crossbow as he was with a sword. He felled a second vampire, leaving me to engage the last four. I took down one before a huge gray werewolf leapt at the throat of another vampire.

I was battling the last two vampires when a terrified scream curdled my blood. I spun toward the cliff in time to see a vampire sling Sara over his shoulder and run for the edge. "Sara!" I shouted, lunging at two female vampires who were harder to kill than their brethren.

A black wolf sped past me toward Sara. My gut twisted with the knowledge that he wouldn't reach her in time.

An arrow zipped past my head, and the vampire and Sara crumpled to the ground. She pushed his weight off her and got to her feet, looking dazed.

A vampire ran at me, and I drove my sword into her heart as I shouted, "Sara, run!"

She started toward me and jerked suddenly. Her pain hit me, and I stared in horror at the knife embedded in her chest. Blood quickly soaked her shirtfront, and she stumbled.

"No!" I roared, slashing at the vampire that stood between us. The vampire fell, and I turned to the cliff.

Sara was gone.

I dropped my swords and raced to the edge of the cliff. Below in the foaming surf, I spotted something dark and wavy, seconds before it disappeared beneath the surface.

"Sara!" I bellowed as I dove after her.

I sensed her before my body hit the water. My momentum took me down a dozen or so feet. Then I flipped around and began searching for her. The water was deep, but I could see clearly as I cut through it with strong strokes. I swam to where she should have been and dove to the bottom. I turned in a complete circle, confused. I could feel her nearby, but there was no sign of her.

I could stay underwater longer than a human, but eventually I was forced to come up for air. I broke the surface and sucked in large gulps of air before I headed back down.

It took me several seconds to realize Sara's presence was growing fainter off to my right. An underwater current tugged at me and I followed it, praying it would lead me to her.

The current flowed into a small cove. She was here; I could feel her. But the moment I entered the cove, she vanished. One second I felt her, and the next I felt nothing.

"Sara." I surfaced and called to her over and over as I searched the cove.

Pain crushed my chest when I finally swam back to the base of the cliff. She couldn't be gone. I'd know if she was dead. I felt our bond, strong and alive inside me, and the pain lessened. If she was dead, there would be no bond.

Chris was in the water when I got back to the cliff. Wordlessly, the two of us began searching. We'd covered a half-mile radius before boats arrived to help with the search. Maxwell had alerted the authorities that a girl had fallen into the ocean.

A police boat came, equipped with large search lights since it would be dark soon. They were joined by at least a dozen fishing boats and pleasure craft as word spread and the townspeople came out to help. The police organized the civilians, and they began searching several miles up and down the coast.

It was late into the evening when they called off the search for the night. They planned to come back at first light and resume their search. I heard snatches of a conversation about divers and a recovery operation. They already believed she was dead.

The only reason I left the water was that I knew without a doubt Sara was not there. A rope had been lowered to us from above, and Chris and I used it to pull ourselves up.

Erik's team had shown up before the police, and along with the wolves, they had removed all the vampires before the humans saw them. The team had also set up a temporary campsite in the field near the cliff to use as a base while they searched the woods. Maxwell's best trackers were out there as well looking for any sign of Sara.

Roland and Peter ran up to me as I climbed over the top of the cliff. Their hopeful expressions fell away when they saw my face.

"Nothing?" Roland asked.

"No," I replied harshly. I softened my tone when I saw the pain in their eyes. "We'll find her."

I spent the rest of the night searching the woods. Roland and Peter refused to go home, changing into wolf form to search with me. By dawn, the two of them were exhausted, and I tried to get them to go home, but they wouldn't leave. Finally, we went back to the Mohiri campsite where the wolves curled up on the ground and were asleep in seconds.

I was standing on the cliff, watching the boats resume their search, when Chris joined me. He'd been out in the woods all night too.

"We've covered at least ten square miles of ground so far. Erik rented a boat so he and Raj can search along the shore."

"Good," I replied, barely listening to him. I was racking my brain with the same question that had plagued me all night. How had Sara been there one second and gone the next? It didn't make sense, and I was going to drive myself insane until I had the answer.

Several hundred yards out, the police boat dropped two divers in the water. Chris watched them for a minute then cleared his throat. "Nikolas, we need to think about the possibility that Sara is –"

"She's not dead, Chris," I bit out. "I'd know."

He fell quiet for a few minutes. "We've never really talked about… Is the bond the reason you know she's alive?"

"Yes," I looked at him, trying not to see the sympathy in his eyes. "When I'm near her, I can sense her. I felt her in the water, and then she just vanished. I know she's alive because our bond is still there and it doesn't feel empty. I don't know how to explain it."

He nodded solemnly. "How does someone disappear like that? Could it be some kind of magic hiding her from us?"

"I don't know."

I'd thought about that and a hundred other scenarios throughout the night, but I couldn't find any that were plausible. It would take an extremely powerful glamour to block a Mori bond. Other than the Fae, only a handful of warlocks could be strong enough to pull it off.

Trolls were cousins to the Fae, and they had some Fae abilities, which had given me brief hope that her friend, Remy, had secreted her away to help her. But I could scour this area for a lifetime and never find the trolls' home. They lived in underground caves that were so well warded they were impossible to locate. I also didn't think Remy would let Sara's family and friends suffer unduly, not knowing where she was. He cared about her too much.

Chris pursed his lips. "You should get some food and sleep. You were out all night and you're still wearing your wet clothes."

"I'll sleep after I find her."

"We won't stop looking. And you won't be any good to Sara if you run yourself down. You're immortal, not invincible."

I knew he was right, but I couldn't think about sleep. I had to call Tristan and break the news to him. But first, I had to go see Sara's uncle. I'd promised him I would bring her home, and I'd failed. He deserved to hear it from me, not someone else.

Erik had brought my bag from the safe house, so I was able to change into clean clothes. I needed a shower, but that would have to wait.

Ten minutes later, I parked my bike next to a familiar blue Toyota outside Sara's building. Roland's mother, Judith, opened the door and invited me in.

"Nate's in the living room," she said in a low voice. "He's in bad shape. Max came last night to tell him about Sara."

She grabbed her coat from a rack in the hall. "I need to go to work. I'll be back later to check on him."

I went into the living room where Sara's uncle sat in his wheelchair, staring out the window. He didn't look my way when I came in.

"I keep expecting to see her walking along the wharves," he said hoarsely. "She loves it down there."

"I know." I'd watched her walk on them many times in the last month.

He turned his head toward me, his eyes dark with grief. "She told me she would be home after she gave him what he wanted. She lied so I would leave. She knew she wasn't coming home."

"She loves you and she wanted to keep you safe." I moved into the room and sat on the couch across from him. "And she will come home."

He seemed not to hear my last words. "Maxwell told me you were all there when she…. She wasn't alone."

"She wasn't alone," I assured him. "I don't think Sara could ever be alone, no matter where she goes."

He looked at me as if he was seeing me for the first time. "You're her warrior friend. You were here yesterday."

I nodded. "Nikolas."

He gave me a half smile. "She called you a royal pain in the ass. She also said you were a good person. She trusted you, and Sara didn't trust many people."

I wanted to tell him to stop talking about her in the past tense, but my throat tightened painfully. It was a minute before I could speak.

"Mr. Grey…Nate, do you think you could trust me like she does?"

"I don't know," he said.

I leaned forward and rested my elbows on my knees. "Will you trust me when I tell you Sara is still alive?"

His eyes widened. It was the biggest reaction he'd made since I'd gotten here. "How can you say that? Everyone saw her get stabbed and fall off a cliff. No one could survive that."

"Sara did. She's missing, but she's not dead."

"How-how do you know that?"

"It's a Mohiri thing." I didn't think he was ready to hear that his niece was bonded to a male he'd only met yesterday.

Hope flared in his eyes. "Where is she then?"

"I don't know," I said honestly. "But I won't stop looking for her. We have a team of warriors out there searching for her."

He let out a ragged breath. "I want so much to believe you. When she told me everything the other night, I didn't take it well. It was a lot to take in…but that's no excuse. She was upset when she went upstairs. I worked it all out by the time I came home from Portland, but I never got the chance to tell her that none of it changes how I feel about her."

"She knows, and she loves you too. I was on the phone with her when Haism called to say he had you. All she could think about was getting to you." It was hard to talk about that phone call, but if it eased her uncle's mind, it was worth it.

He gave a jerky nod. "She was so brave when she stood up to those men. Maxwell said she was brave on the cliff too."

I thought about her standing there, surrounded by vampires, telling Eli she couldn't wait to watch him die, seconds before she killed him. It took a person with incredible strength to go through what she had and to keep her composure through it all.

"She's a warrior," I said proudly.

Nate gave me a strange look, and he seemed to be thinking about his next words. "Can I ask you...? Is there something going on between you and Sara?"

"I care for your niece," I said with deliberate vagueness. "But we're not together in that way."

"Okay," he said, though he didn't look like he was convinced.

I stood and pulled a white card from my pocket. "This is my cell number if you want to know how the search is going, or if you need anything at all. I'll be staying at the Beacon Inn."

I walked over and handed the card to him. "Call me anytime."

"Nikolas," he said when I turned to leave. "Judith brought me one of her breakfast casseroles. I wasn't hungry before, but I think I could eat now. Would you like to join me? I guarantee it's better than anything you'll get at the inn."

I smiled for the first time since that call from Sara yesterday. "Thank you. I'd like that."

* * *

An hour later, I stood beside my bike, staring down at my phone, dreading the call I was about to make. With a heavy sigh, I left my bike and started toward the wharves. When I reached the one where Sara and I had talked on my first visit to her, I walked to the end of it. Then I dialed Tristan's number.

"Nikolas, I was just about to call you. How's Sara doing? Is she nervous about today?"

I closed my eyes for a moment, wishing I wasn't about to kill the happiness I heard in his voice. "Tristan, something has happened."

"What?" His tone grew sharp. "Is Sara okay?"

There was no easy way to say it. "Sara's missing."

"Missing? What do you mean?" he demanded.

"Yusri al-Hawwash's men got to her. They took her uncle, and she traded herself for him." Pain lanced through my chest. "I lost her."

"How could this happen? Where were you? Where were Chris and Erik's unit?" Tristan's voice rose with each question until he was almost shouting.

I told him about the frantic phone call from Sara yesterday afternoon, the fight with the vampires on the cliff, her fall into the ocean, and the search that was underway. Reliving the last twenty-four hours was torture, but it was nothing less than I deserved. I'd promised to keep Sara safe, and I'd failed her and Tristan. I never should have entrusted her safety to someone else. I never should have let her out of my sight.

Tristan's voice was choked with emotion when he spoke again. "Could one of the vampires have taken her? Or more of al-Hawwash's men?"

"We killed every vampire on the cliff." I couldn't bring myself to think we might have missed one. "One of Haism's men is unaccounted for, a German male named Gerhard. He left Sara's uncle at the apartment, but he never met up with Haism. Erik's working with Dax to track him down. We need to put people on Yusri al-Hawwash to monitor his communications and activity. If he has Sara, I don't think he will harm her. Without the troll bile, he'll be desperate for a cure and he might think she can help him."

"I'll oversee it myself. The sheik and I have some mutual acquaintances," he replied, sounding like himself again. "I'm sending everyone we can spare to help with the search. What else do you need?"

I needed to hold Sara in my arms and never let her go again. To tell her I was sorry and to beg her for forgiveness.

"Nikolas, are you still there?"

"I'm sorry. Lost in thought." As I watched several boats head out of the harbor, I wondered if they were going to join in the search. Or the recovery effort as I knew they were calling it now.

He exhaled noisily. "How are you so sure she survived the fall from the cliff?"

"Because I know Sara. She's strong and resilient, and if anyone is a survivor, it's her. And…"

"And what? If you know something, please tell me."

I rubbed my jaw, which was covered in two days of beard. God, this wasn't something I wanted to tell Tristan over the phone. It wasn't something I wanted to discuss with him at all, but he had a right to know.

"I know Sara is still alive because I can feel it."

"Feel it?" he repeated slowly. "What are you saying?"

"I'm saying Sara is my mate."

"*What?*" He made a few sounds of disbelief. "Mate? Are you sure?"

"Were you sure when you met Josephine?" I asked.

"Jesus! I need to sit down." I heard him sink into his desk chair. "How long have you known? Is that why she finally agreed to come here?"

I took a deep breath of the salty air. "I've known since the night we met. Sara doesn't know about it yet. She was so set against having anything to do with us in the beginning. I wanted to let her get to know me and trust me before I laid something like this on her."

"That's good," he said, sounding like he was still in shock. "But how is it that she doesn't know? She should feel the bond by now, if it was there."

"It's there. Trust me." I understood his surprise, but I wouldn't allow anyone to question my bond with Sara. "I told you her control of her Mori is unlike anything I've ever seen. I think she can't feel the bond like other females because she is suppressing her demon. But her Mori does recognize mine, and I think on some level Sara feels it too."

There was silence for a long moment. "I'm sorry. Nikolas. I'm not questioning your integrity. A month ago, I didn't know I had a granddaughter, and now I find out she is bonded to you of all people."

I started to speak, and he said, "I mean, you have never made a secret of your desire to remain single. Now after all these years you bond to an orphan, to my granddaughter. Do you...plan to break the bond?"

"No," I said tightly. "Only Sara can break it."

He let out a long breath. "I know I'm handling this all wrong. I can think of no one who would make a finer mate for my granddaughter."

"Thank you." I stared down at the rippling water. "I know she's alive, Tristan. Wherever she is, I *will* find her."

He sighed wearily. "I know you will. Now please, bring my granddaughter home."

CHAPTER 13

"NIKOLAS, COME IN."

I entered the apartment and closed the door behind me. Following Nate into the kitchen, I sat at the table as he rolled his chair to the spot across from me. I couldn't help but notice his pale skin and the dark shadows under his eyes. He'd lost weight as well. Neither of us was eating or sleeping well these days, but he didn't have a demon to bolster his strength.

I gave him a hard stare. "When was the last time you ate? Or slept?"

"I ate" – he looked at the wall clock in the kitchen – "five hours ago." He avoided my question about sleep like he always did.

"Nate, you have to take better care of yourself. What will Sara say when she comes home and sees you like this?"

His green eyes, so much like hers, took on a haunted look. "Nikolas, it's been two weeks."

"I know."

If he asked, I could tell him exactly how many days and hours it had been. I'd spent them searching every stretch of woods and road, every cave and cove for fifty miles. I had driven every street in Portland, praying I'd feel her presence. Our people had used every resource at our disposal, trying to find even a trace of her. It was as if Sara had vanished into thin air.

In the beginning, everyone had joined in the search, despite the tension between the wolves and the dozen or so warriors camping out in town. The pack was upset so many vampires had walked into their territory and attacked someone under their protection. Maxwell had been incensed that the two wolves he'd sent to guard Sara that day had shirked their responsibility, thinking it wasn't their job to protect a Mohiri. Maxwell had assured me their punishment was severe. Cold comfort.

After the third day, people began to say Sara was dead. Wherever I went in town, I could overhear conversations about "that poor girl who

163

drowned." It angered me every time I heard them talk about her that way, but I couldn't stop people from talking.

It was a week before her friends gave up hope. I didn't see much of Roland and Peter after that because Maxwell had them doing extra training. But the few times I saw them it was clear the two of them were grieving.

"Sara's not coming home," Nate said.

"Yes, she is. Don't give up on her."

"I want to believe that more than anything, but I have to face the truth, and so do you." He swallowed hard. "Sara is dead. It's time we both accept it."

"I'm sorry, but I can't do that." As long as the bond was alive, Sara was alive, and I'd search for her forever if that's what it took.

He sighed wearily and looked down at his clasped hands. "Father Glenn came to see me yesterday. He thinks it's time we let people say good-bye to Sara. We're having a memorial service for her tomorrow at St. Patrick's. I thought you might like to be there."

I pushed my chair back and strode to the window. My fingers gripped the edge of the countertop as I stared at the waterfront and tried to rein in my emotions. I didn't know where Sara was, but I knew with absolute certainty she was alive. And no one would ever convince me otherwise.

"You have to let her go. We both do. I don't know how your people cope with grief, but humans need closure. We say good-bye. Then we try to keep going as best we can."

When I didn't respond, he continued. "I know you felt responsible for her, and you blame yourself for what happened. Anyone who's met you knows you did everything in your power to save her. Sara knows that too."

The countertop creaked under my fingers, and I released it before I accidentally pulled it from the wall. Turning, I met Nate's agonized gaze. I didn't want to add to his pain, but I would never accept that Sara was gone forever. My heart would stop beating before I gave up on her.

"I understand why you need to have the service, but I won't be there." My voice was steady, revealing nothing of the storm raging inside me. I walked past him and stopped in the kitchen doorway. "I'm sorry."

I left the apartment and strode back to my hotel where my bike was parked. A few minutes later, I rode past Nate's, heading out of town.

Passing the marina, I spotted the large yacht still moored at the end of the main dock. After Sara disappeared, Roland told us the two of them had narrowly escaped Haism's men and the Hale witch at the marina the night of the storm. They'd gone there to meet her buyer, Malloy, and the men had come after them. He and Sara had escaped by jumping off a boat and hiding under the pier. Roland said he and Sara had honestly believed those men were after Malloy and that they'd just gotten caught up in his trouble.

Chris and I had scoured every inch of al-Hawwash's yacht for clues, anything that would lead us to Sara. Tristan had sent people to go through the sheik's house in Portland, along with many of his other holdings around the world. Tristan believed the sheik had Sara stashed away somewhere, and he had Yusri al-Hawwash living under a microscope these days. The sheik couldn't buy toothpaste without us knowing about it.

I passed the city limit sign, and soon I was on the old mine road. I'd been down this way so many times in the last two weeks that I knew every rock, tree, and bend in the road. I parked in my usual spot and trekked through the woods to the cliff, the last place I'd seen Sara.

When I broke through the trees at the edge of the field, my throat tightened as it did every time I saw the cliff. Memories of that day assailed me, and I relived them all, trying to see what I could have done differently. I'd been through countless battles and I'd never doubted my skills as a warrior. But this one haunted me and left me wondering how I had failed her.

I walked to the edge of the cliff and stared down at the waves pummeling its base. Nate, the werewolves, and the whole town believed Sara had died here, her body swept out to sea. I understood why they'd given up hope; they didn't have a bond telling them she was still alive.

But even without the bond, I'd find it hard to believe that such a spirited, passionate person, who had survived so much, was gone. She'd tried so hard to go unnoticed, not realizing her inner fire drew people to her like a beacon, just as it had called to me before I knew who or what she was.

And now they wanted to say good-bye to her. Tomorrow her family and friends would gather in their church to sing sad hymns and pray for her immortal soul. I couldn't do that, not for Nate or anyone else. It would be a betrayal of the person who I knew was still alive out there, lost and waiting to be found.

"Where are you, Sara?" I asked for what felt like the thousandth time.

For the thousandth time, there was no answer.

*   *   *

Organ music spilled from the open double doors of the church that was filled to overflowing. At least a dozen men stood on the steps because there was no room for them inside. The music stopped and the priest began to speak again, his deep voice amplified by the microphone he was using.

I stood across the street from the church but close enough for my enhanced hearing to pick up the priest's words.

"Our hearts are heavy with sorrow today as we come together to say good-bye to Sara Grey, who was called home into our Lord's embrace. When we lose a child, it's natural for us to question why God would take someone young —"

Pain pricked my chest, and I rubbed the spot over my heart as I tuned out the priest's voice. I didn't know why I had come here, why I would torment myself this way. Watching people gather in a memorial service for someone I knew was alive was senseless.

But I couldn't turn away. Sara's uncle and friends were inside the church, mourning her. I'd watched Nate arrive with Roland and Judith, and it tore at me to see the grief on their faces. I think I stayed because I didn't want them to suffer alone.

The priest stopped talking, and I heard someone else take the mic. I could tell by the voice that she was young, most likely one of Sara's classmates. She spoke for a few minutes, and then someone else started talking. We had a custom like this among my people, where friends and family of a fallen warrior would take turns celebrating the warrior's life. Perhaps we were not as different from humans as I'd thought.

The music began again, and people poured slowly from the church. Nate appeared first, accompanied by Judith and Maxwell. He sat in his chair just outside the door, and people stopped to pay their condolences as they filed out. It looked like the entire pack had shown up, along with most of Sara's school.

Roland and Peter emerged with a young man in a black biker jacket. The man's dark blond hair fell to his shoulders, but it didn't hide the raw grief on his face.

Who was he? A friend? A relative? Or someone who'd been more than a friend to her? The emotions he showed were not those of simple friendship. This man cared about her deeply.

At the bottom of the church steps, the three of them stopped to talk, and Roland laid his hand on the other man's shoulder. The blond man nodded and walked to a classic Harley sitting alone at the end of the parking lot. He straddled the bike and just sat there, his head hung and his shoulders shaking. After a few minutes, he wiped his eyes with his sleeve and drove off.

I looked at the church again as Chris appeared in the doorway. He spoke briefly to Nate before he continued down the steps. Chris believed me when I said Sara was alive, but he'd felt he should be at the service since he was her family. Tristan decided not to come to the service. He said he couldn't bear to watch Sara's friends and family grieve her when she was still alive.

Chris looked my way as he walked to his bike, but he didn't come over. I think he knew the last thing I wanted in that moment was company.

I stood there a few minutes longer, watching the church empty of mourners. When the last strains of organ music filled the air, I turned and walked away.

*   *   *

The wharf was deserted when I started my stroll down to the end of it. No doubt it was because of the cold wind that formed little whitecaps on the water and buffeted the waterfront.

I didn't mind the cold; in fact, I welcomed it because it let me have this spot to myself. Of all the places in New Hastings, this was where I felt closest to Sara. I could see why she loved it here. I'd never been a sentimental person, but lately I found myself looking at things and seeing them through her eyes. She'd probably laugh if she could hear my thoughts now.

I turned my back on the water and faced the waterfront where a handful of people went about their business. Life here had settled back into its normal quiet routine in the three weeks since Sara disappeared. Erik's team was back in Boston, trying to track down the sudden flow of the demon drug *heffion* into the city. A few days ago, Tristan had finally called back the extra unit he'd sent to help with the search for Sara. Only Chris and I stayed in Maine, and he split his time between here and Portland.

From my vantage point, I could see Sara's building at the end of the waterfront. Nate and I had gotten to know each other in recent weeks, and I'd grown to admire and respect him. We talked about his days in the military before his injury and his transition to a much quieter life in New Hastings. He'd confided in me how he'd been scared to death when Sara came to live with him after her father was killed. He'd had no idea how to raise a child, but he'd never regretted his decision. It was easy to see where Sara got her courage and compassion.

I stuck my hands in my pockets and started walking back the way I'd come. When I reached the waterfront, I turned right toward my hotel, but changed my mind and came about. I felt oddly restless, even more than usual, and I didn't want to spend the next few hours holed up in my hotel room.

I checked the time on my phone as I walked toward Nate's. He had invited me to dinner, but that was two hours away. He was doing a bit better lately, but he still looked like he wasn't sure what to do with his life now. Maybe I'd drop by early and –

My Mori fluttered.

The air left my lungs, and I froze mid-stride. Not a minute had gone by since that day on the cliff that I hadn't longed to feel that sensation again. But when the heart wants something so bad, the mind will play tricks on you.

I took another step.

Nothing.

Two more steps.

My Mori shifted and pressed forward. *Solmi?*

My heart began to race. In seconds, I stood outside Nate's door, my hand on the knob. I opened the door and inhaled sharply as her essence surrounded me, filling the empty place inside me.

My Mori's cry of joy was followed by a fierce surge of possessiveness as it sensed our mate. It was all I could do to stay in control as I walked down the hallway to the kitchen.

I stood in the doorway and stared at the girl sitting on a chair with her arms cradling her head on the table. Her long chestnut hair spilled across her arms, hiding her face, but I'd know her anywhere.

She stirred and lifted her head. "How did he take —?"

Her eyes met mine, and I forgot how to speak.

"Nikolas," she whispered.

My chest constricted as a storm of emotions battered me. *She's home; she's safe,* I said half to myself and half to calm the demon straining to get to her. Holding on to my control by a thread, I spoke more sharply than I meant to.

"Where were you?"

She flinched and hugged herself. "Don't look at me like that. It's not like I stabbed myself and jumped off the damn cliff!"

Her pain hit me, and my Mori ceased its struggle. In the next heartbeat, I was on my knees in front of her, touching her face and drowning in her shimmering green eyes.

All these weeks, I'd thought of the things I'd say to her when I found her, but I forgot every one of them when she burst into tears. I gathered her to me and wrapped my arms around her shaking body. Burying my face in her hair, I breathed in her scent and felt my world right itself again.

Her sobs became quiet hiccups, and still I couldn't let her go.

"*Pozhaluysta, prosti menya,*" I pleaded hoarsely. "I promised to keep you safe, and I didn't. I'm sorry."

"No." She pulled away, and I forced myself to let her go. "If you hadn't shown up when you did, Eli would have…"

"Don't think about that." She'd suffered enough at the hands of that bastard. I wasn't going to let him torment her from the grave.

My shock over her sudden reappearance began to wear off, leaving one burning question. Where had she been all these weeks?

"We've been searching that area ever since you disappeared. Where were you?"

"Seelie," she answered quietly.

My brows drew together. I could not have heard that right. "Come again?"

"Turns out I have friends there." Her teary smile was like the sun, driving away the darkness that had hovered over this place since she'd disappeared. "It's kind of complicated."

"Why does that not surprise me?" Something told me I needed to sit for this one, so I grabbed the closest chair and pulled it over in front of hers.

"Well, let's have it. I'm dying to know how a Mori demon ends up in a world where no demon would dare to tread."

She smiled. "Well, it all started the day I met a sylph... Actually no, it started before that with my great-great-great-great-grandmother."

I stared at her, and her mouth turned down.

"Look, I told you it was complicated."

"I'm sorry." I had no idea what she'd been through in the last three weeks, and the last thing I wanted to do was cause her more distress.

She chewed her lip. "I'm honestly not sure *where* to start. Just before I met you, a sylph came to visit me."

My mouth fell open, and she nodded. "I know. Believe me, I was pretty surprised to see an elemental outside my house. She told me her name was Aine, but she never said what she wanted. We talked for a few minutes about my healing power, and then she left."

Her eyes darkened. "I remember falling off the cliff and hitting the water, and then I woke up in a bed in a strange room with vines on the walls and a dirt floor. Aine came in and told me I was in Seelie. She said some selkies found me in the water and called for her help. Aine said only Fae magic could heal me, so they had to take me to Faerie. I-I guess I was in pretty bad shape."

I knew the exact moment they had taken her. I'd never forget how it felt when she vanished in that cove.

Nate came into the kitchen as she spoke. He had the look of a man who had been given a miracle and was afraid to believe it was real. I knew exactly how he felt.

"Aine told me my great-great-great-great-grandmother, Sahine, was undine. Sahine chose to become mortal, and married a human. Only females can be undine, and all of her descendants were male and human – until me. That's where my healing power comes from. I inherited it from Sahine."

My mind spun, and it was all I could do to hide my shock. Sara was part Fae? She had Fae magic *and* a Mori demon inside her. How was that possible? I'd seen a demonstration of her magic when she'd healed Roland. A demon could never withstand that kind of power. Yet somehow hers had.

Things I'd puzzled over began to make sense. In particular, Sara's unprecedented control of her Mori. She must use her power to keep the demon subdued without harming it. I wondered if she even knew she was doing it.

It also explained why she didn't appear to feel our bond like she should. I didn't know what this would mean for us. With proper training, she could become comfortable with her demon. Or she might never open herself up to her Mori.

"Aine didn't want me to leave Seelie," Sara said, jerking me from my thoughts. "She said demons won't be happy to have a half Fae around."

Nate paled in alarm. "You didn't tell me that part. Does this mean you're in more danger?"

"No," I stated with firm conviction. "Because we will keep her safe this time."

"So she's safe here?"

I turned to face Nate. "I have not lied to you since we met, and I won't start now. Until we track down Eli's master, Sara is not safe anywhere except with the Mohiri."

He frowned. "But what if –?"

"I know you don't know much about us, but Sara has family among the Mohiri and they would never harm her. And you would be welcome there as well."

Sara's hand touched mine, sending warmth up my arm.

"Really?" she asked hopefully.

Nate shook his head, and her smile disappeared. "Thank you, that is very generous," he told me regretfully. "But I can't just pick up and leave. I have a new book coming out and a book tour to plan. And truthfully, I don't think I would be comfortable living among people who all look like twenty-year-olds."

"But you could be in danger if the vampires come back," Sara argued fearfully.

"Everyone – including the vampires – thinks you are dead," Nate replied. "If they were coming back, they would have done it by now."

I nodded. "He's right. As long as we get you out of here before anyone discovers the truth, Nate should be safe."

"But I just got back." Tears glittered in her eyes when she looked at him. "I don't want to leave you."

"I don't want you to go, but I would feel better knowing you're safe," he said in a reassuring voice. "And it's not like we can't talk on the phone whenever you want. I'll even come for Christmas if the Mohiri celebrate it."

"We do, and Thanksgiving too," I told them. Her eyes widened, and I smiled. "We are not as different as you think we are."

I watched the play of emotions across her face before she averted her gaze. Even then, I could sense the struggle within her.

Standing, she walked to the window, and I noticed her thin yellow dress and bare feet for the first time. They made her seem smaller, almost fragile, though I knew she was stronger than she appeared. She was afraid to leave what she knew behind, but she would do it to protect the man she loved as a father.

She set her shoulders and spoke without looking away from the window. "I'll go."

I sighed inaudibly as relief washed over me. "You're making the right decision."

"I know." Her voice barely rose above a whisper. "Why do the right things have to be so hard?"

Nate looked at me and gave a slight nod in her direction. I'd admitted weeks ago to caring for his niece, but the man was no fool. He could see there was more between us.

I walked over to stand beside her, just close enough for our arms to touch. "Do you trust me?"

She had to tilt her head to look up at me. "Yes."

I laid my hand over her smaller one on the counter. "It'll be different, but you'll like it there once you get used to it."

She loved being outdoors, and I couldn't wait to see her reaction to the mountains and woods around Westhorne. After seeing her overflowing bookcases upstairs, I had a feeling she was also going to like the library Tristan had spent years building.

"You'll be able to talk to Nate and your friends as much as you want, and they can visit you there. You already know Chris and me, and you have Mohiri family as well."

Her hand tensed. "Madeline's father? I don't think I'm ready to…"

"Don't worry. He understands, and he'll give you all the time you need."

It would hurt Tristan not to be able to be there for her when she arrived, but his granddaughter's happiness was more important to him.

She was quiet for a moment. "You and Chris live there too?"

"Yes, when we're not on a job." For the last few years, I'd been on the road more than I was at Westhorne. Suddenly, the idea of spending more time at home was very appealing. I'd talk to Tristan about that when we got there.

Our eyes were drawn to the window when a familiar blue car screeched to a stop outside. Roland and Peter jumped out, and we could hear their feet pounding on the stairs.

Sara let out a sound that was between a laugh and a sob and ran to meet them in the hallway. I smiled as they burst through the front door and Roland swung her up into a rib-crushing hug.

My Mori growled at the sight of another male touching Sara, even though it had accepted Roland as her friend.

"I need to make a call. I'll be right outside," I told Sara as I moved toward the front door. I was reluctant to let her out of my sight so soon after getting her back, but I could see she was close to being overwhelmed by everything.

I closed the door behind me and leaned against it, allowing my guard to drop for the first time since I'd walked into the kitchen. I let out a shaky breath as I looked up at the cloudless sky.

Thank you.

My chest felt light when I took out my phone and dialed Tristan's number. He was heading to the Council meeting in India today, and I hoped he hadn't left already.

"Nikolas, you just caught me," he said when he answered. "I was about to walk out the door."

I didn't beat around the bush. "I have news."

The line went silent for a moment. "Is she…?"

"She's back, Tristan. She's safe."

"What?" His voice shook. "How…? You found her?"

"She came home on her own. I'll explain it when I see you. It's not something we can discuss over the phone."

"Is she okay?"

I laughed gruffly. "She's perfect, and I'm bringing her home."

Tristan exhaled. "The plane will be there in a few hours. I'll notify the Council that I'll be a day or two late for the meetings. I wish I could cancel my trip," he said regretfully.

We both knew he wouldn't. The Council oversaw crucial Mohiri business, and they couldn't put their job on hold because too much depended on them. The safety and prosperity of our people came above the personal lives of the Council members. It was a vow they took when they joined the Council.

"We'll stay here tonight and leave tomorrow," I told him. "Sara returned only an hour ago, and she's dealing with a lot. She needs a night with Nate."

"He's welcome here as well."

"I told them that, but he wants to stay in Maine. He'll visit during the holidays."

"I look forward to meeting him," Tristan replied sincerely. It sounded like he was typing on his keyboard. The man was always busy. "I'm sending word to the pilot to change his flight plan. Do you have enough security there tonight?"

"I'm calling Erik's team back from Boston as backup until we get on the plane. Chris is in Portland, so he can be here in an hour. I'm also going to ask Maxwell to provide protection. Two of her werewolf friends are already inside with her."

"Are you sure it's safe for her to stay in the apartment after what happened?"

I looked down at several blackened spots on the landing, a burnt offering from the last unwelcome person who tried to enter the apartment.

"The building is warded with troll magic, so it's the safest location for her tonight."

"Troll magic," he repeated in wonder. "My granddaughter is an extraordinary person. I'm eager to get to know her."

"Yes, she is." My smile dimmed. "I need to tell you she's still not ready to meet her Mohiri family. She needs a little time to adjust first."

"I understand," he said sadly. "I only want her to be happy."

"We'll make sure she is."

He cleared his throat. "Does Sara know yet about the bond?"

I rubbed my jaw. "No. I'm going to wait until we get to Westhorne and give her some time to settle in first." I needed to think of the best way to broach the delicate subject with her. She trusted me and I believed she cared for me, but was she ready to see me as more than a protector and a friend?

"That's a wise idea," Tristan said. "I know you'll do what is best for her."

"I will," I replied roughly. I would do whatever it took to ensure her happiness.

"Well, I need to call the Council and inform them I'll be late because my granddaughter is coming home," he said, and I could tell he wore a wide smile. "I'll see you and Sara tomorrow, my friend."

"Tomorrow."

CHAPTER 14

I HEARD A soft gasp from the back seat when we pulled into the hanger. Sara had been quiet during the drive from New Hastings, and Chris and I had left her to her thoughts. Now, she leaned forward to stare through the windshield at the jet waiting for us.

"You guys own a plane?" she asked incredulously.

Chris chuckled as he put the SUV in park. "I told you we would travel in style."

She made a face. "I thought you meant we'd be flying first class."

"We are. Every seat on the jet is first class." He unbuckled his seat belt and reached for his door. "And look, no lines."

She sank back against her seat. "Roland and Peter are not going to believe this."

I smiled at the wonder that had replaced the unease in her voice. Getting out of the vehicle, I opened her door. "Come on, they're waiting for us."

She slid out and walked to the jet steps. At the bottom, she hesitated a moment, and then she grasped the handrail and entered the jet.

"This is amazing," she breathed when I followed her inside. She sank down in the wide window seat in the first row and ran her hands over the soft leather arms. "I figured you guys had money, but this is unbelievable."

"It's your money too." I turned back to the door. "I'm going to help them load your things, and then we'll take off."

"Okay," she said quietly, and I could hear the nervousness she was trying to hide.

Five minutes later, everything was onboard, and Chris, Erik, and I climbed into the jet. Chris and Erik went to the back, and I let the pilot know we were ready for takeoff. Then I took the seat next to Sara.

"Can you tell me where we're going now?" she asked.

"Idaho."

"Idaho?" She frowned. "I don't know much about Idaho except they grow potatoes."

I laughed. "Westhorne is about an hour north of Boise, close to the mountains. We don't grow potatoes, but we have lots of trees and rivers. The closest town is Butler Falls, which is five miles away."

"Wow, it sounds isolated," she said dejectedly. "I guess you guys like your privacy."

"We do, but you'll find it's not as isolated as it sounds. I think you'll like it there."

The jet pulled out of the hanger and taxied to a runway. Sara's hands gripped the arms of her seat as she peered out the window. When we took off and the landing gear left the ground, her eyes closed tightly. I hid my amusement. Was the girl who had fought vampires and tamed hellhounds afraid of flying?

"Don't like to fly?"

She made a face. "Ask me that in a few hours."

"First time?"

"Yeah."

"Relax and enjoy it." She'd lived a sheltered life in New Hastings, and this was just one of so many firsts she would experience over her lifetime. I wanted to be there for them all.

She looked out the window and became quiet as she watched Portland grow smaller. She'd been quiet on the ride from New Hastings too. Her brave face couldn't conceal her pain and turmoil from me as we'd driven away from everything she knew. I wished I could ease her hurt, but I knew she had to go through this, to accept what had to be done in order to move on to her new life.

The last twenty-four hours had been hard on her. She'd come home thinking she'd been gone two days, only to discover it had been three weeks and everyone she knew thought she was dead. Not just dead; they'd had a memorial service for her.

Before that information had time to sink in, she'd had to start packing her possessions for her move away from everyone she cared about. Roland and Peter had stayed to help. I'd given them and Nate space to spend their last night together, while I made arrangements for our travel.

My Mori and I were so happy to have her back that neither of us had minded sleeping on the couch while the boys stayed upstairs with Sara. I'd lain awake for hours, listening to their soft murmurs, and long after the apartment had grown quiet, I'd heard her tossing restlessly in her bed.

The pilot turned off the seat belt sign. I unbuckled mine and turned to Sara. "Would you like something to…?"

My voice trailed off at the sight of her closed eyes and slightly parted lips. Her face was paler than normal and shadows rested beneath her eyes.

My heart constricted. A day ago, I didn't know if I'd ever see her again, and now here she was sleeping peacefully beside me.

She shivered and I fetched a blanket from a storage compartment to cover her. Unable to leave her, I grabbed a book from my bag and sat beside her to read. It was a futile effort because I could barely focus on the words with her so close.

When she shifted in her sleep and turned toward me to rest her head on my shoulder, I gave up all pretense of reading.

By the end of the flight, she was lying across the wide seat with her head on my lap, letting out an occasional soft snore that made me smile. I'd flown all over the world, but no flight had ever been as pleasurable as this one.

When the plane began to descend, I gently lifted her into a sitting position. Something told me she would be embarrassed if she awoke to find herself lying on me. She must have been exhausted, because she didn't stir until the jet touched down in Boise.

The jet taxied into the hanger where a cargo van, a white Ford Expedition, and four warriors waited for us. We exited the plane, and I introduced Sara to Seamus, Niall, Ben, and Ambrose before they set to loading her things into the van. Then Ben, Ambrose, and Erik climbed into the van while the rest of us piled into the SUV.

Sara fell quiet again, sitting between Chris and me in the back. As we drove through Boise, Chris pointed out buildings and landmarks and kept up a light banter until she relaxed.

It was almost dark when we reached Butler Falls and took the turnoff for Westhorne. I watched Sara's face when her new home came into view. Her eyes moved over the large stone building, which had lights shining from many of the windows, to the snowcapped mountains rising behind it. Tristan and I had chosen this location when we set out from Virginia to form a new stronghold over one hundred and fifty years ago, and we had worked side-by-side to help build the place that was now our home.

"What do you think?" I asked.

She gave me a small smile. "It's prettier than I expected."

Chris grinned. "What did you expect – barracks and barbed wire?"

"Close," she admitted, and laughter filled the vehicle.

We pulled up to the front entrance of the main building, and I felt Sara tense beside me when the door opened. I expected to see Tristan even though he'd told me he would give Sara time to settle in before he introduced himself.

A dark-haired warrior appeared in the doorway and walked down the steps to the SUV. Callum had come to Westhorne a year ago, and I'd heard he was an excellent trainer. I spent so much time away that I didn't know him all that well.

I exited the vehicle, and Sara climbed out to stand beside me. Callum nodded a greeting to me and looked at Sara.

"Sara, welcome to Westhorne," he said in a Scottish brogue, extending his hand to her. "My name is Callum, and I'm here to help you get settled in and to answer any questions you have."

Sara smiled and shook his hand. "It's nice to meet you."

Mine, my Mori rumbled unhappily.

I took a step forward, half blocking her from Callum's view.

"I thought Claire was going to be here." Tristan had said he would have the female warrior greet Sara, to help put her at ease.

"Something came up, so Claire asked me to step in."

Callum addressed Sara. "Claire said to tell you she would give you the grand tour tomorrow. Now, why don't I show you to your room?"

My Mori growled.

"I'll show her to her room," I said brusquely.

I ignored the surprised looks Callum, Seamus, and Niall gave me. It was no secret I didn't fraternize with orphans or trainees unless I had to. But I had no intention of explaining my actions to them or anyone else.

Sara looked from Callum to me. "Is everything okay?" she asked.

Chris moved to her other side and shot me a warning look. "Just a little misunderstanding," he told her. He looked at Callum. "What room is she in?"

Callum looked like he was about to say something and thought better of it. "Third floor of the north wing. Last room on the left."

I laid a hand on the small of Sara's back. "Come with me. Chris and the others will bring your things."

When she didn't move away from my touch, my Mori calmed and the tension left my body. We entered the building, and I heard her soft intake of breath as she looked around. I supposed compared to her home, the main hallway might seem a bit grand with its marble floor and chandelier.

Most people were at dinner, so we didn't encounter anyone as we ascended the stairs to her floor. I knew the trainees lived in this wing, but I'd never been up here until now.

At the end of the hallway, I opened the door and flicked on the light.

"Welcome to your new home," I said as she entered the spacious room and looked around.

She walked to the window, and her expression told me she was more impressed by the mountain view than by her luxurious accommodations.

"It's very nice," she said quietly.

Chris entered the room, followed by the other warriors, all bearing boxes and suitcases. Seamus had to duck under the door frame with the three boxes he carried. He set the boxes in the small living room and observed the load they'd brought up.

"How much clothing does one wee lass need?"

Sara smiled. "Those are books, not clothes."

"Like we don't have enough books here."

"These are *my* books."

For a moment, I saw sadness in her eyes, but she shook it off. "Thank you for bringing up my things."

Niall slapped his twin on the back of the head and gave her a playful bow. "Anytime, lass."

The others left and I found myself alone with her. She looked around as if she wasn't sure what to do next.

"Are you hungry?" I asked.

"A little."

I knew she was lying. She hadn't eaten on the flight and had to be starving. "They're serving dinner now. Would you like to join me?"

Relief flashed in her eyes, and her smile sent warmth through me.

"Do I have time to change and clean up a bit?"

"Take all the time you need." I walked to the door. "I could use a bit of cleaning up too. How about I come back for you in half an hour?"

"Okay."

I closed the door behind me and headed for my apartment to shower and change. My chest felt light for the first time in weeks, and I looked forward to our first evening together at Westhorne.

I knew Sara was homesick and missing her uncle and friends. I'd do everything in my power to make her happy here and to help her transition to her new life.

Knowing Tristan, he had already made preparations for her Mohiri education, and I needed to let him know I intended to be involved in her training. I'd still do my job, but I planned to spend more time at Westhorne. Sara was my first priority now, and her happiness came above all else.

* * *

"Half Fae," Tristan said for about the fourth time since he'd shown up at my door thirty minutes ago. I wondered if I'd worn that same shocked expression when Sara told her story.

"Now you know why I didn't want to tell you over the phone."

He let out a long breath. "How is it possible for a demon to survive surrounded by Fae magic? From what you've told me about her healing the werewolf, her magic is already quite strong."

I shook my head. "I don't know. She must use her Fae magic to keep the Mori under control without harming it. That's how she's been able to survive all these years, where anyone else would have gone insane. That's also why she doesn't feel our bond like she should."

I'd had a lot of time to think about Sara's Mori on the flight from Maine, and I believed once she learned not to fear her demon, she would open herself up to it.

"Incredible."

I smiled. "Yes, she is."

"I wish I could have been there to meet her today. How is she doing?"

"Good. We had dinner, and then Claire came by to show her around. Sara said she was going to call Nate when she got back to her room."

The dining hall had been almost empty by the time we arrived, and we'd had a nice quiet meal. Chris had joined us, and though I would have preferred to have Sara to myself, I knew seeing his familiar face made her more comfortable.

"After everything that's happened, it's hard to believe she's really here."

"I know what you mean." I was half afraid I'd wake up and find myself back in my hotel room in New Hastings, still wondering if I'd ever see her again.

"Thank you for bringing my granddaughter home, Nikolas," Tristan said in a voice thick with emotion.

"You don't have to thank me. I'd do anything for her."

"I know you would." He seemed distracted for a moment. "I wish I didn't have to leave tomorrow for India. I hate not being here for her."

I understood his reluctance to leave, but I knew he'd never shirk his duties. "You'll only be gone a week, and it's not like Sara will be alone. I'll be here, and I think Chris is sticking around for a week or so."

He patted the arm of his chair. "You plan to stay at Westhorne for a while then?"

My brows drew together. "My mate is here."

"She doesn't know she is your mate."

I folded my arms across my chest. "Not yet. I'll tell her when I think she is ready."

Tristan pursed his lips. "And until then?"

I didn't know where he was going with these questions, and I didn't like the direction our conversation was taking. "Until then, I'll be whatever she needs me to be."

"Sara is going to need help from all of us to adjust to her new life. I don't mean just you, me, and Chris. She will have training and studies, and she'll get to know the people living here."

He leaned forward, resting his elbows on his knees. "Are you going to be okay with that, with her being around other males?"

My Mori shifted restlessly.

"I can see the answer in your expression." Tristan clasped his hands and gave me a searching look. "What happened outside earlier with Callum?"

"What do you mean?"

"I couldn't be there to greet my granddaughter, but I was able to watch her arrival on the security cameras. You became aggressive with Callum for speaking to Sara."

I scowled. "I was not aggressive. And I was expecting Claire to be there, not a male I barely know."

He shook his head. "You became territorial, moving in front of her and forcing him to take a step back. You may not have noticed, but everyone else did. And it upset Sara."

I started to argue but stopped, remembering Sara's face and her asking if everything was okay.

"As for you not knowing Callum, there will always be males you don't know. I understand how it feels to be bonded, trust me, but you can't growl at every male who gets near Sara. We have four male trainees here, and she'll be studying with them. Will you get angry when they talk to her or when they have to touch her in training exercises?"

I had no answer for him because he was right. I *was* feeling possessive. I'd just gotten Sara back after the worst three weeks of my life, and I didn't want to share her with anyone, least of all another male.

But more than that, I didn't want to upset her or to make the transition to her life here more stressful than it already was. I'd taken her from what she knew and thrust her into a completely different lifestyle. She hadn't said it, but I could see in her face and her subdued behavior since we left Maine that she was feeling overwhelmed.

Tristan leaned back with a heavy sigh, and I knew I was not going to like what he said next. I was right.

"I think it would be best for Sara and you if you give her some space for a few weeks, maybe a month. Let her have time to settle in here and adjust, and to get to know people without any…complications."

My body stiffened. "You want me to leave her for a month? Do you know what you're asking?"

"I do," he said apologetically. "And I understand why you're angry. I remember how hard it was to be away from Josephine before we completed our bond."

"And yet you ask this of me."

He rubbed his jaw unhappily. "I don't want to, and the decision is up to you. But can you honestly tell me you'll be able to act normally when other males go near her? Will you be able to keep your feelings hidden until she is ready to learn the truth?"

The anger drained out of me. "I don't know."

"Believe me, Nikolas, if I thought there was a better way to do this, I'd suggest it. You're one of my closest friends, and I hate to cause you pain. But Sara is my granddaughter, and her well-being must come first."

I ignored the weight on my chest and the outrage pouring from my Mori. "You're right. Her happiness is all that matters."

"A month is all I ask."

I took a deep breath. "I want to be kept updated on how she's doing. And when I return in a month, I will take over her training."

He didn't try to hide his surprise. "You've never wanted anything to do with training."

"This is different."

"I suppose it is." He smiled. "Well, if anything, it'll be interesting to watch."

"Who will oversee her training while I'm gone?" I was hoping he'd say Claire, though I knew she handled more administrative tasks these days, helping Tristan run Westhorne.

Tristan had that look again, the one that said I wasn't going to be happy with his answer.

"I think the best trainer to start her with is Callum."

"No."

He held up a hand. "Listen to me before you get worked up. Callum is the best trainer we have at Westhorne, and all the trainees like him. You can't object to someone you barely know."

Remembering the handsome Scotsman smiling at Sara, I crossed my arms. "I can."

A smile tugged at his lips, and I scowled. How was any of this amusing?

"Nikolas, I think there is something you should know about Callum that will make you less opposed to him."

"Is he mated?" Because I couldn't think of anything else that would make me agree to him as Sara's trainer.

"No. I believe he was in a relationship that ended right before he moved here last year."

"Then he is single."

"He is also gay."

My eyebrows shot up.

"Callum's a good man, Nikolas, and a fine trainer. In this situation, I think he is the perfect one to pair with Sara until you get back."

I dragged my hand through my hair, knowing I had no arguments left. "Okay."

"Good." Tristan looked relieved to have it settled. "When will you leave?"

"Tomorrow."

Erik had located one of Eli's places in Portland, where they found some Vegas addresses. I'd planned to ask Geoffrey to check them out, but hunting in Vegas had never sounded more appealing. I had a feeling I'd need to work off a lot of aggression in the next four weeks.

*　*　*

"Goddamnit, Nikolas, do you know what time it is?"

I almost smiled at the grumbling coming out of my phone. Chris was an easygoing guy – unless you woke him up in the predawn after a night of drinking with Seamus and Niall.

My own mood wasn't much better after a sleepless night with an agitated Mori. Last night, when I had agreed to go away for a month, I'd planned to tell Sara over breakfast that I was leaving. But if she saw me like this, she'd know something was wrong. And I might not be able to make myself leave.

"Change of plans. Meet me in half an hour."

More groaning and swearing came out of the phone.

"You can follow me later if you need a few hours."

He muttered something about bonds and impatient males before he hung up.

Thirty minutes later, I left my apartment and made my way to the third floor of the north wing. The building was quiet, and I made no sound as I walked down the hallway and stopped at the last door on the left. I could feel Sara inside, and I pictured her sleeping in her bed, dark hair spilling over her pillow. In a few hours, she would awaken to start her first day at Westhorne, and I was sorry I would miss it.

My phone vibrated, and I knew it was Chris, letting me know he was ready to go.

I laid my hand against the door. *Sleep well, moy malen'kiy voin.*

Chris met me in the garage where the motorcycles were stored. Our bikes were being shipped from Maine, but we kept backups here. We stored our gear and weapons, and within minutes, we were driving through the gates. I didn't look back because it was hard enough leaving her.

Solmi, my Mori wailed angrily as we left Westhorne and our mate behind us.

We rode for three hours before we stopped for breakfast at a roadside diner.

After I ate, I went outside and called Dax about an idea I'd had during the ride here. I hoped it would make Sara happy and maybe ease her anger at me for leaving the way I had.

Dax laughed. "You've lost your mind."

"Maybe."

"Okay. I'll get back to you in a few hours."

It was late afternoon when Chris and I pulled into the driveway of one of our two Vegas safe houses. Geoffrey, who oversaw all of our operations here, came up from the basement to greet us when we entered the house and dropped our bags in the foyer.

"Nikolas, Chris, it's been a while," the black warrior said as we walked into the living room. "What brings you to Nevada?"

Chris sat on the couch and stretched out his legs under the coffee table. "We heard you guys are having all the fun out here."

Geoffrey went into the kitchen and returned with three cold beers. Handing one to each of us, he sat on the other end of the couch.

"Well, there's lots of fun to go around; I promise you that. Feels like half the vampires on the west coast suddenly decided to vacation in Sin City."

I stood by the window. "How long has it been like that?"

"About a month." He rubbed his bald head. "I know they've got to be nesting here, but I'll be damned if I can find them. There are a ton of places to hide in Vegas."

"Then you're in luck because we might know a few places to start looking." I took a long swig from my beer, my black mood lightening a fraction. I couldn't think of a better way to ease some of the tension coiled inside me than to kill vampires.

Geoffrey's eyes gleamed. "Half my guys are out on a recon job. You want to wait until they get back?"

I almost said no, but common sense prevailed. Going off half-cocked in my current frame of mind would be foolhardy and dangerous, and I had no intention of dying anytime soon.

"Yes," I said as my phone vibrated.

It was a text from Dax. **Minneapolis. Here's the number.** A phone number appeared on my screen.

Thanks, I wrote back.

Anytime.

I set my beer down on the coffee table and dialed the number Dax had sent. A female's voice answered, and I immediately got to the reason for my call.

She sucked in a sharp breath. "You want us to send them to *Westhorne?*

"Yes."

"But they're... This is a high security facility, and we're much better equipped to house such beasts."

It sounded like she was typing on a computer keyboard. "We had to lock them up in a separate part of the building because they make the other creatures nervous."

"Then you should be happy when I take them off your hands."

She refused to back down easily. "Does Lord Tristan approve of this request?"

I couldn't fault the warrior for doing her job. "Feel free to call Tristan, but I expect those beasts to be on a transport for Idaho by the end of the week."

I hung up and smiled. I hadn't let Tristan know what I was doing, and I suspected I'd be hearing from him within the hour. But if I couldn't be with Sara, I would do my damnedest to make sure she was happy. Something told me those two hellhounds would do that.

Chris gave me a wide-eyed look. "Did you just order them to send those two monsters to Westhorne?"

I shrugged and sat in the chair across from him. "They belong to Sara, and she'd be upset if they were locked away in a place like that."

He let out a choked laugh. "They're hellhounds, Nikolas. Tristan will have to lock them in the menagerie. He might throw you in with them when he gets his hands on you."

"They're better off in the menagerie than in Minneapolis. They'll be close to Sara, and she'll make sure they're well cared for."

He smiled wryly. "Yeah. Until they get loose and eat someone."

"She'll have them eating out of her hand in a day."

He coughed into his beer. "You willing to make a wager on that?"

It was my turn to laugh because I knew Sara a lot better than he did. "Name it."

"Hmmm." He thought for a moment. "My new knife set for your favorite sword."

I raised an eyebrow. "You sure about that, my friend? I know you love those knives."

"And I plan to keep them."

Geoffrey had been silent since my phone call. He looked from me to Chris. "What am I missing here?"

Smirking at Chris, I picked up my beer. "I just acquired a new set of throwing knives."

CHAPTER 15

"THIS IS THE last one." I walked up to the large bonfire and tossed a body on top of the pile there. The stench of burning flesh assailed me, despite the wind blowing across the desert, and I held my breath until I put a safe distance between the fire and me.

"Thank Jesus," groaned Noah, one of Geoffrey's warriors. "I don't think I've ever lugged around that many dead suckers."

Abigail, the only female warrior on the team, stared at the fire. "Twenty-six vampires. I've never heard of a nest that big." She looked across the fire at me. "Have you?"

"Yes, but it's rare. Usually they are new vampires. You don't often see that many older vampires living in the same nest."

Mature vampires were territorial over their nests and didn't play well with others their age. Younger vampires were weaker and more easily led, so it was common for an older vampire to surround themselves with younger ones.

It was the second nest we'd cleaned out this week. The first one was much smaller – five vampires holed up in an apartment in Spring Valley – but one of the vampires we'd interrogated had led us to the larger nest. All in all, it had been a productive week.

My phone vibrated, and I knew it was Tristan before I saw his name. He called me every other day with updates on Sara, which he received from Claire. His trip to India had been extended by a few days, and he'd flown back last night, eager to finally meet his granddaughter.

I felt a pang of envy that he was with her while I was seven hundred miles away in another state. I'd kept busy in the week and a half since I'd left Westhorne, but no matter what I did, it couldn't assuage the lingering ache in my chest. It didn't help that my Mori constantly barraged me with angry longing and images of our mate from the last time we saw her. The only time the demon eased up was when I was killing vampires.

I walked away from the fire as I put the phone to my ear. "You're back."

"Yes, and I see you've been busy. I'm looking at a report that just came in and I'm sure the numbers must be wrong. It says you took out a nest of twenty-six vampires last night."

"That's right." I stopped walking and turned to look at the group of warriors near the fire a hundred feet away. "We're just finishing the cleanup now, in fact."

Tristan let out a low whistle. "I take it you took lots of backup this time."

"You can let the Council know I went in with two heavily armed units. It was completely by the book."

He laughed. "You've never done anything by the book in your life."

My lips twitched. "Okay. It was close."

"I'll be sure to make a note of that."

There was silence for a moment until I asked, "Have you seen her?"

"Yes." A note of wonder filled his voice. "I just watched her... I'm not even sure how to describe it."

Having spent so much time with Sara in Maine, I could only imagine what stunt she'd pulled to make one of the most composed warriors I'd ever known speechless.

"Well, don't leave me in suspense. What has she gotten into this time?"

He took a deep breath and let it out. "Callum and I were walking to the arena when I saw Sara come out of the woods with Seamus and Niall. She likes to walk alone in the woods, and they keep an eye on her."

"She loves being outdoors," I said almost to myself. It was one of the reasons I'd known she would like our valley. The Irishmen were good warriors, and I was glad to have them watching over her. Knowing how much Sara valued her independence, she probably wasn't as happy about them.

"So, what happened?"

"What happened was that those two beasts got loose."

My stomach lurched. "Is Sara okay?"

Tristan let out a hearty laugh. "If by *okay*, you mean did she step in front of two charging hellhounds and command them to stop, then, yes, she's perfectly fine. And then she ordered me and my warriors to lower our weapons because we were upsetting her dogs."

I pictured Sara standing in front of the hellhounds, defending them from the warriors, just as she had put herself between me and her troll friend. She was fiercely protective of those she cared about.

"What did you do?"

"What could we do? We lowered our swords." He laughed again. "I think we were all in shock. One minute, we were prepared to fight for her life, and in the next, she had those beasts fawning over her with their tails wagging. Then she made Seamus take her to the menagerie so she could make sure her hellhounds were being treated well."

I smiled at the images his story created. Sara was already making her mark at Westhorne. I had a feeling life at the stronghold would never be the same.

Tristan exhaled loudly. "You told me about the things she did in Maine, but seeing it…"

"I know."

"I can't wait to get to know her. Don't worry; I won't push her. I want her to be happy here."

I smiled. "Just let her know that her family is ready to meet her when she is. She might surprise you."

Sara harbored a lot of anger toward Madeline, but she hadn't been able to hide her interest when I told her she had a Mohiri grandfather. Once she saw Tristan was nothing like his daughter, she'd open up to him.

"I'll do that." His chair squeaked as he settled back in it. "Did you find anything in that nest last night?"

I watched the warriors who had started digging a pit in which to bury the burnt vampire bodies. "Not yet. We tended to the humans and dropped them at the hospital. We're headed back to the building when we're done here. If there is anything in that place that'll lead us to Eli's Master, I'll find it."

"The Council is making the hunt for this vampire a priority. We're organizing a special task force that will focus solely on searching for him."

"Who did you get to lead the team?" Normally, I would have been one of the first people approached for a job like this, having hunted three Masters and killed two of them. Tristan wouldn't have asked me to lead this one because he knew I could not leave Sara for that long.

"Mateo Ruiz is going to head it up. I believe you and he have worked together a few times."

Mateo and I met on a Master hunt in Bolivia many years ago, and I'd never known a more ruthless hunter. When he was five, his entire village, including his human mother, was wiped out by a Master. The only reason Mateo had survived the attack was because his mother had sent him to a Catholic mission ten miles away for help banishing his "demons." The Mohiri found Mateo when they came to investigate the attack.

Since then, Mateo had devoted his life to one cause: hunting Masters. He had four Master kills to his name, a feat surpassed only by Tristan, who had been around a few hundred years longer.

"Yes. If anyone can find this vampire, it's Mateo."

"I agree." He paused for a moment. "I told the Council about Sara. They needed to be made aware of her unique situation."

"And?" I asked tightly.

"We decided the task force should have the information. Maybe it will help them figure out why the Master wants Sara."

The less people who knew about Sara, the better. But Mateo was discreet and I trusted him. I was still worried, however, with any other plans the Council might have.

"I can guess why you're so quiet," Tristan said. "The Council has some concerns about Sara's power, but I made it clear that my granddaughter is off-limits. They won't press me on this."

"Good." The Council and I didn't agree on a lot of things, but we'd always been on the same side. If they believed they were going to have any say in Sara's life, they were in for a rude awakening.

There was a beep on the line followed by Tristan's sigh. "Speaking of the Council. Back less than twenty-four hours and already they are calling. I have a feeling my phone is going to be busy for the next few months."

I started walking back to the others. "I'll let you know if we find anything at the nest."

"Great. And someone from the task force should be reaching out to you soon. Going forward, you'll give any information you find to them as well."

"Sounds good."

* * *

"You have a visitor." Chris walked into the garage where I was cleaning my gear. I wiped down my weapons after every job, but to keep them in the best condition, I polished the blades daily with a light coating of oil.

I ran a cloth over my blade. "Who is it?"

"She's from the task force. She's here for an update."

"Geoffrey has everything she needs."

"But I'd much rather talk to you," said a warm English voice.

My head came up and I stared at the blonde warrior standing in the doorway behind Chris. A smile spread across my face, and I laid aside my sword so I could stand.

"Viv! Why didn't you tell me you were coming to Vegas?"

"I only found out myself last night." She entered the garage and walked over to hug me.

My Mori cringed away from her, surprising me by its reaction to someone I'd known my entire life. Then I realized Viv was the first female I'd touched since I met Sara.

I gave her a quick hug and stepped back, earning a puzzled look from her.

"So you're on the task force?" I asked as we walked back into the house.

She sank gracefully onto the couch. "Tristan called yesterday and asked me to be part of it. I'm surprised he didn't tell you."

"He probably thought it would be nice if you surprised me instead."

"A good surprise, I hope."

I smiled. "You know I love seeing you. I assume you're here on business."

She laughed. "I always mix business with pleasure, you know that. Have you eaten? I'm starving."

"Not yet."

"Good. Let's go out. There are a ton of great restaurants in this city." Her blue eyes sparkled. "Or we could go to my hotel and order room service. I'm staying at the Palms and the accommodations there are wonderful."

The thought of being with anyone besides Sara caused an unpleasant sensation in my gut and made my Mori growl.

I shook my head. "How about Japanese instead? I know a great place you'll like."

"Japanese would be perfect."

Her smile faltered a little, and I realized my tone had been a bit cool. I immediately regretted it. Vivian was one of my closest friends, and she deserved better.

I extended my arm to her, and she took it, letting me pull her to her feet.

"I'm sorry, Viv. I've been in a foul mood for a few days."

Chris let out a bark of laughter as he passed us, heading for the stairs. "A few days. Sure."

I ignored him. "I'd love to have dinner with you."

Her warm smile returned. "Only if you tell me what's causing your bad mood."

"I will." There was very little the two of us hadn't been able to talk about over the years. We would never be intimate again, but our friendship was important to me, and I valued her advice and her opinions.

"Good. Let's go then, because I'm famished."

We went outside, and I chuckled when I saw the red Aston Martin sitting in the driveway. Vivian had a weakness for fast cars, and she didn't believe in being inconspicuous.

She insisted on driving, and she was grinning when we pulled up to the valet parking at the restaurant. "God, I love this car."

The valet's eyes gleamed when she handed him her key along with a hundred. "Take good care of her for me."

"Yes, ma'am!"

"You treat your cars better than you treat your men," I teased as we walked into the restaurant.

Her rich laugh drew the attention of people nearby. "She's not mine yet, but I think I'm in love."

At my request, the hostess seated us in one of the restaurant's small private dining rooms. A waitress came, and we ordered enough sushi to sink a boat, along with two bottles of their best sake.

The girl looked from me to Vivian. She was no doubt trying to figure out where someone as slender as my companion was going to put all that food. I hid my smile. Mohiri females' appetites rivaled the males', and Vivian loved sushi.

The waitress left, returning a few minutes later with our wine. Vivian filled our cups, and we toasted our friendship before we drank, a custom she'd started the first time we drank together back in our training days.

We talked about the task force while we waited for our food. Vivian was staying in Vegas for two days before she met up with Mateo and the rest of the team in Portland. The Master was interested in Sara and Madeline, so Mateo wanted to start the search where Sara grew up.

"I'm curious," Vivian said after the waitress brought a large tray of food and left us to our meal. "Why aren't you leading the task force instead of Mateo? Don't get me wrong. Mateo is in a league of his own, but this is Tristan's granddaughter. I should think you would have insisted on going after the Master based on that fact alone."

I thought about the best way to answer. "Tristan didn't ask me to be on the task force because he knew I couldn't be away from Westhorne for that long."

She let out a laugh. "What do you mean? You leave for months on end. You're away from Westhorne now."

"Only for a month. I'll be going back in a few weeks."

Her eyebrow arched. "Does this have anything to do with the bad mood you've been in?"

"Yes." I laid my chopsticks on my plate and met her inquisitive gaze. "I found my mate."

Vivian choked on her sake.

I probably should have waited until after she'd drunk to spring the news on her.

"Good one," she wheezed, her eyes watering.

I waited for her to catch her breath. "I'm not joking. I bonded with someone."

"You..." She stared at me. "You're serious."

I nodded.

"But when? Who? It's only been two months since I last saw you, and you've been in Maine that whole time with..." Her eyes widened. "Oh my God. Tristan's granddaughter?"

"Yes."

She put a hand over her mouth. A second later, she dissolved into laughter. My scowl only made her laugh harder until tears streamed down her face. It was a full five minutes before she could look at me without losing it again.

"And you wonder why I'm in a mood," I muttered, reaching for the sake bottle.

"Oh, Nikolas, forgive me." She dabbed at her eyes with her napkin. "But you would laugh too if you were in my shoes."

"Probably," I admitted grudgingly.

The two of us had always joked about which of us would "fall" first. I don't think either of us expected it to be me. I thought about Sara curled up beside me on the plane, and a smile came unbidden to my lips. Suddenly, I couldn't remember why I'd resisted the idea of a mate for so long.

"Wow."

"What?"

"If you'd ever smiled like that for me, I'd have fallen head over heels for you." She stared at me in wonder. "You love her."

"Yes."

Her eyes glistened with fresh tears. "Look what you've done to me. I'm crying like a school girl."

I picked up my phone. "I should take a picture or no one will ever believe me."

"Don't you dare!" She rolled up her napkin and threw it at me.

Chuckling, I caught it and tossed it back to her.

She grew serious. "Tell me you're happy. I've known people who bonded and weren't happy so they broke the bond. I don't want that for you."

I refilled our cups as I thought about how to answer.

"It's complicated, but yes, I'm happy." Or I would be when I could finally tell Sara the truth.

"Do your parents know?"

"God, no. You know what my mother is like."

Vivian laughed again. "She's going to be ecstatic. And she's going to make my life impossible after this."

I gave her a questioning look.

"When she tells my mother you've settled down, I'll never hear the end of it." She sipped her wine. "What's your mate like? I want to hear everything about her and your time in Maine."

I leaned back in my chair and smiled at her. "How long do you have?"

"As long as it takes."

We continued our meal, and over the next two hours, I described seeing Sara for the first time and the moment I knew she was my mate. I told Viv about Eli, his obsession with Sara, and my frustration at not being able to find him. Vivian made comments every now and then, but for the most part, she listened. Her eyes filled with disbelief and awe as I related the events of the last month, and I could imagine how it must sound to someone who hadn't been there and was hearing it all at once.

My voice grew gruff when I spoke about the day Eli finally found Sara and how she'd disappeared. Vivian reached across the table and laid her hand on mine as I talked about the search for Sara and the agonizing three weeks that followed.

I told her about Sara's sudden return and her story about where she'd been all that time. Being on the task force, Vivian already knew about Sara's Fae heritage, and it felt good not to have to keep that from her.

"Sara must be very special to win your heart. And she doesn't know how you feel?"

"I think she knows I care for her, but not how much. She knows nothing of the bond."

Understanding dawned in her eyes. "Being away from her must be hell for you. Why aren't you with her now, making her fall madly in love with you?"

"She's been through so much, and leaving home was hard on her. I'm giving her time to adjust to her new life before I tell her the truth."

Vivian leaned forward. "Your expression tells me leaving was not your idea."

"It wasn't."

I told her about my reaction to Callum and about Tristan asking me to leave for a month.

"As much as I hate to see you hurting, I have to agree with Tristan. You're intimidating enough without adding the emotions of a bonded male. No one would dare to approach Sara with you glowering over her shoulder."

She smiled brightly. "But when the month is up, go get your girl and sweep her off her feet. There is no way any female could resist you for long."

"You don't know Sara," I replied dryly. "But she's worth the wait."

"Okay, now I *really* have to meet this girl."

I folded my arms across my chest. "You know, you seem to know a lot about bonded males for someone who's avoided relationships as much as I have."

Her smile faded. She pressed her lips together and looked away from me. I was not expecting the next words to come out of her mouth.

"That's because I've experienced it firsthand."

My jaw dropped. "You bonded with someone?"

"It was a long time ago, and no one you know. I met him in Germany in my third year out of training, and we felt the bond immediately."

She let out a short laugh. "He was an arrogant piece of work, and I couldn't stand him. He thought courting me meant talking about him and telling me I no longer needed to be a warrior. I broke the bond a week after

I met him, and I haven't seen him since."

I stared at her. "All these years, why did you never say anything?"

She lifted a shoulder. "It's not something I like to remember."

"If you were hurting, I would have been there for you, had I known." She would do the same for me.

"It was uncomfortable, but I never let the bond grow, and it dissolved a few months after I left. I wasn't in pain; trust me on that. He probably wasn't happy at first, but he didn't pursue it." Her smile returned. "It was nothing like what you have with Sara."

The waitress came with our check. I paid it, and we left the restaurant.

"I'm going to miss our time together," Vivian said wistfully as we waited for the valet to bring the car around. "But I'm happy for you, Nikolas."

"Thanks, Viv."

She nudged me with her shoulder. "You know, there are going to be a lot of disappointed women when word gets out that you've mated."

I laughed. "They'll get over it."

The valet arrived with the car, and we headed back to the safe house. At the house, Vivian put the car in park and looked at me.

"Well, you seem to be in a better mood, so I'd say my job here is done."

I smiled at her. "I'm glad you came by."

Chris came out of the house and walked up to my side of the car. "Hey, you two planning to sit here gabbing all night?"

"You have something better in mind?" Vivian asked.

"We just got word about another nest with at least a dozen vampires. We're heading out in five minutes."

"After dinner entertainment. You guys think of everything." Vivian grinned at me. "What do you say, Nikolas? It'll be just like old times."

I smiled and reached for the door. "Let's go."

*   *   *

"Nikolas, your timing is perfect."

"Why is that?" I walked to my bike in the parking lot of the steakhouse where Chris ate at least twice a week.

Tristan's chair creaked as he settled into it. "I just got back to the office. Sara and I had our first dinner together tonight."

"How was it?"

I was happy he and Sara were getting to know each other, but I couldn't help feeling envious of him. I wanted to be the one sharing meals with my mate.

"It was very nice. I can tell she's still a bit uncertain about me, but I can't blame her after what her mother did. We're taking it slow.

"I'm glad she has you." I stood beside my bike and waved for Chris to go on without me. "How is she?"

"Good. She's still adjusting and getting to know people. It's a big change for her, and she misses you."

My chest fluttered. "She said that?"

Tristan let out a breath. "No. She tries to hide it behind her anger, but I can see it when your name comes up."

"I should have waited to say good-bye to her." She'd deserved some kind of explanation for me leaving, instead of waking up to find me gone. I didn't blame her for being upset with me. She probably thought I didn't care for her at all.

"You should have said good-bye," he agreed. "I still stand by my reason for asking you to leave for a month, but I think we both could have handled it better. I was feeling a little overprotective when she got here, and I didn't stop to think how it would hurt her if you left. I should have asked you to delay leaving for a day or two."

"What's done is done," I said. "I'll make it up to her when I come home."

I hated hearing she was hurting, and my first instinct was to grab my stuff and head back to Westhorne tonight. But I'd left to help her settle in without me hovering. If I went home now, it would mean I'd put her through that for no reason.

"How's her training coming along?"

"She's struggling, but it hasn't been that long." He chuckled. "Yesterday, she had her first training with Celine, and probably her last."

Sara and Celine? I wasn't sure whether to be alarmed or amused. "What happened?"

"Each trainee was supposed to hunt and kill two bazerats. According to Celine, Sara refused to kill them, threw a knife at her, and incited the class to not perform the task."

I shook my head. "Sara wouldn't throw a knife at someone unless they were a threat."

"Celine can be a bit dramatic. Sara told me she threw the knife on the ground. But she did admit to telling the other trainees it was easier to kill something than to catch it."

I let out a laugh. "That sounds like Sara, all right."

He laughed with me. "She can hold her own against Celine. I don't think you need to worry about her."

"I think that comes with the bond."

"I know. And I know this isn't easy for you either. But it won't be much longer."

I stared at the lights of the Strip and wished I was looking at the mountains back home instead.

"Less than two weeks, and then I'm coming home."

*   *   *

Geoffrey walked with me to my bike. "You guys sure you don't want to stick around for another few weeks? This place is a lot more exciting than Oregon."

"I think it's time for a change of scenery." I stowed away my stuff. "Chris wants to visit Longstone before we head back to Idaho."

The other warrior held out his hand. "It's been good working with you again. Come back anytime."

I shook his hand and mounted my bike. My Mori shifted impatiently as I waited for Chris. It had been three weeks since I'd seen Sara, and I still had a week to go, but my demon was excited we'd be closer to her. I was too. A few days in Longstone might help to ease my restlessness until it was time to go back to Westhorne.

Chris came out of the house and said good-bye to Geoffrey. Then the two of us were on our way. Neither of us talked much during the ride, except when we stopped to eat at noon. Chris was looking forward to going home again, and I was happy to be closing the distance between me and Sara.

We had just crossed into Oregon late that afternoon when my phone rang. Tristan called every second day to let me know how Sara was doing, so I knew it was him before I answered.

"You're late," I said lightly.

"Yes, it's been a bit crazy here today."

The strain in his voice instantly put me on alert. "What happened? Is it Sara?"

"She's okay," he rushed to assure me. "There was an incident in Boise today with her and three of the other trainees."

"What the hell was she doing in Boise?"

"She needed a day out, so I sent her and some of the other trainees with Seamus and Niall. They went shopping, and they were planning to watch movies then go to dinner."

My hands gripped the handlebars. "What happened?"

"Lamprey demons attacked the movie theater they were in. Several humans were injured as well. Sara and the others managed to kill all the demons before Seamus and Niall got to them. No one was badly hurt, and they've all been treated by the healers."

I heard what he said, but all I could think was Sara was hurt enough to need a healer.

I started looking for the first exit that would take me east to Idaho. "I'll be there in a few hours."

"There's no need for you to come home," Tristan said. "Sara's safe. I knew you'd want to know what happened."

"I appreciate you letting me know, but I need to see for myself that she's all right." It would take a horde of vampires to keep me away from Westhorne tonight.

He sighed quietly. "Just take your time. She's asleep, and she should be out until morning."

"Asleep? I thought you said she was okay."

"She is. The healers wanted her to stay overnight in the medical ward, and they gave her something to help her sleep."

If the healers wanted Sara to stay for observation, that meant she'd been bitten. Lamprey demons were vicious, and their bites could cause serious infections. The thought of her in pain made my stomach twist.

"I promise you she's fine," Tristan said when I didn't speak. "I just saw her."

"Okay." Some of the tension left my body because I knew Tristan would not deceive me. "I'll see you soon."

I hung up and called Chris to let him know what had happened. We were only two hours from Longstone so I suggested he continue his trip, but he said it could wait.

It was just after eight when we reached Westhorne. Tristan met us in the main hall, and walked with me to the medical ward.

"She has an infection and a fever, but the drugs are taking care of it," he said in a low voice as we entered the east wing.

At the door to Sara's room, I stopped to look at the girl lying on the hospital bed. Her dark hair spread across the pillow, and damp tendrils clung to her pale face that glistened with a fine sheet of sweat. She wore a hospital gown, and her blankets were twisted around her legs. Shivers racked her slender frame, and she curled into a ball.

Solmi, my Mori cried, and I shared its anguish at seeing her in pain.

I went to the bed and disentangled the sheets around her legs. They were damp and cold, which was why she'd pushed them off her.

A healer name Margot appeared beside me with a fresh gown and blankets. Tristan and I turned away while she changed Sara's gown and tucked the warm blankets around her shivering body. Margot checked Sara's vitals and wiped her face with a cloth before she turned to me.

"She's almost through the worst of it," Margot said in a hushed voice so she didn't disturb Sara. "I've never seen anyone fight off a lamprey infection this quickly."

"She's a fighter," I replied, relieved she was on the mend. I had a suspicion Sara's Fae power might have something to do with her ability to fight a demon infection.

"I need to check on my other patient. Olivia isn't healing as quickly as Sara. I'll be back shortly."

"I'll stay with Sara, so you don't need to rush."

Margot looked surprised, but she merely nodded and left the room.

Tristan walked up to the bed. The two of us looked at Sara, who had stopped shivering and seemed to be sleeping peacefully.

"She's tougher than either of us gives her credit for," he said softly, his admiration evident. "She fought a lamprey demon with her bare hands *after* she was bitten by one of them."

My head jerked toward him. "She killed it?"

He nodded and motioned for us to move to the other side of the room so we didn't disturb her.

"She told me she used her Fae magic to destroy it, but she had no idea she could do that. All the others saw was an exploding demon. They have no idea what she did." Tristan chuckled. "She's something else. I thought to comfort her after her ordeal, and she told me Jordan was scarier than a dozen demon worms."

"Jordan?"

"She's one of the trainees and quite skilled with a sword. I'm glad she was there."

I remembered the blonde trainee who made the others look like amateurs, and I was happy to hear Sara had made friends.

"I'll leave her in your care and check in on her tomorrow. It's good to have you back, Nikolas."

"It's good to be back."

Tristan left and I settled into a chair beside the bed. Not long after, Sara began to toss and kick her covers off again. Her face grew flushed and hot to the touch, a sign of the fever burning through her.

I ran a cloth under cold water and used it to wipe her face and neck as she mumbled incoherently. I tended to her like that for an hour before she quieted again.

Margot came in to check on her, but I was already doing everything that could be done. I kept up my ministrations, and over the next few hours, I changed the blankets two more times before the fever subsided.

It was long past midnight when I sat near the bed again and laid my hand over Sara's smaller one. She was no longer tossing, and her color looked better. Her hand clasped mine, and I laced our fingers together, smiling as she sighed and tugged our joined hands to her chest.

She murmured in her sleep, and my heart squeezed when she whispered my name. I adjusted her blankets with my free hand, letting my fingers linger against her cool cheek.

I'm here, Sara, and I promise I won't leave you again.

CHAPTER 16

I LEFT THE medical ward at seven o'clock and searched out Tristan, who was already at work in his office.

"How's she doing?" he asked when I sat in one of the visitor chairs.

"Still sleeping. Margot said she'll have a headache when she wakes up. But other than that, she'll be okay."

He laid aside the papers he'd been studying and clasped his hands on the desk. "I assume the reason for this early visit is to tell me you're back for good."

"Yes."

He nodded, clearly unsurprised by my statement.

"And I'm taking over her training."

I expected an argument, but he smiled instead.

"Sara hasn't responded to Callum's training like I'd hoped. I think it's because she fears her Mori. She knows you and she trusts you. Maybe working with you will help her get past whatever is holding her back."

I thought back to the time Sara had given herself over to her demon to save the young trolls. That experience had terrified her, and she probably remembered it every time she tried to open herself up to her Mori. Someone with her level of control wasn't going to let her guard down easily after that.

"I agree. I have some ideas for things we can try to help her."

"Good." Tristan leaned back in his chair. "Though I don't think she will be too happy with her new trainer at first."

I smiled, anticipating her reaction when she found out I was staying on and replacing Callum as her trainer. "I want to be the one to tell her."

Tristan laughed. "Okay, but don't say I didn't warn you. She's still angry with you."

"She'll forgive me," I said confidently, remembering the way she'd reached for me in her sleep.

"She will," he agreed, "but she'll make you earn it."

"I have no doubt."

He grew serious. "I still believe you leaving was the right thing to do, but I'm glad you're back. Sara's made some friends and she's tried to find her place here, but she's not happy. She misses her uncle and friends back home, and it's clear she misses you, though she'll never admit it. I think you're exactly what she needs now."

"Good, because I have no intention of leaving again."

"I don't think…" He paused, contemplating his next words.

"I'm going to speak frankly. I think it's too soon to tell Sara about the bond. Can I ask that you give her a little more time? Train her and get to know each other better, but hold off on anything more serious. Just for a little while longer."

I didn't like anyone telling me how to handle my personal affairs, especially when it came to Sara. I wanted to tell her about us, to court her, but I'd never push her into something she wasn't ready for.

If it had been anyone but Tristan, I would have told them to stay out of my business. But Tristan was a close and trusted friend, and Sara's grandfather. I knew he spoke with her best interests in mind, just as he had when he asked me to leave here for a month.

"I'll hold off on telling her as long as you don't try to keep us apart again," I said.

"I can't promise I won't be an overprotective grandfather at times, but I won't try to come between you." He smiled wryly. "Unless you need a referee."

The two of us laughed because that was a possibility.

"You haven't even been to your apartment yet, have you?"

I looked down at the clothes I'd been wearing for a day. "I had more important things to do."

"What are your plans for this morning?"

"I'm going to get cleaned up, and then I'm planning to talk to Callum about Sara's training."

Tristan raised an eyebrow, and I laughed.

"I only want to ask him what they've worked on so far. I promise to behave."

"When are you going to let Sara know you're back?"

"This afternoon. Margot said she'll sleep for a few more hours, and I don't want to do this in the medical ward."

"I'm sure Sara wouldn't want that either." He shuffled a stack of papers on his desk. "I have some business to take care of, but Chris and I are sparring at noon. Why don't you join us? I promise to go easy on you."

Chuckling, I stood. "You're on, old man."

I stopped by the medical ward to check on Sara before I went to my apartment to shower and change. I spent an hour tending to my weapons, and as I polished my swords, my eyes wandered around my living room.

I'd always enjoyed my Spartan yet comfortable home, but for the first time I wondered how it would look to a woman, to Sara. Would she find it too austere and lacking a feminine touch? Would she feel at home here with my things, and with me?

I imagined her curled up on my couch with her sketchbook on her lap, her books and drawings filling every available surface. I'd never been one to indulge in reverie, but the idea of her belongings here among mine brought a smile to my face.

*   *   *

When I entered the arena at noon, I was surprised to see that Tristan and Chris weren't alone. Seamus and Niall were there along with at least a dozen other warriors, including Erik.

I walked over to Erik. "How long are you here for?"

"A week or so. I thought you were in Vegas."

"I was. Just got in last night."

He gave me one of his signature half smiles. "I guess even Vegas was dull after Maine, huh?"

"Like a resort vacation," Chris quipped, joining us.

I looked toward the door as three more warriors entered. "So I take it this is not a normal sparring session."

"Tristan thought it would be more fun to have a little competition," Chris said. "And once word got out you were back, everyone wanted to participate."

The arena wasn't a large building, although the domed roof gave it the appearance of being bigger than it was. Within thirty minutes, the bleacher-style seats were half full of warriors waiting for their turn to show off their swordsmanship.

Excited whispers reached me, and I glanced at the small group of trainees crowded together near the main door. I knew Sara wasn't among them before I looked, and I wondered if she was coming. I'd called the medical ward on the way here and found out she'd been released. After Maine, it felt strange to be in the same place as her and not know where she was.

Tristan called for everyone to clear the floor and asked who wanted to go first. When Seamus and Niall stepped forward, people laughed. The brothers often bantered about who was the better fighter, but they were identical in more than looks. A more evenly matched pair I'd never met, and neither of them would want to concede defeat.

We took a few minutes to organize the matches. As expected, more than one warrior asked to duel with Tristan and me, so we agreed to three matches apiece. An air of anticipation filled the room when Tristan called out the order of the dueling pairs, and he and I were fourth in line to duel each other.

My phone rang just as Seamus and Niall squared off. I smiled when I saw it was my parents, and I left the noisy building by the back door to walk toward the river. My mother spent the next twenty minutes talking about her best friend's new grandson and asking if I'd met any nice girls. I didn't tell her about Sara because I was half afraid she'd be on the next plane to the states. The last thing Sara needed was my well-meaning and determined mother swooping down on her before she even knew about us.

I walked back to the arena after we ended the call. As I neared the building I felt Sara's presence, and I knew she was inside. My pulse quickened in anticipation of seeing her again.

I knew exactly where Sara was when I entered the building, but I resisted the urge to look at her. If Tristan was right and she was still upset with me for leaving, she wouldn't have a warm welcome for me. I smiled, looking forward to changing her mind about that.

"You ready to lose?" I asked Tristan.

He saluted me with his sword. "Something tells me you're going to show off for a certain young lady."

I grinned as we faced each other. Without warning, his sword came up, and I moved to block his attack. His eyes sparkled with laughter, and my smirk told him it was the last jump he'd get on me.

I struck next. Tristan parried and deftly launched a counter attack. The clang of steel filled the air as we danced around each other.

The best swordsman I'd ever fought was Desmund, a brilliant fighter before the Hale witch had crippled his mind. Tristan was the second best. He might spend his days running a stronghold and handling Council business, but he obviously hadn't let his fighting skills get rusty.

The only way to defeat an opponent as good as Tristan was to keep him constantly on the defensive. I thrust, he parried, and I struck again before he could recover. I knew if I let up for one second, he would take the advantage, and I had no intention of losing. The determination on his face said he was going to make me work for my win.

I feinted to my left, and he moved swiftly to block me. Our eyes met and realization dawned in his a split second before I brought my sword around and touched the tip to his chest.

Applause rose up around us as he bowed and conceded defeat.

"Lucky shot," he joked when he slapped my back.

"You wish," I retorted.

We moved aside to allow the next pair to take over. I glanced at Sara and saw her talking to the blond trainee named Jordan. I couldn't see her face, so it was hard to know what she was feeling.

"You think it's safe to go over there?"

Tristan laughed quietly. "Are you feeling brave, my friend?"

"Very."

I knew Sara. She hated to draw attention to herself, so she'd refrain from yelling at me – for the moment. Actually, now that I thought about it, this was the perfect time and place for our reunion.

"Come on then. I'm looking forward to this."

I shouldered him as we started toward her. "You know, you're taking an awful lot of pleasure in this, considering it was your idea for me to go away in the first place."

"You're right," he replied with a barely concealed grin. "But how often does one see Nikolas Danshov get the cold shoulder from a woman?"

I was about to retort when I looked up and my gaze met Sara's. She appeared to be fully recovered from her illness, and not nearly as impressed by my fighting prowess as her friends. A familiar fire blazed in her green eyes, igniting a matching heat in my gut. Even angry, she managed to steal my breath and make me forget everyone else in the room.

"Showing off as usual I see," said a laughing male voice.

I stopped walking to turn to a black warrior with short dreadlocks. "I'm surprised you left your computers long enough to watch."

Dax chuckled and held up a tablet. "I'm never offline."

It took me several seconds to realize Sara's presence was moving away from me. I turned to the group of trainees to find she was no longer with them.

Chagrin filled me, but it was replaced by wry humor when I saw the door close behind a girl with long dark hair. I'd counted on her not wanting to cause a scene, but I'd forgotten how good she was at slipping away under our noses. Next time, I'd have to outmaneuver her.

I smiled and saluted the closed door with my sword. *Touché*.

*   *   *

"Good choice," Chris commented when I reached for a double burger from the buffet. "Avoid the spaghetti. It'll be less messy when she dumps your dinner on your head."

I laughed and looked behind me at the girl sitting on the far side of the room. Sara had her back to me, and she was saying something to her friend Jordan, waving her slice of pizza in the air for emphasis. I glanced down at my gray sweater and wondered if pizza sauce came out of wool.

I grabbed a soda and picked up my tray. "You coming?"

"No thanks. I prefer to watch the show from a safe distance. Scared?"

I scoffed and turned toward the two girls who seemed too caught up in their conversation to notice my approach.

I was a dozen feet from the table when Jordan saw me and broke off mid-sentence. She looked down at her plate as I pulled out the chair beside Sara.

"You don't mind if I join you, do you?" I asked then sat before Sara could say no. I deliberately moved my chair close to hers, and I was rewarded for my efforts when she turned her head to scowl at me. Her face was so close I felt her warm breath on my cheek.

"You…" She pulled back. "Let me guess, no one else will eat with you."

I smiled in satisfaction. She might be angry with me, but she felt something else too. I remembered Vivian's words about sweeping my girl off her feet. I might have to move slowly with Sara, but that didn't mean I couldn't enjoy myself.

"I seem to remember you being a lot nicer the last time we had dinner together."

She huffed. "Like I had a choice. You guys wouldn't let me out of your sight that night."

I realized she was thinking about our last night in Maine. But I had another night in mind. It was the first time she'd let her guard down and seemed at ease with me.

"Actually, I was thinking about the night of the storm when the power went out."

She looked away, but not before I saw color creep into her cheeks. So I wasn't imagining it; there had been something between us that night.

"People change," she said as she reached for her tray.

"I hear you're having some difficulty in training," I said before she could run away again. "I thought perhaps you might want to talk about it."

"No thank you," she replied shortly, but she made no move to leave.

Sensing I shouldn't push her too hard, I turned my attention to her dinner companion instead. "Jordan, right? I hear you're pretty lethal with a blade."

She blushed and nodded mutely.

"She is," Sara said. "You should have seen her last night, taking on those lamprey demons. If it wasn't for her, we probably would have been demon chow."

My Mori growled at the mention of the danger she'd been in less than a day ago, and my body tensed in response. Watching her toss and cry out as fever raged through her body was not an experience I ever wanted to repeat.

An elbow jabbed me sharply in the ribs. "Quit scowling before you scare off my new friend."

It was impossible to stay upset with her looking so adorably stern. "I certainly wouldn't want to do that. At least this one doesn't shed," I teased.

I hid my smile as I picked up my burger and took a huge bite. I couldn't remember when food had tasted so good.

Sara turned to Jordan, who looked like she wasn't sure what to make of the two of us.

"Just ignore him. He has to ruin at least one meal for me before he disappears on another one of his missions."

"You didn't hear?" I asked, enjoying myself immensely. "Maybe you would have if you hadn't *disappeared* this afternoon."

"Hear what?" Sara asked warily.

"I'm not going anywhere for the next month at least."

Her brows drew together. "What? Sick of hunting already?"

"No, I just have another job at the moment." I watched her face closely as I shared my news. "I'm your new trainer."

Surprise crossed her face, followed by dismay. Her reaction didn't bother me because I understood where it came from. She thought I'd abandoned her, and she was trying to push me away so she didn't get hurt. But I'd worked too hard to break down her walls to let her retreat behind them again.

"I am *not* training with you," she blurted, turning to search the room for Tristan, no doubt.

"It was Tristan's idea," I lied, guessing she'd accept it easier if it came from him. "He thinks it might help you to work with someone you know."

She glowered at me. "Since when do you work with trainees, or follow orders for that matter? Don't you have more orphans to rescue?"

"After you, I have a much greater respect for the people who usually handle those jobs. I agree with Tristan on this. We need to try a different approach with your training."

"A few days ago, Tristan mentioned a guy in India who he thought might be able to help me," she said hopefully.

"Janak?" I laughed, imagining Sara working with the quiet Indian man who relied heavily on Buddhist meditation and prayer in his teachings. "Janak's a nice guy, but way too soft for this. One session with you and he'd be on the first plane back to India."

She crossed her arms. "So, what is your brilliant plan, to harass me until I get so pissed off that I sic my demon on you?"

I polished off my burger before I responded. After my discussion with Callum earlier, I had a better idea of what would and wouldn't work with Sara. She probably expected more of the same training, but I had something else in mind.

She shifted impatiently beside me, and I smiled behind my napkin. Laying it on my tray, I said, "If that's what it takes, but I think something else will work better for you."

Her eyes widened with barely concealed interest. "What?"

I stood and reached for my tray. "Get some sleep tonight because training starts tomorrow."

A smile curved my lips as I walked away. I could have answered her, but it was much more entertaining to see her flustered expression.

Chris joined me outside the dining hall. "You're looking pleased with yourself. And you don't need a change of clothes, so I assume it went well. Did you tell her you were taking over her training?"

"Yes, and she wasn't happy about it."

"She'll try to get out of it," he said. "And you know Tristan is too soft-hearted when it comes to her. He'll give in if she begs him."

I chuckled. "That's why I asked him to be *unavailable* tonight."

He shook his head. "If she finds out you did that, she'll set those beasts after you."

"Let's hope she doesn't find out then."

I started toward the south wing, and he fell into step beside me.

"You working tonight?" he asked.

"I'm meeting with Dax to talk about upgrading security."

Westhorne had never been breached, but I wasn't taking chances with Sara's safety. Tristan hadn't objected when I told him my plans, so I knew he had concerns too.

"You know what they say about all work and no play," said a sultry voice from behind us.

Chris and I turned to face Celine, who looked as beautiful as always in a long, green dress that hugged her body. She tossed her black hair over her shoulder and gave me a warm smile.

"Nikolas, Chris, it's so wonderful to see you again."

"Hello, Celine." I returned her smile. "Tristan said you were back for a few months."

She laughed softly. "And what perfect timing. You're always away when I come to visit. Maybe we can catch up while you're here."

I ignored Chris's quiet snort. "I'm afraid I won't have much free time. I'm going to be working with Tristan and Dax a lot."

"But surely you can spare some time for an old *friend*," she said suggestively.

It was the same game she and I played every time we saw each other. She tried to remind me that at one time we were more than friends, and I gently deflected her advances.

"I'm sure he'll make time for *you*," Chris told her with a note of amusement in his voice.

I had a strong urge to cuff my best friend in the head. If anyone knew how long I'd evaded Celine's attempts to rekindle our brief affair, it was Chris. The look I gave him promised retribution.

"We're on our way to the security center if you'd like to join us," I said. I had no intention of getting involved with her, but we were longtime acquaintances. "What have you been up to since we last saw you?"

If I knew only one thing about Celine, it was how much she loved being the center of attention. She regaled us with stories about her travels in Europe for the last year and her short-lived liaison with a member of the Belgian royal family.

"I'm surprised you gave all that up to come here," Chris said.

"America has its appeal," she answered with a meaningful smile.

We'd been standing outside the security center for twenty minutes. The door opened and Dax came out carrying a laptop. He glanced at Celine then looked at me.

"Nikolas, I wondered if you'd forgotten our meeting. We can reschedule if you're busy."

I shook my head. "I'd rather get started tonight if you still have time."

"Okay." He held up the laptop. "I was going to run this to Claire's office, but I can do that later."

I turned to Celine. "I hope you'll excuse me. Duty calls."

"Of course." She laid a hand on my arm. "I look forward to seeing more of you during my visit."

My Mori shifted uneasily, its feelings clear. It didn't want any female but our mate touching us. I felt the same way, but courtesy kept me from pulling away. Celine had no idea I had bonded with Sara. If she knew, she wouldn't be coming on to me.

Celine smiled at Chris and Dax before sauntering down the hallway. When she was out of sight, Dax whistled softly.

"You lucky bastard. You know, this stuff can wait until tomorrow if you'd like."

"No, this is too important to put off."

He gave me a look that said he thought I was nuts. "Okay, if that's what you want."

I opened the door to the security center. "Let's get to work."

CHAPTER 17

I ENTERED THE dining hall, looking forward to spending time with Sara today. I didn't expect her to feel the same way, but I planned to change that before the day was over. I was going to start with training and see where it went from there.

I thought she might respond better to me as a trainer, so I was all business when I reached the table where she sat with Jordan and another girl.

"Ready to start training?"

Sara nodded without speaking.

"Come with me then." I turned away and left the room to wait for her in the main hall. She came out a minute later, looking nervous but resigned.

When I started for the main entrance, she said, "We're not using a training room?"

I looked back at her. "I thought we'd go outdoors. Would you rather stay inside?"

"No," she replied quickly and hurried to catch up.

Outside, we walked around the building and I steered us toward the woods.

"Where are we going?"

"For a walk," I replied without looking at her. Seamus had told me about how many times he and Niall had caught Sara heading for the small lake on the property. I suspected she missed the ocean and was looking for a body of water to make her feel less homesick. I couldn't think of a better place to start her training.

She harrumphed softly, "I think I should tell you that when I go for walks, I usually end up brought back in chains."

Her wry tone made it hard to keep a straight face. "I think we'll be fine."

We walked in silence for a while before I tried to get her talking. "Other than the problem with your training, how are you doing here?"

"It's not home," she answered sharply, but I could hear the hurt in her voice.

I looked at her, and she stared straight ahead.

"I know you miss Nate and your friends, but it's not like you won't see them again. And you aren't alone here. You've made some new friends, and you have Tristan and Chris and me."

"Until you go off on one of your missions again."

"Are you trying to tell me that you missed me?" I couldn't keep the smile from my face. She wouldn't be angry if she didn't care.

"No."

"I have no plans to go anywhere for the next month so you are stuck with me for a while," I said, hoping to reassure her.

"Lucky me," she grumbled, and I laughed, glad that she seemed more at ease.

"Where did you go?"

"It was a job, clearing out some nests," I answered soberly. "Nothing you want to hear about."

"You were looking for the Master, weren't you?"

"You don't need to worry about him anymore," I said.

My words only upset her more. She stopped short and put her hands on her hips.

How did I make her understand that she no longer had to fear the Master? We would find and eliminate him, and all she had to do was train and settle into her new life.

"I'm not a child, Nikolas, and I deserve to know what is going on. If you can't be open with me, you can go find someone else to train."

I let out a harsh breath and grabbed her wrist when she turned to go back the way we'd come. "I see you are still the same pain in the ass."

"Takes one to know one."

I couldn't see her face, but I heard the smile in her voice.

"We found where we believe Eli was staying in Portland, and there were signs that the Master could be in Nevada. It's not surprising since Vegas is the perfect place for vampires to blend in and hunt. We hit a nest in Henderson and that led us to two more nests near Vegas, but none of them gave us anything useful about the Master. Whoever he is, he is well hidden and his followers have no idea where he is."

She looked at me expectantly. "So, what happens now?"

"Now we train while someone else looks for him. A Master is no small matter, and the Council has made it a priority to find him. They've already sent extra teams to the US dedicated to hunting him. It is only a matter of time before he is found."

We continued our walk until she let out a small gasp and broke into a run. I followed at a normal pace and found her standing at the edge of the lake, glowing with happiness.

I knew how she felt seeing the lake for the first time. I discovered this place a few days after Tristan and I came to the valley, and I used to come here to swim and be alone. I'd even considered building a small house here, but I'd never gotten around to it. It pleased me to know she loved it here too.

"This is incredible," she gushed. "I can't believe people don't come here all the time."

I smiled. "Not everyone loves the woods as much as you do."

"Then why did you bring me here?"

"Because I'm not like everyone else." I sat on a rock and motioned for her to take the one next to me. "Let's talk."

She sat hesitantly. "I thought we were going to train."

"We will, but first I want to talk about your training. Callum told me you don't seem to want to use your Mori strength or speed."

"You talked to him about me?" she asked defensively.

"Of course. I needed to understand the problem so we can fix it."

Talking to Callum had been a good idea. He might not have been the right trainer for Sara, but he was observant. He'd told me she was sensitive about her Mori whenever he tried to talk to her about it, and he suspected she was afraid of the demon. In his defense, he had no idea about Sara's history or her unique ancestry, which made him unqualified to help her get past her fear.

She gave me a skeptical look. "You think you know what my problem is?"

"I have several theories. The first is that you are so used to suppressing your Mori that you don't know how to do anything else. Demons are afraid of Fae magic, which explains why your Mori doesn't fight for control like mine would if I kept it locked away. You need to learn to loosen your control just as you would exercise any muscle. It takes practice."

"That's it then?"

"That is one theory." My gaze locked with hers. "My other theory is that you are afraid."

She rubbed her hands on her jeans. "Why…would I be afraid?"

"I was there in the wine cellar, Sara, and I saw what happened when you let your demon out. I also saw the fear on your face when I asked you about it the next day. It terrified you how close the demon came to controlling you. But that would never have happened." I hated bringing up that night in Portland, but she had to face her fears if she was going to conquer them.

She paled and turned her face away. "You're wrong. It almost did."

"No, it didn't. Look at me."

Her eyes met mine again, and I saw her distress.

"I would not have let it take you," I said firmly.

"But if you hadn't gotten there when you did, I –"

"You would have done it on your own. You're a lot stronger than you give yourself credit for. The demon might have gained control for a short time, but you would not have let it stay that way."

Hope sparked in her eyes. "How can you know that?"

"Because I know *you*. You are one of the most willful people I've ever met, and it would take a lot more than a demon to control you. That I know from experience."

She gave me a small smile. "Are you going to train me to fight without my demon?"

"Today we are going to start with the basics. You will learn to open yourself to your Mori safely."

She leaned away from me. "I can't –"

"Yes, you can. This is something every one of us learns to do, and you will, too. You are a lot stronger than the rest of us were when we started."

I took her hand in mine, hoping my touch would ease her fear. "Do you trust me?"

She nodded.

"And you know that I would never let anything harm you, right?"

"Yes," she answered without hesitancy or doubt, and it pleased me to know she had such faith in me after all she'd been through.

I released her hand reluctantly. "Good. It might be easier if you tell me how it is that you are able to control your demon. How do you keep your Mori separate from your Fae power?"

Her brows drew together, and it was a moment before she answered. "It's hard to explain. I can feel the demon in my head and sense its thoughts, or rather its emotions, if that makes sense."

I nodded.

"When I was little I used to hear its voice whispering in my mind, kind of like a song you get stuck in your head and it won't go away no matter what you think about. I think I was five or six when it first tried to come out, and it scared me so much that I accidentally released my power, which I had no idea about until that day. The beast – that's what I used to call my demon before you told me what it was – was afraid of my power and it pulled into the back of my mind to get away from it. I was scared to death and I had no idea what was going on with me, but I knew I'd done something to make the creepy voice in my head quiet."

Her eyes took on a faraway look. "It wasn't until I found an injured robin and the power burst out of me to heal the bird's wing that I realized what I could really do. After that, I had to learn to keep my power locked away and only call on it when I needed it and also how to tap into it to keep the beast – I mean the demon – caged in the back of my mind. The only times the demon seemed to wake up was when I did a healing and drained my power. That used to happen all the time in the beginning, but it doesn't happen anymore."

Hearing her talk about her childhood and how she'd had to learn to deal with a Mori demon *and* emerging Fae powers on her own, my respect for her grew tenfold.

"I don't know if I am more amazed by your level of control or that you learned it at such a young age with no guidance or training. Are you consciously doing it?"

She shrugged, looking more at ease. "In the beginning I did, and it was hard as hell. I lost control of my power all the time because I had to focus on keeping the beast – demon – quiet. Now, it's like breathing. I don't have to think about it unless I use too much power and get weak. Then the demon starts to move and I have to use force with it. How do you do it?"

I laughed, trying to think of how to explain it to her. "Not like that. You talk about your Mori and your Fae power like they are parts of you that you move as easily as an arm or a leg. For the rest of us, there is no real separation between us and our demons. My Mori and I are joined completely, and I feel its thoughts and emotions as easily as my own."

"How can you control it if it's that much a part of you?" she asked as if she couldn't conceive such a thing.

"I learned from a young age to suppress the demon's natural urges just like you would any craving. But unlike you, I can't block it completely, and I'm always aware of my Mori because together we make one person."

She shook her head. "I don't think I could live like that."

"And I couldn't live any other way. Now I understand why it's so difficult for you to tap into your Mori's strength. You keep it bound so tightly you aren't even aware of its presence half the time. We need to show you how to get to know it."

She clenched the bottom of her hoodie. "How do we do that?"

She wasn't going to like my next words, but there was only one way to move forward.

"You said you keep it locked in a part of your mind, right? You need to loosen your hold on it and connect with it."

She shot to her feet, her eyes fearful. "I can't do that. You don't understand how it felt when I let it out before."

She was right. I'd lost control of my Mori as a child, but I'd never given myself up completely to the demon. I could only imagine how frightening that had been for her.

But she had won in that battle of wills, and her demon hadn't forgotten that. She just needed to believe in her own strength.

"It won't be like that this time because we won't let it. Trust me."

I held my hand out to her, and she let me tug her down to sit on the rock again.

"Take it slowly. Just open up a little and remember that you are the stronger one."

She gave me a puzzled look. "I thought the whole purpose of this is to tap into the demon because it has all the strength and speed."

"Physically yes, but mentally you are stronger, and your Mori knows that."

There was still doubt in her eyes as she closed them. Her brow furrowed as if she was deep in concentration. Minutes ticked by. Several times she flinched then took a deep breath, and I could sense the struggle going on inside her.

Her jaw clenched, and I gave her hand a small squeeze to let her know I was here. She relaxed for a few seconds before she jerked and cried out.

I cradled her cold face in my hands. "Look at me."

She opened her eyes, and the fear in them made all my protective instincts come roaring to life. But this was one battle I could not fight for her.

"I know this feels wrong and frightening to you, but that is only because you aren't used to it. Don't run from it, and don't push it away. Feel your Mori, get to know it, and let it get to know you."

She closed her eyes again. I went back to holding her hand and watching her for any sign she was in trouble. She sat quietly, her expression unreadable, and the only movement was her breathing. Every now and then her eyelids flickered, but she was so still she could have been in a trance. As long as she didn't appear distressed or afraid, I was willing to sit beside her and wait.

A jumble of emotions suddenly came through the bond, and I sensed it was coming from her demon. My Mori pressed forward. *Solmi?*

"Sara, are you okay?"

She didn't answer, and I squeezed her hand, worried she might be in trouble. "Sara, talk to me."

Her eyes opened, and I held back my sigh of relief. "Are you okay?"

"Yes. This is so weird and kind of intense."

I smiled. "I imagine it is. I think that's enough for now."

"But I just started."

"You've been at it for over an hour."

Her mouth fell open. "I have?"

"Yes, and you don't want to overdo it." I knew from experience that learning to work with your demon could be mentally and physically draining.

"Okay." She closed her eyes, and when she opened them again a minute later, they brimmed with tears.

"Sara?" I asked, afraid the demon had hurt her.

She wiped her eyes. "I'm fine. It was just…not what I expected."

I relaxed when I could sense no pain from her. "What happened?"

"We talked a little. Well, I did most of the talking." She went to stand by the lake. "I can't describe it. What is it like for you?"

I hid my astonishment, not wanting to upset her. How did you have a conversation with your Mori?

"I feel my Mori's thoughts, but they are almost like my own thoughts. I don't talk to it like I would to another person."

Her face fell. "Oh."

"Don't do that." I walked over to stand beside her. "You've made great progress, considering your fear when we started."

"I know." She looked at the water. "It's just…never mind."

"Tell me."

She bent to pick up some stones and began tossing them into the water, creating ripples across the glassy surface. When she spoke again, I could hear the frustration and loneliness in her voice.

"Nothing about me is normal. I'm probably the only one of my kind in existence, and I don't fit in here like the other trainees. I can't fight, and I hate killing. What kind of warrior doesn't like killing? I don't even connect with my Mori the way the rest of you do."

I took one of the stones from her hand and skipped it across the lake as I thought about what to say to ease her mind.

"Your Fae blood does make you different, but that doesn't mean you are not as much a Mohiri as the rest of us. And there is nothing wrong with not wanting to kill."

She sighed dejectedly. "My Mori is afraid of me. I bet you don't have to worry about that with yours."

"No, and that will change for you once you and your Mori learn to join. Trust me; all it wants is to be one with you. Without that, it has no purpose."

She looked at me, her eyes troubled. "It said my power burns it. I promised not to hurt it again, but what if my Fae power keeps getting stronger?"

"*Is* your power getting stronger?"

I'd been so happy to have her back I hadn't considered the implications of her being half Fae. Would her power grow? What would happen to her Mori if her Fae side became more dominant?

"Yes."

"Tell me," I urged gently.

"It's hard to explain because I'm not sure what is going on. A couple of times, I felt a cold spot in my chest right where I was stabbed." She rubbed her arms. "And my power's been acting up. At first, it was small stuff like making the leaves move and a bottle of Coke almost exploding. Then we had a training exercise with bazerats, and when I touched one of them it freaked out and my power shocked it."

"What happened to the bazerat?" I asked with a mix of fascination and concern. Tristan had mentioned a training session with bazerats, but he hadn't given me much detail.

"I didn't want to hurt it," she said miserably. "I knocked it out and the other one too. Celine wanted me to kill the bazerats, but those creatures were terrified of us."

I didn't try to hide my surprise. "You felt sorry for demons?"

She lifted her chin. "I didn't find out until later that bazerats are demons, but I still wouldn't have killed them just because someone thought it would be fun."

I pictured her standing up to Celine, who did not like being challenged, especially by other women. But when Sara believed in something, no amount of pressure would sway her.

Sara chewed her lip. "And then I killed the lamprey demon, but I did that on purpose. It was me or him, and I figured if I could hurt one demon, I could hurt another. I think I expected to knock it out like I did with the bazerat. I didn't know it would explode like that."

I wasn't sure what to think about the things she'd shared with me. It was clear her power was growing and it was deadly to demons. A tiny cold knot of fear formed in my stomach. What would happen to her own demon if her power continued to grow?

"Have you told anyone else about this?" I asked, keeping my tone light.

"Only Tristan and Roland."

"Good. Keep it between us for now, and let me know if it happens again."

She met my gaze fearfully. "You didn't answer my question. Will my Fae power hurt my Mori? Could I hurt another Mohiri?"

"Honestly, I don't know." I said the only thing I could think of, and I hoped I was right. "The way I see it, you've had the two of them inside you your whole life, and if you were going to hurt your Mori, you would have done it by now. Did you feel like your demon was in danger when you had these flare-ups?"

"No."

"There's your answer then. Let's not worry about that unless we need to."

She visibly relaxed, and I felt better as well. If she was able to shield her Mori when she used her Fae power, she could continue to do that as her power got stronger.

"What now?" she asked.

She needed a change of pace after the emotional session, and I had just the thing in mind. There was nothing like nature and some good old fashioned exercise to clear your head.

"Now we do some other training."

She stared at me warily. "What kind of training?"

I removed my sword and sweater, and laid them on my rock. Turning back to her, I said, "Nothing difficult. How about we go for a run?"

She burst out laughing. "You expect me to keep up with you?"

I smiled. "I'll try to dial it back a bit."

She made a face and stretched her legs. "Gee, I feel so special. How long will it take me to be as fast as you?"

Distracted by the way her jeans hugged her backside as she warmed up, I almost forgot to answer her. "About a hundred years or so."

I wished I hadn't spoken when she abandoned her stretching to stare at me. "A hundred years?"

"Give or take a few. Your Mori will give you strength, but it'll be a long time before you develop that kind of speed. Didn't anyone explain that to you?"

"I think Callum was too busy trying to get me to use my Mori to go over that stuff. But what you're saying doesn't make sense. How can warriors fight vampires if they can't keep up with them?"

I crossed my arms, wondering if Tristan knew about the serious gap in her education, something I planned to rectify, starting today.

"Apparently there is a lot they haven't told you. How much do you know about vampires and how they are made?"

"I know a vampire drinks from someone and forces the person to drink their blood and that's how the demon is passed into the new host. It takes three or four days for the new demon to grow strong enough to take control of the person. Oh, and only mature vampires can make another vampire."

"That's all true, but did you also know that new vampires are weak and their strength grows over time?" I asked.

She shook her head, her eyes wide in disbelief.

Her lack of knowledge angered me. One of the first things she should have been taught here was how vampires matured and how to tell a young vampire from an older one. That knowledge had saved many warriors' lives in battle.

"They are stronger than a human, but no match for a trained warrior, and it takes them almost as long as it does us to develop the kind of speed you've seen. Most of the vampires we saw in Maine were mature, and it's unusual to see that many mature vampires together. Many of the vampires warriors deal with don't have that kind of strength or speed."

"I knew baby vamps were weak, but I thought that only lasted a few months," she said, looking very relieved to hear that was not the case.

"We're going to need to add some studies to your training. We'll start this afternoon."

Normally, we had people who handled the trainees' studies, but I was reluctant to entrust her education to anyone else. I told myself it had absolutely nothing to do with the fact that it gave me a reason to spend more time with her.

"But right now, how about that run?" I said.

"Okay."

We ran the whole perimeter of the lake, which was roughly five miles. I slowed so she could keep pace with me, and I wasn't surprised she never fell behind. She'd spent half her life outdoors with werewolves and trolls, and she'd probably had to push herself to keep up with them.

By the time we finished our run, she was winded but glowing. I made a note to run in the woods with her whenever I could.

She was quiet but no longer withdrawn as we walked back to the stronghold. At the main entrance, I opened the door for her.

"Get some lunch and rest for a bit. We'll meet up again at two."

"Okay," she said, looking at ease after our morning together.

I remembered then that I had planned to give her a gift for her first training session. I removed the knife I carried on my hip and held it out to her.

"Here. This is to replace the knife you lost."

She unsheathed the knife and touched the pattern on the handle. The pleasure on her face told me I'd chosen the right gift.

"You did great today," I told her.

"Thanks," she blurted, turning away like she was embarrassed by my praise.

I opened my mouth to tell her she had earned it, but one of the trainees chose that moment to come racing into the main hall.

"Shut the door! Shut the door before they get out!" he shouted frantically.

I slammed the door shut when I saw a small white creature careening toward us. The kark changed course and flew up to the high arched ceiling.

"What is it?" Sara asked, tilting her head to look at the kark.

The trainee's reply was drowned out by the sounds of an entire flock of karks headed in our direction. Karks were not dangerous to us, but I pulled Sara behind me anyway as they filled the main hall.

A warrior named Sahir ran into the hall, followed by a group of trainees. Sahir took care of the menagerie, and he helped educate the trainees on the many species in the world and how to handle them.

One of the boys had a sword, and I almost laughed out loud at the sight of him swinging the weapon at the tiny karks whipping around his head.

"Don't hurt them!" Sahir lunged for the boy. "Do you realize how long it takes to breed karks? We can't kill them."

"What the hell are we supposed to do with them?" the boy yelled.

"We have to round them up somehow."

Sara ran over to Sahir. "How do you catch them?" she asked him.

"Normally you'd use a spray made from scarab demon pheromone. Karks can't resist it. Unfortunately, this batch was not supposed to hatch yet, and I didn't see a bottle of spray in the crates."

I frowned. Karks were hard to breed, and the people who handled them were fastidious about their care. No one would ship a batch of eggs without making sure the pheromone was packed with them.

Sahir shouted something about getting a sedative to calm the karks, and then he ran from the hall, leaving us with a few hundred frantic karks.

The only word I could use to describe the scene in the hall was chaos. Trainees ran around, trying unsuccessfully to catch the creatures as Chris and a dozen other warriors ran into the hall and stared in shock.

"What in God's name is going on here?" Tristan bellowed from the second floor landing, before he descended the stairs with Celine. "Who is responsible for this?" he shouted above the noise when he reached the main floor. "Where is Sahir?"

"He went to get some kind of sedative to knock them out," Sara told him.

Tristan stared angrily at the mess around him. "How did this happen?"

Sara shook her head and pointed at the other trainees. "Ask them. I was with Nikolas."

Jordan stepped forward. "It was an accident. We laid all the eggs out after breakfast and turned them as Sahir instructed. We just went back to turn them again and they were all hatched."

"I want these things caged before they make an even bigger mess," Tristan ordered, joining us at the center of the hall.

Celine squealed and started hopping around and trying to get kark dung from her hair. I had to turn away so she wouldn't see me struggling not to laugh.

Sara didn't try to hide her amusement, although her laugh was cut short when she got a whiff of the stuff. Her eyes watered, and she covered her nose and mouth.

I was grinning when my eyes met Tristan's, and after a few seconds, his scowl turned into a smile. He shook his head and looked around the hall that was going to require several cleaning crews after the karks were rounded up.

"They must be getting tired," one of the boys said. "Should we try to catch them now?"

I looked where he was pointing and saw Sara holding a sleeping kark while several dozen of the creatures rested on surfaces around her. Having seen what she could do to a werewolf and two hellhounds, I knew she had to be doing the same thing now.

Walking over to her, I said in a low voice, "Are you doing this?"

"Yes, but I'm not sure how long it will work on them. I hope Sahir gets here soon."

"Someone needs to be reprimanded for this disaster," Celine said when she and Tristan walked over to us.

I didn't bother to tell her there was no one to blame for this one. She was too upset about the white dung clinging to her hair to listen to reason.

One of the boys ran up to us carrying mesh equipment bags. "Will these do?"

"Good idea!" Sara smiled at him and called out to the other trainees to help them.

They managed to get all the sleeping creatures in the bags, but that didn't help with the hundreds of karks flying around the room. It got decidedly worse when the situation became too much for the newly hatched karks, and they began to defecate everywhere. Tristan threw up his arms, and he, Chris, and I stood together watching the spectacle.

When Sara and one of the other trainees collided with Celine, and the three of them went down in a tangle of arms and legs, it was all I could do not to laugh.

Sara sat up covered in stinking kark dung and muttered, "Ah hell," and I had to stifle the bark of laughter that almost slipped out. I'd just spent the morning getting her to warm up to me, and I had no desire to start over.

I moved to help her up, but Chris beat me to it. So I went to assist Celine instead. She clung to my arm for a moment then let go when she looked down and saw the filth covering her.

"If anyone needs me, I'll be soaking in my tub for the next two hours," Celine announced, giving me a look that said I was welcome to join her.

This was a new situation for me; propositioned by a former lover while my mate, who didn't know she was my mate, stood several feet away. I looked at Tristan and Chris, who were laughing openly, and Chris mouthed, *Good luck with that.* It was all so absurd that I could only shake my head and laugh.

Sahir chose that moment to arrive with the sedative. "Sorry it took so long. I had to dilute the sedative and transfer it to a spray canister so it will reach them."

To illustrate, he lifted the nozzle and lightly sprayed two karks. It took about a minute for the sedative to kick in and bring the karks down.

Sara picked one up and smiled at Sahir. "It worked!"

Sahir turned to Tristan. "I diluted this, but it still might knock people out if they breathe too much of it. We should clear the hall before I spray more of it."

Tristan ordered everyone from the hall. He looked at me as we walked to the nearest common room. "Do you want to join me this afternoon on a call with the task force? After we both clean up, of course."

"Can we do it around five? Sara and I are working on her studies after lunch."

He gave me a puzzled look. "Her studies?"

"Yes, it seems we overlooked that part of her training. She didn't even know how vampires matured until I told her."

Tristan looked abashed. "She is the same age as the other trainees who have all had schooling. I didn't stop to think that Sara —"

A cry of pain came from the hall.

Sara.

CHAPTER 18

I RACED BACK to the hall in time to see a mass of white bodies swarming around someone who was trying to run away from them. She cried out, and my stomach lurched when I realized the creatures were attacking her.

I dove through the karks and wrapped my body around Sara to protect her from the impact as we hit the marble floor. We landed with her on top of me, and I swiftly rolled us over so she was on the bottom. A second later, we were covered in crazed karks, and I expected to feel their sharp little teeth in my back. But they completely ignored me and seemed obsessed with getting to Sara.

Sahir ran toward us. "If I spray them, I might get you too."

"I don't give a damn. Just do it," I ordered.

He lifted the nozzle, and I lowered my head to Sara's. "Cover your mouth and nose. Sahir is going to spray around us."

She buried her face in my sweater, and I pulled her to me as tightly as I could.

"There are too many of them," Sahir called.

"Keep spraying us."

I'd pick Sara up and make a run for it, but there were too many of the creatures, and they were in a frenzy to get to Sara.

"I can't. It'll poison you two if I spray more around you," he argued. "I'll do what I can to reduce their numbers. What the hell is wrong with them? Why are they only going after her?"

"I don't know."

Karks didn't attack people without provocation. There was only one thing that made them behave this way. I lowered my head and enhanced my demon senses to smell Sara's hair. It stunk of kark but nothing suspicious. Next I sniffed at her hoodie and picked up a faint, foreign odor mingled with the kark feces. "Something smells off here."

Sara made a noise. "You think?"

I had to get the hoodie off her. If it had even a drop of scarab pheromone on it, the flock wouldn't stop until they devoured it and anything touching it. I grabbed the bottom and began pulling it up.

"What are you doing?" she squeaked.

I continued pulling the hoodie up her torso. "I think something on your clothes is making the karks behave like this. I can detect something that doesn't smell like you or their droppings."

If she'd had scarab pheromone on her when we entered the hall, the karks would have attacked her then. That meant she would have had to come into contact with it since we got here, and the only way for that to happen would be for someone to spray her with it. The idea that anyone at Westhorne would want to harm her seemed preposterous, but I was taking no chances.

She stopped struggling, and I yanked the piece of clothing off her and threw it across the room. Dozens of karks attacked the hoodie.

"Jesus, look at that," Sahir shouted.

Chills ran through me as I watched the tiny karks tearing into the fabric. That could have been Sara if I hadn't reached her in time.

Sahir pointed at us. "They're still trying to get to her. Whatever it is, it has to be on her T-shirt, too."

"I know." I took a breath and lifted my head to look down at Sara, who was shivering beneath me. I hated to do this, knowing how modest she was, but there was no other way.

"Sara —"

Panic flared in her eyes. "No way! Forget it! We can make a run for it."

"There are too many of them. As soon as I get off you, they'll attack you."

Her head moved from side to side. "I don't care. I am *not* taking off my clothes."

I sighed heavily. So much for her warming up to me; I'd be lucky if she looked at me for a week after this.

"I'm sorry but this is no time for modesty. It's just your shirt, and I'll cover you."

She bit her lip and looked away from me, reaching for her shirt. I wanted to say something to ease her discomfort, but I knew she wouldn't want to hear it.

"Stand back, boys. Time for the girls to show you how it's done," a girl yelled. "Let her rip, Liv."

A hard spray of icy water hit my back and moved over us, making Sara sputter and press her face into my chest. It took me a second to realize someone had turned the fire hose on us.

There was no holding back the laughter this time. Christ, life with Sara would never be dull.

"I'm glad you're enjoying yourself," Sara muttered, pushing at me.

I grinned at her. "Immensely."

Reluctantly, I moved off her and stood. I reached down and lifted her to her feet.

The hall was a disaster. Every surface was covered in karks or kark dung, and there was half an inch of water on the floor.

I looked at the blonde girl holding the fire hose. Jordan smirked and turned the powerful spray on us again before attacking the few karks left in the air.

"Hey!" Sara yelled.

Jordan's grin was anything but apologetic. "Sorry, had to make sure I didn't miss any of it. Hey, it worked, didn't it?"

"I think that's enough, Jordan," Tristan said as he and the other warriors returned to the hall and looked around at the mess.

He looked at Sara and me. "Are you two okay?"

We nodded, and he turned to Sahir. "Sahir, what could have caused this?"

I went to the hoodie and yanked it out from under a pile of unconscious karks. "Something on her clothes attracted them. Look at this."

"Have that garment examined. I want to know exactly what happened here," Tristan ordered angrily.

I had a pretty damn good idea what had happened, but I didn't want to voice my suspicions until I knew for sure.

Tristan called for someone to gather up the karks and start cleaning up. He came over to us, his eyes full of concern for Sara.

"Are you sure you're okay?" he asked her.

She rubbed her arms. "I'm fine."

Jordan walked up to us, grinning mischievously. "Sara, you look like you just won a wet T-shirt contest."

"What?" Sara said in a choked voice.

I looked sideways at her to see her tugging on the wet fabric of her yellow T-shirt that was molded to her breasts and tight stomach like a second skin. My breath caught and heat flared in my belly. I had never wanted to touch a woman as much as I did in that moment.

I caught movement out of the corner of my eye, and I looked up to see half the males in the room staring at Sara.

A fierce surge of possessiveness filled me. My Mori growled, and I almost echoed it, as I stepped in front of Sara to shield her from the others' eyes.

The other warriors wisely averted their gaze when I glared at them. The only one who didn't turn away was Jordan, who appeared to be having the time of her life.

Sara moved to stand beside me again. Her T-shirt no longer clung to her, and she had her arms folded across her chest.

I started to ask her if she was okay, but Tristan spoke first.

"Nikolas, we need to talk when you have a minute."

I didn't need to ask what he wanted to discuss. I hadn't exactly been subtle when I'd stared everyone down. But I wasn't going to apologize for protecting Sara's modesty.

"If you don't need me, I'd like to get cleaned up," Sara said wearily.

"Take the rest of the day off," Tristan told her. "Do you need to see a healer?"

"No, I just need a long shower."

He smiled warmly at her. "Go on then. You too, Jordan and Olivia. I think you've earned an afternoon off."

Sara mumbled a "thank you" to me then practically ran up the stairs to the north wing. I waited until she was out of sight before I faced Tristan.

"You wanted to talk?"

He nodded then grimaced. "Why don't we both get cleaned up and meet at my place in thirty minutes?"

"Make that an hour." I held up Sara's destroyed hoodie. "I want to get this to the lab so they can start running tests."

"Good idea. I'll walk with you."

He cut to the chase as soon as we were out of earshot of the hall. "You need to rein in your emotions."

"I'm in control."

"You were territorial back there, and everyone saw it. If they don't know about the bond after that, they will soon if you keep it up. Do you want her to hear about it from someone else?"

God, no. That was the last thing I wanted.

"Did I upset her?"

"I think she was embarrassed, but not by you. I'm more concerned about what others might say to her."

I exhaled slowly. "You're right. I'll keep it under control from now on. Are you coming to the lab with me?"

"No. I just wanted a few minutes to talk. Let me know what they find."

I gripped the hoodie tightly. "I'm pretty sure I know what they'll find. Karks only behave like that for one reason."

His eyes flicked to the hoodie. "Scarab pheromone?"

"I smelled something, but it was impossible to identify with the kark stench. I'm handling the investigation myself, and I'll know something by tonight."

He nodded approvingly. "Good. I'll talk to you later then. I'm having a family dinner with Sara and Chris this evening. We think she's ready to know he's her cousin. You're welcome to join us."

As much as I loved spending time with Sara, I wanted her to form strong bonds with her Mohiri family. And I knew how much it meant to Tristan as well. It was best to give her this time alone with them.

"Thanks. You three do the family thing, and I'll come by around eight."

He smiled. "I'll see you then."

Tristan left, and I entered the medical ward. Our lab wasn't state of the art like those at some other strongholds, but they would be able to tell if there was scarab pheromone or some other chemical on the hoodie. If the karks hadn't devoured it all.

Margot was on duty again, and she started running tests immediately on the tattered hoodie. I told her to test for the pheromone first, and she said it would take at least two hours. She promised she would call me as soon as the results were in.

I hurried to my apartment to shower and change, and then I went in search of Dax. I found the security guy at his favorite spot, in front of a bank of computer monitors in the security center.

"Two visits in as many days. People are gonna start talking soon," he quipped when I grabbed a chair and rolled it over to sit by him. He grinned. "You know, I don't think we ever worked together as much as we have in the last few months."

I chuckled. "That's because a certain orphan has a special talent for finding trouble."

"True that." He tapped a few keys on his keyboard. "Let me guess, you want to see security footage from the kark thing."

"Yes."

Most of our security cameras were outside, but we had two in the main hall. Dax brought up the feeds and went back to the moment Sara and I entered the hall. I watched me hand her the knife and smile when she turned away.

Seconds later, the boy ran into the hall, followed by the flock of karks and everyone else. Soon it was difficult to hear people above the flapping and squeaking, and the scene below was partially obscured by the tiny winged creatures.

I kept my eyes on Sara and anyone she came close to before the karks attacked her. Aside from Tristan, Chris, and me, she came into contact with Celine and one of the boys when the three of them had fallen to the floor. I had Dax replay that piece several times, but I could see nothing suspicious, not that I expected to. Celine might have a reputation for disliking other women, but she would never harm another Mohiri. The boy was clumsy and awkward, and seemed eager to help.

Dax snickered as we watched for the fifth time as Sara backed into Celine and they tumbled to the floor. "That girl is after my own heart."

I laughed. "She's something else, all right."

My smile vanished when we reached the part where the karks began attacking Sara, a few at first and then dozens of them. She cried out and stumbled, trying to escape them. And then I ran into the hall and covered her with my body. Watching the karks try to burrow under me to get to Sara made my blood run cold. If I hadn't gotten to her in time –

"You want to keep going?"

"I've seen enough."

Dax stopped the playback. "Did you find what you were looking for?"

"No. I thought I'd figure out why the karks attacked Sara and no one else, but I can't see anything here that explains it."

I rubbed my jaw and thought about where Sara could have picked up the pheromone, if indeed that was what I'd smelled on her hoodie. Could it have been on her clothes before we entered the building?

Once again, I dismissed that idea. If Sara had walked into the hall with scarab pheromone on her clothes, the flock would have attacked her as soon as they caught the scent. So how the hell had she come into contact with it?

Leaning back in my chair, I stared at the monitor that now showed the ongoing cleanup in the main hall. Was it possible that I was making something out of nothing? Where was the motive? Why would another Mohiri want to hurt Sara? I was so used to protecting her. Maybe I was seeing a threat where none existed.

I pushed my chair back and stood. A glance at the time on the monitor told me I had at least an hour before the lab's pheromone test would be done. The results would tell me if I was overreacting or not. I hoped I was.

*　　*　　*

It was just after eight that night when I arrived at Tristan's door to talk to him about the kark incident and the results of the lab tests. I felt Sara's presence inside, and I was a little worried about seeing her after my behavior in the hall. I was trying to take my time with her, and I didn't want her upset by this.

I rapped on the door. A moment later, it was opened by Tristan.

"Nikolas, come in. We just finished dinner."

My eyes went to Sara as soon as I entered the apartment, and my stomach did a strange flip when I saw her. Instead of her usual attire, she wore a lacy pink top that complimented her sun-kissed skin. Her hair flowed in soft waves around her shoulders, and her face was flushed from laughter. Her green eyes met mine demurely before she glanced away.

Remembering my talk with Tristan, I schooled my expression before she could see the effect she had on me. I turned my gaze to Chris, who gave me a knowing smile.

"I'll leave so you guys can take care of business," Sara said quietly, a note of discomfort in her voice that could only have been caused by my arrival.

Damn it, I *had* upset her this morning. Or someone had mentioned it to her. Only yesterday, I'd told Tristan I could train her and be around her without revealing my true feelings, and I'd already caused her distress.

Tristan shook his head when she moved to stand. "No, this concerns you. Nikolas has been investigating the kark attack."

He looked at me expectantly. "I assume you have something for us."

I sat on the couch, very aware of the girl sitting three feet away, and the fact that she averted her eyes when I looked at her.

"We examined Sara's shirt. The karks destroyed one side of it, so we focused on the scraps of fabric left there and found traces of what looks like scarab pheromone. The only way Sara could have gotten it on her clothes is if someone put it there."

"I cannot believe anyone inside these walls would try to hurt one of our own," Tristan said, no longer smiling.

I met his skeptical stare. "I find it hard to believe as well, but the evidence speaks for itself. Sahir said he found it odd there was no pheromone spray in the crates with the shipment of eggs. It's likely someone took it out before he searched them."

Chris leaned forward. "Why would anyone here target Sara?" He looked at her. "Your beasties didn't snack on someone, did they?"

"Ha, ha." She grew serious. "It's not like I don't have enemies out there."

"Out there, yes, but not in here," Tristan replied confidently. "And we've found nothing to indicate the vampires believe you are still alive. Even if they did, there is no way a Mohiri would betray one of their own people for a vampire."

The idea of someone here betraying Sara to our enemies seemed unthinkable. But God help anyone who caused her harm, Mohiri or otherwise.

"I agree," I said, looking at Sara. "There must be another motive."

Chris pursed his lips. "Trainees have been known to prank each other. They were brutal back in my day. Perhaps one of them did this as a practical joke and it got out of hand."

"I don't know any of them that well, but they've all been nice to me," Sara said, looking genuinely confused. "I really can't see one of them doing something that would hurt me."

"Jordan? Nice?" Chris gave her a disbelieving smile.

She shrugged. "She has her moments. I like her actually. I took her to meet Hugo and Woolf today, and they didn't go all growly on her so she must be okay."

I nodded in approval. "Jordan will make a great warrior one day. You could learn a lot from her."

If I could have picked a friend for Sara, it would have been the blonde trainee, but not just because she was a skilled fighter. Sara didn't open up to people easily, but she'd looked happy the few times I'd seen her with the other girl.

"She is already teaching me a lot," Sara said. She stood and looked at Tristan. "I should get going. I need to call Nate because I forgot to ask him yesterday if he's still coming for Thanksgiving."

Tristan chuckled. "I doubt you could keep him away. I've already arranged for the plane to pick him up in Portland in two weeks."

Her eyes sparkled. "I can't wait for you guys to meet each other."

They walked to the door. Chris and I followed.

"I'm looking forward to it, too," Tristan told her. "He sounds like a nice person on the phone."

Sara stopped walking. "You talked to Nate?"

"We speak at least once a week. You didn't know?"

She wore a small frown. "No. What do you talk about? You don't even know each other."

Tristan darted a look at me before he answered her.

"We are getting to know each other. He wants to make sure you are happy here; he knows how much you miss your friends back home. The last time we spoke he wanted to know if you'd started dating anyone yet. Apparently, the boys back home were not to your liking."

I almost growled at Tristan. Why was he talking to her about dating other males when he knew she was bonded to me?

A flush crept into Sara's cheeks. "Excuse me while I go kill my uncle."

Grinning, Tristan opened the door for her. "I will see you tomorrow."

Sara turned to Chris and me. "Good night."

"I'll walk with you so we can talk about tomorrow's training," I said, although training was the last thing on my mind. I wanted some time alone with her to get back to where we were this morning before the kark incident.

Tristan raised a hand to stop me from following her. "Actually, I need to speak with you, Nikolas, if you don't mind."

I would have glared at him if Sara hadn't been looking at me. Instead, I just nodded.

"I will walk my sweet little cousin out." Chris pulled on her hair playfully, and she smacked his hand. He chuckled. "Just trying to make up for all the years I missed out on."

She gave him a warning smile. "Before you get any ideas, Dimples, I should remind you my best friends are boys and I know many forms of retaliation. I even picked up a few tricks from Remy."

He winked. "I've learned to never underestimate a girl with troll friends."

Sara rolled her eyes and looked at Tristan and me. "I'll see you later."

"Tomorrow," I replied.

Tristan shut the door, and I rounded on him right away. "What was that about?"

He walked back to the living room, unfazed by my outburst. "I needed to talk to you."

"Why are you and Nate discussing Sara's relationships?" I followed him and sat across from him. "You said you wouldn't interfere."

Tristan sighed. "I was only relating to her what we talked about. And Nate actually mentioned you specifically when he asked if she was spending time with anyone. He suspects there is something between you."

I relaxed. "I spent time with Nate when Sara was missing. He's a smart man, and I'm not surprised he picked up on my feelings for her."

"He speaks fondly of you. I think he is just concerned about Sara getting involved in a serious relationship. To you, she is a young woman, but to Nate, she is still his little girl."

"And she is your granddaughter. I understand you are both protective of her, but she is my mate. Nate doesn't know what that means, but you do."

"I do," he replied wistfully. "But Sara is still so young."

"She is almost eighteen, two years younger than Josephine was when you bonded with her."

"Yes, but Josephine was raised a Mohiri, and she knew about bonding and mating before she met me."

I kept my anger in check. "What are you saying? We've already agreed that I would hold off on telling her about us. Are you asking me to stay away from her?"

"No. You need her, and she needs you even if she doesn't understand why."

"But."

"No buts. I promised I wouldn't come between you, and I won't. I know how much you care for Sara, and I trust you to do what's best for her."

"Is this why you asked to talk to me?"

"I actually wanted to ask how Sara's first training session went this morning."

I smiled. "Very good. We talked for a while, and then she spent some time getting to know her Mori."

His brow arched. "Getting to know it?"

"I know how it sounds, but Sara thinks of her Mori as a separate part of her. She's only connected with it once before, and the experience terrified her because the demon tried to dominate her. That's why she can't tap into her Mori's power. We are starting slow, getting her past her fear before we move on to traditional training."

I didn't go into the details of our session. Sara had shared personal things with me today. I'd asked her to trust me, and I would not betray that trust.

Tristan nodded, pleased. "It sounds like you've made a lot of progress already."

"I think so."

He ran a hand through his hair. "Crazy day. Remember when it used to be so quiet here?"

A laugh burst from me. "I hear it's a lot quieter in Maine these days."

"You weren't kidding when you said trouble knows how to find Sara."

"I'm pretty sure I said *she* knows how to find trouble. I just didn't expect it to happen here."

Tristan sobered. "Do you honestly believe one of our own would try to harm her?"

"I don't know," I said. "Has anyone here shown animosity toward her?"

"Not that I've seen."

I'd spent the afternoon scrutinizing the possible motives of anyone who'd been close enough to put the scarab pheromone on Sara's clothes. Celine desired me, and it was possible she was jealous of the time I spent with Sara, but physically attacking someone wasn't Celine's way. She'd consider it beneath her.

"From what I've seen, Sara interacts mainly with the other trainees, and they all seem to like her." For a moment Tristan stared out the window thoughtfully, and I wondered what he was thinking. "I just can't see anyone here wanting to hurt her. Maybe Chris is right, and it was a prank."

"Maybe."

If he was right, I hoped the prankster had learned a lesson about pulling such a dangerous stunt. If they hadn't, they'd have to deal with me.

And I wasn't laughing.

CHAPTER 19

"SO, ARE WE done training for now?"

I sat on one of the arena seats and motioned for Sara to sit beside me. "We'll take a short break, and then I want to try something new."

She'd spent the last hour working with her Mori, and I was pleased to see her progressing so quickly. Yesterday, she'd been afraid of her demon, and today she had allowed it to connect with her for a short while, even tapping into its strength to help her lift heavy weights. She still had a long way to go, and merging with her demon was hard on her, though she pushed through it.

She joined me on the seats, and I was glad to see she was comfortable with me again. We sat in companionable silence for a few minutes before she spoke.

"Can I ask you something? You know all about my life, but you never talk about yours. What was it like where you grew up? Where is your family now?"

Her sudden interest in my background filled me with pleasure. "I grew up in a military stronghold just outside Saint Petersburg. Miroslav Fortress is nothing like Westhorne. It's surrounded by high stone walls and run more like a military base, although there were a number of families like mine there. My parents were advisors to the Council and very involved in planning military operations, so it was necessary for us to live there instead of in one of the family compounds."

She wrinkled her nose. "It doesn't sound like a fun place to live."

I understood her reaction, knowing how much she loved her freedom and being outside. She found Westhorne, with its wide-open space and miles of forest, restrictive.

"It was actually a very good life, and we had a lot more luxuries and conveniences than most people had at the time. Back then, even the wealthy didn't have running water, indoor plumbing, or indoor gas lighting, just to name a few.

"My parents were busy and travelled a lot, but they were very loving, and one of them always stayed home while the other travelled. They pushed me hard in my training and schoolwork, but I knew they were preparing me for the dangers I would face when I became a warrior."

"So, you're an only child?"

"Yes."

She gave me a little grin. "Well, that explains a lot."

I couldn't hold a scowl. I loved seeing this side of her.

"Did you have many friends? What did you do for fun?" she asked.

"I had a few good friends over the years. Most families moved when the parents were transferred to other strongholds and others moved in. I don't think I was ever lonely."

I smiled as I thought back to those days. "I liked to watch the warriors train, and I spent a lot of time hanging around the training grounds. They all taught me how to fight and use weapons. By the time I started formal training, I was so advanced they had to place me with the senior trainees."

"I bet your parents were very proud of you."

"They were; they still are."

She toyed with her ponytail, making me remember how her hair had framed her face last night when she'd worn it loose. My hands itched to reach over and free it from its binds, to run my fingers through the silky waves.

It took me a moment to realize she had asked me a question, something about why my family had left Russia.

"My sire was asked to assume leadership of a key military compound outside London when its leader was killed in a raid. We lived there for eight years before my parents were asked to help establish several new strongholds in North America. By then, I was a full warrior and I found the wildness of this continent appealing, so I tagged along."

"Where are your parents now?"

"They went back to Russia about fifty years ago. My sire is the leader of Miroslav Fortress now. My mother was offered leadership of another stronghold, but she did not want to be separated from him. I see them at least once a year."

She looked around the room then back at me. "So, um, what do you do for fun besides killing vampires and bossing people around?"

I studied her, wondering what had brought on this new curiosity about me. Not that I was complaining.

"Come on, you have to do something for fun," she pressed. "Do you read? Watch TV? Knit?"

"I read sometimes."

A fire lit in her eyes. "Me too. What do you like to read?"

"Anything by Hemmingway. Some Vonnegut, Scott."

"My dad's favorite Hemingway book was *The Old Man and the Sea*," she replied with a nostalgic smile. "What else do you like to do? For some reason I can't see you sitting around watching TV."

"Why not?" She was right, but I was curious about her impression of me.

She gave me an appraising look. "You could never sit back and watch the action. Plus, your sword would probably get snagged in the couch."

I chuckled. "I don't watch television or movies. I enjoy music, but not the music that is popular today. Dylan, the Who, the Stones – those are more my style."

"The sixties, huh?" she said, surprising me. Her eyes widened, and she smirked. "If you tell me you went to Woodstock, I may have to rethink this badass warrior thing you have going on."

I laughed at her description of me. "Actually, I was at Woodstock, along with Chris and about two dozen other warriors. Half the people there were either stoned or drunk, making it the ideal feeding ground for vampires and a few other demons. We were too busy to enjoy the music."

Her eyes gleamed with amusement. "I can't imagine you and Chris dressed in sixties clothes, especially what they wore at Woodstock."

"They had leather jackets and jeans in the sixties. Although, Chris joked about becoming a hippie after that week."

She huffed softly. "By the way, why didn't you tell me Chris was my cousin? What if I'd started crushing on him like every other girl back home?"

The thought of her being attracted to any other male sent a ripple of jealousy through me, but I quashed it. I wasn't going to let irrational emotions ruin this time with her.

"You were spooked when you learned what you were, and I thought it was too soon to introduce you to your Mohiri family. If it makes you feel better, Chris didn't know at first either."

"Just promise, no more keeping things from me."

"Ask me anything and I'll give you an honest answer."

My Mori shifted, filling me with longing. It wanted me to tell her the truth about the bond so we could be with our mate. But the demon acted on instinct, and it didn't understand why I waited.

She didn't say anything, and I knew it was time to get back to training. If the lamprey and kark attacks had taught me anything, it was that Sara needed to learn to defend herself. She had a long way to go before she reached the other trainees' level, but she had one weapon they didn't have. She only had to learn to wield it.

"You ready to try something different?"

She leaned forward eagerly. "Like what?"

I turned in my seat to face her. "I've been thinking about what you told me yesterday about your power getting stronger. You were worried it might hurt your demon or another Mohiri, but I don't think it will, at least not intentionally. The bazerats and lamprey demons were in their true form, which made them more vulnerable to your power."

I took her hand. "Our demons live inside us and are shielded by our bodies. I think *that*, and the fact that you also have a Mori inside you, is why your power is not flaring up right now."

She eased out of my grasp, looking slightly flustered. I wondered if it was my touch or my words that affected her.

"Was that what you wanted to try?" she asked.

I hid a smile. "Not quite. We know your power doesn't react instinctively to me, but I want to find out if you can use it against me consciously."

"What?" She leapt up and backed away, her eyes wide with horror. "Are you crazy? I could kill you."

"You won't," I reassured her.

"You don't know that!" She paled and shook her head. "You didn't see what I did to that demon in Boise. If you had, you wouldn't even suggest this."

I stood slowly. "I saw the pictures our guys took before they cleaned it up."

Her voice shook. "Then why the hell would you ask me to try to do that to you?"

"I'm not asking you to do that."

She took another step back, ready to bolt.

I held up my hands. "Listen to me. I think your power reacts when you are frightened or in danger, and you don't believe it, but you *can* control it. You were in mortal danger when the lamprey demon attacked you, and you knew you had to kill or be killed, so you did what you had to do to survive. You may have been afraid when you were in here with the bazerats, but you never really felt like you were in real danger, did you? Not with everyone outside."

She didn't answer, but I saw her relax slightly as my words sank in.

"You've been using your power to heal creatures most of your life and you know how to manipulate it and how to release it in controlled bursts, right?"

She nodded.

"It's the same power; you just used it offensively with the demons. I think you can learn to use your power as a weapon if you start thinking of it as one and the same."

Hope flared in her eyes for a few seconds before it turned to panic. "I can't… I can't do it…"

I gently gripped her stiff shoulders. "This really frightens you, doesn't it?"

Her head jerked.

"All the more reason for you to learn to master it. If you don't, it will control you instead, and we both know how much you hate being controlled." I smiled. "You trust me, right?"

She averted her gaze. "Yes."

"And I trust you with my life."

Her eyes flew back to mine, and I saw her surprise, her uncertainty.

"I trust you, Sara, and I know you won't hurt me," I said confidently.

"Yes, but –"

"You were afraid to connect with your Mori at first, but you did it and now you no longer fear it. This is no different."

I took her hands and laid them over my heart to show my faith in her. "Start slow and see what happens. You can pull away anytime you need to."

"Okay, but not here." She took her hands from my chest and reached for one of my hands instead.

"Do you feel anything?" she asked after a minute.

I shook my head, and she tried again. Still nothing. Her hands began to glow. I stared at them in amazement. "Your hands feel warmer. What are you doing?"

"I'm sending my power to them like I do when I do a healing." Her brow furrowed, and she let go of my hand. "I don't think this is going to work. I only know how to heal things, and I don't know what I did to those demons."

I'd suspected this was the case, but I'd wanted to start where she was comfortable before I suggested something more aggressive.

"Your offensive power only surfaces when there is a demon nearby, but it doesn't sense my Mori," I said.

Relief filled her eyes. "That's a good thing though, right?"

"It is as long as we keep our demons restrained, but what happens if we allow them closer to the surface?" I replied, already calling my demon forth.

She tried to pull away, but I captured her hands again as I stared into her startled eyes.

"Nikolas, whatever you are thinking is a really bad idea," she said fearfully.

I watched in fascination as tiny blue sparks moved over her face and made strands of her hair lift into the air. My eyes met hers, and I sucked in a breath at the golden specks shimmering in the green of her eyes.

Sara ripped her hands from mine, her wild eyes telling me my theory was right. Now I needed to show her why I trusted her with my life. Her natural instinct to protect those she cared about was too strong for her to harm me.

She backed away. "Nikolas, please stop. I don't want to do this. I don't want to hurt you."

Using my demon speed, I moved out of sight behind her. Before she could turn, I grabbed her shoulders to startle a reaction from her.

She screamed, and a buzzing tingle raced up my arms.

A second later, I was airborne.

I hit the wooden seats with enough force to punch the air from my lungs. The arm of one of the seats jabbed me hard in the ribs before I rolled backward onto the floor, dazed with the faint smell of ozone filling my nostrils.

I lay still for a moment, trying to clear the fog in my head and taking stock of my aches. There was definitely gunna paste and a trip to the healing baths in my near future.

Hands shook me, and I heard a frantic voice saying my name.

I opened my eyes to find her leaning over me. She was so close that my first thought was how easy it would be to reach up and pull her mouth down on mine. The thought brought a smile to my lips.

"I said you could do it."

Her mouth gaped, and she stared at me.

"You jerk! You...you asshole!" she shouted as her small fist punched me in the chest. Then she was up and running for the door.

I beat her to it, and she ran into my chest. She tried to go around me, but I captured her arms and refused to let her go.

"Sara, we needed to test your power to see if you can use it at will, and now we know."

She glared at me through her tears. "At will? I almost fried your ass! If I hadn't pulled it back in time, you'd be singing a different tune. No, actually, you'd probably be dead."

"But you did control it, as I knew you would. You want to know how I knew that?"

I released her, and she folded her arms across her chest. "Please, educate me."

I met her angry glower with a smile. "I know because if there is one thing I have learned about you, it's that you are incapable of hurting someone – unless they are trying to hurt you or someone you care about. Then all bets are off."

She looked away from me, and her voice was hoarse when she said, "You scared the hell out of me. I thought..."

Warmth flooded my chest at the emotion in her voice. Did I hear something more than friendly affection, or was it wishful thinking?

"I'm sorry," I said softly. "I didn't want to frighten you, but the only way to get you to show your power was to expose you to a demon and to put you on the defensive. Now we know what you can do, and we can work with that and teach you to call on it when you need it."

"I am *never* doing that again," she declared.

"Not that, no." I was glad to see anger replace her fear. "We won't have to try anything that drastic next time."

"Next time?" She glared at me. "What part of *never* do you not understand?"

I met her angry gaze. "So you refuse to use your power on me again, no matter what I do?"

"That's right."

"And how will you stop it?" I asked, although I already knew the answer.

She frowned. "What do you mean?"

"If I bring my Mori out again and come after you, what's to stop your power from attacking me again?"

She shifted restlessly from one foot to the other. "*I* will stop it."

"How?"

"I just will, okay?" she snapped. "I know what it is now, and I won't let it get away from me again."

I watched as the impact of her declaration hit her. Her expression went from indignation to confusion to chagrin, all within the space of a minute. She wasn't happy with my methods, but she had to admit they were effective. In forcing her to use her power, I'd shown her she could control it.

"So now that we have that settled, why don't we try something easy that doesn't involve throwing me across the room? If you are up for it, that is."

She scowled at me and marched over to where we'd been working with the weights. "Fine, but don't blame me if I knock you on your butt again. And you owe me for making me believe I killed you."

Her refusal to concede gracefully made me laugh as I joined her. I could only imagine what she was going to ask for. "Okay. What do you want?"

She smiled mischievously. "I need to go into town this week to pick up a bunch of stuff for Oscar before he gets here."

"Oscar?"

"My cat. Nate is bringing him when he comes for Thanksgiving."

"Oh."

At first I was a little disappointed that all she wanted was a ride to the pet store. But then I realized this was a great opportunity to spend time with her outside of training.

Over the next hour, we worked on her power. She threatened to walk out if I tried to get her to use it on me again, so we had to make do without a demon. It made for a frustrating session for her, but I wouldn't let her stop until she managed to call on her power and produce a few sparks. Her little smile as we left the arena told me she was pleased by how far she'd come in only an hour.

"When do you want to go into town?" I asked as I opened the door for her.

"Can we go this weekend?"

"I think we can arrange that," I said, already thinking about places to eat in Butler Falls.

She stopped walking and turned to me. "Chris told me you were the one who had Hugo and Woolf sent here. Thank you for doing that."

"You don't have to thank me. They belong with you."

We walked across the lawn. To my left, I spotted one of the trainees practicing with a sword near the trees. It was the boy who had helped Sara gather up the karks yesterday.

"That boy is going to cut his own head off," I said, watching him fumble with the weapon several times. When he saw me looking his way, he almost dropped the sword.

"Can I exchange the trip into town for something else?" Sara blurted, drawing my attention back to her.

"You don't want to go into town?"

She bit her lip. "I do, but I want something more now."

"All right, let's have it." If it meant more time with her, I was all for it.

"I want you to teach Michael not to cut off his head."

Who? It took me a moment to realize she was referring to the boy with the sword.

She lifted a shoulder. "He needs a lesson in sword fighting a lot more than I need a ride to town. Besides, you have no idea how much this will mean to him. He looks up to you a lot."

I glanced at the boy. Sara was willing to give up her trip to town just to make him happy. Her capacity for kindness never ceased to amaze me.

"If that's what you want."

She smiled. "It is."

"Okay, I'll see what I can do for him, but no promises. And I'll still take you into town." I wasn't quite as willing to give up our time together.

"Thanks!"

Her hug took me completely by surprise. Before I could react to her arms around my waist, she released me and set off toward the main building. I stared after her until she disappeared around the corner.

Shaking my head, I turned to Michael, who was picking his sword up from the ground. I smiled as I started toward the boy. If giving her friend a sword lesson was enough to earn a hug from Sara, I'd volunteer to train the whole damn group next time.

* * *

That afternoon, instead of working with Sara on her studies, I stood at the window in my apartment, waiting for her to leave the menagerie with her hellhounds. Aside from a fleeting moment in the cellar of the house in Portland, I hadn't seen her interact with the beasts.

Sahir, who had over half a century of experience working with creatures, had assured Tristan Sara was safe with the hellhounds. That didn't stop me from being uneasy about her going off alone with them in the woods.

The door to the menagerie opened and Sara emerged, alone. She walked a few steps then turned back to the door and said something.

My hands gripped the windowsill when two massive black bodies hurled toward her. Sara only laughed as the hellhounds ran around her in circles, pressing against her like overgrown puppies.

I released the breath I was holding when she motioned with her hand and both hellhounds heeled on either side of her like well-trained dogs.

I watched them disappear into the trees before I turned away from the window. My first instinct was to follow them and make sure Sara was safe. I pushed that thought aside. It was obvious the beasts adored her, and hellhounds would protect their master with their lives.

I spent the rest of the afternoon with Tristan and Chris, going over the reports of vampire activity around the country. In the last month, there had been more attacks and sightings than we normally saw in half a year. We all suspected it was the work of Eli's Master, but the behavior was out of character for a vampire Master.

Every Master I'd hunted had been careful to hide their presence, because the last thing they wanted was to draw the attention of the Mohiri. It didn't matter how strong a vampire was; they would eventually die at the end of a Mohiri sword. So why was this one suddenly making his presence known after staying hidden so well all these years?

I felt torn when I thought about the warriors who were out there hunting the Master. He was responsible for so much pain in Sara's life, and I wanted to be the one to end his life, to make him pay for her suffering.

But a hunt could take months, even years, and I couldn't be away from Sara that long – not that I wanted to be. The need to be close to her was almost a physical one, and it got stronger every time I saw her. It was my Mori's way of ensuring I spent time with her, thus strengthening our bond.

When the light began to fade, and Sahir hadn't called to let us know Sara had returned, I headed outside with Chris to watch for her.

"She's most likely enjoying her taste of freedom and just lost track of time," Chris said.

"I know." But I worried anyway.

A few minutes later, she walked out of the woods with the hellhounds. Even through the gathering dusk I could see her happy smile when she gave us a quick wave and headed straight to the menagerie.

Chris waved a hand in her direction. "Safe and sound. You worry too much, my friend."

"You will too when it's your mate going off alone."

One corner of his mouth lifted. "Not gonna happen."

"That's what I thought too. The last person I expected or wanted to find when I walked into that bar was my mate." Now, I couldn't imagine my life without her.

He shook his head. "You never expected to find your mate. I, on the other hand, am well aware that I could have potential mates out there, and I am doing my best to avoid that trap for as long as possible."

I laughed at his choice of words. "I may not have wanted it at first, but I never felt trapped. I could have left if I'd wanted to."

"Right," he scoffed.

"Hello," called Seamus as he and Niall walked out of the woods, no doubt back from watching over Sara during her walk.

"Just the lads we were hoping to see," Niall said as they approached us. "How about a few hands of poker tonight?"

"Unless you have plans," Seamus added, giving me a meaningful look.

I raised an eyebrow, and he chuckled.

"Celine was looking for you at lunch, and she had that determined look in her eye."

I groaned inwardly. I had managed to avoid Celine for the most part since I returned, but she didn't give up easily.

"What time does the game start?"

The brothers laughed and said we were meeting at Niall's at seven. They headed into the main building, and I looked at Chris.

"Feel like sparring for an hour?"

He snorted softly. "You mean hiding, don't you?"

"Something like that."

∗   ∗   ∗

"I have to say I'm surprised to see the two of you sticking around for more than a few days." Niall tossed two chips on top of the pile in the middle of the table. "Especially you, Nikolas. Can't remember the last time you stayed here more than a week."

I added chips to his. "Thought it was time for a change of pace."

"Uh-huh." Seamus snickered. "Or a vacation after running around Maine after a certain wee lass. Word is she led you guys on a merry chase."

"You could say that." Chris studied his cards before he threw them down. He leaned back in his chair and smiled at Seamus. "I've learned never to underestimate my little cousin."

Seamus snorted loudly. "You two must be going soft. We've had no trouble with her since she came here. She tried to go off alone a few times, but we brought her back."

"She wouldn't have given us the slip in Maine," Niall stated with a lopsided grin. "Right, bro?"

"Right."

I laughed off their gibes. Niall and Seamus were fine warriors, but they were no match for Sara, even on a good day. Put them all together on her turf, and they'd be singing a different tune.

Niall laid his cards face up on the table. "Read 'em and weep, lads."

Seamus harrumphed and threw down his own cards.

I spread out my straight next to Niall's three queens, and he swore.

"You are the luckiest son of a bitch. You know that?"

I smiled because he didn't know how right he was.

Chris dealt the next hand, and I went to pour another glass of Niall's Scotch. When I came back to the table, Seamus peered at me over his cards.

"So, I heard a rumor about you working with the trainees. That true?"

"Only with Sara," I said. "Tristan and I decided she would do better with someone she knows."

Seamus tossed down two of his cards. "Hell. I'd train her if Tristan asked me. Wouldn't mind seeing that pretty face every day."

I studied my cards, pretending not to hear him.

"Maybe I should offer to work with her," he said. "Free you up so you can get back to doing what you love."

My jaw tightened.

"You go kill things, and I'll show the lass some Irish moves. Win-win situation for both of us, right?"

The cards in my hand began to buckle.

"Ha!" Seamus gave Niall a victorious grin. "Pay up, bro."

Niall's mouth turned down. "You don't even like that album."

"I said it wasn't my favorite one, but you know I like all of Johnny Cash's stuff."

"Since when?"

I stared at the two brothers with a mix of irritation and confusion.

"What are you two going on about?" Chris asked.

Seamus looked at me with a smug expression. "I told Niall you had it bad for the lass. He said she was too young and sweet to interest you. We made a friendly wager, which he just lost."

"You don't have proof he's into her," Niall argued. "He just might not want your ugly mug around her."

Seamus snorted. "You do realize we're identical twins."

"I'm still better looking."

I shook my head at them, used to their sibling banter. "Are we playing this hand or not?"

"Sure." Seamus exchanged a look with his brother. "Let's make this more interesting. Best hand gets to train Sara tomorrow."

"Seamus," Chris said with a note of warning in his voice.

I set my cards down, trying to ignore the heat rising in my chest. Seamus and I had been friends for years, and I knew he was only baiting me for fun.

"I have a better idea. Let's duel over it."

Seamus stared at me for a moment before he shook his head. "I like all my parts right where they are."

"Good, that's settled." I picked up my cards.

No one mentioned Sara again, and the four of us had an enjoyable evening. Seamus and Niall would have played poker all night, but I left at ten to take a walk around the grounds, something I did most nights before I retired.

I was walking back from the river when Celine intercepted me. Most women I knew would have pretended it was a chance encounter. Not Celine.

"Have you been avoiding me, Nikolas?" she asked in a husky voice as we walked back to the main building.

"I've been busy since I got back," I replied without answering her question.

"So I see. I hear you've been working with Tristan's granddaughter. How sweet of you to help that unfortunate girl."

She stopped walking, forcing me to stop out of courtesy. Her lips curled into a smile. "Why don't you join me in one of my training sessions this week? The other trainees would be thrilled to work with the great Nikolas Danshov."

"I'll see if I can fit it in. I'm sure the boys would rather have you as a trainer though."

She laughed and put a hand on my shoulder. "I think the two of us could give them a lesson they'd never forget."

My Mori shifted angrily, not enjoying her closeness. It need not have worried. There was only one female whose touch I wanted, and nothing would change that. Soon everyone else would know it too, and Celine would have no choice but to end her futile pursuit of me.

"Nikolas, I was hoping to find you out here." Tristan strode toward us, his shrewd gaze sizing up the situation. "I wanted to talk to you about a job."

I frowned, stepping away from Celine. "I'm not taking on new jobs right now."

He stopped and greeted Celine before looking at me again. "It's in Boise, and it'll take less than a day. Why don't we go to my office so I can tell you about it?"

I nodded, and we bade Celine good night. She smiled graciously because she was a warrior first and foremost, and she understood the importance of our work.

"Is there really a job in Boise, or did you just say that to give me an excuse to leave?" I asked as the two of us entered the building.

Tristan chuckled. "There is a job, but we could have discussed it tomorrow. You looked like you could use a rescue."

I followed him into his office. "I guess I owe you one. Tell me about this job."

CHAPTER 20

"YOU BUSY TOMORROW?" I asked Chris when he sat with Tristan and me at breakfast the next morning.

"Nothing I can't reschedule. What do you have in mind?"

"We have a warlock selling bad spells in Boise," Tristan said. "Nothing too dangerous, but three people have been hurt using his magic. I'd like you two to have a kind word with him before it gets out of hand."

Chris shrugged. "Sure. I'm up for a day trip. But why didn't you get the Boise team to talk to him?"

Tristan smiled. "The Boise team is fairly young, and you two have more experience dealing with warlocks."

"Good morning, gentlemen."

"Morning," the three of us answered as Celine laid her tray next to mine and took the seat beside me.

Celine said something to me, but I was distracted when I sensed Sara's arrival. I glanced around, but she wasn't in the room yet.

We'd had a great session yesterday, and I looked forward to spending today with her. This morning, I planned to take her back to the lake because she'd enjoyed it so much the last time. After lunch, we were going to spend a few hours on her studies. She'd learned a lot from her friend Remy, but there was so much she didn't know.

"Nikolas?"

I looked at Celine, who looked a little annoyed that I'd been ignoring her.

"I'm sorry. What did you say?"

"I asked if you had given any thought to joining me in one of my training sessions." She leaned in. "I'm sure Chris wouldn't mind working with Sara one afternoon this week to free you up."

Chris's smile was full of mischief. "I'd love to teach my little cousin a few tricks."

Movement behind him drew my eyes to the door, just in time to see Sara's back as she hurried from the dining hall.

I stared after her. Sara didn't skip breakfast. Was she ill?

She'd looked okay when we parted ways yesterday, but I hadn't seen her since. Had I pushed her too hard in training? Maybe I should have gone to see her after dinner.

"Excuse me." I stood and picked up my tray, ignoring the surprised faces of my breakfast companions. I dropped my tray in one of the bins and turned toward the door.

My eyes fell on a side table piled high with baskets of muffins and pastries, and I snatched up a blueberry muffin wrapped in plastic. I'd seen Sara eating these all the time back in New Hastings, so I knew she liked them.

Something told me she had gone outside, so I left by the main entrance and looked around for her. I didn't see or feel her, but she couldn't have gone far. Knowing her love of the woods, I started toward them until I picked up her presence off to my right, in the direction of the river.

The sight of her sitting on the riverbank, with her forehead resting on her knees, which were drawn close to her chest, caused my stomach to tighten. She looked so small and lost against the backdrop of the foaming water, and all I wanted to do was take her in my arms and comfort her.

She didn't look up when I approached, and my steps faltered when I felt pain coming through our bond.

"Are you okay?" I asked.

She started in surprise, but she didn't answer.

I walked over to stand beside her. "You left without eating, and you can't train on an empty stomach. These are your favorite, right?"

Her head tilted back, and she stared at the muffin I held out to her. "Thanks," she said quietly, taking it from my hand without looking at me.

"Are you going to tell me what is wrong with you?" Something had upset her, and I wished she felt like she could talk to me.

"I'm fine."

I sat beside her. "I think I know you well enough to know that is not true."

"I didn't sleep last night and I'm tired," she said thickly, still not meeting my eyes.

"Is that all? You sound upset."

I could sense she was distressed, and I didn't believe it had anything to do with a bad night's sleep. Frustration gnawed at me. I hated seeing her like this and not knowing how to help her.

She lifted her head to stare at the river. "Not getting any sleep messes me up."

Maybe forcing her to use her power on me yesterday had affected her more than she'd let on. She'd told me once that using her power weakened her, and I'd seen the effects of it when she'd healed Roland. She'd looked okay when we parted ways, but she could have been hiding it. Sara was very good at keeping things to herself.

"Perhaps we overdid it yesterday in training," I suggested.

She nodded. "Maybe you're right."

What she needed was a day out. She'd been here a month, training almost every day. The one time she'd gotten a day away, she'd been attacked and spent the night in the medical ward. And I'd been pushing her in training. She needed a break.

"We'll skip training today. Is there anything else you want to do instead? We could take that trip to town."

There was a short pause, and I thought she was going to say yes.

"I think I'll eat my muffin, and then I'll go take Hugo and Woolf for a walk."

I felt a small pang of disappointment, but I pushed it away. Her needs were all that mattered. She was upset and being with the hounds comforted her.

I got to my feet. "Just as long as you don't do anything to tire yourself too much. I'll see you later."

I walked a few steps before she called, "See you, and thanks again for the muffin."

"Anytime," I called back with a smile.

Free from my plans for the day, I found Tristan and told him I'd visit the warlock today instead of tomorrow. Chris and I drove to Boise and found the warlock's residence that had been hastily vacated. Warlocks had a lot of tricks up their sleeves, and this one apparently knew when someone was looking for him. We spent the next day and a half tracking him down and getting him to clean up his mess.

It was a day longer than I'd planned to be away from Sara, and I caught myself speeding more than once on the drive back to Westhorne. It still amazed me how my life had changed since I met her. A few months ago, I'd thought nothing of being on the road for weeks, sometimes months, at a time. Now I could only think about getting back to her.

We made it back in time for dinner. I checked in with Tristan to let him know the warlock problem was resolved, and then I headed for the dining hall.

Sara and Jordan were leaving just as I entered, and Sara gave me a small smile. She appeared to be in better spirits and no longer upset by whatever had been bothering her yesterday.

After dinner, Chris and I went to the arena to spar. We fought for an hour before Chris lowered his sword and declared he'd had enough.

He rubbed his shoulder. "We need to find a better way for you to work off some of that aggression."

"What aggression?"

Chris snorted. "You've been wound up for two days. I thought being back here would improve your mood, but my aching shoulder says otherwise."

I started to shake my head and stopped because he was right; I *was* wound up. Every minute I spent with Sara strengthened our bond and intensified my need to be with her. It was a constant struggle to be what she needed and not reveal my true feelings for her. Being away from her had been hard for me and my Mori.

"I can guess your mood has something to do with my little cousin. You two on the outs?"

"No. She just needed a break." I told him about our training session two days ago when I'd tricked her into using her power on me. "I think I pushed her too hard."

Chris whistled. "You are a braver man than I am. I heard what she did to that lamprey demon."

"It was a risk, but a worthwhile one. She can't fight or use a sword yet, but she has this powerful weapon inside her. She's afraid of using it because she thinks she'll hurt one of us. Now she knows how to call on her power and how to control it, and she doesn't have to be afraid of harming us."

"I'm impressed."

"She is impressive," I agreed.

"I'm talking about you. Who knew you had a trainer hidden inside of you all this time?"

I laughed. "Only for her."

"Trainees everywhere will be sad to hear that," he quipped as we walked to the door.

I followed him outside and came to a halt when I saw Sara and Sahir walking quickly toward the menagerie.

"Where's the fire?" Chris called.

"The young griffin we got in today is in distress, and Sara is going to help me with her," Sahir replied.

Griffins were intelligent creatures, but also vicious when they felt threatened. I'd watched one rip apart a dozen poachers that had stupidly tried to raid its nest after I'd warned them to stay away. A young griffin could be even more dangerous if they were frightened.

"Griffin wrangling? Another one of your talents, Cousin?" Chris said.

"Griffins can be very dangerous when they are cornered. Sara is not going in there unprotected," I said firmly, walking over to them.

Sara frowned at me. "She's just a child, Nikolas."

I stepped between her and the menagerie. "That child could easily rip a grizzly bear apart with her claws."

She raised an eyebrow. "So could the troll you thought was going to kill me."

Sahir stared at us. "Troll?"

"I'll tell you about him later," she said. "Let's take care of your griffin first."

"Not without us," I said.

Sara huffed and rolled her eyes. "Fine, but you better not frighten her. You two can stay by the door unless the *vicious* griffin attacks me."

Chris snickered and leaned toward me to whisper loudly. "I think she's gotten bossy since she came here. What have you been teaching her?"

Scowling, I pushed him away and followed Sara into the menagerie. I took up a position near the door where I could watch her and jump in if necessary.

Chris didn't speak when he stood beside me, but his tight grip on his sword told me he was worried too despite his joking.

Sara and Sahir moved toward the cages. She stopped to pet the hellhounds and called a greeting to the wyvern from a safe distance.

My whole body tensed as Sara walked past the cages toward the center of the building. At the same time, I couldn't help but be amazed by her composure and her lack of fear. You would think she was approaching a baby bird that had fallen from its nest, not a creature that could kill a man with one swipe of its powerful paw.

Despite the instinct that screamed for me to pull her away from this new threat, I did nothing but watch her. I didn't understand the effect Sara had on creatures, but I had to trust she knew what she was doing.

She stopped and looked up, and my gaze followed hers to the small griffin perched in the rafters of the domed building. The griffin's feathers were filthy and dull, and it had a bare spot on its neck where some of its feathers had fallen out. Judging by its size, I guessed it to be no more than four or five years of age.

"Wow, oh, wow," Sara said in an awed voice, staring raptly at the griffin.

"Sara, this is Minuet," Sahir told her in a soft voice.

"She's incredible."

He nodded grimly. "She won't be that way for long if we don't get her down from there and get her to eat something."

"Right, sorry. I've just never seen anything like her." She walked over to sit on the floor with her back against the bars of an empty cage. "Sahir, could you stand with the others so you don't frighten her?"

He stayed where he was. "What are you going to do?"

"I'm just going to talk to her for a bit."

I took a step forward when he left her and walked toward us.

He shook his head and held up a hand to stop me. "She'll be okay," he whispered confidently.

Sara's soothing voice filled the room. "I hope you don't mind me keeping you company, Minuet. I bet it's pretty scary and lonely for you here. I know how you feel. I miss my family, too."

The griffin shifted restlessly but made no move to leave her perch.

"Minuet, would you like to hear a story about a girl who got lost far away from her family?" Sara asked softly. "Kind of like you, I guess. It has a happy ending, I promise.

"The girl's name was...um...Mary, and one day she disappeared, and none of her friends or family knew where she'd gone. They all thought she was lost to them forever. But what they didn't know was that Mary was very sick, so sick she almost died, and some good faeries had taken Mary home with them to heal her.

"For a long time, Mary lay in a deep sleep while the faeries worked their magic on her. And then one day, she woke up and found herself in the most amazing place she had ever seen.

"Mary was lying in the softest bed you could ever imagine, surrounded by walls made of vines and pretty flowers. Then the vines moved and in walked the most beautiful red-haired sylph who told Mary they had healed her.

"Then she shocked Mary by telling her that she was actually half faerie, which was why the faeries had saved her. She took Mary outside and gave her the most delicious food and drink, then took her on a walk to show her a place so beautiful it brought tears to Mary's eyes.

"Mary and her new friend talked for a long time, and the sylph told her this was her home now if she chose to stay. Mary looked around her and knew she might never feel as safe or as content as she did at that moment. She could have that forever if she gave up her life in the human world and stayed in Faerie."

I should have been watching the griffin, but I couldn't tear my eyes from Sara's face as she described her time in Faerie. The joy in her eyes when she remembered the experience caused an ache to start up in my chest. In Faerie she had been safe and pampered, and she never had to worry about the dangers of this world. Was I selfish for wanting her here with me instead of in that beautiful, safe place?

Movement from above drew my attention, and I sucked in a sharp breath as the griffin stepped off the rafter and flew in a small circle before descending to land near Sara.

I raised my sword and took a step toward Sara before Chris grabbed my arm.

"Look at the griffin," he whispered. "It's not upset."

He was right. The griffin stood quietly, watching Sara with interest. But there was nothing threatening in its stance.

Sara went on with her story as if there wasn't a griffin standing a few feet away. I tried to listen, but all of my attention was on the creature. It looked calm now, but griffins were unpredictable. If it attacked, I'd only have a second to reach Sara.

The griffin let out a small squawk, and I realized Sara had stopped talking.

"I know it's scary being away from home," she said in a crooning voice. "I don't know if you can understand me, but I promise you're safe here with us until we find your family."

It took all of my strength not to move when the griffin began to walk toward Sara. It stood over her for several long seconds before it lowered its head and rubbed its face against Sara's. It was a gesture of affection shared only among griffins of the same flock. Then it turned away and marched into the cage across from where Sara sat.

Sara stood and walked over to quietly shut the cage door. Her face glowed when she turned and smiled at us.

Chris found his voice first. "I thought I'd seen it all when I met the troll, but this…"

"Sara, do you realize what just happened?" Sahir croaked.

She frowned and shook her head.

"She marked you with her scent. To her you are one of her flock now. I-I have never seen anything like it."

Grinning, she started toward us. "So, I'm like an honorary griffin? Cool."

She gave me a smug look. "See, piece of cake."

I heard a scratching sound, and it took me several seconds to realize it was coming from the wyvern. My eyes flew back to Sara, and my gut wrenched sickly when I saw how close she was to its cage.

I dropped my sword and ran as flames spewed from between the bars of the cage. A second later, I reached her and spun her away. I wasn't fast enough to prevent the flames from touching her, and I held her against me with one arm while I smothered the fire on her sleeve with my free hand. The smell of seared flesh filled my nose as Sara cried out in pain.

Blood pounded in my ears, and I fought to control the fear simmering below my skin. If I had been one second slower…

Sahir ran toward us. "Sara, are you okay?"

"Goddamnit, Sahir, I told you it wasn't safe in here for her," I roared at the warrior, who came up short. "That thing could have killed her."

"It's not his fault," Sara rasped in a pain-filled voice. "I was careless. I got too close."

"The hell it's not," I bit out. "He should never have allowed you in here."

Chris moved toward us. "Nikolas."

I looked at him and saw the warning in his eyes, the same one he'd given me when I almost lost it the night Sara was hurt by the crocotta.

Sanity returned and I loosened my hold on her, but I kept an arm around her waist. Touching her was the only thing calming my Mori right now.

Sara tried to pull away. "D-don't blame Sahir for this. I'm old enough to make my own decisions." She glared up at me. "Let me go."

I ignored her demand. All I could think about was how close she had come to being engulfed in flames. "You can't keep taking risks like this."

"Would you just get the hell over yourself?" she yelled, pulling hard.

I released her so she didn't injure herself further.

She whirled to face me, her eyes flashing with pain and fury. "You don't get to say where I can go or how I spend my time. And I'm not some weakling you need to jump in and save all the time."

I gave her a disbelieving look. I wasn't trying to control her life. I just couldn't stand to see her put herself in danger. Like just now.

"Okay, you just did and I'm grateful, but that doesn't give you the right to yell at everyone or treat me like I'm useless. If that's all you think of me, I wish you'd just stayed away."

The hurt in her voice cooled my own anger. I took a step toward her.

"I didn't say you were —"

"Just forget it." She put up her good arm and let out a whimper of pain.

"We need to get you to the medical ward," I said, taking another step toward her.

She turned away from me. "I don't need your help. I can get there on my own."

I followed her. "I'm coming with you."

"No, you're not. Just leave me alone." She walked stiffly to the door and pushed it open, the set of her shoulders matching the anger in her eyes.

I stayed behind her as she ran to the main building, and I followed her into the medical ward where she was immediately whisked away by one of the healers. I paced the ward for almost thirty minutes before the healer came out of the room and assured me Sara was no longer in pain.

"You can go in now, if you want to," she said.

I thanked her and went to Sara's room. I knew she didn't want to see me, but I needed to clear up a few things between us. And I needed to see for myself that she was okay.

Sara was lying on the exam table with her arm resting beside her, wrapped in gauze. Her face was paler than usual, but she didn't appear to be in pain.

She saw it was me and turned her face away to look at the ceiling.

"I'm really not up to arguing with you again, Nikolas."

I stayed by the door, not wanting to upset her, but unable to leave. "I wanted to make sure you were okay."

"I'm fine. I've had worse injuries, remember?"

"I remember," I said, my voice rough as I recalled her standing at the edge of a cliff with a knife in her chest.

She sat up, her legs hanging over the edge of the table, and held up her arm. "Look, all taken care of. I'll be as good as new in no time."

Her words were light, but I could sense her discomfort, and I cursed myself for being the cause of it. I'd come home, looking forward to seeing her, and all I'd done was upset her.

"You don't have to stay with me," she said quietly. "The healer said I'm fine."

"I'm sorry for yelling at you." My gaze held her surprised one. "I never meant to make you feel useless. It just angers me to see you taking risks like that."

Her nostrils flared slightly. "What do you expect me to do – hide out in my room so I don't get hurt? I can't be safe all the time. You have to realize that I will get hurt sometimes, especially if I become a warrior."

The thought of her being hurt again made my jaw clench. "I thought you didn't want to be a warrior."

"What am I training for, if not to become one? Isn't that what we do?"

Her agitation pulled at me through our bond, and I walked toward her. "I'm teaching you to defend yourself if you ever need it, not to go out looking for trouble."

"I'm not looking for trouble, and that thing with Alex was a freak accident. It could have happened to anyone." She looked away, her voice cracking. "Why is it so hard for you to believe I can take care of myself? I'm not a child, you know."

I stopped in front of her. She lifted her head, her face flushed, and her beautiful green eyes pulling the air from my lungs.

"No, you are not a child," I said gruffly.

A voice in my head told me to stop, but the need to be close to her, to touch her, was too strong. She didn't move when I lifted my hand. Her breath hitched, but her eyes never left mine as I brushed the pad of my thumb gently over her jaw. I imagined my mouth moving along her skin to finally taste her soft lips. Need tightened my gut, and my body almost trembled from the strain of denying myself what I had craved for so long.

"Sara," I whispered hoarsely. I closed my eyes and rested my forehead against hers, fighting my excited Mori and my own desire. I didn't have the strength to pull away, not unless she asked me to.

"Yell at me. Tell me to go," I said, even as I silently begged her to ask me to stay.

She pulled back slightly and laid her palms against my chest. I waited for her to push me away.

"Nikolas, I..." she breathed, and in those two words I heard confusion and doubt.

But no withdrawal.

I cupped her chin and lifted her face to mine. The innocent desire in her eyes punched me square in the chest, and my Mori came roaring to life.

Mine, it growled, reaching for its mate.

Her Mori answered, and she leaned in. Her lips parted, and her fingers curled in the front of my sweater.

Placing a hand on either side of her face, I gently tugged her to me until my lips grazed hers. Her bottom lip trembled when I kissed it softly, and I slanted my mouth to claim hers at last. Her lips parted slightly in silent invitation, and I pulled her closer as I coaxed her mouth open and deepened the kiss.

When her tongue shyly touched mine, a fire began low in my belly and I had to suppress a groan. Her timid eagerness told me this was her first kiss, and I reveled in the knowledge that no other man had tasted her mouth. She was mine, just as I was hers. My heart knew it, our Mori knew it, and one day soon, she would know it too.

It took most of my willpower to break the kiss. I pulled back just far enough to look into her eyes, and close enough to feel her warm breath mingling with mine. One kiss from her would never be enough, and already I craved her lips. But first, I needed to make sure she was okay. I didn't want to rush her into anything she wasn't ready for.

She wore a bewildered expression, which quickly turned to shock as her eyes widened and she gasped softly.

Her reaction was like cold water dousing my desire. I'd sworn to myself and Tristan I would take things slowly with Sara, to spend time with her and let her get to know me better before I took the next step. She'd been injured and emotional, and I'd taken advantage, even if I hadn't meant to. She deserved better than that.

Releasing her, I stepped back. "I'm sorry. I did not mean to..."

She flinched and looked down, her cheeks rosy with embarrassment.

My chest ached as self-loathing filled me. It killed me to see her in distress and to know I had caused it.

"Sara —"

"No." She whispered the word, but I could hear the tears in her voice.

Every part of me wanted to reach out to her, but it felt like a chasm stretched between us. I stood there for a long moment, waiting for her to meet my eyes again. But she refused to look at me.

"I'm sorry," I said softly before I turned and walked away from her.

It was the hardest thing I had ever done.

CHAPTER 21

I PULLED MY sword from the dead vampire and stepped over him to the large winding staircase. Halfway up the stairs, I heard a muted scream from somewhere on the first floor, but I resumed my silent climb to the second floor. The others would handle whatever was happening down here. I had a more important mission to tend to.

The vampire came at me as soon as my foot touched the landing. He was fast, but not as fast as I was, and I sliced him across the midsection before he could reach me.

He cried out and grabbed at his stomach as he stumbled backward. Hate blazed in his eyes as I advanced on him. He turned to run, and I decapitated him before he took a step. His body crumpled to the floor as his head rolled down the stairs.

I looked both ways at the row of closed doors on the second floor. Standing still, I let my Mori hearing search for movement.

To my left, I picked up a muffled cry. With grim determination, I moved down the hallway and came to a stop in front of one of the doors. I listened again. From inside the room, I heard a child's frightened sob.

I stared at the door, planning my next move. There would be at least one vampire in the room, if not more, but if I waited for the others to reach me, it might be too late for the children.

A sound behind me alerted me to the arrival of another vampire. I spun to face him and saw the shock on his face as my sword went through his chest.

He let out a gurgling cry as I withdrew my blade. Instead of plunging it in him again to finish him off, I grabbed him by the shoulders and hurled him through the closed door.

The door crashed inward and slammed against the wall as the vampire landed in a heap at the feet of a female vampire crouched in the middle of the room. The blonde vampire showed me her bloody fangs and held her clawed hands defensively in front of her. Blood dripped from her chin, and I feared I was too late.

A whimper to my right had me glancing at the two young children huddled in the middle of the large bed. We'd gotten word two days ago from Salt Lake City that a pair of orphans had been found. But before the team could retrieve them, vampires had gotten to them. No one, especially not me, had expected to find them alive.

The boy had his arms wrapped protectively around his twin sister, whose face was buried against his neck. The shoulder of her top was blood-soaked, and her body shook from her sobs. Long dark hair spilled down her back, looking so much like Sara's that I almost shook from the fury boiling inside me.

I gave the vampire my full attention.

She licked blood from the corner of her mouth and sneered at me. "You interrupted my meal. Such a delicacy, young Mohiri blood. So sweet and rich."

"Consider it your last supper," I answered coldly, not rising to the bait.

Her brows drew together slightly when she realized she wasn't going to goad me into making a rash move. She began to walk around me in a wide circle. Her slow, practiced movements told me she was more deadly than the others I'd killed in the house. She wouldn't die as easily, but she *was* going to die today.

I watched her eyes, and I saw them flick to my left a split second before she blurred.

A burst of speed from my Mori saved me from her attack, although her claws managed to score my upper arms. She didn't escape unscathed either, screaming when my blade cut a deep furrow in her chest.

Most vampires would need a few seconds to recover from such a strike. This one whirled almost instantly and flew at me again.

There was no time to bring up my sword, so I caught her and flung her across the room. She slammed into the wall so hard the plaster crumbled.

She was back on her feet in less than a second, but her smile was less confident. "You're a strong one, but I'm no fledgling. Once I'm done with you, I'm going to drain those two little morsels."

My gaze flicked to the two children, and I found the boy watching me with fear-glazed eyes. No child should have to endure what these two had suffered. Their mother had been slaughtered before their eyes, and they'd spent the last two days being terrorized by her killer. It was a wonder they were still alive.

I smiled at the vampire's false bravado. She might be old and as strong as me, but I'd spent my life hunting her kind. "Let's get this over with then."

Her grin faltered, and I saw it in her eyes the moment she shifted from fight to flight mode. The only reason vampires like her lived this long was because they ran when faced with a real threat.

When she feinted toward the door, I was ready for her, and I was at the window a second before she reached it. My sword came up as she flew over my head and crashed through the glass. She screamed as she fell, and I looked through the broken pane to see her writhing on the lawn as two warriors sped around the corner.

"Take care of that for me, and send Paulette up," I said before I turned and stepped over the pair of severed legs on the floor.

I turned from the window as Chris ran into the room. He stared with wonder at the boy and girl on the bed. I understood his disbelief. It was rare that we recovered an orphan once they'd been taken by a vampire. That both twins had survived was nothing short of a miracle.

"They're injured but alive," I told Chris. "Do we have a healer on the team?"

"Paulette will know what to do."

The blonde warrior ran into the room, followed by another female warrior I didn't know. Paulette approached the bed slowly and crouched beside it. She smiled at the boy, who watched her with wary eyes. The girl still had her face hidden in her brother's shirt.

"Hey there," she said gently. "I'm Paulette. You're Colin, right?"

The boy nodded, and I knew he and his sister were in good hands. I walked out of the room with Chris trailing me.

He didn't speak until we were back on the first floor.

"You were supposed to wait for the team." He waved at the four vampires I'd dispatched a little while ago. "You couldn't save one for me?"

"If I'd waited, those children would be dead."

He had no argument for that.

I wiped my blade on the nearest vampire's pants and walked outside. Taking a deep breath of cool night air, I waited for the satisfaction that always filled me after a successful job. My Mori was quiet, sated from our seven vampire kills, but I felt none of the usual gratification. If anything, I was more wound up than when I'd arrived.

I'd come here desperately needing an outlet for my frustration and to put some distance between Sara and me. Not because I didn't want to be near her, but because I wanted it too much. Kissing her and feeling her respond to me had only intensified my need to be with her. Since the moment I left her in the medical ward, her absence was a physical ache in my chest, and my body felt like a wire strung too taut.

"You two must have had a hell of a falling out."

I looked sideways at Chris, who had come out to stand beside me. "Who?"

He rolled his eyes. "Oh, I don't know. Maybe the only person who can put you in a mood like the one you've been in since we left home. What happened after you left the menagerie that night?"

"Nothing happened." Chris was my best friend, but there was no way I was sharing something so private with him.

"Okay," he drawled. "Then I guess we'll be heading home now that the job is done. The Council will be so delighted you saved the children they'll probably forget to scold you for ignoring their orders."

I scowled and started walking to my bike, which I'd left at the end of the street. "Maybe the Council should get out of their offices every now and then, and remember what it's like in the real world."

He snorted softly. "You should tell them that."

"Maybe I will."

We reached my bike, and I stowed away my sword before I straddled the seat. "I'm going to spend another day or two here. I'll catch up with you later."

Chris gave me an understanding smile. "I'll see you at home."

*　　*　　*

I barely noticed my surroundings as I drove through Boise the next evening. My mind was too preoccupied, thinking about the long overdue conversation I needed to have with Sara when I got home. I didn't know if she was ready to hear the truth, but she deserved to know what was happening between us. There was no going back to the way things were, not after I'd kissed her.

Remorse filled me over the way I'd left her. I should have tried to talk to her, if not that night, then the next day. I'd thought I was doing the right thing by leaving and giving us both some space.

I realized now that I'd left because I'd been afraid she wanted nothing to do with me. If I'd been thinking clearly, I would have realized that no one responded to a kiss the way she had if they weren't attracted to the other person. Maybe I'd misread her reaction, and what I'd taken as distress had really been the confusion of a girl receiving her first kiss.

I'm such an idiot, I thought for the hundredth time since I left Salt Lake City. I wouldn't blame Sara if she refused to speak to me for another week. How had I managed to screw things up so badly?

A mocking laugh burst from me. I had known many women in my lifetime, and I'd always been confident and sure of myself with them. One kiss from Sara and I was fumbling like a prepubescent teen.

It was after ten when I pulled into the garage at Westhorne. Grabbing my bag and sword, I walked to the main building, wondering what Sara was doing at that moment. I'd only been gone for three days, but it felt like much longer. I was going to drop my stuff off at my place, and then I was going to find her and make things right between us.

The first place I went was her room. Not finding her there, I checked the common rooms, the library, and the menagerie. I was frowning when I entered the main hall again. It was a Saturday night, but there weren't a lot of places she would go. Maybe she was with Jordan in the other girl's room.

Disappointment pricked my chest. It looked like our talk was going to have to wait until tomorrow.

"Hey man, I thought you were in Utah."

I turned to Dax. "Change of plans."

He held up the tablet he carried. "You must have a sixth sense for trouble. We had a vampire attack in town tonight."

"An attack in Butler Falls? Are you sure?" No vampire would be stupid enough to hunt so close to one of our strongholds.

"It's the real deal, all right." He tapped on his tablet. "Chris went to check it out, and he confirmed it. Tristan's gone to town too on account of the trainees being at a party there. I'm surprised you didn't pass him –"

Icy fingers touched the back of my neck. "Sara is in town?"

"Yeah. No worries though. The party is out at a farm on Old Creek Road, and the attack happened on the other side of town. Besides, Tristan and the others are there by now."

I reached for his tablet, and he relinquished it. On it was a map of Butler Falls, zoomed in to an address on Old Creek Road. Handing the tablet back, I turned to the door.

A minute later, I was speeding toward town, dread knotting my stomach. Butler Falls hadn't had a vampire attack since we moved in next door. And now they had their first one on the night Sara was there. It was just too much of a coincidence.

I shouldn't have left Westhorne. If anything happened to Sara, I'd never forgive myself.

I couldn't help but think about the last time I'd raced to find her. I'd been too late, and I'd almost lost her. What if I was too late again? What if Tristan hadn't reached her in time?

My chest felt like it was in a vise, and my Mori was in a state of high agitation by the time I pulled into the farm's long driveway and spotted two of our SUVs. I parked behind them and strode toward the house. The sounds of laugher and music coming from the place eased my mind a little, but I wouldn't relax until I saw Sara and knew she was okay.

I was almost to the house when I spotted lights moving over at the barn. Instinct had me moving in that direction instead, and I let out a breath when I suddenly sensed Sara's presence nearby. Some of the trainees stood outside with Seamus and Niall, but there was no sign of Sara or Tristan.

I came up short when Callum walked out of the barn with an

unconscious human male over his shoulder. When Jordan appeared behind him in blood-splattered clothes and carrying a bloody knife, my heart began to pound against my ribs.

Movement in the barn entrance drew my eye, and I stared at the girl emerging from the shadows. Her clothes were covered in blood. She stumbled and would have fallen if not for Tristan. He held her up and offered to carry her.

I was too late.

Roaring filled my ears, and a deep-red veil fell over my vision as my tenuous hold on my Mori snapped.

Solmi, the demon roared ferociously, its distress and rage blending with mine. My body shook from the white hot rage consuming me. The urge to destroy anything that threatened my mate overpowered me.

Sara stopped walking and looked at me, and my gaze locked on her. A part of me registered she was well enough to stand, but all I could focus on was her pale face and torn, bloody clothes. The need to touch her, to comfort her, and to reassure myself she was okay was unbearable, and it was all I could do not to go to her and crush her to me. The pain and confusion in her eyes were all that stayed me and kept my Mori in check.

She walked briskly toward me…but then she veered to go around me.

Mine, my Mori growled, and an answering sound rumbled in my chest.

She stopped abruptly to stare at me. "Did you just growl at me?"

"Nikolas, she is okay."

I heard Tristan's words, but it was difficult to focus on anything except the girl standing too far away from me. My Mori was close to losing it, and she was the only thing keeping us together.

Tristan spoke again. "Sara, listen to me. You need to walk toward him, talk to him, and let him know you are okay."

"I don't understand." Her gaze remained locked with mine, and I could see fear creep into her eyes. "Can't he see that from here?" she asked.

"No," Tristan answered calmly. "You need to get a lot closer. He won't hurt you. If there is anyone here who is safe from him, it is you."

I wanted to speak, to tell her I would never hurt her, but I was locked in a power struggle with my demon. My Mori would not harm her, but it might hurt someone else. Sara wouldn't forgive me if that happened. I'd never forgive myself. All I could do was hold myself as still as possible as she closed the distance between us.

She stopped a few feet away and gave me a tentative smile. "Look, Nikolas, I'm perfectly fine, see? Okay, I've looked better, but that's beside the point."

My enhanced senses recognized her sunshine scent beneath the coppery smell of the blood that covered her clothes. *Mine*, the demon snarled again.

I gritted my teeth from the superhuman effort to control the demon side of me that was feral in its need to claim our mate, to take her away and make her ours.

I was only vaguely aware that Sara and Tristan were talking. Then she moved forward until she was close enough for me to see her lips tremble and hear her rapid heartbeat.

An eternity later, I felt her cold hand slide into mine, and I grasped it like a lifeline. If she pulled away now, I didn't think I could bear it.

"Let go!"

I stared down at her in confusion when she hit me in the chest with her free hand.

Then she slapped my cheek hard. "Nikolas, snap out of it! You're breaking my hand."

The pain in her voice penetrated the red haze in my mind, and I released her hand. But if I didn't touch her I'd go insane. I enfolded her tightly in my arms and buried my face in her hair, breathing in her warm scent like it was oxygen to my starved lungs.

Her arms wrapped around my waist, and I sighed as her hands rubbed my back gently.

"Hcy, it's okay. I'm here," she said softly, her touch and voice a cooling balm for the rage burning through me.

It took a while for my Mori to calm, and for the rage to recede enough for me to realize what I'd done. Shame settled like nausea in my gut as I thought about what I'd put her through and how close I'd come to losing control completely.

I looked over her head at the group who stood frozen, watching us. Their shocked faces told me they knew exactly what had just happened and why.

Sara was the only one here who still didn't know about our bond, but it wouldn't stay that way for long. I had come home tonight intending to tell her everything, but not like this. This was the worst possible way for her to learn the truth about us.

I released her as Tristan approached us. She took a step back and looked up at me with eyes full of tender concern.

My stomach knotted. Would she still look at me that way an hour from now?

"Nikolas, we need to get Sara and the others home."

I nodded at Tristan.

Sara's searching gaze moved from me to Tristan, and I knew she was waiting for one of us to tell her what was going on. But this was not the place for that conversation. I'd take her home so she could get cleaned up, and then I'd explain it all to her.

When neither of us spoke, she let out a soft sigh of frustration and stepped around me to walk to the driveway. I fell in behind her, intending to ride with her in one of the vehicles. Someone else could take my bike home.

She approached the second SUV and climbed into the back seat. I moved toward the other door until Tristan laid a hand on my arm.

"I think you need to let me do this," he said quietly.

"She should hear it from me."

Tristan might be her grandsire, but Sara and I shared a bond and a history. It was my place to tell her about us.

"Before tonight, I would have agreed with you. But she's been through too much with the vampire attack and now this."

The rage threatened to surface again. "Is she hurt?"

"No. They were young vampires, and Sara and Jordan killed them. The blood you saw on her is the vampires'."

I unclenched my hands. "I have to be with her."

"Nikolas, listen to me. You are both overly emotional right now. Sara is confused and upset, and you just went into a full rage. You know you're not in the right frame of mind to talk to her about something so delicate. And she will be even more upset if we make her wait until tomorrow to hear the truth."

He sighed heavily. "I know this is hard for you, but given the situation, I'm probably the best person to talk to her."

I opened my mouth to object, but the words died on my tongue. He was right. I was still worked up, and the last thing I wanted was to upset Sara, though it killed me that she was going to hear the truth from someone else.

Tristan laid a hand on my shoulder, and then he walked to the SUV and got inside. A minute later, Seamus and Niall climbed into the front.

I strode to my bike and moved it aside so the SUV could back out of the driveway. I stayed behind them for most of the drive back to Westhorne, but I went on ahead when we reached the main gate. I wanted to be there when she arrived, to reassure her I was in control and she didn't need to fear me.

The SUV pulled up in front of the main steps, and Tristan got out. He reached in to assist Sara from the car.

She emerged, looking pale and exhausted, and I had to force myself to stay where I was. She looked at me before Tristan led her up the steps into the main hall. It was enough for me to see the apprehension in her eyes, and I cursed myself again for doing that to her.

I rubbed the back of my neck and looked around, at a loss as to what to do now. It was going to be a long night.

I was still standing outside ten minutes later when Chris arrived.

He gave me a wry smile. "You look like hell."

"You heard?"

"I saw. I was in the barn when you decided to have your meltdown."

I grimaced. "How bad was it?"

"Bad, but it could have been a lot worse. You got it under control."

"Because of her," I admitted, remembering Sara's arms around my waist as she'd talked to me. Even after I'd frightened her, she'd come to me, comforted me.

"Well, it won't do you any good to stand around here. You're only going to get worked up again. I'd suggest a good sparring session, but in your mood, I might not come out of it with all my parts."

He pointed to the garage. "Let's go for a ride."

I shook my head. "I can't leave. Sara might —"

"Tristan will take care of Sara, and she's not going to talk to you tonight."

I scowled at him.

"You know that's how she copes with change. She avoids dealing with it until she can handle it. She'll talk to you when she's ready."

"I don't know, Chris. She's never looked at me that way."

He shook his head. "She's confused and overwhelmed, that's all. Did you know she killed a vampire right before we all got there?"

"Tristan told me." Pride surged in me in spite of the part of me that struggled with the knowledge that she'd fought a vampire.

"She's tougher than she looks, Nikolas. And she cares about you. Anyone with eyes can see that. Give her some time."

I looked up at the light shining from the second story windows belonging to Tristan's apartment. I should be the one with her, telling her about us.

"God, I really messed up."

"You aren't the first bonded male to lose it, and you certainly won't be the last. Standing here torturing yourself is helping no one."

"You're right." I made myself turn away from the building. "Let's ride."

CHAPTER 22

I WAITED UNTIL noon the next day before I knocked on Tristan's door. I could feel Sara inside the apartment and knew she'd stayed there all night. I hadn't seen Tristan yet today, so I had no idea how their talk had gone or how she'd reacted to the news about the bond. I couldn't forget how lost she'd looked when she arrived here last night. I needed to make sure she was okay.

Tristan didn't look surprised to see me when he opened the door. "She's still asleep," he said quietly as he motioned for me to come in.

"Still?"

His brow creased in concern. "I don't think she slept well. I heard her moving around for a long time after she went to bed."

I hadn't slept well either. My apartment was two doors down from Tristan's, close enough for me to feel Sara nearby. Not being able to go to her had me prowling around the apartment like a caged tiger all night.

"I'll come back in an hour."

He shook his head and gave me a regretful look. "She is not ready to see you. Last night was a shock to her, and she needs some time to process it."

His words didn't come as a surprise, but they hurt.

"I frightened her. I need to talk to her, to explain."

"Sara knows you would never harm her, and she's the only one who wasn't afraid of you last night. You and I both knew she would be upset when she learned about the bond, which is why we agreed to wait to tell her."

I threw up a hand. "I did wait. I left for almost three weeks."

He raised an eyebrow. "When you returned and asked to train her, you said you could keep your distance. Kissing her is not what I'd call *keeping your distance*."

"I didn't mean for that to happen...not yet." I raked my fingers through my hair. "We argued, and we got caught up in the moment. I'm sorry for the way I handled it, but I'm not sorry for kissing her. I came home last night, intending to tell her everything."

His sympathetic look was worse than his anger. I wanted to ask him about their conversation, but all I said was, "How is she?"

"Like I said, it was a lot for her to take in, and she's hurt that we kept it from her. Give her a few days."

"I'll give her whatever she needs. You know that."

"I do." Tristan glanced over at the guest room door. "I think she knows it too."

I turned to the door. "I'd better leave before she wakes. I'll be working with Dax today if you need me."

I didn't know if anything could take my mind off Sara, but I had to try. I had a feeling I was going to be a very busy man until she was ready to talk to me again.

Dax and I spent the afternoon going through the constant stream of reports from our people all over the country. I was grateful for the distraction, but the higher than usual number of vampire attacks was troubling. I scoured the feeds for missing teenage girls, or anything that might indicate the Master was still searching for Sara. I found nothing that pointed to her, but I wouldn't be happy until that vampire was dead.

If Dax wondered about my extended presence in the security center, he didn't say anything. Neither did he mention what had happened last night, though I was sure everyone at Westhorne had heard the story by now. Gossip didn't bother me. Neither did stares. My only concern was Sara, and how she was handling everything. Since I couldn't go to her, I buried myself in work.

Tristan came looking for me late in the afternoon, and we walked outside to talk.

"How is she?" I asked.

"Good. Better than last night, but still a bit shaken up. She said some things that you need to know."

My gut hardened at his serious expression, but his next words were the last ones I expected.

"Sara told me she can sense when vampires are near. It's how she knew there were vampires at the party last night."

I was sure I had heard him wrong. "Sense them?"

"She gets a cold feeling in her chest. Apparently, her sylph friend came to visit her a few days ago, and the sylph thinks it's because of the vampire blood on the knife Sara was stabbed with. It does make sense that Sara's Fae side would react differently to demon blood."

I didn't hide my shock. "You're serious."

He nodded grimly. "That's not all. She said she's sensed vampires three times since she moved here, but she didn't know what was happening until last night."

I frowned. "That's impossible. There is no way vampires could have gotten close to her here."

Tristan shrugged, but didn't look convinced. "She sensed one out in the woods and one near the theater in Boise. It's not inconceivable for there to be vampires in Boise, so I asked Chris to look into it. I would have said none would come near this place before last night. Now, I'm wondering if Sara was right. I'm adding an extra patrol to tighten security."

"*Khristu*. If she's right…"

"It doesn't mean they know she's here. Those could have been coincidences."

We stopped walking at the edge of the trees, and I faced him. "I don't believe in coincidences when it comes to Sara."

He let out a slow breath. "There's more."

I steeled myself. "Tell me."

"Sara used her Fae power on one of the vampires last night. It wasn't enough to kill him, but it incapacitated him long enough for her to finish him off with a knife." Tristan stared at me. "Why don't you look surprised?"

"Because she and I spent some time working on that a few days ago. I think, with practice, she'll be able to call on her magic whenever she wants."

Tristan nodded thoughtfully. "It could be a powerful weapon against vampires if her Fae magic gets stronger."

"It's already helped save her life." I stared across the wide expanse of lawn, my mind working. "She doesn't like to use her power on me, so I'll need to figure out the best course of training for…"

I trailed off at his unhappy expression. "What?"

He took a deep breath. "Sara asked to train with Callum again."

"No."

"Maybe we should —"

"I'm her trainer." The thought of her wanting to work with someone else made my stomach harden. "Callum doesn't understand her. He has no idea what she is."

"I know, and I told her you were the best trainer for her. But if she's not comfortable working with you, I have to respect her wishes."

"She didn't want to work with me when I first offered, and you had no issue with it then."

He knew as well as I that no one cared more about her training than I did. No one could reach her like I could.

"That was before she knew everything." Tristan ran a hand through his hair. "I have to ask that you step back and let this blow over."

My jaw clenched. "We're bonded, Tristan. This is not going to *blow over*."

He rubbed his eyes. "I'm sorry. That came out wrong. I'm in a difficult position here, Nikolas. I don't want to upset you, but Sara is my granddaughter. I know I said I wouldn't come between you, but I feel I have to intercede this time. Sara will train with Callum…for now."

His phone rang, and he looked down at the screen with a weary sigh. "Council business. I can call them back later if you want to talk."

"I don't think talking will resolve anything," I said brusquely, suddenly overcome with the need to get out of there for a few hours.

"Where are you going?" Tristan asked as I turned to the garage.

"Out."

I rode for hours, covering every back road and highway within fifty miles. As much as I needed the freedom of the road, I couldn't bring myself to go too far from Sara. It still amazed me how much my life had changed since I met her. Not so long ago, I couldn't conceive the idea of me wanting to stay at Westhorne for longer than a week at a time. Or the thought that my life could revolve around one person whose happiness meant more to me than my own.

It was close to midnight when I got back to the stronghold. The building was quiet as I headed for my apartment. I slowed walking past Tristan's door, but I knew immediately Sara was no longer there. I wasn't sure if it was a good or bad thing, not being able to feel her nearby.

An hour later, I gave up on sleep. Pushing aside my bed covers. I donned a T-shirt and sweats, grabbed my phone, and went to sit on the couch. My long ride hadn't brought me answers as I'd hoped it would, but there was one place I could always turn to for guidance. If there ever was a time I needed my parents' wisdom, it was now.

My sire answered the video call after three rings. It was morning there, and he usually spent the first part of his day in his home office.

"Nikolas, we were not expecting a call from you for another week."

"I know. Did I catch you at a bad time?"

He settled back in his chair. "It's never a bad time to talk to you. I was just catching up on some reports, and I could use a break." He glanced down at the corner of the computer screen and frowned. "It's quite late there. Is everything okay with you?"

"I'm well," I assured him. As well as I could be under the circumstances.

"But something is bothering you. I can tell."

I didn't answer, suddenly unsure of how to tell him the reason for my call. For months, I'd kept the true nature of my relationship with Sara a secret from my parents. Now I was not only going to tell them about the bond, but I had to admit how badly I'd messed things up.

"Mikhail, I think we should –" My mother entered the room behind my sire and came up short, a smile lighting up her face. "Nikolas!"

"Hello, *Mama*."

She pulled up a chair and sat beside my sire, who laid an arm across her shoulders. Her eyes studied my face with a mother's scrutiny.

"You look tired…and troubled. What's wrong?"

I let out a slow breath. "I need to tell you both something and to ask for your advice."

Her brow furrowed. "It must be serious for you to call so early."

"It is." I searched for the right words, but there was no way to tell them my news that wouldn't shock them.

"I've bonded with someone."

My sire stared at me.

My mother's hand went to her mouth, and her eyes welled with tears. "Bonded?" she whispered.

"Yes."

I'd expected her to be emotional at the news, but I wasn't prepared when she dissolved into tears. I watched helplessly as my sire pulled her into his arms and rubbed her back.

"Our son has a mate," she sobbed against his chest.

"Yes, my love," he said tenderly.

A few minutes passed before she pulled away from him and patted her eyes dry. Her smile was radiant when she faced me again.

"I'm so happy for you. Who is she? Do we know her?"

"Her name is Sara, and she is –"

"Sara?" My mother straightened up in her chair. "Tristan's granddaughter?"

"Yes." I wasn't surprised she made the connection so fast. Tristan must talk about Sara all the time.

"She's the orphan you found in Maine," my sire said slowly. "But that was several months ago."

"She is not yet eighteen. She must have been too young to bond then," my mother told him. "To think, the orphan Nikolas saved would turn out to be his mate."

"That's not how it happened," I said, earning confused looks from both of them. "We bonded the night I met her."

"You've been bonded for months…and you are just telling us now? Why, Nikolas?" my mother asked in quiet disappointment.

"It's a long story."

She reached for my sire's hand. "Tell us."

I started at the night Chris and I went to the Attic, describing how I met Sara and recognized her as a potential mate. I told them about the weeks in Maine, and my frustration over her refusal to leave despite the danger to her. How the bond had grown between us even though Sara hadn't known about it. How it felt like my heart had been torn from my chest when she disappeared and everyone but me had believed she was dead.

"Oh, Nikolas." My mother's eyes misted again. "Why did you not say anything?"

"I don't know. At first, I thought about walking away from the bond."

My mother gasped softly, and I smiled. "You know I never wanted a serious relationship. But it wasn't long before I couldn't leave."

My sire nodded. "When you find the one, your heart knows before your head does."

"So Sara is half Fae, and that is why she can't feel the bond?" my mother asked.

"She uses her Fae magic to suppress her Mori. We've been working on it, and she's made some progress in the last few weeks."

"Incredible."

"It was hard for her to leave her home to come to Westhorne, so Tristan and I decided to let her settle in here before I told her the truth about us."

My mother held up a hand. "She still doesn't know about the bond? But it's been months. You should be showing all the signs of a bonded male. How have you hidden that from her?"

"It hasn't been easy." I dragged a hand through my hair. "She found out last night...and it didn't go as I'd hoped."

My sire leaned forward. "What happened?"

"We had a misunderstanding a few days ago. It was my fault. I left on a job, and I came back last night, planning to tell her everything. And I..." Shame filled me, and I couldn't meet their eyes. "Something happened, and I thought she was hurt."

"You went into a rage." My sire's voice was full of understanding.

"She was at a party in town with the other trainees, and they were attacked by young vampires. Sara and another girl killed the vampires before anyone could reach them. I got there after Tristan, and all I could see was Sara covered in blood. I lost it."

"Did you hurt anyone?" my mother asked gently.

I met her eyes again. "No. Sara brought me out of it. But she was upset, and she wanted to know why I'd been like that. Tristan took her home and explained the bond to her. Now she doesn't want to see me. I've made such a mess of things."

She shook her head. "I'm sure there are things you could have handled better, but I haven't met a bonded male who hasn't behaved irrationally at least one time. It's the nature of the bond."

My sire chuckled. "I wasn't exactly a model of good behavior when I met your mother. I'm still amazed she didn't put me on my ass and run like hell."

"I was tempted a time or two." She arched an eyebrow at him. "But you had some redeeming qualities."

I looked from my mother to my sire. "I thought you had a smooth courtship."

My parents had met in the Australian Outback in seventeen eighty-nine. She'd been on an expedition to study the weerlak population there, and he was with the unit sent to back them up. They mated less than two months later.

The two of them laughed.

"I knew the moment I met Mikhail he was the one, but I refused to have anything to do with him at first. He thought the expedition was too dangerous for me, as if I wasn't a trained warrior. I told him to go away and come back when he was ready to see me as an equal."

"I stayed, of course," my sire added, laughing. "I was determined to keep my mate safe. All I did was entertain my unit and the expedition members. The more I pressed, the more Irina resisted. It took me a while to learn that pushing her was getting us nowhere."

She leaned over to kiss his cheek. "And I'm so glad you figured that out, my love."

"How is it that you've never told me this?"

It was somewhat comforting to know that even my devoted parents' relationship had started out rocky, although maybe not as rocky as mine and Sara's.

My mother lifted a shoulder. "It didn't seem important. Once you complete the bond, none of that matters."

"I have no idea what Sara feels about us or if she even wants this bond. Tristan said she's hurt that I didn't tell her, and I don't blame her."

I rubbed my chest where a familiar ache had started up again. "She won't see me, and she's asked to train with someone else. The last thing I want is to pressure her, but how can I fix this if I can't talk to her?"

"Sara's had many changes in her life these last few months, and from what you told us, she's resisted most of them," my mother said. "But you've been there for her through all of them, and it sounds like she cares for you. Be there for her now, and give her time to work out her feelings."

"Don't push her to talk about your relationship, because that's the surest way to send her running," my sire added. "But let her know you aren't going anywhere. Sometimes, a woman just needs to know that."

"Mikhail's right. Just be patient. Sara will talk to you when she is ready."

"I can do that."

"I know you can. Now go get some sleep." My mother smiled. "And, Nikolas, I can't wait to meet my new daughter."

*   *   *

The door to the training room was closed when I approached it, but I knew Sara was already inside. I'd talked to Callum earlier, and he'd agreed I was a better trainer for her. I decided it was best not to tell her about the change in trainers because I didn't want her finding a way to get out of it.

She needed me as a trainer, even if she didn't want to admit it. If she went back to working with Callum, it would be a step backward for her. She had only just begun to connect with her Mori and to tap into her power, and Callum couldn't help her with those things. I just had to convince her I was right.

Her back was to the door when I opened it. I hadn't seen her since Saturday night, and I hadn't realized how much I'd missed her until this moment.

Her smile faded when she saw it was me. "I'm waiting for Callum."

I shifted into trainer mode as I shut the door. "Callum and I talked, and we agreed that I will continue to train you."

"I didn't agree to that. I'd rather work with —"

I took a step toward her, and she backed up. Her physical withdrawal was like a punch in the gut.

"Don't do that," I said quietly. "I would never hurt you."

"I know. I just think it would be best if I trained with some other people."

"No one here can teach you anything I can't." I saw in her eyes that she knew I was right. But that didn't stop her from shifting nervously from one foot to the other. I hated to see her like this, and my resolve slipped. "We both know what this is about."

She looked away from me. "I don't want to talk about it."

"We have to talk about it sometime," I said gently.

"But not now. Please."

Her pleading tone made my chest tighten, and I backed off. "Let's train then."

"Okay."

Her relief was apparent, and I tried not to let it bother me. At least she hadn't refused outright to train with me.

"What do you want to work on?" I asked her.

A gleam entered her eyes. "I want you to teach me how to fight. I can have all the demon strength I want, but it's totally useless if I don't even know how to throw a punch correctly."

I started to object, to tell her she wasn't ready for combat training, but she spoke before I could.

"Listen, I have to learn to protect myself. I'm supposed to train to be a warrior, right?" A flush rose in her cheeks. "If you're going to get mad every time I mention it, this is not going to work. I'd rather not waste my time."

"You need to condition your body and spend more time getting used to working with your demon before you learn fighting techniques."

"Can't I do both?" she asked hopefully. "The bad guys aren't going to wait for me to catch up with everyone else. Couldn't I learn some moves and do that other stuff at the same time?"

The image of her emerging from the barn covered in blood filled my mind.

"See, there you go again." She glared at me. "Callum wouldn't think twice about teaching me to fight. He'd have no problem giving me a few bruises and throwing me across a room."

"He throws you around?" I asked darkly.

"Gah!" She moved past me toward the door. If she left, it would be even harder to get her to work with me again.

"I'll teach you a few strikes and blocks, and then we will put you through a workout to see how much work we have to do."

She stopped and gave me a look of surprise.

"We'll spend time on your fighting technique and your workouts every day. Once you have mastered the basics, we'll move on to more difficult moves."

I had her full attention now. Suppressing a smile, I went to the center of the room and pointed at a spot in front of me. After a brief hesitation, she joined me.

All right, moy malen'kiy voin. Let's see what you're made of.

Two hours later, I watched her lean shakily against the wall, her breath coming in quick pants, and her hair damp with sweat. I'd put her through a grueling workout to see how long she'd last, one that would have knocked any trainee on their ass, but she stubbornly refused to give in.

I hung her discarded skipping rope on a hook to hide my smile. "Ready to call it quits for today?"

"No, just catching my breath," she replied in a voice that trembled with exhaustion. "What's next?"

Admiration filled me. She could barely stand, yet she would push on rather than admit she was tired.

I began stacking the weights we'd used. "I think that's enough for now. You don't want to overdo it in your first session."

"Okay," she said weakly, failing to hide the relief in her voice.

I grinned at the wall. "Tomorrow we'll start working with the bag."

"Yay," she muttered.

I waited until the door closed, and then I laughed for the first time in days.

*   *   *

Sara returned for training the next day, which told me she'd given up the idea of going back to working with Callum. She'd been okay yesterday once we got into the workout, so I kept the training as businesslike as possible to prevent any discomfort for her. It worked, and we had a good session.

The day after that, she opened up to me about her fight with the vampires.

"I zapped a vampire at the barn."

I set down the weights I was holding and turned to her, waiting for her to say more.

"Tristan told you?" she asked.

"Yes."

She bit her lip. "Why didn't you say something?"

I leaned against the wall. "I figured you would tell me when you were ready, and when you felt like you could trust me again."

Her eyes met mine. "I never stopped trusting you."

The weight on my chest eased a little at her earnest declaration. Knowing I hadn't lost her trust gave me hope, and it was a step toward regaining what I'd had with her. I would not push her for more than that. Instead, I turned the conversation back to a more neutral subject.

"Do you want to tell me what happened? Tristan said you were able to sense them."

She nodded. "Derek was showing us the loft because he's turning it into an art studio. We were about to go back to the house when I got this cold feeling in my chest. I've felt it before, but never that bad. I could barely breathe. Then Derek's friend Seth showed up. I didn't know he was a vampire, not until I saw his claws growing. It got kind of crazy after that. Derek got knocked out, and Jordan killed Seth."

She rubbed her breastbone absently. "And then I felt the cold again. That's when I realized what it meant."

"What happened next?"

"Seth's girlfriend Dana showed up with another vampire. Jordan took Dana, and I took the other one. I fought him with my knife until I lost it. Then I jumped on his back to hold him so Jordan could finish him off. But when my hands touched his face, my power shocked him. He fell down, and I used a knife to kill him."

She gave me a frustrated look. "I tried to call on the power like we practiced, but it wouldn't come until I touched him. Then it just jumped out of me like it did with the other demons. I don't understand why it burned him, but it didn't burn you."

"A vamhir demon is always close to the surface because it controls the body. You couldn't feel my demon until I called it forth."

I was proud of her, but it was hard to move past the thought of her being so close to a vampire, especially after Eli. But a trainer wouldn't dwell on those things, and that was all I could be to her until she was ready for more.

"This is good. It means you have a built-in defense against vampires, young ones at least. We need to keep working on it to make sure it is reliable."

"What about my vampire radar?" she asked hopefully. "Can we go somewhere and test it?"

"Not until we spend a lot more time on your training. There will be plenty of time to test your other abilities."

"Okay," she conceded. "When can we work on my power again?"

I picked up a jump rope, pleased she wanted to work with me. "Let's finish your workout and we'll meet up after lunch for your other training."

Our days took on a routine after that. We did physical training in the mornings, and after lunch we focused on improving her control over her power. With each day that passed, her combat moves grew more precise and she seemed less tired at the end of our workouts.

It was her progress with her Fae power that impressed me the most. I didn't know if her power was growing stronger or if she was getting better at wielding it, but it was clear where her real strength lay. I was torn between wanting to see what she could do against a real threat and hoping she never had to use it to protect herself again.

Although Sara and I spent our mornings and afternoons together, we never talked about anything besides her training. And we didn't see each other outside of training, except in passing. It was like a wall had been erected between us and we grew further apart each day.

My mother called every other day to see how I was doing. Every time we talked, she reminded me the strongest matings usually started out rocky and that Sara would come around if I continued to be patient. I appreciated her advice, and I didn't press Sara, but it felt like Sara was slowly slipping away from me.

It was clear Sara wasn't happy either. When I saw her with her friends, her smiles weren't as bright and she didn't laugh. I hoped Nate's upcoming visit would cheer her up. I even considered inviting Roland and Peter here to spend time with her. I'd do whatever it took to make her happy.

On Saturday evening, I left the security center, and I was headed for the dining hall when I heard laughter ahead of me. I slowed my approach and watched Sara and Chris walk through the main hall, their arms laden with shopping bags. Chris carried a bucket of cat litter in one hand and a piece of cat furniture in the other. He said something to Sara, and she grinned at him, looking happy for the first time in a week.

I waited for them to go up the stairs to her room before I continued on to the dining hall. I was glad to find it almost empty because I wasn't in the mood for company. I grabbed a plate of food and sat alone, trying not to think about how it should have been me to take Sara to town. It should have been me to make her smile like that.

I was so lost in thought that I didn't realize someone had entered the dining hall until I heard a sound on the other side of the room. I groaned inwardly when I recognized Celine, who was taking several bottles of Perrier from one of the glass refrigerators. I hadn't talked to her since I got back last weekend, and I assumed she was keeping a polite distance like everyone else.

I didn't think she had spotted me yet, but she would as soon as she turned around. And then...

"Nikolas, why are you sitting in here alone?"

I sighed and put on a smile. "Got caught up in work. You know how it is."

She was quiet for a moment before she walked over to my table. For once, the sultry expression was gone, replaced by one of concern.

"I heard what happened. How are you?"

"I'm good. Thanks for asking."

"Do you mind if I join you?" she asked almost demurely.

I waved a hand at the chair across from me. "Not at all."

She set her bottles down on the table and sat with her hands on her lap. This reserved Celine was one I hadn't seen before, and I wasn't sure what to make of it.

"I feel I should apologize to you."

I gave her a puzzled look. "Why?"

Her brows drew together delicately. "If I'd known you were bonded, I would not have pursued you since you came home."

I started to speak, but she held up a hand.

"Please, let me finish. You know I've been attracted to you since our week in New York. I've never exactly hidden my desire to resume a relationship with you."

I smiled, unsure how to respond.

"But had I known you were bonded, I wouldn't have come on so strong. You've been very gracious about my advances, and I want to apologize for any discomfort I caused you."

"You don't have to apologize. You couldn't have known, and this hasn't exactly been a normal bonding."

Celine reached across the table. Then she seemed to think better of it and withdrew her hand. "Are you okay? Forgive me for intruding, but you don't look happy."

"No one ever said bonding was easy."

"I suppose not, but I don't think you're supposed to be miserable either."

I shrugged. "I'm more worried about her happiness. This hasn't been easy on her."

Celine's mouth pursed. "She is unusually young to be bonded. Perhaps too young to deal with this."

I nodded absently because I had worried about the same thing more than once in the last week.

She stood and picked up her bottles of water. "I do care about you, Nikolas, and I only want you to be happy."

"Thank you. I wish the same for you."

Her flirty smile was back as she walked away. "I'm suffering a disappointment at the moment, but I'm sure I'll rebound in no time."

"I'm sure you will," I called after her.

CHAPTER 23

"I THINK THAT'S all of them." Tristan tossed a stack of papers down on the coffee table and rolled his shoulders. "I remember when I used to get five to ten reports a week. I get twice that many every day now."

I rubbed the back of my neck, which ached from hours poring over the detailed field reports. "Dax and I have been trying to come up with some kind of pattern to explain why the vampires have been active in certain cities more than others. LA and Vegas have been hit the hardest, but we're also seeing higher activity in Houston and San Diego."

"All western cities." Tristan leaned back in his chair.

I nodded. "I talked to Maxwell Kelly yesterday, and he said it's been so quiet in Maine he went back to normal patrols. He said the whole East Coast is quiet."

Tristan stared at the reports. "I don't know if that's good or bad news at this point."

"It's definitely not good for the western half," I said. "Did you know Stefan Price was spotted in Albuquerque last night?"

"Stefan Price?"

I understood his surprise. Price was an old vampire, over one hundred and fifty years old, and we had been trying to catch him for the last seventy-five years. He was a strong bastard and skilled at evading us.

"There hasn't been a Price sighting in years. Word was he went to South America."

I shrugged. "Looks like he's back."

Tristan swore softly and stood. "I'll have to let the Council know."

"And that's my cue to leave." I got up and opened the door. Instead of leaving, I turned back to Tristan. "Have you talked to Sara today? She was upset in training this morning, but she wouldn't talk about it."

"Yes." He sighed heavily. "Nate's taken ill with pneumonia, and he can't come for the holiday."

"We can send one of the healers to him. He can still make it for Thanksgiving dinner." Sara would be crushed if Nate couldn't be here.

Tristan shook his head. "I offered, but he's not comfortable with non-human medicine. He said he'll come as soon as he's fit to travel."

"Sara's been looking forward to his visit for weeks. This must be killing her, especially on top of everything else."

"I know, but she's strong. She'll be okay –"

"She's not okay, Tristan," I said harshly, thinking about the pain Sara must be in. "Nothing about this is okay. I've never seen her so unhappy. I wanted her to know about us, but this is all wrong. This is not what I wanted for her."

He nodded gravely. "This hasn't been easy on either of you."

"I don't care about me. She's miserable. I can't stand to see her like this. I'd rather she break the bond and be free than be tied to someone she doesn't want."

"You don't mean that." Tristan came over and laid a hand on my shoulder. "It's only been a week, though I'm sure it feels like much longer to you. Sara does care about you, and she's trying to understand all of this. She's seventeen, and she just found out she's bonded to you. She probably doesn't know how to talk to you about it."

Some of the tension left my body. "I'll wait until after the holiday. If she doesn't come to me by then, I'm going to her. We have to work this out one way or the other."

*   *   *

After my talk with Tristan, the last person I expected to see two hours later when I came back from the security center was Sara. She was standing in the hallway, facing the other end, and so lost in thought she didn't hear me approach.

"Sara?"

She gasped and spun around, and I caught her before she fell. Her eyes met mine, and she looked as surprised as I was.

I let her go. "What are you doing here? Were you looking for me?"

Her mouth opened and closed, and a panicked look entered her eyes. "N-no," she uttered, stumbling past me.

What the hell? I caught her again and turned her to face me. That was when I got a whiff of alcohol coming from her. Didn't she know that faeries couldn't handle human alcohol?

"What is wrong with you? Are you drunk?"

"No!" She jerked her arms out of my hold and immediately began to turn a sickly shade of green. A hand came up to cover her mouth. "Oh, I don't feel good."

Something told me I was the last person she wanted to see her like this, but that couldn't be helped now. I picked her up as gently as I could and carried her to my apartment. Inside, I went straight to the bathroom and set her down on the floor. She fell to her knees in front of the toilet and began to vomit.

I stood behind her, holding her hair back, and I was assailed by the sour odor of alcohol, which left no doubt as to what she'd been up to before she came here.

"Oh God, I'm dying," she moaned piteously then retched again.

I smiled, remembering the few times in my life when I'd overindulged in spirits. Sara wasn't soon going to forget this experience.

She raised her head a few inches. "Please, go away and let me die in peace."

Not a chance. I grabbed a cloth and ran it under cold water. Squeezing the water from it, I carried it over and lifted her hair to lay it across the back of her neck. She let out a sigh before she threw up again.

Eventually, the vomiting stopped, and she flushed the toilet with a trembling hand. I went to the sink to wet the cloth again, and I turned around to find her huddled against the tub.

Suppressing a smile, I sat on my haunches and lifted her chin so I could wash her face. She didn't protest, which told me how miserable she was.

"Do you need to throw up again?" I asked.

She shook her head and rested her forehead on her knees, which were drawn up to her chest. It made her look so small and helpless, and all I wanted to do was hold her. Instead, I went to the cabinet and took out a can of gunna paste.

She pushed at my hand when I held the paste to her lips. She hated this stuff, but it was a lot better than the monster hangover she'd have in the morning without it.

"Trust me; you'll be glad for it tomorrow."

She opened her mouth and obediently took the paste, and her expression as she swallowed had me fighting back a laugh.

"Okay, let's get you off this floor."

I scooped her up in my arms and carried her into the living room where I set her down on one end of the couch. I sat on the other end and watched her as she leaned her head against the armrest with her eyes closed. Now that I had her here, there was so much I wanted to say to her, but I didn't know if she was up to talking.

"Were you coming to see me?" I prodded gently.

A nod.

Her silent admission drew another smile from me. "And you had to get drunk first?" I teased.

"The trainees had a party," she said hoarsely.

My smile grew. "Were you coming to invite me?"

She lifted her head, but didn't look at me. "No, I —"

"Take your time," I said when she struggled with her next words. I'd waited a long time to talk to her. What were a few more minutes?

"I..." She swallowed hard, and her voice shook. "I wanted to let you know that...that you're free. I'm going to break the bond."

Pain tore through me, and it felt like someone had shoved a red hot poker into my gut. My Mori howled, making it hard to speak.

"What?"

She looked at me, and I couldn't bear the misery on her face. I stared at the window, trying to breathe and control my wailing demon.

"I'm sorry. I know I'm handling this all wrong," she said in a trembling voice.

"Don't apologize. I don't think there is an easy way to do something like this."

I took a deep breath, trying to accept what was happening. I'd feared she might not want the bond, but deep down, I'd never believed she would break it.

The poker twisted deeper when I realized I'd have to leave here tonight. I could never see her, never hold her again. People said the bond faded completely when the couple was apart long enough, but my heart belonged to Sara. In my mind, she would always be my mate.

"This is why you were upset in training today," I said numbly.

"No, that was something else."

I steeled myself. It made no sense to stay here and torture myself further, but I had to know. "What made you wait until now to tell me? We see each other every day."

"I-I overheard you talking to Tristan tonight." Her voice cracked. "You said you wanted to break the bond."

I jerked my head in her direction. "What are you talking about?"

Her shoulders were hunched and her eyes dark with pain. "You told Tristan you were miserable and that you didn't want this to happen. I didn't mean to listen, and I only heard bits of it. And then Celine said..."

Celine? I swore silently. "What did Celine say?"

"She said it wasn't fair to hold you to a bond you didn't want, and that you were too honorable to break it."

Hope fluttered in my chest. Was she saying —?

A wave of pain came through the bond. Sara covered her face with her hands and began to cry.

"I'm s-sorry," she sobbed brokenly. "I never meant to h-hurt you."

"Damn it." I never should have let things go this far without talking to her. I'd only ended up hurting her more.

I moved to the center of the couch and pulled her into my arms. My chest constricted when I thought of how close I'd come to never being able to hold her like this.

"Celine had no right to say that to you," I said against her hair. "And you misunderstood what you heard me say to Tristan. I told him I never wanted you to find out the way you did, and that I would rather you break the bond than see you unhappy because of it."

She grew very still against me. "You don't want to break the bond?"

"No."

Her breath hitched. "You don't?"

"Do you?" I asked, not sure if I was ready to hear her answer.

I tried not to be discouraged when she didn't respond. She hadn't said yes, so that had to mean something. "You don't have to answer right now," I told her softly.

My words didn't have the effect I intended. She started to cry again.

I tightened my embrace. "I'm sorry you had to learn about it all this way. The last thing I wanted was for you to get hurt."

After a few minutes she stopped crying and hiccupped. "Why didn't you tell me about the bond back in New Hastings?"

Because I was afraid you'd run from me and I'd lose you.

"If I'd told you the truth back then, you never would have come here, and I needed you to be safe."

She sniffled quietly. "Tristan told me the bond makes you overprotective. Maybe you would feel different if we broke it. You wouldn't have to worry about me all the time."

I rested my chin on top of her head. How did I explain that it wasn't just the bond that made me protective and that nothing would change how I felt about her? Things were too fragile and uncertain between us right now for her to learn the depth of my feelings for her.

"I'll always care about you. Don't you know that by now?"

She nodded, and the band around my heart loosened a little.

"What are you thinking? Talk to me," I said gently.

Her voice came out as a raspy whisper. "I don't know what to think anymore. I mean, we've been fighting since we met, and I know you weren't exactly happy to meet me in the first place. My life is a mess and I'll never be a warrior like...Celine."

It was true that I'd been surly when we met, but that had lasted only a few days. And not once had I been unhappy about finding her. I wanted to reassure her about that, but first I had to make sure she was clear on one thing.

"Sara, I don't want you to be like Celine."

"But how do you know what you want? How do you know if what you feel comes from you or from a Mori thing you have no control over?"

I sighed because I knew she, having barely connected to her own demon, couldn't understand how my Mori and I lived together in one body.

"My Mori and I share our minds and emotions, but I always know the difference."

"I'm so confused," she said hoarsely. "I don't understand any of this. It's like I have no control over my life anymore. I'm scared."

My fingers toyed with her hair. "I felt the same way at first."

"You were scared?"

I laughed softly at the disbelief in her voice. "It scared the hell out of me when I saw you in that club and felt something between us. I'd never experienced anything like it, and I wasn't prepared to feel that way for anyone, let alone an orphan I found in a bar. I wanted to stay with you and get far away from you at the same time. I tried to leave, but I couldn't."

My voice grew rough. "And when I saw you in the hands of that vampire…"

Her hand came up and rested over my heart, soothing me. I closed my eyes and banished the memory of Eli holding her against him in that alley.

She cleared her throat. "You said you were confused and scared at first. You aren't anymore?"

"No, I'm not. Yes, it started with my Mori in that bar, but it wasn't long before I realized there was more to you than you let people see. You drove me nuts when you were so stubborn and reckless, and you have an uncanny ability to find trouble. At the same time, I couldn't help but admire your independent spirit and how fiercely protective you were of your friends."

I smiled over her head. "You were an untrained orphan with no apparent abilities, standing your own against a Mohiri warrior while defending two werewolves and a troll. You were something to behold. I didn't want to feel anything more than responsibility for you, but you made it impossible not to."

She was quiet for a long moment. "I felt something too when we met. It was like I knew you somehow even though we'd never met. My life was turned upside down that night in more ways than one. Then you came to see me and I resented you for telling me what I was and for changing everything. I did some pretty stupid things and I hated that you were right about them. I hated that you wouldn't go away and let me be the way I used to be. I thought you were arrogant and bossy and determined to drive me insane."

I almost laughed at her description of me. Leaning down, I spoke close to her ear. "If this is a declaration of love, I'm not getting a warm fuzzy feeling about it."

"I'm not finished!" she said in a rush, and I grinned, loving that I had this effect on her. "Even when I was angry at you, I knew everything you did was to protect me and I always felt safe with you. It was strange. I didn't trust people easily, but I trusted you almost immediately. But I don't think it was until that day at the cliff, before you showed up, that I realized I felt something more. I was alone and expecting to die, and all I could think about was the people I'd never see again. You were one of them."

Her admission made the last week fall away. She might not be where I was in our relationship, but there was no denying we had something strong between us.

She shifted slightly in my arms. "And...I did miss you when you left me here, and it hurt because I thought you were glad to be free of me."

Regret stabbed at me again. "I shouldn't have left the way I did. I should have waited a few days for you to settle in and told you I was leaving for a while."

She was quiet for another long moment. "What do we do now...about this, us?"

"What do you want to do?" As long as we were together, that was all that mattered to me.

"I don't know. I mean..." She exhaled slowly. "When Tristan told me about the bond, I was upset that you kept it from me, and I admit I kind of freaked. Don't take this the wrong way after what we just shared, but we've only known each other for a few months. I like you a lot, but how are we supposed to know if we want to spend forever together. Forever is a long time."

My grin was back. She was adorable when she was flustered.

"You like me a lot?"

"Sometimes," she muttered.

"Forever *is* a long time, but we don't have to think about that right now. Let's just take it slow and see what happens. Just promise you'll talk to me if you have questions or doubts, instead of listening to other people."

She nodded. "I promise."

"Good. Now, do you want to tell me what was bothering you in training today if it wasn't this?"

I already knew she'd been upset about Nate, but I wanted her to tell me. She needed to know she could come to me for anything.

"Nate can't come for Thanksgiving. He called yesterday and said he has pneumonia and he's not allowed to travel." Her voice cracked, and I could tell she was trying not to cry again. "I wanted to go to him, but he wouldn't let me. Now he's going to be alone and sick at Thanksgiving. We've always spent it together."

I rubbed her back, and she curled into me more.

"I'm sorry. I know how much you were looking forward to his visit."

"It won't be the same without him." She wiped her eyes. "God, I can't stop crying tonight."

"Then it's a good thing my shirts don't shrink when they get wet," I teased.

She answered with a soft hiccup. I chuckled and kissed her lightly on the top of the head, something I'd wanted to do since I'd pulled her into my arms. I was rewarded by her arms slipping around my waist. Contentment flowed through me, and I couldn't fathom how I had lived my whole life without this, without her.

I began to rub her back again, and she sighed.

"Do you feel better?"

She yawned. "Yes, but I'm never touching tequila again."

I couldn't stop the laughter that spilled from me. "If I'd known you were going on a drinking binge, I would have told you that Faeries have very little tolerance for human alcohol, unlike the rest of us. Looks like you inherited that trait from your Fae family."

"Great, now you tell me," she grumbled halfheartedly. "Some trainer you are."

"Actually a good trainer lets you make mistakes at first so you learn never to repeat them."

"Then you are the best trainer ever."

I laughed again, enjoying the playful banter with her. "How did you ever get by without me?"

"I have no idea," she murmured sleepily.

We fell silent, and I continued to rub her back as I savored the freedom to hold her as I'd always wanted. She made no move to leave my arms, and eventually her breathing evened out and her arms grew limp around my waist.

A part of me said I should wake her or carry her back to her room, but the selfish part of me didn't want to let her go.

It wasn't much of an argument.

I moved until I was stretched out on the couch with her tucked into my side. She muttered something unintelligible and snuggled against me.

If the last week had been hell, then this was heaven.

Wrapping my arms more tightly around her, I brushed my lips against her forehead.

"I love you, Sara."

*   *   *

The sky was streaked with pink when I woke. For a second, I thought last night had been a dream, until I felt the warm body lying on top of me. I gazed at the sleeping girl sprawled across my chest and smiled at the way her fingers were curled in my sweater, as if she was afraid to let me go. I was okay with that. I'd be content to stay here like this with her all day.

Sara moved until her face nuzzled my throat. Her warm lips against my skin sent heat shooting straight to my belly. It didn't help that her soft body was suddenly pressed intimately against mine.

I bit back a groan and shifted slightly to get comfortable, praying she didn't wake up until my body started behaving. Last night she'd said she wanted a relationship as long as we took it slow. She was most definitely not ready to know how much I wanted her.

I gazed out the window at the tops of the trees, heavy with snow from an overnight storm. I was filled with a sense of peace, and amazement at how my life had changed in the last twelve hours. If Sara hadn't overheard my conversation with Tristan, if Celine hadn't interfered, she might not have come to me to break the bond, and we might never have worked things out. I wouldn't be lying here now, holding her as she slept.

I was angry when Sara told me what Celine had said, but now I could only feel gratitude. Celine had unwittingly sent Sara into my arms, giving me the greatest gift I could have asked for.

An hour after I awoke, Sara began to stir. I smiled when she let out a sigh and snuggled against me again. I was tempted to let her go back to sleep, but I was also certain she would be embarrassed walking back to her room after everyone woke up. It wasn't as if I could give her my clothes to wear, as much as I liked the idea of her in one of my shirts.

"Good morning," I said in a low voice.

She went very still. "Morning."

"How do you feel?"

"Good, considering," she replied in a husky voice.

I fought back a laugh. "Considering the gallon of alcohol you threw up, you mean?"

"Ugh, don't remind me," she grumbled. She sat up with a small groan and presented me with her profile as she combed her fingers through her hair.

I wanted to tell her she couldn't be more beautiful to me.

"Are you going to look at me?" I asked after several minutes of her staring at the window.

"I hadn't planned on it."

Chuckling, I sat up, facing her at the other end of the couch. "You know you can't avoid me forever."

"What makes you think I can't?"

I remembered what she'd said last night, and my smile grew. "Because you like me...*a lot.*"

That got the reaction I wanted. She shot me a glare that might have looked fiercer if she wasn't blushing prettily.

"See, that didn't take long," I teased, earning another hard stare.

"Shut up."

Her attempt at a scowl drew another laugh from me, and I wanted nothing more than to reach over and pull her into my arms again.

"Are you okay? With us?" I asked her.

She nodded shyly. "Are you…okay with it?"

"Yes," I said even though *okay* couldn't come close to how I felt in that moment.

She jumped to her feet and blurted, "Excuse me; I need to use your bathroom and about a bottle of mouthwash."

I couldn't hold back my knowing smirk. "Help yourself."

She shut herself in the bathroom, and I got up and went to see what I had in my refrigerator to offer her. I didn't keep much food there, but I had plenty of water and juice. Looking around my rarely-used kitchen, I had an idea to invite Sara for dinner soon. I wasn't much of a cook, but the kitchen could make anything.

The knock at my door surprised me because it was still fairly early. I opened it, and Tristan entered looking worried.

"Jordan just told me Sara left their party last night and never returned. I went to Sara's room, and her bed hasn't been slept in. She's upset about Nate. You don't think she –?"

I put up a hand. "Sara's fine. She's here with me."

"With you?" His eyes swept over the living room and landed on my bedroom door.

"Yes, with me. She got a little too drunk at the party and came to see me. She was in no shape to go anywhere."

Tristan frowned. "You should have taken her back to her room or to my place. People will see her leaving here and –"

"And think a bonded couple spent the night together," I said. "My relationship with Sara is no one's business but ours."

He pressed his lips together. "Is she okay?"

"Why don't you see for yourself?" I walked over and knocked on the bathroom door. "Sara, do you mind coming out here for a minute?"

"Sure," she called hesitantly.

She emerged from the bathroom, and her eyes immediately went to Tristan. A flush crept up her cheeks, and she blurted, "Nothing happened. I got drunk and Nikolas took care of me. That's it."

"Nikolas already explained it to me," Tristan said. "And I told him he should have brought you back to your own room or to my apartment down the hall."

I smiled at her, trying to ease her discomfort. "And I told him that whatever transpires between the two of us is no one's business but ours."

Tristan sighed. "Sara is not yet eighteen, Nikolas, and her uncle trusts me to take care of her. That includes her virtue and –"

"Oh my God, you did not just go there!" she yelled at him, and he darted a glance at me for help.

I had to swallow a laugh, which earned me a scorching look from Sara. For once, I was staying quiet.

Tristan, on the other hand, kept digging that grave.

"I'm sorry. I don't mean to embarrass you, but in your situation, you cannot take sex lightly. It would —"

She made a choked sound and fled.

"Sara, wait," I called, but the only answer I got was the door slamming behind her.

I turned and slapped Tristan on the back. "Great job, Grandpa."

He gave me a sheepish look. "I didn't handle that well."

"You think?" I sank down on the couch, my eyes falling on Sara's shoes beneath the coffee table. "I just hope she remembers to be mad at you and not me this time."

He took the spot Sara had vacated. "I take it you and she worked things out."

"Yes."

"Good." He gave me a questioning look, and I smiled.

"We're together and we're taking it slow," was all I said.

His brows drew together. "Not that I want you to rush into anything, but does Sara know this will get more difficult for you the longer you wait?"

"No, and we're not telling her," I stated firmly. "I'm fine as long as I'm with her."

He nodded then sighed. "Do you think she'll forgive me by dinner?"

I laughed at his forlorn expression. "Maybe, as long as you don't bring up her virtue again."

He groaned. "Never again. And quit smirking."

CHAPTER 24

THE DINING HALL was already full by the time I walked in, and after a quick scan of the room, I located Sara sitting beside Tristan at the back of the room. Our gazes met, and her expectant look told me she'd been waiting for me.

I would have been here sooner if I hadn't spent the last thirty minutes on the phone with my mother, who was overjoyed Sara and I had finally talked things out. Even the news that Sara and I were taking it slow couldn't dim my mother's happiness. Or mine.

I started toward Sara and realized someone was sitting on her left. When I saw who it was, I almost tripped on my own feet. What the hell was Desmund doing here? I hadn't seen him in years, and the last I'd heard, he was still unstable, yelling at anyone other than Tristan who went near the second floor of the east wing.

After the Hale witch attack, Desmund spent half the last century in confinement at a facility in India. Once he'd recovered as much as he could, Tristan had brought him here to live because they were old friends.

Desmund and I had never been friends, but he'd been one hell of a warrior before the attack. He'd sacrificed himself to save his team from the Hale witch, and you had to respect a man who did that.

He looked well enough now, but no one recovered from a Hale witch attack. And I didn't like how close he was sitting to Sara, as if they were old friends.

"Hey," Sara said when I took the chair across from her. She smiled sweetly, and for a moment I forgot everyone else in the room.

"Hey," I answered, glad to see her smiling. I'd worried she wouldn't be able to enjoy the dinner without Nate.

"Tristan, Chris," I said before I turned to Desmund. I noticed his eyes were clear and his clothes and hair were impeccable. He looked very much like the Desmund Ashworth I knew before, with the same arrogant gleam in his eyes. The transformation was startling.

"I'm surprised to see you here."

He laughed. "As am I, but I am feeling quite like my old self again of late. It's miraculous really."

A suspicion hit me, and I looked at the only person I knew who'd fought off a Hale witch. Someone who also had the *miraculous* power to heal, and who was apparently keeping secrets again.

Sara tried to give me an innocent smile, and failed.

"Is that so?" I said slowly. "I wonder what could have caused it."

One corner of Desmund's mouth lifted as he placed his hand over Sara's. She looked surprised, but she didn't pull away, telling me they were well acquainted.

"If I could credit it to anything, it would be my charming little friend here. I cannot tell you how much I have enjoyed our evenings together."

I knew Desmund was playing with me, but the sight of his hand covering Sara's did not sit well with me or my Mori. I bit back a comment, not wanting to ruin Sara's first holiday here.

"We play checkers," Sara said quickly. "One of these days I might actually beat him."

"Checkers. How quaint," said Celine as she took the chair on my right, reminding me that I needed to have a talk with her about her conversation with Sara.

But not tonight. Tonight I was spending my first Thanksgiving with Sara, and nothing was going to spoil it for us.

Celine laughed. "Although, I can think of much more *entertaining* ways to spend an evening."

So could I. After dinner, I planned for Sara and I to spend more time alone together taking it slow. *Maybe not too slow.* If I had my way, there'd be kissing involved.

"Ah, the beautiful Celine," Desmund drawled, sounding like his old self. "Did I ever tell you that you remind me of a courtesan I knew once in King George's court? She was stunning to look upon and much sought after."

"You flatter me, Desmund. Was she someone of noble birth?"

He took a sip from his water glass. "No, but I believe she serviced a duke or two."

Sara choked on her water and went red in the face. Without missing a beat, Tristan patted her back while he sought to pacify Celine after Desmund's well-aimed insult.

"Celine, I have a Beaujolais that would go lovely with this meal. If I remember correctly, you prefer French wines."

"That would be lovely, Tristan," she replied in a tight voice.

Dinner went smoothly after that. The wine arrived, and Tristan offered some to Sara. I didn't try to hide my smile when she turned a little green and waved away the bottle. I had a feeling it would be a long time before she touched alcohol again.

Conversation at the table inevitably came around to Council talk. One of the older members had just found his mate after six hundred years on this Earth, and he wanted to step down to spend time with his new mate. Now people were wondering who was going to be invited to take his place on the Council. If Tristan knew who the choices were, he wasn't saying.

The meal was almost over when Ben came to our table and spoke quietly to Tristan.

Tristan frowned and stood, looking slightly perplexed. "Please, excuse me. Something needs my attention. I'm sure I'll be back before you finish your pie."

He walked out, and I turned to meet Sara's questioning gaze.

"The rest of the world doesn't take a holiday when we do," I told her. Although, it wouldn't hurt the Council to go one day without talking to Tristan.

She nodded, but didn't resume eating. Less than a minute later, she laid down her napkin and stood. "Excuse me."

I stood, along with Chris and Desmund. "Is everything all right?" I asked her.

"Yes. I just... I need to check on something," she said hurriedly. "I'll be back in a little bit."

Celine made a sound. "She's fine, gentlemen. She doesn't need an escort to go to the ladies' room."

Sara smiled at us. "She's right. Please, finish your dessert."

Reluctantly, I sat. I'd known Sara long enough to tell when something was bothering her. What I couldn't figure out was why she was concerned about Tristan leaving. I knew she wasn't going to the restroom, and I could think of no other reason for her to suddenly excuse herself.

I looked at the others. Chris had gone back to eating his pie, and Desmund was swirling his glass of wine thoughtfully. Neither of them looked concerned. Maybe I was overreacting.

"So Desmund, how did you and Sara become such good friends?" Chris asked. At the other warrior's raised eyebrow, he shrugged. "It's no secret you like to keep to yourself...or did."

"I *was* keeping to myself when she decided to invade my library one night. I tried to convince her to go somewhere else and read, but she didn't take the hint." He smiled fondly. "She kept coming back, and I found myself quite taken with her."

Chris grinned. "Knowing you both, I can only imagine how your first meeting went."

Desmund's eyes sparkled with amusement. "She called me *Lestat* and told me I smelled old and musty."

Chris and I laughed, and Desmund joined in. I pictured Sara standing her own against him. She would have given him as good as she got. A girl who befriended trolls would not be cowed by a surly warrior, even one as bad-tempered as Desmund.

Later, I'd get her to tell me how she'd healed him when our people had tried unsuccessfully for centuries to heal Hale witch victims. What she'd done was nothing short of –

I sucked in a sharp breath as a wave of pain and grief washed over me. *Sara.*

I leapt to my feet, sending my chair skidding away from me.

"What –?" Chris started to ask, but I was already running for the door.

The front door was open, and I ran outside. At the top of the steps, I stopped and stared at the scene below. At the bottom of the steps Sara, Tristan, and Ben stood facing a white van parked in the driveway. Beside the van, Nate stood in front of his wheelchair.

Nate took a step away from the chair and raised his arms. "Look, I can walk again. Aren't you happy for me?" he asked Sara.

The horrible truth hit me as Tristan and Ben moved quickly to grab Nate and hold him between them.

Nate merely smiled and flashed his new fangs at Sara. "I have a message for you from the Master. Eli was his favorite and he was very upset to lose him. The Master thinks it's only fair that, since you took one he loved, he should take someone you love."

Sara staggered, and I was behind her in an instant to catch her before she fell.

"I'm here, *malyutka*," I said as another blast of pain hit me.

She tensed and tried to pull away, but I wrapped my arms more tightly around her.

"It's me, Sara. I've got you," I said softly. I wasn't sure if she even heard me, but she stopped struggling and stood quietly in my arms.

"Nikolas, it's good to see you again."

I raised my eyes to the man I'd come to respect and think of as a friend. Sorrow filled me. "I wish I could say the same. I'm sorry this happened to you, Nate."

He grinned. "Don't be. I've never felt so whole or so strong."

Seamus and Niall arrived, and Nate stood quietly as they placed thick iron cuffs on his wrists. The twins cast pitying glances at Sara before they began to lead her uncle away.

"What…will you do with him?" she asked brokenly.

"What do you think they will do?" Nate jeered at her, and I felt her stiffen. "You are vampire killers, after all."

"We will question him about the Master," Tristan said vaguely.

"And then?"

He looked at me, and I could see how much it weighed on him to say his next words.

"He will die. I promise it will be quick and…"

Sara sagged in my arms, and I held her against me. "Let's get you inside."

She shook her head weakly. "No, I need… I need to be there."

"It won't happen today," Tristan said gently. "It usually takes a few days to get them to talk. He won't hold out long without…sustenance."

A shudder went through Sara. I wanted to tell Tristan to stop, but she needed to know why she couldn't be there. She was suffering enough. There was no way I was putting her through the horror of seeing her uncle starved and screaming for blood.

Desmund appeared beside us and spoke to Sara with uncharacteristic tenderness. "You are turning blue from the cold, little one. Let Nikolas take you inside, please."

She nodded, and we turned to the steps where everyone from the dining hall was gathered. Sara faltered, and I moved to pick her up and carry her inside.

"No," she whispered, gripping my hand instead.

I led her inside, and the crowd parted for us as we passed. I planned to take her to my apartment, but she moved toward her floor as if on autopilot. When we entered her room I expected her to cry, but she curled up on her side on her bed, hugging her knees. She shivered violently, and I grabbed the quilt at the foot of the bed and covered her. I watched her helplessly, and I would have taken her pain into me if I could.

A soft knock on the door heralded Tristan's arrival. He entered and looked at the small form huddled beneath the quilt.

"How is she?" he asked in a low voice.

I stepped outside to talk to him.

"She's in shock."

Worry darkened his eyes. "Should we send for a healer?"

"All they can do is sedate her. I'll take care of her."

He dragged a hand through his hair. "God, if I had only known. This will kill her."

"No, it won't," I said fiercely. "I won't let it." Nate's death would haunt Sara for a long time, but she was a survivor. And I'd be beside her every step of the way.

"Is there anything I can do?" he asked desperately.

"Find out what he knows and end it quickly," I said in a low voice.

The longer Nate was alive in this state, the longer it would be before Sara could begin the grieving process. I wouldn't extend her suffering one minute longer than necessary.

He nodded grimly. "I'm on my way to see him now. I wanted to check on her first."

I didn't envy him his job tonight. He'd formed a friendship with Nate over the last month. Now he had to interrogate and most likely torture the vampire that used to be his friend.

As soon as Tristan left, I pulled out my cell phone and called the one person who could help Sara through this. Roland was her best friend, and he'd known Nate his whole life. As much as I wanted to be the one she turned to, she needed Roland more now.

"Nikolas?" Roland said slowly. "Did you dial the wrong number?"

"No." I lowered my voice. "Something has happened."

"What?" he demanded. "Is Sara okay?"

"Sara is okay, physically at least."

His voice rose. "What the hell does that mean? What happened to her?"

"What's going on?" asked a voice in the background that I recognized as Peter's.

I let out a deep breath. "It's Nate. He just showed up here as a vampire."

"Oh, fuck no!" he cried. I heard him repeat what I'd told him to Peter. "Did you…?"

"We have him locked up for now, but we'll kill him in a few days."

"Oh, God. This'll destroy her. She'll blame herself."

I stared at the closed door to her room. "That's why she needs all of us now. Can you come here?"

"Yes," he said without hesitation. "It might take us a day because of the holiday."

"Don't worry about that. I'll send our jet to pick up you and Peter in Portland," I told him. "I'll have someone call you to let you know when to be there."

"Okay. Tell Sara we'll be there as soon as we can."

I hung up and called Claire to ask her to arrange for the jet to pick up Sara's friends in Portland. Then I turned off my phone and entered the room again.

Kicking off my shoes, I lifted the quilt and lay down behind Sara. She whimpered when I curled my body around hers, and the sound tore at my heart.

"I'm so sorry, Sara," I whispered against her hair.

The nightmares began an hour later. All I could do was hold her as she tossed fitfully and called out for her father and Nate. In the early hours of the morning, she cried Nate's name and began to sob uncontrollably against my chest. I rubbed her back and whispered soothing words to her until she quieted again.

The sky was light when I eased her out of my arms and left the bed. She was finally sleeping soundly after her restless night, so I hoped she'd sleep for a few more hours.

I hated to leave her, but there were things that had to be done. Nate's arrival last night proved the Master knew Sara was alive and at Westhorne, and he wasn't playing around. We had to find out what Nate knew, and then we had to come up with a plan to keep Sara safe.

I met Jordan in the hallway. She was carrying a covered tray, and she came up short when I stepped out of Sara's room.

"I thought Sara might be hungry," she explained.

"She's still asleep, but she might want some food when she wakes up. Maybe you could stay with her while I take care of a few things."

"Sure."

I opened the door and closed it behind her. Then I went in search of Tristan, who was in his office, looking like he'd been put through the wringer.

"How's Sara?" he asked as soon as I entered.

"She had a rough night, but she's sleeping now. Jordan's with her." I sank into one of the chairs in front of his desk. "Did you find out anything from Nate?"

"No, and I don't think we will. It looks like he was compelled by a much stronger vampire, his maker most likely."

I nodded. The vampires knew we'd question Nate, and they wouldn't have wanted to take a chance of us learning something important from him. He'd been nothing more than a way to hurt Sara since the Master couldn't get to her.

"They know where she is," I said.

"Yes." Tristan rested his arms on the desk. "We might have to consider moving her to a different location."

"So you think it's no longer safe here for her?" I'd asked myself that question a number of times last night, but I wanted to hear his thoughts.

"No stronghold has ever been breached, and we've added extra security since Sara came. This time yesterday I would have said she was absolutely safe here. Nate changed that."

I sighed wearily. "I'll talk to her about it in a few days. She can't handle anything else now."

"You're right." He let out a ragged breath. "She was so happy to see Nate, and then he stood up. God, the look on her face. It'll haunt me forever."

"That's what they wanted, to cut her as deeply as possible. It's going to take a long time for her to heal from this."

It was hard enough for her, knowing that Nate and her friends would age and die, but for Nate to go this way. This never should have happened.

My hands clenched the arms of my chair. "I should have known those bastards would go after Nate to get to her. I promised Sara they'd both be safe, and I failed them both."

Tristan shook his head. "*We* failed them. I was so happy my granddaughter was here I didn't do my duty as a warrior. I should have left someone in Maine to watch over Nate until we caught the Master."

"And now Sara and Nate are paying the price." I rubbed my jaw, which was covered in a day-old beard. "I've never seen her like this, Tristan. I don't know what to do."

"Be there. That's all you can do. The bond will help. She has a strong connection to you, and it will let her know she's not alone."

He clasped his hands. "Claire told me you sent for the werewolves."

I frowned. "Is that a problem?"

"No. I'm glad you did it. Sara talks about them like they're family, and she'll need them, especially after Nate's gone."

"About that." I leaned forward in my chair. "I want to give him a proper burial. I know that's not how we dispose of vampires, but this is Nate."

"I agree." He wrote something on a notepad. "I'll arrange for cremation, and we can have a celebration of life ceremony here."

"She'll appreciate that."

Tristan finished writing and pushed his chair back. "I'm going to see Nate again. Do you want to come with me?"

"Yes." The last thing I wanted to do was see Nate as a vampire and chained to a wall. But I owed it to him and to Sara to be there.

The cells and interrogation rooms were located in the lowest level of the main building, and they were specially constructed to contain even the strongest vampire. The stone walls and floor were two feet thick and reinforced with silver mesh. There were no windows, and the only door was warded by an ancient Druid spell.

Ben was standing guard when we got there, and he smiled grimly at us as he took a set of keys from his pocket and unlocked the door to the cells.

"What's it been like down here?" I asked him.

"He's screamed for blood a few times, but other than that he's been quiet."

We stepped into the hallway that housed the cells and closed the door behind us. We'd only taken a few steps when Nate's voice came from the cell at the end.

"Tristan, back so soon? And who do I smell with you? Nikolas, maybe?"

"Hello, Nate." I stepped up to the barred window and flipped the light switch to illuminate his cell.

Nate stood chained by his hands and feet to the back wall. He smiled and rattled one of his chains. "When you asked me to visit, I had no idea the accommodations here were so grand, I should have come a lot sooner."

"I wish you had," I said regretfully.

Seeing him like this doubled the weight lying on my chest. Nate had been a good man, a loving father to Sara, and he never should have come to this end.

"Well, I'm here now." He licked one of his fangs. His eyes were the coal black of a new vampire, and they glittered with hatred.

"I was hoping Sara would come to visit me. Where is my dear little niece?"

"Busy." If I had my way, she'd never see him like this.

He sighed dramatically. "And I was really looking forward to spending some quality time with her, talking about the good old days. Maybe she'd give me a taste of that fine faerie blood. I hear there is nothing like it."

My jaw clenched, and I reached for the door handle.

"Don't." Tristan laid a hand on my shoulder. "He's trying to provoke you."

I dropped my hand and stared at the creature that used to be Nate Grey. It had his memories and his body, but it was nothing like the man. Prior to today, I'd never known anyone before they became a vampire. I'd never thought about the person they'd been, or how much of them was left after the demon took over their body. It was clear to me now that nothing of them remained.

"What happened to you?" I asked him.

He laughed coldly. "I should think that's obvious."

"Yes, but I bet you want to tell us all about it." If there was one thing I knew about vampires, it was how arrogant they were. They loved to talk about themselves. And the younger the vampire, the cockier they were.

"Wouldn't you like to know?" he taunted. "I didn't tell Tristan the ten times he asked me. Why would I tell you?"

I shrugged. "I figured you'd enjoy telling us how you became strong and whole again."

"Like you care. You just want to know who she was."

"She?"

His mouth closed, and he scowled at me.

"A woman, huh? Bet she was beautiful too."

He remained silent.

I wet my lips. "It's kind of dry down here, isn't it? You must be getting thirsty by now."

"I'm fine," he lied as his eyes took on a hungry gleam.

"We have a few pints of blood upstairs in the medical ward if you change your mind. I'm sure it's not as good as blood fresh from the vein, but it'll still taste pretty damn good going down."

He swallowed convulsively, his eyes dipping to my throat.

I continued to taunt him. "I heard new vampires have to drink twice a day. When did you last have blood? Definitely over twelve hours ago. I have a feeling you're going to get mighty parched in the next few hours."

The vampire said nothing.

I looked at Tristan. "I think we're done here."

"I want to see Sara," Nate said.

"I want my friend back," I called over my shoulder. "Looks like neither of us will get what we want."

"I know her. She'll want to see her uncle before...well, you know."

"You know nothing about her, vampire," I said more calmly than I felt. "And you're not her uncle."

"Maybe not, but I might be more inclined to talk to her. If she asks me nicely."

Tristan motioned for me to go back to the outer room.

"That's as much as I could get out of him last night, except for the fact that his maker was a female," he said once we were out of earshot of the vampire. "He keeps asking to see Sara."

I crossed my arms. "That's not going to happen. I won't let that thing torment her for one second more than it already has."

"I don't want that either, but he's right about her. She's going to want to see him before he dies."

I opened my mouth to object, but he spoke first. "You know Sara. No matter how much pain she's in, she's going to need to say good-bye to Nate. We can't stop her from seeing him if she wants to."

My stomach twisted at the thought of her in the same room with the vampire, and the pain it would cause her. *Khristu, hasn't she been through enough?*

"She's not going to see him without me," I said in a tone that brooked no argument.

"Or me," he replied. He looked at the door to the cells. "I'm going to move him to one of the interrogation rooms. He's a lot thirstier today, so I might get something out of him if I tempt him with blood."

His expression of distaste made it clear how he felt about working on the vampire again. Last night could not have been easy for him.

"I'll do it," I said. I wanted to go back to Sara, but Jordan would stay with her. It was important that we find out what the vampire knew, and it wasn't fair to put that on Tristan.

"We'll do it together," he said gratefully. "I don't know how long you could be alone with him before he goaded you into killing him."

"You're probably right."

He opened the door again. "Let's get this over with then."

* * *

I stood on the front steps as the black Expedition pulled up with Niall behind the wheel. The front passenger door opened, and Roland jumped out. Peter climbed out of the back seat, and the two of them went to the rear to grab their large duffle bags.

The SUV drove away, and the boys turned to me.

"Welcome to Westhorne," I said, walking down the steps. "Thanks for coming so soon."

"Thanks for calling us. We would have been here last night if we could." Roland hefted his bag on his shoulder. "Where's Sara?"

"I think she's walking her hounds."

When I'd gone back to her room earlier, I'd found a note from Jordan saying Sara had gone to the menagerie. I'd called there and Sahir told me she had taken Hugo and Woolf out. I didn't worry that she'd go far. Plus, Tristan had doubled the patrols last night.

Peter glanced around nervously. "Oh yeah, the hellhounds."

I smiled and pointed to the door. "You can wait in the main hall while I go find her."

Roland shivered. "Thanks. It's bloody cold in Idaho."

I left them in the hall and started across the snow-covered lawn until movement near the river caught my eye. I headed toward the small figure strolling aimlessly along the bank, looking so pale and lost that my heart ached for her.

She stopped and turned toward me as I drew near, and her sad eyes warmed as her mouth formed a ghost of a smile. I took her in my arms, letting my body warm her chilled one as we stood quietly for a long moment.

I pulled back to look down at her. "How are you holding up?"

"I'm okay," she lied bleakly.

I took her cold hand and started back toward the main building. I hadn't told her about her friends coming because she needed a happy surprise.

"Come, I have something for you."

"What is it?" she asked with mild curiosity.

I squeezed her hand. "I know nothing can take away your pain or undo what's happened. But if you could have anything else right now, what would it be?"

Without hesitation, she said, "I'd want –"

"Sara!" shouted Roland as he tore around the corner of the building.

"Roland!" A sob tore from her throat, and she threw herself at her friend who hugged her as if they hadn't seen each other in years. As soon as Roland let her go, Peter wrapped her in a hug.

"How did you guys get here?" she asked tearfully when Peter had set her on her feet again.

Roland's smile faded. "Nikolas called me last night and told me you needed us. He had a private jet pick us up in Portland this morning. He told us about Nate. I'm so sorry, Sara."

She pressed her lips together and nodded.

"I'll let you three catch up." Seeing them together, I knew her friends were exactly what she needed now.

Sara caught my hand as I turned to leave. "Thank you," she said hoarsely as a tear escaped and ran down her face.

I wiped the wetness away and gave her a tender smile. "I'll be close if you need me."

I had to force myself to leave her, even though I knew she was in good hands. All afternoon, my thoughts returned to her, and I worried how she was doing. It had to be unbearable, knowing Nate was close by and waiting to hear when he was going to die. The sooner we took care of that, the better. After working on him for two hours, I was sure we'd gotten all we could from him. Keeping him alive was only prolonging Sara's pain.

That evening, I ate a quick meal in the dining hall, keenly aware of Sara's absence. As soon as I finished, I headed for her room to check on her. No one answered my knock so I went to Roland's room, which was right across the hall from hers.

"Hey, what's up?" he asked.

"Is Sara with you?"

"No. She was tired after dinner and went to lie down for a while."

I went back to Sara's door and knocked again. When there was no answer, I opened the door and looked inside. The bed was rumpled, but there was no sign of her.

Worry gnawed at me and I headed back downstairs. Maybe she'd gone to the menagerie again. She seemed to find comfort in being with the hellhounds.

I reached the first floor, and nearly collided with Tristan in the main hall.

"Nikolas," he said in a rush, and his fearful expression set off alarm bells in my head. "Ben just called. Sara knocked him out and locked herself in with Nate."

I didn't wait to hear what he said next. My heart pounded against my ribs as I sped down to the lower level. I burst into the outer room and found Ben sitting on the floor, still looking slightly dazed from the jolt Sara had given him.

"She's in there," he said weakly, pointing at the door to the cells.

I tried the door, but it was locked. "Where are the keys?"

"She took them." Ben rested his face in his hands. "What the hell did she do to me?"

Tristan caught up to me, carrying the other set of keys. He unlocked the door, and the two of us ran to the cell at the end of the hallway.

The cell door was locked, and inside the room, Sara stood a foot from the vampire that was still chained to the wall. The vampire's cocky sneer had been replaced by a look of fear. I understood why when I saw blue sparks move through Sara's hair.

"Sara, no!" Tristan shouted. "Whatever you're planning to do, you have to stop."

"I'm going to kill a vampire," she replied thickly.

Tristan gripped the bars in the window. "Listen to me, Sara; you don't want to do this. Killing a vampire is one thing, but if you kill Nate, it will haunt you forever."

"He's not Nate. He's a monster," she said as her hair began to float around her shoulders.

"Yes, he is, but you will see only Nate's face when you remember this," Tristan told her. "Nate would not want that for you."

"I —"

"Sara, open the door," I said in a gentle but firm voice.

Her hands began to glow in response. The vampire shrank away from her, his eyes wide with terror.

She laid her hands on his chest, and he screamed.

Grabbing the keys from Tristan, I fitted one into the lock. I had to stop her. No matter what she said, she would never come back from killing Nate.

The door swung open and I moved toward Sara, only to be hit by a blast of power unlike anything I'd felt from her. I slammed into the wall by the door with enough force to make my ears ring.

I opened my eyes and was nearly blinded by the brilliant white sphere that now encased Sara and the vampire.

"Jesus Christ," Tristan uttered as I got to my feet.

"Sara." I started toward her, and I made it two feet before I came up against a pulsing wall of energy that burned me the longer I pushed at it.

Tristan grabbed me by the shoulders and dragged me backward out of the room. "Nikolas, stop. You're only hurting yourself."

I pulled out of his grasp. "She's in there with a goddamn vampire. I have to get to her."

Turning back to the room, I tried to look at the ball of light, but it was like staring into the sun. I couldn't see Sara or the vampire, and that scared the hell out of me. All I could do was stand here helplessly and imagine the worst.

"Sara's doing this, whatever it is," Tristan said.

No sooner had the words left his mouth than the sphere sent out another pulse that pushed us back several steps.

Then it was gone, leaving Sara and the vampire lying motionless on the stone floor.

CHAPTER 25

SOLMI, MY MORI wailed.

For one terrifying moment, I thought I'd lost her. It wasn't until I sank to my knees beside her and pulled her into my arms that I realized the bond was still there.

"Sara?" I called to her as I checked her pulse and breathing. *Thank you,* I prayed silently when I felt her warm breath against my face.

I patted her cheek. "Sara, can you hear me?"

Nothing, not even an eyelid flicker.

I rose to my feet with her cradled in my arms. "I need to get her to the healers."

Tristan didn't respond.

I looked at him and found him staring at the vampire sprawled on the floor. The shock on Tristan's face had me following his gaze to the vampire looking up at us with a confused expression that made him look almost human again. It took me several seconds to realize he was on the floor instead of chained to the wall and that his shackles were gone.

"It can't be," Tristan breathed. "It's not possible."

"What?" I asked harshly.

"Look at him, Nikolas. Look at his eyes."

I stared down at the vampire, who turned his head until his green eyes, so much like Sara's, met mine. I sucked in a sharp breath.

"Nikolas?" he said weakly, struggling to sit up. "What happened?"

"Nate?"

He sat leaning against the wall and breathing hard from the effort. "I feel like I have the hangover from hell."

Tristan and I exchanged a look.

"Nate, you don't look well," Tristan said slowly. "I'll get you some blood."

"Blood?" A look of revulsion crossed Nate's face, followed soon after by shock. He ran a hand over his mouth, feeling for the fangs he no longer had.

"I-I'm not…that thing is gone… Please, tell me this is real."

"It's real." Tristan looked like he was still in shock. "What can you remember?"

Nate rubbed his temples. "Bits and pieces. It's coming back slowly. I remember talking to Sara. I think I was chained to the wall and…"

He looked up at the girl in my arms and fear filled his eyes. "Sara! Oh, God. What did I do to her?"

"I think whatever she did to you caused this." I looked down at her unconscious form. "I'm going to take her to the healers. Tristan, are you okay here?"

"Yes, although I'm not sure exactly what to do now."

I left him trying to figure out what to do about Nate and rushed to the medical ward. The healers on duty had me lay Sara on a table, and then they got to work examining her. I left the room just long enough for them to remove her clothing and dress her in a hospital gown.

"What's wrong with her?" I asked when I returned.

"We're not sure," one of the healers replied. "All her vitals look good, and she doesn't appear to have any physical injuries. Can you tell us how she came to be like this?"

I shut the door. "Sara is half Fae."

The healers looked at me like I'd lost my mind.

"It's true." I gave them a quick overview of her history. "Her magic affects demons as any Fae's magic would. You heard about her uncle showing up yesterday as a vampire?"

They nodded, looking incapable of speech.

"Sara used her power on him, and it looks like he's human again. And she ended up like this."

One of the healers crossed her arms and fixed me with a hard stare. "Is this some kind of prank?"

"Do I look like I'm joking around?" I ground out. "You know as much as I do about what happened. Now help her."

"Her uncle really is human again?" the other healer asked.

"We think so. Tristan's with him now."

She shook her head in disbelief and waved a hand at Sara. "I don't know much about Fae physiology, but if she used that much magic and she's only half Fae, she could be in shock. She does have a Mori, yes?"

"Yes. We're bonded."

"Ah." Her eyes lit with understanding. "It's possible then that her magic was too much for her Mori and she passed out because of it. We'll observe her and hope she wakes up soon."

"That's it? That's all you can do for her?"

"Nikolas, we've never had a patient like Sara before, and quite frankly, neither of us knows what to do beyond this point. Let's give it a little time and see what happens."

We moved Sara to a bed so she'd be more comfortable. The healers left and I sat by the bed, holding her hand and watching for any sign she was coming around.

Twenty minutes later, Tristan and Ben walked past the door, supporting Nate between them. They put him in one of the rooms, and soon I heard the healers' exclamations as they saw what could be the world's first ex-vampire. I still wasn't sure I believed it myself, and I'd been there.

I squeezed Sara's hand. "You have some explaining to do when you wake up."

"How is she?" Tristan asked from the doorway.

"She's still out. They think she might be in some kind of shock."

He came over to stand at the foot of the bed. "I'm not surprised after what she did. Jesus, what did she do?"

"So Nate is human again?" The words sounded surreal to my ears.

"As far as I can tell. Silver doesn't burn him, and he looked ill when we offered him blood. The healers are checking him now."

I gazed down at Sara's still face. She looked so peaceful she could have been sleeping.

"Is it safe to have him so close to Sara?"

Tristan nodded. "We have a restraint on him as a precaution, and I'm leaving someone outside his door."

"How's he dealing with all this?" I asked.

Tristan exhaled loudly. "He's in shock too. He keeps asking if this is real and if Sara is okay."

"She will be. She has to be," I said roughly.

"Didn't she say healings made her tired? And you said she passed out after healing her werewolf friend. This could be her body's way of recharging after using so much power."

Hope surged in me. "Then she should wake up in a few hours."

There was a commotion outside and a frantic voice said, "Where's Sara?"

Roland and Peter burst into the room followed by Jordan. Roland went around to the other side of the bed to look down at Sara. "What happened to her?"

"She used a lot of power for a healing, and it knocked her out," I said.

Roland frowned. "What the hell did she heal, an elephant?"

"Nate."

"Nate?" His eyes narrowed.

"But Nate's a vampire," Peter cut in.

"Not anymore," Tristan said. "At least we don't think he is."

"What?" Roland croaked. "That...that's impossible."

"I don't think Sara knows that word." I caressed the back of her hand with my thumb as I told them what had happened downstairs. "He's next door. Go see for yourselves."

I stayed with Sara while the rest of them went to see Nate, but I could hear murmurs, followed by the boys' voices raised in excitement. Then there was a shuffling sound, and a healer shouted something. Tristan called out that everything was under control.

What the hell was going on over there?

Jordan came in and flopped down onto a chair near the door. "Well, you don't see something like that every day."

"What happened?"

"Sara's friends stripped down like they were at a spring break party and changed to wolf form. Then they started sniffing her uncle all over. Apparently, they can always smell a vampire when they are in their fur. They said he's definitely human again. Although, he might need therapy after this. I never realized how big a werewolf is in person. Pictures don't do them justice."

"Nothing ever matches the real thing."

"Yeah," she said thoughtfully. "And they must work out a lot. Nice butts. I mean before they went all furry. But don't tell them I said that."

A laugh slipped out. I could see why Sara liked her. "Your secret is safe with me."

Jordan grew quiet for a long moment. "Is she going to be all right?"

"Yes." I wouldn't accept anything else.

Sara didn't wake up that night or the next day. The healers had no answers, and I tried not to be angry because I knew this was a unique situation. But with each passing hour, I grew more afraid she might not come back.

Tristan and I began to talk about what to do if she didn't wake up soon. He knew a few powerful healers who were not Mohiri, and he was already trying to track them down. I wished there was a way to contact Sara's sylph friend. If her condition was the result of her Fae power, the faerie should know what to do.

Nate had been given the apartment next to Tristan's, but he stayed in the medical ward to be close to Sara. He'd started eating food again and continued to ask about Sara. Roland and Peter spent a lot of time with him, and Tristan paid him regular visits. I went to visit him twice, and it warmed me to see the old Nate again.

Tristan and I asked him a lot of questions about his short time as a vampire. He remembered meeting a female vampire, but not her name or face. He couldn't recall much from the change except the pain. He'd been compelled to forget anything that might lead us to the Master.

"I remember talking to Sara on the phone a few days before Thanksgiving. I was already...changing then. I remember the trip here and talking to you outside with Sara..."

His voice broke, and it was a few minutes before he could talk again. "The things I said to her... I told her Daniel's death was her fault, and that I never wanted her. I-I didn't mean it. I love her like she's my own daughter."

"It was the vampire talking," I told him. "Sara knows that, and she'll be too happy to have you back to care about anything else."

If only she would wake up.

Sara had a steady stream of visitors as well. Roland and Peter were in and out all day along with Jordan. Tristan and Chris came by regularly to check on her, as did Seamus, Niall, and Sahir.

Even Desmund left his rooms to come spend time with her. He brought an ancient stereo, which he set up in a corner of the room, and a stack of classical albums. He informed me that Sara liked Tchaikovsky and hearing the soothing music might help her.

I was willing to try anything at that point.

The second day dawned with me pleading with Sara to open her eyes.

"Please, come back to me," I implored as I rubbed her hand between mine. "I almost lost you once. Don't do this to me again."

I knew the more time that passed, the lower her chances were of coming out of her coma. The healers had stopped saying it could happen any minute now, and they looked more worried each time they came to check on her.

Roland arrived at noon. He walked up to the bed then made a face. "Dude, you're a mess. You need a shower."

"I'll shower after she wakes up," I said without looking at him.

"She might not want to if her nose is as good as mine."

I looked down at the clothes I'd been wearing for two days. He was right. I didn't want Sara to see me like this when she woke up.

I let go of her hand and stood. "Stay with her. I won't be long."

When I got back to Sara's hospital room twenty minutes later, I found Roland and Peter plugging in an iPod and a pair of speakers.

Roland pointed at Desmund's stereo. "Sara might like that stuff, but it's not her favorite music. She needs some good old classic rock. That's her thing."

Tristan walked in an hour later with one of the healers. I stalked toward them, determined to either get some answers or to find someone else to help Sara.

"It's been two damn days. Why hasn't she woken up?"

"Physically, there is nothing wrong with her," the healer said. "All I can guess is that her mind needs to heal from the trauma she suffered, and she will wake when she is ready."

"You guess?" I needed more than a guess. I needed someone to tell me what the hell was wrong with my mate.

Tristan raised a hand. "Nikolas, calm down. There is nothing to be gained from yelling at the healers. None of us has seen anything like this before."

Roland snorted. "Dude, I wouldn't want to wake up either with you shouting like that."

Peter pointed at Sara. "I think I just saw her eyes move!"

Roland leaned down over Sara. "Sara, it's Roland. Can you hear me?"

He let out a whoop. "There! Her lips moved. See, Pete, I told you the music was a good idea."

I pushed the two of them out of the way and took her hand in mine. "Sara? It's time to wake up, *moy malen'kiy voin.*"

"Ah, is our beauty still sleeping?" Desmund said from behind me. "Perhaps a kiss from her prince is all she needs."

I gritted my teeth. "This is no time for your humor, Desmund."

Desmund scoffed. "On the contrary, laughter is just what she needs. It is far too gloomy in here…and what is that awful noise?"

"Hey, she likes this music," Roland said defensively.

Roland, Peter, and Desmund began to argue, and I was about to order them all from the room when…

"Stop it."

My breath caught, and I looked down as Sara's eyelids flickered.

And then her beautiful green eyes were gazing into mine.

"Hi," she rasped, that one word melting the icy knot that had been lodged in my stomach for two days.

"Hi, yourself."

Her eyes narrowed in confusion. "What's going on? Why is everyone in my room?"

She coughed, and I picked up a glass of water from the table by the bed. Lifting her head, I held the glass to her lips so she could drink.

"Hey, how are you feeling?" Roland asked. "You scared the crap out of us."

"Roland? What are you doing here?"

He glanced at me. "You don't remember?"

"No, I…" She made a choked sound and buried her face in her hands.

"Oh God, I killed Nate."

"No, Sara, he's okay," I told her, but she was too distraught to hear me.

She began to gasp for air, and I pulled her into my arms to calm her. She pressed her face into the crook of my shoulder, and her heartbreaking cries filled the room.

"Shhh. It's okay, Sara. Nate's alive," I said to her over and over.

Her sobs stopped suddenly, and she pulled back to stare at me. "What did you say?"

"Nate is alive," I repeated.

She shook her head. "That's not possible. I killed him. I felt him die."

Tristan came over to stand beside me. "You killed the vampire. We have no idea what you did in that room, but Nate is alive."

"You're not making any sense," she cried. "How can the vampire be alive if I killed him?"

"Sara, the vampire is not alive. Nate is," I said. "Nate is human again."

"What?" Her stunned gaze went to everyone in the room. "Human? He's human...and alive?"

"He smells human to us," Peter said.

Sara reached for Roland who stood on her other side. "You've seen him?" she asked, her voice rising.

"Ow!" He pulled out of her grasp and rubbed his arm. "Demon strength, remember. We've seen him a few times. And you should know that he —"

"Where is he? I want to see him." She sat up quickly and almost fell out of bed.

I caught her and gently pushed her back against the pillow. "Hold on. You're too weak to go anywhere."

I looked at Roland to tell him to get Nate, but Sara began to struggle against me.

"Let me go! I have to see Nate," she shouted frantically. "Let go of me, Nikolas, or I swear I'll never speak to you again."

"You never did like to be told what to do," Nate said from the doorway.

Sara went still. Then she strained to see past the people standing around the bed. "Nate?" she said hoarsely.

Nate approached the bed, and I moved back to let him get close to Sara. "Hey, kiddo," Nate said.

She broke down, and he pulled her into his arms. I could see that he was shaking too as he held her close and spoke to her.

Sara pulled back from him with a loud gasp. "Nate, you're walking!"

He laughed like a man with a new lease on life. In truth, that's exactly what he'd received, though he'd had to go through hell to earn it.

"Tristan says my spine was healed when the vampire demon possessed me. And then you killed the demon."

Sara sank back to the bed. "I don't understand any of this."

"What do you remember?" Tristan asked.

"Sara has been unconscious for two days, and this is obviously overtaxing her," the healer cut in. "Perhaps we should let her rest before —"

"No. I've been asleep long enough." Sara sat up again and pulled Nate down to sit beside her. She looked around the room, and her mouth parted in surprise. "Desmund? I thought you hated coming downstairs."

I smiled. Something told me the disdainful English warrior would do almost anything for Sara.

He walked over to her. "Well, they would not accommodate me by moving you upstairs, so I was forced to spend time in this depressing ward."

He lifted her hand to his lips, and I felt foolish for being jealous of a gay man. "Welcome back, little one. And if you worry us like that again, I will lock you up myself for the next fifty years."

"Get in line." For once, Desmund and I were in total agreement.

"I will go and let you catch up with your family and friends," he told her. "Come see me when you are feeling better."

After Desmund left, Tristan said, "Sara, do you feel up to telling us what happened? What you did has never been done before, at least it's never been recorded in our history. I don't know where to begin to try to understand it."

She lifted her hands and let them fall back to the blanket. "I didn't know I could do that. I knew I could kill demons, but I never dreamed it was possible to make a vampire human again."

Biting her lip, she looked up at Nate with tormented eyes. "I was so upset and angry about what happened to you. I went down there to kill you, not to save you."

"I know," he replied kindly. "I remember everything, especially the horrible things I…the vampire said to you. I know you did what you had to do."

Roland raised a hand to get her attention. "What exactly did you do?"

She took a deep breath. "Like I said, I planned to kill the vampire. The first time I hit him with my power it was enough to knock him out. While I was connected to him, I could see the vamhir demon attached to Nate's heart. I was going to hit it again, but then I heard its thoughts. Actually, I think they were its memories."

My eyes met Tristan's, and I was sure the shock I saw in his was mirrored in mine. She'd seen a live vamhir demon inside a human host, and heard its thoughts?

Tristan cut in. "You understood what it was saying?"

She nodded. "Bits and pieces."

"Only our oldest scholars can understand demon tongue, and they spend centuries learning it," he told her.

"But we can understand our Mori demons," she argued.

"The Mori demon was chosen to create our race because it is compatible with humans," he explained. "Our demons are born inside us, and we learn to communicate with them as we grow."

She looked at me. "You mean my Mori talks in a whole other language and I didn't even know it?"

I nodded.

"What happened after you heard the demon?" Peter asked.

"Then I saw —" She looked at Nate. "I saw your memories of me. Then I saw you being changed and the pain you went through. I couldn't let you suffer anymore. I held your heart, and I felt it stop. I thought you died."

Her voice broke. I wanted to hold her and soothe away her pain, but it was Nate she needed in that moment.

"I think I did die, but then I felt something pulling at me. It was so bright and warm that I honestly thought I must be looking at an angel. Then heat spread through me and it got so hot I thought I was going to burn from the inside out. The next thing I knew, I woke up on the floor of the cell with Tristan standing over me, looking like he was going to finish the job."

Tristan wore a serious expression. "I almost did. But then I saw his eyes, and I knew something was different, especially after what I'd witnessed."

"What did you see?" she asked him.

He moved closer to the bed. "We unlocked the door, but before Nikolas and I could get to you, you sent out enough energy to throw us across the room. You and Nate were inside some kind of energy sphere that glowed so brightly it was impossible to look at directly. We couldn't get within five feet of it without it pushing us back. I've seen many things in my life, but nothing like that."

Her mouth dropped open, an indication she hadn't been aware of everything she'd done in the cell.

"You didn't actually see what I did to Nate?" she asked.

"No," he said. "You were like that for a minute, and then the sphere disappeared and you both fell to the floor. Whatever it was, it melted the irons on Nate's arms and legs without leaving a mark on him."

"A minute?" she echoed in disbelief. "It felt like it was a lot longer than that."

"Yes, it did," I agreed gruffly, remembering how helpless I'd felt not being able to get to her.

Roland smiled. "You learned some new tricks since the last time we saw you."

"This makes what she did to you look like nothing," Peter quipped.

"No kidding."

Sara laughed, and everyone in the room smiled. It felt like it had been forever since I'd heard that sound.

Roland thought so too. "It's good to hear that again."

"It feels good," she said happily. She looked at Nate. "You're staying here until they get the Master, right?"

Tristan had already offered Nate a home here, and it hadn't taken much convincing to get him to stay after his ordeal. He wasn't sure he could ever live in his old apartment again.

"I guess I can write as well here as I can anywhere else," Nate told her. "Of course, I'll need to get my computer and things from home."

"And don't forget Daisy and –" A look of horror entered her eyes. "Nate, where are Daisy and Oscar? You didn't…?"

"No!" he exclaimed, aghast. "They ran away as soon as I went home after I was attacked."

Peter jumped in. "They're fine. Dad and Uncle Brendan went to check out your place and they saw Oscar outside. He wouldn't come near them so Aunt Judith put out some food for him."

"And Mom took Daisy to our place," Roland reassured her.

"Thanks," Sara said hoarsely.

"Why don't we let Sara and Nate have some time alone together?" Tristan said. "I'm sure they have a lot to talk about."

Sara held out a hand. "Wait. What about Ben? Is he okay?"

Tristan smiled. "Ben is fine, although he is a bit put out about being taken down so easily. He understands you were very distraught and not thinking straight."

"I'll apologize to him as soon as I see him," she said.

"I think Ben would rather you not bring it up again," I said lightly. The young warrior had taken plenty of ribbing the last two days for letting a new trainee get the better of him.

"Maybe I should be the one to apologize to him for helping you hone that particular skill in the first place."

Tristan gave the two of us a mild scolding look. "Perhaps I should learn exactly what goes on in your training sessions. But right now, Sara needs to rest and talk to Nate. We'll discuss her training in a few days."

I didn't respond. Sara's training was my responsibility, and I'd remind Tristan of that when we talked.

Plus, I was proud of Sara. She shouldn't have used her power against another Mohiri, but she'd also demonstrated how strong and controlled she'd become in such a short time. I could only imagine what she'd be able to do in six months or a year.

Sara leaned forward. "Can I go back to my room? We'd be a lot more comfortable there."

"You should stay here, close to the healers, for a few more hours," I said.

"Okay, but only for a few hours. Then I need to get out of this ward. I've spent way too much time here the last month."

"I've given Nate the apartment next to mine," Tristan said. "It has two large bedrooms, so you can move in with him if you want to."

I knew she was going to decline his offer before she spoke. She'd objected to Tristan talking about her love life. There was no way she was going to live with Nate next door to Tristan.

And if I had my way, the next person she lived with would be me.

"If you don't mind, I'd like to stay with the other trainees," she said to Nate. "We'll see each other all the time anyway."

Everyone left until it was just Sara, Nate, and me. I knew they needed time alone, but it wasn't easy to leave her so soon after she'd finally awakened.

"I'll be close if you need anything." I leaned in to kiss her forehead. "Later, you and I are going to talk about what will happen if you ever pull something like that again."

CHAPTER 26

"MAYBE YOU'LL GET home faster if you ditch the bike and run."

Chris's chuckle came through the speaker of my helmet, and I smiled in return. Maybe I *was* going a little fast, but I was looking forward to getting some alone time at last with Sara tonight. She'd been with either Nate or Roland and Peter since she woke up yesterday, and I hadn't wanted to intrude on their reunion.

But now I needed time with her. I'd stopped by her room earlier to tell her I'd see her tonight, and her shy smile had told me she was looking forward to it, too.

I rounded the last curve in the road, and the tall gates of Westhorne came into view. A pit of dread formed in my stomach when I saw the gates hanging open with no security lights on and no one in sight.

"Chris," I said.

"I see it," he answered, all traces of humor gone.

Instead of driving through the gates, we stopped on the road and grabbed our swords from their scabbards. With a blade in each hand, I strode through the gates. I didn't try to be quiet because if there was someone hostile on the inside, they'd heard the bikes and knew we were there.

A vampire flew out of the darkness before I'd taken a dozen steps inside the gates. He was fast, but my heightened hearing warned me of the attack.

I moved to the side, and his claws shredded the sleeve of my leather jacket as he went past me.

I spun to face him and saw Chris engaged in battle with a second vampire as seven more came around the corner of the gatehouse. My gut twisted.

Westhorne was under attack.

Sara. I was too far from the main building to sense her, and not knowing where she was or if she was safe made cold fear flood my chest.

The vampire laughed. "Let's do this, warrior. I have a stronghold to destroy for my Master. Then I'm going to celebrate with some fine young Mohiri blood."

My Mori roared, and a familiar rage ignited in me.

The vampire was still laughing when one of my blades cut him in half at the waist. He screamed and tried to hold in his intestines before his two halves collapsed to the snow-covered ground. His feet landed near his head, and he screamed again when he realized he was in two pieces. A downward swing of my blade ended him. I would have left him to suffer, but a vampire can regenerate if they are put back together. This one was never coming back.

Two more vampires rushed me, and their speed told me they were not young. I was faster and stronger, but they made up for that in numbers. One came at me from the front, and I slashed a blade across his chest before I whirled to confront the one attacking from the back. My sword whistled through the air as the vampire lunged for me, and I felt it connect with flesh.

The vampire shrieked and staggered backward, holding up two stumps where his hands had been. "Take him!" he screeched.

The remaining vampires advanced with more caution. Two went after Chris, who had killed his opponent, and the other four came at me. I brandished my swords. It was going to be a fight, but I'd faced tougher odds. And this time they threatened my mate. I could taste the bloodlust in my throat.

Shouts came from the stronghold, followed by the unmistakable sounds of battle. My heart rammed into my ribs at the knowledge Sara was in there somewhere.

"Nikolas," Chris bellowed.

I spun back to the fight as a vampire dove at me. He hit me full in the chest, and the two of us went down. We hit the paved driveway, and I disentangled myself from him and rolled away, still gripping my swords.

I lay on my back and swung the sword in my right hand as the vampire jumped at me again. The blade cut a deep wound in his midsection, and he soared past me to land on his back several feet away.

"Need some help?"

Desmund appeared out of nowhere to stand over me, wearing his signature arrogant smile and carrying a sword I was sure had not been used in many years.

He didn't wait for me to answer. He went after the nearest vampire, moving so fast, only my demon sight allowed me to track him. Blood sprayed, and the vampire's head flew through the air to hit the stone gatehouse wall with a sickening crunch.

"What took you so long?" I gritted, moving to finish off the vampire on the ground.

Desmund smirked and went after another vampire. "I couldn't find the right sword to go with this outfit."

Chris grunted in pain, and I looked over to see him go down under three vampires. Desmund ran to him and lifted a vampire off him like it weighed nothing. With incredible strength, he threw the vampire in the air and skewered it through the heart.

Another vampire came at me, and I fought him as Desmund made short work of the two left on top of Chris. I dispatched mine and glanced at Chris, who was getting to his feet and holding his shoulder.

"You okay?" I asked him.

"Yeah. Got me in my sword arm, but I can still fight."

A girl's scream pierced the air, and my heart nearly exploded from my chest. *Sara.* I had to find her, protect her.

Eight more vampires came through the open gates. The three of us turned as one to face them, but Chris had trouble holding his sword. I couldn't leave him and Desmund here to fight these vampires alone. Battling my most primal instinct to find and protect my mate, I did the only thing I could.

"Chris," I bit out as more shouts and screams came from the stronghold. "Will you find Sara? Desmund and I can handle this."

"I'll find her," he said fiercely.

The moment he left, the vampires surrounded us. At least half of them were mature, and I had to wonder how so many older vampires were working together like this.

Desmund looked sideways at me. "Try to keep up."

The two of us fought wordlessly, and the only sounds came from the vampires who shouted at each other and screamed when they fell under one of our swords. The younger ones died first, and the older ones proved why they had survived this long.

I tried not to think of Sara. Worrying about her fate only distracted me, and one second of distraction was all a vampire needed to take me down. Desmund and I could be the only thing between these bastards and her. We couldn't let one of them get past us.

When loud roars came from somewhere behind the main building, Desmund and I, and the four remaining vampires, all stopped and stared in that direction.

Khristu! What were my people facing now? I prayed Chris had gotten to Sara in time, even as I began to imagine the worst.

My Mori roared and pushed forward, and I let it have what it wanted. Its excitement filled my mind as its strength flooded my body. A red haze fell over my vision, and I struck out at the nearest of the two vampires circling me. He darted to the side and right into the path of my other sword, which found its mark. I pulled my blade free from his chest, and he crumpled to the ground.

"Now it's you and me," I taunted my last opponent. I gave him no time to respond before I was on him, my sword slicing cleanly through his neck. His eyes bugged as his head flew from his body to roll across the blood stained snow.

I spun to face the next vampire and found Desmund dispatching the last one. Blood roared in my ears as I looked around at the dozen or more vampire bodies littering the ground.

"Now that was refreshing." Desmund's voice broke the sudden silence that had fallen over the grounds.

He looked at me and sighed. "You'd best go find your mate before you lose it altogether."

I sped toward the main building. I was almost at the front entrance when I felt Sara off to one side. I rounded a corner of the building and sucked in a sharp breath at the sight of her. She stood with Chris, Jordan, and the werewolves in the middle of a bloody battlefield, surrounded by vampire bodies and dead crocotta.

My eyes narrowed as I strode toward her, fighting to stay in control. She was bloody but alive, and that was all that mattered.

I threw down my swords and grabbed her shoulders. "Are you hurt?" I growled, trembling from the effort to keep it together.

"I'm okay, Nikolas; we all are." She laid her hands against my chest, and her touch immediately began to calm me.

Then she stood on her toes and whispered, "Please, don't freak out on me, okay? I don't think I can take it right now."

The feel of her body pressed against mine and the sound of her husky voice fed my need for her. I crushed her to me, my mouth capturing hers hungrily, demanding. She filled my senses like a drug, and I wanted more.

She made a soft sound, and her arms crept around my neck as her lips parted under mine. My heart raced when our tongues met, and I began to explore her sweet mouth. Her surrender to the kiss made my body burn for her, while my heart rejoiced at her response and the way she clung to me as if she didn't want to let me go.

Mine, my Mori whispered, and I felt the bond expand. No words could describe the emotions that filled me when our demons connected for the first time. It left me stunned and humbled that this beautiful, passionate woman was mine.

I almost protested when Sara ended the kiss and pulled away from me. But then I saw her blushing cheeks and realized we were not alone.

Jordan whistled. "Wow, I think you guys melted the snow."

"Shut up," Sara retorted.

I hid my satisfied smile.

Chris gave me a tired grin. "You missed all the fun."

He wobbled, and Sara moved to support him. I gently pushed her aside and hooked his arm around my shoulder. I couldn't see any serious injuries on him, but he looked like he'd been put through the ringer a few times.

Sara went to help a boy up from the ground, and my body stiffened when I saw the white markings on his face. A Hale witch? That explained how the vampires were able to breach our defenses.

"I can guess what happened," I bit out.

Chris coughed. "No, you can't, my friend. You really can't. Now, can you please get me somewhere I can lie down before I pass out?"

I nodded and looked at the others, my eyes falling on Sara's bloody clothes. "It looks like you all could use a trip to the healers."

She saw me looking and tried to brush it off. "It's just a scratch. I can hardly feel it. We have to go find the people who were out on patrol. They ran into this guy, and we need to get to them as soon as possible."

My eyes narrowed on the Hale witch who couldn't be older than sixteen. If he'd attacked our sentries, God only knew what shape they were in.

Tristan approached with Desmund and Celine, and I was relieved to see them all looking well except for a few scratches.

"We will find them," Tristan said with barely suppressed anger. "I am relieved to see you are all safe. Go to the healers and I'll talk to you when I get back. Maybe we can piece together exactly what happened here tonight."

"It was Michael," Sara blurted. "He helped the vampires."

"Michael?" Tristan repeated, looking as stunned as I felt.

She had to be mistaken. That kid couldn't even make eye contact with his own people, let alone associate with vampires.

"Little bastard led us right to them," Jordan spat. "If he's not dead, I call dibs on finishing the job."

"Why would Michael do that?" Tristan asked, almost to himself.

Sara wrung her hands. "It's not his fault. The vampires got to him somehow and convinced him they had his twin brother, Matthew. They promised to let him go if Michael helped them."

Jordan scoffed. "Still no excuse to betray everyone you know."

"He's messed up, Jordan," Sara replied with a hint of sadness in her voice.

I stared at her. Was she actually defending the person who had betrayed her to her enemy?

Celine stepped forward. "Where is he now?"

"In the woods over by the menagerie, about fifty yards in," Sara said.

"What were you doing in the woods at night?" I asked, trying not to be angry. After what had happened to Nate, why would she risk herself like that?

"Michael tricked us. He told me Hugo and Woolf got out again and that Sahir had sent him to get me."

"And you believed him?" Celine asked.

"He's Michael. Why wouldn't I believe him?" Sara shot back defensively.

"What happened then?" Tristan asked.

"I was in my room with Roland, Peter, and Jordan when Michael came to me. They went with me to look for Hugo and Woolf. All of a sudden, we were surrounded by vampires."

She swallowed. "Then Michael told them I was the one they wanted."

I swore furiously and fought to keep my anger in check.

Sara let out a shuddering breath. "One of the vampires hit him pretty hard, and I'm not sure if he's alive. We had to leave him."

"We'll find him if he's still out there," Tristan promised her. "You go to the healers. Nikolas, we could use your help if we have men down out there."

Nodding, I passed Chris off to Jordan. Sara looked ready to fall down, and I was pretty sure it was sheer stubbornness keeping her on her feet.

My first instinct was to pick her up and carry her to the medical ward. But we never left a warrior down in the field. The need to take care of my mate warred with the sense of duty ingrained in me since birth.

She gave me a reassuring smile. I didn't want to let her out of my sight, but she would not allow me to stay with her while people were suffering and needed my help.

It was the thought of our warriors lying in the snow, defenseless and in pain, that made me leave Sara. As Chris would say, I needed to think like a warrior now and not like a mate. She was safe and others needed me.

We ran into Erik as we neared the woods. He had a few cuts and bruises, but he looked fine otherwise. Tristan relayed what Sara had told us about Michael's location, and Erik set off to find the boy.

"Who was out on patrol tonight?" I asked Tristan as we entered the woods.

"Seamus, Niall, Ben, and Kenneth."

We walked for several minutes before Tristan stopped.

"We'll cover more ground if we split up. Nikolas and Desmund, you two go toward the lake. Seamus and Niall should be in that area. Celine and I will head toward the road to look for Ben and Kenneth."

The four of us broke into pairs and headed off in opposite directions. Neither Desmund nor I were inclined to speak, and the woods were quiet except for the crunch of our feet on the snow.

We were almost at the lake when we found one of the twins facedown in the snow. I rolled him over, afraid of what I'd find. It was Niall, and he was alive but catatonic.

Hoisting him on my shoulders in a fireman's hold, I said, "Seamus has to be close by."

Desmund didn't respond, and I turned to find him looking at Niall with an unreadable expression. If anyone understood what Niall was going through, it was him. I only hoped he kept it together until we got our warriors home.

"Desmund?"

He shuddered and turned away to continue the search. Ten minutes later, we found Seamus on the lake shore in the same condition as his brother. Wordlessly, Desmund slung the warrior over his shoulder and we headed home.

Halfway there, we met up with Tristan and Celine, who were both carrying warriors. Ben moaned and thrashed, making it difficult for Tristan to keep a grip on him.

Kenneth was a dead weight on Celine's shoulders, and she shook her head sadly when I looked at her.

We were a solemn group when we got back to the stronghold. Celine took Kenneth to the morgue, and the rest of us went directly to the medical ward.

The ward was full of injured people, and they cleared a path for us when we entered carrying the fallen warriors. A healer directed us to put them in one of the larger rooms where we laid each of them on an exam table.

The healers set to work on the warriors, although everyone knew there was little they could do for them. My heart was heavy as I looked at Seamus's and Niall's still forms. I'd been friends with the brothers for half a century, and it was hard seeing them like this. And Ben was so young, barely five years out of training. To die in battle was one thing, but to be felled in such a cowardly way...

A commotion at the door tore my gaze from the injured warriors, and I looked up as Sara pushed through the crowd, dragging the young Hale witch behind her, her face hard with purpose.

People drew back as they passed, fear and revulsion on their faces at the sight of the witch. Sara shoved her way into the room and pushed the witch toward Ben, whom the healers were trying to restrain before he hurt himself. The healers backed up when Sara and the witch reached the table.

"Fix them," Sara commanded. Her voice cracked, but anger flashed in her eyes. One of her arms was bandaged, but otherwise she was uninjured.

Obediently, the witch stepped up and laid a hand on Ben's forehead. Murmurs spread through the crowd as the warrior ceased his struggles and lay quietly on the table.

"He will sleep now, and when he wakes he will be well," the witch told Sara.

They went to the twins so the witch could heal them as well. A collective sigh went through the room when he was done.

Two warriors came to take the witch, and I was surprised when the boy looked to Sara for reassurance. She smiled and nodded at him, and he meekly let them lead him away. We were fortunate he was so young. An adult Hale witch would not have surrendered as easily, and might not have helped the people he'd hurt.

I started toward Sara when someone called my name. I looked around and saw Chris waving from a bed in one of the rooms.

"You going to stay in bed all day?" I quipped when I entered his room.

He grunted. "You'd be on your back too if a Hale witch tried to scramble your brain."

My humor fled. "What happened out there?"

"I found Sara and Jordan out back, and I was running to them when the bastard got me." He grimaced. "It was the worst pain I've ever felt, like my head was going to explode. It was only for a few seconds, but I thought I would go insane. Then Sara screamed and jumped on me, and I passed out. I don't know what she did, but she saved me and crippled the witch at the same time. I would've been a goner if not for her."

"So would a lot of people."

There was no telling how many of our people the witch would have hurt if she hadn't stopped him, and it most likely would have changed the outcome of the attack. The vampires had come here for Sara, and she'd taken out their biggest weapon by herself.

Chris let out a breath. "She had a bloody Hale witch cowering on the ground. I've never seen anything like it."

"And then?"

I didn't know if I wanted to hear more. Judging by the number of bodies I'd seen when I found Sara, she'd been right in the thick of the battle.

"We tried to get to the garages, but at least a dozen vampires showed up with three crocotta. I honestly didn't expect us to make it. I couldn't fight. Sara, Jordan, and the werewolves held them off until the hellhounds arrived with the wyvern and the griffin."

He made a face. "I saw that wyvern coming at us, and I was sure we were dead. But he ignored us and went after the crocotta and vampires. If I didn't know better, I'd say he was protecting us. Jesus, what a night." He sank back against his pillow. "Did you know we lost two trainees?"

I shook my head grimly. "Who told you?"

"Sara and Jordan. They watched the girl die. The boy was already dead when they got there."

"Vampire?"

"Yes. Sara and Jordan killed him. I'm amazed they're still standing after all they went through out there."

"*Khristu!*" I paced the small room. "I promised her she would be safe here, and she's been hurt more times since she came here than she was in Maine. She could have died tonight."

"No one could have predicted something like this would happen. When was the last time vampires, or anything else for that matter, attacked one of our strongholds?"

"I don't know."

Someone shouted, and two of the trainees ran in, carrying Sahir between them. Sara ran up and stood outside the exam room with the boys while the healers worked on Sahir. She looked exhausted, but her anxious expression told me she wasn't leaving until her friend was out of danger.

An hour later, I saw her sagging against the wall, barely able to stand, and I decided I'd held back long enough.

"You should be in bed," I told her.

She tried to hold back a yawn. "I'm fine."

"You're practically asleep on your feet. There is nothing else you can do here tonight. If you don't rest, you'll end up in here yourself."

"Okay."

I expected her to argue. The fact that she gave in easily told me how tired she was.

She moved away from the wall and wobbled.

I reached for her, and she put up a hand.

"I can walk. I'm tired, Nikolas, not weak."

Her indignant expression drew a chuckle from me. "Sara, no one who knew you would ever accuse you of being weak. Come on, I'll walk you to your room."

She nodded, and we headed for the stairs. Except for the medical ward, the main floor of the building was deserted.

"I've never seen it this empty here," she said as we passed through the main hall.

"They're outside, cleaning up," I told her, and she shuddered. She was quiet as we climbed the stairs to her floor.

"You're sure you would not feel better staying with Nate tonight?" What I really wanted was to take her back to my apartment. But she was covered in dirt and blood, and she'd want her own shower and bed after the ordeal.

"I'm sure."

She turned to me when we reached her door, and I saw how hard she was trying not to cry in front of me.

"You were amazing tonight," I said, earning a small smile.

"Really?"

"The whole time I was out there all I could think about was getting to you. And then I find you standing in the middle of it all, surrounded by bodies. I heard what you did. Don't ever tell me again that you're not a warrior."

"I did have a lot of help." Her eyes grew troubled. "I was worried about you, too."

I moved toward her, intending to ask if she wanted me to stay. The exhaustion I saw on her face stopped me. I touched her face and tucked her hair behind her ear. "Try to get some sleep."

"I will," she whispered as she opened the door.

As soon as the door closed behind her, I went to my place for a quick shower. Then I went looking for Tristan. But he was closeted in his office on an emergency conference call with the Council.

I found out from Claire that in addition to Kenneth and the two trainees – Olivia and Mark – we'd lost Phillip and Jay, who had been on duty at the gate. The three warriors were young, and I didn't know them or Olivia and Mark, but their deaths came as a blow.

I decided to go out and help with the cleanup, but a faint wave of pain across the bond had me heading for Sara's room instead. Outside her door, I heard her crying and felt her pain, and I didn't hesitate.

She was on the couch, her face pressed against her knees and her shoulders shaking. I sat beside her, and she made a small wounded sound and threw herself into my arms.

"I can't do this anymore," she sobbed against my chest. "I can't bear all these people getting hurt because of me."

I should have known she'd blame herself for the attack. I never should have left her alone.

"None of this was your fault. No one expected the vampires to try something like this. If you have to blame anyone, blame me. I promised you and Nate that you would be safe here."

"I can't blame you," she said between hiccups. "You all could have died tonight. I couldn't bear it if…"

She started to cry again, and I held her closer.

"Nothing will happen to us. Now that we know the lengths this vampire will go to, we will step up security and put every resource we have into finding him. I will never let them take you. That is one promise I will take to my grave."

A shudder went through her. "Don't say that!"

I had no reply, not one she wanted to hear. The simple truth was that she was everything to me, and I'd willingly trade my life for hers.

I held her and rubbed her back as she quieted, and her body slowly relaxed against mine. Her hair was still a little damp from her shower, and her familiar sunshine scent surrounded me.

When she sighed softly, I said, "Feeling better?"

She nodded, and I unwillingly let her go.

"Would you...stay just a little longer?" she asked hoarsely.

My stomach fluttered. "I'll be here as long as you need me."

I moved us until I reclined against one end of the couch with her lying against me. Then I adjusted the quilt she'd been wearing until it covered us. Her head rested on my chest, and one of her legs was across mine as she snuggled against me. I closed my eyes as a sense of peace filled me and my Mori.

"Go to sleep, *moy malen'kiy voin*," I said softly. "You've earned it."

She huffed softly. "You're always saying stuff in Russian. What did you just say?"

A small laugh escaped me. "It means 'my little warrior.'"

"I'm not that little," she murmured. "You're my warrior too."

I wrapped my arms more tightly around her. *Yes, I am.*

She was asleep within minutes, no surprise considering all she'd been through in the last few hours. I looked down at her delicate features, relaxed in sleep, and pictured her fighting alongside her friends tonight. As much as I wanted to protect her, I could already see her growing into the warrior she'd be someday. It filled me with pride and scared the hell out of me at the same time. I wasn't prepared to see her in battle. Maybe after a year or two of intense training. Maybe.

Sara shivered and cried out softly. I rubbed her back and pressed my lips to her forehead.

"No more bad dreams," I whispered. She'd had far too many of those lately.

She relaxed again, and I closed my eyes. I should be outside helping with the cleanup, but I couldn't make myself leave her. I'd waited days to be alone with her again, and nothing short of another attack would force me out of her arms tonight.

I soon realized her couch was shorter than mine, and not the most comfortable bed for a six foot two warrior. Careful not to jostle Sara, I got up and carried her to the bed. I laid her on top of the covers and went to turn off the TV and grab her quilt. When I lay down beside her, she turned to sprawl across me before I had even covered us with the quilt.

Smiling, I pulled her close and joined her in sleep.

CHAPTER 27

"HARD TO BELIEVE, isn't it?"

I looked sideways at Chris, who had joined me on what had been a battlefield twelve hours ago. The snow was more red than white, and there were three blackened circles where piles of vampire and crocotta bodies had been burnt.

I'd gotten up at dawn to assist with the job of loading the burnt remains on a truck so they could be taken miles away and disposed of. We would not desecrate our home by burying the bodies in our woods. It had been violated enough just having them here last night.

"I never thought I'd see this day," I admitted grimly. "It kills me to say it, but Westhorne is no longer safe, at least not for Sara. As long as she's here, the Master will keep coming."

"I think you're right." His gaze swept the grounds. "Whatever you decide to do, I'm in. No one will get to our girl without going through us."

"Thanks, Chris. I knew I could count on you."

"Yeah. Besides, my life would be unbearably dull without you two."

I smiled. "It's hard to remember what life was like before Sara."

"Very, very quiet," he said, and we both laughed. The sound felt wrong after what had happened here last night.

Chris sobered. "Tristan called in three units to help with security until the Council sends more warriors. I'm going out on patrol until reinforcements get here. Want to join me?"

"Yeah."

It would be good to go out and stretch my legs a bit. I didn't need to get my sword. Like every other warrior here, I was wearing mine wherever I went today. Westhorne was still on alert. Although the chances of a daytime attack were unlikely, we were putting nothing past this Master.

It was late morning when we returned to find the stronghold a lot more crowded than it had been when we left. The twenty well-armed warriors were a welcome sight to everyone at Westhorne, and they immediately went to work, organizing themselves into patrols.

I was on my way to find Sara when Tristan stopped me in the hallway.

"I'm going to see Michael. He's asking for Sara, so I'm going to ask her if she wants to talk to him."

"Not without me."

Michael had betrayed Sara and almost cost her her life. There was no way she was going into the same room with him unless I was there.

Tristan nodded. "I thought you'd say that."

The medical ward was quiet after last night's craziness. The healers had done an exemplary job of handling the dozens of injured pouring in here after the attack.

The worst were Sahir and the three who'd been attacked by the witch. I'd checked in on them this morning and found out they were all doing well. Ben had already been released, and Seamus and Niall would be good to go later this afternoon.

Only Sahir had to stay for another day or two. He had almost been killed by two vampires at the menagerie before he'd somehow managed to free the creatures. The wyvern had thanked him by saving his life.

I wasn't surprised to hear Sara's voice coming from Sahir's room. Tristan went to get her, and I entered Michael's room to find Celine there. We hadn't spoken about what she'd said to Sara, and I'd decided to let it go with everything else going on here the last week, first with Nate and then last night's attack.

I hadn't forgotten it was Celine's interference that was partially responsible for sending Sara right into my arms. I found it hard to be angry about that.

Michael sat on the bed, propped up with pillows, his wrist chained to the bed rail. He gave me a fearful look and ducked his head when I took up a position by the door.

It was hard to believe this frail young boy was responsible for the deaths of five people. If not for Jordan, Roland, and Peter, he would have caused Sara's death as well. Sara thought he was mentally ill, but I wasn't sure I could forgive him for what he'd done to her.

Sara entered the room behind Tristan, looking rested and recovered. Her eyes found mine, but she looked away when Michael spoke to her.

"You came? I didn't think you would."

"I wasn't sure I would come either." There was no anger in her voice, only sadness.

She walked over to the bed. "How are you feeling?"

"O-okay," he stammered. "Sara, I-I'm sorry for what I did to you. I know you won't forgive me, but I want you to know that I didn't ever want to hurt you."

"You didn't hurt just me, Michael," she corrected him in an accusing tone. "Olivia and Mark are dead."

"Oh, God!" Michael began to cry wretchedly. "No one was supposed to die. They said if I gave them you, they would give me Matthew."

"And you believed them?" she asked in disbelief.

"I had to. I messed up everything else, and it was my last chance of getting Matthew back."

Everything else?

Tristan stepped forward. "What do you mean? What did you mess up?"

Michael wouldn't meet Tristan's stern gaze. "I-I was supposed to scare Sara and make her leave. I did things to make her want to go, but she never did."

"What things?" Sara stared at him. "Did you have anything to do with us getting attacked in the movie theater?"

He ducked his head. "I only told them what movie you were going to see. I didn't know they would sic demons on all those people."

My gut hardened in anger, but I stayed where I was. Losing my temper was not going to help us.

Sara looked a lot calmer than I felt. "What about the vampires at the party we went to? Did you tell them we would be there?"

"I didn't even know you were going to a party. I swear," he said.

"What else did you do?" Tristan asked.

"I gave Sara some drex venom," Michael answered in a small voice.

He looked at Sara. "It was supposed to make you sad and depressed so you'd want to leave. It's not supposed to make people sick. I didn't know what to do when you got so sick."

I looked from Sara to Tristan. She'd been ill? When? Why hadn't Tristan told me?

Drex demon venom made people have hallucinations. It normally didn't make them sick. But then most people weren't half Fae... I swore silently. Demon blood and venom were poisonous to the Fae. It was no wonder Sara had gotten sick.

"You did that to me?" Sara asked in disbelief.

Celine spoke for the first time. "Where on Earth did you get drex venom?"

"They keep a lot of venoms in the medical ward for making antidotes," Michael replied.

It was hard to stay calm when I thought about how many kinds of demon venom we had here. If he'd used too much drex venom, or if he'd used a different one Sara couldn't fight off, she might have died. It didn't matter that he had no idea she was half Fae. He could have killed her.

"What else did you do?" I bit out.

He flinched and looked down at his lap. A minute or two passed before he answered.

"I-I let the hellhounds out so they would scare her. I did it when there were lots of warriors around to keep her from getting hurt."

Tristan sent me a warning look before he addressed Michael. "How did you do that without anyone seeing you?"

"They let me hang out in the control room sometimes," he told us. "And I saw Ben entering in his security code when he was on duty. After that, it was easy to log on from my laptop."

I thought back to all the times I'd been in the security center with Dax since I'd returned. I had seen Michael in there on at least one occasion. Dax hadn't seemed to mind, so I hadn't mentioned it.

"You set the karks on me, didn't you?" Sara asked accusingly.

Michael bit his lip. "I sprayed some scarab demon pheromone on you. I used just a drop to get them worked up. I had no idea they'd go nuts like that."

It was all I could do to keep my anger in check. For weeks, this boy had played dangerous games with Sara's life. People were dead because of him, and Sara could have been one of them.

Sara threw up her arms. "I don't get it! The vampires wanted me dead and you had so many chances to finish me off. Why didn't you just kill me and be done with it?"

He gave her a horrified look. "I couldn't do that. I never wanted to hurt you at all. I just wanted you to leave so they would see I did what they asked me and let Matthew go. And they said they wanted you alive."

She stared at him as if she didn't recognize him. "So after all that, they suddenly decided to come here to get me themselves. Why?"

He looked away from us at the far wall. "They asked about your uncle...and I told them he was human again. They wanted to know how, but I didn't know how it happened. That's when they told me I had to bring you to them or Matthew would die."

A needle of ice stabled my chest. If they knew Sara could make vampires human, they'd do anything to get their hands on her. I had to take her away from here as soon as possible.

I'd take her to Miroslav. It was the most fortified stronghold in the world, and the Master would have no idea where we were. It was a bit early to introduce Sara to my parents, but –

"No!" Michael's screams pulled me from my thoughts. "He's alive and now he's going to die because I couldn't give them you. This is all your fault. Why couldn't you just leave? *You* killed him, Sara! You killed my brother."

Sara's eyes filled with tears, and she backed away from the bed with her hand covering her mouth. Two healers ran past her and sedated the crazed boy.

I started toward her, but she shook her head.

"What will you do with him now?" she asked Tristan hoarsely.

"We have a facility in Mumbai where they've had some success rehabilitating some of the older orphans we've found. I'll contact Janek and have him take Michael there." He raked a hand through his hair. "Sara, what he said…"

"He's delusional, I know."

Celine stood. "Please tell me it's not that easy to get to our children and turn them against us."

Sara turned to glare at her. "He's sick and they used that against him. How about a little compassion?"

Celine huffed. "You expect me to show compassion to the person who betrayed us?"

"The welfare of the boy was our responsibility, Celine, and we failed him," Tristan said wearily. "I don't believe our young people are at risk. This was a special case. And I think we should continue this conversation elsewhere."

"I'm done here," Celine said, striding from the room.

Sara followed her out. I stopped Tristan before he could do the same.

"Michael told the vampires what Sara did to Nate. This changes everything."

He looked back regretfully at the unconscious boy. "I know."

I lowered my voice as we left the room. "If they know what Sara did to Nate, they will stop at nothing to get to her."

"I've already spoken to the rest of the Council. We are doubling our force here and bringing in five special teams to hunt this vampire."

"It's not enough," I argued. "You saw the small army he was able to assemble and send against us. One child Hale witch brought down half our sentries without blinking. I'm shocked it hasn't been tried before. You can be sure they will try to use them again now that they know how effective they are. And the only person who can go up against a Hale witch is the one we are trying to keep safe."

Tristan stopped walking. "What do you propose?"

I looked at Sara who was waiting for us in the main ward. She wasn't going to be happy with my plan, but she'd see it made sense once she had time to think about it.

"We need to move her to a new location, somewhere known only to a handful of us. Overseas would be best."

Shock crossed her face, but she quickly recovered. "Hold on. I'm not moving again, especially not to some strange place where I'll be on lockdown twenty-four seven."

"Nikolas makes a good point, Sara," Tristan said in a conciliatory tone.

"It would not be permanent, just until we deal with this Master."

She crossed her arms. "That could take years. I am not going to spend the rest of my life running and hiding while you two hunt this vampire. Forget it."

"Actually, I will be coming with you." As much as I wanted this vampire dead, I couldn't be away from her that long. I didn't want to, and my Mori would never allow it.

My words were meant to reassure her, but if anything, they made her angrier.

"So, I'll be back to having a bodyguard again. Why don't we invite Chris along, too, and it'll be just like old times?"

Ah, so that was it. She'd hated us watching over her back in Maine, and she thought it would be like that again. She had no idea how different it would be.

I tried to diffuse her anger with humor. "We can bring Chris if you'd like. He likes to travel abroad."

"What if I *don't* like to travel abroad?" she shot back.

"You can hardly say that when you've never left US soil. I'm sure we can find plenty of places you will enjoy. We can even bring your two beasts if you want."

I'd travelled all over the world, and there were hundreds of places I wanted to show her. We could spend years travelling and never visit the same place twice.

Tristan laid a hand on her arm. "This would be the best way to keep you safe. I promise we will do whatever we can to end this and bring you home soon."

"But what about Nate?" she asked desperately. "I just got him back. I can't leave him like this, especially if he'll be in danger here."

Tristan smiled. "I've already told Nate he has a home with us as long as he wants to stay. But if he wants to go with you, he has that option."

Her chin quivered. "How can you expect me to run away like a coward and leave everyone else here to face this? Please don't ask me to do that."

"No one here would ever call you cowardly, Sara, especially after what you did last night," Tristan said. "But being a warrior means you must also know when to retreat. This is one of those times."

She gave a jerky nod, but I saw the hurt on her face as she turned away. God, I'd handled this all wrong. I should have waited until we were alone and explained it better.

"Sara, please understand," Tristan said to her retreating back.

"I'll talk to her. She'll come around," I said.

She spun back to us, her eyes blazing. "I will never be okay with this or having no control over my own life. If you don't know that, then you don't know me at all."

Tristan heaved a sigh after she left. "That went well."

"I should have known she'd react like this. She blames herself for the attack and her friends dying."

His brows drew together. "Why would she think that was her fault?"

"Because the vampires were after her," I said as we left the medical ward and walked toward his office.

"I'll talk to her."

"No, I'll go see her." I had to be the one to talk to her and explain. "She's upset now. I'll give her a few hours to cool down."

Tristan shook his head. "I think this might take more than a few hours."

"I know." I rubbed my eyes. "I screwed up. But it doesn't change what we have to do."

He opened his office door and I followed him inside. I sank into a chair as he went to his desk and fired up his computer.

"I'll start making arrangements," he said. "When do you think you'll leave?"

"Day after tomorrow. I don't think we can wait longer than that."

He tapped several keys on his keyboard. "Are you going straight to Miroslav?"

"Yes."

"Does Irina know you're bringing Sara there?"

"Not yet." I smiled, imagining my mother's reaction when I told her. She would be ecstatic to hear I was coming home with my mate. I already knew she'd love Sara.

Tristan chuckled. "Well, if anyone can get Sara to forgive you, it's your mother. No one can resist her for long."

"I hope so." I rubbed my jaw. "I'll need all the help I can get on this one."

CHAPTER 28

I CLOSED MY apartment door with a weary sigh and walked into the bathroom, pulling off clothes as I went. I needed a shower and a clear head before I went to see Sara again.

I'd spent the last two hours with Tristan, making plans for Sara's and my departure from Westhorne tomorrow morning. We were leaving nothing to chance. Instead of driving to Boise, a helicopter would pick us up here and take us to the airport. Chris and Erik would accompany us, and six more warriors would be waiting for us at the hangar. Sara and I were taking the jet to Saint Petersburg where a heavily armed escort would take us to Miroslav.

The plan was perfect except for one thing. Sara still wasn't talking to me. I'd gone to her room twice, and though I knew she was inside, she refused to answer the door. This morning she came out to see Roland and Peter off, but she'd disappeared again before I could catch her. I knew she was hurting and angry, and I wished I could give her time to accept what had to be done. But the longer we stayed here, the more dangerous it was for her.

The first thing I had to do when I saw her was apologize for being an insensitive ass yesterday. She blamed herself for the vampire attack, and I'd basically told her she wasn't strong enough to stay and fight with everyone else. My fear for her had overridden my judgement, and I'd said all the wrong things. Sara was one of the strongest people I knew, and I'd tell her that as many times as I had to until she believed me.

I left the bathroom and walked into the bedroom, toweling my hair dry. I pulled on a pair of jeans and searched the dresser for my favorite blue T-shirt. Strange. I was sure I'd seen it there this morning. Frowning, I grabbed a gray one instead, pulled on a pair of shoes, and turned to leave the bedroom.

I came up short when I spotted a white envelope laying on my pillow. I stared at it suspiciously as I walked over to pick it up. When I saw my name written on the front, my suspicion turned into foreboding. I didn't need to know Sara's handwriting to know this was from her.

With a sinking feeling in my gut, I took out the single sheet of paper and unfolded it.

Nikolas,

I know you'll be angry when you read this, but please try to understand why I have to do this. I don't blame you and Tristan for being worried about me, but I can't just run away and hide this time. If the Master can't find me, he'll hurt someone I care about. I can't live with that.

I know where Madeline is, and I'm going to make her tell me what she knows about the Master. I'm not going alone, and I have people helping me. I promise I'll call you as soon as I talk to Madeline.

I hate leaving with things the way they are between us, but please believe this has nothing to do with us or our bond. I don't want to leave at all, but I have no choice. I won't bother asking you not to come after me because I know you too well.

I'll miss you.
Sara

P.S. Please tell Seamus and Niall I'm sorry.

I read the letter a second and third time before the meaning of it really hit me. Sara had taken off to find her mother. Half the vampires in the country were hunting her, and she was out there alone.

Fear slammed into me, and my legs threatened to give out. *Sara, what have you done?*

I ran from my place and burst into Tristan's apartment without knocking. He and Chris were having dinner, and they jumped up in alarm.

"Sara's gone." I held up the letter. "She went to find Madeline on her own."

Tristan came over, and I handed him the letter.

"Oh, dear God," he breathed as he read it. "How could she know where her mother is?"

"I don't know, but we have to stop her," I ground out.

"I left her with the twins no more than half an hour ago," Chris said. "They were going to the menagerie."

He read the letter over Tristan's shoulder. "What does she mean by 'tell Seamus and Niall I'm sorry'?"

329

I turned to the door. "I think we're about to find out."

"Why is she with Seamus and Niall?" Tristan asked as we ran across the lawn.

"I asked them to stay near her until we leave. I didn't want to take a chance of someone sneaking past our security again." I think a part of me also worried she might try something like this.

The menagerie was dark when we reached it, and we could hear the twins yelling and swearing before I opened the door.

"Get us out of this goddamn thing," Niall bellowed when we found him and his brother locked in the wyvern's cage.

Chris went to the office to turn on the lights and release the cage locks.

"Where is Sara?" I demanded, afraid I already knew the answer.

"The lass got the drop on us," Seamus said as the cage door clicked open. "I'm sorry, Nikolas."

"Bloody hell." Niall grunted in disgust as he tried to wipe something from his pants. All he succeeded in doing was making green streaks of what I suspected was wyvern dung.

"She and that blonde hellion played us," he griped. "She used that faerie magic on us, took our radios, and dragged us in here."

"How long ago?" They couldn't have gotten far on foot, and we'd know if they'd tried to take one of the vehicles.

Seamus glanced at his watch. "Thirty minutes."

I turned to Tristan, but he was already on his phone.

"Dax, alert all the sentries that Sara and Jordan are out in the woods," he ordered. "And send whoever you can find out here to help us search for them."

The four of them followed me outside and into the woods. We spread out to search, and I used my Mori speed to run toward the road. There was only one road in and out of Westhorne, and the girls would have to take it to get to town.

My demon sight allowed me to see in the dark, and I reached the road in no time. I followed it for several miles, expecting to sense Sara at any moment, but I couldn't feel her. Was it possible they'd arranged for someone to pick them up? What if someone had grabbed them? A chill went through me as I realized she might be miles away already.

I sped back to the stronghold. Minutes later, I tore down the driveway on my bike. The guard on the gate saw me coming and opened it before I reached it.

Butler Falls was five miles away, and the girls would have to go through it to reach the highway. Sara wasn't going to stay in town long, knowing I'd be looking for her. There were no buses or taxis in or out of the town, so they must have had a ride lined up. I'd learned not to underestimate Sara when it came to making a getaway.

My hands tightened on the handlebars. Obviously I hadn't learned that lesson well enough or I never would have let her out of my sight.

I had covered half the small town by the time Chris found me. Together, we searched the rest of town. It was soon apparent the girls were not here. I would have sensed Sara by now.

"Boise?" Chris asked when we stopped at a gas station to plan our next move.

"Yes. Let Tristan know where we're going. I'll call Dax."

The security guy picked up immediately. "I take it you haven't found them."

"Not yet. I need you to monitor all the flights, trains, and buses out of Boise for Sara and Jordan."

Dax laughed. "Is that all? I'll need to pull in some help."

"I don't care how many people you have working on it. This is your first priority."

"Got it. Anything else?"

"Check car rental places too. They might find a way to rent a car."

I looked over at Chris. "Chris, you and Callum brought Roland and Peter to the airport this morning, right?"

He lowered his phone. "Yes."

"Do we know if they got on the plane?"

Chris frowned. "No, we dropped them at the front entrance."

I swore softly. "The four of them are together."

"You sure? It sounded to me like Roland was glad you were taking Sara away."

"This is Sara we're talking about. Roland would do almost anything for her."

"You're right."

I put my phone to my ear again. "Dax, can you find out if Roland Greene and Peter Kelly got on their flight today? Claire will know the flight number."

"Sure thing."

"Thanks. Chris and I are heading to Boise. Call me as soon as you have something."

I hung up and called Roland's and then Peter's numbers. Neither of them answered, adding to my suspicion they were with Sara.

Chris reached for his helmet "You know what I don't get? Why does Sara suddenly think she can find Madeline when no one else can?"

"I've been trying to figure that out myself. She said in her note that she had people helping her."

I knew Sara had been involved in the online underworld community when she lived in Maine, but I'd assumed she'd given all that up when she came to Westhorne. Could she have been secretly searching for her mother all along? And if Sara did manage to find Madeline, did she really expect her mother to tell her about the Master when Madeline could have called her father and given him that information?

"Sara's always been very resourceful," Chris said. "No telling what she's up to."

"That's what I'm afraid of."

It took us forty-five minutes to reach Boise. We spent an hour checking out places in the city where Sara and Jordan could be while we waited to hear from Dax. I drove by the train and bus stations and went up to the front entrance of the airport terminal, but I couldn't pick up Sara's presence at any of them.

Frustration and worry were riding me hard by the time Dax called to inform me Roland and Peter hadn't boarded their flight to Maine. It offered some comfort to know Sara wasn't alone. But Jordan and the werewolves could do little against the Master if he found them before we did.

"I'm going to text you the boys' cell numbers. See if you can track their phones."

Dax snorted. "If? Give me five minutes."

It took him less than four minutes to locate the cell phones. "They're headed east on I-84, and they're two hours ahead of you. My guess is they're going to Salt Lake City. I'll let you know if they change direction."

"Thanks, Dax. Let Tristan know we're going to Salt Lake. Do we have anyone down there now?"

"I think we have two guys there. The rest came here after the attack."

"Tell them we're coming that way and to be on the lookout for Sara and Jordan."

"Will do."

I let Chris know where we were going then let out a deep breath. Finally, a break. If we made good time, we could close the distance and catch up with them tonight. All I wanted now was to find Sara. We'd work out the rest of our problems when I knew she was safe.

Four hours later, we passed the city limit sign for Salt Lake City, and I called Dax to find out where the boys' phones were.

"They're at an RV park just north of town," he said.

"An RV park?"

"Looks like the place has cabins for rent. Maybe they figured no one would look for them there."

"Okay. We'll check it out."

It didn't take long to find the park. As soon as I saw the middle-aged couple sitting by a fire outside their RV, I knew Sara and her friends must have stashed their phones on the vehicle to throw us off their trail. And we'd fallen for it.

Disappointment and worry gnawed at me. What if they'd dumped the phones in Boise and we'd been on a wild goose chase this whole time? They could be anywhere by now.

"What do you want to do?" Chris asked when I voiced my concerns to him.

I thought for a moment. "It's late. If they're here, they've likely found a hotel room for the night. I'm going to drive past every hotel in the city and see if I can sense her."

"Try the cheaper places first," he suggested. "I doubt they'll stay at one of the bigger hotels."

The airport wasn't far from us and there were a number of hotels in that area, so we headed there first. We circled half a dozen hotels with no luck. I knew it was a long shot, but I didn't know what else to do.

My Mori quivered.

I inhaled sharply. *She's here.*

The sensation faded. Heart pounding, I found the closest intersection and pulled a U-turn, my tires leaving marks on the asphalt as I raced back the way I'd come.

Find her, I begged my Mori.

I felt it again, stronger this time. Up ahead on the left I could see a sign for a Motel 6. That had to be it. The closer I got to it, the stronger her presence was.

Horns blared as I cut across several lanes of traffic to get to the hotel. I pulled into the parking lot, and suddenly her presence began to fade again.

I peeled out of the lot and back onto the street, but I couldn't tell what direction she'd gone. I couldn't lose her. I might never find her again.

I drove without direction, changing course only when I sensed her again. It happened three times, and then she was gone.

For the next two hours, I searched in an ever-widening circle, but I didn't sense her. My mind and body felt weighed down when I finally admitted to myself that I'd lost her again.

Chris and I stayed at the safe house that night. I would have driven around all night if he hadn't pointed out that I'd drop from exhaustion in a few days if I didn't slow down. He was right. I would have driven myself into the ground if I'd been left alone. I wouldn't help Sara that way.

I didn't get much sleep either way. I lay in bed wondering what had brought Sara to Salt Lake City. Did she think her mother was here? I hadn't seen Madeline in over fifty years, so I had no idea what she could be up to or why she'd be here. Madeline had never cared for Idaho or the mountains, always saying she wished we lived somewhere sunnier. I could see her living in a place like California, but not Utah.

I was still mulling it over the next morning as I resumed my slow search of the city. Short of sensing Sara nearby, there was little to go on. One of the local warriors knew a warlock in the city who might be able to do a locator spell if she was still here, and I had an appointment with him that afternoon.

When my phone rang midmorning, my pulse jumped when I saw Tristan's name, and I prayed he had good news.

"Tristan, tell me you have her."

"No, but she's okay. She just called a few minutes ago."

Relief filled me. "What did she say?"

"She wanted us to know that she was with Jordan, Roland, and Peter, and the four of them were on their way to see Madeline." Tristan let out a slow breath. "She said Madeline was a few hundred miles from her. Could she really know where her mother is?"

"She seems to think she does. What else did she say?"

"She said as soon as she talks to Madeline, she'll call us to come get her and Jordan."

I stared at the mountains rising up behind the city. If Sara thought she was a few hundred miles from Madeline, then Madeline couldn't be in Salt Lake City. What was a few hundred miles from here?

"I asked her if she wanted to talk to you, and she said she knew you weren't here."

"She knew I'd come after her," I said. "Did you trace the call?"

"I tried, but she blocked me somehow," he said in frustration. "She left her phone and laptop here, so someone must have helped her, someone who knows how to hide from us. She planned this well. She said she'd call back in a few days and hung up."

"She was here in Salt Lake last night. I sensed her, but she disappeared before I could find her." I rubbed at the dull ache that had started in my chest after I'd come so close to Sara and lost her. Was it possible she could sense me the way I sensed her? That would explain how she had evaded me last night.

"Then she could still be there," Tristan said hopefully. "I'm going to send back the unit that came from there. They know the city, and they'll be able to help you search. We'll find her, Nikolas."

"I know," I said fiercely.

The question was, would we find her before she found trouble?

* * *

"I can't believe it. Someone finally took that bastard down."

"Are you serious? Do you know I hunted him for four damn years without a glimpse of him?"

"Well, he's dust now."

"Who is dust?" I asked, walking into the safe house, back from chasing down another dead end. It was our second day in Salt Lake, and I was certain Sara was no longer in the city. The warlock I'd seen couldn't find her with a locater spell, which meant she'd most likely left the area. And I didn't have a single lead on where she could be.

Two warriors from the local unit stood in the living room. Martin, a cheerful Englishman with a buzz cut, grinned at me.

"Stefan Price. Someone took him out last night in New Mexico."

My eyebrows shot up. Killing Stefan Price was on the bucket list of half the warriors in the country. It was right up there with killing a Master, because he was almost as elusive and as deadly as one. Whoever had bagged him was going to bask in the glory of that kill for years.

"Who killed him?" I wondered if it was someone I knew.

"No one knows," Martin replied. "The Albuquerque guys said it happened at Orias's place out in the desert, and it was some female warrior. The rumor is she's Mohiri, but she couldn't be one of ours."

"Why not?"

"Well according to a witness, she was short." Martin chuckled. "Have you ever seen a short Mohiri female?"

"Only one." My stomach fluttered. *No. It can't be her.* "What else did they say about her?"

Martin scratched his chin. "Not much. Just that she was short with long dark hair. Oh, and she supposedly had a werewolf with her. She was probably a were– Hey, what's wrong?"

I pulled my phone from my pocket as I raced upstairs. "Chris, where are you?"

"Down in the control room. What's up?"

"Sara's in Albuquerque. I'm leaving in two minutes."

I grabbed my saddle bag and stuffed my clothes in it. We always kept a few changes of clothing stored on our bikes in case we had to go somewhere in a hurry.

Like chasing down runaway mates.

Chris appeared in the doorway. "Albuquerque? How do you know?"

I picked up my bag and looked at him. "Did you hear Stefan Price was killed last night?"

"I just heard. What does that have to do with Sara?"

"Sara killed him."

The thought of her anywhere near that monster sent chills down my spine. Her power was growing, but she wasn't strong enough to take down a vampire that old. Still, I knew in my gut it was her.

"Sara?" Chris followed me when I left the room. "Why would you think she killed him?"

I stopped at the top of the stairs to face him. "Martin said a Mohiri female took Price down. A short Mohiri girl with long dark hair and a werewolf."

Chris stared at me. "Jesus."

"Grab your stuff. We're going to New Mexico."

I'd driven all over the country, sometimes going for twenty-four hours at a stretch, but the trip to Albuquerque was one of the longest rides of my life. I couldn't stop thinking about Sara facing down Stefan Price. Had she really killed him? Had she been afraid? Hurt? Very few people could emerge unscathed from a fight with a vampire as strong as Price.

I tried not to think of her wounded and in pain somewhere. Instead, I wondered what could have brought her to Orias's of all places. Orias was one of the most powerful warlocks in the country, so the Mohiri knew him well. We kept an eye on anyone who could raise a higher demon, which was where warlocks got most of their power.

Unlike most warlocks, who were very selective in their clients, Orias dealt with anyone who could pay his exorbitant fees, and he prided himself on his discretion and his clean business establishment. He mostly did protection spells and glamours, and he liked to gather information that others might find valuable. He had proven to be a useful source of information to us on occasion, so as long as he stayed clean, we had no problem with him.

Why would Sara need to see such a powerful warlock? Had she gone to him looking for a locator spell for Madeline? Those spells were difficult and expensive. Where would she have gotten the money to pay for it?

We didn't stop when we reached Albuquerque, heading directly for Orias's place in the desert. The warlock was wealthy enough to live in a California mansion, yet he chose to live out in the middle of nowhere. When asked about it, he always said being around too many people and other magic affected his work. Out here, away from civilization, he did his best work.

I'd been to Orias's more than once, a good thing since he kept the place well-hidden with his glamours. I knew I was there when I crossed the small wooden bridge that marked the front of his property. As soon as my tires hit the dirt on the other side, a large two-story adobe building came into view.

Normally, the building was lit up, but it was oddly dark tonight with only one light shining from his office on the second floor. There were no cars out front either, which meant he was not seeing clients tonight. Good. I was in no mood to wait.

The front door was unlocked, mainly because few people were stupid enough to attack a warlock like Orias in his home. Chris and I passed through the dark waiting area, walking down the short hallway and up a flight of stairs to the second floor.

Orias's door was open, and he called to us before we reached the top of the stairs.

"Nikolas Danshov and Christian Kent, what an honor to have you in my humble establishment again."

I laughed and entered his office where Orias and his assistant Paulina were going through financial statements. She excused herself when we entered. Everyone believed she was just the receptionist, but Paulina helped Orias run this place. She enjoyed playing the receptionist role during business hours.

"Humble indeed," I said.

Orias chuckled. Tall with long black hair and a hawkish appearance, he looked like a thirty-five-year-old man of Native American descent. Looks could be deceiving. I knew he was well over one hundred years old, possibly even as old as me.

He stood and extended a hand to us then waved to the visitor chairs. "Please, have a seat and tell me what I can do for you, although I can guess the reason for your visit."

I gave him a questioning look, and he smiled.

"When a vampire like Stefan Price dies in your place of business, you expect the Mohiri to show up and ask questions."

"Is that why you're closed tonight?" Chris asked.

The warlock made a face. "We are closed because that little incident scared the hell out of my regular clients. They are afraid to come because Stefan had many followers who are no doubt upset about his untimely passing. No one wants to be here in case the vampires come looking for answers."

"You don't seem worried," Chris said.

Orias shrugged. "I'm not happy about the situation. Having someone die on the premises is not good for business, as you can see. But I don't think I have anything to fear from the vampires. No one has ever attacked me and lived to speak of it."

I watched Orias closely. He spoke and acted as if this whole thing was merely an inconvenience, but I could see uneasiness and anger simmering below the surface of his cool façade. Something – or someone – had unsettled the normally composed warlock. I knew only one person who had an infallible ability for attracting the kind of trouble that came with fangs and claws.

"Tell us what happened last night," I said, careful to hide my personal interest. "I take it Price was a client of yours?"

He cleared his throat. "Stefan used my services a few times over the years. He never bothered to make appointments, so I don't know why he came last night."

"And the girl?" I asked casually.

"Girl?"

I raised an eyebrow.

"Oh, the girl, the one who killed Stefan." He gave me a rueful smile.

"Forgive me. It's been a long twenty-four hours."

I nodded. "Was she a client as well? Who was she?"

"She was a new client, yes," he said after a short hesitation. "I'm afraid I can't give you her name. Client confidentiality."

"Tell us what happened between her and the vampire," I said. It wasn't a request. He was being evasive about the girl, which made me more determined to find out who she was.

He leaned forward and clasped his hands on the desk. "I didn't see the actual fight. I was here in my office, and I heard shouting. By the time I got to the waiting area, Stefan was dead and she was standing over him. They wrecked my waiting area and frightened off all my clients."

Only many years of experience kept me in my chair. Orias was being deliberately vague, and I wanted to shake the whole story out of him.

"Did she say anything after she killed the vampire?" Chris asked.

"Yes. I asked her if she knew who she'd just killed, and she said no. Then she left."

"That's it?" I asked the warlock. "Was the girl injured in the fight?"

He frowned. "Why are you so interested in the girl? I thought you were here because of Stefan Price."

I met his gaze directly. "Word has it she was Mohiri, and we always like to know where our people are."

He opened his mouth, and a strained look crossed his face.

"Believe me, gentlemen, I wish I could tell you more, but the nature of my, um, contract with her, prevents me from sharing her identity with you."

I almost growled my frustration at him. He had always been more than willing to help out the Mohiri when we asked for it. What was different about this time?

"Can you tell us where the girl went when she left here?" I asked.

He shook his head. "That I do not know. I'm sorry."

My hands gripped the arms of the chair. Sara had been here last night. I knew it, and Orias knew it. What I didn't know was why he wouldn't just say it.

"Thank you, Orias," Chris said, giving me a sideways look. "If you don't mind, we'd like to ask Paulina a few questions before we leave."

He smiled, looking almost relieved. "Of course. Send her up when you're done."

We said good-bye to him and went back to the waiting area where Paulina sat behind the reception desk, working on her computer.

"All done?" she asked pleasantly.

"Almost," I said. "May we ask you about last night?"

"Certainly. What would you like to know?"

I looked at the room that bore no sign of a fight. Orias must have used magic to repair the damage.

"What can you tell us about what happened here last night? More specifically, about the girl who killed Stefan Price."

Paulina folded her hands in her lap. "The girl and her friends came in asking to see Orias. They didn't have an appointment, but he agreed to see them."

"Friends?" Chris said.

She nodded. "There was another girl and two young men."

My breath caught. I was right. Sara *was* here last night.

"Do you know why they wanted to see Orias?"

"No. They were in his office for about half an hour, but he never told me what they wanted. They were leaving when Stefan Price arrived."

She smiled apologetically. "I couldn't see much from over here, but I heard him say something about a child out without her protectors. He grabbed the dark-haired girl and threw one of the boys across the room. Next thing I know, there's a werewolf coming through the door, and the girl has Stefan on his knees. Then Stefan was dead with a knife sticking from his chest. It all happened so fast."

My stomach knotted. "Were any of them hurt, other than the vampire?"

Paulina thought about it. "I don't think so. Orias gave the girl a towel, but that could have been to wipe Stefan's blood off her hands. If she'd been badly injured, he would have healed her."

Chris sat on the corner of her desk. "Did they say where they were going when they left here?"

"No. Oh wait. I think someone mentioned Los Angeles. Does that help?"

"More than you know." I smiled at her. "As always, you've been a big help."

"My pleasure." She motioned for us to lean in. "Between you and me, I'm glad she killed him. I hate vampires, and that one always scared the hell out of me. Orias wouldn't like to hear me say that about the clients."

"About that," I said in a low voice. "Do you know why Orias wouldn't tell us about the girl? He didn't care about you telling us."

She frowned. "He's been acting strange ever since they left. I don't know what happened up in his office, but it's almost like he *can't* talk about it. I asked who they were, and he just shook his head and went back to his office."

I looked at Chris, who shrugged. What could Sara and the others have said to the warlock to keep him from talking? He was a businessman above all else, but where would they have gotten the kind of money it would take to buy his silence?

I straightened and held out a hand to her. "Thank you, Paulina."

"Anytime, Mr. Danshov. I hope you find your girl."

"I will."

Chris and I waited until we were a mile away from Orias's before we said anything.

"Did you find that whole thing as strange as I did?" he asked.

"Yes." I maneuvered around a large pothole in the dirt road. "But at least we know where the four of them are headed next."

Chris made a sound. "I still can't believe Sara took down Price. But if she hadn't, we might never have known they were here."

"That's true." She and I were going to have a long talk when I found her, but for now I was relieved she was okay and that I knew where to look for her next.

I glanced at the time. "It's a good eleven hours to LA. We can be there by 9:00 a.m."

Chris's groan filled my headset. "Nikolas, we just drove for nine hours straight. I need food and a few hours of sleep before I hit the road again. So do you."

"If Sara's in LA, we need to –"

"Sara's proven pretty resourceful so far," he cut in. "And she has Jordan and two werewolves with her. She'll be in better shape than you if you keep up this pace. Let's stay in Albuquerque tonight and head out first thing in the morning. I'll call the LA units and let them know to be on the lookout."

I opened my mouth to argue, but he said, "I won't pretend to know how hard this is for you, but you're acting with your heart now and not your head. You haven't eaten since this morning, and you've barely slept since we left home. If you leave for LA now, you'll spend tomorrow passed out in one of the safe houses. Not even your Mori can keep you going indefinitely."

I ground my teeth together. Chris's reasoning was sound, but that didn't make me feel better about it. All I could think of was finding Sara. All my Mori wanted was for us to find our mate.

"We leave at dawn," I told him.

"Dawn," he agreed.

We ate and then went to the Albuquerque safe house. It was smaller than most and a bit crowded, but it wasn't like we'd be there long. Chris bunked on a couch in the control center, and I took the couch in the living room. I made myself comfortable and closed my eyes, willing sleep to come. The sooner it did, the sooner I could wake up and get on the road again.

I was dozing off when my phone rang, jerking me awake. I reached for it where it lay on the coffee table and stared at the unfamiliar number for a moment before I answered.

"Hello?"

"Hello?" I said again when no one spoke.

There was a breath on the other end, followed by a hush.

I shot to a sitting position. "Sara? Is that you?"

There was no answer. I couldn't sense her, but I knew it was her.

"Sara, talk to me," I pleaded softly.

We hadn't spoken since the morning in the medical ward, and my heart squeezed painfully from the need to hear her voice. I didn't care if she yelled at me, as long as I could hear for myself she was okay.

"Sara?"

The line was silent, and I knew she'd hung up. I sat in the dark, hoping she'd call back, but after half an hour I lay down again. I finally fell asleep with the phone in one hand and my other hand rubbing at the hollow ache in my chest.

CHAPTER 29

"NIKOLAS, YOU HEADING out?"

I grabbed my phone from the counter and looked up as Wayne, one of the warriors stationed in Los Angeles, walked into the kitchen.

"I'm on my way to meet up with Chris and the others at Blue Nyx."

Chris and I had stopped by the club to visit Adele the moment we got to the city two days ago, only to find out the succubus was out of town and not due back until today. Adele knew more about the Los Angeles underworld than anyone else in the city. Two young Mohiri in the company of two werewolves would not go unnoticed for long, and if anyone knew where to find them, it was Adele.

We'd spent the last two days scouring the city, visiting every club, informant, and cheap motel we could think of. LA's supernatural community was the biggest in the country, and there were hundreds of species living here. It also had one of the largest vampire populations, which made me even more desperate to find Sara and get her away from here.

She'd called me again last night. It was a different number and she didn't speak, but my gut told me it was her. I'd spent the short call trying to get her to talk, to no avail. I consoled myself with the knowledge she must be missing me too if she felt the need to call. I wished she would talk to me.

Wayne clipped a knife sheath to his belt. "I just heard that two girls were attacked by a vampire at a motel over near LAX. Everyone else is out, so I'm going over there. I could use some backup."

I immediately thought of Sara and Jordan, and my stomach dropped. "I'll go with you."

Chris and the rest of the team were on route to Blue Nyx when I called to let him know where I was.

"You need me to come there?" he asked.

"No, go talk to Adele. She's our best bet of finding Sara and Jordan if they're here. I'll meet you there." I wasn't going to take the chance of missing the succubus if she decided to leave town again.

The motel was a pay-by-the-hour dump with a flickering neon sign and peeling paint. A prostitute who couldn't be more than sixteen approached me before I'd even shut off my bike, and I sent her on her way with a hundred-dollar bill and a warning. Not that I expected her to heed my advice to go home for the night.

As Wayne and I entered the lobby, a short balding man in a crumpled suit passed by us, reeking of cigarette smoke and sex. I knew before I went to the room on the third floor that Sara wasn't here. She'd never stay in a rat hole like this.

"Prostitutes," Wayne said as we stood in the doorway, looking at the bloody scene. "God, they can't be more than eighteen."

I stared at the two naked girls sprawled across the bed with their throats ripped open, their eyes wide and unseeing. I'd seen so many vampire victims in my lifetime I'd thought I was numb to it. But the sight of these two filled me with revulsion and rage. The longer I went without finding Sara, the more I feared her ending up in the hands of a monster like the one who'd done this. The thought shook me so much I had to leave the motel to calm down.

"The clerk called the police before we got here," Wayne told me when he came outside five minutes later. "They don't usually respond as quickly to this part of town, but they should be here soon."

There wasn't anything we could do for the girls, so we left. Wayne returned to the safe house to monitor activity from the control room, and I went to meet up with Chris at Blue Nyx.

After the scene at the motel, I wasn't in the best of moods when I pulled up behind the black brick building that housed Adele's club.

One of her security guys opened the back door for me when I rapped on it.

"Evening, Dolph."

The seven-foot ogre gave me something that resembled a smile. "Evening, Mr. Danshov."

The club was crowded with the usual patrons: demons, weres, Fae. Adele's was one of the few places in the city where species that never mixed in the real world could party together. Although party was a loose term for what was going on here. It was after midnight, the time when Adele's succubus magic was at its strongest, and when her customers cast off all inhibitions and took part in the real reason they came here.

All around me, I could hear couples and threesomes engaged in sex on the couches in the dark corners. On the dance floor, a blond faerie kissed a voluptuous nymph while one of his brethren pressed against her from

343

behind. Soon the trio would leave the floor and find a corner of their own – or they might not. Faeries were notorious exhibitionists.

I found Chris talking to the bartender while the four warriors who'd accompanied him stood like sentries observing the room.

"How was it at the hotel?" Chris asked.

"Bad. Two dead prostitutes. We left before the police arrived."

He grimaced. "Vampires don't even try to hide their kills anymore."

"I know. It's getting bad out there." I looked up at the window on the second floor that overlooked the club. "Have you seen Adele already?"

"Briefly." He smirked. "I told her you were on the way, and she wanted to wait to see you instead."

"Great," I muttered.

I made my way to Adele's office. A burly ogre named Bruce guarded the door, and he nodded in greeting at me.

"Miss Adele is waiting for you."

Adele was reclining on a couch by the window, and she stood in one fluid movement when I walked in. She wore a silver dress that hugged her like a second skin, and her long blonde hair hung around her shoulders. Silver flashed in her violet eyes, and her skin was flushed from feeding off the sexual energy below.

The Mohiri had a no tolerance policy for Incubi and Succubi that fed off humans because the humans always died from such encounters. We made exceptions for demons like Adele who used her club to feed. Her patrons knew she fed from their energy, and they came here for the high. As long as she stayed clean, she was allowed to live.

"Nikolas," she purred, gliding toward me. "It's been far too long since you visited me."

"Hello, Adele. I see things are well for you."

She inhaled deeply. "Business has never been better."

"Glad to hear it."

"I added two new rooms on this floor, and they are quite luxurious. For my more discreet customers." She stopped in front of me and gave me a sensual smile. "Maybe this time you'll finally accept my invitation to sample the delights of Club Nyx."

Her hand slipped inside my jacket, grazed my abdomen, and then descended to the waist of my jeans. I caught it before it could go any lower and took a step back with a shake of my head.

Adele pouted without a trace of embarrassment and went to pour herself a glass of wine. "Next time, perhaps. What else can I do for you?"

"I'm looking for two Mohiri girls who came to LA two days ago."

Her eyes gleamed. "Two Mohiri girls. Ah, maybe you are looking to sample some delights after all."

I ignored her suggestive comments. "The girls are with two werewolves, so they'll be hard to miss."

Adele lifted a delicate eyebrow. "Mohiri and werewolves. I've seen a lot of things in this city, but that's a new one."

"I take it you haven't heard anything then?" I said with a touch of impatience.

"No, but I've been out of town for the last week. I just got back tonight. I can put out some feelers and see what I come up with."

"Thank you. That would be appreciated."

"Always a pleasure to assist the Mohiri."

She sat on the couch and crossed her legs so the slit in her dress showed bare skin to her hip. "I'm curious though. Since when do *you* track down runaway children?"

"One of them is the granddaughter of a friend."

I wouldn't reveal my true connection to Sara. Adele was an informant, but I didn't trust her beyond that. I had many enemies, and if one of them learned Sara was my mate, they'd hurt her to get to me. I'd do anything to save her.

"I'll be sure to keep an eye out for her then. Los Angeles is not a good place for young Mohiri on their own."

"I know." I smiled. "I'll leave you to your business. You have the Mohiri contact number if you find anything."

"Yes. I'll be in touch as soon as I hear something."

I started for the door, but stopped and turned back to her. "There is someone else I meant to ask you about. You haven't heard anything about Madeline Croix being in LA, have you?"

Her glass stopped halfway to her mouth. "She's the Mohiri who ran off years ago. You still haven't found her?"

"No. I heard recently she might be here, and I figured I'd ask since I was coming to see you anyway."

She licked her lips. "I don't think I've heard about her. I'll ask around, discreetly of course."

I nodded my thanks. "I hope to hear from you soon."

"How did it go?" Chris asked when I rejoined him.

I inclined my head toward the main door, and he followed me outside.

"She hasn't heard anything yet. She said she'll see what she can find out."

He let out a breath. "Well, if anyone can find them in this city, it's Adele. It might take her a few days though."

The meaning in his words was clear. I had to try to be patient for the next day or so. I hadn't exactly been the best company since we left home, something he'd pointed out more than once.

"I asked her about Madeline too, but I didn't say Sara and Madeline are related."

Chris's brow furrowed. "You think Madeline is in LA?"

I shrugged. "Something brought Sara here."

A warrior named Hans walked up to us. "Anton was doing a sweep, and he found three dead vampires less than a block from here. He said we should come check it out."

I wasn't sure what was unusual about dead vampires, but I went anyway. We found Anton in an alley on a quiet street, bent over a body on the ground. When we got closer, I saw it was a dead mox demon. It looked like she'd been fed on by more than one vampire.

"I can't make sense of it," Anton said when we entered the alley. "Look around and tell me what you see."

We did as he asked. Near the mouth of the alley lay a beheaded vampire. From the look of it, he'd been killed by a sword. Further in, I saw two more vampires. One had a crossbow bolt in his crotch, and his head looked like it had been ripped off. The other one was in half a dozen pieces at the back of the alley.

Chris stepped over a severed arm. "It looks like they were taken apart by an angry mob."

"A mob with swords and crossbows?" I asked absently, bending to examine one of the bodies.

I stood and walked over to the mox demon. She had on a flimsy red dress; the kind people wore to a place like Blue Nyx. I'd lay odds she'd come from there before she was attacked. A place like that was bound to draw vampires looking for an easy meal. Most of Adele's customers were in a euphoric, drugged-like state when they left the club, easy prey for a vampire. Since vampires couldn't get past Adele's ogre security, they'd wait for their meals to come to them.

"Demons?" Chris suggested.

"That's my guess." I straightened and looked around the alley. "Who else would come to the aid of a mox demon?"

"Good point."

Anton called for backup, and we spent the next hour removing the bodies. Once we had all the parts bagged and in the van, the other warriors took them to an industrial park to incinerate in a furnace they used often.

Chris and I resumed our new nightly routine of visiting various underworld clubs in the Los Angeles area. The problem with LA was its size. Without a way to track Sara, it could take weeks to find her. I was afraid we didn't have weeks with the escalating violence here.

If Sara was here, she wasn't hiding out in a hotel room. She was out here searching for Madeline. She'd proven she was stronger than we'd thought, but sooner or later, she was going to run into trouble she couldn't handle.

As the night wore on, I found myself checking my phone and wondering if she was going to call again. Even though she hadn't spoken when she'd called the last two nights, it eased my mind a little to know that wherever she was, she was thinking about me.

I'd given up on hearing from her when my phone rang just after 3:00 a.m. It was another unknown number, but I knew it was her before I answered.

"Hello?"

Silence.

I walked down the street, away from the were bar I'd just left.

"Sara? Will you talk to me tonight?"

I wasn't surprised when she didn't answer, but it didn't stop the pang of disappointment. Before now, I hadn't known it was possible to crave the sound of someone's voice. Part of it was the bond that made me need my mate, but a bigger part was me. I missed her.

"Okay." I let out a breath. "Tristan said you sounded tired when you called him today. I know you're not sleeping. You know you can call me anytime, even if you're not ready to talk yet."

I looked up at the sky that would start to lighten in a few short hours. "It's late. You should try to get some sleep. Call me again tomorrow so I know you're all right. And Sara...I need to hear your voice, too."

The line was so quiet I thought she'd hung up. Then, I heard a small sound like a muffled sob. "I'm okay."

I closed my eyes, my shoulders sagging. They were just two whispered words, but they told me she cared and that she was hurting too. She might not be ready to talk things out, but she was reaching out to me.

The silence on the other end of the line told me she was gone. I turned back to the bar with renewed hope warming my chest. Tomorrow, she would call again, and I'd coax a few more words out of her.

If I didn't find her first.

$$* \quad * \quad *$$

"No luck?"

I shook my head as I walked into the safe house control room. "They were there two days ago. Garrett told me Sara sold him some very nice diamonds in exchange for cash and weapons. Roland was with her."

Chris spun in his chair to face me. "Where did Sara get diamonds, and how the hell does she know someone like Leo Garrett?"

"I don't know. I'm almost afraid to find out."

I sank onto a chair and rubbed my eyes. "Garrett's main business is gun running, but his hobby is fencing fine art and jewels. He said a mutual business acquaintance introduced him to Sara, and that she was quite the businesswoman. He wouldn't tell me how much money or diamonds were exchanged, but he said both parties were happy with the deal."

Chris stared at me. "I don't even know what to say."

"You and me both."

He blew out a puff of air. "I take it Garrett didn't know where Sara and Roland are."

"He said he didn't, but who knows with a man like that. I asked Dax to look into him and see if he can find something to lead us to Sara."

A phone rang. Wayne, who was sitting at another computer, answered it. He wore a puzzled expression when he came over to us.

"Westhorne just got an anonymous call from someone claiming to be a friend. He told them there is a pretty nasty gulak demon in Los Angeles named Draegan, who is running drugs and human slaves. The guy wouldn't say how he got our private number, but he said we'd want to check it out."

Chris and I stood at the same time. If there was one thing we hated more than vampires, it was slavers. It didn't surprise me to hear that a gulak was involved. I'd dealt with enough of their kind to know they thought of humans as nothing more than chattel.

"Where can we find this demon?" I asked.

Wayne grinned. "I'll tell you on the way. I'm not missing out on this one."

Instead of riding our bikes, the three of us took one of the Escalades parked in the driveway. Wayne drove us to a tall glass apartment building in West Hollywood.

"Are you sure this is the right place?" I asked him when we entered the pink marble lobby.

Before he could answer, a human security guard called to us from behind a desk. "What's your business here?"

"We're here to see Draegan," I said in a voice that dared him to object.

He looked us over warily and nodded. "Top floor. Apartment 3010."

An unhappy tagg demon opened the door to Draegan's apartment as we approached it. The bald, red-skinned demon glared at us over his large nose and waved us inside.

"This night just keeps getting better," he grumbled as he shut the door and followed us down a short hallway.

The first thing I noticed about the place was it was almost completely white, reminding me of a clean room. It was also trashed. It looked like someone had thrown a party that had gotten out of hand. Way out of hand if the dead ranc demon and two dead gulaks on the floor were any indication.

Down another hallway someone was shouting, but the words were muffled. Based on the deep guttural tone, it was the gulak we had come to see.

Aside from Draegan and the tagg demon, the place appeared to be empty. It looked like Draegan's guests had taken off when the killing started. The question was, who had done the killing? A rival demon perhaps? Gulaks didn't have many friends, and they were often engaged in turf wars.

"What happened to his horns?" Chris asked, drawing my attention to the ranc demon that had charred nubs where his horns should be.

"The short one did it." The tagg demon scowled and bent to pick up an overturned chair. "I knew I smelled something off about her."

Chris frowned. "Was it another demon?"

The tagg demon snorted. "More like a pair of hellions. But I guess you already knew that or you wouldn't be here."

Before I could ask what he meant by his remark, a bellow came from the other end of the apartment.

"Wilhem, you worthless piece of shit! You better not have let anyone else in here tonight or I'm going to wring your fat neck."

Wilhelm swallowed fearfully. "I-I'm sorry, Draegan. I didn't have any choice."

"Like you had no choice when you let those two bitches in here?" Draegan growled. "They killed Crak and Lorne and cheated me. Cheated *me*! No one steals from me and gets away with it. When I find those two, they'll wish they'd never heard my name."

"Um, Draegan," Wilhelm stammered, glancing nervously at us. "You have guests. You might want to —"

"Get rid of them," the gulak roared, his voice coming closer. "I'm busy. Do you know how much I could have gotten for that blood contract? That little bitch owes me big."

Something that sounded like a fist slammed into a wall, and then the gulak thundered into the room. Ignoring us, he picked up a curved blade from a table and strapped it to his waist.

A gravelly laugh rumbled from him. "I can't wait to get my hands on her. She'll pay me back every cent in my bed. And when I'm done with her, I'll sell her to Rhys. He prefers humans, but he won't pass up a chance to sample some young Mohiri flesh."

Blood began to roar in my ears as a growl tore from my throat. Someone said my name, but it sounded far off. All I could see and hear was the gulak demon who would dare touch my mate. I was going to rip the forked tongue from his mouth for the things he'd said about her.

Draegan stared at me with a mix of anger and surprise. "Who the hell are you?"

The tagg demon said something that made Draegan's scaly face turn a sickly gray. He snatched up a long curved sword and bared his teeth at me.

"That bitch...girl came in here and tore up my place," he yelled, backing into the living room. "I didn't touch a hair on her head. Tell him, Wilhelm."

I stalked him. Wilhelm said something, but I'd blocked out everything except the gulak. His words about what he'd planned to do to Sara were stuck on replay in my head, and each time I heard them my body shook from the rage threatening to consume me.

Draegan's legs hit the couch, and he maneuvered around it, never taking his lizard-like eyes from me as I advanced on him. I noticed vaguely that my vision had turned the white room the color of watered-down blood.

Metal flashed. I didn't remember drawing my own sword, but it rose to meet Draegan's blade in a shower of sparks.

He staggered backward from the blow, pain flashing across his face. He might be stronger than every other demon he knew, but brute force would not save him this time.

I struck before he could recover, stripping the scales from his left arm.

He bellowed and swung wildly at me. I deflected it easily and nicked his thigh, then his chest, then his ear. Each cut drew another roar of pain from him and sent droplets of black demon blood across the once pristine room.

He panted heavily, but I pushed him relentlessly, wanting him to suffer for every vile thought he'd had about Sara, wanting him to know exactly who was going to end him.

"I have money, jewels, weapons. Take them all," he cried desperately as his strength began to wane. "I was angry about my men. I never meant to hurt the girl. I swear."

"My mate," I snarled, low and deadly.

"Mate?" he croaked. His eyes darted around the room, but there was no escape for him.

He let out a roar and threw his sword at me. I sidestepped it, and it sank into the wall behind me.

In the next instant, Draegan spun and ran toward the floor-to-ceiling windows, his leathery wings unfurling behind him.

My knife buried itself to the hilt in the gulak's back, pinning one of his wings securely to his body. He flailed and tried to stop his forward rush. Too late.

Glass shattered outward as he flew through the window. The good wing flapped uselessly for a second, and then he was gone. His scream followed him down, ending abruptly when he met the ground.

No one in the apartment moved for several minutes. The roaring in my ears receded, my body stopped trembling, and the room turned white again.

It wasn't until I lowered my sword and walked to the window to look down at what was left of Draegan that Chris came over to stand beside me.

"You okay?" he asked over the wind whistling through the broken window.

I nodded stiffly.

He peered at the dark shape in the courtyard far below. "Wayne, we're going to need a cleanup crew. A big one."

"On it," Wayne called from the other side of the apartment.

Chris looked at me. "I guess that's one way to work off some of that pent-up aggression."

I scowled, and he held up his hands. "Hey, you haven't exactly been Mr. Congeniality for the last week."

"With good reason."

His hands lowered. "I know."

I stared at the sea of lights, and felt a moment of despair. Sara was out there somewhere, and I didn't know what she was doing or if she was safe. Los Angeles was a cesspool of vampire and demon activity. How long did we have before she and her friends ran into another Draegan or Price? How long before they found themselves in a situation they couldn't fight their way out of?

"I have to find her, Chris."

"We will." He looked around the apartment. "What were Sara and Jordan doing in a place like this?"

I inclined my head at the tagg demon, who hadn't moved from his spot. "Maybe he knows."

Chris walked over to the demon. "Can you tell us why the two Mohiri girls came to see Draegan?"

Wilhelm gave a jerky nod. "The dark-haired one told me she was here about a debt. Draegan said it was a blood debt."

"Blood debt? Whose?" *Khristu. Sara, what are you mixed up in?*

"I don't know. She didn't say."

Chris pointed to the three dead demons. "What happened to them?"

Wilhelm's gaze flitted nervously to me as if he was afraid I'd blame him for whatever had gone down earlier tonight. "Draegan passed out from the Glaen, and –"

"Glaen?" Chris and I said together.

Why would a demon touch a Fae drink? It was poison to them.

"It's a game some demons like to play," Wilhelm explained. "They drink shots of Glaen until one passes out. The girl played Draegan for the blood debt. No one's ever beaten Draegan, and Crak and Lorne didn't take it too well. They tried to stop the two girls from leaving, and you can see how that worked out."

I looked around and my gaze fell on a crystal decanter on a side board, containing a luminescent white liquid. Sara had duped a gulak demon into a drinking contest he couldn't possibly win. And no one could have known she was half Fae and immune to the stuff.

Glaen. Jesus. If I wasn't still wound up from my fight with Draegan, I would have laughed at the absurdity of it all.

Wilhelm cleared his throat. "What are you going to do with me?"

I shook my head. "Nothing. You can leave after you help us sort out a few things."

Tagg demons were not aggressive, and they were vegetarians for the most part. Most of them ended up working as servants for other demons. Certainly nothing that deserved a death sentence.

He let out a deep breath. "I'll help however I can, sir."

"We'll bring in some people to go through Draegan's files. You can assist them. Any money you find here is yours as payment for your services."

"Yes, sir!"

The way his eyes lit up told me his former employer kept a substantial amount of money on hand. I didn't care. It wasn't like we needed it.

"Who was this Rhys Draegan mentioned?" I had a suspicion about what he was, and it was hard for me to say the name without wanting to hit something. The thought of Sara anywhere near one of his kind made bile threaten to rise in my throat.

Wilhelm flinched. "Rhys is an incubus. He and Draegan did business a lot."

My fingers tightened around the hilt of my sword. I wanted to bring Draegan back so I could kill him all over again. God only knew how many innocent human girls he had sold to the incubus, or what horrors they had suffered before they died.

"Do you know where I can find this incubus?" I could no longer take my anger out on the gulak, but I would rid the world of his incubus friend. Draegan wasn't the only demon getting a house call from me tonight.

CHAPTER 30

"HOW ARE YOU feeling?"

"Like I've been impaled through the gut by a bloody spear," I grumbled, rubbing my hand over my stomach. The bandage had come off two hours ago, and the wound already looked a week old, but it still hurt like hell. I reached for the can of gunna paste on the coffee table.

Tristan's chuckle came out of the phone. "You're on the mend, all right. Although, Chris told me he almost called for a healer."

I swallowed some paste and scowled at the ceiling. "Chris is as fussy as an old nursemaid."

"He was worried about you. We all were."

"Thanks, but you can stop now."

To prove my point, I sat up, stifling a groan as the movement pulled at my sore stomach muscles. *Son of a bitch.* I planted my feet on the floor and leaned back against the couch cushion, waiting for the gunna paste to do its job.

Tristan's voice grew serious. "I don't remember the last time you were injured this badly. You need to be more careful."

"I'm always careful."

"Not last night. You went in there distracted and nearly got killed."

I started to argue, but he cut me off. "Chris told me what happened with the gulak. You should have taken more time to cool down from your rage before you went after the incubus."

He was probably right, but I was glad I'd gone after Rhys when I had. If I'd waited until today, the human girls he'd been feeding off would have been dead. Two human lives were worth a few hours of pain. So was seeing that bastard's lifeless eyes after I'd killed him.

If I'd been thinking clearly instead of being so focused on taking out the incubus, I would have noticed the booby traps he'd set up in his lair. I was carrying one of the girls through the living room when I heard a click and a whirring sound. It was sheer luck that the spear hit me and not the girl. A few inches higher and she would have been killed.

"Here's something that might improve your mood. Nate and I talked to Sara this afternoon, and she sounded tired but good."

"She's okay?"

I sat up straighter, ignoring the pain in my stomach. She hadn't called last night or today, and I'd been scared something had happened to her after she left Draegan's. Or that she'd been hurt in the fight at his apartment. I'd gotten so used to her calling every night. Not hearing from her left me unsettled. That was the reason I'd been distracted when I got to the incubus's place.

"She's fine. She said she knew we'd be upset if she didn't call today."

I racked my brain, trying to remember the date. I'd lost track of the days since I left Westhorne. "What's special about today?"

He let out a laugh. "Oh, my friend, you *are* a mess. How could you have forgotten Sara's birthday?"

I stared hard at the far wall as I worked through the days in my head. "It's her eighteenth birthday."

Eighteen was a special age for us because it marked our transition into adulthood. It was also the age when most of us became warriors. Before the awful thing with Nate and the attack on Westhorne, I'd planned to take Sara to town for a special birthday dinner, just the two of us.

Regret pricked my chest. I'd be with her right now for her birthday if I hadn't driven her away.

"You're sure she's okay?"

"Yes, from what I could hear. We tried to get her to tell us where she is, but she still won't say." He paused, and I heard him take a breath. "Have you heard about Orias?"

"What about him?"

"I just got word his place was attacked by vampires last night."

My hand tightened on the phone. "Was it payback for Stefan Price?"

"They were asking about the girl who killed him. No one could tell them who she was so they destroyed the place and started killing. I heard Orias killed two vampires, but he couldn't save his receptionist. She and two vrell demons were killed. Orias got away."

I swore and got to my feet. "Paulina was the one who told us Sara might be in Los Angeles. If she told the vampires that, they could be on their way here. I have to find Sara before they do."

"Jesus." It took him a moment to continue. "I'll call the San Diego team and have them head to LA to help with the search."

"Good. Tell them to let me know when they get here. I'm headed out now to start looking again."

"Are you well enough to go out?" he asked in a concerned voice.

"Yes. I've been in worse shape." I'd been down long enough. It would take more than a little stomach pain to keep me in this safe house any longer.

"Be careful out there."

"I will."

I looked around the living room for my gear and keys, but they were nowhere in sight. I was sure I'd left them here last night before we went to Draegan's.

The door to the control room opened, and Chris came out, holding his phone. He walked over and held it out to me.

I gave him a questioning look, but he said nothing. As soon as I took the phone from him, he left the room.

Scowling, I put the phone to my ear. "Hello?"

"Hi."

My heart thudded.

"Sara," I breathed, almost afraid I'd imagined her voice. In the next instant, alarm shot through me. "What's wrong? Are you hurt? Did he hurt you?"

"Chris?" she asked, sounding confused.

"The gulak demon." I clenched my free hand into a fist at the thought of Draegan or one of his cronies laying a hand on her.

"He didn't touch me."

My body relaxed. "You didn't call last night. I didn't know what to think."

"I'm sorry," she said thickly.

I sank down on the couch again. "I'm just glad you're okay and that you're talking to me."

"Me too."

I closed my eyes as her words flowed over me like a healing balm, soothing away my aches and pains. Hearing her voice did more for me than any medicine could.

"I know you're angry with me, but this isn't solving anything. Tell me where you are, and we'll talk this through."

"I'm not angry about that anymore."

"Then tell me where you are," I pressed gently.

There was a brief silence. "If I do, will you try to stop me from looking for Madeline?"

I opened my mouth, unsure of what to say. My gut and my heart told me to take her as far away from this place as possible, but that thinking had driven her away in the first place.

"This is important to me, Nikolas. I've gotten closer than anyone else to finding her, and I can't stop now."

"We'll look for her together," I said. It went against my every instinct, but at least she'd be with me. I'd surround her with a hundred warriors if that was what it took to keep her safe while we tracked down her mother.

"Does that mean you won't have any problem with me going to see warlocks and demons, and anyone else who might lead us to Madeline?"

I thought about Draegan and his incubus friend, and knew I'd never be okay with her going near demons like them. Not without me.

"We'll work something out."

I got up and walked into the control room where Chris sat at one of the computers. He pointed at a monitor and shook his head to let me know they were trying to run a trace and not having much luck.

"You can't trace me. I made sure of it," Sara said softly.

"So I see." I waved a hand at Chris, who was typing on the keyboard. "You picked up a few tricks."

"Yes, and some new friends."

I suspected her new friends were the ones blocking our trace. One day soon, I hoped she'd tell me how she'd come to know someone who could outmaneuver Dax on a computer.

"Listen, I have to go," she said suddenly.

I didn't want her to hang up because I didn't know when I'd hear from her again. "Call me tomorrow," I said as I walked back to the living room.

"I will," she promised, and I thought I could hear a smile in her voice. "Good night."

"Good night. And, Sara, happy birthday."

She didn't respond, and I hoped she'd heard me before she hung up. But it was enough to know she was okay and no longer angry with me.

Chris came into the living room. "I take it you two made up. At least, you're looking better than you did an hour ago."

I stood by the window staring at the dark street. "She still won't tell me where she is."

He let out a short laugh. "And that surprises you? This *is* Sara we're talking about. She's going to make you work for it. At least she's talking to you again."

"I know."

"She'll come around soon. Give her a few days."

If I had a few days to persuade her, I wouldn't mind, but Los Angeles was becoming more dangerous by the day. And if those New Mexico vampires showed up here, it was going to get a lot worse. We were running out of time, and so was Sara.

*   *   *

I opened the bathroom door and walked down the hall to my room with dripping hair, a towel wrapped around my waist, and my phone in my hand.

Shutting the door behind me, I threw the phone on the bed, pulled off the towel, and began to dry my hair.

Tonight, we'd gotten word of a possible nest in Long Beach, and we'd ended up killing six vampires and recovering two human bodies. It was the third nest discovered here in the last two weeks. Los Angeles would soon be overrun at this rate.

The alarm clock beside the bed said 2:00 a.m., making dread coil in my stomach. Sara should have called by now. Last night when she'd called, she'd sounded off. She kept reassuring me she was fine and just a little tired, but my gut told me something was wrong.

Not knowing where she was or if she was okay was killing me. I hadn't slept much since I left Westhorne, but the last two nights, I'd barely closed my eyes.

My phone rang, and I practically dove for it. I didn't know the number, but Sara used a different one each time she called.

"Sara?"

There was a short pause. "No, it's Jordan."

"Jordan?" Alarm raced through me. "What's wrong? Where's Sara?"

"She's here." Jordan's voice caught. "She's really sick. I-I don't know what to do."

Sick? Sara was half Fae and half Mohiri. She shouldn't get sick…unless she'd been poisoned by some kind of demon venom again. "Where are you?"

Jordan didn't answer.

I forced myself to stay calm. The last thing I needed was to scare her away. "She didn't want you to call, so you're afraid she'll be mad at you?"

"Yes."

"But you did the right thing," I said. "You wouldn't have called me if it wasn't serious. Tell me where you are, and we can have healers there in a few hours."

"She won't forgive me for this," Jordan said before she gave me the address.

I was dressed and out the door in under a minute, nearly bowling over Chris in the hallway.

"Where's the fire?" he called as I sped past him.

"Jordan called. Sara's sick."

He ran outside behind me, and the two of us roared away from the safe house. I knew the city well, and it was easy to find the address Jordan had given me. Less than ten minutes later, I pulled up to an old firehouse, and my Mori began to flutter wildly when we sensed Sara inside. Relief washed over me, weakening my knees for a few seconds.

The door opened before I reached it, and a pale-faced Jordan greeted us. She led us up to an apartment on the second floor where Roland, Peter, and another young man stood waiting for us in the living room. I barely saw them, my eyes going to the pile of blankets on the couch.

I pushed past the others and gently lifted the edge of the blankets until I saw Sara. Her face was colorless except for the purple bruises beneath her closed eyes, and she shivered despite all the blankets and the warm apartment.

My hand trembled when I caressed her cheek and brushed a few strands of hair off her face. Touching her was like breathing for the first time in a week, and the persistent pain beneath my breastbone disappeared.

"Sara?" I laid my hand against her cool skin, but she didn't move. "Sara, can you hear me?"

"She's been going in and out like that all day," Roland said. "But this time she wouldn't wake up. We were going to take her to a hospital, but we decided it was best to call you."

"I called Tristan. He's sending the jet." Chris walked into the living room. "How is she?"

"I don't know," I replied roughly. I'd treated countless battle injuries, and I'd never felt as helpless as I did in that moment.

I sat on the edge of the couch with my hand cradling her face. "How did she get like this?"

Jordan came forward. "We don't know. She was fine until two days ago. She woke up with a headache and said she was too tired to get up. I gave her some gunna paste, but it didn't help. Then she started saying how cold it was here, and we wrapped her in blankets. She was worse when she woke up today, and she barely ate anything all day. All she does is sleep."

I frowned. "Two days ago? That's the day after you went to Draegan's."

"Yes."

"What happened there?" I asked. "Why did you go there in the first place?"

"They went to help me…against my wishes."

A young man with dark blond hair stood behind the couch, looking at Sara with an expression of worry and affection that made my Mori growl possessively. The man looked familiar, and it took me a minute to recognize the blond biker from Sara's memorial service. I remembered how grief-stricken he'd looked, and I couldn't help but wonder what his connection was to her, and how he'd come to be with her on the other side of the country.

Roland came over to stand by the blond man. "Nikolas, this is Greg McCoy, a friend of ours from home. Greg, this is Nikolas Danshov. He's Sara's…"

"Mate," I finished for him.

Greg nodded. He didn't smile, but his expression wasn't hostile either. "She told me about you. Don't you think she's a bit too young to be mated or whatever you call it?"

"No." I wasn't about to justify our relationship to him or anyone else. "Where do you come into all of this?"

He scowled at me before he answered. "My uncle died last month, and I came here to take care of his things for my aunt. I ran into Sara and the others a few days ago and asked them to stay here. I didn't like her being out there, staying at hotels. She might have these powers, but LA's a bad place."

At least we agreed on that. "You're human?"

"Yeah."

"Los Angeles isn't particularly safe for humans either."

"I know," he said gruffly.

"What was Sara helping you with?" Chris asked Greg.

Greg rubbed the back of his neck. "Draegan held a blood debt against my uncle. When my uncle died, the debt fell to me. Sara got upset when she found out, and she went to see Draegan without telling me."

I looked at Jordan. "What the hell were you thinking, going to see a gulak demon? Don't you know what he could have done to you?"

Jordan flinched and crossed her arms defensively. "I told her it was a really bad idea, but she wouldn't listen. She would have gone alone if we hadn't gone with her. Besides, Sara can hold her own against a demon. She killed a ranc *and* a gulak that night."

"So I saw. What happened there?"

"We got there around ten. The demon on the door wouldn't let Roland and Peter in, so Sara and I went in alone. Draegan was playing Glaen with some other demons, and when we found out what it was, Sara said she was going to play him for Greg's debt.

"She said Glaen wouldn't hurt her because she's half Fae. She beat Draegan, and he passed out. We started to leave and his goons tried to stop us, so we took care of them. That's it. We came back here, and we haven't left." Jordan bit her lip. "Is-is she going to be all right?"

"Yes." I told her fiercely because I wouldn't accept anything else.

Sara shivered so violently I heard her teeth chatter. I tucked the covers around her, but it didn't help. She whimpered, and the sound tore at my heart.

I stood and kicked off my shoes as I pulled off my jacket and tossed it on the floor. Sara didn't move when I lifted the blankets and positioned my body behind hers on the couch. If she couldn't warm herself, then my Mori would do it for her. I pulled her back against me and wrapped my arms around her to give her as much of my body heat as I could. I ignored everyone in the room as I focused on easing her discomfort.

The others drifted away to talk, leaving Sara and me alone. Long minutes passed before her shivering began to subside, and she relaxed against me with a small sigh.

"You're going to be okay," I whispered against her ear.

My Mori shifted, distressed about its mate, and I could feel it trying to push its strength to Sara through the bond. I knew it was a futile effort. Only a completed bond allowed you to share your Mori's power with your mate. Otherwise, I'd give her whatever she needed to get well.

Time crawled as I waited for Sara to wake up. Every now and then, someone would come over to check on her. I didn't know if it was my body heat or touch helping her, but she seemed to be resting more comfortably.

An hour later, I felt her stirring. She pushed weakly at the blankets covering her and made a small frightened sound.

"Shhh," I murmured.

She grew still. "Nikolas?"

The emotion in her voice when she said my name made my heart constrict. "I'm here," I said softly.

Quiet sobs began to rack her body, and I pulled her closer, wishing I could draw her pain into me.

"Don't cry."

After several minutes, she grew quiet again, except for a few sniffles.

"How do you feel?" I asked.

"Rotten," she said hoarsely. "What's wrong with me?"

I kept my voice calm, not wanting to upset her. "I don't know, but we'll figure it out."

She tried to turn toward me, and I lifted her, wanting to see her face.

Her emerald eyes were full of anguish, and her face was wet with tears. She looked pale and tired, her hair was a mess, and still she was the most beautiful sight I'd ever seen.

Her hand came up to touch my face, her cold fingers softly tracing my lips and stroking my forehead.

I had imagined her touching me this way, but nothing had prepared me for the emotions that crowded my chest and tightened my throat until I could barely breathe. I'd missed her more than I could put into words, and the pain in her eyes told me I hadn't suffered alone.

"I'm sorry I didn't call," she whispered.

I smiled and kissed her forehead, and she laid her head wearily against my chest.

"It's okay," I assured her. "Go back to sleep."

The sound of a phone ringing awoke me two hours later. With Sara safe in my arms, it hadn't taken long for me to succumb to much-needed sleep.

Chris walked over to us and spoke in a low voice. "Tristan wants to talk to you."

I eased out from behind Sara and went into the kitchen where Chris's phone lay on the counter.

"How is she?" Tristan asked as soon as I said hello.

I looked at the small figure buried beneath a mountain of blankets. "I wish I knew. I've never seen her like this."

"She'll be okay. We have some of the best healers in the world, and two of them are on the way to you. Seamus and Niall are with them. They insisted they be the ones to go."

I let out a deep breath. "Tell them to hurry."

"I have Margot on the line now. What are Sara's symptoms?"

"She's cold and sleeps a lot. Jordan said she hasn't been eating since she got sick, and she had a bad headache when it started."

Tristan repeated what I'd said to Margot. The two of them talked for a minute before he came back to me. "There are two demon species in North America that can give you some or all of those symptoms. Sara would have been bitten by one of them to get their venom in her system."

"What demons?"

"Wirm and goccan demons," Tristan said.

I pressed my lips together. Wirm demons were highly venomous, and their bites were fatal to humans. My Mori would protect me if I was ever bitten by one of them, but Sara's Mori wasn't strong enough to help her. And there was no telling how her Fae side would react to a demon bite. Goccan demons lived among humans. They were poisonous, but they tended to keep to themselves. I couldn't remember the last time I'd heard of one of them biting someone.

I called Jordan into the kitchen. "Is there any chance Sara was bitten by a wirm or goccan demon?"

Her eyes widened, and she shook her head. "No. Not a chance."

I released the breath I was holding. "Tristan, did you hear that?"

"Yes. Margot will be there in less than two hours. Try to keep Sara comfortable until then."

I hung up and went back to the living room. Sara was still sleeping soundly, and she didn't stir when I sat on the couch and moved her so her head was on my lap.

"They'll figure out what's wrong with her at Westhorne, right?" Roland asked after a long silence.

"Tristan is sending two healers with the jet," I told him. "I don't want to wait until we get her home."

Chris entered the living room. "Good idea. Do they have any ideas what it could be?"

I shook my head. "There are several species of demon with venom that can cause some of these symptoms, but according to Jordan, they didn't come into contact with any of them."

"Tell us again what happened at the party," Chris said to Jordan.

She repeated what she'd told us earlier. "She didn't eat or drink anything except the Glaen, and the only demons I remember her touching were the ranc and the gulak. The only other demon that got close to us was an incubus."

I stiffened, thinking immediately of Draegan's friend Rhys. "An incubus?"

Jordan snorted and grinned. "Sara would have fried his man parts if he'd touched one of us. Trust me. My girl doesn't mess around."

I smiled at the pride in Jordan's voice. She and Sara had grown close, and I was grateful she'd been with Sara out here. Although, that didn't make me feel better about Sara being anywhere near an incubus.

Chris leaned against the wall by the large window. "How was she after she drank the Glaen? It's a powerful drink from what I hear."

Jordan shrugged. "She was kind of silly, like she was drunk, but not staggering. She even hugged me."

Roland snickered. "Sara hugged you? That must have been some good stuff."

Chris looked at me. "Could her Mori be sick from the Fae drink? She's only half Fae after all."

I'd seen faeries drinking Glaen at Adele's and at other clubs like hers. It was their version of alcohol, and what Jordan was describing was the effects of the drink on them.

"My Mori is fine."

I looked down at Sara, relieved to see she was awake and to hear her Mori was okay. "How are you feeling?"

She made a face. "Same. Thirsty."

Jordan ran to the kitchen and returned with a glass of water and a straw. She held the glass while Sara sipped the water. "Better?" she asked.

Sara smiled wanly. "Yes."

"If it is a venom, it won't take long for the lab to figure out which one," Chris said, distracting me from Sara and Jordan's conversation.

"You guys can identify every type of demon?" Peter asked.

Chris smiled. "It's a necessity in our line of work. We've been cataloguing demons for almost a millennium."

Peter whistled. "Damn."

"Sara, your hand is like ice!" Jordan cried, pulling my attention back to them.

"C-can't get w-warm," Sara stammered, shivering.

I reached out to touch Sara's face as Jordan leapt to her feet. "Nikolas, look at her. I think she's turning blue from cold."

I lifted Sara easily onto my lap and wrapped my arms around her, pushing my body heat into her. Jordan covered us with the blankets as Sara curled into a ball and pressed her shaking body against mine.

When Sara let out a small moan of pain, I knew my heat wasn't enough this time.

"Fill the tub with hot water," I ordered Jordan who ran to do it. I held Sara and rubbed her back and arms while the tub filled. She clutched my shirt and held on to me like she was afraid to let go.

"It's ready," Jordan called.

I stood and let the blankets fall away. Sara cried out as I carried her to the bathroom and set her down in the large claw-foot tub full of hot water. As soon as I sat her in the tub, her weakened body slid down. I caught her before her head went below the surface.

The tub was big enough to fit both of us, so I got in behind her and pulled her back until she rested against my chest, submerged in hot water almost to her neck. I vigorously rubbed her arms, but she continued to shiver uncontrollably. Her head fell forward, and she wept brokenly. I could feel her slipping away from me.

"Stay with me, Sara," I pleaded, hugging her tightly.

"I'm scared," she whispered.

Her words terrified me because she sounded like she was giving up.

"I did not chase you halfway across the country to let you leave me again," I said. "You are one of the strongest, most stubborn people I've ever met, and you are going to beat this. Do you hear me?"

She didn't answer, and I raised my voice. "Do you hear me, Sara?"

"Yes," she mumbled.

Seconds later, I sucked in a breath as the water around us began to fill with golden specks that multiplied before my eyes.

"Look!" Jordan cried.

"What is that?" Roland asked as he and the others pushed into the bathroom to see what was happening.

Jordan smiled broadly. "It's her magic – or the water magic. I'm not sure which."

Chris stood behind Jordan. "Whatever it is, it's helping. Her color is improving."

I'd never seen Sara's water magic, and I stared in awe at the glowing particles that were attaching themselves to her wherever the water touched her. Immediately, her shivering stopped.

She sighed and sagged against me.

"That's it. Hold on, Sara," I said against her cheek. "The healers will be here soon."

Her hand touched mine where it rested on her waist. "Don't leave me," she murmured almost incoherently.

"Never." I vowed, pressing my lips to her temple.

The water continued to glow even after she lost consciousness, and her skin stayed warm to the touch. I remained in the tub with her, afraid to take her away from the magic keeping her warm.

It wasn't until the healers arrived an hour later that I stood and carried her to one of the bedrooms. As soon as I laid her on the bed, Jordan and the healers shooed me from the room so they could dress her in dry clothes.

I paced outside the bedroom door until Margot opened it and gave me a kind smile. "You can bring her to the couch. It's a bit warmer in the living room."

I picked Sara up and brought her to the couch where I covered her in blankets again. Then Margot knelt on the floor beside the couch and checked Sara's vitals.

"We'll hook her to an IV to give her some fluids until we can get her home. The medical ward is being prepped for her now."

"Prepped how?" I asked.

"We're setting up to run blood panels as soon as she gets there so we can test for venoms. The lab has all the known antidotes on hand, so we're prepared in that area. We also have a mobile healing bath we can use to keep her core temp up."

I was reluctant to leave Sara, but I knew I was hovering, and Margot needed space to do her job. I went into the kitchen where Chris and Jordan were talking about the trip home. Seamus and Niall had come with the healers to provide extra security for Sara, and they were outside standing guard now.

Roland and Peter were accompanying us to Westhorne as well because Sara would be distressed if they didn't come with us. Tristan would arrange to fly them to Maine once Sara was out of danger.

"Sara!" Roland shouted.

I ran into the living room to find Sara curled into a ball on the couch, clutching her head and crying out in pain. Margot lay on the floor six feet away, looking dazed, and the other healer stood across the room.

I moved past them toward Sara and came up against a wall of energy that sent electric shocks through my body. I recognized the same power Sara had used on me back at Westhorne.

"Sara," I yelled, trying to push past the barrier that burned the longer I touched it. I watched helplessly as she stiffened and let out a small scream.

The air in the room shifted, and out of nowhere, a tall, blond man appeared near the window. Ignoring the rest of us, he started toward Sara.

I moved to intercept him. "Stay away from her," I snarled.

He kept coming and fixed me with a hard stare. "Let me help her, warrior, if you want her to live."

CHAPTER 31

AS SOON AS he got within two feet of me, I knew what he was. The power he emanated was like Sara's, only much stronger. Faeries couldn't be trusted, but they had saved Sara's life once before.

I stepped aside, and the faerie walked through the wall of energy as if it didn't exist. I tensed as he bent over Sara and laid a hand on her forehead. She let out a gasp and stopped crying. Her hands fell away from her head, and she looked up at the faerie as if she knew him.

"Hello, little cousin. I told you I'd see you again soon."

She blinked. "H-how did you find me?"

He stroked her face as a lover would, and I bit back a growl.

"Your pain is like a beacon to any Fae within fifty miles of here," he said. "I was away from the city or I would have come sooner. I'm going to take care of you now."

"You healed her?" Roland asked hopefully.

"No," the faerie replied without looking away from Sara. "I merely eased her pain. I will take her to Faerie where we will tend to her."

I moved to push through the barrier, only to discover it was gone. Standing close to the couch, I glared at the faerie. "She stays with me."

"Sara needs to be around my kind," he said casually, as if she hadn't just been in agonizing pain a minute ago. "She is going through *liannan*."

"*Liannan*?" I repeated.

He smiled. "Think of it as the Fae equivalent of puberty. Her powers are experiencing a growth spurt, and her body cannot handle the sudden changes. If she was full Fae and had grown up among our kind, this would have happened slowly, over months or years, and she would have been better able to deal with it. We were not sure she could even enter *liannan* since she is half Mohiri and lives outside of Faerie. Only exposure to our kind or a prolonged visit to Faerie should trigger *liannan*. I did not sense it in her when we met, and our brief encounter was not sufficient to cause it."

My stomach twisted. If Sara's Fae power was growing too fast for her body to handle it, what did that mean for her Mori? If her power killed her demon, could she survive without it?

Jordan spoke up. "What about Glaen?"

The faerie raised an eyebrow at her. "What do you know of Glaen?"

Jordan came into the room but kept distance between her and the faerie. "Sara drank a bunch of it at a demon party a few nights ago. She started getting sick a day later."

"Don't forget the times she glowed when she was asleep before she drank the Glaen," Roland added. "No way was that normal."

"It sounds like she was already approaching *liannan*," the faerie said. "Consuming that much of our drink at one time could be a catalyst to someone like her."

"Will she be okay?" Roland asked anxiously.

The faerie smiled down at Sara. "Yes, but she needs proper care."

My eyes met Sara's, and relief coursed through me to see hers free of pain. I'd do whatever I had to do to keep them that way.

"What kind of care?" I asked the faerie.

He looked up at me, and I was surprised to see real concern in his eyes. "She will need to be near our kind, at least until she passes through the most difficult stage. The best place for her is Faerie."

I didn't want to ask, but I had to know. "For how long?"

"I cannot say. It may take weeks or months."

Pain pricked my chest, and my Mori wailed at the thought of being separated from Sara for that long. "Do whatever it takes to help her."

Sara shook her head weakly. "No, I don't want to go to Faerie."

I crouched beside her. "You'll get better faster there."

"I can get better here. Eldeorin will stay here with me." She looked at the faerie. "Won't you?"

He smiled at her. "I will stay if that will put you at ease, Cousin."

"Thank you," she breathed, trying to sit up.

I stood and helped her up. Eldeorin sat close to her and took her hand in his. Instinct drove me hard to tell him to take his hands off her, but I knew his touch was easing her pain.

Sara gave me a weary smile and reached for me. I took her hand, and she pulled me down to sit on her other side. She laid her head on my shoulder and closed her eyes.

I looked over her head at Eldeorin. "It's not safe to stay in this apartment. Can you come to our stronghold?"

He pursed his lips. "That would be unwise. I and others of my kind will have to be near Sara for weeks. I don't think a prolonged Fae presence at a Mohiri stronghold would be received well. And we don't know yet how

Sara's *liannan* might affect your people."

He was right. We'd have a lot of very moody warriors if they had to be exposed to a bunch of faeries for any length of time. Even now, the presence of the faerie was causing my Mori aggravation, and not just because of his closeness to Sara. Chris and Jordan were keeping their distance from him, but I wasn't leaving Sara.

Chris frowned thoughtfully. "None of our safe houses are big enough to hold all of us. We could take a large house for a few months and bring in some people to help with security."

"That is not necessary," Eldeorin said. "I have a place we can use, and it is big enough to accommodate all of us without Fae and Mohiri affecting each other."

It would take more than a big house to stop the Master. "Is it safe?"

He narrowed his eyes at me as if annoyed I would question his security. "It is glamoured and well-fortified with faerie protections. No vampire would dare attack it."

"Where is this place?" I asked him.

"It is near Santa Cruz."

"We can be there in an hour on the jet," Chris said.

I stood and started issuing orders. "Chris, call the pilot and tell him to be ready to leave within the hour. Jordan, pack your things and Sara's."

"We're coming too," Roland declared.

"Be ready to leave here in five minutes," I told him and Peter, knowing Sara would never leave her friends behind.

I looked around the living room. We had six warriors, Jordan, two werewolves, and Eldeorin. That should be more than enough to protect Sara until we reached the faerie's house.

"The pilot said the plane will be ready when we get there," Chris called.

Eldeorin stood. "Now, Cousin, let's get you ready to travel. I could have the two of us there in seconds, but I have a feeling neither you nor your warrior would be happy with that."

He was right. I wasn't letting her out of my sight unless I had no other choice. I watched quietly as he laid his hands on her face, and they glowed like hers did when she healed someone. She let out a small sigh and visibly relaxed against the couch.

"This will keep you comfortable for the journey," Eldeorin said. "I won't need to be in physical contact with you the entire time, but I will stay close."

That was all I needed to hear, and I picked her up, cradling her in my arms.

"I can walk," she protested weakly.

Not a chance. I smiled and held her closer.

Exhaling softly, she rested her head against the crook of my shoulder, her hand touching my chest. Jordan opened the door, and I carried Sara outside where Seamus and Niall waited for us beside two white Escalades. The twins turned to grin at us as we approached.

Sara looked up at me, and I could see the question in her eyes.

My lips twitched. "They volunteered to come. I think they found Westhorne too tame after you left."

Niall started toward us. "Never a dull moment, lass."

"What's this I hear about you giving a beatdown to some gulak demons?" his brother teased.

Sara suddenly went rigid in my arms. I opened my mouth to shout for Eldeorin, but she rasped, "Vampires. Eight."

No one questioned her. Seamus and Niall drew their swords and spun to face the road. Eldeorin appeared beside me, and I thrust Sara into his arms.

"Get her out of here," I commanded, ignoring the protest that burst from her lips.

A second later, they were gone.

Jordan handed me a sword because mine was still strapped to my bike. Chris pulled out two knives, and Jordan gave knives to the two healers. They might have devoted their lives to medicine, but they were also trained warriors.

A mature vampire sped out of the darkness and came up short at the sight of his welcoming party. He obviously hadn't expected to face eight armed warriors and two werewolves.

He veered to the right into the path of Roland and Peter just as they exploded from their clothes into wolf form. The two werewolves were on the vampire before he could scream, tearing him apart with a ferociousness that gave me a new appreciation for Sara's friends.

The rest of the vampires burst upon us, shock registering on their faces. I went after the closest one, my blade laying open his stomach before he knew what had hit him. Another swing of my sword cut off his screams and his head.

The fight was short and brutal as we took advantage of their surprise to cut them down. Several minutes later, we stood in the driveway, looking at the bodies littering the ground.

"Eight," Chris said, counting the bodies. "How did she know that?"

"Your guess is as good as mine." I doubted I'd ever understand how her power worked. "Is everyone okay?"

We had no serious injuries. A few people had scratches, nothing that wouldn't heal in an hour. One of the healers had shoved Sara's human friend into the building to keep him safe.

Roland and Peter went to change into fresh clothes since they'd shredded what they were wearing. I called Wayne and asked him to send people to clean up the mess. The jet was waiting to take us to Santa Cruz, and I didn't want to be away from Sara for a minute longer than necessary.

I walked over to Greg who came outside as we were loading up the SUVs.

"You should get out of here, too. We have no idea if there'll be another attack, and we won't be here to protect you."

He drew himself up. "Don't worry about me. Sara's the one you should be thinking about."

I crossed my arms. "Sara is all I think about."

"Then why was she running around LA in the first place?" he demanded. "I know she thinks she can take care of herself, but this…" He waved angrily at the dead vampires. "This is too much. She said she was in danger, but I had no idea how bad it was. How could you let her leave your stronghold with all these vampires after her?"

I bristled at the accusation in his tone, mainly because he was right. I'd failed to keep Sara safe, and I never should have allowed her to slip away from Westhorne. I wouldn't make that mistake again.

"I don't know you, but I can see you care about Sara," he said. "But that doesn't mean much to me if she gets hurt because you guys can't keep her safe."

"Greg…" Roland said.

Greg waved him off and scowled at me. "I've known Sara a lot longer than you, and I was watching out for her before you even knew she existed. I don't care who or what you are. You'll answer to me if anything happens to her."

Anger surged in me. There was nothing more important to me than Sara's safety and happiness. I didn't need this stranger telling me how to care for my mate, even if he was her friend.

"You don't have to worry about her anymore," I ground out. "Sara is my concern now."

He took a step toward me. "Sara will always be my concern, and *I* watch out for the people I care about."

My hands clenched. If he wasn't a human, I would have punched him for insinuating I cared less for Sara's welfare than he did.

Chris stepped between us and gave me a warning look. "The jet is waiting for us. We need to go."

"Yeah, and Sara will kick your ass if you two fight," Roland added with a smile.

Peter piped up. "And she could probably do it too."

I nodded and turned away before I went against everything I believed in and hit an innocent human. I knew he was only overreacting because he was scared for Sara, but that didn't cool the anger his words stirred.

"Greg's just worried about Sara," Roland said after we climbed into one of the SUVs. "She's like a little sister to him, and it really tore him up when he thought she was dead."

I watched the blond man go back into the apartment. "Is he staying here?"

"No, he's grabbing his stuff and going to stay with his aunt in Dallas for a week. Then he's going to Philly."

"Good."

The flight was short, but I spent every minute wondering how I was going to find Sara when we landed. Eldeorin had said his place was near Santa Cruz, but he hadn't given us the address before he'd left. Was he telling the truth about the house? Even now, Sara could be in Faerie where I would never reach her.

We landed at the San Jose airport where Tristan had several Expeditions waiting for us in a private hangar to take us to Santa Cruz. When we exited the plane, I'm not sure who was more surprised to see a dwarf emerge from behind the parked SUVs.

He bowed when we approached him. "I am Heb. Master Eldeorin bade me give you directions to his home."

I walked over and took the slip of paper he held out to me. The address on it was for place a few miles outside of Santa Cruz.

"Master Eldeorin is awaiting your arrival," the dwarf said. Then he vanished before I could ask him about Sara.

"Let's go," I said to the others.

Seamus, Niall, and the two healers decided to return to Westhorne on the jet, since Sara had little need for them with the faerie to take care of her. The rest of us piled in one of the SUVs, and Chris drove us to the address Heb had given me.

It took forty-five minutes to reach the gates of Eldeorin's estate. We followed a winding driveway to a white mansion with a marble fountain out front.

I was half out of the vehicle when it stopped in front of the main entrance. Heb greeted me at the door and showed me into a large hall where Eldeorin waited for me.

"Where is she?" I demanded, unable to sense Sara in the house.

"She is upstairs, asleep," he said. "She was distraught and unable to control her power so I put her in a healing sleep. She is resting comfortably now."

"A healing sleep?" Was that why I couldn't feel her?

"It's a deep restorative state that will allow her body to adjust to the changes she's going through."

"How long will she be asleep?"

"That will depend on her," he replied in his infuriating calm manner. "She will wake when her body is ready to handle the effects of her *liannan.*"

I looked toward the stairs. "I want to see her."

"Of course. She is on the second floor, last room on the right."

I ran up the stairs. The door to Sara's room was closed, and I opened it slowly. When I saw her lying in the bed, I released a deep breath and started toward her.

A blast of energy slammed into me, stinging my skin and sending me flying into the wall on the other side of the hallway.

A petite red-haired girl appeared in the doorway and shut the door quietly. She kept her distance from me, which told me she was Fae.

"Oh my," she exclaimed. "Are you hurt?"

"I'm fine. What was that?"

She clasped her hands in front of her long blue skirt. "That was Sara's magic. I was afraid this might happen."

"What?" I asked with a growing sense of dread.

"Sara's magic is growing so fast her body cannot contain it. The healing sleep will help her adapt, but for now she will strike at anything demonic that enters her room." She smiled regretfully. "That includes the Mohiri."

My chest tightened at the knowledge I couldn't be with Sara when she needed me. "How long?"

"I do not know. Sara is the first of her kind, so we have no idea how she will progress through *liannan*. But she is strong, and she was advancing well with her magic before *liannan* started. We will have to wait until she wakes to see what happens."

I suddenly realized who the girl was. "You're Aine?"

She smiled sweetly. "Yes. You must be Nikolas. Eldeorin said you would be arriving."

I looked at the closed door. "Tell me the truth. Is she going to come through this?"

"Yes. Eldeorin is our most gifted healer, and he is confident she will survive."

Eldeorin appeared beside Aine wearing an arrogant smile. "I have never lost a patient, and I do not intend to start with my sweet little cousin. Besides, I look forward to having her as a guest in my home and getting to know her better."

I knew he was baiting me because faeries love causing mischief, but that didn't stop my jaw from clenching. I also knew male faeries were indiscriminate, immoral beings with unquenchable sexual appetites.

"I hope you don't mind having at least one other guest," I told him curtly. "I go where Sara goes."

He gave a small bow. "My home is your home for as long as you need to be here."

"Thank you. What happens now?"

Eldeorin smiled. "Now we wait."

*   *   *

Tristan and Nate arrived that evening, and they were upset to learn neither of them could see Sara. Aine had put protections on Sara's room to keep her power from escaping and to keep anyone from entering. She said she would let us know when it was safe for non-demons to enter the room.

The next day, Nate, Roland, and Peter were able to visit Sara, and I watched enviously as they entered the room and closed the door behind them. Roland and Peter came out after an hour, but Nate stayed with her most of the day.

Dinner that night was a lavish affair, except we were served human food instead of faerie food. Nate stared at the dwarf as he brought out the food and filled our glasses. He shook his head after Heb left the dining room.

"Faeries and dwarves. I feel like Sara isn't the only one asleep."

"How is she?" Tristan and I asked together.

"She looks like she's sleeping," Nate said. "Every time I look at her I expect her to open her eyes."

Sara didn't open her eyes that day, or the next, or the one after that.

Aine and Eldeorin spent a lot of time in her room, and all they could say when I asked about Sara was that she was doing well.

"How will this affect her Mori?" I asked Eldeorin on the fourth day. "Will all this power harm it?"

"From what I can see, she has a wall around her demon, keeping it away from her magic. Even in sleep she protects it." He shook his head slowly. "I've never seen anyone like her. I cannot fathom how one can live with Fae magic *and* a demon inside them."

"Neither can I." I'd tried many times to understand how a Mori could survive being constantly surrounded by Fae power.

Unable to be with Sara, I prowled around the estate, growing more ill-tempered by the hour. As the days stretched into a week, with no change in her condition, my fear for her escalated. Even the faeries seemed unsure of what was going on inside her body or when she'd wake up.

Eight days after Sara had entered Eldeorin's healing sleep, Roland burst into the den where I was trying to concentrate on reports Tristan had sent me. We were planning to set up a command center nearby so I could be near Sara and oversee the extra teams the Council was sending to California. Tristan had found two properties for lease within a mile of here, and he was working on procuring the one next door.

"She's awake," Roland shouted.

I stood so fast the desk chair fell over. "You've seen her?"

"No, Heb told me. He said Aine felt Sara waking up."

I was up the stairs and standing outside Sara's door within seconds. Aine appeared at the top of the stairs, carrying a tray of faerie food.

My heart began to pound. "Sara's awake?"

Aine smiled happily. "She is just coming out of the sleep. I'll tend to her and come back when I can."

My body felt weak, and I needed to lean against the opposite wall. I stared at the closed door, wondering what was going on in the room. Was Sara awake now? Was she still in pain? I knew Nate was in there because he spent his days with Sara, but I couldn't hear anything past Aine's faerie wards, even with my Mori hearing.

Roland and Peter showed up, and the three of us paced the hallway, waiting for Aine to reappear with word of Sara. The waiting drove me insane, although it didn't come close to what I'd been through the last week.

"What the hell is taking so long?" Roland griped, making me worry that something was wrong.

At last, the door opened. Aine smiled and beckoned me forward then put up a hand when I reached the doorway. She waved her hand, and suddenly I could feel Sara. My pulse quickened and I stepped into the room.

"No!" Sara cried a second before I felt the sting of Fae power against my face.

Aine ushered me outside and closed the door. "I'm sorry. Sara is awake, and I needed to test her control before I allowed you to see her. She is past the worst of it, but she will need more time to learn to control her magic."

I swallowed my disappointment. She was awake; that was all that mattered. "Is she all right otherwise?"

"Yes. She is a little distraught, but physically she is well."

"I want to talk to her. Is there a phone in her room?"

Aine nodded. "I believe so. I will check."

She disappeared and reappeared a minute later with a phone number.

"Thank you." I pulled out my phone and gave Roland and Peter a look that said I wanted some privacy. They frowned and headed downstairs, followed by the sylph.

I could hear the phone in the room ringing. On the third ring, Nate answered.

"Hello?"

"It's Nikolas. Can I speak to her?"

It felt like an eternity before I heard her tearful voice on the other end. "Nikolas?"

"I'm here," I answered softly, wishing I could hold her and wipe away her tears. "Don't cry."

A small sob escaped her. "I'm sorry."

Nate left the room, closing the door quietly. He gave me a wide smile and went downstairs.

I laid a hand on the door. "You have nothing to apologize for. The faeries explained what is happening with your power."

Her voice rose. "I could have killed you."

"But you didn't," I calmly reassured her.

She was quiet for a moment. "I don't know how long it'll be before I can see you again."

"I know."

I heard the uncertainty, the unspoken question in her voice. Did she really think I would leave her after everything I'd gone through to find her?

"I'm not going anywhere, and we can talk like this whenever you want to. You just focus on getting better."

"I will," she replied, sounding a little more like herself.

"Good. Now tell me, how do you feel?" Fatigue was creeping into her voice, and I didn't want her to overdo it.

"A bit weak," she admitted.

"But you aren't in any pain?"

"No pain. Aine said I'm over the worst of it."

I smiled. "She told me that too."

I heard her muffle a yawn, and I knew it was time to go. For now. "You need to rest."

"I'm fine," she protested weakly.

I laughed. "Liar. Get some sleep. We can talk again when you wake up."

She sighed. "Okay."

I hung up as Roland and Peter appeared at the top of the stairs again.

"Can we go see her now?" Roland asked impatiently.

"Yes, but don't let her overdo it. She needs to rest."

I went back to the den to call Tristan and give him the good news. He'd had to return to Westhorne earlier in the week, but he said he'd come back to California when Sara woke up.

Aine met me in the main hall. "May I have a word with you?" she asked.

"Of course." The sylph had stayed by Sara's side, tirelessly taking care of her for the last week, and she had my deepest gratitude for that.

"Sara will require time and training before she can control her power like she used to. Eldeorin and I will work with her to speed along her recovery."

"She's fortunate to have you two to help her."

Aine smiled and tucked a curl behind her ear. "I wanted to talk to you about the living arrangements here now that Sara is awake. In her current condition, she will have to stay in her room as long as you and your people are in the house. I believe it would help her progress if she could move freely around the house and grounds."

"I didn't think of that." The last thing I wanted was for Sara to be confined to a single room just so I could be near her. I could talk to her on the phone from anywhere.

"We're working on taking a house nearby. Until then, we'll stay at a hotel in town."

"Thank you. Her human uncle and the werewolves may stay. Her power will not harm them."

"Good." Sara would be glad for their company, and I was relieved to know she wouldn't have to be alone with the faeries. They'd cared for her in her time of need, but I didn't think I'd ever be able to trust them completely. Aine maybe, but not Eldeorin.

We ended up moving to the house next door that afternoon, thanks to Tristan pulling some strings and getting us the place with a six-month lease. I hoped it would only be a week or so before we could move back here, but we still needed the other house for our temporary command center.

I talked to Sara twice a day by phone. She was working long hours with Aine and Eldeorin, and each time I spoke to her she sounded tired and frustrated. I kept telling her she was doing great and reminded her that she'd learned to control her power on her own when she was just a little girl. She could do it now with the faeries' help.

Roland and Peter came to visit us and to let me know how Sara was really doing.

"She's getting better every day, but she's working herself way too hard," Roland told me. "And she's not sleeping well."

I understood her inability to sleep. It was an affliction I suffered from as well.

Christmas drew near, and I hated the thought of not being able to spend it with Sara. At our rented house, no one was in the holiday spirit.

Chris spent a few days in Los Angeles with the new teams working there. The vampire presence in California seemed to have doubled in the last two weeks, and we could all guess why. Word had gotten out there were two young Mohiri females in Los Angeles. Between the Master, Stefan Price's followers, and every vampire hoping for a taste of young Mohiri blood, the city was swarming with them.

Two of the teams were coming here after New Year's to set up our new command center. There wasn't much to do around here until then. I itched to go out and hunt down a few vampires to work out some aggression, but I was reluctant to leave Sara so soon after her waking up.

Jordan moped around unhappily, and I tried to get her to tell me how she and Sara had managed to sneak away from Westhorne.

She shook her head. "I'm going to let Sara tell you that one."

"Then tell me what you've been doing since you left home. Why were you in Salt Lake City?"

She pressed her lips together. "Sorry, can't do that."

"Why not?" I'd tried to get the story out of Roland and Peter, too, with no luck. "Is there something you don't want me to know?"

"No. Just feels like betraying her trust, and I don't do that."

Tristan returned from Westhorne on Christmas Eve morning, saying he couldn't bear the thought of spending the holiday without his granddaughter. I told him it was unlikely he'd get to see her even if he was here, but he said we had to have hope.

Late that afternoon, Aine came by unexpectedly to give us the news I'd been waiting for.

"Sara still struggles with using her magic, but she has regained control of it," the sylph explained. "It's safe for you to go to her now. I know she will be happy to see you."

It was a short walk to Eldeorin's house next door, and I felt Sara as I neared the house. I skirted the house and stopped at the edge of the back lawn.

Sara lay on a chaise lounge, her eyes closed and her face turned toward the sun. She wore a small smile and looked so peaceful I almost didn't want to disturb her.

I stood there for a long moment, savoring the sight of her, before I walked across the grass. She didn't stir as I approached or when I sat on my haunches beside the chair.

"Sara," I said in a low voice.

"Hmm?" Her brows drew together, and she turned her face toward me. "Nikolas?" she murmured.

Her eyes opened and stared at me in sleepy confusion. I smiled at her, and the next thing I knew, I was lying on my back in the grass with her on top of me, her arms clinging to my neck.

She rose up on her elbows, her hair forming a curtain around us. Her green eyes moved over my face with a hunger that made pleasure curl in my stomach.

"Miss me?" I asked huskily.

CHAPTER 32

SHE MADE A small choked sound and lowered her head. I realized she was going to kiss me a second before her mouth descended. Her lips moved over mine, soft yet insistent as she boldly traced my mouth with her tongue, sending a jolt of desire through every part of me. My lips parted to let her in, and she answered the invitation with a slow exploring kiss that robbed me of all thoughts except one.

My hands captured her face, and I held her to me, kissing her with a hunger I'd never felt before. Being away from her had been hell. Not knowing if I'd ever be able to touch her again, torture. I wanted nothing more than to carry her upstairs and spend the night making slow exquisite love to her.

"Sara," I whispered reverently against her mouth.

She trembled as my lips moved up her face to her forehead and back again. Breathing hard, I pulled her head down to my chest and held her close. We lay quietly for a moment as I willed my heart to slow down and basked in the pleasure of holding her in my arms.

"I'll take that as a yes," I teased gruffly, still trying to calm my overheated body. "I should go away for another week."

She huffed and pulled out of my arms to rise over me, wearing an adorable scowl that made me want to kiss her again, despite the approaching footsteps. I'd know Chris's walk anywhere, and I silently cursed him for his timing.

"Maybe I should come back later," he said, with barely-suppressed laughter.

"Good idea." My eyes never left Sara's. I was already thinking about tasting her lips again.

"Where is she?" Jordan called, and I almost groaned at the new interruption.

Sara's cheeks turned pink as her friend walked toward us.

"Oh. Well, I guess she's feeling better," Jordan quipped, and I could tell she was grinning as much as Chris. I was glad the two of them were having fun, but I'd be a lot happier if they'd do it somewhere else.

Chris chuckled softly. "Come along, Jordan. Let's give these two some time together."

"But..."

"We'll see you two later," Chris said as they walked away.

I smiled at Sara and noticed the dark shadows under her eyes. "You look tired," I said, lifting her hair away to see her better.

"I haven't been sleeping well." She lowered her body to lay her head on my chest with a shuddering breath. "Are you really here?"

"Yes." The catch in her voice made my chest tighten, and I pulled her closer. "Aine said you've been working hard to get your control back. Looks like she was right."

"She and Eldeorin are so good to me. Eldeorin said I have to start training next week."

"Yes, he told me that." I hoped the faerie made himself scarce until then. I wanted Sara to myself for Christmas, at least as much as possible with everyone else here.

"He didn't say how long it would take," she said slowly, sadness creeping into her voice.

"What's wrong?"

"Nothing," she mumbled.

I rolled to one side so she was lying beside me and made her look at me. "You are a terrible liar. Tell me what's bothering you."

She bit her lip. "I was just wondering how long I'll have to be here. I know you have responsibilities and I don't expect..."

Was that what was worrying her? Did she actually believe I'd leave her here?

"I'm not going anywhere," I said, holding her gaze so she'd see the truth in my eyes. "I may have to leave for a day or two sometimes, but I'll come back."

"Oh," she breathed, a smile lighting up her face.

I arched an eyebrow. "You thought I'd leave you after the chase you led me on?"

She glanced away and inhaled deeply. "I'm sorry I took off the way I did. I was upset, but I should have talked to you instead of running away."

I reached up to stroke her hair, and she brought her eyes back to mine.

"I'm sorry too," I said regretfully. We would have been saved so much pain if I hadn't overreacted that day at Westhorne. "I handled the whole thing badly. I saw how upset you were, and I should have known you would run."

Her lips twitched. "You did know. That's why you had the twins follow me everywhere."

I gave her a wry smile. "A lot of good it did. At least Seamus and Niall won't be making any more wisecracks about how you never would have given them the slip in Maine."

She toyed with the front of my sweater. "How long did it take you to find them and realize we were gone?"

My smile faded as I thought about that day. "About thirty minutes. Then we spent the next thirty scouring the woods. How did you two get past all our sentries?"

Her lips parted in surprise. "Jordan didn't tell you?"

"She said she was going to let you tell that story." I waited for her to start. "Well?"

She looked down. "You promise you won't get angry?"

"I think we're beyond that after everything else that's happened, don't you?"

She nodded and took a breath. "You already know how we got away from Seamus and Niall. I knew it wouldn't take long for you to come after us, and the first place you'd look was the woods. There was no way Jordan and I could outrun you on foot so we rode the river to town."

"You rode a boat down the river? Where did you get a boat?"

"Remember, you promised not to be angry." She gave me a small smile. "We didn't use a boat. I used my magic to float us. And before you start yelling, you should know I'm really good with water magic, and we weren't in any danger. Except maybe from freezing our butts off when we got out. We had dry clothes in plastic bags so we changed into them at the old mill. Then we ran to Derek's to pick up a car Jordan bought from his friend Wes."

I opened my mouth and closed it again. I think I was more scared about her walking around town in the dark than her river stunt. I wanted to say something, but it wouldn't change what was already done.

"Then you drove to Boise to pick up Roland and Peter. What was in Salt Lake City? Jordan and the others wouldn't tell us much about it."

"A friend who set me up with a laptop," she said vaguely, making me curious to know what friends she had in Utah. "You traced Roland's and Peter's cell phones there?"

"Yes."

She made a face. "You almost caught us at our hotel and we had to take off."

"I know, and I spent the better part of a day searching for you there." I didn't like to think about how close I'd come to catching up with her that first day and how I'd let her slip through my fingers. "Why did you go to Albuquerque?"

Her mouth fell open. "How did you know we were in Albuquerque?"

I smirked at her. "You aren't the only one with resources. Although, I have to say yours are impressive to help you get as far as you did with us on your trail." Genius was more like it.

"Aren't you full of yourself?"

Her look of mock chagrin pulled a laugh from me. "I do have some experience in this area."

"What? Chasing runaway...orphans?"

"Among other things." I noticed she hadn't answered my question about why she was in Albuquerque. "Are you going to tell me why you went to New Mexico?"

"Madeline was there," she said with a heavy sigh. "We were so close, and we just missed her. But we got a good lead that she was headed for LA."

Madeline was in Albuquerque? How the hell had Sara gotten that close to her when no one else could?

"Now it's your turn," she said. "How did you know we went there?"

"Let's just say that when a vampire as old as Stefan Price is killed, news travels fast. We've been hunting him for years, but he's always managed to evade us. When we heard a rumor that he was killed by a girl warrior who looked suspiciously like you, we went to Orias's place to check it out for ourselves."

She didn't even try to deny she'd been at the warlock's. "You know Orias?"

"Everyone knows Orias. He's a powerful warlock, but he usually stays under the radar." At least he had until Sara walked into his place. What a coincidence he suddenly suffered from memory loss around the same time? "For some reason he couldn't mention the names of the warrior and her friends or where they'd gone."

She lifted her shoulder. "Warlocks are a strange breed." I had a feeling there was more to the story than she was saying, but I didn't push her.

She raised her hand, and I caught it. "Tell me the truth. Did you kill Stefan Price by yourself?"

I'd mulled over it countless times and couldn't figure out how she could have killed one of the strongest vampires in the country. Or maybe I didn't want to imagine her fighting a vampire like Price.

She nodded. "Roland and Jordan helped, but I did kill him."

"With your power?"

"That and one of Jordan's knives," she said with more than a hint of pride.

I didn't know whether to be horrified or impressed, so I settled for a bit of both. I didn't want to think about her fighting Price, so I locked it away to deal with later. Much later.

I let out a breath. "And then you went to LA, and you met the faerie at Adele's club." That much I'd learned from Eldeorin, and Jordan had confirmed it was true. Although, she'd been strangely vague about it. All she'd said was Sara went to see Adele about Madeline, and Eldeorin went with her to keep her safe from the succubus.

Sara scowled darkly. "You know Adele, too?"

Her reaction filled me with pleasure. "Jealous?"

"No," she blurted.

I pressed my mouth to her fingertips and she flushed, making me want to kiss her again.

"Adele is well-known in the Los Angeles underworld, and she has given us helpful information in the past," I explained.

Sara smiled, looking pleased with herself. "I bet she didn't tell you that she and Madeline are pals or that Madeline goes to visit her once or twice a year."

"She told you that?"

Madeline friends with Adele? I knew the succubus couldn't be trusted completely, but for her to keep this from us, there had to be more to it.

What I really wanted to know was how Sara had pried that information out of her.

Her smile grew. "I told you I was close to finding Madeline."

Footsteps came toward us, and I almost yelled at whomever it was to go away. What did it take for a man to have a few minutes alone with his mate?

"Um, what are you guys doing down there?" Roland asked, his voice full of laughter.

"What does it look like?" Sara retorted.

"Looks like you got started without the mistletoe."

"Mistletoe?" She looked at me with wide eyes. "It's Christmas?"

"Christmas Eve," Roland told her. "And we're getting ready to decorate the tree. You two coming?"

I gave him a look that said we weren't quite done here. "We'll be there in a few minutes."

He turned away with a shrug. "Right."

I looked at Sara, who seemed distracted. "You're quiet all of a sudden."

Her bottom lip quivered. "I can't believe I forgot Christmas."

"You had more important things on your mind," I said gently.

"But I don't have gifts for anyone," she protested, growing agitated. "I need to –"

Moving with demon speed, I had her beneath me before she could blink, caging her with my arms.

"Are you going to run away from me again?" I asked gruffly.

"No," she squeaked.

I smiled. "Then that's all I want."

"Oh."

Her eyes fell to my mouth, and heat coiled in my belly again. I lowered my head until our lips almost touched. "There is one other thing."

My mouth captured hers again, and I lost myself in the long, leisurely kiss that left both of us breathing a little faster. When I lifted my head to look at her, I smiled at her slightly dazed expression.

"We should probably go inside before they come looking for us," I said reluctantly. I was all for spending Christmas Eve like this, but I didn't think the others would agree.

"Oh, okay," she whispered, but her eyes told me she'd be happy to stay right here.

Chuckling, I rolled off her and stood, leaning down to help her up. Her hair was mussed and her face still glowed from our kissing. I ran my fingers through her hair to tidy it, and she brushed grass from her clothes.

She smiled shyly when I took her hand and led her into the house where we were instantly surrounded. Sara's eyes welled up when she saw Tristan, Jordan, and Chris.

I squeezed her hand and said, "Merry Christmas," before she was swept away in a sea of hugs.

"She looks good," Tristan said when he came over to stand with me by the window.

I watched Sara laugh at something Roland said as he passed her. "It's good to see her smiling again."

Chris joined us and handed us glasses of liquor. "For a guy who can't tolerate human alcohol, Eldeorin has an impressive bar selection."

I drank some of the well-aged Scotch and nodded in agreement. I had a suspicion this was one of many places the faerie liked to entertain his human lovers.

"How did it go in LA?" Tristan asked Chris, turning the conversation to work.

"Good. Raoul's unit will be here next week to set up the equipment. Brock's unit is still in New Orleans, but they should be done there by the time we get everything up and running."

"We need everyone we can get," I said, thinking about the reports I'd been going over.

"The Council's sending Hamid Safar to help clean up LA," Tristan told us. "He should be there by now."

"Hamid?" I tore my gaze from Sara, who was on the other side of the room with Jordan, decorating the tree. I was finding it hard to take my eyes off her, but Tristan's announcement was enough to grab my attention.

I hadn't seen the Egyptian warrior in years, mainly because he preferred to work closer to home. He was one of the biggest, fiercest men I'd ever met, and he usually worked alone or with his brother Ammon. If the

Council was sending him here, they were more worried about the situation than they were saying. I'd fought alongside Hamid a few times, and I was glad to have him here.

Chris let out a low laugh. "Hamid's one scary bastard. I don't think we'll have a vampire problem in LA once they see him on their tails."

Tristan said something, but my attention was drawn to Sara again. I found her watching me, her cheeks pink. When she touched her lips, I didn't need to wonder what she was thinking about. I didn't blame her. Every time I thought about kissing her, I wanted to take her and find a private place to pick up where we'd left off.

Tristan's laugh pulled me back to the conversation. He shook his head at me. "Are you sure you'll be able to focus on work with Sara next door?"

I smiled wryly. "I'll do my best."

Chris chuckled. "Give him a break, Tristan. He's been impossible to live with the last few weeks. This is a big improvement."

I raised my glass to him. "Amen to that. If you'll excuse me, I'm going to spend Christmas Eve with my mate."

I set down my glass and walked over to the couch where Sara had gone to sit with Nate.

"California is nothing like Maine, that's for sure," she said wistfully as I approached.

I sat beside her and took one of her hands, lacing my fingers with hers. "We'll go back there someday when this is all over."

"If this is *ever* over," she replied sadly. "I guess we can assume the Master knows I'm no longer at Westhorne."

"Judging by the reports out of Los Angeles I'd say that is a safe assumption," Tristan said as he sat in one of the large chairs.

"How bad is it?" Sara asked him.

"Over twenty attacks on humans in the last week that we know of. The council has dispatched three teams to the area to deal with it."

"Twenty attacks?" she repeated, horrified.

Tristan gave her a stern look. "If the vampires weren't killing in Los Angeles, they'd be killing elsewhere. This is not your fault."

Roland leaned forward in his chair. "I wonder how they knew we were in LA. The vampires we ran into didn't live to tell anyone about it."

"What vampires?" I fixed him with a hard stare. None of them had mentioned seeing any vampires in LA.

"We, um, might have run into a couple after we left Blue Nyx," Sara said when no one else spoke up.

Chris stared at her open-mouthed. "*You* killed the vampires in the alley? So you *were* at the club that night?"

I thought about the vampire bodies we'd found in the alley. We'd been confused because two of them had been torn apart, and one had been killed by a sword. It all made sense now.

"We saw you come in with those other warriors. Eldeorin glamoured us so we could get away." Sara looked at me. "Why weren't you with Chris that night?"

"I was there, just a little too late by the sound of it. We got word that two girls were attacked at a hotel, and I went to check it out."

I silently cursed the faerie and his interference. Sara was half Fae. What had Eldeorin been thinking to allow her to run around alone in a city full of vampires and demons?

"What happened with the vampires?" I asked Sara.

"We were driving back to the hotel when we came across three vampires attacking some people." She waved at the others. "They killed them. I didn't even fight."

"We found the vampires, but no human bodies, just a dead mox demon," Chris said.

"That's because they were attacking demons, not humans," Sara replied.

"You rescued demons?" Tristan's disbelief mirrored mine.

Sara nodded. "A vrell demon and his friend. They were harmless."

I let out a breath. "You don't endanger yourself for demons, no matter what kind they are."

She narrowed her eyes at me, not trying to hide her annoyance. "Not all demons are bad, you know. The guy who gave me the laptop and helped me track Madeline is a vrell demon. He's actually a very nice guy."

Jordan sighed loudly. "We've learned that it's easier if you don't argue with her about this." Sara gave her a look I couldn't see, and Jordan said, "And I guess Kelvan is cool…for a demon."

"And the vampires?"

Jordan shrugged. "They weren't that old, no match for all of us."

"I thought Sara didn't fight them," Nate said.

"I didn't go near them," Sara insisted. "I shot one with a crossbow, and the boys took him out."

I raised an eyebrow at her as Chris said, "A crossbow?"

Roland laughed and Peter snorted.

"Yeah," Roland said. "He started mouthing off to her and she shot him right between the legs."

I remembered the vampire with the crossbow bolt in his crotch. I had to hide my smile. I didn't want them to think I approved of their actions, but at the same time, I wished I'd been there to see Sara shoot him.

"Sara has wicked aim with that thing," Jordan said proudly. "She definitely should start training with one."

"What happened to our weapons anyway?" Sara asked. "Did we leave them at Greg's uncle's place?"

Jordan raised her eyebrows. "You honestly think I'd leave that sword behind? It would take more than a few vamps to separate us."

Her reply made me think about the large group of vampires that had attacked us. I'd been wondering how they could have known where Sara was. There was no question about Jordan, Roland, and Peter's loyalty to her, but what about her biker friend?

"What I would like to know is how vampires knew you were at that apartment in the first place. How well do you know that human who was with you?"

Roland raised a hand. "Dude, don't even go there."

Sara stiffened and tried to pull her hand from mine. I refused to let her go, and she turned her face away from me. "Greg is one of my closest friends from high school, and he would *never* do anything to hurt me."

Roland's eyes met mine. "Greg's a solid guy. He used to watch over Sara like she was his sister. I can't see him betraying her."

Peter nodded. "Especially after she saved his life."

Even Nate came to his defense. "I always thought Greg McCoy was trouble, but he did seem to care for Sara."

"It could have been one of those demons at Draegan's," Jordan suggested. "They all knew Sara was playing Draegan for the blood contract, and one of them could have known who Greg was and where he was staying. I wouldn't put anything past that bunch."

She made a good point. Draegan had to have known where Greg lived so he could collect on the debt. It made sense that he'd told someone else, especially considering how furious he'd been after Sara won the contract back from him.

"It's a good thing you called Nikolas when you did," Nate said. "I don't want to think about what would have happened to you all if he hadn't been there."

Tristan looked at Sara. "Promise us you won't take off like that again."

"I promise."

Heb entered the room carrying a tray of food. He smiled and laid it on the coffee table, telling us dinner would be ready in an hour.

I heard Sara's stomach growl as Roland and Peter went for the food. Grabbing a napkin, I placed some canapés on it and laid it on her lap.

"Thanks," she said softly and began eating.

Roland looked at Tristan. "So what happens now? Are you all going home?"

"Sara has to stay here to train with the faeries," Tristan said. "Jordan and I will return to Westhorne after Christmas. Nate too, unless he wants to stay here."

Jordan's face fell. "I thought I could stay here with Sara."

Tristan shook his head. "Sara will be busy training, and Nikolas is staying with her. You need to continue your own training."

"But I can train here with Sara," she protested.

Sara gave me a nervous look. "I have to do faerie training *and* Mohiri training?"

"We'll pick it up where we left off." I'd either make her a warrior, or too exhausted to think about running off again.

Chris laughed. He knew me too well. "I smell payback."

Jordan gave Sara a pleading look. "You want me to stay, right? We can train together."

"Yes."

Tristan picked up a canapé. "We'll see. I'm not sure of the wisdom in keeping you two girls together. You seem to have a remarkable talent for attracting trouble."

I couldn't agree more, but I also knew how close Sara and Jordan were. I couldn't be with Sara all the time and run the command center, and Jordan would be a good companion for her. Especially since Roland and Peter had been ordered by Maxwell to go home after the holidays.

Jordan grinned. "At least no one could ever accuse us of being dull. Besides, Nikolas will be here. How much trouble could we get into?"

If I'd been eating, I would have choked. Almost everyone in the room howled with laughter, everyone except Sara and Jordan.

"You might want to think about sending a unit here for backup," Chris joked to Tristan.

"You may be right," he agreed.

"Everyone's a comedian," Sara grumbled.

Something told me there'd be no mistletoe kisses for me if I made the remark that was on the tip of my tongue. I wisely kept silent.

Like Tristan had said to Sara once, a good warrior knows when to retreat.

CHAPTER 33

SARA YAWNED BEHIND her hand and smiled at something Roland said. It was late, almost midnight, and Nate, Tristan, and Chris had already retired for the night. I'd expected Sara to go to bed hours ago, considering how tired she was, but she seemed determined to stay up with everyone else.

I took her hands and tugged her to her feet. "Come on," I said, leading her from the room.

"Where are we going?" she asked without resisting.

"You're going to bed. Everyone will still be here in the morning."

Roland and Jordan hooted as we left the room. The fact that Sara didn't blush at their teasing comments told me how tired she was. She was quiet as we walked up the stairs and stopped outside her bedroom door.

When she turned to me, I pulled her into my embrace. She wrapped her arms around my waist, and we stood holding each other for a long moment.

"It's late. You should get some sleep," I said softly.

I was reluctant to let her go, but we'd have all day tomorrow together. Even with everyone here, Eldeorin's house was big enough for us to find a few minutes alone together.

"Stay."

My stomach did a little flip at her unexpected request.

She quickly blushed and looked at my chest. "I don't mean..."

I tilted her face up and brushed her lips with mine. "I know."

As much as I wanted her, I knew she wasn't ready for anything more intimate. When I made love to her, it would be she who initiated it, and she wouldn't be falling asleep on her feet.

I opened her door and followed her into the room, closing the door quietly. She turned around and faced me, twisting the hem of her sweater in her fingers and looking so endearingly flustered I couldn't help but laugh softly.

"Get ready for bed. I'll just stay until you fall asleep."

She smiled and grabbed some clothes, going into her bathroom to change.

I walked around the room, looking at her things: a sketch pad on a small table, an iPod and ear buds on the dresser, a hoodie slung over the back of a chair.

At the balcony, I stopped and listened to the Pacific through the slightly open door. She'd told me once how much she loved the ocean, and I never realized how much she must have missed it in Idaho.

The bathroom door opened, and I watched her enter the bedroom and look around for me. My eyes moved up her bare legs to a familiar navy blue T-shirt that hung almost to her knees. If it hadn't already been my favorite shirt, it was now after seeing her in it.

"I wondered what happened to that T-shirt," I said.

She toyed with the bottom of the shirt, and I almost didn't hear her response.

"It's really comfortable."

I stalked toward her, and she backed up. When we got to the bed, I didn't miss her small intake of breath when I reached around her.

Smiling, I lifted the covers. "In you go."

I pulled the covers over her then kicked off my shoes and lay beside her on top of the blankets. I lifted my arm over her head in silent invitation, and she moved over to snuggle against my side with her head on my shoulder.

Closing my eyes, I played with the end of her hair as I let her soft breathing lull me into a light doze.

"Nikolas?"

"Hmmm?"

"Why haven't you yelled at me for leaving Westhorne?"

My eyes opened, and I frowned at the ceiling. "Do you want me to yell at you?"

She sighed. "No, but you're taking this too well. Are you being nice because I was sick?"

I swallowed a laugh. "Yes, but don't worry. I'm sure you'll give me more reasons to yell soon enough."

She fell silent, and I wondered if she was waiting for me to say more.

"I was furious when I found out you'd left, and all I could think about was what could happen to you out there. I always want to keep you safe, but after the attack I couldn't think of anything but getting you away from there."

I looked down at her, wishing I could see her face. "I'm sorry I made you feel like you had no other choice but to leave. I want you to be able to come to me about anything."

"I'm sorry I left the way I did. I was upset about the attack, and all I wanted to do was fight back," she said hoarsely. "It hurt when you and Tristan said you were taking me away to hide, especially after people were hurt and killed because of me."

"You're not responsible for what happened that night."

"I know, but it's impossible not to feel guilty when some of my friends were killed by vampires who were after me. And I knew it wasn't going to stop and they'd keep coming. Sooner or later, someone I love will die and I can't live with that."

Her voice cracked. "I had to do something to try to end this. I should have told you what I knew about Madeline instead of going after her without you. I kept telling myself I could find her and that she'd run if she saw the Mohiri. But the truth is, I needed to be the one to find her. I needed to feel like I was in control of my life again."

I'd known from the beginning this was as much about Sara's fight for independence as it was about finding Madeline. Since I met her, I'd been driven by my instinct to protect her, at all costs. First, I took her away from everything she knew and brought her to Westhorne. When that didn't prove safe enough, I made the decision to take her to Russia without talking to her first. I'd never stopped to think that I could be the one hurting her the most.

"You've spent most of your life taking care of yourself, and I've spent mine protecting others. It's not easy for either of us to go against our nature. I didn't realize how much I was pushing you to change yours until you left."

"And now?" she asked quietly.

She wasn't going to like what I said no matter how I worded it. "I won't lie to you. I'm not going to try to take you away, but I can't stand to see you in danger either. You're a fighter, but I'm an experienced warrior, and I'm going to do what I have to do to keep you safe."

Her body tensed. "I understand why you feel so protective, but you have to see that I'm not helpless."

"I never thought you were helpless. I just don't think you're ready to face what's out there."

Her powers were growing and one day soon, she'd be a force to be reckoned with, but she hadn't seen a fraction of the ugliness in the world.

She pulled away from me, but I gently refused to let her go. "Let's not fight," I pleaded.

She lay against me again.

I pressed my lips to the top of her head. There had been a time when our disagreements ended with her yelling and walking away from me. We were making progress.

"You should go to sleep. I don't want Nate and Tristan shooting me dirty looks tomorrow when you can't stay awake at Christmas dinner."

She yawned and snuggled against my side. "You'll stay until I fall asleep?"

"I'll stay until I hear snoring."

"I don't snore," she retorted.

I grinned at the indignation in her voice. "Like a motorboat."

"I do *not* snore!" She punctuated her words by poking me in the ribs.

Her playful touch sent warmth through me, and I had to grab her hand before she started something I wouldn't want to stop.

"Okay, it's more like a kitten purring," I said, laughing. "Did I ever tell you how much I like kittens?"

I must have said the right thing because she laid her arm across my stomach and tucked her body as close as the blankets between us would allow.

I waited until I heard her breathing even out before I moved to slip out of her arms. She made a soft sound of protest and threw a leg across mine, her arm tightening around my waist.

"I don't want to leave you either," I whispered to her.

She sighed happily in her sleep, and I wrapped my arms around her again.

"Okay, five more minutes, and then I have to go."

*   *   *

"What the hell?"

A loud, angry male voice jerked me from sleep, and I looked at the blue walls and billowing white curtains in confusion. Then I felt the warm body nestled against me – or actually, on top of me – and I realized where I was.

I looked down as Sara raised her head, and her wide eyes met mine.

A slow smile spread across my face at her sleepy confusion. With her hair wild around her face and her lips still swollen from sleep, she was ravishing.

"Morning," I murmured roughly.

"What are you doing in her bed?" Nate demanded loudly, reminding me what had awoken me from the best sleep I'd had in ages.

Color flooded Sara's face, and she moved off me to bury her head in a pillow. "Oh God," she moaned.

I slid off the bed and looked for the shoes I'd kicked off last night. I picked them up and turned to face Sara's irate uncle standing in the bedroom doorway.

"Good morning, Nate. And Tristan," I added as he appeared behind

Nate.

"Nikolas," Tristan said with a smile.

Nate took a step into the room. "I know you two are in a relationship, but this is inappropriate. Sara just came out of some faerie…coma. The last thing she needs is —"

"Nothing happened!" cried a muffled voice from the bed. "Tell them, Nikolas."

My lips twitched, but I didn't think laughter would help the situation. Schooling my expression, I addressed Nate.

"I walked Sara to her room and stayed to talk. I meant to leave, but I fell asleep."

Nate wasn't appeased. "And you had to get into bed with her to talk to her?"

"No, but I haven't seen Sara in a long time, and I wanted to hold her for a while."

I figured honesty was the best option. I respected Nate more than most humans I'd met, and I considered him a friend. I also knew he didn't understand Mohiri bonding or a bonded male's need to touch his mate. But I wouldn't apologize for spending the night with her. That would mean admitting we'd done something wrong, which we hadn't. Not to mention Sara was eighteen, an adult in both the human and Mohiri worlds.

"He was on the bed, not in it," Sara clarified.

"That doesn't make it right," Nate told the form beneath the covers. "Why are you hiding in there? I want to talk to you."

"No way. I'm not doing this again."

"Again?" Nate glowered at me. "What does she mean by that?"

"It's nothing. She fell asleep on my couch one night back at Westhorne."

I decided not to mention the part where she'd been drinking and ended up sleeping on top of me. I loved her favorite sleeping position, but I probably shouldn't mention that either.

"I might have embarrassed Sara when I showed up at Nikolas's apartment the next morning," Tristan said.

"Hmph," Sara muttered, drawing smiles from Tristan and me as we remembered his disastrous attempt to talk to her about sex. Again, not something to share with Nate in his current mood.

"It was all quite innocent," Tristan assured Nate. "I'm sure this is as well. Nikolas wouldn't try to —"

"Gah!" Sara shrieked. "Out. Everyone out of my room, right now."

"You two leave," Nate said. "I want to talk to Sara."

The bed covers moved, but Sara didn't show her face. "You too, Nate. I am so not talking to you about this."

"Sara…" he began.

"Out," she said again. "Or I'm not coming out of here until tomorrow."

It was an empty threat. I knew there was no way she wouldn't spend Christmas with him and the others. But it worked.

Nate sighed. "Okay. We'll talk later. Do you want breakfast? Heb made all your favorites."

"No thanks. I'm not hungry."

Her stomach growled loudly in protest.

I leaned down to whisper to her. "Liar. I'll send Heb up with some food. Something tells me you're going to need your strength."

She groaned and burrowed deeper in the bed. "You're enjoying this, aren't you?"

I laughed softly. "See you soon."

Straightening, I walked around the bed toward the door. Nate didn't move until I'd left the room and headed downstairs to the kitchen. I found Heb and asked him to bring something to Sara. The dwarf was eager to help and hurried to prepare a tray for her.

Sara came downstairs an hour later, and we all spent the day lounging around and stuffing ourselves on Heb's endless supply of food.

Nate didn't say anything else about finding Sara and me together, but he kept shooting me looks every time I went near Sara. I understood his anger. He'd raised Sara as his daughter, and she'd always be a child to him.

I almost laughed when I walked into the dining room for dinner and saw Sara already seated between Nate and Tristan. She scowled when I smirked and took the chair across from her.

"The food looks amazing," Tristan said, reaching for a platter of roast goose. "The cook outdid himself."

"Yes, everything looks so good." My eyes met Sara's. "I don't know where to start."

She blushed and picked up the mashed potatoes. The heavy glass bowl almost slipped from her hands, and I leaned across the table to grab it. My fingers grazed hers, and warmth coursed through me. Her small intake of breath told me I wasn't the only one affected by the touch.

"You guys going to hog the potatoes or share them with the rest of us?" Roland asked with a devilish smile.

"Let me." I took the bowl from Sara and spooned a generous helping of potatoes onto her plate. Taking some for myself, I passed the bowl to Peter, who sat beside me. Then I reached for the prime rib, which had been cooked to perfection. I asked Sara if she wanted some before I put a slice on her plate.

Heb really had outdone himself. In addition to prime rib and roast goose, there was a ham, a whole roasted salmon, and every side dish you could ask for. The dwarf knew how to feed a party of Mohiri and werewolves.

I wasn't the only one making sure Sara's plate was full. Tristan and Nate took turns placing food from almost every serving dish on her plate until she held up a hand to stop them.

"No more." She laughed and waved a fork at all the food before her. "I'm going to explode if I eat all this."

Peter grinned. "But what a way to go."

Roland cut into his prime rib and sighed. "I'm going to miss Heb's cooking when we go home. He's spoiled me for normal food. Do you think he'd consider coming with us?"

"Do you really have to go?" Sara asked, toying with her food.

Peter grimaced. "Dad's orders. Trust me, if we could stay, we would."

"Yeah, I don't even want to think about what he's going to do to us when we get home," Roland said.

"Will he beat you?" Jordan asked. "I read that some Alphas do that when a pack member disobeys them."

"Maxwell would never do that," Sara declared. "He's tough and he can be scary when he's angry, but he wouldn't beat someone."

"Uncle Max prefers the 'work you until you drop' form of punishment," Roland said. "I don't know what will be worse, him or going back to school and trying to catch up."

"Ugh. I forgot about school." Peter groaned. "Thanks for ruining my appetite, man."

Everyone laughed and the mood at the table lightened, even with Nate's occasional scowls in my direction. Fortunately, by the time dessert came out, he seemed to have forgiven me. That made Sara happy, and anything that made her smile made me happy too.

That night, I walked Sara to her room, and she looked around as if expecting Nate to pop out and start scowling again. I pulled her into my arms and kissed her tenderly before I said good night. I was disappointed, but not surprised when she didn't ask me in. She'd been pretty embarrassed that morning, and she clearly didn't want a repeat.

Two days after Christmas, Tristan and Nate went back to Westhorne. Sara was down for a few hours, but Roland and Peter cheered her up. She told me she hated to think of the boys leaving too, and she got a sad look in her eyes whenever someone brought it up. I was glad Jordan was staying on with us so Sara didn't have to lose all of them at once.

The next week went by quickly. Jordan, Chris, and I had moved back to Eldeorin's on Christmas Day, but Chris and I spent the days next door, getting the place ready for the warriors arriving after New Year's. I saved my evenings for Sara. We were rarely alone, but I enjoyed being with her no matter what we were doing.

I'd planned to spend time with her and get to know her better at Westhorne before everything happened with Nate and then the attack.

Here, Sara was safe inside the faerie protections, and I didn't need to worry about her. I could do my job while she trained and got stronger. And I'd finally be able to court her as she deserved.

Every night, I walked her to her room and kissed her good night as if I was dropping her off after a date. She didn't ask me to stay, and I didn't ask to come in. My Mori was impatient to claim its mate, and so was I, but I was determined to let Sara set the pace.

One person I was happy not to see that week was Eldeorin. Aine came by once a day to visit with Sara, but Eldeorin stayed away. He was supposed to come back in the next few weeks to begin training with Sara. I wasn't sure what that entailed, but if it helped her master her power, I'd put up with him.

Roland and Peter left us the day after New Year's to drive back to Maine. The same day, a truckload of equipment arrived along with the first warrior unit. Chris and I spent all day next door, helping to get the command center in order. By that evening, we had all the systems up and running.

It felt good to be doing familiar work again, and I didn't realize how much I'd missed it until I was back in the middle of it. I wouldn't be going out on jobs as much as the other warriors, but I'd still see some action. At one time, that would not have been enough for me. Being with Sara changed things.

The next afternoon. I came back from the command center to start Sara's combat training, and I found her and Jordan standing near the pool, which was almost frozen solid. The look on Sara's face told me her first day of training with Aine hadn't gone as she'd hoped.

"What happened?"

"Sara froze the whole thing in like two seconds," Jordan said.

"Incredible." I knew Sara could use her power to warm the water around her enough to keep her warm, but to freeze a twenty-thousand-gallon pool?

"No, it's not," Sara said glumly. "I wasn't trying to freeze it, just lower the temperature a little."

"Ah, come on, you have to admit it was funny." Jordan grinned at me. "Chris had his legs in the water. Luckily, he has demon speed or he'd be a popsicle right now."

"Lucky him," Sara muttered.

Jordan let out a small laugh. "Sara was in the middle of the pool, and it took her a while to get free. She's still a bit peeved."

Sara scowled at her. "You would be too. I think my butt is still numb."

A chuckle escaped me, and I couldn't stop my eyes from dropping to her jean-clad backside. I was tempted to ask if she needed me to warm her up, but her glare stopped me.

"I suck. I can't even control my own power anymore," she grumbled, disheartened.

"It's only your first day of training, and Aine said it wouldn't happen overnight. Give yourself some time to get used to it." I laid a hand on her arm. "You can do this."

She gave me a grateful smile. "Thanks."

CHAPTER 34

"EVERYTHING WE'VE SEEN points to a small nest, but watch your backs. I don't want any surprises."

Brock nodded and hefted his weapons bag onto his shoulder. "We'll be in and out before those suckers know we're there. You sure you don't want to come with us? I know how much you *love* to clean out nests."

"Not this time. I have plans tonight." Something a lot more pleasant than killing vampires.

He gave me a knowing smile. "Have fun."

Brock left as Chris walked into the living room we'd turned into the main control room of the command center. Chris spotted me and headed over to where I stood.

"Hamid called. He and Ammon will be here tonight, and they want to talk about the situation in Seattle."

A teenage girl had gone missing two days ago, and the body of another girl had been found in a restaurant dumpster yesterday, drained of blood. Seattle news stations were already talking about a serial killer, but we knew different. So far our guys in Seattle hadn't been able to find a trace of the vampire responsible.

"What time will they get here?"

"Late, I think. You have somewhere to be?"

"I'm taking Sara out."

He smiled broadly. "Well, it's about damn time."

"What's that supposed to mean?"

"Nothing. Just that most males date the girl *before* they start going into rages and chasing her across the country."

I scowled. "In case you haven't noticed, the last few months haven't left a whole lot of opportunities for dating."

"True." He sat on the edge of a table. "Where are you taking her?"

"I don't know. Wherever she wants to go. I thought it would be good for her to get out of the house for a few hours."

Chris nodded in understanding. "She still having a rough time with her Fae training?"

"Yes."

Rough didn't exactly describe Sara's Fae training. In addition to freezing the pool, she'd managed to blow up the gazebo near the lake, create a thunderstorm on the back lawn, and awaken a water dragon sleeping at the bottom of Eldeorin's small lake.

Her training with me was going well, and she continued to surprise me with how fast she picked up the new strikes and kicks I'd taught her. She still didn't like the strength and cardio workouts, but I made her do them every day. I was pushing her hard, but she had a lot of missed years of training to catch up on. I'd rather I be the one to get past her defenses instead of someone out to kill her.

This afternoon, she'd been unusually withdrawn in training. Normally, I could coax a few smiles from her, but she'd been too distracted today to even notice my attempts.

Tonight I planned to take her somewhere nice, just the two of us, and enjoy some good food and conversation. And hopefully get her to tell me what had upset her earlier.

"Have fun." Chris smiled slyly. "I'll let Hamid know you might be a little late."

"Thanks." I headed to the door. "Later."

When I got to Eldeorin's, Jordan informed me that Sara was in her room. I went to my room to change and grab my leather jacket, and then I knocked on Sara's door.

It took a minute for her to answer, and her tangled hair and wrinkled shirt told me she'd been in bed. Her lips parted in surprise, and then her eyes slid down my body to somewhere in the vicinity of my abs. Heat filled me at the realization she was checking me out.

I cleared my throat softly to bring her attention back to my face. I held back a smile at the pink in her cheeks.

"Grab a warm coat. We're going out," I told her.

Her eyes widened hopefully. "We are?"

"If you'd rather stay —"

"No!"

I chuckled as she sped to the closet to grab fresh clothes and disappeared into the bathroom. Her eagerness told me I was right, and this was just what she needed. I needed it too. Our first date was long overdue.

In no time, she stood in front of me again, her face flushed in anticipation. She pulled on her coat as we walked to the stairs.

"Where are we going?"

"I thought you might like to go out to dinner for a change."

We reached the foyer, and I opened the door for her. Her eyes lit up when she saw my Ducati.

"That sounds nice," she breathed.

I helped her don a helmet, explaining how to use the built-in mic so she could talk to me on the ride. Then I straddled the seat and patted the spot behind me.

When she climbed up behind me and her arms slipped around my waist, I forgot all about dinner. I just wanted to ride for hours with her holding on to me like that.

I drove us through the gates and turned toward Santa Cruz. I wished we were going farther than that. Riding my bike had always been one of my greatest pleasures, but nothing came close to having Sara hugging my back, her thighs pressed against mine.

"You okay?" I asked when she began to fidget a few minutes into our ride.

"Yes, but I should have brought gloves with me."

I reached down and laid a hand over one of hers. Damn, she was like ice. I didn't need gloves because my Mori kept me warm. I should have reminded her to bring some for herself.

I needed my hands to drive, but I couldn't stand the thought of her being cold all the way to town. An idea came to me, and I slipped her hand into my jacket pocket. The heat from my body would keep it warm there.

Following my example, she did the same with her other hand. I smiled when I heard her sigh happily.

"Better?"

"Much better."

Her hands rubbed against my stomach as she warmed herself, and I found it hard to concentrate on the road. I inhaled slowly, glad she had no idea about the effect she had on me. As our bond grew stronger, so did my need for her. Every touch from her was pleasure and torture, and it killed me not to be able to be with her as I longed to.

My Mori grumbled unhappily as I denied us yet again. It didn't understand or care about our human emotions; all it wanted was to be with its mate.

Soon, I said to myself as much as to the disgruntled demon.

"Where are we going anyway?" Sara asked.

"Santa Cruz," I replied, glad to think about something else. "What kind of food are you in the mood for?"

"I love Italian, but I'm not picky if you want something else."

"Italian it is."

I knew the perfect place. Chris and I had found an authentic little Italian restaurant last week, and my first thought had been to bring Sara there. I'd seen her and Nate go to dinner a few times at an Italian restaurant in New Hastings so I knew she liked the food.

The place was already busy when we got there, but I managed to get us a table for two by the window. A waiter hurried over to bring rolls and fill our water glasses while we looked at the menu.

"I'll have the linguine," Sara told him quietly.

I handed him our menus. "Lasagna for me."

The waiter left, and Sara chewed her lip, something she did when she was nervous. She looked at the tablecloth, out the window, at the dining room – anywhere but at me. Her shyness was endearing, but I wanted her to be comfortable with me.

"This seems like a nice place," she said.

I picked up a roll. "It is. I've been here before."

"Oh."

"I came here with Chris last week," I said casually as if I hadn't noticed the flash of jealousy in her eyes. Tearing apart my roll, I smirked at her. "You should grab one of these before I eat them all."

She laughed, her eyes sparkling in the candlelight. I smiled and ate half my roll while she buttered one for herself.

"Mmm, this is amazing."

My mouth went dry at the look of rapture on her face, which made me think of things that definitely had nothing to do with food.

Jesus, get a grip. I reached for my water as I searched for something to say.

"I talked to Tristan today. He said Sahir is hoping to use Hugo and Woolf to patrol the grounds."

Her face lit up. "I heard that too. They've been great with him ever since the night of the attack. I'm glad they don't have to be caged all the time now."

"You miss them, don't you?" I said, hearing a little sadness in her voice.

"Yes," she replied wistfully. "But I know Sahir is taking good care of them. He doesn't have a lot to do without Minuet and Alex there."

"The wyvern didn't go as far as you think."

Her eyes rounded, and I nodded. "They've spotted him twice in the mountains near Westhorne. Sahir thinks he's found a cave to live in, and there is plenty of game for him to hunt. They've been too busy with everything else that's been going on to try to catch him. So far he's kept out of sight of the humans, and Tristan said he's going to leave him alone for now, unless he poses a threat to people."

She smiled fondly. "The night of the attack he could have hurt a lot of people, but he only went after the crocotta and vampires. I hope that means he's no longer a danger to humans."

"We'll see." Only Sara would have a soft spot for a creature that had tried to burn her.

The waiter brought our food, and I started on my lasagna. I soon noticed Sara wasn't eating much. Instead, she was looking around the dining room with an almost sad expression.

"Heavy thoughts?" I asked, wondering what had changed her mood.

She gave me an apologetic smile. "Sorry. I was just thinking about New Hastings. It seems like forever since I was there."

"Do you still miss it?" I asked. Her whole life had been in that little town with Nate and her friends. She had only left to keep them safe.

She toyed with her pasta. "Yes, but not as much as I used to. I miss Remy more than anything, but even if I was there, I couldn't see him."

Her voice grew sad as she spoke about her troll friend. There was nothing I could do to fix the rift between her and the trolls, but I could be there for her.

"We can go back again when it's safe. And trolls live a very long time. I'm sure you'll see him again."

Her eyes grew misty, but she looked happier as she resumed eating.

"Other than Maine, where would you like to go?"

She'd been furious when I said I was taking her away. I suspected she'd only said she didn't want to travel out of anger. Sara was too curious about the world to spend her life on one continent. And there were so many places I wanted to show her.

"Everywhere."

I gave her a questioning look, and she laughed.

"Okay not *everywhere*, but there are so many places I'd like to see. Europe, South America, Africa. Sahir told me so much about Africa that I won't be happy until I see one of those sunsets he described."

"I think you'll like Africa. It has more wild animals than even you can tame. And I think we can find you plenty of pretty sunsets."

I pictured her face when she saw Kenya. The Masai Mara National Reserve had some of the best sunsets in the world, not to mention an abundance of wildlife. It was one of a hundred places I couldn't wait to show to her.

She sipped her water thoughtfully. "You've been all over the world. Do you have a favorite place?"

"I was usually too focused on my missions to enjoy a lot of the places I visited." Until I met her, I never realized how much my life revolved around my work. I still loved being a warrior, but she was my life now.

"Maybe we can go back and visit some of them. You can show me Russia."

The thought of showing her my homeland and introducing her to my parents filled me with pleasure. "I'd like that."

She smiled happily. "Tell me about a few of the places you do remember."

I wiped my mouth with my napkin and sat back in my chair. "Let me see. I remember hunting down three sati in the Hunan province in China. They went into the Tianzi Mountain, and we had a devil of a time finding them in there."

"Sati?"

"Think of a gray, hairless chimpanzee with six-inch claws and fangs, and a taste for anything warm-blooded."

"Ugh. I hope you got them."

"We did, but it wasn't easy. It rained, and there was a dense fog over the place the whole time we were there. The sati were able to blend in perfectly. There were four of us, and it took us three days to locate and kill them."

"Sounds like fun," she said dryly.

I shook my head. "That actually wasn't the worst part. We took the dead sati back to the village that had asked for our help. They threw a huge feast to celebrate, and guess what was on the menu."

"No!" She made a face. "You ate it?"

"It would have been an insult to the village not to." I shrugged, trying not to laugh at her look of disgust. "Tasted like chicken."

She pretended to throw her napkin at me. "You're messing with me, aren't you?"

I put a hand over my heart. "Every word is true."

"Was Chris there?"

"No, that was before I came to this country and met Chris."

She leaned forward eagerly. "Tell me about another place you've been. And you can leave out the parts about eating."

I chuckled and told her about the week I'd spent in Venice, hunting down a sea serpent that had made its way into the canals. After that I regaled her with tales of some of my South American adventures. She listened raptly, asking questions and laughing at some of the stories.

"Did you find it boring here in the US after all your travels?"

"I thought I would, but America surprised me. Once I lived here a few years, and Tristan and I became friends, I decided to stay."

She laid down her fork with a sigh. "It must have been something to watch how much the world changed in the last two hundred years. You lived through the Industrial Revolution, the invention of cars, airplanes, television, everything."

I gave her a playful scowl. "Are you calling me old?"

She gave me an impish grin. "Well, you did go to Woodstock."

"True. Now that was an unforgettable time." I smiled as I remembered the craziness of that weekend. "The sixties were the best decade for music."

"How can you say that? The seventies had the best music."

"Says the girl who was born when?" I teased.

"Hey, I know good music when I hear it," she retorted. "Some of the best musicians might have started in the sixties, but they didn't get really good until the seventies."

"Like who?"

"Fleetwood Mac for one. Their earlier stuff is good, but Rumors was their best album. And Eric Clapton didn't go big until he went solo in the seventies."

I nodded. "They're good, but what about musicians like Jim Morrison and Janis Joplin, or the Who and the Stones? I could name dozens of bands that did their best work in the sixties."

She rested her arms on the table, and the gleam in her eyes told me she was ready to argue. We went back and forth, and I enjoyed the debate immensely. Sara knew her music, and she argued as passionately about the subject as she did about everything else she believed in. I could have sat there and talked to her all night.

The waiter came out to ask if we wanted dessert, and instead of declining as most women did on a date, Sara asked for a big piece of tiramisu. When he laid the large serving in front of her, I raised an eyebrow.

"You want some?" she asked, picking up her fork.

"No thanks. Never cared for it."

She narrowed her eyes at me. "How can you not like tiramisu? It's the best dessert ever invented."

She took her time eating the dessert. Watching her close her eyes and savor each bite, I decided I liked tiramisu after all. When she slowly licked the spoon clean, I made a note to bring her here often.

"That was great," she said as we left the restaurant.

"So what would you like to do now?" I asked when we reached the Ducati.

Her eyes lit up. "We aren't going home?"

"Not unless you want to." If she kept looking at me like that, we might stay here all night.

"Can we ride around and see the city?" she asked hopefully.

I looked at her bare hands. "Are you sure you won't be too cold?"

She pulled on her helmet. "Not if I can use your pockets again. How is it that you're so hot...? I mean your skin is hot when mine is cold," she stammered.

I didn't need to see her face to know she was blushing again. Grinning, I fitted my own helmet over my head. "My Mori controls my body temperature. You'll be able to do that too, eventually."

"That'll come in handy," she mumbled.

I sat on the bike, and she climbed up behind me. When she wrapped her arms around me and slid her hands into my pockets, I loved how natural it felt. She was still shy about intimacy, but we'd come a long way since our first meeting in that club in Portland.

I took my time driving us around the city because the temperature had dropped since we'd left Eldeorin's.

"You're not cold, are you?" I asked her.

She tightened her hold on my waist. "No, this is great. It's not as cold at this speed."

"We'll go slower on the way back." I mentally berated myself for not thinking about how cold it would be for her on a bike. "I should have taken one of the SUVs instead."

Her helmet moved between my shoulder blades when she shook her head. "I'd rather ride a motorcycle than in a car. Greg used to give me rides on his bike, and I loved it. I asked him to teach me to ride, but he didn't want to upset Nate."

Hearing about her love of motorcycles pleased me. "I can teach you, if you still want to learn," I said, turning us toward the Boardwalk.

She let out a short laugh. "You'll let me ride your motorcycle?"

I chuckled when I pictured her trying to handle my bike. "No, I'll get you something smaller and less powerful than the Ducati to start on."

"When can we start?" she asked earnestly, pulling another laugh from me.

"Let's focus on your training right now. Besides, I need to find the right bike for you first."

I was already thinking about models that would comfortably fit her smaller frame. Ducati had some smaller models, and so did Harley Davidson. Although, I'd have to start her out on something with a lot less power.

"What is that?" Sara asked, interrupting my train of thought.

"That's the Boardwalk," I said as we approached the amusement park. "The rides are closed, but I thought you might like to walk through it."

"I'd like that."

I parked the bike, and we walked through the park. Sara didn't want to stop at any of the attractions until we found a funnel cake vendor.

"I've never had a funnel cake before," she told me.

"We can't have that." I pulled out some money as she happily told the man what she wanted.

She grinned at me as she held up the chocolate-covered cake. "Thank God for a high metabolism." She took her first bite of the cake and made a happy sound. "This is so good. You sure you don't want some?"

"No, thanks." Watching her enjoy herself was enough for me.

She bit into it again. "You don't know what you're missing."

My breath hitched when her tongue came out to lick her lips, and I wanted to pull her to me and kiss every bit of chocolate from her mouth. I spotted a dribble of chocolate on her chin and reached out to catch it.

Her eyes followed my thumb to my mouth, and I thought I heard a small intake of breath when I sucked the chocolate from my finger.

"You're right; it's delicious."

I took a piece of her cake and ate it, not because I wanted it, but to keep me from grabbing her and making out with her right there in front of everyone.

She quickly finished her cake, and we resumed our stroll to the end of the Boardwalk. She turned to start back, and I stopped her.

"Let's take the beach instead," I suggested.

She nodded, and we made our way down to the sand. Before we'd gone ten feet, I brought up her training, hoping she'd tell me what had been bothering her.

"How is your training with Aine coming along? You haven't talked about it much."

She heaved a sigh. "That's because there's not much to tell. I stopped blowing up stuff, so that's a good thing, I guess. I don't understand why I can heal things but I can't do anything else. Sometimes it feels like I'm going to explode if I don't use my power. It's so frustrating."

I couldn't imagine what it felt like to have all that power inside her, especially now that it had gotten stronger. I wished there was something I could do to help her, but her sylph friend was the only one who could help her with her power.

"Is that why you were upset when you came to training today?" I asked.

She was quiet for a moment. "We were working in the lake, and I was trying to make waves. It used to be so easy for me, and now I can't do it without worrying I'll hurt someone. Aine kept telling me to try again, and I got so frustrated and angry I...yelled at her. And then Eldeorin showed up and asked what was wrong. I got so upset, and that made the two of them fuss over me. I yelled at her, and she tried to make me feel better. I feel awful about it. She's been so good to me and I yelled at her."

I stopped walking and pulled her around to face me. "Aine understands what you're going through. I only wish there was something I could do to help you through this."

Her eyes met mine. "You are doing something. I needed this."

She turned away and we started walking again, but I couldn't stop thinking there was something else on her mind. Was she homesick? Did she miss Roland and Peter? Or Nate?

"What else is troubling you?"

"Nothing," she answered, but I heard the hesitation in her voice.

"Liar," I challenged her.

"It's just that there's not much to do at Eldeorin's. I have my training during the day, but it's kind of boring at night. I'm not used to being idle." She kicked at the sand. "Never mind. It's nothing."

I looked at her bent head and wanted to kick myself. How could I not have noticed how unhappy she was? As work demands had increased, I'd started going to the command center more often. I would have asked her to join me, but I'd thought she preferred to stay at home with Jordan.

"It's not nothing if it's bothering you. I know I've been spending a lot of time next door, and I'm sorry for leaving you alone so much."

"It's not that," she replied quietly. "You have an important job to do, and I don't want to be coddled or entertained. I just need *something* to do. I need to feel useful."

We found a wharf and turned onto it. The wind had a chill to it, but she didn't seem to mind.

I thought about what she'd said, and it bothered me a lot to hear she didn't feel useful. The last thing I'd wanted was to make her feel that way.

"You and Jordan don't have to stay at the house all the time. You can go next door whenever you want."

"Oh." She said the word so softly it was almost lost on the wind.

I glanced at her and caught her look of surprise. I'd invited her to see the command center, hadn't I? The answer to that question made me feel like a total ass.

"The work we're doing concerns you, too. I'm sorry you thought I didn't want you there."

Her lips curved into a small smile. "I should have asked instead of assuming it was off-limits."

We reached the end of the wharf, and she went to the rail to look down at the waves. Watching her, I was reminded again of how at home she was near the ocean. It also reminded me of another day on another wharf and of our rocky start.

I went to stand beside her. "You're not planning on jumping, are you?"

She smiled and shook her head then took a deep breath of ocean air. The wind tossed her hair, and she held it to the side with one hand as she stared out over the dark water. She looked almost content. I hated to make her leave, but we'd been away too long as it was.

"We should be heading back," I said regretfully.

Her smile dimmed a little. "Okay."

She was quieter on the ride back to Eldeorin's, not saying much until we pulled up in front of the house.

"I had a great time tonight," she said as she pulled off her helmet. "Next time I'll remember to bring gloves."

I could still feel her hands against my stomach as I moved closer to smooth her hair. "I don't mind if you forget them."

Her lips parted, and she trembled slightly under my hand. "I guess I should go in. Jordan's probably waiting to grill me about every detail," she said in a breathless voice that made my pulse quicken.

I smiled and lifted her chin. If Jordan wanted details, I'd better make this kiss worth talking about. My stomach fluttered in anticipation as I lowered my head.

"Good, you're back at last."

I swore silently as Sara jerked away from me and whirled to face the faerie who stood several feet away, looking far too pleased with himself.

"What are you doing here?" Sara demanded, sounding as unhappy as I was to see him.

He gave her a smile that was too familiar for my liking. "I've been thinking about the problems you've been having with your magic, and I have an idea that will help you."

She didn't return his smile. "That's great, but shouldn't we talk about it tomorrow when Aine is here?"

He walked toward her, and it was all I could do not to growl at him when he took her hand.

"This is not part of Aine's training," he said with a gleam in his eye. "It's time for you to start your training with me."

Then they disappeared before my eyes.

CHAPTER 35

IT TOOK ME a second to realize what he'd done, and fury replaced my surprise.

"Sara," I yelled as I ran to the back lawn, hoping he'd taken her there, even though I couldn't feel her nearby. When I found no sign of them, I cursed Eldeorin loudly.

Jordan came running from the house. "What happened? Where's Sara?"

"Eldeorin took her," I ground out.

She came up short. "Eldeorin? Where did he take her?"

"I don't know," I snapped.

Her eyes widened and she took a step back, her fearful expression dousing some of my anger.

"I'm sorry. I didn't mean to take it out on you."

"No problem." Her breath came out in a puff. "Just don't do it again. I almost had to go change my pants."

I smiled grimly at her attempt to lighten the mood.

"So he just showed up and took her? Did he say anything?"

"He said it was time for her to start training with him."

"Oh." She smiled. "Then that's what they're doing."

I didn't share her relief. Eldeorin had a whole estate to train Sara on. He had no reason to take her away from here. There was no telling where he'd taken her and what they were doing. Or when he'd see fit to bring her back. Faeries were unpredictable and thoughtless. He'd think nothing of keeping her away for days or weeks if it suited him.

"I know Eldeorin can be a bit much," Jordan began hesitantly. "But he cares for Sara, and he'll keep her safe. And if he tries anything, Sara won't –"

"Not helping, Jordan." I knew exactly how the faerie felt about Sara, and what he'd do, given the chance.

"Sorry," she said sheepishly.

I walked around to the front of the house again, hoping they would appear. They didn't, of course, and I began to pace the driveway in angry strides.

Chris arrived half an hour after Sara and Eldeorin had disappeared. He didn't look surprised to see me looking ready to hit something.

"Jordan called me," he said. "No word yet?"

"No," I said through clenched teeth.

"Jordan wasn't kidding. You are in a scary mood."

I glared at him. "This isn't funny."

He raised an eyebrow, undaunted. "I can tell that by the fact that you're out here wearing a trench in the driveway and Jordan's hiding in the house. Not much makes that girl nervous."

I stopped walking. "She's hiding from me?"

Chris shrugged. "You can get a bit crazy when it comes to Sara. Based on what you look like now, I can only imagine what you were like right after Eldeorin took her."

"I was furious," I admitted, rubbing the back of my neck. "You would be too if a faerie took your mate away."

"Whoa." He put up his hands. "After seeing what you've been through the last four months, I'm never taking a mate."

His vehement tone brought a reluctant smile to my lips. "You won't say that when you bond with someone. All you'll want is to make her your mate. And all you'll think about is her safety and happiness."

He grimaced. "Don't get me wrong; I love my cousin. But if all women make their mates lose their minds like this, then thanks but no thanks."

I started for the house. "I haven't lost my mind, and Sara's not like other women."

"You can say that again."

"All I'm saying is when it happens to you, you won't care about any of that."

He opened the door and entered the foyer ahead of me. "I'll just have to make sure it doesn't happen to me."

"I'm sure there are a lot of mated males who said that once too." I was one of them.

Jordan was waiting for us in the living room. "No sign of her yet?"

"No." I paced the large room as she and Chris speculated about where Sara and Eldeorin could be.

"They could be anywhere," I burst out, my anger returning with each passing minute.

"He won't let anything happen to her," Chris said.

I knew Eldeorin would keep her safe, but –

I sucked in a sharp breath as I felt her return. Then I was at the bottom of the stairs, looking up at her.

"Are you okay?" I asked as she walked down the stairs, looking the same as when she'd left.

Her smile melted my anger. "Better than okay."

She stopped on the bottom step, and I framed her face with my hands, needing to touch her and reassure myself she was unharmed. Her face was slightly flushed, and her eyes seemed to glow with some inner light. She looked happy.

"Where did he take you?"

"We went to a place where there were no people around, and he helped me release my power," she said with a hint of excitement in her voice. "He said I needed to let it out without worrying about hurting you guys."

"Did it help?" I asked, releasing her.

"Yes. I almost feel like my old self again." She reached up to place her hand on my chest, her touch soothing. "I'm sorry if you were worried," she said softly.

"You don't have to apologize." My fingers brushed her face, and her eyes made me forget everything but her and the kiss we'd been denied earlier.

She moistened her lips and leaned toward me in invitation. My other hand lifted, intending to pull her to me. Nothing would come between us this time.

Khristu! I swore inwardly as my cell rang loudly in my pocket. *This better be a goddamn emergency.*

I recognized Raoul's number and sighed. There was no way I couldn't answer it with all that was going on out there. Smiling at Sara, I put the phone to my ear.

"Here."

"Nikolas, it's Raoul. Anders called in from Seattle. They just got back from searching two houses for that missing girl."

"What did they find?"

"No sign of the girl, but a vampire had definitely been nesting in one of the houses," Raoul said. "I told Anders you'd call him back, but if you're busy, I can debrief his team."

"No, I want to talk to them. We'll be there shortly."

Raoul was thorough, but I had more experience tracking down vampires. The smallest detail might lead us to this one and the missing girl. Three days had passed from when the first girl went missing and when her body was found. Time was running out for this one.

I hung up and looked at Sara. "It's still early. Do you want to come see the command center?"

Jordan appeared out of nowhere. "Hell yes, we do."

Sara grinned. "What she said."

I smiled at her as I pocketed my phone. "Grab your coats and we'll head over."

The four of us walked over together, and several warriors nodded to us as they walked by on patrol. Eldeorin's house might be hidden behind faerie glamours and protections, but this one was open to attack.

"How many warriors do you have here?" Sara asked as we entered the house through the main door.

"We have three units working out of this place, plus Chris and me. Half the warriors are out on jobs now."

We walked into the main control room, and Raoul waved me over. Excusing ourselves from the girls, Chris and I went over to the other warrior.

"New recruits?" Raoul joked.

I followed his gaze to Sara and Jordan, who had stopped at one of the computer stations to talk to Dominic. The blond warrior was showing them something on one of his monitors, and the two girls looked fascinated.

"Not unless we have really good hazard insurance," Chris said. He chuckled at Raoul's puzzled look. "Let's just say Sara and Jordan have a unique talent for finding trouble."

Raoul smiled. "I'll make sure to lock up the big weapons."

"Probably a good idea," I said then got down to business. "Is Anders calling back, or am I calling him?"

Raoul handed me a piece of paper with a phone number on it. "He asked that you call him."

The three of us left the control room and closed ourselves in the den to call Seattle. We were five minutes into our call with Anders when a knock came on the door. Chris opened it to admit Hamid and Ammon.

Raoul and I stood to greet the warriors. I was six-two, and Hamid Safar made me feel short next to his six-six height. His shoulders almost spanned the doorway when he entered, and his dark eyes regarded me for several seconds before he nodded.

"Nikolas, it has been a while," he said in accented English.

"I haven't seen you since we hunted that Master together in Spain twelve years ago."

His eyes gleamed. "Ah yes, my first Master kill."

"Which would have been my kill if you hadn't stolen my bike," I retorted good-naturedly.

At the time, I hadn't been as amused. The two of us had tracked the Master to Valencia. While we were talking to a human informant, a truck ran over Hamid's bike, which was parked beside mine. He'd made off with mine before I knew what had happened.

The only reason I hadn't been furious was that Hamid had a personal stake in finding the Master. The vampire had killed Hamid's cousin's mate in Cairo, and nothing was more important to the big Egyptian warrior than his family.

"You guys want to continue this later?" asked a voice from the phone.

"No," Hamid answered brusquely. "Continue, please."

"As I was telling the others, we raided two houses today. One was a bust, but a vampire's been nesting in the second one. We found the body of a transient in the basement, drained."

"Do you have more leads?" I asked him.

"None yet. We caught a young vampire last night, and it didn't take him long to talk. He said he'd heard there was an older vampire grabbing the teenagers." Anders exhaled slowly. "It's getting crazy up here with the press involved and everyone calling this a serial killer."

Hamid walked over to stand by the desk. "Ammon and I will be there tomorrow to assist."

I almost laughed because Hamid didn't assist, and he didn't play well with others. But he was a damn good hunter. If anyone could find this bastard, it was him.

"I thought you wanted to help out in LA," Chris said to him. "Too boring for you?"

Hamid scowled and crossed his arms. "We go where the need is greatest. Children are more important than what is happening in Los Angeles."

"I agree," Chris and I said together.

Chris, Raoul, and I left Hamid and Ammon talking to Anders, and headed back to the control room. I looked for Sara, and I found her and Jordan sitting on a couch that had been pushed against the fireplace. Her eyes met mine, and I smiled at the happiness on her face.

Raoul called me over to discuss the job he and Raj were doing tomorrow. Ever since Sara told me about Adele's friendship with Madeline, we'd been trying to plant surveillance equipment at her house and club. But Adele was no fool, and she used warlock spells to render our devices useless. Raj was working on a way around it, and he and Raoul were going to do a field test.

A burst of feminine laughter filled the room, and I looked over at Sara and Jordan who were clinging to each other and laughing so hard they had tears in their eyes. I raised an eyebrow at Sara, and that just made her laugh more. I shook my head and smiled as I went back to work.

* * *

I walked into the control room, two weeks later, and as usual, my eyes immediately searched for Sara. Since the night of our date, she'd come here almost every evening. Sometimes she read or used her laptop, and other times she got the warriors to teach her about the equipment and share stories about their adventures. I wasn't the only one who liked having her here. It wasn't hard to see the smiles every time she walked in the door.

I didn't see her, which meant she was probably in the kitchen fixing a snack. She never left on her own, always waiting for me to walk her back to the house.

I'd been worried about her walking between the two houses until Eldeorin offered to place a glamour over our rented house and the short strip of road to protect her and Jordan.

"Nikolas, have you heard?" Chris called. He was standing with Raoul and Brock by one of the tracking stations, and the three of them wore puzzled expressions.

I walked over to stand with them. "Heard what?"

"Someone bagged that vampire in Seattle."

"Hamid?"

Since the Egyptian warrior and his brother went to Seattle, two more teenagers had gone missing and Hamid had been like a man obsessed. But this vampire had proven to be adept at hiding their tracks, which meant he or she was older and experienced. Hamid was one of our best hunters, however, and every day I'd expected to hear he had finally caught the vampire.

A week ago, two of the missing teenagers had shown up at Northwest with no memory of where they'd been or who had brought them to the hospital. No vampire would release his victims, so we figured we'd been wrong in thinking they'd been taken by the one who had killed the first girl.

Chris shook his head. "No, it wasn't one of ours. Hamid just found the house the vampire was holed up in. He said someone really did a job on the vampire, and his chest was half burnt, probably from a flamethrower. He also found the body of the girl who went missing two weeks ago."

"Did Hamid have any ideas about who killed the vampire?"

Chris shook his head. "He's still looking around. I didn't want to push him because he was not happy he didn't find the vampire sooner. And you know what he's like when he's not happy."

The four of us laughed as Sara entered the room, carrying a soda. She smiled at us and walked over to sit in her usual spot on the couch. She set the soda down and picked up her laptop, looking engrossed in whatever was on the screen.

I joined her once we finished our discussion about Seattle. "Ready to head home?"

She closed the laptop and smiled up at me. "Sure."

We walked the short distance to Eldeorin's in companionable silence. Jordan was in the living room on her laptop when we got there, and she gleefully informed us she was about to kick Roland's ass in World of Warcraft. Sara rolled her eyes. She didn't share her friends' love of games.

Sara motioned for me to follow her into the kitchen where Heb was cleaning the stove. She greeted the dwarf and went to pull a bottle of water from the fridge. She took a long drink and turned to me.

"I've been meaning to talk to you about something. Do you have time?"

I smiled and led her over to the small breakfast table. "I always have time for you. What's on your mind."

"Remember when I told you I had some friends helping me look for Madeline?"

I frowned. "You mean the ones you refused to tell me anything about?"

I'd tried several times to get her to reveal the names of the people who had not only helped her look for Madeline, but had also blocked us from tracing her when she called. But if there was one thing about Sara, it was her loyalty to those she considered her friends.

She smiled. "Yeah, them. We've been talking, and we're going to start looking for Madeline again."

"You're what?" I didn't know if I was more shocked she was still in contact with those people, or that she thought I'd be okay with her going out there and endangering herself like that again.

She shook her head. "Okay, that came out wrong. Before you blow a gasket, listen to what I have to say."

"Go ahead."

She tapped her fingers on the table. "First off, I'm not talking about me chasing after Madeline like I did before, so you can stop scowling at me like that."

I unfolded my arms and rested them on the table. "You can't blame me for thinking that after what happened in December."

Her face softened and she reached over to take my hand, her touch sending warmth through me. "I promised not to run again, and I meant it. I'm sorry for putting you through that."

"I know." I closed my fingers around hers. "Tell me your idea, and I promise to try to keep all my gaskets in place."

She smiled again. "It was David's idea, actually."

"David?" The name sounded vaguely familiar.

"I guess I should start by telling you about David and Kelvan. They said it was okay, and if you knew Kelvan, you'd know what a big deal it is. He's kind of paranoid, and he doesn't like many people."

She stroked my palm with her finger, distracting me, and I had to make myself pay attention to what she was saying. I could have pulled away, but I craved her touch so much now it would be like giving up air.

"David is the guy I used to talk to online back in Maine. He's the one who told me about Madeline and the Master. We stayed in touch when I moved to Westhorne, and he helped me when I left to look for Madeline. He sent me to his friend Kelvan in Salt Lake City to get a laptop. David and

Kelvan are hackers, and they're really good. The best. Kelvan wrote the software I used to call you from my laptop. He's the reason you couldn't trace me."

"Dax tried everything to break that guy's encryption," I told her. "I think his ego was a little bruised."

Her brows drew together. "Dax?"

"He's the head of security at Westhorne. Wears dreadlocks and always carries a laptop."

"Oh, I remember seeing him there." Amusement lit her eyes. "Tell Dax not to be so hard on himself. Kelvan is a vrell demon, and apparently they're known for their technical skills. Plus, all he does is stay at home and work on his software."

The news that Kelvan was a demon surprised me, and then I remembered Jordan mentioning him at Christmas. He had to be a genius to out-code Dax.

"You have some interesting friends," I said wryly.

"You have no idea. David and Kelvan have been tracking Madeline since November. Don't ask me how they're doing it. They found her in Albuquerque, and Kelvan found out through the demon community that Madeline was going to see Orias."

She gave me an odd look. "Did you know there was a demon community?"

"Yes. Not that they would willingly talk to the Mohiri, or go out of their way to help us."

She made a face. "That's because they're all scared of you guys. You're like the boogeyman and Van Helsing rolled into one."

I quirked an eyebrow at her description of me. "I've been called a lot of things, but never a boogeyman."

"Not to your face," she teased. "Do you know how frustrating it is to try to talk to people who are afraid of you for no reason?"

I gave her a pointed look. "Yes."

"Ha! As if I was afraid of you. You just aggravated me because you wouldn't leave me alone."

I lifted her hand to my lips. "Aren't you glad I'm so persistent?"

A small tremor went through her at my kiss. "Sometimes."

"Tell me about your plan to look for Madeline," I said, releasing her hand. The taste of her skin made me think of things I couldn't have yet.

Her smile was radiant. "It's simple, really. David and Kelvan will keep working their magic, and I'll share what they find with you. If you hear something, you let me know and I'll tell them."

I nodded thoughtfully. The plan was straightforward and didn't involve her leaving the safety of this place.

"Wouldn't it be better if your friends worked directly with Dax?"

Her smile dimmed. "I guess so. They don't trust many people, but I think if I explained it to them…"

"No, forget that," I said, trying to repair my blunder. "You know David and Kelvan, and as you said before, the three of you came closer to Madeline than anyone else. It makes no sense to mess with that."

"You mean that?" she asked breathlessly.

"Yes."

She let out a happy cry, launching herself out of her chair and into my arms. "Thank you," she murmured against my throat before she lifted her head and pressed her lips to mine.

The kiss started out playful, but it quickly became hungry and searching as the feel of her soft curves and the taste of her lips set my already heated body on fire. My arms tightened around her, afraid she'd shift on my lap and feel the evidence of my desire. This wasn't the time or place for her to make that discovery, as much as my body objected to my reasoning.

"You're welcome," I said roughly when she ended the kiss. "Maybe you should go and tell David and Kelvan the good news."

"You're right." She released me and stood, grabbing her laptop off the table. "I can't wait to get started."

I didn't stand. "Keep me posted."

"I will."

I remained seated for a good five minutes before it was safe to get up. Jordan was still in the living room when I passed by, and she called good night to me as I jogged up the stairs.

I entered my room and headed for the bathroom, pulling off clothes as I went. Walking into the shower, I shut the door and turned the water on blast.

"*Khristu!*" I braced my hands against the tile as the cold water flowed over me. This was becoming a nightly routine for me, and every time I stood here, I wondered how much longer I could go on like this. It wasn't just my unfulfilled desire for Sara; it was nature demanding we finish what it had started and complete the bond.

I groaned and turned my face up to the frigid spray, feeling it run down my body in rivulets. Had any bonded male ever gone this long without mating?

I knew the answer to that already. You could delay completing the bond for a period, but only if you maintained a distance between you and your mate, meaning no touching, no kissing, and definitely no sleeping in the same bed with them. I'd passed the point of no return with Sara the moment I'd kissed her back in the medical ward at Westhorne.

But I would wait. Whether or not she felt the bond as I did, I knew she cared deeply for me, and she was affected by my touch too. I'd wait for her to be ready to take the final step, for her to come to me and tell me she

loved me.
    I loved her too much not to.

CHAPTER 36

"YOU GUYS HEAR about that warehouse in Minneapolis?" Raoul called as Chris and I walked toward the control room a week later.

"No, what about it?"

"Last week, a truckload of people showed up at a hospital in Minneapolis, going on about giant lizard people stealing them from their beds and keeping them in cages. The humans were all young – late teens to early twenties – and at first the hospital thought they were a bunch of college kids on drugs. They called in the police to try to make sense of the victims' stories. No one could tell the police exactly where the warehouse was, but they all said someone showed up out of the blue, killed the lizard people, and helped them escape.

"The Minneapolis unit found the warehouse before the police did. Inside, were two dead gulaks and a dead ranc demon. One of them was a gulak master – a big one – and he had a hole burnt through his chest."

"Giant lizard people," Chris said, shaking his head.

"Yeah. They found a bunch of cages too. Looked like the gulaks were running slaves and someone took exception."

Chris frowned. "Couldn't have been a rival demon. They wouldn't have let the humans go."

"That's true," Raoul said.

"How did we not hear about this before now?" Chris asked.

I let out a short laugh. "Because we've been too busy to read the reports from the rest of the country."

"I've been searching the central database for any reports that mention strange incidents like this," Raoul said. "None of these kills were done by our people."

"Do we have any intel on who might be doing this?" I asked as we entered the control room.

As usual, my eyes sought out Sara who was in her spot on the couch. She smiled at me, and I started toward her.

"Whoever they are, they are deadly and fast," Raoul said as he and Chris followed me. "I hate to admit it, but their kill rate is better than ours right now with zero human casualties. They move around a lot too, which makes it impossible to get a lead on them. We have reports coming in from all over the country."

I joined Sara on the couch, and Chris and Raoul grabbed chairs for themselves.

"Are you sure it's the same people?" Chris asked Raoul.

"No, but my gut tells me it is," Raoul replied. "All the strikes have the same feel to them, and the hostiles were killed by some kind of weapon we haven't seen before. The warehouse in Minneapolis, the vampire in Seattle, the nest at the old amusement park in New Jersey. The person shows up, makes the kill and leaves. And each time the victims recovered had no clear memory of their rescuer or what happened to them. It's like someone messed with their memories. Twenty-two people were rescued from the gulak in Minneapolis, and every one of them gave a different description of the person who helped them."

"One person?" I stared at him. "Didn't you say we found a dead gulak master in the warehouse? It would take an experienced warrior to kill a demon that powerful."

Across the room, Raj looked up from his work and laughed. "Maybe we have a rogue warrior taking it on the road."

"Or it could be a human hunter with a new kind of weapon," Brian suggested. "Whoever he is, he has a pair to go into that nest on his own."

Chris laughed. "Maybe we should try to recruit him."

"You guys automatically assume it's a male," Jordan said derisively.

"No offense, Jordan," Raoul said. "But the odds are small that this is a female."

Beside me, Sara spoke for the first time since we'd come in. "Why?"

Raoul smiled at her. "Most females don't have the stomach for that kind of killing."

Jordan shot him an angry glare, and I almost laughed when he rushed to say, "Mohiri females do, but I doubt one of them is behind this. I think we are dealing with someone new."

"Why does it matter who they are as long as they are helping people and killing the bad guys?" Sara asked.

I squeezed her bare foot, which rested against my thigh. "It doesn't as long as they keep a low profile and don't endanger humans. We monitor the police bands in most cities, so we heard about the warehouse in Minneapolis and were able to get it contained before the local authorities arrived."

"It looks like we aren't the only ones with a vigilante at work," Brock said. "We also picked up a story about a village in Mexico that claims an 'angel' appeared out of nowhere to destroy the demons terrorizing their village. One of our teams down there checked it out and found two dead vampires."

I'd heard the story out of Mexico weeks ago, and I hadn't made much of it at the time. But now I wondered if it wasn't the same people who had done some of these other kills. The Mexican vampires had been burnt through the chest as well.

I didn't believe it was one person as Raoul did. More likely it was a group of people trying to make it look like a single vigilante. They had to be highly trained, and whatever weapon they used sounded military-grade. Did we have a group of soldiers going rogue, or had the human government decided to join the war against our common enemy?

"Nikolas."

I looked at Sara as she lifted her laptop and turned it so I could see the screen. On it was a black and white photo of a woman who looked shockingly familiar.

I leaned closer to study the picture. There was no mistaking the face, even with the dark sunglasses and the scarf hiding most of her blonde hair.

Chris got up from his chair to look over my shoulder, and I heard his small intake of breath as he recognized the woman. "It's Madeline. How the hell did they find her?"

"I told you they're the best," Sara said with a little smile of satisfaction.

"Where was this taken?"

My mind reeled from seeing the face I hadn't laid eyes on in fifty years. When Sara had told me she wanted to help David and Kelvan search for Madeline, I don't think I really believed they'd find her again. I should have known not to underestimate Sara or her friends.

"One second." She turned the laptop back to her and typed something.

"Yesterday in Vancouver," she said, reading from the screen. Her excited gaze met mine. "David sent an address where they think she's staying."

I stood and called to Brock. "Have your guys ready to go within the hour."

He jumped up from his chair. "On it."

"Raoul, can you alert the pilot we'll be flying to Vancouver, Canada as soon as he gets clearance?"

One of Brock's team hurried past, and I stopped him. "Calvin, pull up that address and see what we're dealing with."

"Sure thing."

I felt Sara behind me, and I turned to smile at her. "Great work, Sara."

She shrugged. "Thanks, but David did most of the work."

David might have been the muscle behind the work, but I had no doubt who the heart of the operation was. "Why don't you grab your stuff, and I'll walk you and Jordan home before I leave?" I doubted she'd want to stay here at the command center with most of us out on the job.

Her smiled faded. "What do you mean? I'm coming with you."

"It's too dangerous." We had no idea what we were walking into. I didn't think Madeline would try to harm her own people, but she was on the run from a Master. I wasn't taking a chance of Sara being caught in the crossfire if we ran into trouble.

"I can take care of myself, Nikolas," she argued. "Besides, it's only Madeline."

I shook my head, knowing I was about to upset her, but it couldn't be helped. She'd come a long way in training, and she could fight, but not well enough for the kind of trouble we could run into out there. With the strain our incomplete bond was putting on me, I wouldn't be able to endure anything happening to her. One cut and I'd probably lose it.

"You're not ready. We'll handle this."

She crossed her arms and her voice rose. "She's my mother, so if anyone should be there, it's me. I didn't work this hard to find her just so you could leave me behind."

I steeled myself against the anger and hurt on her face. "You can talk to her when we bring her back here."

"So that's it. We're back to you making all the decisions and me having no say at all?" she said in a raw voice that tore at me. "I thought we were in this together."

"We are."

"You mean as long as I'm doing something you don't think is dangerous," she said. "Why have I been working my butt off in training if you're not going to take me seriously?"

"I do take you seriously." I rubbed the back of my neck in frustration. I didn't want to leave her like this, but there was no time to work it out with her now. "Listen, this is not the time or place for this discussion. We'll talk about it when I get back."

"Fine." She turned away from me and picked up her laptop and backpack. Her shoulders were stiff, and her voice wavered when she said, "Chris, will you walk me back?"

I waved Chris off, following her to the door. "I said I'd take you home."

"You have a mission to organize," she said without turning around. "One of the others can make sure I get home."

"Chris can get things ready here." I picked up her coat and she let me help her into it, but she refused to look at me. I didn't know what to say to her, so I didn't say anything.

She didn't speak during the short walk to Eldeorin's, and when we got

Warrior

to the main door, she reached for the handle without looking at me.

I closed my hand around hers to stop her from walking away. I'd handled things wrong again and upset her. I hated the tension stretching between us, especially since I couldn't stay and talk things out.

"I hate to leave you upset, but I have to go. We'll talk when I get back, okay?"

She nodded quietly.

A touch was not enough. I pulled her into my arms, and she came, unresisting.

"I'll see you in a day or two," I said tenderly.

My chest swelled when her arms snaked around my waist.

"Be careful," she whispered.

"Always." It would take an army of vampires to keep me from coming back to her. I tilted her chin toward me and brushed my lips across hers.

I let her go and reached around her to open the door. I waited until she went inside and closed the door behind her before I headed back.

The team was stowing gear in the SUVs when I got there. I grabbed my own bag, which was always packed and ready to go, and climbed behind the wheel of one of the vehicles.

Chris took the passenger seat and gave me a questioning look, but I wasn't in the mood to talk about it. He rested his head against the back of his seat and muttered, "It's going to be a long few days."

The jet was fueled and waiting on clearance when we got to the airport in San Jose. The current situation in the country had prompted Tristan to supply us with our own jet for reasons exactly like this. If you were going to fight an enemy like ours, it helped to have unlimited resources.

While we waited to leave, I called Tristan and filled him in.

"Are you sure it's her?" he asked shakily.

"I won't know for sure until I see her in person, but Chris and I both believe it's her."

"Dear God," he breathed. "After all this time."

I ran a hand through my hair. "Sara said she and her friends would find her. I have to admit I didn't think they would do it this fast."

"How is Sara doing?" he asked. "She says she doesn't care about her mother, but this can't be easy on her."

"I think she's more upset that I left her at home." I remembered her hurt look as she'd closed the door.

"Ah."

"I understand why she wants to be there when we find Madeline, but it's not worth endangering her life."

"You don't think she'll try to follow you?" he asked.

"No." Sara had promised me at Christmas that she wouldn't run off again, and I believed her. Though that wouldn't make her any less upset

421

with me.

I exhaled slowly. It was going to take a lot more than a few kisses to make this up to her.

I thought about calling Roland and asking him to visit, but I already knew that was out of the question. Maxwell wasn't going to let him and Peter leave New Hastings, let alone Maine, until they graduated from school and worked off their punishments.

I could ask Nate to come, but he was finally writing again, and Sara wouldn't want to disrupt him. I could think of no one else, except...

When the idea came to me, I couldn't believe I hadn't thought of him first. If anyone could distract Sara and cheer her up, it was that arrogant Englishman. And he'd do anything for her.

"Tristan, would it be possible for me to speak to Desmund?"

"Desmund? Uh...sure. I'll see if I can find him."

I smiled, imagining the look on Tristan's face. I doubt anyone ever called for the warrior. Desmund had been ill for so long I wasn't sure he knew how to use a phone.

"I'm transferring you to his apartment."

"Thanks," I said before Desmund's phone began to ring.

"Hello?" said a clipped English voice. "Tristan?"

"Nikolas," I corrected him.

There was silence for a moment. "Is Sara okay?"

"She's fine," I assured him. "Listen, are you free for a week or so?"

I figured it would take that long for her to start talking to me again.

"That depends," he replied haughtily. "I'm planning a trip to England, but I suppose I could postpone it if I'm needed here."

"How would you feel about a trip to California first? I'm on my way to Canada for a few days, and Sara's not happy about it. I think a visit from you would cheer her up."

"You want...me to visit your mate while you are away?" he asked slowly. "Are you not worried I'll steal her away from you right under your nose?"

I knew he was trying to get a rise out of me, just like I knew he was going to say yes to my invitation.

"I'm willing to chance it," I retorted dryly.

He took a moment to answer. "I'd love to visit with Sara. When would you like me to be there?"

"Tomorrow, if you can."

"I'll let Tristan know I need to use the plane. Tell Sara I'll see her tomorrow."

"Actually, I think I'll let you surprise her."

Chris waved at me to let me know it was time to take off.

"Listen, I have to go. The plane is waiting for me. Thank you for doing this."

"I would say you owe me, but it's my pleasure."

I hung up and joined the others on the jet. Chris had saved me a seat beside him in the front row, and I sank down into it.

"Did you just invite Desmund to visit?" he asked, looking at me as if I'd lost it.

I shrugged. "Sara likes him, and he'll be good company for her."

He studied my face. "On a scale of one to ten, how angry is she?"

I buckled my seat belt. "I think she's more upset than angry."

"Maybe seeing Madeline will make her forget she's upset with you. She's got years of anger built up for her mother."

I leaned back and closed my eyes. "We can hope."

Two hours later, we touched down in Vancouver. An hour after that, we arrived at the address David had given us. We parked our Suburban three houses away, and Chris and I approached the front of a well-maintained, gray, two-story house. Brock and Tyrelle went around to the back. Will and Calvin stayed with the SUV.

I knocked on the door and waited a minute. There was a light on in the living room, but I could pick up no sounds inside, even when I engaged my demon hearing.

After my second knock went unanswered, as well as the doorbell, we quietly picked the deadbolt and let ourselves in. The interior was clean and tidy, and it looked as if someone had been there within the last twenty-four hours, based on the empty restaurant takeout containers in the trash can. Lipstick smears on a napkin told us at least one woman had been there.

"Looks like we missed them," Brock observed. He looked at me. "What do you want to do?"

I looked around. "See if they left anything behind that will tell us who they are. We'll watch the place for tonight and see if anyone shows."

We left the house as we'd found it, and took shifts watching the place that night. The next morning, we met up at the Vancouver safe house and talked to the local team about the reason for our visit. They had a few suggestions for places we could check out so it wouldn't be a waste of a trip. I wasn't that familiar with the city, and it surprised me to hear they didn't have a big vampire problem like we were facing farther south.

Around mid-morning, Raoul called to pass along another address Sara had gotten from David. We went to check it out and found a stately white house at the end of an older neighborhood lined with tall trees.

Chris went in to scope it out, and he came back a few minutes later to tell us someone was staying there. He believed it could be the woman from the previous address because he found takeout containers from the same Thai restaurant. It was enough to convince me, and I decided to watch the place to see if anyone showed up.

We divided into pairs, with Brock and Will taking the first shift. If Madeline was staying here, the sight of a dark SUV might tip her off that something was going on. So they parked the vehicle on a side street and watched the house from the cover of a small stand of trees.

Chris and I were grabbing a quick dinner nearby when Brock called to tell us there was activity at the house.

"What do you see?" I asked him.

"Silver Audi pulled into the garage. Tinted windows so we couldn't see the driver." He paused. "Light just came on downstairs."

"We're on our way. Call in Calvin and Tyrelle and anyone else who is available. If this is Madeline, I don't want to take any chances of her slipping past us."

Brock was standing at the bottom of the street when we pulled up a few minutes later. I didn't bother hiding the SUV since the person we sought was already in the house. We would soon find out whether or not it was Madeline.

The others joined us, and I told them I'd take the front door while Chris took the back. The rest of them would take up positions around the exterior to make sure no one slipped past us.

They nodded, and we moved in.

I waited until everyone was in position before I walked up to the front door and rang the doorbell. If the person inside wasn't Madeline, I didn't want to scare some unsuspecting human half to death by having armed warriors invade their home.

Focusing my hearing, I picked up faint movement inside. Someone was there, and they were moving around quietly. The thing with older houses is that no matter how well they are kept, they begin to creak after a while, especially the floorboards. I rang again. This time there was no mistaking the sound of a footstep on a noisy stair.

I signaled Brock, who stood at the front corner of the house, to let him know I was going in. Making short work of the lock, I opened the door and went inside.

A small foyer opened into a great room with heavy dark furniture, oriental rugs, and fine art on the walls. Not exactly Madeline's taste – at least not the Madeline I used to know, who had preferred modern styles over traditional. But then, I hadn't seen her in five decades.

Chris entered quietly through the back door. I pointed at the ceiling to let him know I was going upstairs. He nodded and began doing a sweep of the first floor. We'd worked together so much in the last two years that no other communication was needed.

Several of the stairs creaked under my feet, but it wasn't as if the person I sought didn't know I was there. There were five bedrooms, and I searched them all without any luck. A narrow set of stairs led to an open attic, but a quick search of that turned up nothing as well.

I walked back to the top of the stairs and texted Brock, who assured me no one had left the house since we'd entered. So where was the person I'd heard inside?

Abandoning all pretense of stealth, I called for Chris, who ran upstairs, looking as confused as I was.

"They have to be up here," he said, walking to the first doorway on the right. "Unless they sprouted wings and flew away."

The two of us did another search of the second and third floors and met up again in the master bedroom. The room looked undisturbed except for a corner of the bedspread that had been ruffled. I walked over for a closer look. Seeing nothing suspicious, I straightened and looked around the room. Something was off about it, but I wasn't sure what it was.

"What are you looking for?" Chris asked.

"I don't know." I did a three-sixty degree turn. "There's something about this room that…"

I trailed off as it hit me what I was looking at. "This room is shorter than it should be."

His brows drew together, and he looked from one end of the room to the other. "You sure?"

"Positive." I went to the head of the bed, where the cover had been out of place, and felt around the bedframe and nightstand. My fingertip touched a slight depression at the base of the headboard where it connected to the frame. I pressed the area and heard a soft click before a door-sized panel separated from the wall on the other side of the nightstand.

"Damn," Chris said. "We're not getting through that thing."

My lips pressed together when I saw the steel door behind the wall. A panic room. The door was probably an inch thick, and there was no knob of any kind. I'd bet it could only be opened with a remote, and I had a good idea where that remote was.

I glanced at the upper corners of the room, and I wasn't surprised to see a camera in one of them. No doubt, there were cameras all over this place that fed into a security system in that room.

I stood facing the camera, guessing it had an audio feed as well. "Madeline, we just want to talk."

Chris shook his head. "Somehow I don't think it's going to be that easy."

My reply was cut off by the sound of pounding feet below and Brock's hoarse shout. "We've got trouble."

"Jesus Christ!" Calvin yelled. "They're everywhere."

I ran to the window and watched a mob of people surrounding the house.

No, not people. Vampires. Dozens of them.

I blinked, unable to believe my eyes. In my whole life, I'd never seen that many vampires in one place – and working together.

A door slammed, jerking me into action. I took the stairs two at a time and had my sword drawn before I reached the first floor.

"Everyone in?" I shouted as warriors ran to take up defensive positions near the windows and doors.

"All in," Brock confirmed.

Will peered through a closed drape. "Fuck. We're screwed."

"No, we're not." I strode over to the much younger warrior. "They have the numbers, but we're armed. And I guarantee half of them are new."

He nodded and tightened his grip on his sword.

I looked at Brock. "Call Raoul and tell him we're under attack. Tell him we'll hold them off, but we'll need backup ASAP."

Chris came to stand beside me, his sword drawn. He peered out the window and swore. "Bloody Canadians don't do anything small, do they?"

Glass shattered all over the house as the first wave of vampires came. The warriors near the windows took the brunt of the assault, and Chris and I jumped in to even the odds.

I sliced through the throat of one of the two vampires attacking Will, sending a spray of blood across the warrior. He didn't seem to notice, his fear from a few minutes ago swept aside as adrenaline and training kicked in.

A grunt of pain had me spinning to Calvin as he went down with two vampires on top of him. I grabbed one of the vampires by the hair and ripped him away before he could sink his teeth into the warrior's throat.

The vampire sailed across the room and went headfirst into the stone fireplace. Before he could move, one of the Vancouver warriors was there, finishing him off.

I looked back to Calvin to see him on his feet, facing off against the second vampire. Behind him, Tyrelle and Brock were locked in battle with three vampires.

From all over the house came shouts and the sounds of fighting.

The second wave came at us. Vampires poured through the broken windows, and it hit me that this was an organized breach, unlike the one at Westhorne last fall. They'd waited until the first group had engaged us fully before they sent in the second group to overwhelm us. It was a military tactic, and one we used whenever we cleaned out a large nest.

My blade eviscerated one vampire. He fell to his knees, and I spun to the larger threat. This one was faster and stronger. His claws scored my stomach before I could bring my blade around to counter his attack. With so many bodies in the room, it was getting harder to wield my blade. No doubt whoever was commanding this assault knew that too.

I ignored the burning pain in my stomach and drew one of my knives.

The vampire's eyes flicked between my sword and my knife.

My foot slammed into the side of his knee, and the cracking of bone was followed by his scream of pain. He flailed and fell toward me, his claws reaching for my throat. My knife caught him between the ribs, and his momentum did the rest.

Brock yelled, and I whirled to see two vampires trying to pull him through a window.

I leapt over a couch and severed one of the grasping hands with my sword. It was enough for Brock to yank free and fight off the second one.

"Will," Chris shouted from the stairs.

My eyes found Will's unconscious form slung over the shoulder of a big vampire who was carrying him to the closed front door.

A growl burst from my lips, and I let my knife fly as I sped toward them. The blade sank into the back of the vampire's head, and he dropped like a stone.

I caught Will just before his head made contact with the hard tile floor.

There wasn't much I could do for the warrior, except ensure he was still breathing. I dragged him behind a large chair where he was mostly hidden from sight. Then I turned back to the fight.

The punch came out of nowhere. My head snapped back, and I barely had time to recover and block the kick that came next.

I dropped my sword, grabbed the foot inches from my face, and twisted. Instead of the bone breaking, the body attached to the foot spun in the air to strike out at me with its other foot. I released the vampire to protect my head, and he hit the floor on all fours like a cat before he came back to his feet.

I faced my opponent and immediately knew he was the leader of this ambush. Tall and muscular with short-cropped hair, the vampire had been in his mid-twenties when he was made. Judging by the speed with which he moved, that had happened at least fifty years ago. He wore camouflage pants and a black T-shirt, and on his bicep I saw a *Semper Fi* tattoo common among Marines.

We took several seconds to size each other up, and then he struck. His fists blurred as they came at my face and throat.

I blocked them and caught his arm, spinning him toward me. I grasped his shoulders and pushed him down as my knee came up and met his face with a sickening crunch.

Blood sprayed from his broken nose as he grabbed my leg and threw me on my back. In a second, I was on my feet, facing him again.

An arm wrapped around my throat from behind. Instead of trying to pull free, I gripped the arm and flung the vampire over my head. He crashed into the Marine, who batted him away irritably and grinned at me through bloody teeth.

I smiled back.

We began trading strike for strike, kick for kick. He was fast, strong, and he knew how to fight. I couldn't remember the last time I'd fought hand-to-hand with a vampire who could hold their own against me. He even managed to land a few hits, including a kick that most likely bruised a rib or two.

"Nikolas," Chris bellowed over the shouts and screams. "Could use some help when you've finished your fun."

The vampire used the brief distraction to kick out and hook behind my knee to throw me off balance.

I rolled onto my side and bounced up behind him. Grabbing his arm, I yanked it behind his back until I heard his shoulder pop. My other hand pulled my second knife free. I drove the blade between his shoulder blades, straight into his heart.

He jerked and sagged against me. I released him, and he slid to the floor. During our entire fight and his death, he'd never uttered a sound.

I surveyed the room. Two of the Vancouver guys were down but alive. Vampire bodies lay everywhere, but the living ones still outnumbered us two-to-one.

The front door opened, and I saw six vampires file outside as if the pied piper was out there calling to them.

I didn't have time to wonder what they were up to. Chris was at the bottom of the stairs, fighting off three vampires at once. I grabbed my sword off the floor and ran to help him just as two more flew down the stairs.

The two of us fought back-to-back as we'd done a hundred times. All around us, warriors battled with everything they had in them. If we made it through this...

Not if. When. I thought about Sara and the way we'd left things. *Nothing* was going to stop me from getting back to her.

A vampire sped out of a doorway on my left, and this one was not young. He didn't have the fighting skills of the Marine, but he made up for that in sheer speed and strength. It took all my concentration to battle him in the confined space. Unfortunately, that left Chris to handle the others on his own.

A flash of pale gold caught my eye as a blonde female ran past the second floor landing. Madeline.

Son of a bitch. She was making a run for it, and there was nothing I could do to stop her.

The vampire must have seen her too. He broke away from me and ran out the open back door into the night.

Before I could give chase, another jumped in to take his place. Goddamnit. Where the hell were they coming from?

"I'm down," Brock shouted weakly.

"Hold on," I called back.

My sword came down, severing the head of my opponent. I made my way over to Brock through the sea of bodies, killing two vampires that got in my way.

Brock was sitting on the floor with his back against the wall and a hand over the side of his neck. Blood seeped through his fingers, but it was flowing too slowly to be a major artery. I yanked a throw off the back of a chair and pressed it against the wound to staunch the flow of blood.

"Hold this here until we can triage," I told him.

He did as I ordered and gave me a thumbs-up with his free hand.

I took up his sword and went to help the others finish off the bastards. The last one ran past me and out the back door. I gave chase and caught him as he hit the night air. My blade sliced easily through his neck, taking his head from his body.

A second vampire fled through a window and tried to run past me. My sword impaled him before he took two steps.

Silence fell over the yard that was littered with bodies.

A small sound brought my gaze around. Standing in the midst of the dead vampires was a masked figure dressed in black. I could see no weapon, though a burnt body lay at his feet.

"Who are you?" I asked, not really expecting an answer. He wouldn't have hidden his face if he'd wanted me to know his identity. I had a suspicion I was looking at one of our mysterious vigilantes.

"A friend," he replied in a voice that was oddly distorted.

"That doesn't answer my question." I waved at the carnage around us in the yard. "No human could do this. What are you and how did you find us?"

No one but our own people and Sara's friends knew where we'd be tonight. Sara trusted David implicitly, and for his part, he could have betrayed her many times before now if he'd wanted to.

"That is because I am not human," the stranger rasped without enmity. "As for how I found you, I have my ways."

Not human? Warlock then. Who else could cloak themselves and mess with the memories of all the people they'd saved? I took a step toward him, intending to see what was under that mask.

"Nikolas," called a member of the Vancouver team.

"What is it, Devon?"

"We found a tablet and some other things, but she's not here. Looks like she got away."

Before I could answer, a window shattered on the front of the house and a vampire screamed. Thinking of our injured men inside, I raced to the front of the house. When I got there, I found Chris finishing off what I hoped was the last of our attackers.

Chris straightened and pushed his damp hair out of his face. "I think that's it."

"I hope you're right." My eyes fell on a pile of vampire bodies in the driveway. "Your work?"

"I think we can thank our mysterious friend for that."

"Shit."

I sped to the backyard, but it was empty except for dead vampires. I'd been so close. I couldn't believe I'd let him slip through my fingers.

Chris came to stand beside me. "I don't know about you, but I'm going to need a stiff drink – or a bottle – after this one."

"You and me both. But first, we have to clean up this."

He groaned and turned to the house. "Going to be a long night."

CHAPTER 37

ONCE THE SEATTLE team had arrived to take over the cleanup operation in Vancouver, the rest of us took our injured back to the safe house to see to their wounds. There were a few deep lacerations, a couple of broken bones, and one concussion, but we'd all survived. After we'd treated our injuries and showered, the healthier warriors had wanted to drink and celebrate. I'd told them to have fun. I was going home.

It was almost dawn when I let myself into Eldeorin's house. I walked up the stairs and stopped outside Sara's door. I had no intention of going in. I only wanted to feel her nearby, to know she was close and safe before I tried to get some sleep and put this night behind me.

Tomorrow, she and I would talk, and I'd make her understand why I'd had to do what I did. Even if she refused to talk to me for a week, I wouldn't go back and change a thing. If she'd been with us tonight...

A shudder went through me, and the need to see her became too strong to deny. Entering the room, I closed the door softly behind me and walked quietly to the bed.

My chest squeezed at the sight of her sleeping so peacefully and safe. All I wanted to do was crawl into bed with her, take her in my arms, and let her closeness soothe the aches in my body and heart.

I sat on the edge of the bed and caressed her face with a featherlight touch. I didn't want to disturb her sleep; I just needed physical contact after being away from her for two days.

She stirred, her face turning toward my hand. "Nikolas," she murmured drowsily.

"Shhh. Go back to sleep," I whispered, feeling selfish for having woken her. I kissed her forehead. "I'll see you in a few hours."

"Mmm," she said as I started to get up.

Her hands came up and cupped the back of my head, pulling me down

431

to her. Surprise and desire jolted me as she claimed my lips with a hungry desperation that fed my own need for her.

In the next instant, I was lying beside her with my top half covering her as I deepened the kiss. My heart pounded and my brain lost all function as my body responded to her.

I didn't remember pushing the blankets down, just the raw pleasure of running my hand slowly down her side, brushing the curve of her breast through her T-shirt, wanting the barrier between us gone.

Mine, my Mori growled.

Mine, I agreed as my hand found the bare skin of her stomach.

The small gasp against my lips brought me back to my senses so fast my head spun.

Khristu, what am I doing?

It took everything in me to lift my mouth from hers and to stop myself from taking what I craved more than the air in my lungs. I laid my head beside hers and studied her profile as I willed my body and heart to calm down.

My arm still lay across her, and I could feel her chest rise and fall rapidly as her heart hammered in tune with mine. She wanted me too, but it was easy to let desire carry you away. When we made love, it would be because she was ready for that final commitment, and not because she'd been swept away by a moment of passion.

I lifted my head until our eyes met. "I should go." And take a very long, cold shower.

"Okay," she whispered.

The confusion and desire in her eyes were almost too much to take, and I groaned as I touched my forehead to hers. "Jesus, Sara, don't look at me like that or I'll never be able to leave."

"I don't want you to leave," she replied huskily, her breath warm against my face.

I almost groaned again. Did she realize what she was asking and what her words did to me?

"I know, but you're also not ready for where this is headed."

"I…"

Her hesitation told me what she could not put into words, and I was glad I'd made myself stop before it was too late. I wanted her. God, I'd never wanted anyone this much, but I wouldn't take her like this. If I had to be strong for the both of us, I would. Even if it killed me.

I rolled off her and lay, staring at the ceiling. My hand sought out hers, and I entwined our fingers as I thought about what I wanted to say to her.

"I'm sorry about what happened before I left. I didn't handle it well and I hated leaving you upset. I know how important it is to you to find Madeline, and I should have known you'd expect to be there when we brought her in. But I'm also glad I listened to my gut and didn't take you with us." I let out a ragged breath. "This was a rough one."

"I was scared for you," she said in a small voice.

I turned my head toward her. "That's how I felt the whole time I was looking for you. I was afraid something would hurt you before I found you."

Her bottom lip trembled. "I'm sorry."

I didn't want to make her feel bad. I just wanted to make her see what it was like for me.

"I wish I could explain how it feels, this need to protect you, and how crazy it makes me when you're in danger. The bond is a part of me – us – and it's not something I can just turn off. Do you understand what I'm saying?"

"I'm trying to, but it's hard. Put yourself in my shoes. How would you feel if you suddenly lost your freedom and had people telling you what to do? I don't want to be pampered and taken care of. I'm not fragile, and I don't break that easily."

Her sadness made my chest tighten. I placed our joined hands over my heart to ease the ache there.

"I know you're not. Your spirit and independence make you who you are, Sara, and I never want to take them from you."

I understood where she was coming from, and the last thing I wanted to do was change who she was. I'd been training her to be a warrior while asking her to give up the things I valued in my own life.

"All I've known for a long time is how to be a warrior and how to command others. That's worked with everything else in my life. It's taken me a while to learn that won't work with us."

"You figured that out, huh?"

I smiled at her teasing tone because it meant we had passed a big hurdle. We – I – still had a way to go, but this was a big step forward.

"Do you think you'll ever get past it, this overprotectiveness?" she asked.

I sighed as I thought about how to answer. "I'll never stop worrying about your safety, but I think it will get easier."

Her answering smile told me I'd said the right thing. "When I prove I can defend myself, will you treat me like the other warriors?"

I laughed, feeling my chest lighten. "I can safely say I will never see you as one of the other warriors. But I will try to be less of a tyrant. And when you demonstrate you are ready for a mission, I won't stop you from going on one." Chris would probably have to tie me down to help me keep that promise. "I guarantee I won't like it, but I won't hold you back."

"Thank you."

I let go of her hand and put my arm above her head in invitation. She laid her head on my shoulder as I held her against me.

"Do you want to talk about Vancouver?" she asked.

I closed my eyes. "Later. Right now I just want to hold you."

She snuggled into my side. "Okay."

*   *   *

"Nikolas, may I speak with you a moment?"

I looked up from my bike as Desmund walked toward me. He'd been here four days, and in that time, we hadn't spoken much. I'd been busy with work, and I wasn't sure exactly what he did when he wasn't with Sara. Sara was happy to have him here, and Desmund had even been training her a few hours a day. I wanted her to have every advantage, and few people could boast they had trained under one of the greatest warriors of the last five hundred years.

I straightened and wiped my hands on a rag. "What's up?"

"I want to talk about Sara's training. She's not progressing as quickly as she should." He eyed the black grease on my hands with distaste. "She is afraid of her Mori."

"She's not afraid of it, at least, not anymore. She's just not comfortable with it."

His brows drew together. "Training is not supposed to be comfortable."

"I know that." It was my turn to frown. "She's been through a rough time the last two months, and she's made great progress in her Fae and combat training. It's just taking her a bit longer to get used to her demon."

"You don't seem to be in any hurry for that to happen."

I let out a short laugh. "Trust me, Desmund, if there is anyone who wants Sara to join with her Mori, it's me."

More than once, I'd wondered where our relationship would be if she and her Mori were one and she could feel the bond as much as I did. I had a feeling we would have been mated months ago, and I wouldn't be taking cold showers every day.

"Then you will be happy to assist in the special training I've planned for her."

"What training?" I asked.

"Eldeorin and I had a conversation last night about Sara, and we both feel she would do better with the proper…motivation. Namely you."

I raised an eyebrow. "You and Eldeorin. This should be good." I couldn't imagine what the two of them could have cooked up, and I wasn't sure I wanted to know.

"It's quite simple really," he replied smugly. "But it won't work without your assistance."

"What's the plan?" I didn't like Eldeorin, but he did genuinely seem to care for Sara. And Desmund wouldn't do anything to harm her or allow her

434

to be harmed.

"I think it would be more effective if you didn't know beforehand."

His sly smile made me wonder what the hell I'd just agreed to. But if it would help Sara, I'd do it.

"Fine. What time?"

He glanced at his watch. "Half an hour in the training room. Eldeorin will join us there."

"I'll see you then."

He walked away, and I crouched beside the bike again. I could have taken the Ducati to a mechanic for a tune-up, but I enjoyed working on it myself. I didn't think Eldeorin would appreciate me changing the oil in his pristine driveway, not that I cared. I still owed the faerie for taking off with Sara the night of our date.

Twenty minutes later, I went to get cleaned up and headed to the training room. No one was there when I arrived, and I wondered what Desmund had planned for today. Looking around, all I saw was the usual gym equipment.

I was stacking weights when I felt Sara approach. She stopped in the doorway and gave me a puzzled look, but Desmund nudged her into the room.

"Nikolas has agreed to join us today to help with a new training technique I've devised for you. We'll start with our normal routine and take it from there."

Curious about their training, I walked over to stand near the wall and watch. Sara went to the middle of the room and took a few deep breaths as if she was about to lift something heavy. Her shoulders tensed, and she grimaced as she joined with her Mori.

I tried to imagine what she felt and why it bothered her so much to do something so completely natural to me. She'd described it to me once, but it was still hard to grasp.

Desmund spoke to her, and she bent to lift a pair of forty-pound kettlebells. He walked over to join me, leaving her to her weights.

"She has to stay joined with her Mori for the duration of the exercise," he explained. "That is the real work out. The weights just give her something to focus on."

"How long is the exercise?"

"Normally it's thirty minutes, but she's barely lasting that long," he said in a low voice. "Today, I hope to fix that."

I nodded and watched her switch to sixty-pound weights. So far, she appeared to be doing well.

"So Vancouver was bad?" he asked after a few minutes of silence.

I lowered my voice. "Biggest ambush I've ever seen." I told him everything that happened from the time we entered the house to when we killed the last vampire.

"I've never seen them behave that way. There were enough of them to wipe out several teams."

He nodded slowly. "It is unusual to hear of that many vampires working together. I am amazed you did not suffer casualties."

"I am too." I thought about the way some of the vampires had tried to grab warriors and leave with them. That had been bothering me since the attack. "If I didn't know better, I'd think they were trying to capture us, not kill us."

A kettlebell hit the floor on the far side of the room, drawing our attention to Sara. I went to pick it up and bring it back to her.

"Are you okay?" I asked because she looked a little shaken.

She gave me a tight smile. "Great. Sometimes I don't know my own strength."

I set the weight on the floor and joined Desmund again. We watched her resume the exercise for a minute before he spoke.

"You are fortunate then that help arrived."

"Yes," I replied, thinking about the masked man I'd spoken to briefly in the backyard. I was annoyed when he took off, but after I saw the carnage outside, I knew every warrior there probably owed their life to him. "We found almost twenty vampires dead in the street and near the house. I don't know how he knew where we were, but he's the reason we didn't lose anyone. The Seattle team wouldn't have made it in time."

Desmund glanced at Sara to check on her progress. "It sounds like you have a powerful ally out there."

I nodded gravely. "We need one. We are already getting reports of more vampire attacks on our people. The team in Houston nearly lost two warriors last night."

"Did they get help from this vigilante too?"

"No, but it's fortunate they were all experienced warriors. The four of them took on nine vampires and killed seven. The last two got away." According to the warriors, the vampires had seemed more interested in taking hostages than in killing them.

Desmund left me to walk over to Sara, who had set her weights on the floor. She was breathing heavily and a sheen of sweat covered her forehead. A glance at the clock told me she'd been at this for twenty-five minutes.

"You have thirty-five minutes left in this exercise," he said firmly.

"I can't last an hour," she panted. "I can barely do half an hour."

He waved a hand. "Nonsense. You are stronger than that. Continue."

It surprised me when she conceded without further argument. Whatever else I could say about Desmund, he was a good trainer.

Instead of resuming our conversation, he and I watched Sara as she struggled to maintain the connection with her Mori.

At least ten minutes passed before she cried, "I can't." Her body shook from the effort, and her jaw was clenched when she gave me an imploring look.

"She must learn to do this," Desmund said in a low voice before I could go to her.

"Am I late?" Eldeorin walked into the room. He looked at Desmund. "Sorry, I was detained."

"Your timing is perfect," Desmund told him.

"What are you doing here, Eldeorin?" Sara asked through gritted teeth.

The faerie smiled at her. "Desmund and I talked last night about your training, and he mentioned the difficulties you are having with your demon. We came up with something that will help motivate you."

She looked at me, but I was as in the dark as she was. I just hoped they got on with whatever they were going to do. Seeing her in pain was hard enough. Not being able to go to her was torture, and I would not be able to stand back much longer.

"We are going to try something new, and Nikolas has agreed to take part in our little experiment," Desmund said as he walked over to her. "You must stay joined with your Mori until the hour is up. If you don't we will start over, but I don't think that will happen."

"Why?" she asked hoarsely.

In the next instant, Eldeorin was behind me with his hands gripping my shoulders. He was shielding me from the brunt of his power, but an unpleasant tingle spread out from where his hands touched me. It was like a low electrical current, enough to make me grunt in discomfort but not strong enough to cause any damage.

"Stop!" Sara yelled, starting toward us, her eyes wide with fear.

Desmund caught her from behind, holding her arms against her sides. My pulse jumped angrily at the sight of her being restrained, and my Mori growled.

"Your life could one day depend on you joining with your Mori," Desmund said mercilessly. "What if it was one of your friends' lives in danger? Or his? Could you do it then?"

Sara stopped struggling and glared at Eldeorin. Her eyes blazed so hot I wouldn't have been surprised to see smoke rising from his body. "Let him go, or so help me…"

Desmund leaned down. "Imagine that is a vampire instead of the faerie. What will you do?"

Sara didn't respond. Her gaze locked with mine, and I watched her body shake as rage replaced her fear and pain. Being joined with her Mori must be making her feel the bond more intensely. It was an emotion I recognized all too easily, and my heart swelled at the thought of her feeling that way for me.

Eldeorin shifted and sent a small jolt of power into me. I held back my grunt of pain, cursing him silently. I wouldn't be surprised if he was enjoying this.

Something blurred in the middle of the room, and Desmund slammed backward into the far wall. Eldeorin's hands were torn away from me as something hit him hard and sent him sprawling ten feet away. I blinked as the blur became Sara, her face a mask of fury as she stalked toward the faerie.

If there was one thing I knew from experience, it was how to calm a Mori rage. I reached for Sara and pulled her back against me, wrapping my arms firmly around her. She tried to break free, and I put my mouth to her ear. "It's okay, Sara. Calm down."

Her struggles ceased, and she stood quietly in my arms, her chest heaving and her breath coming in angry little pants. The tension in her body told me she was prepared to attack anyone who came near us.

Eldeorin gave her an appraising look as he leaned against the wall. "Fascinating. Sara, are you still joined with your demon?"

"Yes."

"Interesting." Desmund joined us. His hair was out of place, but he didn't seem to notice as he studied Sara.

"I'm glad I could entertain you guys," she bit out.

Eldeorin smiled, unfazed by her anger. "You are not strong enough to throw off a warrior or me with your demon strength. You used your Fae magic."

She huffed. "So?"

"You used it while joined with your demon," he added with a smug look.

"What?" She trembled, and I pulled her closer, my hands rubbing her arms.

"What does that mean?" I asked the faerie.

"I am not sure," he replied with a thoughtful expression. "Sara has told me that her magic hurts her demon. Perhaps she and her demon have adapted. Or perhaps her Mori is safe from her power when they are joined."

Sara had told me more than once she was afraid of her Fae power hurting her demon. I'd been afraid of that too, especially after her *liannan*. If her power couldn't harm her Mori while they were joined, there was nothing to stop them from coming together permanently.

Desmund looked pleased with himself. "Whatever the reason, I was correct in my assumption. You think too much about merging with your Mori, instead of just letting it happen naturally. I thought that giving you something else to focus on would make you forget about the joining."

I had to hand it to him, he'd called this one right. If there was one thing that would make her forget her discomfort, it was seeing someone she cared about in pain. Though I wouldn't gloat too much if I were him. She'd already tossed him once, and her stiff stance told me she'd do it again with little provocation.

"You couldn't have explained it to me instead?" she bit out.

He shrugged. "We thought this would be more effective."

She pulled out of my embrace and gave me a look of betrayal. "I can't believe you went along with this."

I could have told her the truth, that I'd had no idea what they were planning. But she'd made great progress today because of them, and it was apparent she needed their guidance. Making her angrier at the two of them would not help with her training.

"I didn't agree at first, but Desmund made me see that you needed incentive."

She rubbed her arms. "Hurting you is not incentive. It's cruel."

I moved to take her in my arms again, but she backed away.

"You know Eldeorin would not really harm me," I told her, not quite sure I spoke the truth.

"I'm sorry you are upset, little one, but I think you will see this was all for the best," Desmund said. "We've made significant progress in your training today."

Eldeorin scoffed loudly. "It is no wonder she cannot join properly with her demon, the way you coddle her."

He walked toward her. "Everything we do is to help keep you alive, Cousin. I won't apologize for that, just as I did not apologize for our training."

"Apologize for what?" I asked them. Sara never said much about her sessions with Eldeorin, and his comment made me wonder if there was a reason why.

"Nothing," she said shortly.

"Sara did not care for my training techniques either at first," he told me. I waited for him to elaborate, but he left it at that.

I looked at Sara, who was still upset and taking breaths to calm herself. I didn't like knowing I'd been part of making her this way, even though the exercise had benefited her. Sometimes, it was difficult to separate my trainer side from my mate side. Desmund knew that, which was most likely why he hadn't told me what he was planning to do.

"I think that's enough for today," I said. "We'll continue this tomorrow."

Sara practically ran from the room. I wanted to go after her, but I doubted she would want my company.

"That went better than I'd hoped," Desmund said.

I let out a short laugh as I went to put away the weights Sara had been using. "You should count yourself lucky she likes you. I'm surprised she didn't send you through the wall."

After I'd stacked the weights, I looked at Eldeorin. "Why would you need to apologize for your training? What's that about?"

He shrugged. "Sara didn't have faith in her abilities, and she needed to be pushed beyond what she thought she was capable of. Once she started to believe in herself though…" He smiled proudly. "I believe she is the finest protégé I've ever had. Our time together has become the highlight of my week."

I ignored his last comment because he'd only made it to annoy me. "Did you know she'd be able to use her power while joined with her Mori?"

"No, that was a shock to me as well. But then, my little cousin never fails to surprise me."

"At least we have that in common."

He straightened his clothes, which had been ruffled when Sara threw him. "I know you think she is not ready to be a warrior, and by Mohiri standards, you are right. But Sara is also Fae, and she has powers and abilities you'll never be able to comprehend. Don't underestimate her, warrior."

I frowned. "What do you –?"

He vanished before I could finish my question. It was another annoying habit of his.

I looked at Desmund. "What was that about?"

"I couldn't say."

Something told me he knew more than he was letting on, but pushing him would be as fruitful as banging my head against the wall. Desmund gave a whole new meaning to the word obstinate.

"Are you two planning to train her together again?"

"Yes."

I remembered the fury on Sara's face right before she'd sent him flying. "Good luck. If you're going to piss her off like that again, you might want to have a peace offering ready."

He gave me a puzzled look. "What kind of peace offering?"

I set down the last weight and headed for the door. "The kind I'm going to get for her now."

"What's that?" he called after me.

I didn't answer. He'd have to figure this one out on his own, while I went to a certain Italian place and got the biggest piece of tiramisu they had.

CHAPTER 38

"NIKOLAS?"

I pulled my gaze from the rain running down the coffee shop window and looked at Chris. "Sorry, what were you saying?"

"I said I'm going to take a few guys and check out that lead in San Francisco tomorrow. Unless you already put someone else on it."

"No, it's all yours."

We'd gotten a tip yesterday that Adele might be using a third party in San Francisco to communicate with Madeline. I'd planned to send Raoul, but if Chris wanted to go, I had no problem with that.

He sipped his coffee. "This should be an easy recon job. I was thinking it might be a good one for Jordan."

"Jordan? She's still a trainee."

Chris laughed. "Don't let her hear you say that. She'll probably kick your ass just to prove you wrong."

I smiled. "You're probably right."

Jordan had already seen more action than most first-year warriors. She was also one of the best young swordsmen I'd seen, better than I'd been at her age. And just as driven to prove herself. She'd been asking me for weeks to let her go on a job.

"Is that a yes?"

I picked up my coffee. "Yes. She's ready."

I stared at the rain again. Jordan was going to be ecstatic, but I wasn't sure how Sara would take the news. She'd be happy for her friend, but she'd also question why she was the only one not allowed to go on a job. And none of the answers I gave her were going to go over well.

Since our talk the morning after the Vancouver attack, I was more understanding of her need for independence and her struggle to keep her own identity. I couldn't turn off my protectiveness for her, but I could give her room to grow.

I accepted the fact that she would someday be a warrior, as much as that scared the hell out of me, and I was doing everything I could to prepare her for that day. For the last three weeks, I had trained her hard, and I'd watched her work tirelessly with Desmund until he'd left yesterday to go back to Westhorne. She worked with Eldeorin every day now as well, although I still had no idea what went on in their training.

I wished I could say our relationship was progressing as well as her training, but we seemed to be at a standstill. After the morning I'd almost taken things too far, I'd avoided nighttime visits to her room. I wanted her too much, and my willpower was weak when it came to her. Every touch and kiss from her made it harder to keep my resolve to wait.

"You're not listening to a word I'm saying, are you?"

I rubbed my jaw and apologized again. "I'm sorry, Chris. I have a lot on my mind these days."

"I know. May I offer some advice?"

I nodded.

"I don't know what it's like to be bonded, but I can tell when two people are crazy about each other. I can also tell when my best friend is miserable. Go to her and tell her how you feel."

I scowled at my coffee mug. "You think I haven't thought about doing that. She's not ready. She's —"

"She's eighteen."

"I know how old she is."

"No. I mean that despite everything she's been through, Sara's an eighteen-year-old who's probably never been in love before. I guarantee she's a hell of a lot more confused about all of this than you are. And scared."

"Scared?" I knew she was shy about intimacy, but scared?

He gave me a grave smile. "Her mother abandoned her when she was a child. I don't care what Sara says about Madeline, something like that leaves a mark on a person. And then her father was taken from her. I'd be afraid to love someone if that happened to me."

"That's even more reason not to push her and to let her come to me when she's sure."

He sighed. "Did you ever think she might be afraid to say it first, that she's waiting for you?"

I had no answer because the thought hadn't ever occurred to me. I'd been so focused on giving her time and letting her set the pace of our relationship that I hadn't considered she might be waiting for me. Was it possible? Had I been reading her wrong this whole time?

My mind immediately went back over the last month, trying to remember every conversation, every look from her. There had been a few times when it felt like she wanted to tell me something, but I'd thought I'd imagined it. Could she have been trying to open up to me?

Chris shook his head. "Listen, if there's one thing I know about you two, it's that you care deeply for each other. And that you're both stubborn as hell. Okay, maybe I know two things."

"Is there a point in there somewhere?"

"What I'm trying to say is you both want each other, and neither of you is going to say it first. You need to stop holding back and tell that girl how you feel – for everyone's sake. I can't stand to see you two like this."

*   *   *

Work kept me at the command center that night, as it had for most of the week. In the last month, vampires had been attacking Mohiri warriors across the country at an alarming rate. Strongholds had beefed up security, fearful of an attack like the one on Westhorne in early December. Family compounds were the most vulnerable, and some were sending their younger children to strongholds overseas.

I was never so glad to live in a house with faerie protections. I couldn't have done my job properly if I was worried about Sara's safety all day long.

The next morning, Chris and Jordan left just after dawn for San Francisco, and I spent the better part of the day working. I'd planned to have dinner alone with Sara at the house since Chris and Jordan weren't expected back until tomorrow. But we had three teams out on jobs, which meant fewer of us to monitor them.

When Raoul offered to do a food run, I knew my dinner plans would have to be put on hold. But there was no reason why Sara couldn't join us at the command center like she'd been doing almost every day.

I knocked on her bedroom door, and she called for me to come in. Opening the door, I smiled at the sight of her sitting cross-legged on the bed, surrounded by books and papers. I wondered what she was up to. She hated being idle and didn't seem to care much for TV, something we had in common.

"Do you want to come next door with me instead of spending the evening here alone? Raoul is ordering from that Italian place you like."

Her face lit up. "That sounds awesome."

She moved to get up, and a cat meowed. I walked to the bed, looking at the black and gray tabby I hadn't noticed on her lap. Something about the animal looked familiar –

"Is that the cat you had back in Maine?"

She touched the cat's head. "Yes, his name is Oscar."

"How did your cat get here?" I'd been so busy the last week she'd probably told me someone was sending her cat and I'd forgotten.

"Eldeorin took me to the apartment today and I brought Oscar back

443

with me."

"He did what?"

A chill went through me. I had to have heard her wrong. There was no way Eldeorin would take her to Maine where she'd almost died at the hands of vampires.

"It was safe, Nikolas," she said in a rush. "Eldeorin was with me and I didn't go outside."

Safe? Nate had been turned in that apartment, which meant the Master knew about it and was probably watching it somehow. She'd been taken from there once and I'd almost lost her.

My Mori growled furiously at the thought of our mate in danger, and my voice rose along with my anger. "What the hell is wrong with him? He knows New Hastings is not safe for you."

She laid the cat aside and stood on the other side of the bed.

"Is any place safe for me? Other than here where I'm surrounded by Faerie wards, is there any place I can go and be safe? It's a dangerous world for everyone now, not just me."

"Everyone else's safety is not my concern."

"And everyone else doesn't have built-in vampire radar or power like mine. I'm not defenseless, Nikolas, far from it. I've killed more vampires than most trainees do before they become warriors. I'm not saying I'm invincible, just that I'm a lot stronger than you think I am."

"I know you're strong, Sara. *Khristu!*" I raked a hand through my hair, not wanting to think about all the vampires she'd had to kill since I met her. "But we're not talking about a few vampires looking for you. A Master wants you dead. Every time I think about that, it makes me want to forget my promise and take you far away from here."

Her anger faded, and she came around the bed to stand in front of me. She laid her hands on my chest as if she knew her touch was exactly what I needed.

"There is always going to be some vampire or demon that wants us dead because of what we are. They've been trying for a while now, but we're still here. I have no plans to go anywhere. Do you?"

"God, I wish it was that easy." I took her shoulders in my hands, wishing there was a way to make her understand what I was trying to protect her from. "Even with all the things you've seen, you still have no idea how much evil is out there and how bad it can get. And I don't want you to ever have to see that."

She opened her mouth, closed it, and opened it again. "About that. There's something I've been wanting to talk to you about."

The second the words were out of her mouth, my phone rang. I didn't want to answer it because her expression said she was about to share something important with me. A glance at the screen told me it was Raoul, and he wouldn't call unless it was important.

I gave her an apologetic look as I put the phone to my ear. "Nikolas here."

"Nikolas, we've got trouble in San Francisco. Chris's team got hit by a bunch of gulaks at the *wrakk*."

I swore silently and kept my expression neutral, not wanting to alarm Sara. "When?"

"Just a few minutes ago. They're in some kind of standoff now. You want me to take some guys and head up there?"

"No, I'll be there in five minutes. Tell Elijah to assemble his team." I wasn't worried about Chris. He could handle himself. But I'd sent Jordan out today. If anything happened to her on her first job, I didn't think Sara or I would forgive me.

"What's wrong?" Sara asked when I hung up.

"One of our teams called in and said they ran into some trouble," I said calmly. "I'm going to take another team to back them up. It's nothing you have to worry about."

"What team?"

I shook my head. "Sara, you don't have to worry about it."

Panic filled her eyes, and she clutched my arm tightly. "What team, Nikolas?"

"Chris's team."

Her hand flew to her mouth. "Oh God. We have to help them."

"We will," I said confidently. I lifted her chin so her eyes met mine. "Chris knows what he's doing and he'll keep Jordan safe. Raoul said they are pinned down, but no one is hurt. They'll be okay."

She was quiet for a moment, and her normally expressive face was impossible to read. "Go," she burst out. "Do what you need to do."

I kissed her forehead. "I'll call you when I find them."

She and I would resume our talk when I got back, and this time I'd make sure there were no interruptions.

Five minutes later, I was on the Ducati, heading north to San Francisco with Elijah's team following in an SUV. My mind wanted to go in two separate directions. I forced myself to focus on the most important thing now, which was the team's situation and the best way to handle it when I got there.

The San Francisco *wrakk* – or demon marketplace – was located near the waterfront in a nondescript, two-story brick building. I parked my bike out of sight and walked toward the building, ignoring the wind and rain that lashed at me. Elijah's team was ten minutes behind me, having gotten stuck in a traffic jam that I'd maneuvered around. I couldn't wait for them. Gulaks were impatient and violent, and they weren't going to wait around in a standoff for long.

I'd been to a lot of *wrakks* over the years, and they were all laid out pretty much the same – rows of stalls selling everything from food to clothes to medicines and glamours. They were one of the few places demonkind could assemble in public and socialize, and they were heavily warded to keep humans away. They didn't like the Mohiri hanging around either, but they tolerated us. For the most part. Apparently, this wasn't one of those times.

I rounded the corner, and my first indication that something was going down inside was a small vrell demon family huddled by the side of the building. The male, female, and two children wore hats to cover their horns, but I knew what they were right away.

When they saw me, they shied away, moving to the other end of the building, making me think of Sara's comment about the Mohiri being like boogeymen to demons. Funny how I never realized that before, yet she had seen it after only a week of exposure to them. And then she'd scolded me for it.

Thinking about Sara, I smiled and raised my hand in a nonthreatening manner as I approached the demons. It was better to find out exactly what the situation was inside the building before I went in.

I stopped in my tracks as my Mori began to flutter. What the –?

Backing up a step, I looked at the main door to the building. The fluttering grew stronger.

"That's not possible."

Solmi, my demon whispered.

Confusion and a mounting sense of foreboding had me yanking the door open with more force than necessary. The door slammed against the wall, loudly announcing my arrival as I entered the building.

I sucked in a sharp breath when her presence surrounded me. My heart sped up and my throat felt dry as I strode through the mass of demons that scurried out of my way. I scanned the large room, even as my mind argued there was no way Sara could be here, no matter what my Mori was telling me.

The crowd parted and I spotted Chris standing in the middle of the room, wearing an uneasy expression that created a sinking feeling deep in my gut. Behind him, dead gulaks littered the floor, too many to count in a single glance.

"Chris, what the hell is going on here? And why do I feel –?"

Someone moved behind Chris, and I watched in stunned silence as Sara stepped into view.

Dressed in black, she had her hair in a ponytail, but a few strands hung around her face as if they'd been pulled free in a fight.

Blood roared in my ears as the weight of what I was seeing punched me square in the gut.

Chris raised an arm protectively in front of Sara. "Take it easy, Nikolas. She's unharmed."

In the back of my mind, I knew my best friend was trying to protect his cousin. All my Mori saw was a male trying to keep us from our mate. Red spots floated before my eyes.

"Move, Chris."

"Shit," he muttered, standing his ground.

Sara pushed his arm out of the way. She stepped around him to stand several feet away from me, just out of my reach.

Defiant eyes met mine. "Nikolas."

Her lack of fear and the fact that she looked unharmed were the only things keeping my demon in check. But if I didn't touch her soon, I was going to lose control.

I held out my hand. "Come here."

"Listen, I know you're upset, but you don't get to order me around," she said.

I breathed through my nostrils, fighting to calm myself. "Sara, I'm trying very hard not to lose it. I need to…"

Understanding lit her eyes. Without another word, she came to me, and I wrapped my arms tightly around her. The moment her soft body pressed against mine, my Mori quieted and the rage flowed out of me.

"What the hell are you doing here?" I asked harshly when I could speak again.

She inhaled deeply. "I came to help Chris and Jordan."

"Help them?" I asked dumbly, still torn between shock and anger and relief she was unhurt.

"I didn't think you'd get here in time." Her words were muffled against my chest. "I had to come."

I loosened my arms so I could see her. "How did you get here?"

The answer hit me before she spoke, and my anger came roaring back as I scanned the room for the faerie. "I'll kill him."

Her chin lifted. "No, you won't."

My gaze swung back to her. "The hell I won't. He's supposed to be teaching you, not putting you in danger."

She pulled away from me, and I let my arms fall to my sides. I thought she was going to put distance between us, but she stayed within arm's reach and met my gaze unflinchingly.

"I asked him to bring me."

"And he should have said no. You could have been killed." I knew Eldeorin was a bit outlandish, but I never believed he would endanger her this way.

"Look around, Nikolas." Her voice rose, and she waved her arm at the dead gulaks. "Most of the demons on the floor were put there by me. The team was in more danger of being killed than I was."

I glanced at the carnage around us, counting at least eight large gulaks and a drex demon. "*You* did this?"

"Yes." She crossed her arms. "And it's not the first time."

"What do you mean?"

I already knew about the demons at Draegan's place. Had she not told me everything that had happened while we were separated?

Her eyes locked with mine. "I mean I've killed a lot of demons and vampires. All over the country."

I stared at the dead gulaks, all of which were three times her size. And deadly. My gaze moved to Chris who gave me a small nod, his mouth set in a firm line.

"*Iisus Khristos!* Please, tell me you're joking," I said harshly.

She shook her head slowly. "I wouldn't joke about that."

"*Ya ne mogu v eto poverit'!*" I burst out, my stomach churning just imagining the risks she'd taken. All the times I'd thought she was safe at Eldeorin's, he was taking her out and exposing her to the very things I was fighting to protect her from.

I gripped her arms. "What in God's name were you thinking? Do you have any idea what could have happened to you out there?"

"I wasn't alone. Eldeorin was with me every time," she argued.

"And that makes it okay? You've barely begun your training. You have no business being in any of those places."

She glared at me. "You had no problem with Jordan coming here."

"Jordan's been training since she could hold a sword, and she can –"

"Can what? Defend herself?" Her face flushed in anger, but there was no mistaking the hurt in her voice. "I'm never going to be like Jordan or any other warrior no matter how much I train, Nikolas. But I'm strong, a lot stronger than you give me credit for. You saw what I did in Vancouver. Eldeorin was with me, but over half of those kills were mine."

Vancouver? But that would mean…

Who are you?

A friend.

"*Sukin syn!* That was you in the backyard?"

She'd stood fifteen feet away from me, and I hadn't sensed her presence or recognized her. Of course – Eldeorin and his goddamn glamours.

"Yes."

I thought about all the reports of the mysterious vigilante who seemed to appear out of nowhere and killed with a weapon we hadn't seen before. A Fae weapon, as it turned out.

"All this time. Why didn't you tell me?"

"Because I knew you'd react this way. Eldeorin told me I had to learn to use my power as a weapon, and he was right. I needed this." Her voice lowered. "I've been trying for weeks to tell you the truth, but I didn't know how. I almost told you today, but you got the call to come here."

I remembered the occasions she'd been with us at the command center when we'd discussed the vigilante. She'd never said a word or had given any hint she knew who the person was. After everything we'd been through, she should have been able to tell me anything. Did she not trust me at all?

She exhaled slowly. "It started out as training, but then I realized I could make a real difference."

I released her, not sure what to think or how to feel. "I can't believe this. How could you keep this from me?"

Her voice grew softer, imploring. "I didn't want to. I hated not telling you."

I turned away from her because her pleading eyes made it impossible to think.

"Nikolas?" she said quietly.

"I need a minute, Sara," I replied more harshly than I meant to. I had to put some space between us before I said something in anger that I couldn't take back.

She didn't follow or call after me when I left the building and let the heavy door slam shut behind me. Outside, the rain and wind had picked up, a perfect accompaniment to the turbulence inside me. I set off down the street with no destination in mind, just the need to walk. It wasn't as if I could go far. I was furious with her and my chest ached from her deception, and yet all I could see was the tears shimmering in her eyes before I left.

Sara is the vigilante.

Maybe if I said the words enough I'd accept them. Maybe then I could accept that the woman I loved, the person I'd lived with in the same house for months, had kept something so important from me. It made me question everything about us, about her. She knew how much I worried about her safety. Why would she do this?

Because she knew you'd never think she was ready, a tiny voice whispered in my head.

I tried to ignore it, but it got louder and more insistent. How many times since I met her had I told her she needed to be protected? How many times had I said she wasn't strong enough to protect herself? And how many times had she told me she didn't want to be coddled and she couldn't live like that?

Eldeorin had told me weeks ago that I judged Sara's fighting skills by Mohiri standards and that I had no idea how strong she really was. I'd watched some of her training with Aine from a distance, so I knew her power was not something to take lightly. I'd just never thought she'd advanced this far.

I'd seen some of the vigilante's kills and heard the stories about her fighting skills. I'd talked to warriors who might have died in recent vampire attacks if the vigilante hadn't shown up out of nowhere to fight beside them.

I stopped walking and turned back toward the building. Releasing a ragged breath, I wondered what really upset me more: Sara keeping this from me, or that she'd been out there fighting vampires, and demons, and God only knew what else. If Jordan had turned out to be the vigilante and the one keeping secrets from us, would I have reacted this way?

I didn't need to think about it for long to come up with the answer.

The truth was I knew Sara was strong, and I'd known the night of the attack on Westhorne she'd one day be a force to be reckoned with. But I'd also been happy to keep her tucked away at Eldeorin's the last few months, where I could do my job and not have to fear for her safety. I'd told her it wasn't safe out here, and yet I'd been okay with sending a trainee out into the field.

Because Jordan's not my mate.

And there was the crux of this whole situation. Sara was my mate, and it was impossible for me to separate logic from emotion when it came to her. No matter how good a fighter she was or how well she could defend herself, my heart and my Mori couldn't see past the need to protect her. If anything happened to her, life would cease to have meaning for me.

I grimaced as I arrived back at the door of the building. Now that I'd admitted the truth to myself, where did that leave Sara and me? I would *not* lose her over this, but I didn't know how we were going to move past it.

I opened the door and entered the building more quietly this time. I tried not to look at the dead demons, but my eyes went to them anyway. I pictured Sara being mauled by a gulak or drex demon. And then I thought about what Draegan had planned to do to her before I'd killed him. Fear twisted my gut, and my Mori grew agitated again.

Everyone was pretty much where I'd left them. Sara watched me approach and drew her shoulders up as if steeling herself for the worst.

"Just tell me you're done with this," I said when I stood in front of her.

She frowned. "Done?"

"No more rogue...vigilante...or whatever." I understood her need to fight and to help others, but I didn't know how to deal with the thought of her going off alone.

She took a breath. "What if this is what I'm supposed to do, just like you're supposed to be a warrior?"

"It's too dangerous," I replied without thinking.

"It'll always be dangerous, Nikolas," she shot back. "I was there in Vancouver, remember? You and Chris put your lives in danger all the time. Soon Jordan will be a warrior and she will too. Are you going to hold her back and tell her it's too dangerous for her?"

"Khristu!" I dragged my hand through my hair. I was saying all the wrong things again, and my Mori wasn't helping. All it wanted was to protect our mate no matter how good a warrior she was. "I don't want to hold you back, but every instinct I have is telling me I need to keep you safe."

I waited for her to be angry, to yell at me. I deserved it after the way I'd spoken to her. What I didn't expect was the look of total defeat that crossed her face.

"I understand," she said tonelessly as she turned away.

I'd never seen her like this, and it sent a cold shiver across the back of my neck. "Where are you going?"

"I'm going home," she replied without looking back. "I can't do this anymore."

"Can't do what?" I asked, alarmed by the sudden change in her.

"Love you."

The words were whispered so softly that for a second I thought I'd imagined them.

My heart thudded as I caught her hand and gently pulled her back around to face me. She wouldn't look at me, so I lifted her chin until I could see her tear-filled eyes.

"You love me?" I asked in a raw voice.

Her tears spilled over.

"Yes."

CHAPTER 39

OVERCOME WITH EMOTION, my mouth covered hers. She reached for me at the same time, pulling my head down to her. I tasted her tears on our lips as I poured all my love and months of longing into the kiss. When I felt the faint joy of her Mori through our bond, it was like finding a lost piece of me.

I lifted my head and used my thumbs to brush away her tears, humbled by the love shining in her eyes.

"*Ya lyublyu tebya*," I whispered gruffly.

It took me a second to realize I'd professed my love to her in Russian and she had no idea what I was saying. Smiling at my blunder, I took her face in my hands.

"I love you."

Her smile stole my breath. "I love you, too," she said huskily.

My lips captured hers again in a slow, lingering kiss. Then I wrapped her tightly in my arms and buried my face in her hair. I didn't think I could ever let her go from my arms again.

"I wasn't sure if you…" she whispered.

"And I didn't think you were ready to hear it. I was waiting for you to say something, to let me know you felt the same way."

God, I was such a fool. I should have told her how I felt months ago. I could have saved us both so much lost time.

"How…long?" she asked hesitantly.

I pulled back, and she looked up at me. Unable to stop touching her, my hand came up to caress her cheek.

"I was lost the first moment I saw you at that club in Portland. I just didn't know it yet. Before I even knew who or what you were, I was drawn to you. At first, I told myself it was my responsibility to protect you. But the more time I spent with you, even when we were arguing, the more I knew what I felt for you was anything but duty. I don't think I knew how deep my feelings were until that day you traded yourself for Nate."

I took a ragged breath. "That ride from Portland was the longest of my life."

Pain flashed in her eyes, and she leaned into my hand. "I'm sorry I put you through that."

I brushed the lose tendrils of hair from her face. "I know. Your courage is one of the first things I came to love about you, and I should have known you'd do anything to protect Nate and your friends."

"And you," she declared fiercely.

I hugged her tightly again, half afraid none of this was real.

Sara made a small sound of embarrassment and buried her face against my chest. It took me a moment to realize why.

"They left." I'd noticed we were alone after our first kiss, and I figured it was Chris's doing. Jordan would have wanted ringside seats.

"What?" Sara murmured.

I smiled, wanting to kiss her until she couldn't think of anything else.

"Chris and the others. They went outside."

"Oh."

I took her hand and led her to a nearby bench. She sat on one end, but that was too much distance for my liking. Scooping her into my arms, I settled her on my lap.

She sighed happily and nestled against me, her fingers toying with the fabric of my shirt.

"I was so busy trying to push you away that I refused to admit I felt anything for you at first," she said softly. "I didn't know for sure that I loved you until Thanksgiving, but I think I started to fall for you at my apartment the night of the storm."

"Was it my mad cooking skills?" I teased, even though my mind reeled from the discovery she'd loved me all this time.

She laughed softly. "It was the first time I saw a different side of you, and you weren't bossing me around for once."

I stroked her hair. "We've come a long way since that night."

"Yes, but you're still trying to boss me around," she retorted playfully.

"And you still make me want to tie your ass to a chair to keep you out of trouble."

She snorted delicately. "Ha, you can try."

I looked at a dead drex demon ten feet away and grimaced. "Sara, I hate the idea of you out there fighting, and I doubt I'll ever be okay with it. I don't think any male would be okay with the woman he loves putting herself in danger."

She grew quiet. "Do you know what it's like for me when you go away on a job, especially with the way things are now? I don't sleep, and I spend every minute praying we don't get word that you're in trouble – or worse. It's torture. That night we heard you were under attack in Vancouver, I almost lost it. I almost lost you. Seeing you in danger kills me."

I knew she stayed at the command center whenever I had to leave on a job, and she refused to go home until I returned. After Raoul had told me that, I'd started calling her to let her know I was okay. But I hadn't realized what she was going through until now.

"I never thought about how hard that was for you. I've spent my whole life being a warrior and not much else. Before you, I didn't have someone waiting for me when the job was done or worrying about my safety."

She let out a deep breath. "This is new for both of us, and we're going to have to learn to deal with it."

"Something tells me you're going to cope with this a lot better than I will."

She touched my jaw to get me to look at her. "We'll figure it out together. Knowing us, it won't be easy, but I'll try if you will."

Easier said than done. "I'll try, but I can't promise to have any civil words for the faerie."

She made a face. "I've had a few choice words for him myself. At first I didn't like his idea of training because he pushed me out of my comfort zone. He always had more faith in my abilities than I had, and he kept pushing until I believed in myself too. He's been a good mentor and a friend to me, and he always has my back."

I tried not to be jealous of the affection in her voice when she talked about the faerie. "You like spending time with him."

She smiled. "Sometimes, but I like being with you more."

My lips met hers again. "Good answer."

She rested her head against my shoulder again and surveyed the damage in the room. After a moment, she sighed and sat up straighter. "I guess we should get this mess cleaned up."

I reluctantly released her and looked around the deserted market.

"I'm sure Chris has already called for a cleanup crew. We should probably put one on speed dial for you."

She scowled at me, but Jordan's voice cut off whatever she was going to say.

"Hey, is it safe to come in now? We're freezing our butts off out here."

Sara smiled at me. "All good."

Jordan breezed into the building with Chris behind her, both of them grinning at us.

"Thank God!" Jordan wrinkled her nose at us. "Well, you two look disgustingly happy. And it's about damn time."

"Amen," Chris said. "I called in a crew to help with this mess. I told them they might need extra guys."

I laughed at the look Sara gave him before she walked away to talk to some of the vendors who had returned to their stalls. She walked around, conversing with them as if she hung out in *wrakks* every day. I'd never seen her around demons, and it struck me how quickly she put them at ease. I couldn't hear their conversations, but I saw it in their posture and the smiles and nods they gave her.

I also noticed her outfit for the first time. Dressed in tight black jeans, a black T-shirt, and combat boots, she looked ready to kick ass and take names. I could barely take my eyes off her.

"Hey, Romeo?" A hand waved in front of my face. "I hate to interrupt your ogling, but duty calls."

I tore my gaze from Sara to glower at Chris. "I don't ogle."

"Right." He shook his head and walked away, stepping over several gru-eels flopping around on the wet concrete. "Jesus, what a mess."

"You want to give me the rundown?"

He picked up his sword and shook the gore from it before he wiped it on the body of a ranc demon.

"It was quiet here until the gulaks arrived – eight of the bastards with the drex demon. As soon as they saw us, they cornered the three of us in the loading bay and started talking about delivering us to some vampires for cash."

He waved at Will, who was limping with a strip of cloth wrapped around his thigh. "We fought them off, and Will took a gulak claw to the leg. Jordan was ready to take on the whole lot of them herself, and she might have tried if those damn ranc demons hadn't arrived with flamethrowers."

I looked at a dead gulak with bulking eyes and his tongue hanging out. "Skip to the part where Sara made her big entrance."

"How do you know she didn't come in quietly like a ninja?"

My eyebrows rose.

Chris laughed. "Honestly, it was kind of hard to see her at first with the wall of gulaks in the way. I heard her fight with one of them, and then I saw her when the rest of the gulaks turned to look. She took down a gulak with her bare hands. I have to say I was pretty damn impressed, and I had no idea it was her at that point.

"After that, all hell broke loose. She knocked over the gru-eel tank, but I was too busy fighting to see what happened. Then it was over, and she was standing there. I knew it was the vigilante, and I went up to her to thank her for helping us. She shocked the hell out of me when she showed me who she really was. Jordan wasn't surprised, of course."

"Of course." I looked over at Sara and Jordan talking to a quellar demon. Those two were as thick as thieves. I wasn't surprised Sara had confided in Jordan.

"So, you okay with all of this now?"

I raked both hands through my hair. "What do you think?"

"I think there's a case of Macallan in your future."

"I think you may be right."

I watched Sara say something to the quellar demon who was looking at a piece of paper in his hand. Then she and Jordan walked over to join us.

"Giving out your number, Sara?" Chris teased. "He doesn't seem like your type."

Her eyes met mine. "He's not."

Heat curled in my gut. *Mine*, growled my Mori.

"You ready to get out of here?" I asked her, looking forward to getting her home and spending some time alone with her.

"Yes." She glanced around. "It looks like my ride left, so you're stuck with me."

A smile curved my lips. For once that accursed faerie had done something right.

"Something tells me he doesn't mind one bit," Jordan said slyly.

Sara and Jordan walked ahead of Chris and me to the open door. Jordan went through, but Sara slowed and put up her hands as if she was pushing through a heavy curtain.

I gave her a questioning look when we got outside, and she made a face.

"Demon wards and Fae blood don't mix."

Outside, two black Escalades had been pulled up to the front of the building. Chris spoke to Will, who said he was staying with Elijah's team to help with the cleanup, and then the four of us went to one of the SUVs. Sara and I climbed into the back seat, and I took her hand in mine as Chris started the vehicle.

Jordan immediately launched into the story about what had happened in the *wrakk*, although her version was a lot more colorful and entertaining than Chris's telling.

"When that ugly lizard grabbed me, I wanted to cut his male bits off, but *he* held me back," she griped, tossing Chris a sour look.

"You might have been able to take him, but you're not fireproof," he argued. "And those ranc demons looked way too trigger-happy."

"*Might* have?" She made a huffing sound.

Chris rolled his eyes. "You got to kill him, didn't you?"

Sara grinned at me. I wanted to lean over and kiss her.

"What were you guys doing in a demon market in the first place?" she asked them.

"We discovered Adele has been sending letters to someone there," Chris said. "We thought it was worth checking out."

She snorted softly. "People still send letters?"

"People who suspect their electronic communications are being monitored," I told her. So far, Adele had proven to be very good at evading any attempts to listen in on hers.

Chris nodded. "And who have something to hide."

"Did you find anything?" Sara asked with a note of excitement in her voice.

"We found the demon she was sending them to. He said he was paid to drop them in a mailbox. Inside the envelope was another envelope with an address and postage. Unfortunately, every time he tries to remember the address he draws a blank."

She looked at me. "Some kind of memory spell?"

"Looks like it," Chris answered. "Adele is proving to be more covert than we gave her credit for."

Sara made a sound of disgust. "So I'm learning. And I bet it's Madeline she's writing to. Turns out they have been friends for a lot longer than she let on to us."

My eyebrows shot up. "How do you know that?"

She smiled as if she had a great secret to tell. "I brought a box of Madeline's things back with me from New Hastings today and –"

Jordan whipped around in her seat to gape at Sara. "Whoa! Hold up. You went to Maine? Today? How the hell did that happen?"

Her eyes flicked to me. "And why is Nikolas not freaking out about it?"

Why indeed? Most likely because I'd temporarily forgotten about it after learning she was the vigilante and hearing her tell me she loved me. Jesus, had that all happened in the last hour?

Sara lifted a shoulder. "Eldeorin took me there and we didn't stay long. I found a box of things belonging to Madeline that Nate had mentioned last fall. I was going to give them to Tristan, but I wanted to look through them first."

Jordan's gaze swung back to me. "And you were okay with her going there?"

"I didn't know until after she got back."

"We were in the middle of discussing it when he got the call that you guys were in trouble," Sara said.

"Discussing it. Riiight," Jordan drawled.

"What did you find in the box, Sara?" Chris asked, reminding me of the books and papers scattered across her bed.

"Pictures of Madeline and Adele that were taken back in the seventies," she said dryly. "And they look pretty chummy in them."

I nodded thoughtfully. "That would have been just a few years after Madeline left Westhorne."

Now that I thought about it, I wasn't surprised to hear that she and Adele were friends. Madeline had wanted to rebel against her life, and what better way than to befriend someone like Adele?

"Looks like we need to pay Adele another visit, Nikolas," Chris said.

"Not without me," Sara declared.

Jordan nodded. "Or me."

Sara's expression told me she wasn't going to back down. After all I'd seen and heard today, I knew she could take care of herself, even if my gut lurched every time I thought about it.

"We'll go see her tomorrow."

*   *   *

"Heb, do you have a fire hose around here?"

The dwarf blinked at Jordan and shook his head. "No, miss. Master Eldeorin's home is impervious to fire."

She waved her dessert fork at me. "Yeah, but he's not, and he's going to combust if he keeps staring at her like that."

Chris barked a laugh, and across from me, Sara's cheeks turned pink.

I chuckled and watched as she demurely lifted her eyes to mine. The warmth in her gaze told me I wasn't the only one wishing it was just the two of us there.

As much as I enjoyed Chris and Jordan's company, all I wanted was to take Sara somewhere private and kiss her until neither of us could think straight.

But then, the night was still young.

When we'd returned home, my plan had been to take Sara out to her favorite Italian place and then spend the rest of the evening making up. But Jordan had protested that we had to have a celebratory dinner, so here we were.

"Hello? Earth to the lovebirds."

I smiled at Jordan who smirked back at me. It was impossible not to like this girl, and I could see why she and Sara had hit it off. They were different in many ways, but they had the same fiery spirit and passion for what they believed in. Jordan was good for Sara, even though the two of them did share an uncanny talent for trouble.

"I asked if you are going next door after dinner," she said.

"No."

Sara's lips parted in surprise. "I thought you had to work."

"Raoul can handle things for a few hours, and I told him to call me if something comes up."

She gave me a radiant smile as she laid down her napkin. "I'm glad."

I stood and looked out the window at the moonlit lawn. "It's a nice night. Would you like to take a walk with me?"

She pushed back her chair. "I just need to grab my coat."

"Don't mind us. We'll just entertain ourselves," Jordan quipped as Sara ran from the room.

458

Laughing, Chris stood as well. "Come on, Jordan. Let's go write up the report for today."

Her face fell. "Report?"

"All part of the job," I told her. "You'll get used to them after the first hundred or so."

"Ugh." She made a face. "Why can't we just kill vampires and let someone else do the paperwork?"

Chris and I exchanged grins because we'd been saying the same thing for many years. I had a feeling Jordan was going to give the Council more heartburn than I ever had.

"Field reports are also used to keep track of our kills," I told her. "You'll be entered into the central warrior database today."

"Really?" She jumped up from the table. "Let's go, Blondie. We have a report to do."

Sara appeared in the doorway as they were leaving. We used the French doors in the dining room to exit to the back lawn. It was a cool, clear night, and we could hear the waves crashing against the base of the cliff the house was built on. We turned away from the cliff, and I took her hand in mine as we walked toward the gazebo that had been rebuilt on the other side of the small lake.

Sara gasped in pleasure when we entered the small building and it lit up with thousands of faerie lights. "Wow, it's beautiful here."

Eldeorin's light display was impressive, but it paled next to the picture she made as she stood by the rail looking at the lake.

I wrapped my arms around her from behind, blocking her from the small breeze that blew off the ocean. "Are you warm enough?"

She leaned back against me. "Yes."

She was quiet for a moment. "What do you think would have happened if someone else had found me in Maine? Or if I'd been found when I was little?"

I brushed my lips against her hair. "What do you mean?" The thought of someone else finding her in Maine didn't sit well with me, but that was a moot point now.

She shrugged. "I mean, who knows when we would have met? I would have been just another orphan, and you might never have noticed me."

I laughed and hugged her tighter. "I'm pretty sure I would have noticed you."

I'd often wondered how different our relationship would have started out if she'd been raised at Westhorne. I would have known her already, and she would have understood bonding and what was happening between us.

A warm breeze suddenly blew over us. Sara turned in my arms, tilting her face up to me as her hands stroked my abdomen through my sweater. Her bold caress took me by surprise and sent heat curling in my stomach.

"Sara?"

Her smile was seductive and shy at the same time. "Will you kiss me?" she asked huskily.

"You never have to ask me that."

I framed her face with my hands and captured her mouth with mine. She opened to me without coaxing, kissing me back with a passionate abandon she'd never shown before. In all my previous sexual encounters I'd been the seducer, but I'd never known a woman who could unravel me so completely with a kiss.

I sucked in a sharp breath, and a groan formed deep in my throat when her hands slid beneath my sweater to trace the muscles of my stomach. Fire raced through my veins and pooled low in my belly as her fingers moved over my bare skin, branding me and marking me as hers.

Deepening the kiss, I let my hands slide down her shoulders to the front of her coat. I undid the top buttons, needing to be closer to her. One of my hands slipped inside and cupped her perfect breast through her shirt and bra.

She moaned softly against my mouth, and I –

I stared in confusion at the moon reflecting off the lake as the wind cooled my heated skin. Sara was in my arms, but her back was to me as it had been a few minutes ago. I felt disoriented and...aroused?

Shock rippled through me. What the hell was going on?

"Sara? What just happened?"

She turned to face me, wearing an apologetic smile. "Eldeorin paid us a visit. He put you in some kind of dream state."

"Khristu!"

That son of a bitch. Only Eldeorin would toy with someone's private thoughts that way.

"I really don't like that faerie."

"Eldeorin's a bit outrageous, but he does have a good heart." She reached up to touch my face. "You'll be happy to know that he's gone to Faerie for a few weeks."

"This must be my lucky day," I muttered, trying to shake off the very real aftereffects of the not-so-real dream.

She smiled up at me. "Best day ever."

Her expression was so like the one from the dream, I thought for a second I was back in that place. I lowered my head and kissed her long and slow, with all the reverence she deserved. Her hands curled in my hair, and her lips were pliant and sweet under mine.

The kiss only fanned the flames created by the dream, but I'd already decided not to take it beyond this tonight. Today had been an emotional rollercoaster for us, and I wasn't going to overwhelm her with the heavy emotions of sex.

As much as I wanted her, I also wanted her first time and the last step in our bonding to be perfect. And I really didn't want it to happen in Eldeorin's home. I wouldn't put it past that bastard to pop in and say hi in the middle of our lovemaking.

I'd have to figure something out soon though. Neither I nor my Mori could bear to be apart from our mate for much longer.

I lifted my head and gazed at the desire in her green eyes. God, if she kept looking at me like that, I was going to forget everything else, take her back to her room, and not leave until we were good and truly mated.

My phone rang, startling us both. I wasn't sure if the groan I let out was one of relief or frustration. Perhaps a bit of both.

"Nikolas here."

"Hey, sorry to interrupt your evening," Raoul said. "Brock just called. He said you wanted to talk to him as soon as he found something."

"I'll be there in twenty minutes."

For the last week, Brock had been watching Adele's home and club, and he was the one who'd given us the San Francisco lead. If he had any news, I wanted to hear it firsthand.

"Duty calls," Sara said, not hiding the disappointment in her voice.

"Sorry. One of our teams reported in with some intel and I need to be there. I wasn't expecting to hear from them today."

"You don't need to apologize. It's your job."

We walked back to the house, and the closer we got to it, the more unwilling I was to leave her.

"Do you want to come to the command center with me?" I asked her.

"Yes," she blurted.

Everyone gave us knowing smiles when we entered the control room, but Sara seemed too happy to notice. She sat on the couch with Jordan while I made some calls, and I found her asleep there when I finished up an hour later. I wasn't surprised after the exciting day she'd had.

Raoul came to stand beside me. "Is she really the vigilante?" he asked in a hushed voice.

"Yes."

His breath came out in a whoosh. "I thought Chris and Jordan were messing with me. I still can't believe it."

"You and me both."

"But she's so…small. How did she do it?"

I watched her sleeping, curled up on her side with her hands tucked beneath her chin. She was the picture of innocence, and she looked so vulnerable and young. But beneath that soft exterior was a fighter who would do anything to protect the people she loved.

"She's a warrior."

CHAPTER 40

"NIKOLAS, WHAT A pleasant surprise! How can I be of service to you tonight?"

Adele smiled invitingly up at me from the couch in her office. Wearing a long red dress, she looked more ready to attend a cocktail party than lounge in her club.

Her eyes widened. "And Eldeorin's little cousin? This *is* a surprise."

"Hello, Adele," Sara said coolly, coming to stand close to my side in a clear display of possessiveness.

Behind me, Jordan snickered and Chris chuckled softly.

"Adele, do you have –?" Adele's bathroom door opened, and who should emerge but Orias. The warlock did a double take when he saw Sara, and he almost dropped the satchel in his hands.

"You!" he barked at Sara, making me wonder again what had happened when she visited him in New Mexico.

"Nice to see you again, Orias," she replied in a sweet voice.

He glared at her and held on to the satchel like it held his life savings. "Because of you, I have no home and no business, and every vampire in New Mexico wants me dead. You are a menace!"

She crossed her arms and returned his dark look. "Maybe you should be more careful about the people you do business with."

"Yeah, and you shouldn't have tied us up either," Jordan added irately.

My stare returned to Orias, and he visibly recoiled. He hadn't mentioned that tidbit when I spoke to him back in December.

Sara touched my arm. "He was going to turn us over to Tristan for the reward money," she explained.

"And you upset my demon so much that it took me a week to get him to calm down," Orias whined, stroking the satchel that must hold his demon. "I wish I'd never laid eyes on you."

"*This* is the girl who killed Stefan Price?" Adele looked from Sara to Orias, wearing an expression of disbelief. "You didn't tell me she was Fae."

The warlock huffed indignantly. "She's not Fae. She's Mohiri. And I couldn't tell you because *she* put a gag on me."

A gag? My eyes went to Sara who merely shrugged. What the hell had happened between these two? And how did she stop a warlock like Orias from doing whatever he wanted?

"But that means you are not Fae as you and Eldeorin led me to believe." Adele narrowed her eyes at Sara. "What game are you playing?"

"This is not a game to me."

"Why did you lie to me?" the succubus demanded.

My body tensed. Adele usually kept a cool head about her and stayed out of trouble, but Succubi were known for their tempers. And they were incredibly strong.

Undaunted, Sara strode over and threw several old photos on the coffee table. "I could ask you the same question," she said coldly as Adele leaned forward to peer at them.

Adele picked them up carefully, handling them like they were valuable heirlooms. "Where did you get these?"

"From a box of things my mother left behind," Sara told her.

"Your mother? What would your mother be doing with…?" Adele's mouth fell open, and she stared at Sara. "You are Madeline's daughter."

"Yes."

I looked at Sara. She claimed she didn't feel anything for her mother, but the trace of bitterness in her voice said otherwise. I wondered if she even knew it was there.

"You look nothing like her," Adele commented, studying Sara's face.

"I know."

"Madeline's daughter," Adele breathed, settling back against the couch. "Pardon me for staring, but in all the years I've known her, she never once spoke of a daughter. I knew she was married to a human for a few years, but not that there was a child."

Apparently, that part of Madeline's life was something she'd kept from everyone, even her closest friends. And judging by the fondness in Adele's voice, she and Madeline were very close.

"I'm not a child anymore."

Adele's shrewd eyes met mine. "So it would seem."

Now that the introductions were over, it was time to get to the reason for our visit. I pointed to the photos Adele still held. "Tell us about your history with Madeline."

She stared at the photos then looked at Sara. "The story I told you about Madeline saving my life from a vampire was true. That happened years after we met. It was nineteen seventy-one and I was living in San

Diego when I met Madeline at a party. We were the only non-humans there, and we were drawn to each other's company. We hit it off immediately and spent the next few months partying and having fun. It was the best summer of my life."

Her story rang true and sounded exactly like the Madeline I knew. She'd always loved the beach and talked about California. San Diego would have been the ideal scene for her.

Adele's brows drew together. "She surprised me when she said she was enrolling in college in Maine of all places. Madeline was more adventurous than academic, and she liked warm sunny places. It was around that time that I lost touch with her for a few years. She sent a few letters, but she stopped visiting altogether for about four years. One day she reappeared and told me she'd gotten married, but it hadn't worked out. She never said his name."

Adele stood and walked over to pour herself some wine. "Would you care for a drink?" she asked us.

When we declined, she went back to her couch. "Madeline was different after that, quieter. Sometimes she got a sad look in her eyes, but when I questioned her she never wanted to talk about it. I figured she still cared for her human ex-husband and I left it at that. She continued to travel and return here three or four times a year, until about ten years ago. I barely see her these days."

"What did she tell you about the Master she was running from?" Sara asked in a hard voice.

Hearing about her parents had obviously upset her, though she was trying not to show it. I would have taken her hand, but I sensed she needed to be strong in front of Adele.

"Madeline told me she'd had a run-in with a Master, but she didn't say more than that." Adele's eye twitched, belying her fear. No demon, not even a powerful succubus, wanted to talk about a Master, lest he find out and come asking questions.

"Were you selling Madeline glamours to hide her from the vampires?" Sara asked Orias.

Why hadn't I made that connection? I'd known Adele and Orias were friends, and he was the one who'd sent Sara to Adele to look for Madeline. Which raised yet another question. Why would he help Sara if she'd upset him so much during her visit?

"My glamours are the best," he replied haughtily. "Only Fae magic is better."

I looked at Adele. "Our sources tell us that Madeline was on her way here to Los Angeles in December, around the time Sara paid you a visit."

"She came to see me at my home that same night. I told her there was a faerie youngling asking after her on behalf of her daughter, and she asked me if I was joking. She left the next morning, and I haven't seen or heard from her since."

Adele set her glass down and stood. "This has been lovely, but I'm afraid I must beg you to excuse me. I have a lot of work to do before the club opens in a few hours."

I nodded. "Thank you for your time."

"Anytime," she replied smoothly.

Taking Sara's arm, I turned her toward the door. My eyes met Chris's, and he gave me a tiny nod.

"But…"

Sara started to protest, but I led her outside before she could call Adele out for lying to us.

We left the office, and Chris shut the door. I let go of Sara, and she spun to face me.

"What are you doing? She knows exactly where Madeline is."

"Yes, and we are the last people she is going to tell," I replied evenly. "It's clear she and Madeline are very close, and she is not going to betray her friend."

Sara's face fell. "But she's our only connection to Madeline."

"I didn't say we were giving up."

I smiled as I took her arm, and we started down the stairs. It was time to show her there was more to being a warrior than killing vampires.

"Adele's probably on the phone with Madeline right now, warning her about us," Sara grumbled once we hit the street.

"And that is exactly what we want her to do."

I opened the back door of the SUV for her. Jordan jumped in on the other side, and Chris and I took the front with me behind the wheel.

Behind us, Elijah's team sat in two more SUVs as backup. Los Angeles was still a very dangerous place, even with the extra teams of warriors, including Hamid and Ammon, working to clean it up. I'd spent an hour this morning explaining that to Sara and trying to convince her to stay behind today.

She was quick to remind me that not only did she have vampire radar, but she could crisp one of them faster than I could say toast. It was hard to argue with that, having seen the results of her vigilante work, but it was going to take me a while to get used to it.

"Are we good, Chris?" I asked.

He pulled out the phone Raj had given him before we left the command center. When he turned it on, I could see Raj's surveillance app was already running.

He grinned at me. "We're in."

"What is that?" Sara asked, peering over his shoulder.

He tapped the screen. "That is the signal from the transmitter I left in

Adele's office."

Jordan leaned forward. "Wait. Didn't you guys say you couldn't bug her place because she uses warlock magic to detect them and short them out?"

I started the engine. "These aren't normal transmitters. Raj loaned us one of his prototypes to test out. So far it appears to be working." Raj was going to be thrilled when he heard his project was a success.

"How do you know?" Sara asked.

Chris held up the phone. "Green means the transmitter is working and the signal is good."

"What do the dots mean?"

He pointed to the screen. "That blue dot tells us that someone is using the land line in Adele's office. The red dot means that my receiver is recording it."

"Recording it?" Sara repeated breathlessly.

He waved the phone at her. "Why don't we see who the lovely Adele was in such a hurry to call?"

Sara squealed and hugged his neck. "You are a genius!"

"I have my moments."

He pressed a button, and we all quieted as Adele's voice filled the car.

"Orias, would you be a dear and make sure our Mohiri friends didn't leave a little gift for me?"

"Your wards should take care of that," the warlock answered.

"It never hurts to be thorough."

I knew by the static that poured from the speaker that Orias was using his magic to do a sweep of the office. A minute later he said, "If they did leave something, it's no longer working."

I heard Adele pick up her phone, her long nails tapping against the buttons as she dialed. I enhanced my hearing so I was just able to pick out a voice on the other end.

"Hello."

I couldn't identify the voice, but Adele's next words left no doubt about who it was.

"Darling, you will never believe who just left my office. Nikolas Danshov...and your daughter."

There was a pause. "My daughter?"

"Yes, your daughter, Sara." Adele sounded a little hurt. "Why did you never tell me you had a child?"

"You know I don't like to talk about that time in my life."

"I understand wanting to leave the past behind, but you could have told your oldest friend. God knows we've shared everything else."

"What...is she like?" Madeline asked.

Adele laughed. "She doesn't look like you, but she certainly has your fire. And she is an inquisitive little thing. She wanted to know all about my friendship with you."

"Did you tell them you knew me?"

A sigh. "I didn't have much choice. She showed up with pictures of us from that summer in San Diego. I could hardly lie about them."

Madeline's voice rose. "You didn't tell them about —"

"Of course, I didn't tell them about that. How can you even ask?"

"If they found out we're friends they'll find me next. I need to move again," Madeline said.

"No, I think you should stay where you are for now," Adele argued. "No one knows I own that place, and they'd never expect you to go there."

"Maybe I should go see Orias again," Madeline suggested.

"Orias's glamour is good for another month at least. Here, talk to him yourself."

"Madeline, stop worrying," Orias said confidently. "None but a faerie could see through my magic."

The voice on the other end grew so faint I couldn't make out the words. It had to be his magic interfering with the connection.

"Haven't my glamours kept you hidden all these years?" he said.

Madeline said something I couldn't hear.

"As I've told you many times, no one's magic is strong enough to undo that. I'm the strongest warlock I know, and I've been trying for years. No, I'm not giving up. I'll let you know if I come up with anything."

He handed the phone back to Adele.

"Stop worrying, darling," she crooned. "Orias and I have your back as always. Now I have to go and open the club. I'll catch up with you in a few days. Night."

Chris turned off the recording when Adele began discussing club business with her bartender. He looked at me. "What do you think?"

"I think we need to take a closer look into Adele's real estate holdings."

I put the vehicle in drive, wishing Adele or Madeline had given us some hint about where Madeline was. I glanced at Sara in the rearview mirror to see how she was after hearing Adele talk to her mother. But Sara appeared to be more thoughtful than upset.

"Why would Adele say that no one would expect Madeline to be wherever she is?" she asked. "Is there a place Madeline would not want to go?"

"Wherever the Master is would be my first guess," Jordan said.

Chris shook his head. "Madeline wouldn't be foolish enough to hide near the Master. She's evaded him this long by being smarter than that."

"She doesn't want us to find her either, so maybe she's hiding near one of our strongholds," Jordan said. "Hell, maybe she's in Boise."

I nodded. "That is a possibility."

Perhaps that was how Madeline had hidden from everyone all this time.

The Master wouldn't want to get too near one of our strongholds, and we wouldn't think to look that close to home.

"We should narrow our search to places near our compounds, see if Adele has property in any of them."

Chris called Raoul and told him to dig around more in Adele's holdings. Raoul worked closely with Dax, so I knew I didn't have to call the security guy. If anyone could find something, it was Dax.

As soon as Chris hung up, Sara took out her phone and called her friend David, who had also been privy to her vigilante activities. She'd assured me that David had not been happy about it, and he had asked her more than once to stop.

I didn't need my Mori hearing to pick out what David was saying. I listened to them talk about Adele's properties in New York, Miami, and San Diego, places we already knew about. Sara told him Madeline might be hiding out at a property we didn't know about. David said he'd see what he could find and get back to us. I had to admit, the guy was dedicated to finding Madeline.

"Something else I'd like to know is what Orias has been trying to undo for years for Madeline," Chris said almost to himself.

"I'd like to know that myself. Orias is a powerful warlock. If he can't undo something, it must be very strong magic."

I thought back to the exchange between Sara and the warlock. "By the way, what was he talking about back there when he said you put a gag on him? And what did you do to his demon?"

She gave me a sheepish smile. "Oh, that. I might have made him take a binding oath that prevented him from telling anyone we were there."

I frowned. "What kind of oath?"

"You ever hear of the White Oath?" she asked.

I shook my head, not sure I wanted to know.

"When a warlock takes the White Oath, he can't break it, even if you torture him. It's the only oath that can hold them to their word. It's something I learned from Remy."

I stared at her. It was one thing to know about such an oath, but to make a warlock like Orias take it was a gutsy move. Most people wouldn't dare try to coerce someone who got his power from an upper demon.

"And what did you do to upset his demon?" I asked her.

Jordan made a sound of disgust. "That bastard had the rest of us tied up, so Sara took his demon hostage until he let us go."

Chris's expression of disbelief mirrored mine as he turned to look at Sara. "You took an upper demon hostage? This I have to hear."

So did I.

"It wasn't like I actually saw the demon. Orias already had it trapped in a lamp. I took the lamp and shook it up a little." She smiled mischievously.

"Demons really don't like Fae magic."

"No, I would guess not," I said dryly as a cold tingle ran down my spine. I'd had a small taste of her power, and that had been before her *liannan*. I could only imagine how it would feel to a demon trapped in a lamp.

I didn't want to think about what might have happened if the demon had escaped its prison. Mori demons were strong, but upper demons were the most powerful of demon kind, which was why warlocks wanted them.

"How do you fit a demon in a lamp anyway?" Jordan mused out loud.

"It takes a spell cast by a very crafty and powerful warlock."

I'd witnessed the ritual, and it was complicated and dangerous. More than once I'd been called to deal with a demon summoning gone bad. Those never ended well for the warlock. It was almost impossible to kill summoned demons in their non-corporeal form, so you had to send them back to their dimension. Not an easy feat, and one that only an experienced warlock or shaman could handle. In fact, we'd called on Orias many times over the years to assist in that area.

"If Madeline is using his glamours, how was Sara's friend David able to get that picture of her in Vancouver?" Chris asked.

"Orias told us his spells only last a month because they are so strong," Sara replied. "Maybe we were able to catch her as one was wearing off."

He nodded. "Makes sense. Let's hope she is between glamours when we find her or we'll never be able to recognize her."

"No problem. I can see through his magic."

What? I stared at Sara over my shoulder. "You can?"

"I can see through all glamours," she said as if it was no big deal. "I thought you knew that."

I turned my attention back to the road. "You forgot to share that piece of information with us."

"She saw right through the glamour Orias had on his place in New Mexico," Jordan told us. "The rest of us couldn't see a thing, and we thought she was nuts when she said there was a building there."

I shook my head, not sure why I was still surprised by her revelations.

"Sara, when we get home, we're going to have a long talk about all the things you've *forgotten* to mention."

She and Jordan shared a laugh. Chris snickered, and I gave him a pained look.

He held up his hands. "Don't look at me. You're the one who told Tristan it was okay for the two of them to stay together."

Sara's phone rang. She spoke to David for a minute then put him on speaker so the rest of us could hear their conversation.

"So here is what we found. In the last year, Adele has flown to Las Vegas twice by private charter. She stayed there for three days on one trip and five on another."

"Maybe she just likes to gamble," Jordan said.

"Maybe. What I do know is she didn't stay at any of the big hotels during her trips, and she doesn't strike me as a person who would charter a jet only to stay in a cheap hotel."

"She's not." Sara replied. "Where do you think she stayed?"

"We think she has a residence there," David said. "If anyone can find it, Kelvan can. You can't hide much from him once he's on your trail."

Las Vegas? It made sense. The place was crawling with vampires and Mohiri. No one would think to look for Madeline there, as long as she stayed out of sight.

"How long do you think it will take?" Chris asked him.

"Oh yeah!" David hooted. "I think this is a new record for him."

"He found something?" Sara asked breathlessly.

David typed something. "Adele owns a luxury condo in Las Vegas, overlooking the Strip. She bought it three years ago under the name Elizabeth Cummings."

"What makes you think this woman and Adele are the same person?" I asked.

"Elizabeth Cummings is one of the identities Adele used before she took her current one," he said. "Succubi have to create a new identity every few decades, especially if they are a businesswoman like Adele. She went by Elizabeth Cummings back in the forties."

"How the hell did you find that?" Chris asked. "Even our records on her don't go back that far."

David chuckled. "Yours don't, but demons have their own archives."

I'd been impressed by Sara and her friends when they found Madeline in Vancouver, but this gave me a whole new level of respect for them. It wasn't lost on me that we wouldn't have found this information without the help of a demon Sara had befriended. No demon would have come forth and offered to help us otherwise.

Sara laughed. "You guys are scary sometimes, you know that? I'm *really* glad you're on my side."

"We decided it was more fun to use our power for good instead of evil," he retorted.

Jordan leaned forward and grabbed the back of my seat.

"So, are we going to Vegas?"

CHAPTER 41

"ARE YOU READY?"

Sara turned away from the tall glass building to look at me. "I've been ready for this for a long time."

Her smile didn't hide the uncertainty in her eyes, not that anyone could blame her for what she was feeling. In a few minutes, she was going to come face-to-face with the mother who'd abandoned her. She kept saying she only wanted to see Madeline to ask her about the Master, but I could feel her pain, even if she didn't realize it was there.

I looked at Geoffrey over the hood of the SUV, and he nodded to let me know his team would take up watch outside. He'd met us at McCarren Airport to provide us with an escort and extra backup. Vegas was a dangerous place these days, and Sara wouldn't be here at all if it was up to me. But she wanted to be the one to talk to Madeline, and God knew she'd earned that right.

We walk into the building's marble lobby, followed closely by Chris and Jordan, with Elijah and Noah taking up the lead. Sara was quiet as we took the elevator up to the forty-second floor. I reached for her hand and gave it a reassuring squeeze when we got off the elevator and walked the short distance to Adele's condo.

Sara and I stood in front of the door, and everyone else stayed a few yards away. I rang the doorbell, and we waited. After a minute, I knocked.

"Madeline, we've had our people watching this place, so we know you're in there," I called to her. "We just want to talk."

When no one came to the door, Sara impatiently stepped in front of me.

"An hour of your time, and we'll be out of your life forever. You owe me that much...*Mom*."

The locks disengaged, and the door opened an inch.

"I'm sorry but you have the wrong address," said a female voice I didn't recognize. "My name is Claire and I have no children."

"Now that really hurts," Sara replied with thinly veiled sarcasm.

The woman started to shut the door. "I don't know who you are, but I'm calling the police if you don't leave."

Sara put a hand on the door and leaned in. "Before you do that, I think you should know I can see through glamours…even Orias's."

There was a sharp inhale before the door shut. A few seconds later, it opened fully to reveal a tall, thirtysomething brunette wearing blue pants and a cream-colored top. If I didn't know better, I would never guess she was Madeline.

"Come in," she said stiffly.

She locked the door after we entered and led us into a living room with large windows overlooking the Strip. Sara and I sat on a leather couch while Madeline took the chair.

She studied Sara for a moment before she spoke. "You look like Daniel."

"I know," Sara said, unsmiling. I tried to imagine what she was feeling, but her face was almost expressionless.

Madeline looked at me. "It's been a long time, Nikolas."

I smiled. "It has. I'd say you look well, but I can't see past the glamour."

She frowned and looked at Sara again. "And how is it that you can? Did Orias give you something to see past it? Did he tell you where I was? I know Adele would never betray me."

Sara shook her head. "Orias and I are not exactly on the best of terms, and Adele didn't give you up. She is amazingly loyal to you."

"Then how did you find me? How can you see me now?" Madeline demanded.

"Some very resourceful friends of mine found you for me. As for how I can see you, that's irrelevant." She stared intently at her mother. "You know the identity of a Master and we want to know who he is."

Madeline shook her head, and Sara's voice grew hard.

"He had my dad killed. *Your* husband. He's spent the last six months trying to kill me and everyone I love. I know family means nothing to you, but you must have felt something for my dad once upon a time."

Madeline blanched. "You know nothing about what I felt for him."

Sara's hands clenched tightly in her lap. I wanted to reach over and offer the comfort of my touch, but I stayed where I was. She needed to do this her own way.

"You're right. I don't. I don't know how you can love someone and hurt them so completely. I don't know how you can stand back while they are murdered and let the one responsible walk free so he can destroy other families. I have no idea what a person who does something like that is feeling. So why don't you enlighten me?"

472

For a moment, Madeline looked like she was at a loss for words. "I know you are angry because I left you –"

Sara's angry laugh cut her off. "I don't even remember you. My dad gave me all the love I needed until *they* took him from me. You have the information I need to find them, and that is the *only* reason I'm here now."

No one spoke for a long moment.

"I loved him," Madeline said softly.

"What?"

"Your father. I met him in college. I knew he was human and it could never work between us, but he was… He had a way of making you feel like you were the only person in his world."

She cleared her throat delicately. "I should not have married him, but I was in love, and I couldn't think of leaving him. I knew it wouldn't be long before he realized I was different, so a month before our wedding, I told him what I was."

"He knew what you were?" Sara asked in surprise.

Madeline had to have loved Sara's father deeply to expose herself to him like that. The Madeline I'd known had always been too shallow for those kinds of feelings. But then, love had a way of changing a person. I knew that firsthand.

"I told him I was Mohiri, but not about my Mori because I didn't think he could cope with that," Madeline said. "It was a struggle for him to learn about the real world, but he said what I was didn't matter to him. Even when I said I would not age, he wanted me to stay. So we got married. Those two years were the happiest of my life."

She looked almost regretful for what she was about to say next.

"I was content with just the two of us, but Daniel wanted a child. He talked about how wonderful it would be, and I loved him so much that I let myself believe it was what I wanted, too. The day you were born, he was the happiest I'd ever seen him. I thought that would be enough for me to be happy too, but I was wrong. I loved my daughter – you, but being a mother wasn't something I had ever wanted. I did it for two years, and then I couldn't handle it anymore."

I could stay quiet no longer. "You left your child with a human who had no idea what would happen to her when her Mori emerged."

Madeline flinched at my harsh tone. "I could sense no Mori in her. I thought she was human like her father."

She looked at Sara, her eyes sad. "I came back sometimes to see how the two of you were doing, but neither of you knew it. If I'd seen a sign that you were different, I would have gone to your father. You looked happy together."

Sara swallowed hard. "We were happy. Until he was killed."

Madeline's face became pinched. "I went to him and warned him he might be in danger. He didn't believe me. The last thing I wanted was for him to get hurt."

"He didn't get hurt, Madeline. He got murdered."

The pain in Sara's voice pulled at me. It was all I could do not to slide over and put an arm around her.

Madeline lurched from her chair and went to the window. Outside, rain was coming down in torrents, blurring the city lights.

"Part of me died that day," she said hoarsely. "No matter what had happened between us, Daniel was the only man I ever loved."

"Did you even care about what happened to your daughter after he died?" I asked.

I understood her pain over losing the man she loved. I'd go crazy if anything happened to Sara. But Madeline was a mother. She should have protected her daughter above all else.

She scowled at me. "Of course I did! Sara disappeared after her father died, and there was no trace of her. I thought she had died, too, at first. I don't know why I forgot about Daniel's brother, Nate, but it was years later when I remembered him."

Sara had told me Aine had erased all traces of her after her father was killed to keep her safe from the vampires. That was why the newspaper articles had no mention of a child, and people forgot Daniel had a brother. Even Sara's own mother had forgotten about him.

I rested my arms on my knees. "Tell us about the Master."

Madeline's face turned ashen. "I-I can't."

"Yes, you can." Sara's voice rose. "Why are you protecting him?"

Madeline began to pace, her face tight with fear. "I'm not protecting him. You don't understand. I can't tell you because I don't know who he is."

"You're lying. A day before my dad was killed, you went to visit a friend of yours in Portland and you told him you knew about the Master."

Madeline stared at her. "Jiro Ito? How do you know about him?"

"His son, David, was there and he overheard you talking to his father. You said you knew the identity of a Master, and you needed the money he was holding for you so you could disappear."

"Jiro's son was there?" She paused as if she was trying to remember that day. "He misunderstood what I said. I told Jiro that a Master was after me because I'd seen him, but that I didn't know who he was."

"That makes no sense," Sara argued. "If you saw him, you can describe him. And how did you come to see him in the first place or even know he was a Master?"

The air was thick with fear when Madeline sat again and began to tell us her story.

"I was in New York to see Adele, who was opening a new night club there, and I ended up at a party on the Upper East Side. I –"

She swallowed convulsively, real terror in her eyes. "Something happened to me at the party. One minute I was having a drink, and the next I woke up in a cage in the basement of a place I didn't know. There were vampires everywhere, but none of them talked to me until one named Eli came in. He taunted me about being his Master's new toy. When I heard the word 'Master' I knew I was dead."

"Khristu!"

"A few hours later, they took me upstairs to meet the Master. I remember walking into a room and seeing him sitting by the fireplace." Her voice faltered. "I remember every minute I was tortured by him for two days. I remember wishing to die. But I can't remember anything about him."

"I'm sorry," Sara said softly. "Did they drug you to make you forget?"

Madeline shook her head. "He compelled me to forget him."

Sara turned her shocked gaze to me. "But we can't be compelled by vampires. Can we?"

"A Master is not a normal vampire," I reminded her. The vamhir demon in a Master was much stronger than those in a normal vampire. No one knew what made them so powerful, but they could compel other vampires and most demons, including ours.

Madeline trembled. "He made sure I remembered everything about my time there, except him. He said he was going to enjoy playing with me for a long time."

Lightning lit up the room, and Sara jumped. The three of us were on edge after hearing Madeline's story.

"How did you escape?" I asked Madeline kindly, seeing how difficult this was for her.

"I didn't. He released me."

I stared at her in disbelief.

"He let you go?" Sara asked.

Madeline's voice cracked. "Something happened. I don't know what. I was chained in his sitting room and I heard voices outside. Then he came in and said something that made me go to sleep. I woke up in Central Park filled with an overwhelming urge to run. The first thing I did was go to Portland to warn Daniel. I've been running ever since."

"Madeline, why didn't you go home?" I asked her. "Tristan would do anything to keep you safe."

"Whatever *he* did to me made me afraid to trust anyone, especially the Mohiri. Adele is my closest friend, and I can't even trust her completely."

For a moment, anger replaced the fear in her eyes. "He stole that from me. He released me from my chains, but he still robbed me of my freedom. Until I can get rid of this compulsion, I'll never be free."

I swore silently as the meaning of her words sank in. Sara was going to be devastated when she realized it, too. We'd chased Madeline for months, and she would never be able to tell us who the Master was.

"Orias is trying to find a way to break the Master's compulsion, isn't he?" Sara asked her.

"He's been working on it for ten years, but nothing can break it."

"The only thing that can break a Master's compulsion is his death," I said.

Sara paled as realization set in. "She can't tell us where he is unless she can break the compulsion, but in order to break it he has to die?"

"Yes."

Her shoulders sagged, and she looked away. It killed me to see her disappointment after all she'd been through to find Madeline.

"Are you okay?" I asked her.

She made a brave attempt at a smile.

"We'll find him," I promised. "It'll just take a little longer than we thought."

"So you are Mohiri after all," Madeline said, reminding me of her presence. "I'm glad you found our people, Sara."

Sara's smile was real this time. "Actually, it was Nikolas who found me."

She placed her hand between us on the couch, and I covered it with mine. I gave her hand a light squeeze, and she laced our fingers together.

Madeline stared at our joined hands and gave us a questioning look. When neither of us spoke, she said, "What will you do now?"

I smiled at Sara. "We'll keep looking. Keep fighting."

"We found you. We'll find him, too," Sara said. She let go of my hand as she stood. "We should be going."

Madeline nodded and walked us to the door.

"Sara, for what it's worth, I really did love your father. And I loved you, too. I still do."

Despite her anger at Madeline and her terrible disappointment, Sara raised her hand graciously to her mother, reminding me again why I loved her so much.

"Thank you for talking to us. I hope Orias can find a way to help you," she said sincerely.

Madeline took the offered hand, her voice cracking. "Thank you."

"Good-bye, Madeline," Sara said then walked out.

I nodded at Madeline as I followed Sara, and I felt a surge of pity for the woman. She'd given up everyone she loved in her life because of her selfishness: the father who adored her, the husband who had worshiped her, and the daughter who would have loved her unconditionally.

Not getting to know her daughter was her greatest loss. Sara had such a capacity for love and a light within her that made the world a brighter place.

Madeline could have had that love freely, but she'd thrown it away.

I would never take the love I'd been given for granted, and every day God gave me with Sara, I'd make sure she knew it.

Jordan came up to us as soon as the door closed. "What did she say?"

"Not here," I said, seeing how tired Sara looked. "We'll talk outside."

We dashed through the rain and climbed into the SUV. Sara was subdued on the seat beside me, so I filled the others in as Geoffrey drove us back to the hangar at the airport. When we got there, Sara went directly into the plane, and I went to talk to our pilot.

"The tower said there are some big storms coming through, backing up air traffic," the pilot said apologetically. "We probably won't get clearance to leave for three or four hours."

"Come back to the safe house for the night," Geoffrey suggested. "It's better than hanging around here."

I told the others about the change in plans and went to find Sara. She was reclined in a seat in the last row with her eyes closed. I was loath to disturb her, but she couldn't stay here all night.

I said her name as I sat beside her. She opened her eyes and gave me a questioning look.

"We've got some bad electrical storms moving through the area, so we're grounded for a few hours, at least. Geoffrey's team has a safe house nearby, and we're going to wait out the storm there. It's more comfortable than an airport hangar."

"Okay."

"You did well tonight." I brushed damp hair from her face. "I know that was harder for you than you're letting on."

"It was," she whispered.

I didn't think I'd ever seen her this disheartened, and I wasn't sure what to say to help her feel better. Her reticence told me she didn't want to talk about it yet, so I'd wait until she was ready.

"Come on."

I stood and held out my hand to her. She let me help her out of the seat and quietly followed me to the SUV. Jordan gave her a worried look, and I smiled at the other girl to let her know Sara was okay.

The safe house was the same one Chris and I had stayed at in the fall. The rain was coming down in heavy sheets so Geoffrey pulled into the garage. Normally, he wouldn't bother, but I think even he was worried about Sara, who hadn't spoken since we left the plane.

"How is she?" Chris asked in a low voice as Sara entered the house ahead of us.

"It wasn't easy for her. She needs some time."

"So what now?"

I shrugged. "Now we start over. Madeline said she was grabbed by the

Master in New York City. He could be long gone by now, but it's as good a place to start as any."

When we entered the house, Sara was nowhere in sight, although I could sense her nearby. I talked to Chris and Geoffrey for a minute, and then I called Vivian to fill her in on what Madeline had told us about the Master. We talked for a few minutes, and then I went to look for Sara.

It wasn't hard to find her in the den off the main hallway. I entered the dark room and sat on my haunches in front of the couch where she lay.

"Why are you hiding in here alone?" I asked, though I already knew the answer.

"If I was hiding, I'd be behind the couch."

I smiled at her attempt at levity. "You'd never hide behind a couch."

"True," she said with a sad smile. "There is no dignity in lying in dust bunnies."

"Want some company?"

I'd understand if she wanted to be alone, but the pain I felt through the bond told me that wasn't the case. She was hurting, and all I wanted to do was ease her pain.

"Behind the couch?"

"Wherever you want."

"Yes," she said softly.

She started to sit up, but I had other plans. The leather couch wasn't really big enough for two people, a fact which worked in my favor. I lay on my side behind her, using one arm to pillow her head and wrapping the other around her waist to pull her back against me. Her curves fit my body like she'd been made for me.

"Comfortable?" I asked when she relaxed against me.

"Yes," she whispered.

"Do you want to talk about her?"

At first, I didn't think she was going to respond. I was content to hold her until she was ready to talk.

"She wasn't what I expected. I pity her. Except for Adele, she has no one, and she spends her life running and afraid and regretting the love she gave up. I think of her and I realize how lucky I am to have you and everyone else in my life."

"That's not luck," I said. "You have so many people who love you because you're a good person. Madeline was always selfish. She proved that when she left home the way she did, and with her behavior since then. I'm not saying she deserves the things that have happened to her, but I do believe she brought most of them on herself. That you can feel sad for her after all you've been through shows how kind you are."

She was quiet for a moment. "Can I ask you something?"

"Anything."

She drew in a deep breath. "How do you always know when I need you?"

My heart squeezed, and I pulled her closer. "When you're hurting, I feel it."

"You do?"

I smiled at the wonder in her voice and leaned in to kiss her forehead. "Yes. So don't ever try to hide your pain from me."

"Why can't I do the same with you?"

"You will, someday."

One day soon we were going to complete the bond, and nothing would ever come between us again. She would never have to question my love for her because she'd feel it without me uttering a word.

She snuggled closer to me. "I love you, Nikolas."

I cupped her chin and turned her face toward mine. "I love you too, *moy malen'kiy voin*," I said before I kissed her tenderly.

She closed her eyes. After several minutes passed, I thought she'd fallen asleep, until she spoke softly.

"What do we do now?"

"I don't know," I said honestly. "But we'll figure it out together. Like you told Madeline, you found her when no one else could. We'll go back to California and come up with a plan for what to do next."

Maybe we could enlist the help of her friend David. He'd proven to be an invaluable ally, and he was the one who'd ultimately lead us to Madeline. If I could convince him to work with Dax, there was no telling what the two of them could do.

"I don't want to go back to California."

Her hoarse declaration took me by surprise. "Where do you want to go?"

She turned in my arms until she was on her back. Lightning lit up the room, revealing the tears gathering in her eyes.

"Can we go home?"

Home. I had a sudden image of her things spread around my apartment. Our apartment.

"I thought you'd never ask."

I lowered my head to brush my lips across hers. Her hand came up to hold the back of my neck, and the tender kiss turned into a sensual exploration that left us both breathing a little faster.

She protested softly when I broke the kiss, but she deserved a lot more than heated groping on a couch. Tomorrow, we were going home. Tomorrow night, I was going to make love to her in our bed and sleep with her in my arms. And that was worth waiting for.

CHAPTER 42

I STAYED WITH Sara until she fell asleep, and then I went to notify the pilot we would be flying to Boise instead of California. After that, I called Raoul and asked him to have our things and Sara's cat sent on to Westhorne. He was also going to take over running the command center, but they were going to move it to Los Angeles now that they didn't need to be close to Eldeorin's house.

"You coming with us to Westhorne or heading back to California?" I asked Chris after all the arrangements had been made. All we were waiting for now was word from the pilot that we could depart.

"I'll make sure you two lovebirds get home safe and sound, and then I'll probably go back to LA by way of Longstone."

He gave me a sly look. "Something tells me you won't be leaving home again for a while."

I didn't disagree with him. Males stayed close to their mates for the first year or so after completing the bond, and I had a feeling I wasn't going to be any different. That didn't mean we had to stay at Westhorne, however, and I hoped to persuade Sara to take a trip to Russia to meet my parents. I'd be sure to phrase it a lot differently this time.

"Is Sara comfortable in the den?" Geoffrey asked. "She's welcome to use my bedroom until you leave."

"Thanks, but it shouldn't be much longer."

I heard running feet a second before Sara screamed, "Vampires!"

I ran to her as she burst into the living room. "Where? How many?"

"Everywhere," she gasped. "At least fifteen."

Fifteen? Jesus, it was another ambush.

"How does she know that?" Geoffrey demanded.

"No time to explain. Get ready."

Chris and I grabbed our weapons. I went back to Sara, and he ran to take up a position by the large window.

"Chris?" I asked as I strapped on my knife belt.

"Nothing yet."

I began issuing orders, not caring this was Geoffrey's command. I was taking no chances with Sara and Jordan here, even if they had proven themselves to be more than capable fighters.

"We have at least fifteen hostiles incoming," I shouted as warriors spilled into the living room. "Jordan and Abigail, you're with Chris. Elijah, you, Joseph, and Noah cover upstairs. Travis and Oliver, take the kitchen. Geoffrey and I will cover the back."

"What about me?" Sara asked.

Geoffrey held out a sword to her. "Can you fight?"

She put up her hands. "Not with that thing."

I touched her arm. "Sara, you stay with me. Do not leave my sight."

For once she didn't argue. Grabbing a knife from Geoffrey, she followed us just as a window broke at the back of the house. We ran into the den to see two vampires come through the window. My blood chilled at the thought that Sara had been sleeping in here a few minutes ago.

I went after the first vampire, letting Geoffrey worry about the second one. There wasn't a lot of fighting room in the den so I had to watch where I put my sword. Sara stayed by the door where I could see her out of the corner of my eye as I fought.

The vampire looked surprised to see two armed warriors waiting for him. I took advantage of his hesitation and sliced open his gut. Then I brought my blade around again and took his head from his shoulders.

As soon as he went down, two more vampires leapt through the window. I checked to see where Sara was before I moved in to meet the newest threat. They were faster than the first one, but there was no way they were getting past me with Sara standing a few feet away.

Over the thunder and rain, I could hear screams and fighting in the rest of the house, but I blocked them out to concentrate on the two vampires circling me.

The nearest one feinted at me from my left, and his friend tried to use that as an opportunity to come in from my right. My sword flashed, but there was barely enough room to swing with any force.

The vampires realized that too, and they smiled, showing me their fangs.

Holding my sword in one hand, I unsheathed my long knife with my other hand.

In the hallway, a vampire screamed.

Sara.

Someone crashed into a wall. Fear knotted my stomach, and I spun to the empty doorway, forgetting the danger behind me.

A familiar figure ran past the door toward the living room. I started after her.

"Nikolas," Geoffrey grunted.

I turned back to the room just as both vampires came at me at once. Desperate to finish the fight, I brought both blades up – my sword to block and my knife to maim.

The vampire on my left screamed as my knife plunged between his ribs. The strike was too low to hit his heart, but it still had to hurt like the devil.

He staggered back, and I spun to the one who had tried to get past my sword. Blood dripped from one of his hands where four of his fingers used to be.

He snarled and lunged at me again, and I used his forward momentum against him. My sword came down, cutting his arm off at the shoulder. Before he could scream in pain, I skewered him through the heart.

I turned back to the one I'd knifed as he started to regain his footing. I leapt at him, striking out with the knife again. This time my aim was perfect, and he sank to the floor in a heap.

Leaving Geoffrey to finish off his opponent, I raced into the hallway where a dead vampire was crumpled against the wall.

"Sara?" I shouted, running toward the front of the house.

A vampire jumped out of the hall bathroom, directly into my path. I was moving so fast I slammed into him, knocking us both off balance.

Dropping my sword, I wrapped an arm around his neck and snapped it. He went limp, but he'd be back on his feet in thirty minutes if I left him like that. I picked up my sword and finished the job.

Heart pounding, I ran into the living room to find half a dozen dead vampires and no sign of Sara. People stood in front of the broken window staring in shock at something on the front lawn.

No. A bellow of rage tore from my throat. People scattered as I ran to the window and jumped through it. Ignoring the bodies littering the ground, my gaze zeroed in on Sara. My knees weakened when I saw her standing there, looking unharmed.

She didn't move as I strode to her. Trembling, I pulled her into my arms, needing to reassure my Mori and myself she was okay. Her arms immediately crept up around my neck, pulling my head down to her.

"I love you," she said. Then her lips met mine.

Her touch dismantled my rage, and her kiss set me aflame with a different kind of heat. I crushed her to me, my hands roving over her back, only vaguely aware of the rain plastering our hair and clothes to our bodies. She clung to me, wrapping her legs around my waist as she made me forget everything but the two of us.

My sanity returned to me, and I separated our mouths, breathing harshly. "You were supposed to stay with me."

Her look was anything but apologetic. "You didn't need my help, and someone had to save Chris's ass. Again."

I opened my mouth, but all that came out was a groan. *She's going to be the death of me.*

I rested my forehead against hers. "Now I know why Nate's going gray. At this rate, I'll be white before him."

She smiled evilly. "Well, there's always *Clairol for Men.*"

I stared at her, and she burst into laughter before she burrowed her face against my throat. Her hot breath on my skin made me extremely thankful for the cold rain drenching us.

Chris walked up to us, chuckling and shaking his head. "Do you two want us to give you some privacy?"

I grinned at him as Sara lifted her head to say something.

Her eyes widened, and she looked down as if realizing for the first time where she was.

Satisfaction filled me, knowing I'd done that to her. Her eyes lifted to mine, and I smiled as my hands slid down to cup her firm bottom.

"On second thought, this might be worth a few gray hairs."

Her brows came together in an unconvincing scowl, and she removed her legs from around my waist.

Ignoring her silent demand to be set down, I held her for a moment, relishing the feel of her body flush against mine.

Her scowl deepened as I lowered her to the ground. Unable to resist, I kissed her nose before finally letting her go.

Geoffrey walked across the lawn toward us, his mouth set in a grim line.

"How many?" I asked him.

"Fifteen." He rubbed his head and stared at the bodies on the grass. "Jesus! If you and your team hadn't been here, it would have been a massacre."

"Or maybe they came *because* we were here," Chris said.

"How did you know?" Geoffrey asked Sara. "You said fifteen were coming. How could you possibly guess that?"

"I wasn't guessing..." Her eyes narrowed, and she rubbed her chest. "I was wrong. There were sixteen. There's still one here."

Elijah stood in the doorway. "The house is clear."

"Chris, can you and Elijah do a sweep out here to be safe?" I asked as Sara walked toward the house, her lips pursed in concentration.

I followed her because her intuition, or radar as she called it, was never wrong.

She entered the house and stood motionless for several seconds. Then she pointed at the closed door to the basement where the control room was located. "There."

Geoffrey shook his head. "There's no way for anyone to get in down there. The basement windows are all too small."

She put her hands on her hips. "Then one tried to go out that way and got trapped, because there is a vampire in that basement."

He looked at me, and I nodded.

"We'll have to flush him out," he said. "Abigail and I will go down, and the rest of you keep an eye on this door in case he comes through it."

"We need to find out how they found this place and if they knew who was here," I reminded him. "Unless you're in immediate danger, do not kill him."

I looked at Sara. "I don't suppose it would do any good to ask you to let the others handle this one."

She put up her hands and walked to the far side of the living room. "I've done enough killing for one night. This one is all yours."

The other warriors and I formed a semicircle in front of the basement door. Geoffrey opened the door, and he and Abigail disappeared through it.

Seconds later, a female vampire's scream was followed by the sounds of a struggle and a crash. The vampire cried out in pain.

"We have her," Geoffrey called.

The rest of us relaxed, and I went to stand by Sara.

"What will they do with her?" she asked, still watching the basement door.

"They'll confine her and wait until she gets hungry to see if she'll talk."

I looked through the window as the other Vegas team came roaring up in an SUV. The four warriors leapt out and dashed into the house. They skidded to a stop when they saw the damage.

"Goddamn!" Evan, a dark-haired warrior with short, spiked hair, let out a whistle. "We missed all the action."

"Fuck the action." Jackson ran past us to the stairs. "If my *Martin* has a scratch on it, I'm going to find some vampire ass to kick."

I grinned at the blond warrior who loved his guitar almost as much as he loved his mother.

Chris waved me over, and the two of us righted an overturned couch. Then we went outside to drag bodies from the front lawn to the garage. The last thing we needed was for someone to drive by and see a pile of bodies on the lawn before we could dispose of them. We were lucky as it was that the houses on this street were spaced far apart, and that no one had come to investigate. Lucky too that the storm had probably camouflaged most of the noise.

Sara was standing where I'd left her when I went back to the living room. The cleanup was underway, and she looked around as if she wasn't sure what she was supposed to be doing.

"Are we staying here?" she asked me.

"We're leaving once we help get the place secured. The rest of them will pack up and move to another safe house in the morning."

I would have left for the airport with her already, but the chances of another attack on the safe house were slim, especially now that all the warriors were here. The place was trashed, but it was probably the safest place in Vegas tonight.

It took all of us working together for two hours to clear out the bodies and cover most of the windows to keep the rain out. Sara and Jordan worked alongside us, neither of them complaining about the hard work, though I knew it had to be tiring after their long day and the attack.

Sara had been put through an emotional wringer in the last twelve hours, and I had no idea how she kept going. I hoped this was the last of the excitement for us until we got home.

As we were finishing up, the pilot called to let me know we could leave in the next hour.

I looked around for Sara. I couldn't wait to get her out of this city.

She came down the stairs a few minutes later, wearing dry clothes someone had loaned her. I hid my smile when I saw the rolled-up legs of her borrowed jeans.

She looked tired but otherwise okay as I made my way over to her.

"The storm is letting up, and the pilot says we can take off in an hour or so," I told her. "I'm going to call Tristan, and then we'll head over to the airport."

"Okay." Her smile told me I wasn't the only one eager to leave.

I took out my cell phone and frowned when I saw there was no signal, most likely due to the severe storms. I walked out to the covered deck at the back of the house to call Tristan, who still didn't know we were coming home or that we'd talked to Madeline. I'd called him from the plane to tell him we were on the way to Las Vegas and that we had a lead on Madeline. But so much had happened since then I hadn't been able to update him.

The vampire screamed as I stepped outside and closed the door behind me. Geoffrey and Abigail had been down in the basement with her this whole time, questioning her, and I could imagine what interrogation tactics they were using now. Silver probably. It was clean, easy, and effective. None of us liked that part of our job, but you had to do unpleasant things when you fought a war like this one.

Someone shouted inside the house. It was followed by a second one, and then a third.

I ran inside and down the hall to the living room as the vampire screamed again, closer this time.

The first thing I saw was Geoffrey coming through the open basement door. Then I saw the crowd gathered in front of the kitchen, bodies crouched in attack positions.

A pit opened in my stomach. I pushed my way through the warriors to the kitchen as a flash lit up the room, and the vampire sagged against Sara.

"Damn it, Sara. There are a dozen warriors here. You couldn't let one of them handle this?"

Her glare told me what she thought of my question. "Look at her, Nikolas. She's even smaller than I am. Do you think I can't handle one little vampire?"

Jackson spoke up. "Don't answer that, my man. It's a trap."

I shot him a hard look, though he had a point. Not that it was a trap, but that Sara *was* capable of holding her own against the vampire. Arguing with her just because I still had trouble with her fighting was not going to help. It would only make her think I doubted her in front of everyone.

The vampire moaned, alerting me to the fact she was not unconscious.

"We need to get her secured again before she comes to," I said to Geoffrey as he and I entered the kitchen. "How the hell did she escape in the first place?"

He rubbed his jaw. "She picked the lock on the shackles. I don't know how she did it. Most vampires can't handle silver that long."

Sara smiled wanly. "Desperation will make you do a lot of things you couldn't do before."

Evan joined us in the kitchen, and he and Geoffrey moved to take the vampire from Sara.

"Good job, Sara. We'll take her now," Geoffrey said.

The vampire woke up and bared her fangs at us as she tried to twist away from Sara. Before anyone could grab her, Sara sent another jolt of power into her, knocking her out again. The ease with which she handled the vampire and the control she displayed impressed the hell out of me.

Even more impressive was how cool-headed and fearless she was, holding a vampire in her arms. Every warrior there, myself included, was tense and ready to jump in at the slightest provocation. Sara could have been holding a life-sized doll for all it seemed to affect her.

Geoffrey whistled under his breath. "That's some trick."

"You should see me pull a rabbit from a hat," she joked.

Several people laughed, but the mood was still tense as Geoffrey and Evan took the vampire by the arms and relieved Sara of her burden.

"We'll make sure this one doesn't get loose again," Geoffrey said firmly. "Not sure if she's worth keeping, though."

"Why?" Sara asked.

He shrugged. "Some vampires break. Most don't. After a while you can tell the ones that will."

Jordan entered the kitchen. "Then why waste your time with her?"

"Because they can't take the chance of not getting information out of her," I explained.

"Wait," Sara called as Geoffrey and Evan dragged the vampire away. "Maybe I can get something out of her."

Geoffrey gave her a skeptical look. "How?"

I shook my head. "No."

I knew what it would take to get this vampire to crack, and Sara was too softhearted to do what needed to be done, even to a vampire. She had a weapon we didn't have, but that wouldn't help when she remembered this tomorrow or a year from now.

She gave me a puzzled look. "Nikolas, you said they need information. And it's not like she can hurt me."

I laid my hands on her shoulders. "You don't have the stomach for torture, and that's what it will take."

"Maybe not." She chewed her lip. "I could connect with the demon."

My stomach rolled as fear shot through me. "Absolutely not. Do I need to remind you what happened the last time you did that?" The memory of her lying on that cell floor after she'd healed Nate would haunt me for the rest of my life.

"No," she said slowly. "But I'm a *lot* stronger than I was that time, and I know what to expect now."

"No."

She laid her hands on my chest. "I know you're worried, but I've come so far since that thing with Nate. I've spent months working with Aine and Eldeorin, and I know what I can do."

My heart, my Mori, and every instinct yelled at me to take her away from here. In that moment, I relived every torturous hour spent waiting for her to wake up and not knowing if she would. The only thing that had made it bearable back then was knowing she had saved Nate. This wasn't the same. This was a random vampire who *might* have information we wanted. It wasn't worth the risk.

I looked into her eyes, which pleaded with me to trust her. She was confident she could do this, just as I was sure of myself as a warrior. And her power was much stronger than it had been back then, not to mention the control she'd displayed a few minutes ago.

"Sara has powers and abilities you'll never be able to comprehend. Don't underestimate her, warrior."

Eldeorin's words came back to me. As much as I hated to agree with him on anything, he was right in this. As a Mohiri, I couldn't understand her power, and that scared me because I'd never know if she was ready to face a situation like this one. I had to trust her to know.

I rested my forehead against hers. "Promise me you'll be careful."

"I promise."

"I mean it, Sara." I pulled back to look into her eyes. "If I have to sit by a hospital bed for another two days, I really will lock you up."

"That won't happen. Trust me."

Her smile did not reassure me. I let go of her shoulders and stepped back.

"What do we need to do?"

She waved at the kitchen floor near the island. "Just lay her here on the floor, and I'll do the rest."

I turned to Geoffrey. "Do as she asks."

He shot me a look that said he expected some answers later. When I nodded, he and Evan laid the vampire where Sara wanted her.

Sara looked at the vampire and then at me and the other warriors. "I need some room to do this. Can you all move to the living room?"

I was the last one out, and I stood outside the archway, refusing to go a step farther. Jordan stood beside me while the other warriors crowded in behind us, curious to see what Sara was going to do to the vampire.

Ignoring her audience, Sara knelt on the floor and placed her hands on the vampire's chest. Immediately, her hands began to glow, causing gasps and exclamations behind me.

The vampire opened her eyes, and I took a step into the kitchen. Sara's glow intensified, and the vampire's face contorted into a hideous silent scream.

"What the fuck?" Jackson croaked.

My body tensed and my stomach turned to rock as I waited for what would come next.

The glow coming from Sara's hand expanded until her whole body was encased in soft white light. Unlike before, when her power had exploded from her, it billowed out from her in undulating waves like a giant soap bubble that slowly enveloped her and the vampire.

"What the hell is that?" someone asked.

"What is she?" Geoffrey breathed.

Jordan looked up at me, her eyes wide with awe. "I heard about it, but I never imagined..."

"I know."

My eyes went back to the two shapes that were still visible but distorted through the bubble. Sara didn't move, but every now and then the vampire twitched as if it was being electrocuted.

Minutes ticked by. What was happening in there? Sara hadn't actually talked to the vamhir demon inside Nate; she'd seen and heard its memories. Was she doing that now, or was she trying to talk to it? Was it even possible for her to communicate with the demon in that way?

I shifted restlessly. She'd been connected to Nate for no more than a minute. At least five had passed since she laid her hands on the vampire.

The bubble suddenly grew brighter and hotter until it was impossible to look upon and unbearable to be near, forcing us to retreat several feet.

My throat went dry when I found myself shielding my eyes against the same sphere of light I'd seen in Nate's cell.

Oh God. I knew what she was about to do, and I was powerless to stop it.

"Holy Mother!" someone said as the sphere pulsed and the lights in the house flickered.

And then it was gone.

CHAPTER 43

SARA WAS SLUMPED motionless across the vampire, neither of them moving.

My heart stuttered as I knelt beside them and lifted her off the vampire. Turning her in my arms, I laid her on the tile floor. With shaking hands, I checked for a heartbeat, and I sagged when I felt her strong pulse.

A girl screamed.

I looked over into the terrified brown eyes of the vampire – no, the human girl – as she sat up and scrambled backward to cower against the cupboards. Wailing, she curled into a tight ball with her arms wrapped around her head.

No one approached her. Everyone seemed at a loss about what to do.

All I cared about was Sara.

"Sara, wake up." I patted her cheeks and gave her a gentle shake.

No response.

I brushed the hair from her face. "You promised you wouldn't do this. You need to open your eyes."

Nothing.

Desperately, I leaned over her and cupped her face with my hands. "Goddamnit, Sara, do not do this to me again."

Her eyelids flickered. Dazed green eyes stared into mine.

"Why am I on the floor?"

The relief that washed over me would have sent me to my knees, had I been standing. I hugged her to me, burying my face in her hair.

"Fifty years. I'm locking you up for the next fifty goddamn years."

"Can't breathe," she wheezed.

I lowered her to the floor and studied her face. "How do you feel?"

"Great." She blinked in confusion. "My butt is cold."

I smiled, almost giddy with relief. "We can't have that."

Sitting on the floor, I swept her up to settle her onto my lap. "Better?"

"Much better."

She let out a deep breath and leaned into me as if she hadn't the strength to do anything else. That was fine by me because I didn't want to let her go.

Our happy reunion was soon interrupted by the sobs of the girl Sara had healed. Sara pulled away to look behind me, letting out a gasp when she saw the girl. She tried to stand, but I held her close.

"It's not safe."

She touched my face. "Yes, it is. Trust me. She won't hurt anyone else."

I looked between her and the girl, unsure of what to do. The girl might not be a vampire anymore, but there was no telling what state her mind was in after decades of being trapped in her own body with a demon.

I released Sara, and she crawled over to the girl, approaching her slowly like you would a wounded animal. When she was a foot away, she stopped and spoke softly to the girl.

"Shhh, it's okay. You're safe now and no one is going to hurt you."

The girl began to cry harder. Sara reached out to lay a hand on her shoulder. "My name is Sara," she said in a soothing tone. "I know you're scared and confused, and I swear I won't let anything hurt you. I'm just going to sit here with you until you're feeling a little better."

She sat on the floor beside the girl, her hand rubbing the girl's back. The girl looked more terrified than threatening, but I wasn't leaving Sara alone with her.

"Sara?" I called to her softly.

She smiled reassuringly and shivered. "We're good. Can I get a blanket for her?"

Jordan ran and got two blankets – one for Sara and one for the girl. Out in the living room, everyone else stared at Sara and the weeping girl, whispering among themselves.

I didn't blame them. It was my second time witnessing this miracle, and I still couldn't believe it. Aside from Chris, Jordan, and me, no one here knew what Sara was or what she could do. We were filling people in on a need-to-know basis. This was going to be one of those situations.

At one point, Sara inclined her head toward the living room, but I shook my head firmly. Their questions could wait. Sara and her new charge were more important.

Slowly, the girl quieted, inching closer to Sara until her head was in Sara's lap. Sara stroked her hair like a mother comforting a frightened child. It made me think of Sara with our future children. She was going to be an incredible and loving mother someday – after I had her to myself for a few decades.

When Sara started showing signs of discomfort, I picked up the sleeping girl and laid her on the loveseat in the living room. I had no idea what we were going to do with her when she woke up, but the way Sara hovered over her told me she was already feeling protective of the girl.

Geoffrey looked shaken when he came to stand beside Sara and me. "Is she really human again?"

"Yes," Sara said.

He stared at the girl who had been a vampire an hour ago. "That's...not possible."

Sara gave me a pleading look.

"Geoffrey, let's talk in the kitchen so we don't disturb the girl," I said.

"We can go downstairs if you don't want to be overheard."

"The kitchen will do." I wasn't letting Sara out of my sight. I didn't care if this place was crawling with warriors.

"What just happened?" Geoffrey asked when we entered the kitchen. "I feel like I just watched a Copperfield show. I'm not sure what to believe."

"You just watched a vampire become human again."

"But —"

"I know what you're going to say. I didn't believe it myself the first time I saw it."

His mouth fell open. "You've seen this before?"

I stood so I could see Sara sitting on the foot of the loveseat. "This is the second time it's happened. The first was in November at Westhorne."

"How? How does she do it? Is she even a Mohiri?"

I watched Chris walk over to talk to Sara.

"Sara is half Mohiri and half Fae."

He shook his head. "That's impossible. Fae and demons don't mix. There's no way one of us could be with a faerie even if we wanted to."

I exhaled slowly. Then I explained how Sara's ancestor was undine and all of the descendants had been male until Sara. Sara's father had been a human, making him fully compatible with Madeline.

I gave him a brief overview of Sara's power, what had happened to Nate, and how Sara had made her uncle human again.

To his credit, Geoffrey managed to keep his questions to a minimum, although it was clear he was bursting with curiosity.

"This...is just incredible. Think of what it could mean for us. Sara could —"

"No. You saw how it knocked her out. Last time she was out for two days, and we didn't know if she was going to wake up at all."

I had a feeling Sara would disagree with me, and that this wouldn't be her last vampire healing. She cared too much about people to not want to help them if she could. I also had a feeling she and I were going to be having long discussions about it.

"So what will you do with her? The vampire...I mean, girl?"

Sara looked over at me and smiled. She seemed tired but otherwise okay. We should be on our flight to Boise by now. But there was no way Sara would leave until we knew what shape the girl was in, and we figured out what to do with her.

"We'll watch her tonight and see where we are tomorrow. I guess that means we'll be your guests for a few more hours."

"No problem. It looks like we're just about ready to head over to the Henderson safe house."

We went back to the living room. "How is she?" I asked Sara.

"Still asleep."

Geoffrey studied the sleeping girl. "Do you think she'll be able to talk to us when she wakes up?"

"I have no idea," Sara replied softly.

"We'll have to question her," he persisted. "There's no telling what information she can give us about the attack tonight."

He had a point. I could only imagine what this girl could tell us after being a vampire for decades. That was, if she could talk at all.

Sara pressed her lips together. "I can tell you that your warriors were followed here from a casino two days ago. The vampires had no idea the rest of us would be here when they attacked this place."

Geoffrey sucked in a sharp breath. "She told you that?"

Sara hesitated before answering. "Yes. That's all she said."

"Son of a bitch." He called to Evan. "Evan, weren't you guys at the Mirage two days ago?"

Evan frowned. "No, that was Tyler's team. Why?"

Geoffrey swore loudly, something he rarely did. "Sorry for that," he said to Sara. "I need to contact Tyler. His team is out on a job right now. Excuse me."

As soon as he stalked off, Sara said, "I think we should move her somewhere quieter. She'll be scared if she wakes up and sees all these strange people."

I nodded. "We'll take her to the new safe house. You need to rest, too."

She smothered a yawn. "We all do."

Thirty minutes later, we piled into the crowded SUVs and made the short drive to the other safe house. The house was slightly larger than the one we'd left, which was good considering how many of us were staying there. Tyler's team, who lived at the house, offered to give up some of their rooms for Sara, Jordan, and the girl whose name we didn't know yet.

Chris carried the girl during the ride over, and he laid her on the bed in one of the upstairs bedrooms. Sara refused to leave her, until I sent Jordan to kick her out of the room with orders to get some sleep.

It was after three in the morning when I went upstairs to check on Sara. I found her asleep in the room next to the one the girl was in. When I reached for the comforter to cover her up, she woke and pulled me down to her.

"Stay," she murmured sleepily.

I kicked off my shoes and lay beside her, pulling the comforter over us. In moments, she was sound asleep again with an arm around my waist and a leg thrown across my thighs.

Smiling, I closed my eyes to get in a few hours of much-needed sleep.

*   *   *

"How is the girl doing?" Tristan asked.

It was the second time he'd called today. He was genuinely concerned for Emma, Sara's new charge, but I could tell he was more worried about us staying in Vegas another day, especially after the attack on the first safe house. I didn't blame him. I felt the same way.

"Better. Sara's been with her since this morning. Emma's talking, and she managed to eat something."

"That's incredible. When you told me last night what Sara did, I have to admit, I wasn't sure what to expect in the way of recovery. Nate was a vampire for a week, but the girl had been one for decades."

"Twenty-one years."

I leaned against the wall by the living room window and watched Jordan walk down the stairs, carrying empty dinner plates. She'd brought lunch and dinner to Sara and Emma, who had stayed in Emma's room all day.

At first, I'd stayed in the upstairs hallway, not quite ready to trust Emma. But after a while, it was clear she wasn't a threat. I stuck around long enough to learn Emma had been changed by Eli and to hear what she'd suffered at his hands. I knew it had to be difficult for Sara to hear those things, but she didn't leave the room once.

"And she's only seventeen?" Tristan's voice was full of concern. "We'll have to make some arrangements to help her. She can't go home, and we can't leave her alone in the world without protection."

"I think Sara's going to want to bring her home with us, if Emma agrees to come."

"Good. I'll have the room next to Sara's prepared for her so she'll be more comfortable."

I didn't bother to tell him Sara would be moving into my apartment when we got home. I hadn't asked her yet, but I could be very persuasive. I smiled to myself. I couldn't wait to get her home and start convincing her to live with me.

"When do you think you'll leave Vegas?" Tristan asked, pulling me from my more pleasant train of thought.

"Tomorrow, I hope. Day after at the latest." I'd leave tonight if I could, but Emma was still too fragile to travel.

"And how is Sara holding up? She's been through a lot in the last two days."

I glanced up at the ceiling, wondering what Sara and Emma were talking about now. "She's doing well with all of it. Meeting Madeline was hard on her, but I think it was good for her too. She's ready to move on now."

His sigh was audible. I'd called him last night after we got to the new safe house to fill him in on everything that had happened since we arrived in Las Vegas. He was excited we'd found Madeline, but hearing about her reason for leaving Sara and her life since hadn't been easy for him. Neither was the fact that Madeline seemed to have no plans to reconnect with her family.

"I'm glad Sara got the closure she needs," he said quietly. "And it'll be great to have her and Jordan home again. This place is not the same without them."

I let out a laugh. "You say that now."

He chuckled. "They are quite the pair, aren't they?"

Jordan came out of the kitchen and waved to me before she went to join the warriors sparring in the backyard.

"I've been meaning to talk to you about Jordan, actually. She handled herself like a pro last night. Took down two vampires. I think she's ready."

"High praise, coming from you."

Jordan's laughter floated back to me, and I smiled. "She's trained with Chris and me for the last two months, and Desmund when he was here. She's a skilled swordsman, and she keeps her head in a fight. And honestly, I think she'd be bored to death if she had to go back to Westhorne and train for another six months."

He was quiet for a moment. "I see no reason to hold her back. I'll inform the Council, and we can have the ceremony when you get home. Do you want to tell her?"

"No, I'll let you have the honor."

"And what about Sara? When will she be ready to become a warrior?"

I ran a hand through my hair. "Sooner than I'd like."

He laughed. "You sound resigned. Has she finally worn you down?"

"More like she proved me wrong. You should have seen her with that vampire, Tristan. She was incredible, even though she scared the hell out of me."

"I wish I could have seen it."

"I don't know how I'm going to get used to the idea of her fighting, but she's already a warrior in her own right."

He exhaled slowly. "You'll never get used to it, but you'll learn to live with it as every bonded male before you has done. Myself included."

I nodded unhappily. "Well, I guess it could be worse."

"How's that?"

"Can you imagine what the man who bonds with Jordan is in for?"

Tristan let out a bark of laughter. "Well, that's one way to put it all into perspective."

Through the window in the back door, I saw Jordan disarm one of the warriors. From the astonished look on his face, he hadn't meant for it to happen. Boisterous laughter followed as she handed him his sword with a little bow.

Sara was going to miss Jordan at Westhorne. I had no doubt the two would keep in touch, but Jordan wouldn't be content to stay in one place for long. Sara wanted to see the world, but she would always be drawn back to home and family.

"I should go see how Sara's doing," I said. "She's been up there all day."

"Okay. I'll see you in a day or two."

I ended the call and climbed the stairs to the second floor. Down the hallway, I could hear the soft murmur of voices coming from Emma's room. It was a good sign that Emma was still talking, but Sara had to be tired.

Ten minutes later, Sara left the room and closed the door quietly behind her. She saw me waiting for her and walked straight into my arms, hugging me like she was afraid to let go. When her tears came, I rubbed her back and told her how amazing and strong she was.

When she stopped crying, she let me lead her into her room. I shut the door, and we lay together on the bed, talking in low voices so we didn't disturb Emma.

"I don't know what I'm doing," she said as she toyed with the buttons on my shirt. "Emma's been through hell. What if I say the wrong thing to her? Maybe we should find someone to help her."

I stroked her hair. "She trusts you, and she feels safe with you. I don't think anyone else can do more than that."

She let out a shuddering breath. "I'm so glad you're here with me."

"Wouldn't be anywhere else."

We stayed like that for the rest of the night. The next morning, Sara went back to Emma and convinced her to talk to Chris about the vampire activity in Las Vegas. Emma gave him a lot of helpful information, including the location of two nests no one had known about.

Unfortunately, she could tell us nothing about the Master, although she told Sara she was sure she must have met him. Eli had taken her everywhere with him in the first few years she was a vampire. According to Emma, the Master compelled every vampire to forget him when they left his house.

A day later, Sara, Jordan, Chris, Emma, and I finally boarded the jet for the flight to Boise. Emma sat timidly in her seat, but Sara was full of happy energy and couldn't sit still until the pilot told us to take our seats. She sat beside Emma, and the two of them talked quietly.

I sat two rows ahead of them, reading a Tom Clancy paperback one of the guys at the safe house had given me. The story was engrossing, but not enough to keep my mind off what was going to happen between Sara and me when we got home. I smiled, glad no one could read my mind.

"It can't be."

Sara's shocked voice had me out of my seat and beside her in seconds. "What's wrong?"

Emma shrank away from me like I'd yelled at her. I realized I was glaring, and I looked at Sara instead.

Sara held up a notepad with a trembling hand. "This," she said breathlessly. "This is his house."

"Whose house?"

Her eyes were lit with excitement. "The Master's."

"What are you talking about?" I took the notepad and stared at the drawing on the paper. It was a large stone house with turrets and a lot of windows. Sara had drawn it in great detail.

I looked at Sara. "Did she tell you that?"

Sara's voice shook. "No. I drew it from memory, from a memory I took from the vamhir demon before I killed it."

"You took the demon's memory?" asked Jordan, who had crowded in behind me.

Sara and I hadn't talked about what had happened when she was connected with the vamhir demon. All she'd told us was how the vampires had found the safe house, and that the vamhir demon hadn't known who the Master was.

Sara stared past me as if she was remembering something. "I asked it about the Master and it showed me this house. I forgot about it with everything else that happened."

Chris patted my arm, and I handed him the notepad. He stared at it for a long moment. "How do you know this is the Master's house?"

Sara lifted her shoulders. "I don't for sure, but something feels off about it. Emma feels it, too."

"It gives me the creeps, and it seems familiar," Emma said in a small voice.

"I told you what Emma said about the Master being so paranoid that he compels other vampires to forget him. Eli took her with him when he visited the Master and she was compelled to forget." Sara's face was slightly flushed when she looked at me. "But no one can erase your mind that completely, and I think I found a memory he missed."

Chris let out a breath. "Jesus, if that's true..."

The conviction in Sara's eyes was all the proof I needed. We could be holding the first tangible lead to the Master since we'd learned of his existence. It might take a while to track down the house, but Dax could do it.

I looked at Chris. "We need to get this to our guys as soon as possible."

"Already on it."

He and Sara took pictures of the drawing with their phones. "I'm sending this to David," Sara said. "If anyone can find this house, it's him and Kelvan."

Somehow, I didn't doubt that.

The mood for the rest of the flight was one of nervous excitement. More than ever, I wanted to get Sara home. I let out a relieved sigh when we touched down in Boise.

Seamus and Niall were waiting beside a large black SUV when we pulled into the hangar. Seamus smirked at Sara. "Look who finally decided to come home."

"I heard it was too boring here without me," she retorted with a grin.

Everyone but Emma laughed as we piled into the vehicle. She was even quieter than normal as she sat in the back between Sara and Jordan. I smiled when I heard the two of them telling her about Westhorne.

Up front, the conversation centered around the work we'd been doing in California, and what had been happening at Westhorne in our absence.

Seamus and Niall told us about all the new security measures Dax had put in place, including new boundary sensors that were a combination of technology and warlock magic. Raj had gotten the idea when he was developing the listening devices, and he'd been working on a prototype with an Indian warlock he knew. The new sensors were designed to detect a vampire if one got within scanning range. They'd been tested in a lab, but so far none of the ones at Westhorne had picked up anything.

"And how do you like having the hellhounds loose on the grounds?" I asked them.

Seamus snickered. "One of the monsters took a liking to Niall. Follows him whenever he's out of patrol."

"One of these days, you'll find my bones picked clean in the woods," Niall said glumly. "You won't be laughing then."

"They probably won't leave any bones behind," his brother said not-so-helpfully.

Niall scowled. "You wouldn't joke if it was —"

"Vampires!" Sara choked out.

I turned around in my seat in time to see a large white cargo van with darkened windows slam into the back of the SUV.

"Son of a bitch!" Seamus shouted as the SUV swerved precariously on an icy patch of road. Everyone was thrown forward, and I automatically reached for Sara to steady her. Emma screamed, and Sara and Jordan covered her with their bodies at the van sped up again.

Seamus hit the gas and we shot forward, but it was too late. The van hit us hard.

"Jesus Christ!" Niall bellowed as the tires lost purchase on the ice and we skidded off the shoulder of the road.

The ten-foot embankment was steep, and we rolled over twice, hitting the trees hard at the bottom.

My only thought was of Sara. Before the vehicle had come to a complete stop, I tore off my seat belt and reached for her. "Sara? Are you hurt?"

She winced but shook her head. "No."

"Stay with Emma," I told her as Chris and I went for the weapons stored beneath the seat cushion. Sara couldn't handle a sword, but she could use her power to hold off a vampire if one tried to get inside the SUV. Emma looked like she was in shock. Sara would keep her safe.

I wanted to hug her, to tell her to be careful, but there was no time. The slamming of car doors above us told me our attackers were coming for us. Sword in hand, I climbed out the window and flew up the embankment.

I met the first two vampires on the shoulder of the road, and I tore through one of them before he knew what hit him. Chris was right beside me, and he went after the second vampire as Seamus and Niall held off six more.

As I moved in to help the twins, Jordan sped past me and jumped into the fray. She ducked under Niall's arm and put her sword through the chest of a female vampire before she could attack the other warrior. Pulling her sword free, she whirled to meet the next vampire.

A tall vampire blurred out of sight and reappeared behind me. I saw him coming and spun away before he could punch through my back. Older vampires had the strength to rip a spinal cord out, but I wasn't going out that way.

I came around and sliced through his arm at the elbow. He hissed in pain but didn't retreat like a younger vampire would have. Moving fast, he swiped at my throat with his remaining hand. At the same time, someone grabbed my shoulders from behind.

I went down to one knee and threw my new attacker over my shoulder into the one-armed vampire. He staggered off balance, and before he could right himself, I plunged my blade into his heart.

The vampire I'd thrown hit the ground and rolled to his feet. I started toward him when the screech of tires cut through the sounds of fighting. A second van stopped, and another eight vampires spilled out.

I looked back to the one I'd been fighting. He was gone.

Sara.

Her presence began to fade. I tore down the incline to the SUV to find it empty. Movement nearby led me to Emma, who was hidden behind some bushes.

"Where is Sara?" I demanded.

She pointed into the woods. I looked down and saw the indentation where she'd fallen and the tracks in the snow. *God, no.*

CHAPTER 44

I SPED THROUGH the trees, moving so fast over the ground my feet barely disturbed the snow. It took me a minute to sense her again, and another to catch up to them.

The vampire I'd let escape had Sara pinned on her stomach with her face pressed into the snow. She wasn't moving.

I plowed into him so hard he flew twenty feet and slammed into a tree. I was on him before he could recover from the blow. My sword went for his chest, but he managed to roll to one side. He screeched when the blade slid through his ribs. I withdrew quickly and struck again. This time my blade found its mark, and he collapsed into the snow.

I raced back to Sara and threw down my bloody sword. Grasping her shoulders, I rolled her over, afraid of what I'd find.

She took a wheezing breath and coughed.

Relief warred with the fear in my chest. "Sara!"

Her eyes opened, and she croaked, "Nikolas."

I wanted to crush her in my arms, but there was no time. That vampire had gone for Sara and taken her instead of trying to kill her back at the road. Part of me had hoped it was a random attack on the Mohiri. Now I knew what they really wanted.

Grabbing my sword, I picked her up and got to my feet. "It's an ambush. I have to get you out of here."

"What about the others?" she cried.

"It's you they want." I'd die before I let them take her.

"But Emma —"

Five vampires appeared from the trees in front of us. I set Sara on her feet, not taking my eyes off the new threat. They were mature or close to it based on how fast they'd arrived. I'd taken on five vampires at once, but not five mature ones.

I pushed Sara behind me, hoping she was recovered enough to use her power. Something told me our attackers weren't going to come at us one at a time.

A ghostly white light spread across the snow to illuminate the clearing, drawing the vampires' attention to Sara. I didn't want them looking at her, but it provided a distraction we desperately needed.

I struck first, my blade taking off a vampire's arm. He screamed, and he and three of his friends started to circle me while the last one went for Sara. I sent up a silent prayer that she was back to full strength. Even a mature vampire was no match for her power.

A vampire came at me, moving so fast only my demon sight saved me. I ducked to one side and slashed him across both thighs, deep enough to sever tendons and touch bone. He went down howling, but as old as he was, he'd heal within minutes.

Behind me, a vampire roared in pain. I spun to see one backhand Sara with enough force to knock out a human. In the next moment, she retaliated when her glowing hand made contact with his chest.

I heard someone come at me from behind, and claws ripped into the back of my leather jacket. As I threw him off me, Sara went after her downed vampire.

Two more vampires stepped from the woods.

"Sara, look out!" I shouted.

Rage erupted inside me. I welcomed the red haze that dropped down over my vision and the roaring that filled my ears as my Mori's aggression took over.

The vampire I'd thrown off went for my stomach. He was dead before he touched me, his head flying into a snowbank. Two more flew at me, but my mind was too crazed to register them as a threat. One, I sent headfirst into a large rock. The second, I gutted from his navel to his throat.

The first one gained his footing just as a furious roar split the air and the trees around us shook. Everyone stared at the large winged creature diving from the sky, flames shooting from its snout.

The wyvern went straight for the two vampires stalking Sara. No one else moved as it engulfed the female vampire in flames. She was still screaming when Alex snatched up the male in his powerful claws and tore him to pieces.

Blood and flesh rained down on us as the wyvern circled the clearing. I tore my gaze from him as the vampire whose thighs I'd cut leapt back to his feet, fully healed. He looked ready for payback, but their numbers had dropped drastically, and I was fueled by pure rage now.

Alex dove again. I prayed he wouldn't mistake Sara or me for the enemy. He rose into the air again, and I waited for the fresh shower of blood as I swung at the closest vampire.

I gasped as I felt Sara's presence pulling away from me. I stared around the clearing, but she was nowhere in sight.

Sound above me drew my eyes to the sky. Fear exploded in my chest when I looked up in time to see Sara disappear over the tops of the trees in the wyvern's claws.

"Sara!" I bellowed.

The rage consumed me, and I lost all conscious thought. When I came to, I was standing in the clearing, surrounded by at least a dozen bodies. More vampires must have arrived while I was out of it. I didn't know how much time had passed. All I could think of was finding Sara.

I set off in the direction the wyvern had flown, trying not to think about the overwhelming odds against me finding Sara out here. There were hundreds of miles to cover, and Alex left no tracks to follow.

I headed north toward the mountains. Tristan had said they believed Alex was living in a cave up there. He could be taking Sara there. It was all I had to go on. I prayed I was right and that I got to her in time.

Stop. She'll be okay.

If it had been anyone else, I'd have little hope of their survival with the wyvern. Sara wasn't just anyone. She had a gift for connecting with creatures. I'd seen it in her friendship with the troll, the devotion of her hellhounds, and the adoration of the young griffin. Even the wyvern had come to help her the night we were attacked at Westhorne. He could have flown off, but he'd gone straight for Sara, according to the stories I'd heard about that night. Just like he went for the vampires attacking her back in the clearing.

Using my Mori speed, I moved quickly over the ground. My enhanced vision pierced the heavy snow and the approaching dusk, searching for any sign of Sara and the wyvern. My hearing picked up every crack of a branch, every movement.

I wanted to call to Sara, but I didn't know if there were vampires out here searching for her too. A mature vampire could move as quickly and as quietly as me, and I couldn't take the chance of leading one to her. I'd feel her once I got close enough.

When the woods began to darken and the snow turned to sleet, a new fear settled in my chest. It was close to freezing, and the temperature was going to plummet once it got dark. Sara wasn't dressed for this weather, and her Mori couldn't regulate her body temperature to keep her warm. If she couldn't find adequate shelter, she could die from exposure before I found her.

I'd been searching for well over an hour when my nose caught the scent of blood nearby. My stomach lurched as I veered left toward the blood, and I braced myself for what I might find. But it was just the remains of some small animal – a fox, judging by the tuffs of red fur on the bloody snow.

The sound of water ahead made me stop and visualize a map of the terrain. A large river ran through this area, alongside several game trails. If the wyvern lived within a few miles, he'd come here to hunt. I looked down at the bloody patch of snow and set off running toward the river.

I came out of the trees beside the roaring water and began making my way upriver. Minutes later, I felt a rush of excitement when I came upon a patch of beaten down snow at the base of a large boulder. Footprints, too small to belong to a man, led away from the rock, heading upstream. It was Sara. It had to be.

The freezing rain was coming down hard, spurring me to go faster. If Sara was walking, she couldn't be badly hurt, but she wouldn't last long in this weather. Even my Mori was working hard to keep me warm against the freezing onslaught.

Above the rain and the roar of the river I heard what sounded like a growl. I thought my ears were playing tricks on me, until I peered through the darkness and saw a shape circling in the air a quarter of a mile upriver.

Ten steps later, I felt the faintest brush against my mind.

I sped over the uneven ground, her presence growing ever stronger. I'd almost reached the bend in the river when my name carried to me on the wind.

My heart thundered. She knew I was near.

I rounded the bend, and a pit opened in my stomach when I saw her lying facedown in the snow less than one hundred yards from a small cabin.

"Sara!" I yelled, dropping to my knees beside her.

"Sara, wake up," I ordered as I checked her breathing and pulse. They were weak, but she was alive. "Stay, with me."

Her mouth opened, and she mumbled something that sounded like my name.

"Sara, oh God."

I crushed her to me. Above us, the wyvern growled as it flew in circles like it was guarding her. It must have sensed I wasn't a threat to her because it didn't attack.

"Are you hurt?" I asked her. When she didn't respond I shook her gently. "Sara, talk to me."

"C-cold," she muttered.

I felt her jeans. "*Khristu*, you're soaked through."

I picked her up and stood. I had to get her warm and out of those clothes. "I've got you. You need to stay awake for me."

"Okay," she said weakly.

In seconds, we were at the cabin perched on the edge of the river. One twist was all it took to break the padlock on the door. I shoved it open and carried Sara inside, kicking the door shut behind me.

My eyes saw well enough in the darkness of the cabin to pick out a pair of twin beds. I sat Sara on the closest bed. A scan of the room revealed an oil lantern on a small table, and I went to light it.

"Nikolas?" Sara called fearfully.

"I'm here."

I struck a match and put it to the wick, thankful that whoever owned the cabin kept it well maintained. The lantern flared to life, and I left it on the table to go to the fireplace where kindling had already been arranged for a fire. It took no time to get a good blaze putting off heat into the small room.

Now to get her out of those wet clothes. She didn't protest when I peeled off her small coat and removed her shirt, boots, and jeans. Her skin had a bluish tint, and she was shivering violently by the time I got her outer clothes off.

"Jesus, your skin is like ice," I said when my hand brushed her thigh.

I got to my feet and pulled off my coat and shirt. My Mori already knew what I wanted, and it increased my body temperature as I pulled her up and pressed her body against mine. She stood like a life-size doll while I rubbed her arms and back to get her circulation going again. Her lack of response scared me, even though I knew it was normal for someone suffering from hypothermia. She'd be herself again as soon as I got her core temperature up.

She sighed softly when her skin began to warm. Relief washed over me, and I looked around the room to see if there was anything dry for her to wear. Between the two beds stood a large wooden chest that looked promising.

I sat her on the bed and opened the chest. Inside were homemade quilts and two pillows. I grabbed a thick quilt, wrapped it around her, and carried her over to the fire. There was a small rug on the floor, and I set her down on it.

"It will warm up in here soon," I promised her.

I added more wood to the fire, and then I went outside to bring in some of the chopped firewood I'd seen in a small lean-to by the side of the cabin. Freezing rain lashed my bare back as I filled my arms with wood. Ignoring the discomfort, I made three trips, creating a good-sized pile near the hearth. It was turning into a real storm out here, and I needed to make sure Sara stayed warm all night.

On my last trip outside, I heard the flap of wings and the scratch of claws on shingles. Looking up, I saw the wyvern perched on top of the cabin like a sentry. He turned his head and stared at me for a moment before he settled down with his head under his wing.

Shaking my head, I walked around the cabin to make sure it was as secure as it could be. It was small but made of logs, and storm shutters covered the two windows. The thick door wouldn't keep out a determined vampire, but it would provide ample protection from the weather. I hadn't run across a single vampire while I was searching for Sara, so I doubted there were any nearby. If by chance, one did find this place, the wyvern would make him think twice about paying a visit.

I went back inside and pulled the bolt to lock us in. The cabin had warmed considerably since I set the fire, and I was glad to see Sara was starting to get some color back into her cheeks.

Wind shook the cabin. Sara looked up at the ceiling when the beams creaked.

"It's the wyvern," I told her as I added wood to the fire. "I think it's guarding you."

If I hadn't seen it myself, I might not have believed it. Wyverns could be trained to hunt vampires, but they were unpredictable, and only the most experienced handlers worked with them. Even a well-trained wyvern didn't protect someone of its own accord. I was deeply grateful for this one. He'd saved Sara's life when he carried her away, whether or not he knew what he was doing.

Sara pulled the quilt up to her chin, reminding me she still needed dry clothes. There were no clothes in the chest, so I went to a tall cabinet in the corner where I found several folded men's flannel shirts. I grabbed one and a towel and went back to kneel in front of her.

She didn't speak when I pushed the quilt off her shoulders. As I dressed her in the shirt, I was aware of the curve of her breasts above her bra, but my only thought was getting her warm. I buttoned the shirt and smiled when I saw how it engulfed her. If she stood, it would probably come to mid-thigh.

Reaching for one arm then the other, I rolled up the sleeves for her. That done, I covered her with the quilt again and sat behind her to dry her hair with the towel. I stretched out my legs on either side of her and shifted us so she was facing the fire. Then I took up the towel and began to use it on her hair.

Neither of us spoke for several minutes. The longer we sat there, the more I dwelled on how close I'd come to losing her. My throat tightened, and I wanted to hug her to me until the pain in my chest went away.

"When I saw the wyvern carry you away I thought I'd lost you," I said roughly. "And then I saw you lying in the snow."

Her voice was as raw as mine when she spoke. "How did you find me?"

"I killed the rest of the vampires and headed in the direction the wyvern went with you. I can cover a lot of ground on foot, but there are hundreds of square miles of forest out here, and he didn't leave a trail."

I closed my eyes, not wanting to think about how I would have missed her had I gone in a different direction.

"It was sheer luck that I found where he landed by the river. The broken branches and footprints in the snow told me what way you'd gone."

"What about the others? Do you think they're okay?"

I stopped toweling. "Yes. Half the vampires went after you. Chris and the others would have been able to handle the rest. I'm sure Chris contacted Westhorne, and Tristan has half of the stronghold out there looking for us by now."

"I promised Emma I would keep her safe, and I left her there," she said in a heavy voice.

I resumed drying her hair. "You didn't leave her; you were taken. Emma will understand."

She leaned back against me with a sigh. "Do you think we'll be safe here?"

"I don't think we have anything to worry about. If any vampires did survive and somehow manage to find us, they are not getting past the wyvern."

She fell silent again, and I finished drying her hair. It was still a little damp, but the fire would take care of that soon. I tossed the wet towel on the rough wooden floor and laid my hands on her shoulders.

"How do you feel?"

"One of the vampires shot me with a dart and now I can't use my power," she said in a choked voice.

Alarm filled me. They shot her?

"What do you mean? It's gone?" I asked, keeping my voice steady.

She swallowed. "It's there but I can't touch it or use it. What if…?"

I put my arms around her, holding her close. The knowledge that vampires had a drug to disable her power scared the hell out of me. But I couldn't let her see that.

"We'll contact Eldeorin when we get home. It's obviously something that affects Fae magic, and he'll know what to do."

I felt her body relax.

"I thought you didn't like him," she said.

"For you, I'll tolerate him." Unable to resist the bare skin so close to my lips, I kissed her throat beneath her ear.

Her breath hitched, and my body instantly warmed in response. I imagined laying her down beside the fire and removing that shirt I'd dressed her in.

Groaning inwardly, I stood and put more wood on the fire. Then I went to one of the twin beds. It was colder over on this side of the room, but the mattress would make a comfortable bed for Sara by the fire. I planned to stay awake all night to keep watch.

I looked at her and forgot what I was thinking. Framed by the fire, her damp hair fell around her shoulders in wild disarray. With the quilt hanging off one shoulder and a bare thigh peeking out from the bottom, she was a vision of sweet seduction.

But it was the look she gave me that stole my breath and made my pulse race. Emerald eyes met mine before they moved down my body to linger on my bare stomach. Her gaze was like a caress against my skin, and my body hardened in response.

Tearing my eyes from her, I turned to the bed to hide the evidence of her effect on me. I forced my heart to slow its crazy dance as I lifted the mattress and carried it over to the hearth. Then I went to the chest and took out a pillow, a blanket, and a quilt.

"It's warmer over here," I explained as I made up her bed, glad for something to distract me.

After the bed was made, I lifted the blanket for her, trying not to look at her naked legs as she dropped her quilt and got into the bed. I covered her and went to the door. Opening it, I looked outside, relishing the freezing air against my heated flesh.

I locked the door again and doused the lantern since we didn't need it with the fire. I could see well enough without either. I went back to sit on the floor beside her, keeping her between me and the fire. My wet jeans were uncomfortable, but I'd suffered a lot worse conditions.

"Aren't you cold?"

I pulled the quilt up to her chin. "My Mori keeps me warm."

Her eyelids lowered. "Oh. I was just…"

I stopped moving. "What?"

She bit her lip and raised her eyes to mine again, and the shy hope on her face made my breath catch. "We can share."

"My jeans are wet," I said huskily, my throat dry. Did she mean…?

"You could…take them off."

Her whispered words fanned the fire already burning inside me. Desire made my voice gruff. "Are you sure?"

"Yes."

I studied her face. She looked nervous but unafraid, and love shone in her eyes. I wanted her more than I'd thought was possible to want someone. I'd fantasized about her and longed to complete our bond. She was offering me both, and I found myself too humbled to speak.

Standing, I kicked off my wet boots. Her eyes followed me, and my breath quickened at the thought of her watching me undress. When I undid the button of my jeans, she turned her head toward the fire, sending a little pang of disappointment through me. I wanted her eyes on me, but I also understood her shyness. Tonight, we'd get to know each other in the way only a mated couple could, and she'd never again have reason to be shy with me.

I pushed the wet jeans down my legs. They landed with a soft thump, and I stepped out of them. My boxers followed, and I stood there for a moment before I knelt and lifted the quilt to lie beside her on the narrow mattress. I turned on my side, facing her with my head supported by my hand, and watched her profile as she stared at the fire.

"Sara."

She swallowed. "Yes."

I used my free hand to turn her face toward me. Wordlessly, I captured her mouth in a slow, deliberate kiss. Into every brush of my lips against hers, I poured my adoration and love for her.

I kissed her until her body relaxed beneath me. Raising my head, I looked at her as my fingers traced the planes of her face. My throat tightened at the love and trust in her eyes, and I didn't think there were words to express my feelings for her.

"Being a warrior is all I've ever known, all I ever wanted. I thought I didn't need anything else. And then I found you, and it was like finding the other half of me that I didn't know was missing. You make me whole, Sara."

"My warrior," she said softly, her eyes sparkling with tears. "I used to think the empty place in my heart was from losing my dad. But I was wrong. My heart was just waiting for you to come and fill it up."

I claimed her lips again. Her fingers weaved through my hair to cling to me, matching my hunger with her own. Our breaths came in small pants, and she set my blood on fire until I ached from the need to possess her.

Mine, my Mori growled impatiently, demanding I finally take what was ours. It strained against my control, wanting to be free to claim its mate.

"Mmmm," Sara protested when I broke the kiss. She tried to pull me back down to her, but I stopped her.

"Do you want this?" I searched her eyes for some sign she wasn't ready.

"Yes," she breathed.

"We can wait until —"

She touched my face. "Nikolas, I don't want to wait. All I want is you."

I trembled with desire as I rose up on one elbow to look at her. My body and my demon were ready for her, but her first time should be a slow, sensual awakening, something she would treasure.

I brushed my fingers against her brow then let them trail down her flushed cheek, across her full lips, and down her throat. When I reached the quilt, I eased it off her, letting it pool at her feet. I allowed my greedy gaze to pass over her bare legs and the shirt that had ridden up to the tops of her thighs, before I lifted my eyes to hers again.

Her eyes widened slightly when my fingers freed the first button of her shirt. A blush stole across her face, and her irises turned a deeper shade of green. I watched her as I slowly undid each button, savoring the way her lips parted in anticipation and her breath quickened.

When I released the last button, the shirt fell open. Still looking into her eyes, I laid my hand on her taut stomach. She sucked in a breath, sending a jolt of desire through me.

Jesus, she was killing me and she hadn't even touched me yet.

I looked down as I began my exploration of her body, watching my hand touch her the way I'd wanted to for so long. My fingers skimmed across her stomach and over the top of her white lace bra to where her heart fluttered wildly.

"God, you're beautiful," I whispered, lowering my head to kiss her breast where it peeked tantalizingly above the top of her bra. I wanted the barrier between us gone, but I reminded myself I had to take this slow. I consoled myself by tasting her skin, feathering kisses across her breasts. She arched, baring her throat to me, and I eagerly moved my lips along the creamy column to cover her mouth once more.

My heart threatened to burst from my chest as I rose up to look into her eyes. "Sara Grey, you've owned my heart from the moment I met you. My body and soul are yours if you'll have them."

Her eyes welled. "Yes, if it means forever with you."

I groaned and kissed her hungrily as my hand slipped inside the lacy material of her bra to cup her soft breast. She made a small sound of pleasure against my mouth that nearly drove me out of my mind.

My fingers moved to the front of the bra, lingering there for what seemed like forever before I released the clasp. Gently I eased the cups aside, baring her breasts to me. *Khristu*, she was as perfect as I'd imagined. I lowered my mouth to one breast, cherishing it slowly, then moved to do the same to the other.

Her soft moans brought a smile of pure male satisfaction to my lips and stoked my own desire even higher. My hand shook as it moved down her abdomen to the top of her matching panties. She made no protest when I hooked my fingers in the material and slid them off her. Then I lifted her easily, freeing her from her shirt and bra as well.

I looked up at her to make sure she was okay, and her passion-glazed eyes told me all I needed to know.

"You good?" I asked huskily.

She nodded and bit her lip. "I've never…"

"I know."

I leaned in, and my tongue traced the soft fullness of her lips before dipping inside. God, I could never get enough of kissing her.

When I lifted my head again, I saw uncertainty in her eyes. I took her hands and placed them against my chest.

"I…don't know what to do," she whispered.

"Just touch me any way you want. Whatever you do will be heaven for me."

Her coy smile almost pulled a growl from me. Then her hands began to explore me, and I was lost.

Her touch was tentative at first as she caressed my chest and shoulders, and ran her fingers along my arms. I made a sound to let her know how much I loved her hands on me, and she grew bolder, letting them trail down my spine. When her hand grazed my backside, I groaned, forgetting for a moment that I was supposed to be the one pleasuring her.

Knowing I couldn't last much longer with her touching me that way, I resumed my exploration of her body. My hands and lips worshiped her soft curves, kissing and touching her until both of us were panting and covered in a fine sheen of sweat.

"Nikolas," she whispered desperately.

I rose over her, covering her body with mine, and resting my weight on my elbows. She shifted so I lay between her thighs and gave me the most beautiful smile I'd ever seen.

"I love you," she said softly, entwining her arms around the back of my neck.

I brushed my lips against hers. "I love you, too."

"Then make me yours."

I joined with her, whispering over and over how much I adored her as I made slow love to her. When our bodies found release, our bond opened like a flower blossoming in the sun. In that moment, I was undone by her and remade into a new man. A warrior still, but a mate and a lover first. And I felt complete.

Later, I lay beside her, gazing down at her as she slept. Her hair was spread across the pillow, and her cheeks still bore a slight flush from our lovemaking. I pulled the quilt up over her chest to keep her warm, and she snuggled against me, whispering my name.

I wanted nothing more than to kiss her awake and make love to her again, but she needed her sleep after today. I held her close and listened to the storm raging outside. A few times, I heard the wyvern walking around on the roof, and I knew we were safe here for tonight. But I stayed awake just in case. I wouldn't relax completely until we were home.

When the fire began to die down, I eased out of Sara's arms and added more wood. Then I draped our wet clothes over two chairs and moved them closer to the fire to dry.

All night, I lay awake with her in my arms, wonder filling me every time I looked at her sleeping face. What had I done to deserve this beautiful woman? She was everything I could ask for in a mate: loving and passionate, brave and strong. And she was mine, forever.

Mine, my sated Mori whispered.

The storm blew itself out in the early hours of the morning. When I peered out just before dawn, everything was coated in a thick layer of ice. I noticed the wyvern had left, probably to hunt. Or he thought Sara was no longer in danger.

As I dressed in my dry clothes, I watched Sara, who still slept soundly. If we were at home, I would wake her up slowly and spend our first day as a mated couple making love to her. But daylight was approaching, and Tristan would be searching for us. I needed to get her home, and then we'd make up for lost time.

I let her sleep as long as I could, and then I lay beside her. Raising myself on my elbow, I caressed her face softly, reluctant to wake her, but dying to kiss her again.

When my finger touched her lips, she stretched and a sensual smile curved her lush mouth. Her eyes opened sleepily, and I smiled as I lowered my head to kiss her.

"Morning," she said in a husky voice.

I rose up to meet her eyes. *Good morning, moy malen'kiy voin,* I said, testing our bond for the first time.

Her brow furrowed, and then her eyes widened. *Nikolas?*

Pleasure filled me at hearing her voice in my mind. I smiled at her. *One of the perks of being mated.*

"Mated." She stared at me, her face full of the same wonder I'd been feeling all night.

Through the bond, I felt a swell of love and happiness – and a trickle of something else. I knew what it was when I saw a blush creep across her cheeks. My beautiful mate was remembering last night – in detail, I hoped.

"Can you read my mind?" she blurted.

I lifted an eyebrow. "No. But that blush makes me wish I could."

Her mouth fell open, and she ducked her head, pressing her face against my chest.

Chuckling, I wrapped my free arm around her, pulling her close. I leaned down to touch my lips to her ear. "I love waking up with you in my arms."

She looked up at me and surprised me when she tugged me down and proceeded to kiss the hell out of me. Her mouth was soft and insistent, her tongue teasing as she wantonly seduced me. Through the bond, I felt her desire, and my body stirred in response.

I pulled out of the kiss and growled at her sensual smile. "If you keep looking at me like that, we'll never leave this cabin. In fact, I might have to find the owner and buy it from him."

Her stomach rumbled. "Can we bring food next time? I'm starving."

A laugh burst from me. Reluctantly, I stood and handed her clothes I'd hung to dry last night.

"Your shirt and jeans are dry, but your boots are still wet," I said as I gave them to her. I didn't add that her bra and panties were somewhere in the tangle of quilts.

As she dressed, I went to the small cabinet in the corner, which served as a kitchen, and took out the food I'd found earlier. I kept my back to her until I heard her finish.

I carried my meager offering to her. Canned tuna, saltines, and bottled water was not the breakfast I would have given her the morning after our mating, but it was all I had.

I sat beside her on the mattress. "Not exactly a five-star breakfast."

She smiled warmly. "It's perfect."

I spread some tuna on a cracker for her. "It'll be daylight soon. The storm's over, so we should head out as soon as it's light enough."

"How far is it to the road?" she asked before she popped the cracker into her mouth.

"About fifteen miles. I won't be surprised if we run into some of our people on the way." I had expected Tristan and Chris to find us by now. But then, the storm would have wiped out all our tracks, and it was a large area to search.

I gave her another cracker. "We'll be home before you know it."

I watched her as she ate. She looked well recovered from yesterday's ordeal, and she hadn't mentioned the problem with her power.

"How do you feel today? Is there any change in your magic?"

She looked away as if she was testing it, and then she let out a shaky laugh. "I think it's getting better. Whatever they shot me with must be wearing off."

"Good. That means we won't have to call the faerie." Although, I'd put up with Eldeorin if she needed him.

She smirked playfully. "Jealous?"

"I might have been a little jealous once or twice." I thought about last night and smiled with satisfaction. "But I got the girl."

She leaned over and pressed a quick kiss on my lips. "You always had the girl."

When she went to pull away, I grabbed her and kissed her again.

We finished our food and got up to tidy the cabin. I doused the fire and put the mattress back on the bed. Before we left, I stuck some money under the lantern to pay for the busted lock and food.

The storm might have passed, but the temperature hadn't risen much yet. Our breath came out in steamy puffs, and Sara rubbed her bare hands together. I couldn't find any gloves in the cabin, and I worried about the long walk ahead of us.

The cold wasn't our only problem. The snow was deep and crusted over, and her legs would tire quickly trudging through it.

"It's going to be rough walking with the snow iced over. Climb on my back, and I'll carry you."

She snorted softly. "You can't carry me fifteen miles."

"Are you willing to bet on that?" I challenged, already thinking of my prize.

"I don't know." She treated me to a saucy smile. "What will you give me if I win?"

I laughed at her playfulness and reached for her. "Anything you —"

It took me a second to recognize the sharp sting near my shoulder blade. Blood roared in my ears, and my vision dimmed.

"Sara…run," I croaked as I fell.

"Nikolas!" she screamed.

My last thought before darkness took me was that I'd failed her.

CHAPTER 45

"TIME TO WAKE up, my darling."

Sara?

I pushed upward from the dark void toward the sound of a female voice. A hand stroked my forehead, but the touch felt wrong. Something was off.

"That's it. Open your eyes."

The voice was familiar in a distant way, as if I hadn't heard it in a long time. But it was also one I knew well. I struggled to focus on it, and slowly, from the mists of my memory, a face appeared. Heart shaped with mischievous blue eyes. Long blonde hair.

"Elena?" I mumbled, finding it hard to concentrate.

It had been a while since I'd thought about Tristan's little sister. For years, I'd carried the guilt over her death with me. In recent years, I'd thought of her less, and hardly at all since I met Sara. Maybe protecting Tristan's granddaughter and keeping her safe had absolved me of the guilt of not saving his beloved sister.

But you didn't protect Sara, taunted a voice in my head. *You failed her.*

"You do remember me," Elena crooned, her fingers caressing my jaw. "Oh, I've missed you so much."

Can't be Elena. Elena is dead.

"Sara?"

The fingers stopped moving.

"Nikolas, open your eyes," commanded a hard voice that was not Sara's. "Look at me."

I forced my lids to rise. The light hurt my eyes, and I closed them again. What the hell was wrong with me?

"Here, my love." A lamp clicked. "Try now."

My eyes opened again. The light was less harsh, and above me a face swam into view. I blinked a few times to clear my vision. The face grew sharper, the features coming into focus.

I stared at the face of the young girl who had died over one hundred and fifty years ago. Tristan's sister looked as she had the last time I saw her, except there was a hardness in her face, a malice in her eyes that hadn't been there before.

"Hello, Nikolas." She picked up my hand and held it between both of hers. I could feel her touch, but my arm was lifeless when I tried to move it.

"Elena? You're not real."

Her smile was as sweet as I remembered. "Oh, I'm very real."

"How?" My mind was still fuzzy, and I couldn't make sense of what I saw. "You died. I...helped bury you."

"No, my love." She stood and twirled beside the bed I lay on. "See? I'm as alive as you are. And now we can finally be together."

"Together?" Something faint brushed against my mind. Like a curtain lifting, the fog in my brain dissipated.

Sara. The cabin. The prick of a dart. Her screaming my name.

Oh God, Sara. The vampires had found us and knocked me out. Where had they taken us? Where was Sara? I concentrated on our bond and felt her nearby, not in the next room but close enough to know she was still alive.

Sara? I called to her. *Sara, can you hear me?*

Nothing.

Was she hurt? Afraid? What had they done to her?

"Nikolas, are you even listening to me?"

I stared at Elena who had come to sit on the bed again. The sinking feeling in my gut turned into horror as I put the pieces together.

Vampires had captured us.

Elena was a vampire.

"It's not possible. You can't be... A Mohiri can't become a vampire."

She smiled, and this time, two dainty fangs appeared at the corners of her mouth. "Oh, but you can. It's rather painful, of course, but entirely possible if the right vampire does it."

"Jesus, Elena." My chest ached for Tristan and the memory of the girl I used to know. All this time, we'd believed she was dead. The vampires must have put her clothes on a human girl and burned the body so we wouldn't recognize it. They knew we'd come for her if we thought she was still alive.

"I'm so sorry." She was alive, but becoming a vampire was a fate worse than death.

Her smile faded. "You should be. I suffered a lot more than you will. You're fortunate you are mine, and that I'm a better Master than my old one."

"Master?" It took a moment for her words to register. Shock tore

516

through me, leaving a solid lump of ice in my stomach. "It's you?"

"Yes."

"But how?" Masters were very old and powerful. How could she have become one so fast?

She patted my arm. "That's a story I'm saving for when my dear niece joins us."

Fear threatened to suffocate me. "What have you done with Sara?"

The gleam in her eyes was pure evil. "She's well – for now. She's enjoying my special guest accommodations, which I'm afraid are not as nice as yours. I must say, she's an intriguing little thing. I quite enjoyed talking to her, although she had no idea who I was."

She laughed gleefully. "Do you know she actually tried to comfort me, thinking I was a scared little human girl in the cell next to hers? She even told me we were all getting out of here. Endlessly entertaining, my niece."

I swallowed dryly. "Why her?"

"That is something else I'm saving for our little reunion." She glanced at a clock on the wall. "Oh dear, look at the time. We have to get ready for the party I've planned in your honor."

I tried to rise, but whatever drug they had used on me left my body as weak as a newborn's.

Elena leaned over me, and I realized I was shirtless. "Don't worry, my love. You'll be strong again very soon." She kissed my jaw, and a shudder went through me. Pushing my head to one side, she ran her tongue down my throat.

I gasped when her fangs pierced my skin. She latched on to me, drinking my blood in long pulls, and I was helpless to stop her.

In my entire life, I'd never been bitten by a vampire, until now. Revulsion twisted my stomach as she made little moaning sounds and slowly drained me.

I was close to passing out when she released me and lifted her head. She closed her eyes and licked her lips like she had just sampled a fine wine.

"I've waited so long to taste you, and you are better than I dreamed. We're going to have so much fun together. But first, we have other business to take care of."

She stood and went to the door. "Ava."

A red-haired female vampire and a dark-haired male appeared in the doorway.

"Take Nikolas to the drawing room, and then bring my niece up. I'll be along shortly."

"Yes, Master," the female said.

The male vampire hoisted me over his shoulder and followed the female down a flight of stairs to the first floor of the house. Between the drugs in my system and the blood loss, I had trouble holding on to consciousness. I fought the darkness threatening to swallow me. I couldn't leave Sara to face this horror alone.

God, Elena. My mind had trouble coming to terms with Tristan's sister being a vampire. Not just a vampire, but the Master. The person responsible for so much pain and death, the person who had killed Sara's father and tried to destroy her life was someone I'd once loved as a sister.

We passed through a set of French doors, and the vampire dumped me on a rug in the center of the room. Around me, I heard the murmur of many voices. Vampires.

I heard the clank of metal, and then I found myself on my knees, shackled and chained. I struggled to stay upright when my body tried to slump. Closing my eyes, I saw a picture of Sara smiling at me as we left the cabin. I focused on her face and drew strength from it to keep my body upright.

Sara? I called to her. I had to tell her about Elena, had to tell her to find a way to escape before...

I'm here, Nikolas. I'm coming to you.

Coming to me? No! Elena...Elena was going to hurt her. She couldn't come here.

No, you have to run. The Master...

I slumped as a wave of dizziness hit me. In my mind, I thought I heard Sara calling my name, but I was too disoriented to respond. It was all I could do to stay awake.

"Nikolas!"

A gentle hand lifted my head, and her presence surrounded me like a warm blanket. I tried to tell her to run, but the words wouldn't come.

"I'm here." Her lips brushed mine, and she wrapped her arms around me protectively. *I love you, Nikolas. Stay with me.*

"Sara," I rasped. She was the most precious thing in my life, and I'd failed her. She deserved a long life full of love and happiness, but she was going to die here surrounded by evil.

She pulled back to look at me. *What have they done to you?*

"How very touching," said a male vampire sitting in front of us.

Sara released me and stood to face the vampire. I reached for her, but the chains held me back.

"Sebastian, how many times have I asked you not to sit in my chair?" said a sweet voice laced with malevolence.

The room grew quiet.

Sara took a step back and turned to look at Elena. I managed to grab hold of her hand.

"We meet at last, Sara Grey," Elena said with barely concealed excitement. "Or maybe I should say, *niece.*"

"Elena, please," I croaked.

Sara gripped my hand in both of hers, and I cursed my weak body. More than any other time, she needed me to stand beside her, and I could barely hold my head up. If I had any strength in me, I would give it all to her. I'd do anything to save her from what was going to happen.

"Please what, Nikolas?" Elena asked with cold glee as she walked around us to sit in a large chair in front of me. "I've waited a long time to hear you beg, so make it good."

I raised my eyes to her glittering blue ones. "This is between you and me. Let her go and I'll do whatever you want."

Sara clung to my hand. "No!"

"She's such a loyal little thing, isn't she?" Elena jeered. "How loyal do you think she'll be when she hears how you abandoned me and left me in the hands of a monster?"

"He didn't abandon you," Sara said. "He and Tristan looked everywhere for you. They thought you died."

"They didn't look hard enough!" Elena glared at me, her face contorted with rage. "For weeks I prayed you would come for me, Nikolas, but you never did. Week after week, month after month, the Master used me, tortured me, and drank from me until I was almost dry. He was a sadistic animal, and for two years he kept me chained in his chambers, two years of living hell while my loving brother and friend lived their happy little lives."

For one moment, instead of the vampire, I saw the agonized face of the young girl who used to be vibrant and happy and alive. I couldn't bear to think of her suffering like that at the hands of a vampire. If I'd known, if I'd had a single clue she might be alive, I never would have stopped looking for her. Tristan and I would have devoted our lives to finding her and bringing her home.

"One day the Master got bored and decided I'd be a more fun plaything if I was a vampire. Only I already had a demon inside of me."

Elena leaned forward, her clawed hands gripping the chair so hard it threatened to break. "Do you know what it feels like to have two demons fighting to the death inside your body? Do you know how agonizing it is when your Mori dies, Nikolas?"

I couldn't imagine the horror she'd been through. "Elena…"

I choked as powerful hands wrapped around my throat and lifted me as far as the chains would allow. Elena snarled, her face inches from mine. "You talk when I say you can talk."

"Stop!" Sara screamed. "You're killing him."

Elena struck her so hard Sara fell to the floor. I tried to yell out, but I could get no air into my lungs.

She released me, and I fell backward, no longer able to support my weight on my knees.

Sara let out a sob and crawled to me. She pulled my head into her lap and stroked my face as my lungs filled with air again.

Elena circled us and continued her story as if she hadn't almost killed me.

"The Master was so pleased with himself because he was able to change a Mohiri into a vampire. I was his favorite pet and his prized possession, and he showed me off every chance he got. He liked to dress me up in pretty clothes and pamper me. I was a life-sized doll he could take out and play with whenever he wanted. He loved how small and weak I was, and he told me every day that I belonged to him forever."

She crouched in front of us, her eyes gleaming with insanity. "But he was wrong. I was a lot stronger than I let him see, and I was biding my time, waiting years for the perfect moment. That arrogant bastard was so sure of his superiority that he got complacent. One night he didn't bother to lock me up after he'd finished playing with me, and that was the opportunity I'd been waiting for. I killed him while he slept and drank him dry."

She smiled as if she was having a fond memory. "Did you know that is the only way to become a Master? His children, his wealth, and power all became mine. After years of being a slave I was free and powerful, and it felt incredible. My old family had deserted me, so I began to create a new one."

My blood turned to ice when she began toying with Sara's hair. Elena wasn't just powerful; she was demented and volatile, and she could kill Sara without blinking.

"I spent months searching for the perfect human to become my firstborn. Eli was special," she said with eerie softness. She leaned close to Sara. "You will pay for his death a thousand times over."

Sara shuddered and hugged me tighter. Her fear flowed to me across our bond.

I covered her hand with mine. *Be brave, moy malen'kiy voin.*

She's insane, Nikolas. I'm scared.

No matter what happens, I'm here with you, I vowed.

I sent my love through the bond and her body relaxed slightly as it filled her.

She looked at Elena. "Why did you send Eli to kill my father? He was nothing to you."

Elena laughed. "Your father *was* nothing to me, but he meant something to my dear niece, Madeline."

"You killed him to get to Madeline?" Sara asked as Elena went back to her chair. Her voice was laced with pain and fury.

Elena arranged her skirt around her. "I killed him, not because she loved him, but because of the child she could have with him. It wasn't until ten years later that I learned I had been too late and a child already existed."

A child? Elena had disappeared long before Madeline was born. Why would she want Madeline's daughter? Did she hate Tristan so much she wanted to destroy his family?

"But why? Why did you care so much if they had a child?" Sara pressed.

Elena hesitated before answering. "I was having a party and Madeline was my guest of honor. You should have seen her face when she realized who I was. Priceless. Of course, I compelled her to forget me before I let her go." She giggled. "I even made her think I was a male."

"You let her go?" Sara asked.

"Nothing like a little hunt to spice up a party." She pursed her lips unhappily. "Madeline proved to be more evasive than I gave her credit for. One of my guests was a warlock named Azar who was known for his gift of sight. Azar stupidly waited until after Madeline had gone to tell me he'd had a vision when he saw her. He told me that Madeline's half-blood daughter would destroy me."

I didn't put much faith in prophecies because I'd never seen one come to pass. But Elena was insane, and she obviously believed the warlock. If she thought Sara was her biggest threat, she wouldn't let her niece live long. I had to get Sara out of here.

Elena lifted a shoulder. "Needless to say, I was quite upset Azar hadn't shared that piece of information *before* I released Madeline. I discovered aged warlock is a very fine drink."

She laughed at her own joke. "We managed to pick up Madeline's trail, and followed her to Portland, which is how we found her human husband. Oddly, Eli saw no sign of a child even though he went to the house you lived in. It wasn't until Eli found you in Portland last fall that we learned what you really were. I had no idea someone like you could even exist. But here you are."

She stood and looked at the red-haired vampire. "I am bored with this chatter. I think it's time we get the festivities underway. Ava?"

The female came over.

"Has everything been prepared as I asked?" Elena asked her.

"Yes, Master."

"Wonderful." Elena smiled at us. "Today is a very special day for me, and it wouldn't be possible without the two of you."

Dread filled me, but I hid it from Sara, not wanting her to sense it through our bond. I could already feel her mounting fear.

Nikolas.

Be strong.

I sat up with Sara's help. "What are you planning, Elena?" It was better to know what was coming, to prepare ourselves.

She came over and stroked my face as a lover would, not the person about to kill me. "Why, today is my wedding day. All I needed was my groom."

"What?" Sara's fear immediately turned to rage, and I had to hold her back when she tried to jump at Elena.

Elena ran her fingers through my hair, and I hid my revulsion, not wanting to set her off.

"I have been waiting for you for a long time, Nikolas. For months, my children have tried to bring you to me. I had to find Sara because of Azar's pesky prediction. But *you* are my real prize."

Sara grew rigid in my arms as the meaning of Elena's words hit us. I sent her reassurance through the bond, but a bonded female could be as crazy as a male if her mate was threatened.

Elena continued as if she hadn't noticed anything. "You are a magnificent warrior, and you will make an even more magnificent vampire and a fitting mate for me."

"No!"

Sara leapt out of my arms and would have reached Elena if two vampires hadn't grabbed her first. She twisted in their hold, her eyes blazing despite my attempts to calm her.

"You can't have him," she shouted.

Elena smiled indulgently. "Sara, what you don't understand is that Nikolas and I were always destined to be together. He loved me, and we would have been mated if I hadn't been taken from him. Isn't that right, my love?"

I didn't want to anger her, but I could never profess that kind of love for her. If something happened to Sara or me, my last words would not be a lie.

"I loved you, Elena, but as a sister. I grieved your death as a brother grieves his sibling."

She shook her head. "That's not true. We were perfect together. If we'd had more time together, the bond would have grown."

I didn't know what to say so I said nothing.

Her smile returned. "That's all in the past. Today we'll start over and create a new bond."

Sara tried to lunge at her again. "Nikolas will never bond with you. He's mine."

Elena sneered at Sara. "Just because he is your protector, does not mean he belongs to you, you silly child."

"He's not my protector," Sara growled. "He's my mate."

"No!" Elena stomped her foot. "You're mine, Nikolas, not this half breed's. When you become a vampire your Mori will die and the bond with her will be severed. Then we will be together forever."

I shook my head in horror. Sever the bond with Sara? I'd rather die than lose her that way.

Elena stood over me. "My wedding gift to you will be her. You will be very thirsty after the change. Her blood will be our wedding drink."

My stomach lurched. If she managed to do what she said, the vamhir demon would take over my body. I'd be trapped as it killed Sara, and the last thing she'd see was my face as it drained her. I'd spend the rest of my life in hell.

Sara, you need to get out of here. Use your power, I pleaded. I could get through what was to come if she was safe.

I can't. They drugged me again.

"Take her out of my sight until the ceremony," Elena ordered. "Everyone leave us. I wish to be alone with my groom."

The two vampires dragged Sara away. She struggled against them and called my name.

Fight, Sara. Try to use your power. You're stronger than they are.

Her screams rang in my ears after she was gone. I closed my eyes and prayed.

God, please give her the strength to survive this.

CHAPTER 46

ELENA KNELT AND released my shackles. "I think I'd like our reunion to be somewhere a little more private. Wouldn't you like that too, my love?"

Not waiting for an answer, she picked me up as if I weighed nothing and carried me from the room. At the end of the hallway, she opened the door to what had to be her private suite, based on its size, opulence, and the heavy shutters over the windows.

She laid me on the canopy bed, and I tested my strength, which was slowly returning. If I'd been taken alone, I'd wait until was I strong enough and try to fight my way out. Or at least cut the head off the snake. But I couldn't risk Sara's life. There had to be a way to get her out of here.

"Alone at last." Elena knelt on the bed beside me and forced my arms above my head. Cold metal closed around my wrists as she secured me.

She sat back on her heels and ran a hand across my chest. "I love my children, but being a parent can be so unbearably tedious at times. I do what I can to amuse myself. I've lost count of the lovers I've had."

She smiled. "Are you shocked to hear that? Even women have needs, Nikolas. I prefer the blood of human girls, and I like my males strong and virile. But not one of my lovers could ever compare to you."

Her hand slid down to my stomach and trailed along the top of my jeans. I swallowed down my abhorrence of her touch. The longer she was distracted with me, the longer she'd leave Sara alone.

"I want you," she murmured, kissing my jaw. "But as much as I enjoy a reluctant male, I want you willing when we consummate our bond. It'll be so much more pleasurable for us both."

"How can there be a bond without our Mori?" I asked as if I cared, when all I wanted to do was keep her occupied as long as possible.

She waved it off. "When two people are meant to be soul mates, the bond will always be there. You'll see."

I thought about Sara and knew Elena was right. No matter what happened to me, I'd always love Sara. My Mori could die, and I could be trapped in a vampire's body, but my heart and my soul would always belong to her.

"Before we can bond and begin our life together, you have to be reborn as my mate." Elena rose up over me, straddling my hips. "I've dreamed of this moment for so long. It's hard to believe we are really here."

She rubbed her hands against my chest. "You look so calm, so brave. Such a warrior. I've made hundreds of vampires, and they all begged for their pathetic human lives before the change. You won't beg, will you?"

I met her stare. "No."

"Good. Let's begin then, shall we?"

I closed my eyes and thought of Sara. *I love you.*

"No. Look at me," Elena ordered. "I won't have you thinking about that half-breed when I make you. I'm the one you will see."

I opened my eyes and stared defiantly at her. She had me at her mercy, but she would not break me. She might be the face in front of my eyes, but it was Sara who filled my heart and Sara's touch I felt on my skin.

She leaned down and turned my head to one side. I braced myself.

"I wish I could tell you this won't hurt." She licked the bite mark she'd made earlier. "But you haven't felt pain until you've felt your Mori die. All I can promise is that it will be quick. Most vampires take days to change, unless they are made by a Master. Our blood is much stronger, and it will make your vamhir grow quickly. Tonight you will be reborn."

I knew it was coming, but I still wasn't prepared for her strike and the awful pulling sensation of her drinking my blood. She lay on top of me, writhing with pleasure as she drank until I was sure she had lost control and was going to drain me dry.

When my heart slowed and my vision darkened, she lifted her head and smiled. "Perfect. Now you're ready."

She bit her wrist and held it over my mouth. I pressed my lips together in a last attempt to fight her, but she pinched the sides of my jaw with her other hand and forced my mouth open.

I gagged when the warm blood hit the back of my tongue and ran down my throat. I tried to cough it up, but there was too much, and I couldn't move my head to spit it out. Despair rose up in me, for Sara, who would be alone in this hellish place and who would be forced to see me become the thing she despised the most.

"There." Elena removed her wrist and wiped away the blood that had run down my chin. Her eyes glowed with excitement when she smiled at me. "Soon, it will begin. But don't worry, my love. I'll be with you through it all."

She curled up against my side with her head on my shoulder. Her hand stroked my chest as she told me what our new life would be like.

"You will be insatiable at first, but I will provide you with all the warm bodies you can drink. I want my mate to be strong and happy. Then you will lead the army we'll build against the Mohiri. You know all their locations, their defenses, and how they think. And you are a magnificent fighter."

"No," I slurred.

"Shhh. You will feel different about it soon." She kissed my chest. "If you'd like, we can change some of your friends. Maybe even Tristan. Would that please you? Actually, I like that idea very much. I'd love to be reunited with my dear brother. And the three of us will hunt down Madeline and make her pay for the trouble she's caused me."

She sighed happily. "It will be the perfect life. And we'll celebrate every victory with our sweet little Sara. I plan to keep her around for many, many years."

No, my mind screamed because my voice no longer worked. *Sara? Sara? You have to run. You have to get out of here.*

There was no answer.

Then the pain hit.

My Mori screamed as blinding, white-hot pain unlike anything I'd felt before shot through my head. I couldn't breathe, my throat and chest felt as if they were on fire, and I was sure my eyes were going to burn in their sockets. My body arched off the bed, but there was no escaping the agony consuming me.

Something moved beneath my ribs, and cold tentacles reached for my heart. I fought my bonds, but my body was too weak.

The pain subsided, and I dropped back to the bed. Sweat coated my face, and my eyes hurt so much I couldn't open them.

"I'm here," Elena crooned, touching my face. "I know it hurts, my love, but it will pass."

The vamhir demon moved in my chest again, and my whole being recoiled at the thought of having that thing inside me and of what I would become.

Fight, I ordered my Mori. *Don't let it take us.*

Elena and her Mori were young when she was changed. My Mori was old and very strong. It would fight the younger demon and win. Elena would realize she couldn't make me into a vampire.

Too soon, the next wave of pain crashed over me, and I lost all thought. My Mori's screams echoed in my head as it fought the other demon invading our body. My body convulsed, and I thought the pain would never end.

A hand brushed damp hair out of my face. "Don't fight it, my warrior.

You will only prolong the pain."

I shook my head weakly at her words. *Not your warrior. I belong to Sara.*

This time when the pain came, I screamed Sara's name.

And then, blessed darkness came for me.

*   *   *

Pain woke me. I opened my eyes and stared up at the night sky in confusion. I was outdoors, lying on something cold and hard. Stone. I tried to move, but someone held my arms above my head. I tilted my head and saw a female vampire in a red dress. Another female, similarly attired, held my feet. In my weakened state, it didn't require much effort for them to restrain me. I looked down at my body now dressed in a black tuxedo.

"You're awake at last."

Elena came into view, wearing a white dress and a tiara with a veil attached. A wedding gown. We were dressed as a bride and groom, and we were surrounded by vampires dressed like wedding guests.

She leaned down to press a kiss to my lips. "You're doing so well, my love."

"Sara?" I croaked.

Elena's mouth hardened. "She will be along shortly. She is my wedding present to you, after all."

Nikolas?

Sara's voice filled my head, and I felt her coming toward me.

Sara. No, she couldn't come here. It would kill her. *I don't want you to see this.*

Warmth and love flowed through the bond. *Whatever happens, we'll face it together.*

I felt her fear but also her courage as she drew near. My Mori called to its mate as the crowd parted for her.

"Oh, God," she cried.

I turned my head to see her. She was dressed in a flowing emerald dress, and her chestnut hair lay around her shoulders in soft waves. She was a vision, an angel in the midst of hell.

"My beautiful little warrior," I said in a voice raw from pain. *Look away, Sara. Please.*

Elena clapped her hands, drawing all eyes but mine to her. I watched Sara.

"My children, we are gathered here for a very happy event. Tonight, I will take a mate."

The vampires applauded and cheered. Sara stood frozen.

Elena called for silence. "The transformation has begun, and in a few hours my mate will be born."

Sara stared at me. "No," she screamed, her pain slicing through my own.

She fought against the red-haired female holding her arm. The vampire released her, and she ran to me.

Her hands cupped my face, and I sighed at her touch.

"I'm here, Nikolas. I won't leave you." *Fight it. Your Mori is strong. You can defeat this thing.*

I felt the next surge of crippling pain coming, and I tried to close off the bond and block her from it. But I couldn't hide the tremors that racked my body or keep the grimace from my face.

She wiped the sweat from my face. *Listen to me, Nikolas. I've seen vamhir demons, and they're weak. They control through pain. Fight the pain, and you'll beat it.*

I opened my eyes to look at her. I had to prepare her for the worst. She already knew I loved her, but I had to make sure she knew I would never stop.

"I'll fight until my last breath for you. But if this thing takes my body, I want you to remember that my soul belongs to you. No matter what the demon does or says, I love you. I will always love only you."

"I'll fight too. I promise," she whispered.

Her eyes widened, and a burst of excitement came through the bond. *Nikolas, my power is coming back. Just hold on a little longer, and I'll be strong enough for both of us.*

My heart leapt. Her power wasn't strong enough to take on a Master and houseful of vampires, but she could use it to escape. I would die knowing she was safe.

You can't save me and fight Elena. Use your power to get away from here.

Her eyes widened in horror. *No, I won't leave you.*

Get out of here, Sara, I pleaded desperately. *Get help and come back for me.*

She shook her head, her eyes welling with tears. "It'll be too late."

I opened my mouth to speak, but Elena grabbed Sara's shoulder.

"You two have had plenty of time to say your good-byes. It's time to get on with my wedding."

"Wait, Elena, please." I gave her a beseeching look.

She smiled, but it didn't reach her eyes. "Yes, my love?"

"One kiss before you take her."

Her face twisted into an ugly snarl. "You're *my* groom, Nikolas. You don't kiss another girl on your wedding day."

I summoned a smile for her. "Just a good-bye kiss. You will have all the rest."

"Oh," she simpered. "Very well. One kiss."

"My arms?" This would be the last time I touched Sara, and I needed to hold her.

"Fine. Get on with it," Elena snapped.

"Nikolas, what are you doing?" Sara whispered when I wrapped my arms around her.

I smiled to hide my intentions. If she knew what I planned, she'd fight me. She would never try to save herself as long as I was here. That left only one thing for me to do.

But first, I would hold my beautiful little warrior and kiss her one last time.

I brushed her hair aside and framed her face with my hands, pulling her down to me. Our lips met, and I coaxed hers open to deepen the kiss and to lose myself in her.

She whimpered, her hot tears falling on my face. I wouldn't give in to my grief over the life stolen from us. This moment was about her. She would survive this, and her last memory of me would be full of love and tenderness.

She stifled a sob, and I kissed away the tears streaming down her cheeks as I memorized her sweet face.

"Shhh, don't cry. It'll be okay."

"It'll never be okay." She pressed her face against my throat, and I held her tightly as she cried.

My heart ached, not because of the demon attacking it, but for her. She'd grieve when I was gone, but someday she'd be happy again. Tristan and Nate and all of the people who loved her would be there to make sure of it. The knowledge she would go on filled me with a sense of peace and acceptance.

Elena's hard voice cut through the silence. "Time's up."

Sara started to pull away, but I held her tightly as I opened myself completely to my Mori. Our mate needed us, and we worked for the last time to give her the final gift of our love.

"Be strong, Sara. Live – for me."

I felt her shock and heard her gasp when I pushed everything I had through our bond. My speed and strength, coupled with her power, would give her what she needed to escape this place. Where I was going, I didn't need it.

My arms went slack.

She staggered backward, her face drained of color. "What have you done?"

I could barely see her through the dark haze descending over me. *I love you*, I thought groggily, glad she was the last thing I would see of this life.

My Mori cried out and became silent. In my chest, the vamhir demon surged to claim my dying body. I shuddered and convulsed under the attack, but the demon was too late. There would soon be no life left in this body for it to use.

Someone shook me. From a long way off, Sara screamed, "You promised you'd fight! You said you wouldn't leave me."

Hands hit my chest, and my body jerked as if hit by an electric current.

The demon in my chest stopped moving.

I felt my heart slow and my breathing grow shallow as coldness spread through me.

*　*　*

A roar penetrated the cold darkness I floated in. There was something about the sound, a mix of pure grief and rage, that tugged at my chest. Someone was in a lot of pain, and I wanted to go to them. But my body refused to move.

"Jesus, did you see that?"

"I'm not sure what I saw."

"She disappeared into thin air. What they say must be true."

"What's that?"

"That she's half Fae?"

The voices sounded garbled like I was underwater. That must be why they made no sense.

Why was I underwater? And how was I breathing? But I couldn't be breathing. I was dead.

"What's going on out there? Can you see anything?"

"No. There's some kind of ice wall blocking them."

"Ice wall? Go check it out."

"Tristan asked us to stay with him."

"You think she can kill a Master."

"After what I just saw, all my money is on her."

Her? Sara. My beautiful little warrior. I would have given anything to stay with her. But I had to leave so she could live.

Hearing she was with Tristan sent warmth through my cold body. She was safe with the people she loved.

It grew quiet again in the blackness. I'd never felt so alone. My Mori had always been a part of me, and it felt wrong not having it here with me. Was this how Sara felt when she wasn't joined with her Mori? How did she stand the aloneness?

The vamhir demon was dead too, killed by Sara. And I was completely alone. I hated it here, but it was a small price to pay for her life.

The darkness rippled and pulled at me. My head rested on something warm, and a hand touched my face. Her hand. But how could she be here in this place with me?

"Sara, we have to —"

"No. Leave us alone."

"No one is going to take him from you. Let us move you both somewhere warmer."

"Nikolas doesn't get cold."

"Nikolas would want you to take care of yourself. You can't stay out here."

"He needs me. I won't leave him."

"Here, little one."

More warmth wrapped around me. *I'm here, Nikolas. I won't let them take you from me.*

The voice came to me, not out of the darkness, but from inside my head. But that was impossible, unless…

Solmi, whispered a voice so faint I thought I'd imagined it. A voice I'd never thought to hear again. Hope flared in my cold chest as I searched for the missing part of me.

I'd known a warrior once who had been so gravely injured in battle everyone thought he was dead. What we hadn't known was that his Mori had gone into a kind of stasis to regenerate itself.

Sara's voice came to me again. *You would have been so proud of me, Nikolas.*

I am proud of you, I wanted to say.

In the back of my mind, something stirred, another consciousness awakening. I reached for it, and it slowly moved toward me. It sank into me quietly, and the loneliness I'd been feeling disappeared.

My Mori was alive.

And so was I.

I'm here, Sara, I tried to say, but no words came. The connection was still there between us, but my Mori was too weak. Like the rest of me.

My heart beat slowly in my chest, and my breath was shallow. My body and my demon had been through a lot, but my Mori was quickly repairing us. With each second that passed, I could feel my Mori growing stronger and the bond opening.

My Mori reached out to its mate. Across our bond, Sara's Mori answered.

Her hands began to stroke my face again, and her voice came to me as clear as if she'd spoken out loud.

I don't know if I can bear this. I'm not as strong as you thought I was, Nikolas. I'm so lost without you.

The pain in her voice was too much to bear. I couldn't move, but I had to let her know I was coming back to her. I imagined how it felt to hold her in my arms, and then I sent that warmth and love to her.

Oh, Nikolas.

Sara, I called.

Nikolas?

My chest tightened. She'd heard me.

I'm here, Sara.

Oh God, I am going crazy, she moaned.

Feel my face, Sara, I ordered softly.

Her warm hand pressed against my cheek. She sucked in a sharp breath and bent over me until I felt her warm breath on my face.

She jerked upright. "He's alive!"

"No, Sara, he's gone," Tristan said in a voice rough with emotion.

Sara moved. I didn't know what was happening, but Tristan yelled, "Jesus Christ, he's breathing."

"Get the healers," Chris shouted to someone. "We need to move him inside."

Someone lifted me and carried me indoors to lay me on what felt like a bed. I felt Sara beside me the entire time.

I'm here, Nikolas, she called.

Healers arrived, and I was poked and prodded. The only touch I needed was Sara's, but I couldn't tell them that.

After a few minutes, Sara screamed, "Just help him, goddammit!"

I'm not going anywhere, Sara, I said to calm her fears.

If you do, I'll never forgive you.

A needle pricked my chest. Warmth spread quickly through me and my foot twitched.

"He's suffered some trauma around his heart, but nothing that won't heal," said one of the healers. "He should wake up soon. He's very strong."

"Yes, he is," Sara said.

Someone covered me with blankets, and Chris said, "You two are definitely meant for each other. I don't know which one of you is more stubborn."

"Him," Sara replied. She sat beside me on the bed and took my hand.

A jumble of emotions poured through the bond, and I knew she was crying. I forced my hand to move and cover hers as I sent reassurance to her.

Shhh, don't cry.

She sniffled. *Then you better hurry up and get better, because I'm a bit of a basket case right now.*

I tried to smile. *I'd heal a lot faster if I could hold my mate.*

She let out a small sob and lay down beside me with her head on my chest. Peace washed over me. The only thing that could make this better was being able to hold her.

"Is this real?" she whispered hoarsely. "Because if I'm dreaming, I never want to wake up."

It's real. I'm here, moy malen'kiy voin.

"How is this possible? I felt you die."

There was so much to explain to her. *You killed the vamhir demon. My Mori just needed time to recover. You brought me back.*

She began to cry once more. "Please, don't leave me again."

I lifted my arm slowly and wrapped it around her. "Never," I promised as I pulled her close.

She cried herself to sleep not long after, and I was happy to lie there and hold her as my strength returned.

Chris came in to check on us and to let me know we'd leave when I was recovered enough to travel. With so many warriors there and the Master dead, there was no fear of any vampires who might have escaped coming back.

Plus, Tristan had to make arrangements for his sister's body. I didn't need to ask what shape he was in. My happiness dimmed when I thought about the grief my friend must be feeling.

"Who killed her?" I asked Chris quietly, not wanting to wake Sara. "Please tell me Tristan didn't have to do it."

"You don't know? Shit, of course you don't."

"Know what?"

He raked a hand through his hair and pulled a chair up to the bed. "It was Sara. When we got here, she and Elena were fighting. From the look of the place, Sara had already killed a bunch of them."

He let out a puff of air. "We were stunned when we walked in and saw Elena. But Sara was so calm it was eerie. Elena took off, but she couldn't outrun Sara."

"Sara caught up to her?" I'd given her my strength and speed, but even I couldn't run down a Master.

"Let's just say Sara's Fae side came out to play. I thought you in a rage was scary, but you have nothing on her."

Sara whimpered in her sleep. I stroked her face, and she quieted.

I looked at Chris, who was smiling at us.

"You mated, didn't you?"

I kissed the top of her head. "How did you know?"

"Only a mated female can get *that* pissed off. And my little cousin gives the word a whole new meaning."

"Tell me."

"Like I said, Elena ran, but Sara didn't chase her. She transported like the faeries do, and Elena ran right into her."

"You're serious?" My mouth was hanging open, but I didn't care.

He laughed. "I couldn't make this stuff up if I tried. Sara and Elena were out on the lake behind this place. We went after them, but Sara put up a wall of ice around her and Elena. We tried to get inside, but we couldn't even put a chip in it. It had to be full of Sara's magic or Elena would have been able to punch through it.

"They were in there a few minutes before the wall came down. Sara walked out of it, and Elena was dead. Sara cut her head off somehow. I didn't see a weapon, and Sara was too out of it to tell us what happened in there."

"*Khristu.*"

Chris grew somber. "Sara told us Elena killed you. What happened?"

In a low voice, I told him what I could remember from the time I woke up here to when I thought I was dying. The only part I skimmed over was when Elena gave me her blood to start the change. It wasn't something I wanted to remember, let alone talk about.

He swore softly. "If we'd found this place a day sooner…"

"It's not your fault, so stop blaming yourself."

I looked down at Sara. I'd give anything to save her from what she'd suffered here. But she was alive and safe, and the Master was dead. Despite everything, I felt incredibly blessed.

He stood. "You look like you could use some rest too. I'll be down the hall if you need anything."

"Thanks, Chris."

"Anytime, my friend."

I pulled the blankets up over Sara's shoulders and held her close, thinking about what Chris had told me. After the torment and grief Elena had caused her, it was fitting that Sara had been the one to kill Elena.

I couldn't believe all of this had started because of some warlock's premonition. A premonition Elena had set into motion when she'd killed Sara's father. By doing so, she had brought about her own destruction. And she'd set me on the path to finding my mate.

Sara jerked awake. "Nikolas!"

I rubbed her back. "Shhh, I'm here."

"I thought…" She hugged me tightly. "I thought I dreamed it and you were…"

I brushed my lips against her forehead, and she turned her face toward mine.

"I'm never leaving you again, remember?" I said softly. "You'll be so sick of seeing my face you'll tell me to go away."

Her sad smile made my chest ache, and I knew it would be a while before both of us healed from this. But we were together, and we'd create so many happy memories there would be no room for the bad ones. I'd make sure of it.

She looked at the window, and a shiver went through her.

"Are you cold?"

"No. I hate this place."

"So do I." I sat up, lifting her into my arms as I stood. My muscles were still a little weak, but I had more than enough strength to carry her.

"What are you doing? You need to lie down."

I smiled at her. "I'll lie down when we get home."

Her face brightened. "Home?"

"Home."

I kissed her and carried her from the room.

CHAPTER 47

I OPENED THE refrigerator door and studied the contents. No milk, no eggs, no bread. We really needed to order some groceries today. Unfortunately, that wasn't going to help me with my current dilemma.

I pulled on some clothes and quietly let myself out of the apartment – and tripped over the massive body lying in the hallway. I smothered a curse and managed to catch myself before I hit the wall and woke up the whole floor.

Hugo raised his head and stared at me. He and his brother had been beside themselves when Sara came home almost two weeks ago. At first, they'd refused to let her out of their sight, and I'd had to endure two hellhounds sleeping in our bedroom.

After three days, even Sara agreed our apartment was too small for them, and she'd made them sleep outside the door. They didn't like it, but they had the run of the whole place now, and people no longer jumped when they ran into one of the hounds in the hallways.

"Morning, boy." I walked past him, and a few seconds later, I heard the scratch of his claws on the floor as he followed me. Woolf stayed in his spot on the other side of the door.

It was early, so not a lot of people were on the go yet. The few I saw looked amused when they spotted my furry companion. No matter where Sara and I went on the grounds, one of the hellhounds was with us. It was like the pair of them had decided I was Sara's so I belonged to them too. Sara thought it was adorable. Whatever made her smile was okay with me.

I entered the dining hall and went to the buffet to pile food on a tray. Soon I had enough French toast, waffles, scrambled eggs, sausages, bacon, and hash browns to feed a family of four. I added some fresh milk and orange juice because Sara liked them both, cutlery, and a blueberry muffin.

Hugo whined. When I looked at him, he licked his chops and wagged

535

his tail so hard his whole body moved from side to side.

Shaking my head, I grabbed half a dozen sausages and tossed them to him one at a time. When he was done, his tongue hung out and he gave me a toothy grin that would make a vampire wet his pants.

"Is this some kind of male bonding thing?"

I spun to glare at the blond faerie standing several feet away.

Hugo growled, and Eldeorin waved a hand at him. The hellhound sat back on his haunches, staring straight ahead as if he were in a trance. One of Eldeorin's "waking dreams," if I wasn't mistaken.

"What are you doing here?" I asked, not happy to see him but not entirely surprised he was here. He'd shown up immediately after we got home, having gotten word somehow that Sara was in trouble. He hadn't stayed long, but he told us he'd be back when it was time to resume her training.

"Just checking in on my little cousin. I'm happy to see she looks much improved." He smirked. "I never would have pegged her as a stomach sleeper."

"Stay the hell out of our bedroom," I growled at him.

He chuckled. "Chill out, warrior. I have better things to do than watch you two make little demons. There's this pair of French twins who can —"

"Faerie," I ground out.

He rolled his eyes. "Bonded males. No fun at all."

I laid my tray on the nearest table. "Is there a reason for this conversation other than to annoy me?"

His expression grew serious. "There is, actually. I think we've only scratched the surface of what Sara can do. I plan to resume training with her when she's recovered from her ordeal. Physically she is ready, but emotionally she has some healing to do first."

I nodded gravely, thinking about all the nights she'd woken up screaming my name in the last two weeks. I'd hold her and talk to her until she calmed, and then we'd make love. Afterward, she'd fall asleep again in my arms.

It had taken her almost a week to talk about what had happened that night with Elena, and her nightmares seemed less intense since she'd opened up. Last night she hadn't woken at all, and I hoped the worst was over.

"I know the Master is dead, but there are others out there who will fear Sara if they learn what she can do. By Fae standards, she's still a child, and we protect our children."

My stomach tightened. "She won't go to Faerie."

"I know. That's why I'm here to offer my protection."

"What kind of protection?"

He smiled. "Relax. I have no plans to hang around here. I'm going to ward this valley against vampires. Someday, when she's strong enough, I'll teach Sara to do it. Until then, I'll take care of it. It won't harm your demons or affect your people in any way."

"That's very generous of you." Even with all the additional security measures at Westhorne, I worried this place wasn't safe enough for Sara. There were a lot of vampires gunning for her, especially after she'd killed their Master. It was one of the reasons she'd agreed to take an extended trip to Russia with me this summer. The other reason was that my parents were dying to meet Sara. If we didn't go to them, they'd come here.

Eldeorin shrugged. "As I said, we protect our children. Now if you'll excuse me, I'll take care of the wards. And then I might visit those charming French twins…"

He disappeared mid-sentence. Hugo let out a snort and sniffed the air with a low growl.

"Yeah, I don't like him either." I picked up my tray. "Let's go feed our girl."

The apartment was quiet when I let myself in. I left Hugo and Woolf guarding the door. They were a wonderful deterrent to a well-meaning uncle and grandfather who loved to visit unannounced.

In the bedroom, I set the tray down on the nightstand. I sat on the bed and leaned down to the shape buried beneath the covers.

"Good morning, beautiful."

"Too early," she groaned from under the blanket. "Go away. I don't want to get up."

I laughed and pulled the covers down, revealing sleepy green eyes and tousled hair. Unable to resist, I leaned in for a quick kiss.

"Who said anything about getting up? I thought we'd have breakfast in bed this morning."

Her eyes widened, and she smiled. "You made breakfast?"

"No. All we have in the fridge is apples and an open can of tuna. Although, you do like tuna, if I remember. Maybe I should see if we have saltines."

She laughed and sat up, propping herself against the pillows. She was wearing my blue T-shirt again, and my body warmed at the sight of her in it.

"I don't think Oscar will be happy if we eat his tuna." Her stomach growled noisily. "But something smells amazing."

I set the tray down on her lap. "Your breakfast."

She stared at the food and burst out laughing. "Are we expecting company, or are you trying to fatten me up?"

"No and no."

I broke off a piece of bacon and put it to her lips. She ate it obediently, and I picked up a wedge of French toast dipped in syrup.

She smiled. "Mmmm, I could get used to this."

"Good, because I like doing it."

"But you have to eat, too." She lifted a forkful of eggs to my mouth and grinned when half the egg landed in my lap. "Oops. Maybe we should feed ourselves."

Chuckling, I ate the food left on the fork, and we started on our large breakfast. When she was done, she leaned back into the pillows with a contented sigh, leaving me to finish the meal. I loved moments like this when she looked happy and unburdened by bad memories.

"You remembered!"

She reached for the wrapped blueberry muffin, her smile doing funny things to my stomach. She leaned across the tray and pressed a quick kiss to my lips.

"Have I told you lately how much I love you?"

I smiled. "I think you might have said it a few times last night."

Her cheeks went an enticing shade of pink that told me exactly what she was thinking about. God, what had I ever done to deserve her?

Averting her eyes, she pushed the tray off her lap and climbed out of bed, holding the muffin. I followed her into the living room, watching how close the bottom of my T-shirt came to her curved behind.

I need to buy smaller shirts.

"Breakfast, boys," she called as she removed the plastic wrap from the muffin.

I heard a small shuffling sound and a squeak near the large teak chest under the window. The chest used to hold weapons, until Sara had decided it would make the perfect home for the three imps I'd discovered under her bed as we were packing up her old room. As I'd stared at the imps, she'd explained how they'd stowed away in her boxes from Maine and had been living in her room ever since. She'd given me a pleading look I could never refuse, which was why I now lived with a trio of imps.

In our world, imps were considered vermin, but Sara treated them with the same kindness she showed every other creature she encountered. She'd even named them, and unbelievably, the little fiends responded to their new names.

She knelt on the floor as a six-inch, pale, bald demon stepped out from behind the chest. She'd made a small hole in the back for them to get in and out of their new home.

"Verne, why am I not surprised to see you first? I swear you have a hollow leg."

The imp looked down at the legs showing beneath his loincloth. He shook one leg then the other before he frowned at Sara, who laughed softly.

"Never mind."

She broke the muffin into three pieces and held one out to him. I watched in wonder as he walked over and took it from her. The first time she'd done that, I'd been worried the little demon would bite her. But he'd seemed as taken with her as everyone else was.

"Where are Eliot and Orwell? Ah, there you are."

Two faces peeked out from behind the chest. More shy than the first one, they hesitated before creeping forward to get their food. The three of them scurried back into their home with their meal.

Sara went to the kitchen to throw the plastic wrap in the garbage, and I glanced around the apartment that was now full of her things. A drawing of her father hung on one wall, and photos of him, Nate, Roland, and Peter adorned the mantle. A red throw hung from one arm of the couch, and one of her paperbacks lay beside mine on the coffee table where we'd left them when we went to bed last night.

All the years I'd lived here, this had been my private place to unwind and keep my possessions. But I'd never realized what was missing until Sara moved in. Now, it felt like a home.

She came up behind me and slipped her arms around my waist. "You look deep in thought."

I smiled and turned to wrap my arms around her. "I was thinking about all the books you brought with you. How many classic authors do you like?"

"I don't know." She furrowed her brow. "Why?"

"You already have Hugo, Woolf, Oscar, Verne, Eliot, and Orwell. I'm wondering how many more pets you plan to get, and if we'll need a bigger place."

She laughed and tugged me over to the couch. "No more for a while, I promise," she said as she pulled the throw over her bare legs.

I sat beside her and lifted her legs onto my lap. "So what are your plans for today?"

"Jordan and I are getting together with Chris for archery lessons at ten. Then I have lunch with Nate, and I'm spending the afternoon with Emma. We're going to the lake to paint. Well, she'll paint. I'm going to draw."

"How's Emma doing?"

Emma looked healthier than she'd been when we found her, but she was withdrawn and she had regular anxiety attacks. Not that anyone could blame her after what she'd been through. Sara spent a lot of time with her and was slowly pulling Emma out of her shell.

Sara sighed. "Good, but I'm not sure she'll ever feel completely at home here. She says she'd like to find some small place to settle in when she's ready to leave. She seems so lost. I want to help her, but I'm not sure how."

I rubbed her leg. "You've been a great friend to her, and I can see a difference in her since we got home. It's going to take a while after all she's been through, but she's strong."

"She is."

I didn't like the sadness that had crept into her voice, and I had just the thing to cheer her up. I'd planned to give it to her tonight, but now was as good a time as any.

"Wait here." I lifted her legs and stood.

"What are you up to?" she called when I went into the bedroom.

I opened the top drawer of my dresser and retrieved the brown manila envelope I'd placed there yesterday evening. Thinking of her reaction when she saw what was inside, I smiled as I returned to the living room.

"You're looking very pleased with yourself," she said when I joined her on the couch again. Her eyes went to the envelope, and she gave me a questioning look. "What's that?"

I handed it to her. "Open it."

Her eyes narrowed suspiciously as she took the envelope and opened it. I watched her face closely when she reached inside and pulled out several sheets of paper.

She stared at the first one for a long moment before her mouth fell open and her gaze flew to mine.

"Is this...?" Her voice cracked as her eyes began to shimmer with tears.

"...the deed to your building in New Hastings," I finished for her. "Nate and I talked, and he was thinking about selling. So I —"

She launched herself at me, straddling my lap to kiss me until both of us needed to come up for air.

"I love you, I love you, I love you," she sang, hugging me tightly. "I can't believe you bought me a whole building."

I nuzzled her throat. "I'd buy you a whole block if you asked me to."

"I don't want a whole block." She lifted her head to look at me. "Why didn't you guys tell me?"

I lifted a corner of my mouth. "And miss out on that reaction? Not a chance."

She looked down at the papers that were now slightly crumpled in her hand. "When can we go visit? It should be safe there now, right?"

"How about this weekend?"

Her head whipped up. "Are you serious?"

I nodded, and she squealed. This time she tossed the papers on the couch before she took my face in her hands and kissed me senseless.

"Thank you," she whispered against my lips.

"No thanks necessary." I gave her a lazy smile and settled my hands on her hips. "Just kiss me like that every day for the rest of our lives."

"Deal."

She laid her head on my shoulder, and I rubbed my hand up and down her back.

"My mother called again this morning. She's dying to meet you. I'm not sure if she'll be able to wait until this summer."

"I know I said I wanted to wait to talk to her in person, but we can call her today if you think that'll make her happy."

I smiled, thinking about my mother's reaction when my mate called her.

"Yeah, that will make her very happy. And maybe she'll stop calling me at 5:00 a.m."

Sara chuckled. "Well, she *has* waited a long time for her son to find a mate."

"So have I." I lifted her chin and looked into her eyes. "I waited almost two hundred years for you. I just didn't know what I was waiting for until I found you."

She gave me a teary smile. "I bet you never expected it to be this crazy. Was it worth it?"

"Every. Single. Second." I punctuated each word with a kiss.

She toyed with the hair at the back of my head, sending a shiver through me. I could live a hundred lifetimes and never tire of her touch.

"When I look back at everything that's happened, it feels unreal sometimes," she said. "It's been an adventure, hasn't it?"

I kissed her mouth and her throat, and her breath hitched when my lips found the swell of her breast. I lifted my head to smile at her. A familiar fire burned in her eyes, and an answering one blazed inside of me.

"No, *moy malen'kiy voin.* Our adventure is just beginning."

~ The End ~